DEAN KOONTZ'S
FRANKENSTEIN

DEAN KOONTZ'S
FRANKENSTEIN

Prodigal Son
City of Night
Dead and Alive

Dean Koontz

DEAN KOONTZ'S FRANKENSTEIN: PRODIGAL SON Copyright © 2005 by Dean Koontz
  Publication History: Bantam Dell mass market paperback, February 2005
DEAN KOONTZ'S FRANKENSTEIN: CITY OF NIGHT Copyright © 2005 by Dean Koontz
  Publication History: Bantam Dell mass market paperback, August 2005
DEAN KOONTZ'S FRANKENSTEIN: DEAD AND ALIVE Copyright © 2009 by Dean Koontz
  Publication History: Bantam Books mass market paperback, July 2009

First Direct Brands, Inc. Printing: July 2010

Published by arrangement with
Bantam Books
A Division of Random House, Inc.
New York, New York

Visit The Literary Guild Book Club online at www.literaryguild.com

ISBN 978-1-61664-482-6

Printed in the United States of America.

CONTENTS

DEAN KOONTZ'S
FRANKENSTEIN
PRODIGAL SON

FIRST . . .

Although I'm a chatty kind of guy, never before have I found it necessary to explain up front how a book came to be written. In the case of the series originally known as *Dean Koontz's Frankenstein*, a few words of explanation seem necessary.

I wrote a script for a sixty-minute television-series pilot with this title. A producer and I made a deal for the pilot plus episodes to be broadcast on USA Network. Because he liked my script, Martin Scorsese—the legendary director—signed on as executive producer. A hot young director, also enamored of the script, signed on as well. At the request of USA Network, I wrote a two-hour version. On the basis of this script, a wonderful cast was assembled.

Then USA Network and the producer decided that major changes must be made. I had no interest in the show in its new form, and I withdrew from association with it. I wished them well—and turned to the task of realizing the original concept in book form. I hoped *both* versions would succeed in their different media.

Subsequently, Marty Scorsese also expressed the desire to exit the series. I am grateful to Marty for being so enthusiastic and insightful about the show we wanted to make. For a man of his accomplishments, he is refreshingly humble, the very definition of grace, and anchored to real-world values in a business where many are not.

I would also like to thank the late Philip K. Dick, great writer and nice man, who twenty-three years ago shared with me the story of asking for "something too exotic for the menu" in his favorite Chinese restaurant. I've finally found a novel in which the anecdote fits. The entrée that sent Phil fleeing makes Victor Frankenstein lick his lips.

The first two volumes of this series were originally published with the bylines of co-writers. Each gentleman did his job well, but I discovered another character flaw in myself (it's a long list): I am not able to collaborate. I have sat alone at the keyboard for so many years that alone is the only way I know how to do this. Given a good first draft from a co-author, I nevertheless strike out in my own direction. I should have known. As a kid in school, I never got a positive mark in the plays-well-with-others column.

For the power of man to make himself what he pleases means, as we have seen, the power of some men to make other men what THEY *please.*

—C. S. Lewis, *The Abolition of Man*

ROMBUK MONASTERY
TIBET

CHAPTER 1

DEUCALION SELDOM SLEPT, but when he did, he dreamed. Every dream was a nightmare. None frightened him. He was the spawn of nightmares, after all; and he had been toughened by a life of terror.

During the afternoon, napping in his simple cell, he dreamed that a surgeon opened his abdomen to insert a mysterious, squirming mass. Awake but manacled to the surgical table, Deucalion could only endure the procedure.

After he had been sewn shut, he felt something crawling inside his body cavity, as though curious, exploring.

From behind his mask, the surgeon said, "A messenger approaches. Life changes with a letter."

He woke from the dream and knew that it had been prophetic. He possessed no psychic power of a classic nature, but sometimes omens came in his sleep.

IN THESE MOUNTAINS OF TIBET, a fiery sunset conjured a mirage of molten gold from the glaciers and the snowfields. A serrated blade of Himalayan peaks, with Everest at its hilt, cut the sky.

Far from civilization, this vast panorama soothed Deucalion. For several years, he had preferred to avoid people, except for Buddhist monks in this windswept rooftop of the world.

Although he had not killed for a long time, he still harbored the capacity for homicidal fury. Here he strove always to suppress his darker urges, sought calm, and hoped to find true peace.

From an open stone balcony of the whitewashed monastery, as he gazed at the sun-splashed ice pack, he considered, not for the first time, that these two elements, fire and ice, defined his life.

At his side, an elderly monk, Nebo, asked, "Are you looking at the mountains—or beyond them, to what you left behind?"

Although Deucalion had learned to speak several Tibetan dialects during his lengthy sojourn here, he and the old monk often spoke English, for it afforded them privacy.

"I don't miss much of that world. The sea. The sound of shore birds. A few friends. Cheez-Its."

"Cheeses? We have cheese here."

Deucalion smiled and pronounced the word more clearly than he'd done previously. "Cheez-Its are cheddar-flavored crackers. Here in this monastery we seek enlightenment, meaning, purpose . . . God. Yet often the humblest things of daily life, the small pleasures, seem to define existence for me. I'm afraid I'm a shallow student, Nebo."

Pulling his wool robe closer about himself as wintry breezes bit, Nebo said, "To the contrary. Never have I had one less shallow than you. Just hearing about Cheez-Its, I myself am intrigued."

A voluminous wool robe covered Deucalion's scarred patchwork body, though even the harshest cold rarely bothered him.

The mandala-shaped Rombuk monastery—an architectural wonder of brick walls, soaring towers, and graceful roofs—clung precariously to a barren mountainside: imposing, majestic, hidden from the world. Waterfalls of steps spilled down the sides of the square towers, to the base of the main levels, granting access to interior courtyards.

Brilliant yellow, white, red, green, and blue prayer flags, representing the elements, flapped in the breeze. Carefully written sutras adorned the flags, so that each time the fabric waved in the wind, a prayer was symbolically sent in the direction of Heaven.

Despite Deucalion's size and strange appearance, the monks had accepted him. He absorbed their teaching and filtered it through his singular experience. In time, they had come to him with philosophical questions, seeking his unique perspective.

They didn't know who he was, but they understood intuitively that he was no normal man.

Deucalion stood for a long time without speaking. Nebo waited beside him. Time had little meaning in the clockless world of the monks, and after two hundred years of life, with perhaps more than that ahead of him, Deucalion often lived with no awareness of time.

Prayer wheels clicked, stirred by breezes. In a call to sunset prayer, one monk stood in the window of a high tower, blowing on a shell trumpet. Deep inside the monastery, chants began to resonate through the cold stone.

Deucalion stared down into the canyons full of purple twilight, east of the monastery. From some of Rombuk's windows, one might fall more than a thousand feet to the rocks.

Out of that gloaming, a distant figure approached.

"A messenger," he said. "The surgeon in the dream spoke truth."

The old monk could not at first see the visitor. His eyes, the color of vinegar, seemed to have been faded by the unfiltered sun of extreme altitude. Then they widened. "We must meet him at the gates."

SALAMANDERS OF TORCHLIGHT crawled the ironbound beams of the main gate and the surrounding brick walls.

Just inside the gates, standing in the open-air outer ward, the messenger regarded Deucalion with awe. "Yeti," he whispered, which was the name that the Sherpas had coined for the abominable snowman.

Words escaping him on plumes of frosted breath, Nebo said, "Is it custom now to precede a message with a rude remark?"

Having once been pursued like a beast, having lived two hundred years as the ultimate outsider, Deucalion was inoculated against all meanness. He was incapable of taking offense.

"Were I a yeti," he said, speaking in the messenger's language, "I might be as tall as this." He stood six feet six. "I might be muscled this solidly. But I would be much hairier, don't you think?"

"I . . . I suppose so."

"A yeti never shaves." Leaning close, as if imparting a secret, Deucalion said, "Under all that hair, a yeti has *very* sensitive skin. Pink, soft . . . quick to take a rash from a razor blade."

Summoning courage, the messenger asked, "Then what are you?"

"Big Foot," Deucalion said in English, and Nebo laughed, but the messenger did not understand.

Made nervous by the monk's laughter, shivering not only because of the icy air, the young man held out a scuffed goatskin packet knotted tightly with a leather thong. "Here. Inside. For you."

Deucalion curled one powerful finger around the leather thong, snapped it, and unfolded the goatskin wrapping to reveal an envelope inside, a wrinkled and stained letter long in transit.

The return address was in New Orleans. The name was that of an old and trusted friend, Ben Jonas.

Still glancing surreptitiously and nervously at the ravaged half of Deucalion's face, the messenger evidently decided that the company of a yeti would be preferable to a return trip in darkness through the bitter-cold mountain pass. "May I have shelter for the night?"

"Anyone who comes to these gates," Nebo assured him, "may have whatever he needs. If we had them, I would even give you Cheez-Its."

From the outer ward, they ascended the stone ramp through the inner gate. Two young monks with lanterns arrived as if in answer to a telepathic summons to escort the messenger to guest quarters.

In the candlelit reception hall, in an alcove that smelled of sandal-wood and incense, Deucalion read the letter. Ben's handwritten words conveyed a momentous message in neatly penned blue ink.

With the letter came a clipping from a newspaper, the *New Orleans Times-Picayune*. The headline and the text mattered less to Deucalion than the photograph that accompanied them.

Although nightmares could not frighten him, though he had long ago ceased to fear any man, his hand shook. The brittle clipping made a crisp, scurrying-insect sound in his trembling fingers.

"Bad news?" asked Nebo. "Has someone died?"

"Worse. Someone is still *alive*." Deucalion stared in disbelief at the photograph, which felt colder than ice. "I must leave Rombuk."

This statement clearly saddened Nebo. "I had taken comfort for some time that you would be the one to say the prayers at my death."

"You're too full of piss to die anytime soon," Deucalion said. "As preserved as a pickle in vinegar. Besides, I am perhaps the last one on Earth to whom God would listen."

"Or perhaps the first," said Nebo with an enigmatic but knowing smile. "All right. If you intend to walk again in the world beyond these mountains, first allow me to give you a gift."

LIKE WAXY STALAGMITES, yellow candles rose from golden holders, softly brightening the room. Gracing the walls were painted mandalas, geometric designs enclosed in a circle, representing the cosmos.

Reclining in a chair padded with thin red silk cushions, Deucalion stared at a ceiling of carved and painted lotus blossoms.

Nebo sat at an angle to him, leaning over him, studying his face with the attention of a scholar deciphering intricate sutra scrolls.

During his decades in carnivals, Deucalion had been accepted by carnies as though nothing about him was remarkable. They, too, were all outsiders by choice or by necessity.

He'd made a good living working the freak shows, which were called ten-in-ones because they offered ten exhibits under one tent.

On his small stage, he had sat in profile, the handsome side of his face turned to the sawdust aisle along which the marks traveled from act to act, from fat lady to rubber man. When they gathered before him, puzzling over why he was included in such a show, he turned to reveal the ruined side of his face.

Grown men gasped and shuddered. Women fainted, though fewer as the decades passed. Only adults eighteen and older were admitted, because children, seeing him, might be traumatized for life.

Face fully revealed, he had stood and removed his shirt to show them his body to the waist. The keloid scars, the enduring welts from primitive metal sutures, the strange excrescences . . .

Now beside Nebo stood a tray that held an array of thin steel needles and tiny vials of inks in many colors. With nimble skill, the monk tattooed Deucalion's face.

"This is my gift to you, a pattern of protection." Nebo leaned over to inspect his work, then began an even more intricate tracing in dark blues, blacks, greens.

Deucalion did not wince, nor would he have cried out at the stings of a thousand wasps. "Are you creating a puzzle on my face?"

"The puzzle *is* your face." The monk smiled down at his work and at the uneven canvas on which he imprinted his rich designs.

Dripping color, dripping blood, needles pricked, gleamed, and clicked together when, at times, Nebo used two at once.

"With this much pattern, I should offer something for the pain. The monastery has opium, though we do not often condone its use."

"I don't fear pain," Deucalion said. "Life is an ocean of pain."

"Life outside of here, perhaps."

"Even here we bring our memories with us."

The old monk selected a vial of crimson ink, adding to the pattern, disguising grotesque concavities and broken planes, creating an illusion of normalcy under the decorative motifs.

The work continued in heavy silence until Nebo said, "This will serve as a diversion for the curious eye. Of course, not even such a detailed pattern will conceal everything."

Deucalion reached up to touch the stinging tattoo that covered the surface of the cracked-mirror scar tissue. "I'll live by night and by distraction, as so often I have before."

After inserting stoppers in the ink vials, wiping his needles on a cloth, the monk said, "Once more before you leave . . . the coin?"

Sitting up straighter in his chair, Deucalion plucked a silver coin from midair with his right hand.

Nebo watched as Deucalion turned the coin across his knuckles—*walked* it, as magicians say—exhibiting remarkable dexterity considering the great size and brutal appearance of his hands.

That much, any good magician could have done.

With thumb and forefinger, Deucalion snapped the coin into the air. Candlelight winked off the piece as it flipped high.

Deucalion snatched it from the air, clutching it in his fist ... opened his hand to show it empty.

Any good magician could have done this, too, and could have then produced the coin from behind Nebo's ear, which Deucalion also did.

The monk was mystified, however, by what came next.

Deucalion snapped the coin into the air again. Candlelight winked off it. Then before Nebo's eyes, the coin just ... vanished.

At the apex of its arc, turning head to tail to head, it turned out of existence. The coin didn't fall to the floor. Deucalion's hands were not near it when it disappeared.

Nebo had seen this illusion many times. He had watched it from a distance of inches, yet he couldn't say what happened to the coin.

He had often meditated on this illusion. To no avail.

Now Nebo shook his head. "Is it truly magic, or just a trick?"

Smiling, Deucalion said, "And what is the sound of one hand clapping?"

"Even after all these years, you're still a mystery."

"As is life itself."

Nebo scanned the ceiling, as if expecting to see the coin stuck to one of the carved and painted lotus blossoms. Lowering his stare to Deucalion once more, he said, "Your friend in America addressed your letter to seven different names."

"I've used many more than that."

"Police trouble?"

"Not for a long time. Just ... always seeking a new beginning."

"Deucalion ... ," the monk said.

"A name from old mythology—not known to many people anymore." He rose from the chair, ignoring the throbbing pain of countless pinpricks.

The old man turned his face upward. "In America, will you return to the carnival life?"

"Carnivals have no place for me. There aren't freak shows anymore, not like in the old days. They're politically incorrect."

"Back when there were freak shows, what was your act?"

Deucalion turned from the candlelit mandalas on the wall, his newly tattooed face hidden in shadows. When he spoke, a subtle pulse of luminosity passed through his eyes, like the throb of lightning hidden behind thick clouds.

"They called me ... the Monster."

NEW ORLEANS

CHAPTER 2

MORNING RUSH-HOUR TRAFFIC on the I-10 Expressway flowed as languidly as the Mississippi River that wound through New Orleans.

When Detective Carson O'Connor got off the expressway in the suburb of Metairie, intending to use surface streets to make better time, the morning took a turn for the worse.

Stopped interminably at an intersection, she impatiently kneaded the steering wheel of her plainwrap sedan. To dispel a growing sense of suffocation, she rolled down the window.

Already the morning streets were griddles. None of the airheads on the TV news, however, would try to cook an egg on the pavement. Even journalism school left them with enough brain cells to realize that on these streets you could flash-fry even ice cream.

Carson liked the heat but not the humidity. Maybe one day she'd move somewhere nicer, hot but dry, like Arizona. Or Nevada. Or Hell.

Without advancing a foot, she watched the minute change on the dashboard clock display—then spotted the reason for the jam-up.

Two young hoods in gang colors lingered in the crosswalk to block traffic each time the light turned green. Three others worked the line, car to car, tapping on windows, extorting payoffs.

"Clean your windshield. Two bucks."

Like a patter of semiautomatic gunfire, car doors locked one after another as the young entrepreneurs made their sales pitch, but no car could move forward until the driver paid the tariff.

The apparent leader appeared at Carson's window, smug and full of false good humor. "Clean your windshield, lady."

He held a filthy rag that looked as if it had been fished out of one of the city's many weedy canals.

A thin white scar on one darkly tanned cheek was puckered at several suture points, suggesting that he'd gotten into a knife fight on a day when the ER physician had been Dr. Frankenstein. His wispy beard implied testosterone deficiency.

Getting a second, closer look at Carson, Scarface grinned. "Hey, pretty lady. What you doin' in these shabby wheels? You was made for Mercedes." He lifted one of the wipers and let it slap back onto the windshield. "Hello, where's your mind? Not that a long-legged fresh like you *needs* a mind."

An unmarked sedan had advantages in low-profile detective work; however, back when she'd driven a black-and-white patrol car, Carson had never been bothered by crap like this.

"You're breaking the law," she told him.

"Somebody in a *mood* this mornin'."

"The windshield's clean. This is extortion."

"I charge two bucks to clean it."

"I advise you to step back from the car."

The kid lifted his rag, prepared to smear the windshield. "Two bucks to clean it, three bucks *not* to clean it. Most ladies, whether they're male or female ladies, take option two."

Carson unbuckled her seatbelt. "I asked you to step back from the car."

Instead of retreating, Scarface leaned into the window, inches from her. Breath sweetened by a morning joint, soured by gum disease. "Gimme three bucks, your phone number, a nice apology—and maybe I don't mess with your fine face."

Carson grabbed the gink's left ear, twisted it hard enough to crack cartilage, and slammed his head sideways against the door post. His howl sounded less like that of a wolf than like that of an infant.

She let go of his ear and, exiting the sedan, opened the door into him with enough force to knock him off his feet.

As he sprawled backward, rapping his head on the pavement hard enough to summon constellations to an inner planetarium, she planted one foot on his crotch, grinding down just enough to make him squirm and to pin him in place for fear that she'd make paste of his jewels.

Shoving her police ID toward his face, she said, "My phone number is nine-one-one."

Among the hostage cars, heads up and alert, Scarface's four ace kools were looking at him, at her, stunned and angry but also amused. The guy under her foot was a homey, and a humiliation to one home boy was a humiliation to all, even if maybe he was a little bit of what they called *hook homey,* a phony.

To the nearest of Scarface's friends, Carson said, "Stall it out, shit-head, unless you want a hole in your doo-rag."

The gink under her foot tried to crab-walk away, but she stepped down harder. Tears sprang to his eyes, and he chose submission over the prospect of three days with an ice pack between his legs.

In spite of her warning, two of the other four gangbangers began to edge toward her.

Almost with the nimbleness of prestidigitation, Carson put away her ID and produced the pistol from her holster.

"Check it out, this lady under my foot, he's been scratched"—which meant embarrassed—"but none of you has. Nothin' here for you but two years in stir, maybe lit up and crippled for life."

They didn't split, but they stopped moving closer.

Carson knew they were less concerned about her pistol than about the fact that she talked the talk. Since she knew the lingo, they assumed—correctly—that she had been in situations like this before, lots of them, and still looked prime, and wasn't afraid.

Even the dumbest gangbanger—and few would win a dime on *Wheel of Fortune*—could read her credentials and calculate the odds.

"Best to break, best to book," she said, advising them to leave. "You insist on bumping titties, you're gonna lose."

Ahead of her plainwrap sedan, closer to the intersection, cars began to move. Whether or not they could see what was happening in their rearview mirrors, the drivers sensed the shakedown had ended.

As the cars around them began to roll, the young entrepreneurs decided there was no point to lingering when their customer base had moved on. They whidded away like walleyed horses stampeded by the crack of thunder.

Under her foot, the windshield-washer couldn't quite bring himself to admit defeat. "Hey, bitch, your badge, it said *homicide*. You can't touch me! I ain't killed nobody."

"What a moron," she said, holstering the pistol.

"You can't call me a moron. I graduated high school."

"You did not."

"I *almost* did."

Before the creep—predictably—took offense at her impolite characterization of his mental acuity and threatened to sue for insensitivity, Carson's cell phone rang.

"Detective O'Connor," she answered.

When she heard who was calling and why, she took her foot off the gangbanger.

"Beat it," she told him. "Get your sorry ass out of the street."

"You ain't lockin' me?"

"You're not worth the paperwork." She returned to her phone call.

Groaning, he got to his feet, one hand clutching the crotch of his low-rider pants as if he were a two-year-old overwhelmed by the need to pee.

He was one of those who didn't learn from experience. Instead of hobbling away to find his friends, telling them a wild story about how he'd gotten the best of the cop bitch after all and had punched out her teeth, he stood there holding himself, ragging her about abusive treatment, as though his whining and threats would wring from her a sudden sweat of remorse.

As Carson concluded the call, pressed END, and pocketed the phone, the offended extortionist said, "Thing is, I know your name now, so I can find out where you live."

"We're obstructing traffic here," she said.

"Come jack you up real good one night, break your legs, your arms, break every finger. You got gas in your kitchen? I'll cook your face on a burner."

"Sounds like fun. I'll open a bottle of wine, make tapas. Only thing is, the face gets cooked on the burner—I'm lookin' at it."

Intimidation was his best tool, but she had a screwhead that it couldn't turn.

"You like tapas?" she asked.

"Bitch, you're crazy as a red-eyed rat on meth."

"Probably," she agreed.

He backed away from her.

With a wink, she said, "I can find out where *you* live."

"You stay away from me."

"You got gas in *your* kitchen?" she asked.

"I mean it, you psycho twat."

"Ah, now you're just draggin' me," Carson said, *draggin'* meaning *sweet-talking.*

The gangbanger dared to turn his back on her and hobble away fast, dodging cars.

Feeling better about the morning, Carson got behind the wheel of the unmarked sedan, pulled her door shut, and drove off to pick up her partner, Michael Maddison.

They had been facing a day of routine investigation, but the phone call changed all that. A dead woman had been found in the City Park lagoon, and by the look of the body, she hadn't accidentally drowned while taking a moonlight swim.

CHAPTER 3

WITHOUT USING HER SIREN and portable flasher, Carson made good time on Veterans Boulevard, through a kaleidoscope of strip malls, lube shops, car dealerships, bank branches, and fast-food franchises.

Farther along, subdivisions of tract homes alternated with corridors of apartment buildings and condos. Here Michael Maddison, thirty and still single, had found a bland apartment that could have been in any city in America.

Bland didn't bother him. Working to the jazz beat and the hoodoo hum of New Orleans, especially as a homicide dick, he claimed that he ended every day in local-color overload. The ordinary apartment was his anchor in reality.

Dressed for work in a Hawaiian shirt, tan sports jacket that covered his shoulder holster, and jeans, Michael had been waiting for her to drive up. He looked wry and easy, but like certain deceptive cocktails, he had a kick.

Carrying a white paper bag in one hand, holding an unbitten doughnut in his mouth with the delicacy of a retriever returning to a hunter with a duck, Michael got into the passenger's seat and pulled the door shut.

Carson said, "What's that growth on your lip?"

Taking the doughnut from between his teeth, intact and barely marked, he said, "Maple-glazed buttermilk."

"Gimme."

Michael offered her the white bag. "One regular glazed, two chocolate. Take your pick."

Ignoring the bag, snatching the doughnut from his hand, Carson said, "I'm crazy for maple."

Tearing off a huge bite, chewing vigorously, she swung the car away from the curb and rocketed into the street.

"I'm crazy for maple, too," Michael said with a sigh.

The yearning in his voice told Carson that he longed not only for the maple-glazed doughnut. For more reasons than merely the maintenance of a professional relationship, she pretended not to notice. "You'll enjoy the regular glazed."

As Carson took Veterans Avenue out of Jefferson Parish into Orleans Parish, intending to catch Pontchartrain Boulevard to Harrison and then head to City Park, Michael rummaged in the doughnut bag, making it clear that he was selecting one of the other treats only from cruel necessity.

As she knew he would, he settled on chocolate—not the glazed that she had imperiously recommended—took a bite, and scrunched the top of the paper bag closed.

Glancing up as Carson cruised through a yellow light an instant before it changed to red, he said, "Ease off the gas and help save the planet. In my church, we start every workday with an hour of sugar and meditation."

"*I* don't belong to the Church of Fat-Assed Detectives. Besides, just got a call—they found number six this morning."

"Six?" Around another bite of chocolate doughnut, he said, "How do they know it's the same perp?"

"More surgery—like the others."

"Liver? Kidney? Feet?"

"She must've had nice hands. They found her in the City Park lagoon, her hands cut off."

CHAPTER 4

PEOPLE CAME TO THE fifteen-hundred-acre City Park to feed the ducks or to relax under the spreading live oaks draped with gray-green curtains of Spanish moss. They enjoyed the well-manicured botanical gardens, the Art Deco fountains and sculptures. Children loved the fairy-tale theme park and the famous wooden flying horses on the antique merry-go-round.

Now spectators gathered to watch a homicide investigation in progress at the lagoon.

As always, Carson was creeped out by these morbidly curious onlookers. They included grandmothers and teenagers, businessmen in suits and grizzled winos sucking cheap blends out of bagged bottles, but she got a *Night of the Living Dead* vibe from every one of them.

Centuries-old oaks loomed over a pool of green water fringed with weeds. Paved paths wound along the edge of the lagoon, connected by gracefully arched stone bridges.

Some rubberneckers had climbed the trees to get a better view past the police tape.

"Doesn't look like the same crowd you see at the opera," Michael said as he and Carson shouldered through the gawkers on the sidewalk and the jogging path. "Or at monster-truck rallies, for that matter."

In the eighteenth and nineteenth centuries, this area had been a popular place for hot-blooded Creoles to engage in duels. They met after sunset, by moonlight, and clashed with thin swords until blood was drawn.

These days, the park remained open at night, but the combatants were not equally armed and matched, as in the old days. Predators stalked prey and felt confident of escaping punishment in this age when civilization seemed to be unraveling.

Now uniformed cops held back the ghouls, any one of whom might have been the killer returned to revel in the aftermath of murder. Behind them, yellow crime-scene tape had been strung like Mardi Gras streamers from oak tree to oak tree, blocking off a section of the running path beside the lagoon.

Michael and Carson were known to many of the attending officers and CSI techs: liked by some, envied by others, loathed by a few.

She had been the youngest ever to make detective, Michael the second youngest. You paid a price for taking a fast track.

You paid a price for your style, too, if it wasn't traditional. And with some of the cynical marking-time-till-pension types, you paid a price if you worked as if you believed that the job was important and that justice mattered.

Just past the yellow tape, Carson stopped and surveyed the scene.

A female corpse floated facedown in the scummy water. Her blond hair fanned out like a nimbus, radiant where tree-filtered Louisiana sunlight dappled it.

Because the sleeves of her dress trapped air, the dead woman's arms floated in full sight, too. They ended in stumps.

"New Orleans," Michael said, quoting a current tourist bureau come-on, "the romance of the bayou."

Waiting for instruction, the CSI techs had not yet entered the scene. They had followed Carson and stood now just the other side of the marked perimeter.

As the investigating detectives, Carson and Michael had to formulate a systematic plan: determine the proper geometry of the search, the subjects and angles of photographs, possible sources of clues . . . .

In this matter, Michael usually deferred to Carson because she had an intuition that, just to annoy her, he called witchy vision.

To the nearest uniform on the crime line, Carson said, "Who was the responding officer?"

"Ned Lohman."

"Where is he?"

"Over there behind those trees."

"Why the hell's he tramping the scene?" she demanded.

As if in answer, Lohman appeared from behind the oaks with two homicide detectives, older models, Jonathan Harker and Dwight Frye.

"Dork and Dink," Michael groaned.

Although too far away to have heard, Harker glowered at them. Frye waved.

"This blows," Carson said.

"Big time," Michael agreed.

She didn't bluster into the scene but waited for the detectives to come to her.

How nice it would have been to shoot the bastards in the knees to spare the site from their blundering. So much more satisfying than a shout or a warning shot.

By the time Harker and Frye reached her, both were smiling and smug.

Ned Lohman, the uniformed officer, had the good sense to avoid her eyes.

Carson held her temper. "This is our baby, let us burp it."

"We were in the area," Frye said, "caught the call."

"Chased the call," Carson suggested.

Frye was a beefy man with an oily look, as if his surname came not from family lineage but from his preferred method of preparing every food he ate.

"O'Connor," he said, "you're the first Irish person I've ever known who wasn't fun to be around."

In a situation like this, which had grown from one bizarre homicide to six killings in a matter of weeks, Carson and her partner would not be the only ones in the department assigned to research particular aspects of the case.

They had caught the first murder, however, and therefore had proprietary interest in associated homicides if and until the killer piled up enough victims to force the establishment of an emergency task force. And at that point, she and Michael would most likely be designated to head that undertaking.

Harker tended to burn easily—from sunshine, from envy, from imagined slights to his competence, from just about anything. The Southern sun had bleached his blond hair nearly white; it lent his face a perpetually parboiled look.

His eyes, as blue as a gas flame, as hard as gemstones, revealed the truth of him that he attempted to disguise with a soft smile. "We needed to move fast, before evidence was lost. In this climate, bodies decompose quickly."

"Oh, don't be so hard on yourself," Michael said. "With a gym membership and a little determination, you'll be looking good again."

Carson drew Ned Lohman aside. Michael joined them as she took out her notebook and said, "Gimme the TPO from your involvement."

"Listen, Detectives, I know you're the whips on this. I told Frye and Harker as much, but they have rank."

"Not your fault," she assured him. "I should know by now that vultures always get to dead meat first. Let's start with the time."

He checked his watch. "Call came in at seven forty-two, which makes it thirty-eight minutes ago. Jogger saw the body, called it in. When I showed up, the guy was standing here running in place to keep his heart rate up."

In recent years, runners with cell phones had found more bodies than any other class of citizens.

"As for place," Officer Lohman continued, "the body's just where the jogger found it. He made no rescue attempt."

"The severed hands," Michael suggested, "were probably a clue that CPR wouldn't be effective."

"The vic is blond, maybe not natural, probably Caucasian. You have any other observations about her?" Carson asked Lohman.

"No. I didn't go near her either, didn't contaminate anything, if that's what you're trying to find out. Haven't seen the face yet, so I can't guess the age."

"Time, place—what about occurrence?" she asked Lohman. "Your first impression was . . . ?"

"Murder. She didn't cut her hands off herself."

"Maybe one," Michael agreed, "but not both."

CHAPTER 5

THE STREETS OF NEW ORLEANS teemed with possibilities: women of every description. A few were beautiful, but even the most alluring were lacking in one way or another.

During his years of searching, Roy Pribeaux had yet to encounter one woman who met his standards in every regard.

He was proud of being a perfectionist. If he had been God, the world would have been a more ordered, less messy place.

Under Roy Almighty, there would have been no ugly or plain people. No mold. No cockroaches or even mosquitoes. Nothing that smelled bad.

Under a blue sky that he could not have improved upon, but in cloying humidity he would not have allowed, Roy strolled along the Riverwalk, the site of the 1984 Louisiana World's Fair, which had been refurbished as a public gathering place and shopping pavilion. He was hunting.

Three young women in tank tops and short shorts sashayed past, laughing together. Two of them checked Roy out.

He met their eyes, boldly ogled their bodies, then dismissed each of them with a glance.

Even after years of searching, he remained an optimist. *She* was out there somewhere, his ideal, and he would find her—even if it had to be one piece at a time.

In this promiscuous society, Roy remained a virgin at thirty-eight, a fact of which he was proud. He was saving himself. For the perfect woman. For love.

Meanwhile, he polished his own perfection. He undertook two hours of physical training every day. Regarding himself as a Renaissance man, he read literature for exactly one hour, studied a new subject for exactly one hour, meditated on the great mysteries and the major issues of his time for another hour every day.

He ate only organic produce. He bought no meat from factory farms. No pollutants tainted him, no pesticides, no radiological residue, and certainly no strange lingering genetic material from bioengineered foods.

Eventually, when he had refined his diet to perfection and when his body was as tuned as an atomic clock, he expected that he would cease to eliminate waste. He would process every morsel so completely that it would be converted entirely to energy, and he would produce no urine, no feces.

Perhaps he would *then* encounter the perfect woman. He often dreamed about the intensity of the sex they would have. As profound as *nuclear fusion*.

Locals loved the Riverwalk, but Roy suspected that most people here today were tourists, considering how they paused to gawk at the caricature artists and street musicians. Locals would not be drawn in such numbers to the stands piled with New Orleans T-shirts.

At a bright red wagon where cotton candy was sold, Roy suddenly halted. The fragrance of hot sugar cast a sweet haze around the cart.

The cotton-candy vendor sat on a stool under a red umbrella. In her twenties, less than plain, with unruly hair. She looked as baggy and as simply made as a Muppet, though without as much personality.

But her eyes. *Her eyes.*

Roy was captivated. Her eyes were priceless gems displayed in a cluttered and dusty case, a striking greenish blue.

The skin around her eyes crinkled alluringly as she caught his attention and smiled. "Can I help you?"

Roy stepped forward. "I'd like something sweet."

"All I've got is cotton candy."

"Not all," he said, marveling at how suave he could be.

She looked puzzled.

Poor thing. He was too smooth for her.

He said, "Yes, cotton candy, please."

She picked up a paper cone and began to twirl it through the spun sugar, wrapping it with a cloud of sugary confection.

"What's your name?" he asked.

She hesitated, seemed embarrassed, averted her eyes. "Candace."

"A girl named Candy is a candy vendor? Is that destiny or just a good sense of humor?"

She blushed. "I prefer Candace. Too many negative connotations for a . . . a heavy woman to be called Candy."

"So you're not an anorexic model, so what? Beauty comes in lots of different packages."

Candace obviously had seldom if ever heard such kind words from an attractive and desirable man like Roy Pribeaux.

If she herself ever thought about a day when she would excrete no wastes, she must know that he was far closer to that goal than she was.

"You have beautiful eyes," he told her. "Strikingly beautiful eyes. The kind a person could look into for years and years."

Her blush intensified, but her shyness was overwhelmed by astonishment to such a degree that she made eye contact with him.

Roy knew he dared not come on to her too strong. After a life of rejection, she'd suspect that he was setting her up for humiliation.

"As a Christian man," he explained, though he had no religious convictions, "I believe God made everyone beautiful in at least one respect, and we need to recognize that beauty. Your eyes are just . . . perfect. They're the windows to your soul."

Putting the cloud of cotton candy on a counter-top holder, she averted her eyes again as though it might be a sin to let him enjoy them too much. "I haven't gone to church since my mother died six years ago."

"I'm sorry to hear that. She must have died so young."

"Cancer," Candace revealed. "I got so angry about it. But now . . . I miss church."

"We could go together sometime, and have coffee after."

She dared his stare again. "Why?"

"Why not?"

"It's just . . . You're so . . ."

Pretending a shyness of his own, he looked away from her. "So not your type? I know to some people I might appear to be shallow—"

"No, please, that's not what I meant." But she couldn't bring herself to explain what she *had* meant.

Roy withdrew a small notepad from his pocket, scribbled with a pen, and tore off a sheet of paper. "Here's my name—Ray Darnell—and my cell-phone number. Maybe you'll change your mind."

Staring at the number and the phony name, Candace said, "I've always been pretty much a . . . private person."

The dear, shy creature.

"I understand," he said. "I've dated very little. I'm too old-fashioned for women these days. They're so . . . bold. I'm embarrassed for them."

When he tried to pay for his cotton candy, she didn't want to take his money. He insisted.

He walked away, nibbling at the confection, feeling her gaze on him. Once out of sight, he threw the cotton candy in a trash can.

Sitting on a bench in the sun, he consulted the notepad. On the last page at the back of it, he kept his checklist. After so much effort here in New Orleans and, previously, elsewhere, he had just yesterday checked off the next-to-last item: *hands.*

Now he put a question mark next to the final item on the list, hoping that he could cross it off soon.

EYES?

CHAPTER 6

HE IS A CHILD of Mercy, Mercy-born and Mercy-raised.

In his windowless room he sits at a table, working with a thick book of crossword puzzles. He never hesitates to consider an answer. Answers come to him instantly, and he rapidly inks letters in the squares, never making an error.

His name is Randal Six because five males have been named Randal and have gone into the world before him. If ever he, too, went into the world, he would be given a last name.

In the tank, before consciousness, he'd been educated by direct-to-brain data downloading. Once brought to life, he had continued to learn during sessions of drug-induced sleep.

He knows nature and civilization in their intricacies, knows the look and smell and sound of places he has never been. Yet his world is largely limited to a single room.

The agents of Mercy call this space his billet, which is a term to describe lodging for a soldier.

In the war against humanity—a secret war now but not destined to remain secret forever—he is an eighteen-year-old who came to life four months ago.

To all outward appearances, he is eighteen, but his knowledge is greater than that of most elderly scholars.

Physically, he is sound. Intellectually, he is advanced.

Emotionally, something is wrong with him.

He does not think of his room as his billet. He thinks of it as his cell.

He himself, however, is his own prison. He lives mostly within himself. He speaks little. He yearns for the world beyond his cell, beyond himself, and yet it frightens him.

Most of the day he spends with crossword puzzles, immersed in the vertical and horizontal patterns of words. The world beyond his quarters is alluring but it is also . . . disorderly, chaotic. He can feel it pressing against the walls, pressing, pressing, and only by focusing on crosswords, only by bringing *order* to the empty boxes by filling them with the *absolutely right* letters can he keep the outer disorder from invading his space.

Recently, he has begun to think that the world frightens him because Father has *programmed* him to be afraid of it. From Father, he has received his education, after all, and his life.

This possibility confuses him. He cannot understand why Father would create him to be . . . dysfunctional. Father seeks perfection in all things.

One thing gives him hope. Out in the world, and not far away, right here in New Orleans, is another like him. Not one of Father's creations, but likewise afflicted.

Randal Six is not alone. If only he could meet his equal, he would better understand himself . . . and be free.

CHAPTER 7

AN OSCILLATING FAN riffled the documents and case notes—held down by makeshift paperweights—on Carson's desk. Beyond the windows, an orange sunset had deepened to crimson, to purple.

Michael was at his desk in the Homicide Division, adjacent to Carson's, occupied by much of the same paperwork. She knew that he was ready to go home, but he usually let her define the workday.

"You checked our doc box lately?" she asked.

"Ten minutes ago," Michael reminded her. "You send me out there one more time, I'm going to eat a get-small mushroom and just *stay* in the doc box until the report shows up."

"We should've had the prelim autopsy on that floater hours ago," she complained.

"And I shoulda been born rich. Go figure."

She consulted photos of cadavers in situ while Michael watched.

The first victim, a young nurse named Shelley Justine, had been murdered elsewhere and dumped beside the London Street Canal. Tests revealed the chemical signature of chloroform in her blood.

After the killer rendered her unconscious, he killed her with a knife to the heart. With exquisite precision he removed her ears. A peptide profile found no elevated endorphin levels in the blood, indicating that the surgery occurred after she was dead. Had she been alive, the pain and terror would have left telltale chemistry.

The second victim, Meg Saville, a tourist from Idaho, had also been chloroformed and knifed while unconscious. The Surgeon—the press's name for him—had neatly sawed off Saville's feet.

"If he'd just *always* take feet," Michael said, "we'd know he was a podiatrist, and we'd have found him by now."

Carson shuffled the next photo to the top of the stack.

The first two victims had been women; however, neither Shelley Justine nor Meg Saville had been molested.

When the third victim was a man, the killer established his bona fides as an equal-opportunity maniac. The body of Bradford Walden—a young bartender from a hole-in-the-wall across the river in Algiers—had been found with the right kidney surgically removed.

The switch to souvenirs of internal origin wasn't troubling—an urge to collect feet and ears was no less disturbing than a fancy for kidneys—but it *was* curious.

Chemical traces of chloroform were found, but this time peptide profiles showed that Walden had been alive and awake for the surgery. Had the chloroform worn off too soon? Or had the killer intentionally let the man wake up? In either case, Walden died in agony, his mouth stuffed with rags and sealed with duct tape to muffle his screams.

The fourth victim, Caroline Beaufort, Loyola University student, had been discovered with both legs missing, her torso propped on an ornate bench at a trolley-car stop in the upscale Garden District. She had been chloroformed and unconscious when murdered.

For his fifth kill, the Surgeon dispensed with the anesthetic. He murdered another man, Alphonse Chaterie, a dry cleaner. He collected Chaterie's liver while the victim was alive and fully awake: not a trace of chloroform.

Most recently, this morning's body in the City Park lagoon was missing both hands.

Four women, two men. Four with chloroform, one without, one set of results pending. Each victim missing one or more body parts. The first three women were killed before the trophies were removed, while the men were alive and conscious for the surgery.

Apparently none of the victims had known any of the others. Thus far no mutual acquaintances had come to light, either.

"He doesn't like to see women suffer, but men in agony are okay with him," Carson said, and not for the first time.

Michael had a new thought. "Maybe the killer's a woman, has more sympathy for her own gender."

"Yeah, right. How many serial killers have ever been women?"

"There've been a few," he said. "But, I am proud to say, men have been a *lot* more successful at it."

Carson wondered, "Is there a fundamental difference between lopping off female body parts and digging out male internal organs?"

"We've been down this road. *Two* serial killers collecting body parts in the same city in the same three-week period? 'Is such a coincidence logical, Mr. Spock?' 'Coincidence, Jim, is just a word superstitious people use to describe complex events that in truth are the mathematically inevitable consequences of a primary cause.'"

Michael made this work a lot less gruesome and more tolerable, but sometimes she wanted to thump him. Hard.

"And what does that mean?" she asked.

He shrugged. "I never did understand Spock."

Appearing as if conjured into a pentagram, Harker dropped an envelope on Carson's desk. "ME's report on the floater. Delivered to my doc box by mistake."

Carson didn't want a push-and-shove with Harker, but she could not let obvious interference pass unremarked. "One more time your foot's on mine, I'll file a complaint with the chief of detectives."

"I'm so afraid," Harker dead-panned. His reddened face glistened with a sheen of sweat. "No ID on the floater yet, but it looks pretty much like she was chloroformed, taken someplace private, and killed with a stiletto to the heart before her hands were taken."

When Harker continued to stand there, the day's sun bottled in his glassy face, Michael said, "And?"

"You've checked out everyone with easy access to chloroform. Researchers doing animal experimentation, employees at medical supply companies . . . But two sites on the Internet offer formulas for making it in the kitchen sink, out of stuff you can buy at the supermarket. I'm just saying this case doesn't fit in any standard box. You're looking for something you've never seen before. To stop this guy, you've got to go to a weirder place—one level below Hell."

Harker turned from them and walked away across the squad room.

Carson and Michael watched him leave. Then Michael said, "What was *that*? It almost seemed like genuine concern for the public."

"He was once a good cop. Maybe a part of him still is."

Michael shook his head. "I liked him better as an asshole."

CHAPTER 8

OUT OF THE LAST of the twilight came Deucalion with a suitcase, in clothes too heavy for the sultry night.

This neighborhood offered markedly less glamour than the French Quarter. Seedy bars, pawn shops, liquor stores, head shops.

Once a grand movie house, the Luxe Theater had become a shabby relic specializing in revivals. On the marquee, unevenly spaced loose plastic letters spelled out the current double feature:

THURS THRU SUNDAY
DON SIEGEL REVIVAL
INVASION OF THE BODY SNATCHERS
HELL IS FOR HEROES

The marquee was dark, the theater closed either for the night or permanently.

Not all of the streetlamps were functioning. Approaching the Luxe, Deucalion found a route of shadows.

He passed a few pedestrians, averting his face without seeming to, and drew attention only for his height.

He slipped into a service walk beside the movie palace. For more than two centuries, he had used back doors or even more arcane entrances.

Behind the theater, a bare bulb in a wire cage above the back door shed light as drab and gray as this litter-strewn alleyway.

Sporting multiple layers of cracked and chipped paint, the door was a scab in the brick wall. Deucalion studied the latch, the lock . . . and decided to use the bell.

He pushed the button, and a loud buzz vibrated through the door. Inside the quiet theater, it must have echoed like a fire alarm.

Moments later, he heard heavy movement inside. He sensed that he was being studied through the fish-eye security lens.

The lock rattled, and the door opened to reveal a sweet face and merry eyes peering out of a prison of flesh. At five feet seven and perhaps three hundred pounds, this guy was twice the man he should have been.

"Are you Jelly Biggs?" Deucalion asked.

"Do I look like I'm not?"

"You're not fat enough."

"When I was a star in the ten-in-one, I weighed almost three hundred more. I'm half the man I used to be."

"Ben sent for me. I'm Deucalion."

"Yeah, I figured. In the old days, a face like yours was gold in the carnival."

"We're both blessed, aren't we?"

Stepping back, motioning Deucalion to enter, Biggs said, "Ben told me a lot about you. He didn't mention the tattoo."

"It's new."

"They're fashionable these days," said Jelly Biggs.

Deucalion stepped across the threshold into a wide but shabby hallway. "And me," he said drily, "I've always been a fashion plate."

BEHIND THE BIG theater screen, the Luxe featured a labyrinth of passages, storage closets, and rooms that no patron had ever visited. With a rolling gait and heavy respiration, Jelly led the way past crates, mildewed cardboard boxes, and moisture-curled posters and stand-ups that promoted old films.

"Ben put seven names on the letter he sent me," Deucalion said.

"You once mentioned Rombuk monastery, so he figured you might still be there, but he didn't know what name you'd be using."

"He shouldn't have shared my names."

"Just knowin' your aliases doesn't mean I can mojo you."

They arrived at a door that wore an armor-thick coat of green paint. Biggs opened it, switched on a light, gestured for Deucalion to enter ahead of him.

A windowless but cozy apartment lay beyond. A kitchenette was adjacent to the combination bedroom and living room. Ben loved books, and two walls were lined with them.

Jelly Biggs said, "It's a sweet place you inherited."

The key word whipped through Deucalion's mind before lashing back with a sharp sting. "Inherited. What do you mean? Where's Ben?"

Jelly looked surprised. "You didn't get my letter?"

"Only his."

Jelly sat on one of the chrome and red-vinyl chairs at the dinette table. It creaked. "Ben was mugged."

The world is an ocean of pain. Deucalion felt the old familiar tide wash through him.

"This isn't the best part of town, and getting worse," Biggs said. "Ben bought the Luxe when he retired from the carnival. The neighborhood was supposed to be turning around. It didn't. The place would be hard to sell these days, so Ben wanted to hold on."

"How did it happen?" Deucalion asked.

"Stabbed. More than twenty times."

Anger, like a long-repressed hunger, rose in Deucalion. Once anger had been his meat, and feasting on it, he had starved.

If he let this anger grow, it would quickly become fury—and devour him. For decades he had kept this lightning in a bottle, securely stoppered, but now he longed to pull the cork.

And then . . . what? Become the monster again? Pursued by mobs with torches, with pitchforks and guns, running, running, running with hounds baying for his blood?

"He was everybody's second father," said Jelly Biggs. "Best damn carnie boss I ever knew."

During the past two centuries, Ben Jonas had been one of a precious handful of people with whom Deucalion had shared his true origins, one of the few he had ever trusted completely.

He said, "He was murdered after he contacted me."

Biggs frowned. "You say that like there's a connection."

"Did they ever find the killer?"

"No. That's not unusual. The letter to you, the mugging—just a coincidence."

At last putting down his suitcase, Deucalion said, "There are no coincidences."

Jelly Biggs looked up from the dinette chair and met Deucalion's eyes. Without a word they understood that in addition to years in the carnival, they shared a view of the world that was as rich with meaning as with mysteries.

Pointing toward the kitchenette, the fat man said, "Besides the theater, Ben left you sixty thousand cash. It's in the freezer."

Deucalion considered this revelation for a moment, then said, "He didn't trust many people."

Jelly shrugged. "What do I need with money when I've got such good looks?"

CHAPTER 9

SHE WAS YOUNG, poor, inexperienced. She'd never had a manicure before, and Roy Pribeaux proposed that he give her one.

"I give myself manicures," he said. "A manicure can be erotic, you know. Just give me a chance. You'll see."

Roy lived in a large loft apartment, the top half of a remodeled old building in the Warehouse District. Many rundown structures in this part of the city had been transformed into expansive apartments for artists.

A printing company and a computer-assembly business shared the main floor below. They existed in another universe, as far as Roy Pribeaux was concerned; he didn't bother them, and they reciprocated.

He needed his privacy, especially when he took a new and special woman to his loft. This time, her name was Elizabeth Lavenza.

As odd as it might seem on a first date—or a tenth, for that matter—to suggest a manicure, he had charmed Elizabeth into it. He knew well that the modern woman responded to sensitivity in men.

First, at the kitchen table, he placed her fingers in a shallow bowl of warm oil to soften both the nails and the cuticles.

Most women also liked men who enjoyed pampering them, and young Elizabeth was no different in this regard.

In addition to sensitivity and a desire to pamper, Roy had a trove of amusing stories and could keep a girl laughing. Elizabeth had a lovely laugh. Poor thing, she had no chance of resisting him.

When her fingertips had soaked long enough, he wiped them with a soft towel.

Using a natural, nonacetone polish remover, he stripped the red color from her nails. Then with gentle strokes of an emery board, he sculpted the tip of each nail into a perfect curve.

He had only begun to trim the cuticles when an embarrassing thing happened: His special cell phone rang, and he knew that the caller had to be Candace. Here he was romancing Elizabeth, and the *other* woman in his life was calling.

He excused himself and hurried into the dining area, where he had left the phone on a table. "Hello?"

"Mr. Darnell?"

"I know that lovely voice," he said softly, moving into the living room, away from Elizabeth. "Is this Candace?"

The cotton-candy vendor laughed nervously. "We talked so little, how could you recognize my voice?"

Standing at one of the tall windows, his back to the kitchen, he said, "Don't you recognize mine?"

He could almost feel the heat of her blush coming down the line when she admitted, "Yes, I do."

"I'm so glad you called," he said in a discreet murmur.

Shyly, she said, "Well, I thought . . . maybe coffee?"

"A get-acquainted coffee. Just say where and when."

He hoped she didn't mean *right now*. Elizabeth was waiting, and he was enjoying giving her the manicure.

"Tomorrow evening?" Candace suggested. "Usually business on the boardwalk dies down after eight o'clock."

"Meet you at the red wagon. I'll be the guy with the big smile."

Unskilled at romance, she said awkwardly, "And . . . I guess I'll be the one with the eyes."

"You sure will," he said. "Such *eyes*."

Roy pressed END. The disposable phone wasn't registered to him. Out of habit, he wiped it clean of prints, tossed it on the sofa.

His modern, austere apartment didn't contain much furniture. His exercise machines were his pride. On the walls were reproductions of Leonardo da Vinci's anatomical sketches, the great man's studies of the perfect human form.

Returning to Elizabeth at the kitchen table, Roy said, "My sister. We talk all the time. We're very close."

When the manicure was complete, he exfoliated the skin of her perfect hands with an aromatic mixture of almond oil, sea salt, and essence of lavender (his own concoction), which he massaged onto her palms, the backs of the hands, the knuckles, the fingers.

Finally, he rinsed each hand, wrapped it in clean white butcher paper, and sealed it in a plastic bag. As he placed the hands in the freezer, he said, "I'm so happy you've come to stay, Elizabeth."

He didn't find it peculiar to be talking to her severed hands. Her hands had been the essence of her. Nothing else of Elizabeth Lavenza had been worth talking about or to. The hands were *her*.

CHAPTER 10

THE LUXE WAS an ornate Deco palace, glamorous in its day, a fit showcase for the movies of William Powell and Myrna Loy, Humphrey Bogart, Ingrid Bergman. Like many a Hollywood face, this glamour had peeled and sagged.

Deucalion accompanied Jelly Biggs down the center aisle, past rows of musty, patched seats.

"Damn DVDs screwed the revival business," Jelly said. "Ben's retirement didn't turn out like he expected."

"Marquee says you're still open Thursday through Sunday."

"Not since Ben died. There's *almost* enough thirty-five-millimeter fanatics to make it worthwhile. But some weekends we run up more expenses than receipts. I didn't want to take responsibility for that since it's become your property."

Deucalion looked up at the screen. The gold and crimson velvet curtains drooped, heavy with dust and creeping mildew. "So . . . you left the carnival when Ben did?"

"When freak shows took a fade, Ben made me theater manager. I got my own apartment here. I hope that won't change . . . assuming you want to keep the place running."

Deucalion pointed to a quarter on the floor. "Finding money is always a sign."

"A sign of what?"

Stooping to pick up the quarter, Deucalion said, "Heads, you're out of a job. Tails, you're out of a job."

"Don't like them odds."

Deucalion snapped the coin into the air, snatched it in midflight. When he opened his fist, the coin had disappeared.

"Neither heads nor tails. A sign for sure, don't you think?"

Instead of relief at having kept his job and home, Jelly's expression was troubled. "I been having a dream about a magician. He's strangely gifted."

"Just a simple trick."

Jelly said, "I'm maybe a little psychic. My dreams sometimes come sorta true."

Deucalion had much he could have said to that, but he remained silent, waiting.

Jelly looked at the moldering drapes, at the threadbare carpet, at the elaborate ceiling, everywhere but at Deucalion. At last he said, "Ben told me some about you, things that don't seem they could be real." He finally met Deucalion's eyes. "Do you have two hearts?"

Deucalion chose not to reply.

"In the dream," Jelly said, "the magician had two hearts . . . and he was stabbed in both."

A flutter of wings overhead drew Deucalion's attention.

"Bird got in yesterday," Jelly said. "A dove, by the look of it. Haven't been able to chase it out."

Deucalion tracked the trapped bird's flight. He knew how it felt.

CHAPTER 11

CARSON LIVED ON A tree-lined street in a house nondescript except for a gingerbread veranda that wrapped three sides.

She parked at the curb because the garage was packed with her parents' belongings, which she never found time to sort through.

On her way to the kitchen door, she paused under an oak draped with Spanish moss. Her work hardened her, wound her tight. Arnie, her brother, needed a *gentle* sister. Sometimes she couldn't decompress during the walk from car to house; she required a moment to herself.

Here in the humid night and the fragrance of jasmine, she found that she couldn't shift into domestic gear. Her nerves were twisted as tight as dreadlocks, and her mind raced. As never before, the scent of jasmine reminded her of the smell of blood.

The recent killings had been so gruesome and had occurred in such rapid succession that she could not put them aside during her personal time. Under normal circumstances, she was seventy percent cop, thirty percent woman and sister; these days, she was all cop, twenty-four/seven.

When Carson entered the kitchen, Vicky Chou had just loaded the dishwasher and switched it on. "Well, I screwed up."

"Don't tell me you put laundry in the dishwasher."

"Worse. With his brisket of beef, I gave him carrots and peas."

"Oh, never orange and green on the same plate, Vicky."

Vicky sighed. "He's got more rules about food than kosher and vegan combined."

On a cop's salary, Carson could not have afforded a live-in caregiver to look after her autistic brother. Vicky took the job in return for room and board—and out of gratitude.

When Vicky's sister, Liane, had been indicted with her boyfriend and two others for conspiracy to commit murder, she seemed helplessly snared in a web of evidence. She'd been innocent. In the process of sending the other three to prison, Carson had cleared Liane.

As a successful medical transcriptionist, Vicky worked flexible hours at home, transcribing microcassettes for physicians. If Arnie had been a more demanding autistic, Vicky might not have been able to keep up with her work, but the boy was mostly quiescent.

Widowed at forty, now forty-five, Vicky was an Asian beauty, smart and sweet and lonely. She wouldn't grieve forever. Someday when she least expected it, a man would come into her life, and the current arrangement would end.

Carson dealt with that possibility the only way that her busy life allowed: She ignored it.

"Other than green and orange together, how was he today?" Carson asked.

"Fixated on the castle. Sometimes it seems to calm him, but at other times . . ." Vicky frowned. "What is he so afraid of?"

"I don't know. I guess . . . life."

BY REMOVING A WALL and combining two of the upstairs bedrooms, Carson had given Arnie the largest room in the house. This seemed only fair because his condition stole from him the rest of the world.

His bed and nightstand were shoved into a corner. A TV occupied a wheeled metal stand. Sometimes he watched cartoons on DVD, the same ones over and over.

The remainder of the room had been devoted to the castle.

Four low sturdy tables formed a twelve-by-eight-foot platform. Upon the tables stood an architectural wonder in Lego blocks.

Few boys of twelve would have been able to create a model castle without a plan, but Arnie had put together a masterpiece: walls and wards, barbican and bastions, ramparts and parapets, turreted towers, the barracks, the chapel, the armory, the castle keep with elaborate bulwark and battlements.

He'd been obsessed with the model for weeks, constructing it in an intense silence. Repeatedly he tore down finished sections only to remodel and improve them.

Most of the time he was on his feet while adding to the castle—an access hole in the table arrangement allowed him to build from within the project as well as from every side—but sometimes, like now, he worked while sitting on a wheeled stool. Carson rolled a second stool to the table and sat to watch.

He was a dark-haired, blue-eyed boy whose looks alone would have ensured him a favored place in the world if he'd not been autistic.

At times like this, when his concentration on a task was total, Arnie would not tolerate anyone being too near to him. If Carson drew closer than four or five feet, he would grow agitated.

When enthralled by a project, he might pass days in silence except for wordless reactions to any attempt to interrupt his work or to invade his personal space.

More than eighteen years separated Carson from Arnie. He'd been born the year that she moved out of her parents' house. Even if he'd been spared from autism, they would not have been as close as many brothers and sisters, for they would have shared so few experiences.

Following the death of their parents four years ago, Carson gained custody of her brother. He had been with her ever since.

For reasons that she could not fully articulate, Carson had come to love this gentle, withdrawn child. She didn't think she could have loved him more if he had been her son rather than her brother.

She hoped that someday there would be a breakthrough either in the treatment of autism in general or in Arnie's particular case. But she knew her hope had little chance of being fulfilled.

Now she pondered the most recent changes he had made to the outer curtain wall of the castle compound. He had fortified it with regularly spaced buttresses that doubled as steep flights of stairs by which defenders could reach the walkways behind the battlements.

Recently Arnie had seemed to be more fearful than usual. Carson could not shake the feeling that he sensed some trouble coming and that he was urgently determined to prepare for it. He could not build a real castle, so he took refuge in this fantasy of a fortress home.

CHAPTER 12

RANDAL SIX CROSSES SPHINX with XENOPHOBE, finishing the last crossword puzzle in the book.

Other collections of puzzles await him. But with the completion of this current book, he is armored against the fearsome disorder of the world. He has earned protection.

He will be safe for a while, although not forever. Disorder builds. Chaos presses at the walls. Eventually he will have to fill more patterns of empty boxes with more judiciously chosen letters for the purpose of denying chaos entrance to his private space.

Temporarily safe, he gets up from the worktable, sits on the edge of his bed, and presses a call button on his nightstand. This will summon lunch.

He is not served meals on a regular schedule because he cannot eat when obsessed with crossword puzzles. He will let food grow cold rather than interrupt the important work of fending off chaos.

A man in white brings his tray and places it on the worktable. While this attendant is present, Randal Six keeps his head bowed to discourage conversation and to prevent eye contact.

Every word he speaks to another person diminishes the protection that he has earned.

Alone again, Randal Six eats his lunch. Very neatly.

The food is white and green, as he likes it. Sliced turkey breast in cream sauce, mashed potatoes, white bread, peas, beans. For dessert, vanilla ice cream with crème de menthe.

When he finishes, he dares to open his door and slide the tray into the corridor. He quickly closes the door again, and feels as safe now as he ever does.

He sits on the edge of his bed and opens his nightstand drawer. The drawer contains a few magazines.

Having been educated by direct-to-brain data downloading, Randal Six is encouraged by Father to open himself to the world, to stay abreast of current events by the more ordinary means of reading various periodicals and newspapers.

He cannot tolerate newspapers. They are unwieldy. The sections become confused; the pages fall out of order.

Worse, the ink. The ink comes off on his hands, as if it is the dirty disorder of the world.

He can wash the ink away with enough soap and hot water in the bathroom that adjoins this chamber, but surely some of it seeps into his pores and thence into his bloodstream. By this means, a newspaper is an agent of contagion, infecting him with the world's disorder.

Among the magazines in the drawer, however, is a story that he tore from a local newspaper three months ago. This is his beacon of hope.

The story concerns a local organization raising research funds to find a cure for autism.

By the strictest definition of the affliction, Randal Six might not have autism. But he suffers from something very much like that sad condition.

Because Father has strongly encouraged him to better understand himself as a first step toward a cure, Randal reads books on the subject. They don't give him the peace he finds in crossword puzzles.

During the first month of his life, when it wasn't yet clear what might be wrong with him, when he had still been able to tolerate newspapers, he read about the local charity for autism research and at once recognized himself in descriptions of the condition. He then realized that he was not alone.

More important, he has seen a photo of another like himself: a boy of twelve, photographed with his sister, a New Orleans police officer.

In the photo, the boy isn't looking at the camera but to one side of it. Randal Six recognizes the evasion.

Incredibly, however, the boy is smiling. He looks happy.

Randal Six has never been happy, not in the four months since he has come out of the creation tank as an eighteen-year-old. Not once. Not for a moment. Occasionally he feels sort of safe . . . but never happy.

Sometimes he sits and stares at the newspaper clipping for hours.

The boy in the photo is Arnie O'Connor. He smiles.

Maybe Arnie is not happy all the time, but he must be happy sometimes.

Arnie has knowledge that Randal needs. Arnie has a secret to happiness. Randal *needs* it so bad he lies awake at night desperately trying to think of some way to get it.

Arnie is in this city, so near. Yet for all practical purposes, he is beyond reach.

In his four months of life, Randal Six has never been outside the walls of Mercy. Just being taken to another floor in this very building for treatment is traumatic.

Another neighborhood of New Orleans is as unaccessible to him as a crater on the moon. Arnie lives with his secret, untouchable.

If only Randal can get to the boy, he will learn the secret of happiness. Perhaps Arnie will not want to share it. That won't matter. Randal will get it from him. Randal will *get* it.

Unlike the vast majority of autistics, Randal Six is capable of extreme violence. His inner rage is almost equal to his fear of the disordered world.

He has hidden this capacity for violence from everyone, even from Father, for he fears that if it is known, something bad will happen to him. He has seen in Father a certain . . . coldness.

He puts the newspaper photo in the drawer once more, under the magazines. In his mind's eye, he stills sees Arnie, smiling Arnie.

Arnie is out there on the moon in New Orleans, and Randal Six is drawn to him like the sea to lunar tides.

CHAPTER 13

IN THE SMALL dimly lighted projection booth, a sprung sofa slumped against one wall, and stacks of paperbacks stood on every flat surface. Evidently Jelly liked to read while the movie ran.

Pointing to a door different from the one by which they had entered, the fat man said, "My apartment's through there. Ben left a special box for you."

While Jelly went to fetch the box, Deucalion was drawn to the old projector, no doubt original to the building. This monstrous piece of machinery featured enormous supply and take-up reels. The 35mm film had to be threaded through a labyrinth of sprockets and guides, into the gap between the high-intensity bulb and the lens.

He studied the adjustment knobs and worked forward until he could peer into the cyclopean eye of the projector. He removed a cover plate to examine the internal gears, wheels, and motors.

Across the balcony, the mezzanine, and the lower seats, this device could cast a bright illusion of life upon the big screen.

Deucalion's own life, in its first decade, had often seemed like a *dark* illusion. With time, however, life had become too real, requiring him to retreat into carnivals, into monasteries.

Returning with an old shoebox full of papers, Jelly halted when he saw Deucalion tinkering with the projector. "Makes me nervous, you messing with that. It's an antique. Hard to get parts or a repairman. That thing is the life's blood of this place."

"It's hemorrhaging." Deucalion replaced the cover to protect the delicate parts. "Logic reveals the secrets of any machine—whether it's a projector, a jet engine, or the universe itself."

"Ben warned me you think too much." Jelly set the shoebox on a stack of entertainment-gossip magazines. "He sent you one newspaper clipping with his letter, right?"

"And it brought me halfway around the world."

Jelly took the lid off the box. "Ben collected lots of this."

Deucalion picked up the top clipping, scanned the photo, then the headline: VICTOR HELIOS GIVES ONE MILLION TO SYMPHONY.

The sight of the man in the photo, virtually unchanged after so much time, jolted Deucalion as before, in the monastery.

SCIMITARS OF LIGHTNING *gut a black-bellied night, and then crashes of thunder shake darkness across the tall casement windows once more. From flickering gas lamps, light capers over the stone walls of a cavernous laboratory. An electric arc crackles between the copper wire-wrapped poles of eldritch equipment. Sparks spray from dangerously overloaded transformers and piston-driven machinery.*

The storm grows more violent, hurling bolt after bolt into the collector rods that stud the tallest towers. The incredible energy is channeled down into—

—him.

He opens his heavy eyelids and sees another's eye magnified by an ocular device resembling a jeweler's loupe. The loupe flips up, and he sees the face of Victor. Young, earnest, hopeful.

In white cap and blood-spattered gown, this creator, this would-be god . . .

HANDS TREMBLING, Deucalion dropped the clipping, which fluttered to the floor of the projection room.

Ben had prepared him for this, but he was shocked anew. Victor alive. *Alive.*

For a century or more, Deucalion had explained his own longevity to himself by the simple fact that he was unique, brought to life by singular means. He might therefore exist beyond the reach of death. He never had a cold, the flu, no ailment or physical complaint.

Victor, however, had been born of man and woman. He should be heir to all the ills of the flesh.

From an inner jacket pocket, Deucalion withdrew a rolled sheet of heavy paper, which he usually kept in his carryall. He slipped the knot of the securing ribbon, unrolled the paper, and stared at it for a moment before showing it to Jelly.

Scrutinizing the pencil portrait, Jelly said, "That's Helios."

"A self-portrait," Deucalion said. "He's . . . talented. I took this from a frame in his study . . . more than two hundred years ago."

Jelly evidently knew enough to receive that statement without surprise.

"I showed this to Ben," Deucalion said. "More than once. That's how he recognized Victor Helios and knew him for who he really is."

Setting aside Victor's self-portrait, Deucalion selected a second clipping from the box and saw a photo of Helios receiving an award from the mayor of New Orleans.

A third clipping: Victor with the district attorney during his election campaign.

A fourth: Victor and his lovely wife, Erika, at a benefit auction.

Victor purchasing a mansion in the Garden District.

Victor endowing a scholarship at Tulane University.

Victor, Victor, *Victor.*

Deucalion did not recall casting aside the clippings or crossing the small room, but he must have done so, for the next thing he knew, he had driven his right fist and then his left into the wall, through the old plaster. As he withdrew his hands, clutching broken lengths of lath, a section of the wall crumbled and collapsed at his feet.

He heard himself roar with anger and anguish, and managed to choke off the cry before he lost control of it.

As he turned to Jelly, Deucalion's vision brightened, dimmed, brightened, and he knew that a subtle pulse of luminosity, like heat lightning behind clouds on a summer night, passed through his eyes. He had seen the phenomenon himself in mirrors.

Wide-eyed, Jelly seemed ready to bolt from the room, but then let out his pent-up breath. "Ben said you'd be upset."

Deucalion almost laughed at the fat man's understatement and aplomb, but he feared that a laugh would morph into a scream of rage. For the first time in many years, he had almost lost control of himself, almost indulged the criminal impulses that had been a part of him from the moment of his creation.

He said, "Do you know what I am?"

Jelly met his eyes, studied the tattoo and the ruin that it only half concealed, considered his hulking size. "Ben . . . he explained. I guess it could be true."

"Believe it," Deucalion advised him. "My origins are a prison graveyard, the cadavers of criminals—combined, revitalized, *reborn.*"

CHAPTER 14

OUTSIDE, THE NIGHT was hot and humid. In Victor Helios's library, the air-conditioning chilled to the extent that a cheerful blaze in the fireplace was necessary.

Fire featured in some of his less pleasant memories. The great windmill. The bombing of Dresden. The Israeli Mossad attack on the secret Venezuelan research complex that he had shared with Mengele in the years after World War II. Nevertheless he liked to read to the accompaniment of a cozy crackling fire.

When, as now, he was perusing medical journals like *The Lancet, JAMA,* and *Emerging Infectious Diseases,* the fire served not merely as ambience but as an expression of his informed scientific opinion. He frequently tore articles from the magazines and tossed them into the flames. Occasionally, he burned entire issues.

As ever, the scientific establishment could teach him nothing. He was far ahead of them. Yet he felt the need to remain aware of advancements in genetics, molecular biology, and associated fields.

He felt the need, as well, for a wine that better complemented the fried walnuts than did the Cabernet that Erika had served with them. Too tannic. A fine Merlot would have been preferable.

She sat in the armchair opposite his, reading poetry. She had become enthralled with Emily Dickinson, which annoyed Victor.

Dickinson had been a fine poet, of course, but she had been God-besotted. Her verses could mislead the naive. Intellectual poison.

Whatever need Erika might have for a god could be satisfied here in this room. Her maker, after all, was her husband.

Physically, he had done a fine job. She was beautiful, graceful, elegant. She looked twenty-five but had been alive only six weeks.

Victor himself, though two hundred and forty, could have passed for forty-five. His youthful appearance had been harder to maintain than hers had been to achieve.

Beauty and grace were not his only criteria for an ideal wife. He also wished her to be socially and intellectually sophisticated.

In this regard, in many small ways, Erika had failed him and had proved slow to learn in spite of direct-to-brain downloads of data that included virtual encyclopedias of etiquette, culinary history, wine appreciation, witticisms, and much else.

Knowledge of a subject did not mean that one could apply that knowledge, of course, but Erika didn't seem to be trying hard enough. The Cabernet instead of the Merlot, Dickinson . . .

Victor had to admit, however, that she was a more appealing and acceptable creature than Erika Three, her immediate predecessor. She might not be the final version—only time would tell—but whatever her faults, Erika Four was not a complete embarrassment.

The drivel in the medical journals and Erika reading Dickinson at last drove him up from his armchair. "I'm in a creative mood. I think I'll spend some time in my studio."

"Do you need my help, darling?"

"No. You stay here, enjoy yourself."

"Listen to this." Her delight was childlike. Before Victor could stop her, she read from Dickinson: "The pedigree of honey / Does not concern the bee / A clover, any time, to him / Is aristocracy."

"Charming," he said. "But for variety, you might read some Thom Gunn and Frederick Seidel."

He could have told her what to read, and she would have obeyed. But he did not desire an automaton for a wife. He wanted her to be free-spirited. Only in sexual matters did he demand utter obedience.

In the immense restaurant-quality kitchen from which staff could serve a sit-down dinner for a hundred without problem, Victor entered the walk-in pantry. The shelves at the back, laden with canned goods, slid aside when he touched a hidden switch.

Beyond the pantry, secreted in the center of the house, lay his windowless studio.

His public labs were at Helios Biovision, the company through which he was known to the world and by which he had earned another fortune atop those he had already accrued in earlier ages.

And in the Hands of Mercy, an abandoned hospital converted to serve his primary work and staffed with men of his making, he pursued the creation of the new race that would replace flawed humanity.

Here, behind the pantry, measuring twenty by fifteen feet, this retreat provided a place for him to work on small experiments, often those on the leading edge of his historic enterprise.

Victor supposed that he was to arcane laboratory equipment what Santa Claus was to gizmo-filled toy workshops.

When Mary Shelley took a local legend based on truth and crafted fiction from it, she'd made Victor a tragic figure and killed him off. He understood her dramatic purpose for giving him a death scene, but he loathed her for portraying him as tragic and as a failure.

Her judgment of his work was arrogant. What else of consequence did *she* ever write? And of the two, who was dead—and who was not?

Although her novel suggested his workplace was a phantasmagoria of gizmos as ominous in appearance as in purpose, she had been vague on details. Not until the first film adaptation of her book did the name Frankenstein become synonymous with the term "mad scientist" and with laboratories buzzing-crackling-humming with frightening widgets, thingums, and doohickeys.

Amusingly, Hollywood had the set design more than half right, not as to the actual machines and objects, but as to ambience. Even the studio behind the pantry had a flavor of Hell with machines.

On the center worktable stood a Lucite tank filled with a milky antibiotic solution. In the tank rested a man's severed head.

Actually, the head wasn't severed. It had never been attached to a body in the first place.

Victor had created it only to serve as a braincase. The head had no hair, and the features were rough, not fully formed.

Support systems serviced it with nutrient-rich, enzyme-balanced, oxygenated blood and drained away metabolic waste through numerous plastic tubes that entered through the neck.

With no need to breathe, the head was almost dead still. But the eyes twitched behind the lids, which suggested that it was dreaming.

The brain within the skull was self-aware but had only the most rudimentary personality, sufficient to the experiment.

Approaching the table, Victor addressed the resident of the open Lucite tank: "Time to work, Karloff."

No one could say that Victor Helios, alias Frankenstein, was a humorless man.

In the head, the eyes opened. They were blue and bloodshot.

Karloff had been selectively educated by direct-to-brain data downloading; therefore, he spoke English. "Ready," he said, his voice thick and hoarse.

"Where is your hand?" Victor asked.

The bloodshot eyes shifted at once to regard a smaller table in a far corner of the room.

There, a living hand lay in a shallow bowl of milky antibiotic solution. As in the case of the head, this five-fingered wonder was served by numerous tubes and by a low-voltage electrical pump that could empower its nerves and, thereby, its musculature.

The systems sustaining the head and those sustaining the hand were independent of each other, sharing no common tubing or wiring.

After reading the status displays on the equipment and making a few adjustments, Victor said, "Karloff, move your thumb."

In the dish, the hand lay motionless. Motionless. And then . . . the thumb twitched, bent at the knuckle, straightened again.

Victor had long sought those genes that might carry the elusive psychic powers that humankind had sometimes experienced but had never been able to control. Recently he had achieved this small success.

This ultimate amputee, Karloff, had just exhibited psychomotor telekenesis, the control of his entirely detached hand strictly by means of mental exertion.

"Give me an arpeggio," Victor said.

In the shallow bowl, the hand raised on the heel of its palm and strummed the air with all fingers, as if plucking at the strings of an invisible harp.

Pleased by this display, Victor said, "Karloff, make a fist."

The hand slowly clenched, tighter, tighter, until the knuckles were sharp and white.

No emotion showed in Karloff's face, yet the hand seemed to be an exquisite expression of anger and the will to violence.

CHAPTER 15

NEW DAY, NEW DEATH. For the second morning in a row, Carson chased breakfast with the discovery of a mutilated corpse.

A TV crew was at the library, hauling gear out of a satellite van, when Carson jammed the brakes, twisted the wheel, and slotted her plainwrap between two black-and-whites that were angled to the curb.

"I break land-speed records getting here," she grumbled, "and the media's already on the scene."

"Bribe the right people," Michael suggested, "and next time you might get the call before Channel 4."

As she and Michael crossed the sidewalk toward the library, a reporter shouted to her, "Detective O'Connor! Is it true the Surgeon cut out a heart this time?"

"Maybe they're so interested," she told Michael, "because none of those bastards *has* a heart."

They hurried up stone steps to the ornate redstone building with gray granite arches and columns.

Admitting them, the police guard at the door said, "It fits the pattern, guys. It's one of his."

"Seven murders in a little over three weeks isn't a pattern anymore," Carson replied. "It's a rampage."

As they entered the reading foyer with the elevated main desk, Michael said, "I should've brought my overdue book."

"You checked out a book? Mr. DVD with a *book*?"

"It was a DVD guide."

Crime-scene techs, police photographers, criminalists, jakes, and personnel from the medical examiner's office served as Indian guides without saying a word. Carson and Michael followed their nods and gestures through a labyrinth of books.

Three quarters of the way along an aisle of stacks, they found Harker and Frye, who were cordoning off the scene with yellow tape.

Establishing that the territory belonged to him and Carson, Michael said, "Yesterday's hand bandit is this morning's thief of hearts."

Frye managed to look greasy *and* blanched. His face had no color. He kept one hand on his expansive gut as if he had eaten some bad pepper shrimp for breakfast.

He said, "Far as I'm concerned, you take the lead on this one. I've lost my taste for the case."

If Harker, too, had a change of heart, his reasons were not identical to Frye's. His face was as boiled red as ever, his eyes as challenging.

Running one hand through his sun-bleached hair, Harker said, "Looks to me like whoever has point position on this is walking a high wire. One mistake on a case this high profile, the media will flush your career down the toilet."

"If that means cooperation instead of competition," Michael said, "we accept."

Carson wasn't as ready as Michael to forgive the toe-tramping they had received from these two, but she said, "Who's the vic?"

"Night security man," Harker said.

While Frye remained behind, Harker ducked under the yellow tape and led them to the end of the aisle, around the corner to another long row of stacks.

The end-stack sign declared ABERRANT PSYCHOLOGY. Thirty feet away, the dead man lay on his back on the floor. The victim looked like a hog halfway through a slaughterhouse.

Carson entered the new aisle but did not proceed into the blood spatter, leaving the wet zone unspoiled for CSI.

As she quietly sized the scene and tried to fit herself to it, planning the approach strategy, Harker said from behind her, "Looks like he cracked the breastbone neat as a surgeon. Went in there with complete professionalism. The guy travels with tools."

Moving to Carson's side, Michael said, "At least we can rule out suicide."

"Almost *looks* like suicide," Carson murmured thoughtfully.

Michael said, "Now, let's remember the fundamentals of this relationship. *You* are the straight man." .

"There was a struggle," Harker said. "The books were pulled off the shelves."

About twenty books were scattered on the floor this side of the dead man. None was open. Some were in stacks of two and three.

"Too neat," she said. "This looks more like someone was *reading* them, then set them aside."

"Maybe Dr. Jekyll was sitting on the floor, researching his own insanity," Michael conjectured, "when the guard discovered him."

"Look at the wet zone," Carson said. "Tightly contained around the body. Not much spatter on the books. No signs of struggle."

"No struggle?" Harker mocked. "Tell that to the guy without a heart."

"His piece is still in his holster," Carson said. "He didn't even draw, let alone get off a shot."

"Chloroform from behind," Michael suggested.

Carson didn't respond at once. During the night, madness had entered the library, carrying a bag of surgical tools. She could hear the soft footsteps of madness, hear its slow soft breathing.

The stench of the victim's blood stirred in Carson's blood a quivering current of fear. Something about this scene, something she could not quite identify, was extraordinary, unprecedented in her experience, and so unnatural as to be almost *super*natural. It spoke first to her emotions rather than to her intellect; it teased her to see it, to know it.

Beside her, Michael whispered, "Here comes that old witchy vision."

Her mouth went dry with fear, her hands suddenly icy. She was no stranger to fear. She could be simultaneously afraid but professional, alert and quick. Sometimes fear sharpened her wits, clarified her thinking.

"Looks more," she said at last, "as if the vic just laid down there and waited to be butchered. Look at his face."

The eyes were open. The features were relaxed, not contorted by terror, by pain.

"Chloroform," Michael suggested again.

Carson shook her head. "He was awake. Look at the eyes. The cast of the mouth. He didn't die unconscious. Look at the hands."

The security guard's left hand lay open at his side, palm up, fingers spread. That position suggested sedation before the murder.

The right hand, however, was clenched tight. Chloroformed, he would have relaxed the fist.

She jotted down these observations in her notebook and then said, "So who found the body?"

"A morning-shift librarian," Harker said. "Nancy Whistler. She's in the women's lav. She won't come out."

CHAPTER 16

THE WOMEN'S REST ROOM smelled of pine-scented disinfectant and White Diamonds perfume. Regular janitorial service was the source of the former, Nancy Whistler of the latter.

A young, pretty woman who put the lie to the stereotypical image of librarians, she wore a clingy summer dress as yellow as daffodils.

She bent to one of the sinks and splashed cold water in her face from a running faucet. She drank from cupped hands, swished the water around her mouth, and spat it out.

"I'm sorry I'm such a mess," she said.

"No problem," Carson assured her.

"I'm afraid to leave here. Every time I think I just *can't* puke again, I do."

"I love this job," Michael told Carson.

"The officers who did a perimeter check tell me there are no signs of forced entry. So you're sure the front door was locked when you arrived for work?" Carson pressed.

"Absolutely. Two deadbolts, both engaged."

"Who else has keys?"

"Ten people. Maybe twelve," said Nancy Whistler. "I can't think names right now."

You could only push a witness so far in the aftermath of her encounter with a bloody corpse. This wasn't a time to be hard-assed.

Carson said, "E-mail a list of keyholders to me. Soon."

"All right, sure. I understand." The librarian grimaced as if she might hurl again. Instead she said, "God, he was such a toad, but he didn't deserve *that*." Michael's raised eyebrows drew an explanation from her: "Bobby Allwine. The guard."

"Define *toad*," Michael requested.

"He was always . . . looking at me, saying inappropriate things. He had a way of coming on to me that was . . . just weird."

"Harassment?"

"No. Nothing forceful. Just weird. As if he didn't *get* a lot of things, the way to act." She shook her head. "And he went to funeral homes for fun."

Carson and Michael exchanged a look, and he said, "Well, who doesn't?"

"Viewings at funeral homes," Whistler clarified. "Memorial services. For people he didn't even know. He went two, three times a week."

"Why?"

"He said he liked to look at dead people in their caskets. Said it . . . relaxed him." She cranked off the water faucet. "Bobby was sort of a geek. But . . . why would someone cut out his heart?"

Michael shrugged. "Souvenir. Sexual gratification. Dinner."

Appalled, repelled, Nancy Whistler bolted for a toilet stall.

To Michael, Carson said, "Oh, nice. Real nice."

CHAPTER 17

PEELING PAINT, crumbling stucco, rusting wrought iron, sagging trumpet vines yellowing in the heat, and a pustulant-looking fungus flourishing in the many cracks in the concrete walkway established a design motif carried out in every aspect of the apartment building.

On the patchy lawn, which looked as if someone had salted it, a sign announced APARTMENT AVAILABLE / ONLY LOSERS NEED APPLY.

Actually, only the first two words were on the sign. The other four didn't have to be spelled out; Carson inferred them from the condition of the place as she parked at the curb.

In addition to the sign, the front lawn actually contained a flock of seven pink flamingos.

"Bet my ass there's a couple plastic gnomes somewhere around here," Michael said.

Someone had painted four of the flamingos other tropical hues—mango green, pineapple yellow—perhaps hoping that a color change would render these lawn ornaments less absurd if not less tacky. The new paint had worn off in places; the pink shone through.

Not because of the implication of borderline poverty but because of the weirdness of the place, it was an ideal building for odd ducks and geeks like Bobby Allwine, he of the stolen heart. They would be drawn here, and in the company of their own kind, no one among them would receive particular attention.

A grizzled old man knelt on the front steps, fixing a railing brace.

"Excuse me. You work here?" Michael asked, flashing his ID.

"No more than I have to." The old man looked Carson up and down appreciatively, but still spoke to Michael. "Who's she?"

"It's bring-your-sister-to-work day at the department. Are you the super here?"

"'Super' don't seem to be a word that fits anyone or anything about this dump. I'm just sort of the jack-of-all around here. You come to see Bobby Allwine's place?"

"News travels fast."

Putting down his screwdriver, getting to his feet, the jack-of-all said, "Good news does. Follow me."

Inside, the public stairwell was narrow, dark, peeling, humid, and malodorous.

The old guy didn't smell so good, either, and as they followed him up to the second floor, Michael said, "I'll never complain about my apartment again."

At the door to 2-D, as he fumbled in his pockets for a passkey, the jack-of-all said, "Heard on the news his liver was cut out."

"It was his heart," Carson said.

"Even better."

"You didn't like Bobby Allwine?"

Unlocking the door, he said, "Hardly knew him. But this makes the apartment worth fifty bucks more." He read their disbelief and assured them, "There's people that'll pay extra."

"Who," Michael asked, "the Addams family?"

"Just people who like some history about a place."

Carson pushed inside the apartment, and when the old man would have followed her, Michael eased him aside and said, "We'll call you when we're done."

The blinds were drawn. The room was uncommonly dark for a bright afternoon.

Carson found the switch for the ceiling fixture and said, "Michael, look at this."

In the living room, the ceiling and walls were painted black. The wood floors, the baseboards, the door and window casings were black, as well. The blinds were black.

The sole piece of furniture was a black vinyl armchair in the center of the room.

Closing the front door behind him, Michael said, "Does Martha Stewart have an emergency design hotline?"

The windows were closed. No air conditioning. The moist heat and the blackness and a tauntingly familiar sweet fragrance made Carson feel slow, stupid.

"What's that smell?" she asked.

"Licorice."

Thick, sweet, pervasive, the aroma was indeed licorice. Though it should have been pleasant, the smell half nauseated Carson.

The black floor had a glossy sheen, unmarred by dust or lint. She wiped a hand along a windowsill, down a door casing, and found no grime.

As it had in the library with Allwine's corpse, fear found Carson, a creeping disquiet that climbed her spine and pressed a cold kiss to the back of her neck.

In the meticulously clean kitchen, Michael hesitated to open the black door of the refrigerator. "This feels like a Jeffrey Dahmer moment, severed heads among the bottles of pickles and mayonnaise, a heart in a OneZip bag."

Even the interior of the refrigerator had been spray-painted black, but it held no heads. Just a coffee cake and a quart of milk.

Most of the cupboards were empty, too. A drawer contained three spoons, two forks, two knives.

According to his employee file, Allwine had lived here for two years. An inventory of his possessions would give the impression that he'd been prepared to leave on a moment's notice and to travel light.

The third room was the bedroom. The ceiling, the walls, and the floor were black. Even the bed and sheets: black. A black nightstand, black lamp, and black radio with glowing green numbers.

"What *is* this place?" Carson wondered.

"Maybe he's a satanist? Or just an over-the-top metal fan."

"No music system. No TV."

Michael found the source of the licorice odor. On the unpadded windowseat sat a tray holding several fat black candles, none burning at the moment. Bending down to sniff, he said, "Scented."

Carson considered the time and effort required to create this unrelieved blackness, and suddenly she thought of Arnie and his Lego castle. Bobby Allwine held a job and interacted with the world, but on some level he was as dysfunctional as her brother.

Arnie was benign, however, whereas judging by the available evidence, Allwine's psychology must be, at the core, malignant.

"This place is worth an extra *hundred* bucks a month," Michael declared.

When Carson switched on the light in the adjacent bathroom, the startling contrast stung her eyes. Paint, floor tile, sink, toilet—everything was a dazzling *white,* assiduously polished. The pungent smell of ammonia allowed no intrusion of the scent of licorice.

Opposite the vanity mirror, hundreds of single-edged razor blades bristled from the wall. Each had been pressed at the same angle into the sheetrock, leaving half of the blade exposed, like a wicked silver fang. Row after row after row of clean, sparkling, unused razor blades.

"Seems like," she said, "the victim was even crazier than his killer."

CHAPTER 18

IN NEW ORLEANS uptown society, formal dinner parties were a political necessity, and Victor took his responsibilities seriously.

Inside the sprawling Garden District mansion, his housekeepers—Christine and Sandra—and his butler, William, had spent the day preparing for the evening's event. They cleaned every room, added flowers and candles, swept the covered porches. Gardeners tended to the lawn, trees, flower beds, and shrubs.

These people were all his creations, made at the Hands of Mercy, and were therefore tireless and efficient.

In the formal dining room, the table was set for twelve with Pratesi linens, Buccelatti silverware, Limoges china, historic Paul Storr silver chargers, and a monumental Storr candelabrum featuring Bacchus and attendants. The sparkle factor was greater—and embodied greater value—than any display case of diamonds at Tiffany's.

The housekeepers and butler awaited their master's inspection. He entered the dining room, already dressed for dinner, and considered the preparations.

"Sandra, you've selected the right china for tonight's guests."

His approval drew a smile from her, though it was uneasy.

"But, William, there are fingerprints on a couple of these glasses."

At once the butler took the indicated glasses away.

Two centerpieces of cream-colored roses flanked the candelabrum, and Victor said of them, "Christine, too much greenery. Strip some of it out to emphasize the blooms."

"I didn't arrange the roses, sir," she said, and seemed to be dismayed to have to reveal that his wife had taken charge of the roses. "Mrs. Helios preferred to do it herself. She read a book on flower arranging."

Victor knew that the staff liked Erika and worried that she should do well.

He sighed. "Redo the arrangements anyway, but don't say anything to my wife." Wistfully, he removed one of the white roses and slowly turned it between thumb and forefinger. He sniffed it, noting that a few of the petals already showed early signs of wilt. "She's so . . . young. She'll learn."

AS THE HOUR drew near, Victor went to the master bedroom suite to determine what had delayed Erika.

He found her in the dressing room, at her vanity. Her shoulder-length bronze hair was as lustrous as silk. The exquisite form and buttery smoothness of her bare shoulders stirred him.

Unfortunately, she had too much enthusiasm for the effects of makeup.

"Erika, you can't improve on perfection."

"I so much want to look nice for you, Victor."

"Then wash most of that stuff off. Let your natural beauty shine through. I've given you everything you need to dazzle."

"How sweet," she said, but she seemed uncertain whether she had been complimented or criticized.

"The city councilman's wife, the university president's wife—none of them will be painted like pop-music divas."

Her smile faltered. Victor believed that directness with a subordinate—or a wife—was always preferable to criticism couched to spare feelings.

Standing close behind her, he slid his hands along her bare shoulders, bent close to smell her hair. He pulled that glorious mane aside, kissed the nape of her neck—and felt her shiver.

He fingered her emerald necklace. "Diamonds would be a better choice. Please change it. For me."

In the vanity mirror, she met his eyes, then lowered her gaze to the array of makeup brushes and bottles before her. She spoke in a whisper: "Your standards for everything are . . . so high."

He kissed her neck again and matched her whisper: "That's why I made you. My wife."

CHAPTER 19

IN THE CAR, on the way to the Quarter for a grab-it dinner in Jackson Square, Carson and Michael ping-ponged the case.

She said, "Allwine wasn't chloroformed."

"We don't have blood results yet."

"Remember his face. He wasn't chloroformed. That makes him and the dry cleaner, Chaterie, the exceptions."

"The other male, Bradford Walden, *was* chloroformed," Michael said. "Otherwise, those three make a set."

"The Surgeon took their internal organs as souvenirs."

"But from the women he only takes ears, feet, hands. . . . Did Nancy Whistler e-mail you that list of people with library keys?"

"Yeah. But after seeing Allwine's apartment, I think he opened the door for the killer, the guy didn't need a key."

"How do you get to that?"

"I don't know. It's just a feeling."

"Let's do some victimology analysis," Michael suggested. "First . . . I've given up on the idea the victims are connected to one another somehow. They're random prey."

"How did you analyze your way to that?"

"Now and then," he said, "I have a feeling of my own."

"Any significance to which body part he takes from any particular victim?"

"Elizabeth Lavenza, swimming without her hands. Are hands of special importance in her life, her work? Is she a pianist? Maybe an artist? Maybe a massage therapist?"

"As you know, she was a clerk in a bookstore."

"Meg Saville, the tourist from Idaho."

"Took her feet."

"She wasn't a ballet dancer. Just a receptionist."

"He takes a nurse's ears, a university student's legs," Carson said. "If there's significance, it's inscrutable."

"He takes the dry cleaner's liver, the bartender's kidney. If he'd carved the bartender's liver, we might build a theory on that."

"Pathetic," she said.

"Totally," he agreed. "The bartender had a Goth lifestyle, and Allwine lived in black. Is that a connection?"

"I didn't get *Goth* from his apartment, just *crazy*."

She parked illegally in Jackson Square, near a Cajun restaurant favored by cops.

Just as they reached the entrance, Harker exited the place with a large bag of takeout, bringing with him the mouthwatering aroma of blackened catfish, reminding Carson that she'd skipped lunch.

As if not in the least surprised to see them, as if picking up in mid-conversation, Harker said, "Word is the mayor might push for a task force as early as the weekend. If we'll be teaming this later, we might as well start swapping thoughts now."

To Harker, Carson said, "Surely you gotta know your reputation. Everyone in the department pegs you and Frye for glory hogs."

"Envy," Harker said dismissively. "We close more cases than anyone."

"Sometimes by popping the suspect," Michael said, referring to a recent officer-involved shooting for which Harker had narrowly avoided being brought up on charges.

Harker's smile was contemptuous. "You want my theory about the library security guard?"

Michael said, "Do I want pancreatic cancer?"

"The black rooms are a death wish," Harker conjectured.

"Damn," Carson said.

"He tried to slash his wrists with each of those razor blades in the bathroom wall," Harker continued. "But he just couldn't find the courage."

"You and Frye went to Allwine's apartment?"

"Yeah. You two," Harker said, "you're *our* babies, and we sometimes feel the need to burp you."

He pushed between them, walked away, glanced back after a few steps. "When you *have* a theory, I'll be happy to listen to it."

To Carson, Michael said, "I've got a short list of hearts *I'd* like to cut out."

CHAPTER 20

AFTER VICTOR LEFT the master suite, Erika slipped into a St. John dress that managed to be sensational yet respectable, subtly sexy but classy.

Standing in front of a full-length mirror in her enormous walk-in closet, which was as big as most master bedrooms, she knew that she looked enchanting, that she would leave an indelible impression on every man at the dinner. Nevertheless, she felt inadequate.

She would have tried other dresses if the first guests had not been scheduled to arrive in mere minutes. Victor expected her to be at his side to greet each arrival, and she dared not fail him.

All of her clothes were behind doors or in drawers along three aisles. She owned literally hundreds of outfits.

She hadn't shopped for any of them. Having created her to his ideal measurements, Victor had purchased everything while she had still been in the tank.

Perhaps he'd bought some of these things for the previous Erika. She didn't like to think about that.

She hoped that someday she would be allowed to shop for herself. When Victor allowed that, she would know she had at last met his standards and earned his trust.

Briefly, she wondered what it would be like not to care what Victor—or anyone—thought of her. To be herself. Independent.

Those were dangerous thoughts. She must repress them.

At the back of the closet, perhaps two hundred pairs of shoes were stored on canted shelves. Although she knew that time was of the essence, she dithered between Gucci and Kate Spade.

Behind her in the closet, something rustled, something thumped.

She turned to look back at the center aisle but saw only closed cherrywood doors behind which hung some of her seasonal wardrobe, and pale yellow carpet. She peeked into the right-hand aisle, then into the left, but they were also deserted.

Refocusing on her dilemma, she finally resolved it by choosing the Kate Spades. Carrying them in one hand, she hurried out of the closet into her dressing room.

Entering, she thought she saw movement from the corner of her eye, on the floor at the open doorway to the bedroom. When she turned her head, nothing was there.

Curious, she went into the bedroom never-theless—just in time to see the silk spread flutter behind something that had just slipped under the king-size bed.

They had no house pets, no dog, no cat.

Victor would be furious if it turned out that a rat had gotten into the house. He had zero tolerance for vermin.

Erika had been made to be cautious of danger but to fear nothing in the extreme—although her programmed respect for her maker came close to fear at times.

If a rat had gotten into the house and if now it hid under the bed, she would not hesitate to snare it and dispose of it.

She set aside the Kate Spades and dropped to her knees beside the bed. She had no doubt that her reflexes were quick enough to snatch a scurrying rat.

When she lifted the spread and looked under the bed, her superb vision required no flashlight. But nothing lurked beneath the boxed springs.

She got to her feet and turned, surveying the room. She sensed that something was here, but she didn't have time to search behind every piece of furniture.

Conscious of time racing rat-fast, she sat on the edge of an armchair, near the fireplace, and pulled on her shoes. They were beautiful, but she would have liked them more if she had bought them herself.

She sat for a moment, listening. Silence. But this was the kind of silence that suggested something might be listening to her as she listened for it.

When she left the master suite for the upstairs hall, she closed the door behind her. It fit tight. Nothing could get under it. If a rat was loose in the bedroom, it couldn't get downstairs to spoil the dinner party.

She descended the grand staircase, and as she reached the foyer, the doorbell rang. The first guests had arrived.

CHAPTER 21

AS ROY PRIBEAUX dressed in black slacks, a pale-blue silk sport jacket, and a white linen shirt for his date with Candace—those *eyes!*—an all-news channel on TV did a segment about the Surgeon.

What an absurd name they had given him. He was a romantic. He was an idealist from a family of idealists. He was a purist. He was many things, but he was not a surgeon.

He knew they were talking about him, though he did not closely follow the media response to his harvests. He hadn't begun his collection of female perfection with the hope that he would become a celebrity. Fame had no appeal for him.

Of course his quest generated public interest for all the wrong reasons. They saw violence, not art. They saw blood, not the work of a dreamer who sought perfection in all things.

He had only contempt for the media and for the audience to which they pandered. Knaves speaking to fools.

Having come from a prominent family of politicians—his father and grandfather had served the city of New Orleans and the state of Louisiana—he had seen with what ease the public could be manipulated by the clever use of envy and fear. His family had been expert at it.

In the process, the Pribeauxs had greatly enriched themselves. His grandfather and father had done so well in public service that Roy himself had never needed to work and never would.

Like great artists during the Renaissance, he had patrons: generations of taxpayers. His inheritance allowed him to devote his life to the pursuit of ideal beauty.

When the TV reporter mentioned the most recent two victims, Roy's attention was suddenly focused by the coupling of an unknown name—Bobby Allwine—with that of Elizabeth Lavenza. He had harvested Elizabeth's lovely hands before consigning the depressingly imperfect remainder of her to the City Park lagoon.

The *heart* had been removed from this Allwine person.

Roy had no interest in hearts. He wasn't about internals. He was about externals. The kind of beauty that moved Roy *was* skin deep.

Furthermore, this Allwine person was a *man*. Roy had no interest in the ideal beauty of men—except in the constant refinement and perfection of his own physique.

Now, standing before the TV, he was further surprised to hear that Allwine was the *third* man whom the Surgeon had murdered. From the others he had taken a kidney and a liver.

These murders were linked to those of the women by the fact that at least one of the male victims had been chloroformed.

Copycat. Misguided imitator. Out there somewhere in New Orleans, an envious fool had been inspired by Roy's murders without understanding the purpose of them.

For a moment, he was offended. Then he realized that the copycat, inevitably less intelligent than Roy himself, would eventually screw up, and the police would pin *all* these killings on the guy. The copycat was Roy's get-out-of-jail-free card.

CHAPTER 22

THE PROJECTION BOOTH might have seemed too small for two men as large—in different ways—as Jelly Biggs and Deucalion. Nevertheless, it became the space they shared when they preferred not to be alone.

The booth was cozy, perhaps because of Jelly's collection of paperback books, perhaps because it felt like a high redoubt above the fray of life.

For extended periods of his long existence, Deucalion had found solitude appealing. One of those periods had ended in Tibet.

Now, with the discovery that Victor was not dead, solitude disturbed Deucalion. He wanted companionship.

As former carnies, he and Jelly had a world of experience in common, tales to tell, nostalgic reminiscences to share. In but one day they found that they fell into easy conversation, and Deucalion suspected that in time they would become true friends.

Yet they fell into silences, as well, for their situation was similar to that of soldiers in a battlefield trench, in the deceptive calm before the mortar fire began. In this condition, they had profound questions to ponder before they were ready to discuss them.

Jelly did his thinking while reading mystery novels of which he was inexpressibly fond. Much of his life, imprisoned in flesh, he had lived vicariously through the police, the private investigators, and the amateur detectives who populated the pages of his favorite genre.

In these mutual silences, Deucalion's reading consisted of the articles about Victor Helios, alias Frankenstein, that Ben had accumulated. He pored through them, trying to accustom himself to the bitter, incredible truth of his creator's continued existence, while also contemplating how best to destroy that pillar of arrogance.

Again and again, he caught himself unconsciously fingering the ruined half of his face until eventually Jelly could not refrain from asking how the damage had been done.

"I angered my maker," Deucalion said.

"We all do," Jelly said, "but not with such consequences."

"My maker isn't yours," Deucalion reminded him.

A life of much solitude and contemplation accustomed Deucalion to silence, but Jelly needed background noise even when reading a novel. In a corner of the projection booth, volume low, stood a TV flickering with images that to Deucalion had no more narrative content than did the flames in a fireplace.

Suddenly something in one of the droning newscast voices caught his attention. *Murders. Body parts missing.*

Deucalion turned up the volume. A homicide detective named Carson O'Connor, beseiged by reporters outside the city library, responded to most of their questions with replies that in different words all amounted to *no comment*.

When the story ended, Deucalion said, "The Surgeon . . . How long has this been going on?"

As a mystery novel aficionado, Jelly was interested in true crime stories, too. He not only knew all the gory details of the Surgeon's murder spree; he also had developed a couple of theories that he felt were superior to any that the police had thus far put forth.

Listening, Deucalion had suspicions of his own that grew from his unique experience.

Most likely, the Surgeon was an ordinary serial killer taking souvenirs. But in a city where the god of the living dead had taken up residence, the Surgeon might be something worse than the usual psychopath.

Returning the clippings to the shoe box, rising to his feet, Deucalion said, "I'm going out."

"Where?"

"To find his house. To see in what style a self-appointed god chooses to live these days."

CHAPTER 23

ILLEGALLY PARKED IN Jackson Square, the hood of the plainwrap sedan served as their dinner table.

Carson and Michael ate corn-battered shrimp, shrimp étouffée with rice, and corn maque choux from take-out containers.

Strolling along the sidewalk were young couples hand-in-hand. Musicians in black suits and porkpie hats hurried past, carrying instrument cases, shouldering between slower-moving older Cajun men in chambray shirts and Justin Wilson hats. Groups of young women showed more skin than common sense, and drag queens enjoyed the goggling of tourists.

Somewhere good jazz was playing. Through the night air wove a tapestry of talk and laughter.

Carson said, "What pisses me off about guys like Harker and Frye—"

"This'll be an epic list," Michael said.

"—is how I let them irritate me."

"They're cheesed off because no one makes detective as young as we did."

"That was three years ago for me. They better adjust soon."

"They'll retire, get shot. One way or another, we'll eventually have *our* chance to be the old cranks."

After savoring a forkful of corn maque choux, Carson said, "It's all about my father."

"Harker and Frye don't care about what your father did or didn't do," Michael assured her.

"You're wrong. Everyone expects that sooner or later it'll turn out I carry the dirty-cop gene, just like they think he did."

Michael shook his head, "I don't for a minute think you carry the dirty-cop gene."

"I don't give a shit what you think, Michael, I *know* what you think. It's what everyone else thinks that makes this job so much harder for me than it ought to be."

"Yeah, well," he said, pretending offense, "I don't give a shit that *you* don't give a shit what I think."

Chagrined, Carson laughed softly. "I'm sorry, man. You're one of a handful of people I *do* care what they think of me."

"You wounded me," he said. "But I'll heal."

"I've worked hard to get where I am." She sighed. "Except where I am is eating another meal on my feet, in the street."

"The food's great," he said, "and I'm glittering company."

"Considering the pay, why *do* we work so hard?"

"We're genuine American heroes."

"Yeah, right."

Michael's cell phone rang. Licking Creole tartar sauce off his lips, he answered the call: "Detective Maddison." When he hung up moments later, he said, "We're invited to the morgue. No music, no dancing. But it might be fun."

CHAPTER 24

CARESSED BY CANDLELIGHT, the chased surfaces of classic silver seemed perpetually about to melt.

With five movers and shakers and their spouses gathered in his dining room, Victor looked forward to stimulating conversation that he could guide subtly into channels that would serve his interests long after the mayor, the city councilman, the university president, and the others had left his table. To Victor, every social occasion was primarily an opportunity to influence political and cultural leaders, discreetly advancing his agenda.

Initially, of course, the talk was of frivolous things, even among such accomplished guests. But Victor fancied himself to be as capable of light chatter as anyone and could enjoy this witty froth because it sharpened his anticipation for meatier discussion.

William and Christine served the soup, the butler holding the tureen while the maid ladled a creamy pink richness into the bowls.

This was Erika's third dinner party in the five weeks since she had risen from the tank, and she exhibited some improvement in her social skills, though less than he had hoped.

He saw her frown as she noticed that the flower arrangements were different from those that she had painstakingly created. She possessed the good sense to say nothing of the change.

When his wife glanced at him, however, Victor said, "The roses are perfect," so she would learn from her error.

City Councilman Watkins, whose once-patrician nose had begun subtly to deform as inhaled cocaine ate away supporting cartilage, used one hand to fan the rising aroma from the bowl to his nostrils. "Erika, the soup smells delicious."

John Watkins's opponent in the next election—Bobby Moreau—was one of Victor's people. With all the dirt about Watkins that Victor could provide, Bobby would romp to victory at the polls. In the months until then, however, it was necessary to flatter Watkins with dinner invitations and to work with him.

"I love lobster bisque," said Pamela Watkins. "Is this your recipe, Erika?"

"No. I found it in a magazine, but I added some spices. I doubt I've improved it, probably the opposite, but I like even lobster bisque to have a little bite."

"Oh, it's divine," the university president's wife declared after her first taste.

This compliment, at once echoed by others, brought a glow of pride to Erika's face, but when she herself raised a spoonful to her mouth, she took it with a soft, protracted slurp.

Appalled, Victor watched her dip the spoon into the bowl once more.

Soup had not been on the menu at either of their previous dinner parties, and Victor had taken a meal with Erika only twice otherwise. Her faux pas surprised and unsettled him.

She sucked in the second spoonful no less noisily than she had the first.

Although none of the guests appeared to notice this ghastly play of tongue and lips, Victor took offense that as his wife she should risk being mocked. Those who might laugh at her behind her back would also laugh at him.

He announced, "The bisque is curdled. William, Christine, please remove it at once."

"Curdled?" the mayor's wife asked, bewildered. "Not mine."

"Curdled," Victor insisted as the servants quickly retrieved the soup bowls. "And you don't want to eat a lobster dish when it might be in any way off."

Stricken, Erika watched as the bowls were removed from the table.

"I'm sorry, Erika," Victor said, into an awkward silence. "This is the first time I've ever found fault with your cooking—or with anything about you."

John Watkins protested, "Mine was delicious."

Although she might not have understood the cause of Victor's action, Erika recovered quickly. "No, John. You've always got my vote for city council. But in culinary matters, I trust Victor. His palate is as refined as any chef's."

Victor felt his clenched jaw relaxing into a genuine smile. In part, Erika had redeemed herself.

CHAPTER 25

THE GRAY VINYL-TILE FLOOR squeaked under Carson's and Michael's shoes. Although subtle, the sounds seemed loud in the otherwise silent hallway.

The forensic pathology unit appeared to be deserted. At this hour, staffing should have been reduced but not this drastically.

They found Jack Rogers where he said he'd be—in Autopsy Room Number 2. With him were the professionally fileted corpse of Bobby Allwine, supine upon a guttered steel table, and a lanky young assistant whom Jack introduced as Luke.

"Trumped up an excuse to send the rest of the night staff home," Jack said. "Didn't want to take a chance of some chatterbox getting a glimpse of what we've got here."

"And what do we have?" Carson asked.

"A miracle," Jack said. "Except I get a squamous feeling, like it's too dark a miracle to have anything to do with God. That's why only Luke and I are here. Luke isn't a gossiping jackass, are you, Luke?"

"No, sir."

Luke's slightly protuberant eyes, long nose, and longer chin gave him a scholarly look, as if books exerted such an attraction on him that they had pulled his features toward the contents of their pages.

Potbellied, with a hound-dog face full of sags and swags that added years to his true age, Jack Rogers looked older now than he usually did. Although his excitement was palpable, his face had a gray tinge.

"Luke's got a good eye for physiological anomalies," Jack said. "He knows his guts."

Luke nodded, taking pride in his boss's praise. "I've just always been interested in viscera since I was a kid."

"With me," Michael said, "it was baseball."

Jack said, "Luke and I completed every phase of the internal xamination. Head, body cavities, neck, respiratory tract—"

"Cardiovascular system," Luke continued, "gastrointestinal tract, biliary tract, pancreas, spleen, adrenals—"

"Urinary tract, reproductive tract, and musculoskeletal system," Jack concluded.

The cadaver on the table certainly appeared to have been well explored.

If the body had not been so fresh, Carson would have wanted to grease her nostrils with Vicks. She could tolerate this lesser stench of violated stomach and intestines.

"Every phase revealed such bizarre anatomy," Jack said, "we're going back through again to see what we might've missed."

"Bizarre? Such as?"

"He had two hearts."

"What do you mean two hearts?"

"Two. The number after one, before three. Uno, *dos*."

"In other words," Luke said earnestly, "twice as many as he should have had."

"We got that part," Michael assured him. "But at the library, we saw Allwine's chest open. You could have parked a Volkswagen in there. If everything's missing, how do you know he had two hearts?"

"For one thing, the associated plumbing," Jack said. "He had the arteries and veins to serve a double pump. The indicators are numerous. They'll all be in my final report. But that's not the only thing weird about Allwine."

"What else?"

"Skull bone's as dense as armor. I burnt out two electric trepanning saws trying to cut through it."

"He had a pair of livers, too," said Luke, "and a twelve-ounce spleen. The average spleen is seven ounces."

"A more extensive lymphatic system than you'll ever see in a textbook," Jack continued. "Plus two organs—I don't even know what they are."

"So he was some kind of freak," Michael said. "He looked normal on the outside. Maybe not a male model, but not the Elephant Man, either. Inside, he's all screwed up."

"Nature is full of freaks," Luke said. "Snakes with two heads. Frogs with five legs. Siamese twins. You'd be surprised how many people are born with six fingers on one hand or the other. But that's not like"—he patted Allwine's bare foot—"our buddy here."

Having trouble getting her mind around the meaning of all this, Carson said, "So what are the odds of this? Ten million to one?"

Wiping the back of his shirt sleeve across his damp brow, Jack Rogers said, "Get real, O'Connor. Nothing like this is possible, period. This isn't mutation. This is *design*."

For a moment she didn't know what to say, and perhaps for the first time ever, even Michael was at a loss for words.

Anticipating them, Jack said, "And don't ask me what I mean by *design*. Damn if I know."

"It's just," Luke elaborated, "that all these things look like they're meant to be . . . improvements."

Carson said, "The Surgeon's other victims . . . you didn't find anything weird in them?"

"Zip, zero, nada. You read the reports."

Such an aura of unreality had descended upon the room that Carson wouldn't have been entirely surprised if the eviscerated cadaver had sat up on the autopsy table and tried to explain itself.

Michael said, "Jack, we'd sure like to embargo your autopsy report on Allwine. File it here but don't send a copy to us. Our doc box is being raided lately, and we don't want anyone else to know about this for . . . say forty-eight hours."

"And don't file it under Allwine's name or the case number where it can be found," Carson suggested. "Blind file it under . . ."

"Munster, Herman," Michael suggested.

Jack Rogers was smart about a lot more things than viscera. The bags under his eyes seemed to darken as he said, "This isn't the only weird thing you've got, is it?"

"Well, you know the crime scene was strange," Carson said.

"That's not all you've got, either."

"His apartment was a freak's crib," Michael revealed. "The guy was as psychologically weird as anything you found inside him."

"What about chloroform?" Carson asked. "Was it used on Allwine?"

"Won't have blood results until tomorrow," Jack said. "But I'm not going out on a limb when I say we won't find chloroform. This guy couldn't have been overcome by it."

"Why not?"

"Given his physiology, it wouldn't have worked as fast on him as on you or me."

"How fast?"

"Hard to say. Five seconds. Ten."

"Besides," Luke offered, "if you tried to clamp a chloroform-soaked cloth over his face, Allwine's reflexes would have been faster than yours . . . or mine."

Jack nodded agreement. "And he would have been *strong*. Far too strong to have been restrained by an ordinary man for a moment, let alone long enough for the chloroform to work."

Remembering the peaceful expression on Bobby Allwine's face when his body lay on the library floor, Carson considered her initial perception that he had welcomed his own murder. She could make no more sense of that hypothesis, however, than she had done earlier.

Moments later, outside in the parking lot, as she and Michael approached the sedan, the light of the moon seemed to ripple through the thick humid air as it might across the surface of a breeze-stirred pond.

Carson remembered Elizabeth Lavenza, handless, floating face-down in the lagoon.

Suddenly she seemed half-drowned in the murky fathoms of this case, and felt an almost panicky need to thrash to the surface and leave the investigation to others.

CHAPTER 26

TO ALL OUTWARD APPEARANCES, Randal Six, Mercy-born and Mercy-raised, has been in various degrees of autistic trance all day, but inwardly he has passed those hours in turmoil.

The previous night, he dreamed of Arnie O'Connor, the boy in the newspaper clipping, the smiling autistic. In the dream, he requested the formula for happiness, but the O'Connor boy mocked him and would not share his secret.

Now Randal Six sits at his desk, at the computer on which he occasionally plays competitive crossword puzzles with gamers in far cities. Word games are not his purpose this evening.

He has found a site on which he can study maps of the city of New Orleans. Because this site also offers a city directory of all property owners, he has been able to learn the address of Detective Carson O'Connor, with whom the selfish Arnie resides.

The number of blocks separating Randal from their house is daunting. So much distance, so many people, untold obstacles, so much *disorder.*

Furthermore, this web site offers three-dimensional maps of the French Quarter, the Garden District, and several other historic areas of the city. Every time he makes use of these more elaborate guides, he is quickly overcome by attacks of agoraphobia.

If he responds with such terror to the *virtual* reality of the cartoon-like dimensional maps, he will be paralyzed by the vastness and chaos of the world itself if ever he steps beyond these walls.

Yet he persists in studying the three-dimensional maps, for he is motivated by intense desire. His desire is to find happiness of the kind that he believes he has seen in the smile of Arnie O'Connor.

In the virtual reality of New Orleans on his computer screen, one street leads to another. Every intersection offers choices. Every block is lined with businesses, residences. Each of them is a choice.

In the real world, a maze of streets might lead him a hundred or a thousand miles. In that journey, he would be confronted with tens of thousands or even hundreds of thousands of *choices*.

The enormity of this challenge overwhelms him once more, and he retreats in a panic to a corner, his back to his room. He cannot move forward. Nothing confronts him except the junction of two walls.

His only choices are to stay facing the corner or turn to the larger room. As long as he doesn't turn, his fear subsides. Here he is safe. Here is order: the simple geometry of two walls meeting.

In time he is somewhat calmed by this pinched vista, but to be fully calmed, he needs his crosswords. In an armchair, Randal Six sits with another collection of puzzles.

He likes crosswords because there are not multiple right choices for each square; only *one* choice will result in the correct solution. All is predestined.

Cross YULETIDE with CHRISTMAS, cross CHRISTMAS with MYRRH. . . . Eventually every square will be filled; all words will be complete and will intersect correctly. The predestined solution will have been achieved. Order. Stasis. Peace.

As he fills the squares with letters, a startling thought occurs to Randal. Perhaps he and the selfish Arnie O'Connor are *predestined* to meet.

If he, Randal Six, is predestined to come face to face with the other boy and to take the precious secret of happiness from him, what seems now like a long harrowing journey to the O'Connor house will prove to be as simple as crossing this small room.

He cannot stop working the crossword, for he desperately needs the temporary peace that its completion will bring him. Nevertheless, as he reads the clues and inks the letters in the empty squares, he considers the possibility that finding happiness by relieving Arnie O'Connor of it might prove to be not a dream but a *destiny*.

CHAPTER 27

DRIVING AWAY FROM the medical examiner's office, into a world transformed by what they had just learned, Carson said, "Two hearts? Strange new organs? Designer freaks?"

"I'm wondering," Michael said, "if I missed a class at the police academy."

"Did Jack smell sober to you?"

"Unfortunately, yeah. Maybe he's nuts."

"He's not nuts."

"People who were perfectly sane on Tuesday sometimes go nuts on Wednesday."

"What people?" she asked.

"I don't know. Stalin."

"Stalin was not perfectly sane on Tuesday. Besides, he wasn't insane, he was evil."

"Jack Rogers isn't evil," Michael said. "If he's not drunk, insane, or evil, I guess we're going to have to believe him."

"You think somehow Luke might be hoaxing old Jack?"

"Luke 'been-interested-in-viscera-since-I-was-a-kid'? First of all, it would be a way elaborate hoax. Second, Jack is smarter than Luke. Third, Luke—he's got about as much sense of humor as a graveyard rat."

A disguise of clouds transformed the full moon into a crescent. The pale flush of streetlamps on glossy magnolia leaves produced an illusion of ice, of a northern climate in balmy New Orleans.

"Nothing is what it seems," Carson said.

"Is that just an observation," Michael asked, "or should I worry about being washed away by a flood of philosophy?"

"My father wasn't a corrupt cop."

"Whatever you say. You knew him best."

"He never stole confiscated drugs out of the evidence lockup."

"The past is past," Michael advised.

Braking to a stop at a red traffic light, she said, "A man's reputation shouldn't have to be destroyed forever by lies. There ought to be a hope of justice, redemption."

Michael chose respectful silence.

"Dad and Mom weren't shot to death by some drug dealer who felt Dad was poaching on his territory. That's all bullshit."

She hadn't spoken aloud of these things in a long time. To do so was painful.

"Dad had discovered something that powerful people preferred to keep secret. He shared it with Mom, which is why she was shot, too. I know he was troubled about something he had seen. I just don't know what it was."

"Carson, we looked at the evidence in his case a hundred times," Michael reminded her, "and we agreed it's too airtight to be real. No file of evidence is ever braided that tight unless it's concocted. In my book, it's proof of a frame. But that's the problem, too."

He was right. The evidence had been crafted not only with the intent of convicting her father postmortem, but to leave no clue as to the identity of those who had crafted it. She had long sought the one loose thread that would unravel it, but no such thread could be found.

As the traffic light turned green, Carson said, "We're not far from my place. I'm sure Vicky's got everything under control, but I feel like I ought to check on Arnie, if that's okay."

"Sure. I could use some of Vicky's bad coffee."

CHAPTER 28

IN THE MASTER BEDROOM of the Helios estate, all was not well.

What Victor wanted from sex exceeded mere pleasure. Furthermore, he did not merely *want* to be satisfied but fully *expected* to be. His expectation was in fact a demand.

According to Victor's philosophy, the world had no dimension but the material. The only rational response to the forces of nature and of human civilization was to attempt to dominate them rather than be humbled by them.

There were serfs and there were masters. He himself would never wear a slave's collar.

If there was no spiritual side to life, then there could be no such thing as love except in the minds of fools; for love is a state of spirit, not of flesh. In his view, tenderness had no place in a sexual relationship.

At its best, sex was a chance for the dominant person to express control of the submissive partner. The fierceness of the dominance and the completeness of the submission led to satisfaction of greater intensity than love could have provided even if love had existed.

Erika Four, like the three before her and like the other brides that he had made for himself, was not a partner in the traditional sense of marriage. To Victor, she was an accoutrement that allowed him to function more effectively in social situations, a defense against the annoyance of women who saw in him the prospect of wealth by marriage, and an instrument of pleasure.

Because pleasure and power were synonymous to him, the intensity of his satisfaction was directly proportional to the cruelty with which he used her. He was often *very* satisfied.

Like all of his modern creations, in a crisis she could block the perception of pain at will. During sex, he did not permit her to do so. Her submission would be more satisfyingly complete and genuine if she were made to suffer.

If he struck her particularly hard, the evidence would be gone in hours, for like all his people, she healed rapidly. Bleeding lasted less than a minute. Cuts healed without scars in a few hours. Bruises sustained in the night would have faded by dawn.

Most of his people were psychologically engineered to be utterly incapable of humiliation, for shame in all its shades grew from an acceptance of the belief that Moral Law lay at the heart of creation. In the war against ordinary humanity, which he would one day launch, he required soldiers without moral compunctions, so certain of their superiority that no ruthlessness would be beyond them.

He allowed Erika humility, however, because from humility arose a quality of innocence. Although he was not entirely sure why this should be the case, the mildest abuse of a delicate sensibility was more thrilling than committing savageries against a woman who lacked all innocence.

He forced her to endure the things that most shamed her because, ironically, the greater her shame and self-disgust, the further she would lower herself and the more obedient she would become. He had made her strong in many ways, but not so strong that he could not break her will and mold her as he wished.

He valued subservience in a wife more if it had been beaten into her than if it had been engineered in the tank, for in the latter case, her slavish obedience felt mechanical and dull.

Although he could remember a time, centuries ago in his youth, when he had felt differently about women and marriage, he could not recall or understand why that young Victor had felt the way he did, what belief had motivated him. He didn't actually try to understand, however, because he had for a long time taken this different road, and there was no going back.

Young Victor had also believed in the power of the human will to bend nature to its desires; and it was that aspect of his early self with which Victor could still identify. All that mattered was the triumph of the will.

What was wrong here in the bedroom was that for once his will failed to bend reality to its desire. He wanted sexual satisfaction, but it eluded him.

His mind kept straying back to the dinner party, to the sight and sound of Erika noisily sucking soup from spoon.

At last he rolled off her, onto his back, defeated.

They stared at the ceiling in silence until she whispered, "I'm sorry."

"Maybe the fault is mine," he said, meaning that perhaps he had made some mistake in the creation of her.

"I don't excite you."

"Usually, yes. Not tonight."

"I'll learn," she promised. "I'll improve."

"Yes," he said, for that was what she must do if she hoped to keep her role, but he had begun to doubt that Erika Four would be the final Erika.

"I'm going to the hospital," he said. "I'm in a creative mood."

"The Hands of Mercy." She shuddered. "I think I dream of it."

"You don't. I spare all of you from dreams of your origins."

"I dream of someplace," she persisted. "Dark and strange and full of death."

"There's your proof that it's not the Hands of Mercy. My labs are full of life."

Both bored with Erika and troubled by the direction of her musings, Victor rose from the bed and went naked into the bathroom.

A jewel in this mounting of gold-plated fixtures and marble-clad walls, he looked at himself in the beveled mirrors and saw something much more than human.

"Perfection," he said, though he knew that he was just shy of that ideal.

Looping through his torso, embedded in his flesh, entwining his ribs, spiraling around his spine, a flexible metallic cord and its associated implants converted simple electrical current—to which he submitted himself twice a day—into a different energy, a stimulating charge that sustained a youthful rate of cellular division and held biological time at bay.

His body was a mass of scars and strange excrescences, but he found them beautiful. They were the consequences of the procedures by which he'd gained immortality; they were the badges of his divinity.

One day he would clone a body from his DNA, enhance it with the many improvements he had developed, expedite its growth, and with the assistance of surgeons of his making, he'd have his brain transferred to that new home.

When that work was finished, he would be the model of physical perfection, but he would miss his scars. They were proof of his persistence, his genius, and the triumph of his will.

Now he got dressed, looking forward to a long night in his main laboratory at the Hands of Mercy.

CHAPTER 29

WHILE CARSON CHECKED on her castle-building brother, Michael stood at a kitchen counter with a mug of Vicky's coffee.

Having just finished cleaning the oven, Vicky Chou said, "How's the java?"

"As bitter as bile," he said.

"But not acidic."

"No," he admitted. "I don't know how you manage to make it bitter without it being acidic, but you do."

She winked. "My secret."

"Stuff's as black as tar. This isn't a mistake. You actually *try* to get it like this, don't you?"

"If it's so terrible," she said, "why do you always drink it?"

"It's a test of my manhood." He took a long swallow that made his face pucker. "I've been doing a lot of thinking lately, but you'll tell me to shut up, you don't want to know."

Washing her hands at the sink, she said, "I *have* to listen to you, Michael. It's part of my job description."

He hesitated but then said, "I've been thinking how things might be if Carson and I weren't partners."

"What things?"

"Between her and me."

"Is there something between you and her?"

"The badge," he said mournfully. "She's too solid a cop, too professional to date a partner."

"The bitch," Vicky said drily.

Michael smiled, sampled the coffee, grimaced. "Problem is, if I changed partners so we could date, I'd miss kicking ass and busting heads together."

"Maybe that's how the two of you relate best."

"There's a depressing thought."

Vicky clearly had more to say, but she clammed up when Carson entered the kitchen.

"Vicky," Carson said, "I know you're good about keeping doors locked. But for a while, let's be even more security conscious."

Frowning, Vicky asked, "What's wrong?"

"This weird case we're on . . . it feels like . . . if we're not careful, it could come home to us, right here." She glanced at Michael. "Does that sound paranoid?"

"No," he said, and finished the rest of the bitter coffee as though the taste of it would make their unsatisfying relationship seem sweeter by comparison.

IN THE CAR AGAIN, as Carson swung away from the curb, Michael popped a breath mint in his mouth to kill the sour stench of Vicky's death brew. "Two hearts . . . organs of unknown purpose . . . I can't get *Invasion of the Body Snatchers* out of my head, pod people growing in the basement."

"It's not aliens."

"Maybe not. Then I think . . . weird cosmic radiation, pollution, genetic engineering, too much mustard in the American diet."

"Psychological profiles and CSI techs won't be worth a damn on this one," Carson said. She yawned. "Long day. Can't think straight anymore. What if I just drive you home and we call it a wrap?"

"Sounds swell. I've got a new pair of monkey-pattern jammies I'm eager to try on."

She took a ramp to the expressway, headed west toward Metairie. The traffic was mercifully light.

They rode in silence for a while, but then he said, "You know, if you ever want to petition the chief of detectives to reopen your dad's case and let us take a whack at it, I'm game."

She shook her head. "Wouldn't do it unless I had something new—a fresh bit of evidence, a different slant on the investigation, something. Otherwise, we'd just be turned down."

"We sneak a copy of the file, review the evidence on our own time, look into it until we turn up the scrap we need."

"Right now," she said wearily, "we don't really have any time of our own."

As they exited the expressway, he said, "The Surgeon case will break. Things will ease up. Just remember, I'm ready when you are."

She smiled. He loved her smile. He didn't see enough of it.

"Thanks, Michael. You're a good guy."

He would have preferred to hear her say that he was the love of her life, but "good guy" was at least a starting point.

When she pulled to the curb in front of his apartment house, she yawned again and said, "I'm beat. Exhausted."

"So exhausted, you can't wait to go straight back to Allwine's apartment."

Her smile was smaller this time. "You read me too well."

"You wouldn't have stopped to check on Arnie if you intended to go home after dropping me off."

"I should know better than to bullshit a homicide dick. It's those black rooms, Michael. I need . . . to work them alone."

"Get in touch with your inner psychic."

"Something like that."

He got out of the car, then leaned in through the open door. "Ditch the twelve-hour days, Carson. There's no one you've got to prove anything to. Not anyone on the force. Not your dad."

"There's me."

He closed the door and watched her drive away. He knew that she was tough enough to take care of herself, but he worried about her.

He almost wished that she were more vulnerable. It half broke his heart that she didn't need him desperately.

CHAPTER 30

ROY PRIBEAUX ENJOYED the date more than he expected. Usually it was an annoying interlude between the planning of the murder and the commission of it.

Candace proved to be shy but charming, genuinely sweet with a dry, self-deprecating sense of humor.

They had coffee in a riverfront café. When they fell at once into easy conversation about a host of subjects, Roy was surprised but also pleased. The lack of any initial awkwardness would more quickly disarm the poor thing.

After a while she asked him exactly what he'd meant the previous night when he'd called himself *a Christian man*. Of what denomination, what commitment?

He knew at once that this was the key with which to unlock her trust and win her heart. He had used the Christian gambit in a couple of other instances, and with the right woman, it had worked as well as the expectation of great sex or even of love.

Why he, an Adonis, should be interested in a schlump like her— that mystery fed her suspicion. It made her wary.

If she believed, however, that he was a man of genuine moral principle who sought a virtuous companion and not just a good hump, she would see him as one with higher standards than physical beauty. She would convince herself that her lovely eyes were enough physical beauty for him and that what he really prized was her innocence, her chastity, her personality, and her piety.

The trick was to divine the brand of Christianity that she had embraced, then convince her that they shared that particular flavor of the faith. If she was a Pentecostal, his approach would have to be far different from that required if she was a Catholic, and *much* different from the worldly and ironic style that he must assume if she was Unitarian.

Fortunately, she proved to be an Episcopalian, which Roy found markedly easier to fake than one of the more passionate sects. He might have been lost if she'd been a Seventh Day Adventist.

She proved to be a reader, too, and especially a fan of C. S. Lewis, one of the finest Christian writers of the century just past.

In his quest to be a Renaissance man, Roy had read Lewis: not all of his many books, but enough. *The Screwtape Letters. The Problem of Pain. A Grief Observed.* Thankfully they had been short volumes.

Dear Candace was so enchanted to have a handsome and interested man as a conversationalist that she overcame her shyness when the subject turned to Lewis. She did most of the talking, and Roy needed only to insert a quote here and a reference there to convince her that his knowledge of the great man's work was encyclopedic.

Another fortunate thing about her being an Episcopalian was that her denomination did not forbid drink or the joy of sensuous music. From the café, he talked her into a jazz club on Jackson Square.

Roy had a capacity for alcohol, but one potent hurricane erased whatever lingering caution Candace might otherwise have harbored.

After the jazz club, when he suggested they take a walk on the levee, her only concern was that it might be closed at this hour.

"It's still open to pedestrians," he assured her. "They just don't keep it lit for the roller skaters and fishermen."

Perhaps she would have hesitated to stroll the unlighted levee if he hadn't been such a strong man, and so good, and capable of protecting her.

They walked toward the river, away from the shopping district and the crowds. The full moon provided more light than he would have liked but also enough to allay any of Candace's lingering concern about their safety.

A brightly decorated riverboat chattered by, its great paddle wheel splashing through warm water. Passengers stood on the decks, sat at tables. This late-night river cruise wouldn't stop at any nearby docks. Roy had checked the schedules, always planning ahead.

They ambled to the end of the pavement atop the breakwater of boulders. Fishermen were more likely to come this far in daylight. As he expected, here in the night, he and Candace were alone.

The lights of the receding riverboat painted serpentine ribbons of oily color on the dark water, and Candace thought this was pretty, and in fact so did Roy, and they watched it for a moment before she turned to him, expecting a chaste kiss, or even one not so chaste.

Instead, he squirted her in the face with the squeeze bottle of chloroform that he had withdrawn from a jacket pocket.

He had found this saturation technique to be far quicker, more effective, and less of a struggle than a soaked cloth. The fluid penetrated her nostrils, splashed her tongue.

Choking, gasping for breath and thereby inhaling the anesthetic, Candace dropped as suddenly and as hard as if she had been shot.

She fell on her side. Roy rolled her onto her back and knelt next to her.

Even in the insistent silvery moonlight, they presented a low profile to anyone who might look this way from a craft on the river. Glancing back the way they had come, Roy saw no other late strollers.

From an inside jacket pocket, he produced a stiletto and a compact kit of scalpels and other instruments.

He didn't need larger tools for this one. The eyes would be simple to extract, though he must be careful not to damage the part of them that he considered to be perfectly beautiful.

With the stiletto, he found her heart and conveyed her from sleep to death with only the faintest liquid sound.

Soon the eyes were his, safely in a small plastic bottle full of saline solution.

On his way back to the lights and the jazz, he was surprised when he suddenly had a taste for cotton candy, not a treat that he had ever before craved. But of course the red wagon was closed and might not open for days.

CHAPTER 31

A NINETEENTH-CENTURY stonemason had chiseled HANDS OF MERCY into a limestone block above the hospital entrance. A weathered image of the Virgin Mary overlooked the front steps.

The hospital had closed long ago, and after the building had been sold to a shell corporation controlled by Victor Helios, the windows had been bricked shut. Steel doors had been installed at every entrance, equipped with both mechanical and electronic locks.

A tall wrought-iron fence surrounded the oak-shaded property, like a stockpile of spears from a full Roman legion. To the rolling electric gate was affixed a sign: PRIVATE WAREHOUSE / NO ADMITTANCE.

Hidden cameras surveyed the grounds, the perimeter. No nuclear weapons storage depot had a larger or more dedicated security force, or one more discreet.

The forbidding structure stood silent. No beam of light escaped it, though here the new rulers of the Earth were designed and made.

A staff of eighty lived and worked within these walls, assisting in experiments in a maze of laboratories. In rooms that had once held hospital patients, newly minted men and women were housed and rapidly educated until they could be infiltrated into the population of the city.

The armored doors of certain other rooms were locked. The creations within them needed to be restrained while being studied.

Victor conducted his most important work in the main laboratory. This vast space had a techno sensibility with some Art Deco style and a dash of Wagnerian grandeur. Glass, stainless steel, white ceramic: All were easy to sterilize if things got . . . messy.

Sleek and arcane equipment, much of which he himself designed and built, lined the chamber, rose out of the floor, depended from the ceiling. Some of the machines hummed, some bubbled, some stood silent and menacing.

In this windowless lab, if he put his wristwatch in a drawer, he could labor long hours, days, without a break. Having improved his physiology and metabolism to the point that he needed little or no sleep, he was able to give himself passionately to his work.

Tonight, as he arrived at his desk, his phone rang. The call came on line five. Of eight lines, the last four—rollovers that served a single number—were reserved for messages and inquiries from those creations with which he had been gradually populating the city.

He picked up the handset. "Yes?"

The caller, a man, was struggling to repress the emotion in his voice, more emotion than Victor ever expected to hear from one of the New Race: "Something is happening to me, Father. Something strange. Maybe something wonderful."

Victor's creations understood that they must contact him only in a crisis. "Which one are you?"

"Help me, Father."

Victor felt diminished by the word *father*. "I'm not your father. Tell me your name."

"I'm confused . . . and sometimes scared."

"I asked for your name."

His creations had not been designed to have the capability to deny him, but this one refused to identify himself: "I've begun to *change*."

"You must tell me your *name*."

"Murder," said the caller. "Murder . . . excites me."

Victor kept the growing concern out of his voice. "No, your mind is fine. I don't make mistakes."

"I'm changing. There's so much to learn from murder."

"Come to me at the Hands of Mercy."

"I don't think so. I've killed three men . . . without remorse."

"Come to me," Victor insisted.

"Your mercy won't extend to one of us who has . . . fallen so far."

A rare queasiness overcame Victor. He wondered if this might be the serial killer who enchanted the media. One of his own creations, breaking programming to commit murder *for no authorized reason?*

"Come to me, and I'll provide whatever guidance you need. There is only compassion for you here."

The electronically disguised voice denied him again. "The most recent one I killed . . . was one of yours."

Victor's alarm grew. One of his creations killing another *by its own decision.* Never had this happened before. A programmed injunction against suicide was knit tightly into their psyches, as was a stern commandment that permitted murder for just two reasons: in self-defense or when instructed by their maker to kill.

"The victim," Victor said. "His name?"

"Allwine. They found his corpse inside the city library this morning."

Victor caught his breath as he considered the implications.

The caller said, "There was nothing to learn from Allwine. He was like me inside. I've got to find it elsewhere, in others."

"Find what?" Victor asked.

"What I need," said the caller, and then hung up.

Victor keyed in *69—and discovered that the caller's phone was blocked for automatic call-back.

Furious, he slammed down the handset.

He sensed a setback.

CHAPTER 32

FOR A WHILE AFTER Victor left for the Hands of Mercy, Erika remained in bed, curled in the fetal position that she'd never known in the creation tank. She waited to see if her depression would pass or thicken into the darker morass of discouragement.

The flux of her emotional states sometimes seemed to have little relation to the experiences from which they proceeded. After sex with Victor, depression always followed without fail, and understandably; but when it *should* have ripened into something like despondency, it sometimes did not. And though her future seemed so bleak that her despondency should have been unshakable, she often shook it off.

Remembering verses by Emily Dickinson could lift her out of gloom: *"Hope" is the thing with feathers— / That perches in the soul— / And sings the tune without the words— / And never stops at all.*

The art on Victor's walls was abstract: oddly juxtaposed blocks of color that loomed oppressively, spatterings of color or smears of gray on black that to Erika seemed like chaos or nullity. In his library, however, were large books of art, and sometimes her mood could be improved simply by immersing herself in a single painting by Albert Bierstadt or Childe Hassam.

She has been taught that she is of the New Race, posthuman, improved, superior. She is all but impervious to disease. She heals rapidly, almost miraculously.

Yet when she needs solace, she finds it in the art and music and poetry of the mere humanity that she and her kind are intended to replace.

When she has been confused, has felt lost, she's found clarity and direction in the writings of imperfect humanity. And the writers are those of whom Victor would especially disapprove.

This puzzles Erika: that a primitive and failed species, infirm humanity, should by its works lift her heart when none of her own kind is able to lift it for her.

She would like to discuss this with others of the New Race, but she is concerned that one of them will think her puzzlement makes her a heretic. All are obedient to Victor by design, but some view him with such reverential fear that they will interpret her questions as doubts, her doubts as betrayals, and will then in turn betray her to her maker.

And so she keeps her questions to herself, for she knows that in a holding tank waits Erika Five.

Abed, with the smell of Victor lingering in the sheets, Erika finds this to be one of the times when poetry will prevent depression from ripening toward despair. *If I shouldn't be alive / When the Robins come / Give the one in Red Cravat / A Memorial crumb.*

She smiled at Dickinson's gentle humor. That smile might have led to others if not for a scrabbling noise under the bed.

Throwing back the sheets, she sat up, breath held, listening.

As though aware of her reaction, the scrabbler went still—or if not still, at least silent, creeping now without a sound.

Having neither heard nor seen any indication of a rat when she and Victor had returned to the bedroom following the departure of their guests, Erika had assumed that she'd been mistaken in thinking one had been here. Or perhaps it had found its way into a wall or a drain and from there to another place in the great house.

Either the vermin was back or it had been here all along, quiet witness to the terrible tax Victor placed upon Erika's right to live.

A moment passed, and then a sound issued from elsewhere in the room. A short-lived furtive rustle.

Shadows veiled the room, were lifted only where the light of a single bedside lamp could reach.

Naked, Erika slipped out of bed and stood, poised and alert.

Although her enhanced eyes made the most of available light, she lacked the penetrating night vision of a cat. Victor was conducting cross-species experiments these days, but she was not one of them.

Desirous of more light, she moved toward a reading lamp beside an armchair.

Before she reached the lamp, she sensed more than heard a thing on the floor scurry past her. Startled, she pulled her left foot back, pivoted on her right, and tried to sight the intruder along the path that instinct told her it must have taken.

When there was nothing to be seen—or at least nothing that she could see—she continued to the reading lamp and switched it on. More light revealed nothing that she hoped to find.

A clatter in the bathroom sounded like the small waste can being knocked over.

That door stood ajar. Darkness lay beyond.

She started toward the bathroom, moving quickly but coming to a stop short of the threshold.

Because members of the New Race were immune to most diseases and healed rapidly, they were afraid of fewer things than were ordinary human beings. That didn't mean they were utter strangers to fear.

Although hard to kill, they were not immortal, and having been made in contempt of God, they could have no hope of a life after this one. Therefore, they feared death.

Conversely, many of them feared *life* because they had no control of their destinies. They were indentured servants to Victor, and there was no sum they could work off to gain their freedom.

They feared life also because they could not surrender it if the burden of serving Victor became too great. They had been created with a deeply embedded psychological injunction against suicide; so if the void appealed to them, they were denied even that.

Here but a step from the bathroom threshold, Erika experienced another kind of fear: of the unknown.

That which is abnormal to nature is a monster, even if it might be beautiful in its way. Erika, created not by nature but by the hand of man, was a lovely monster but a monster nonetheless.

She supposed that monsters should not fear the unknown because, by any reasonable definition, they were part of it. Yet a tingle of apprehension traced the contours of her spine.

Instinct told her that the rat was not a rat, that instead it was a thing unknown.

From the bathroom came a *clink,* a clatter, a metallic rattle, as if something had opened a cabinet and set about exploring the contents in the dark.

Erika's two hearts beat faster. Her mouth went dry. Her palms grew damp. In this vulnerability, but for the double pulse, she was so human, regardless of her origins.

She backed away from the bathroom door.

Her blue silk robe was draped over the armchair. With her gaze fixed on the bathroom door, she slipped into the robe and belted it.

Barefoot, she left the suite, closing the hall door behind her.

As the midnight hour came, she descended through the house of Frankenstein, to the library where, among the many volumes of human thought and hope, she felt safer.

CHAPTER 33

AT VICTOR'S SUMMONS, they came to him in the main lab, two young men as ordinary in appearance as any in New Orleans.

Not all the men of the New Race were handsome. Not all the women were beautiful.

For one thing, when at last he had secretly seeded enough of his creations in society to exterminate the Old Race, humanity would put up a better defense if it could identify its enemy by even the most subtle telltales of appearance. If all members of the New Race looked like gorgeous fodder for the box-office battlefields of Hollywood, their beauty would make them objects of suspicion, subject them to testing and interrogation, and ultimately expose them.

Their infinite variety, on the other hand, would ensure the winning of the war. Their variety, their physical superiority, and their ruthlessness.

Besides, though he sometimes crafted specimens breathtaking in appearance, this enterprise was not fundamentally about beauty. It was at root about power and the establishment of a New Truth.

Consequently, the young men he summoned might be considered extraordinary in appearance only because, considering what they were inside, they looked so common. Their names were Jones and Picou.

He told them about Bobby Allwine in a drawer at the morgue. "His body must disappear tonight. And all confirming evidence—tissue samples, photographs, video."

"The autopsy report, tape recordings?" asked Jones.

"If they're easily found," Victor said. "But by themselves, they confirm nothing."

Picou said, "What about the medical examiner, anyone who might have been there when the body was opened?"

"For now, let them live," Victor said. "Without the body or any evidence, all they'll have is a wild story that'll make them sound like drunks or druggies."

Although they were intellectually capable of greater work than this garbage detail, neither Jones nor Picou complained or found their assignments demeaning. Their patient obedience was the essence of the New Race.

In the revolutionary civilization that Victor was making, as in Aldous Huxley's *Brave New World,* everyone in the social order would have a rank. And all would be content, without envy.

Huxley ordered his world with Alphas at the top, the ruling elite, followed by Betas and Gammas. Brute laborers were designated Epsilons, born to their positions in a designed society.

To Huxley, this vision had been a dystopia. Victor saw it more clearly: utopia.

He'd once met Huxley at a cocktail party. He considered the man to be an officious little prig who worried ridiculously about science becoming a juggernaut and more dogmatic than any religion could hope to be, crushing everything human from humanity. Victor found him to be rich in book knowledge, light on experience, and boring.

Nevertheless, Huxley's nightmare vision served well as Victor's ideal. He would make the Alpha class almost equal to himself, so they would be challenging company and capable of carrying out his plans for the day after humanity had been liquidated, when the Earth would serve as a platform for great accomplishments by a race of posthumans who would work together as industriously as a *hive.*

Now these two Epsilons, Oliver Jones and Byron Picou, set out like two good worker bees, eager to fulfill the roles for which they had been designed and built. They would steal Allwine's remains and dispose of them in a landfill that operated in higher ground outside the city.

The landfill was owned by Victor through another shell company, and it employed only members of the New Race. He regularly required a secure disposal site to bury forever those interesting but failed experiments that must never be discovered by ordinary humans.

Under those mountains of garbage lay a city of the dead. If ever they fossilized and were excavated by paleontologists a million years hence, what mysteries they would present, what nightmares they would inspire.

Although problems existed with the comparatively small hive—as yet only two thousand of the New Race—that he had established here in New Orleans, they would be solved. Week by week he made advances in his science and increased the number in his implacable army. He would soon begin to mass produce the tanks, creating his people not in a laboratory but by the many thousands in much larger facilities that might accurately be called *farms.*

The work was endless but rewarding. The Earth had not been made in a day, but he had the necessary patience to *re*make it.

Now he was thirsty. From a lab refrigerator, he got a Pepsi. A little plate of chocolate chip cookies was in the fridge. He adored chocolate chip cookies. He took two.

CHAPTER 34

SOMEONE HAD PUT a police seal on Bobby Allwine's apartment door. Carson broke it.

This was a minor infraction, considering that the place was not actually a crime scene. Besides, she was, after all, a cop.

Then she used a Lockaid lock-release gun, sold only to police agencies, to spring the deadbolt. She eased the thin pick of the gun into the keyway, under the pin tumblers, and pulled the trigger. She pulled it four times before lodging all the pins at the shear line.

The Lockaid gun was more problematic than breaking the seal. The department owned several. They were kept in the gun locker with spare weapons. You were supposed to requisition one, in writing, through the duty officer each time that you had a legal right to use it.

No detective was authorized to carry a Lockaid gun at all times. Because of a screwup in the requisition process, Carson had come into permanent possession of one—and chose not to reveal that she had it.

She had never used it in violation of anyone's rights, only when it was legal and when precious time would be saved by dispensing with a written requisition. In the current instance, she couldn't violate the rights of Bobby Allwine for the simple reason that he was dead.

Although she liked those old movies, she wasn't a female Dirty Harry. She'd never yet bent a rule far enough to break it, not in a situation of true importance.

She could have awakened the superintendent and gotten a pass key. She would have enjoyed rousting the rude old bastard from his bed.

However, she remembered how he'd looked her up and down, licking his lips. Without Michael present, roused from sleep perhaps induced by wine, the super might try to play grab-ass.

Then she would have to reacquaint him with the effect of a knee to the gonads. That might necessitate an arrest, when all she wanted was to meditate on the meaning of Allwine's black-on-black apartment.

She switched on the living-room ceiling fixture, closed the door behind her, and put the Lockaid gun on the floor.

At midnight, even with a light on, the blackness of the room proved so disorienting that she had half an idea what an astronaut might feel during a space walk, tethered to a shuttle, on the night side of Earth.

The living room offered nothing but the black vinyl armchair. Because it stood alone, it seemed a little like a throne, one that had been built not for earthly royalty but for a middle-rank demon.

Although Allwine had not been killed here, Carson sensed that getting a handle on the psychology of this particular victim would contribute to her understanding of the Surgeon. She sat in his chair.

Harker claimed that the black rooms expressed a death wish, and Carson grudgingly conceded that his interpretation made sense. Like a stopped clock, Harker could be right now and then, although not as often as twice a day.

A death wish did not, however, entirely explain either the décor or Allwine. This black hole was also about *power,* just as real black holes, in far reaches of the universe, exert such gravitational pull that not even light can escape them.

These walls, these ceilings, these floors had not been painted by a man in a state of despair; despair enervated and did not inspire action. She could more easily imagine Allwine blackening these walls in an energetic anger, in a frenzy of rage.

If that was true, then at what had his rage been directed?

The arms of the chair were wide and plumply padded. Under her hands, she felt numerous punctures in the vinyl.

Something pricked her right palm. From the padding beneath a puncture, she extracted a pale crescent: a broken-off fingernail.

A closer look revealed scores of curved punctures.

The chair and the room chilled her as deeply as if she had been sitting on a block of ice in a cooler.

Carson hooked her hands, spread her fingers. She discovered that each of her nails found a corresponding slit in the vinyl.

The upholstery was thick, tough, flexible. Extreme pressure would have been required for fingernails to puncture it.

Logically, despair would not produce the intensity of emotion needed to damage the vinyl. Even rage might not have been sufficient if Allwine had not been, as Jack Rogers had said, inhumanly strong.

She rose, wiping her hands on her jeans. She felt unclean.

In the bedroom, she switched on the lights. The pervasive black surfaces soaked up the illumination.

Someone had opened one of the black blinds. The apartment was such a grim world unto itself that the streetlamps, the distant neon, and the glow of the city seemed out of phase with Allwine's realm, as if they should have existed in different, isolated universes.

Beside the bed, she opened the nightstand drawer, where she discovered Jesus. His face looked out at her from a litter of small pamphlets, His right hand raised in blessing.

From among perhaps a hundred pamphlets, she selected four and discovered that they were memorial booklets of the kind distributed to mourners at funerals. The name of the deceased was different on each, though all came from the Fullbright Funeral Home.

Nancy Whistler, the librarian who had found Allwine's body, said he went to mortuary viewings because he felt at peace there.

She pocketed the four booklets and closed the drawer.

The smell of licorice hung on the air as thick as it had been earlier in the day. Carson couldn't shake the disturbing idea that someone had recently been burning the black candles that stood on a tray on the windowseat.

She crossed to the candles to feel the wax around the wicks, half expecting it to be warm. No. Cold and hard, all of them.

Her impression of the scene beyond the window was unnerving but entirely subjective. Enduring New Orleans hadn't changed. In the grip of creeping paranoia, however, she saw not the festive city that she knew, but an ominous metropolis, an alien place of unnatural angles, throbbing darkness, eerie light.

A reflection of movement on the glass pulled her focus from the city to the surface of the pane. A tall figure stood in the room behind her.

She reached under her jacket, placing her hand upon the 9mm pistol in her shoulder holster. Without drawing it, she turned.

The intruder was tall and powerful, dressed in black. Perhaps he had entered from the living room or from the bathroom, but he seemed to have materialized out of the black wall.

He stood fifteen feet away, where shadows hid his face. His hands hung at his sides—and seemed as big as shovels.

"Who're you?" she demanded. "Where'd you come from?"

"You're Detective O'Connor." His deep voice had a timbre and a resonance that in another man would have conveyed only self-assurance but that, combined with his size, suggested menace. "You were on TV."

"What're you doing here?"

"I go where I want. In two hundred years, I've learned a great deal about locks."

His implication left Carson no choice but to draw her piece. She pointed the muzzle at the floor, but said, "That's criminal trespass. Step into the light."

He did not move.

"Don't be stupid. Move. Into. The. Light."

"I've been trying to do that all my life," he said as he took two steps forward.

She could not have anticipated his face. Handsome on the left, somehow *wrong* on the right side. Over that wrongness, veiling it, was an elaborate design reminiscent of but different from a Maori tattoo.

"The man who lived here," the intruder said, "was in despair. I recognize his pain."

Although he had already stopped, he *loomed* and could have been upon her in two strides, so Carson said, "That's close enough."

"He was not made of God . . . and had no soul. He agonized."

"You have a name? Very carefully, very slowly, show me some ID."

He ignored her order. "Bobby Allwine had no free will. He was in essence a slave. He wanted to die but couldn't take his own life."

If this guy was correct, Harker had nailed it. Each razor blade in the bathroom wall marked a failed attempt at self-destruction.

"We have," the intruder said, "a built-in proscription against suicide."

"We?"

"Allwine was full of fury, too. He wanted to kill his maker. But we are also designed to be incapable of raising a hand against him. I tried long ago . . . and he nearly killed me."

Every modern city has its crazies, and Carson thought she knew all the tropes, but this guy had a different edge from what she had encountered before, and a disturbing intensity.

"I tried going to his house to study it from a distance . . . but if I'd been seen, he might have finished me. So I came here. The case interested me, because of the missing heart. I was in part made from such stolen essentials."

Whether this hulk was the Surgeon or not, he didn't sound like the kind of citizen who made the city safer by being on the streets.

She said, "Too weird. Spread your arms, get on your knees."

Although it must have been a trick of light, she thought a luminous pulse passed through his eyes as he said, "I bow to no one."

CHAPTER 35

I BOW TO NO ONE.

No suspect had ever challenged her in such a poetic fashion.

Wound tight, wary, edging sideways from the window because her back felt exposed, she said, "I wasn't *asking*."

She took a two-hand grip on the pistol, pointed it at him.

"Will you shoot me in the heart?" he asked. "You'll need two rounds."

Allwine lying on the autopsy table. Chest open. The associated plumbing for two hearts.

"I came here thinking Allwine was an innocent man," he said, "torn open to provide the heart for another . . . experiment. But it's not that simple anymore."

He moved, and for an instant she thought he was coming at her: "Don't be stupid."

Instead he went past her to the window. "Every city has its secrets, but none as terrible as this. Your quarry isn't a crazed murderer. Your real enemy is his maker . . . and mine, too."

Still reeling from his apparent claim to have two hearts, she said, "What do you mean, I'll need two rounds?"

"His techniques are more sophisticated now. But he created me with bodies salvaged from a prison graveyard."

When he turned away from the window, facing Carson again, she glimpsed that subtle pulse of luminosity passing through his eyes.

"My one heart from a mad arsonist," he said. "The other from a child molester."

Their positions had been reversed. His back was to the window, hers to the bathroom door. Suddenly she wondered if he'd come alone.

She put herself at an angle to him, trying to watch him directly while keeping the bathroom threshold in her peripheral vision.

This put the door to the living room behind her. She could not cover every approach by which she might be assaulted, overwhelmed.

"My hands were taken from a strangler," he said. "My eyes from an ax murderer. My life force from a thunderstorm. And that strange storm gave me gifts that Victor couldn't grant. For one thing . . ."

He moved so fast that she did not see him take a step. He was at the window but then *right in her face.*

Not since her first days at the police academy, when she'd been in training, had Carson been outmaneuvered, overpowered. Even as he seemed to materialize in front of her, he boldly wrenched the pistol out of her hand—a shot discharged, shattering a window—and then he was around her, behind her.

She *thought* he went behind her, but when she turned, he seemed to have vanished.

Even dressed in black in this black room, he could not make a shadow of himself. He was too big to play chameleon in a dark corner.

His unmistakable voice came from the windowseat—"I'm not the monster anymore"—but when Carson spun to face him, he wasn't there.

Again he spoke, seemingly from the doorway to the living room— "I'm your best hope"—yet when she turned a third time in search of him, she was still alone.

She didn't find him in the living room, either, though she did recover her service pistol. The weapon lay on the floor beside the Lockaid lock-release gun, which she had left there earlier.

The door to the public hallway stood open.

Wishing that her thudding heart would quiet, she ejected the magazine. The telltale gleam of brass confirmed that the weapon was loaded but for the one expended round.

Slamming the magazine into the pistol, she cleared the doorway fast, staying low, weapon in front of her.

The corridor was deserted. She held her breath but did not hear any footsteps thundering down the stairs. All quiet.

Considering the shot that had accidentally discharged, she could be reasonably sure that someone in the apartment across the hall was watching her through the fish-eye lens in that door.

She stepped back into the black hole, snatched up the Lockaid gun, and pulled the door shut. She left the building.

As she reached the bottom of the stairs, she realized that she had not switched off the lights in the apartment. To hell with it. Allwine was too dead to care about his electric bill.

CHAPTER 36

IN A CORNER of the main lab, Randal Six had been strapped in a cruciform posture at the center of a spherical device that resembled one of those exercise machines that could rotate a person on any imaginable axis, the better to stress all muscles equally. This, however, was not an exercise session.

Randal would not move the machine; the machine would move him, and not for the purpose of building mass or maintaining muscle tone. From head to both feet, to the tip of every finger on both hands, he was locked into a precisely determined position.

A rubber wedge in his mouth prevented him from biting his tongue if he suffered convulsions. A chin strap did not allow him to open his mouth and perhaps accidentally swallow the wedge.

These precautions would also effectively muffle his screams.

The Hands of Mercy had been insulated against the escape of any sound that might attract attention. A researcher involved in cutting-edge science, however, Victor could not be too cautious.

And so . . .

The brain is an electrical apparatus. Its wave patterns can be measured with an EEG machine.

After Randal Six had been extensively educated by direct-to-brain data downloading but while the boy had remained unconscious in the forming tank, Victor had established in his creation's brain electrical patterns identical to those found in several autistic people that he had studied.

His hope had been that this would result in Randal being "born" as an eighteen-year-old autistic of a severe variety. This fond hope had been realized.

Having imposed autism upon Randal, Victor sought to restore normal brain function through a variety of techniques. Thus far he had not been successful.

His purpose in reverse-engineering Randal's release from autism was *not* to find a cure. Finding a cure for autism interested him not at all, except that it might be a source of profits if he chose to market it.

Instead, he pursued these experiments because if he could impose and relieve autism at will, he should be able to learn to impose *selected degrees* of it. This might have valuable economic and social benefits.

Imagine a factory worker whose productivity is low due to the boring, repetitive nature of his job. Selective autism might be a means by which said worker could be made to focus *intently* on the task with an obsession that would make him as productive as—but cheaper than—a robot.

The lowest level of Epsilons in the precisely ranked social strata of Victor's ideal society might be little more than machines of meat. They would waste no time in idle chatter with their fellow workers.

Now he threw the switch that activated the spherical device in which Randal Six was strapped. It began to rotate, three revolutions on one axis, five on another, seven on yet another, slowly at first but steadily gaining speed.

A nearby wall contained a high-resolution nine-foot-square plasma screen. A colorful ultrasound display revealed the movement of blood through Randal Six's cerebral veins and arteries as well as the subtlest currents in his cerebrospinal fluid as it circulated between the meninges, through the cerebral ventricles, and in the brain stem.

Victor suspected that with the properly calculated application of extreme centrifugal and centripetal forces, he could establish unnatural conditions in cerebral fluids that would improve his chances of converting Randal's autism-characteristic brainwaves into normal cerebral electrical patterns.

As the machine spun faster, faster, the subject's groans and terrified wordless pleas escalated into screams of anguish and agony. His shrieks would have been annoying if not for the wedge in his mouth and the chin strap.

Victor hoped to achieve a breakthrough before he tested the boy to destruction. So much time would have been wasted if he had to start all over again with Randal Seven.

Sometimes Randal bit the rubber wedge so hard for so long that his teeth sank in it to the gum line, whereafter it had to be cut out of his locked jaws in pieces. This sounded as if it might be one of those occasions.

CHAPTER 37

A WHITE PICKET FENCE met white gateposts inlaid with seashells. The gate itself featured a unicorn motif.

Under Carson's feet, the front walkway twinkled magically as flecks of mica in the flagstones reflected moonlight. Moss between the stones softened her footsteps.

Almost thick enough to feel, the fragrance of the magnolia-tree flowers swagged the air.

The windows of the fairy-tale bungalow were flanked by blue shutters from which had been cut star shapes and crescent moons.

Trellises partially enclosed the front porch, entwined by leafy vines graced with trumpetlike purple blooms.

Kathleen Burke, who lived in this little oasis of fantasy, was a police psychiatrist. Her work demanded logic and reason, but in her private life, she retreated into gentle escapism.

At three o'clock in the morning, the windows revealed no lights.

Carson rang the bell and then at once knocked on the door.

A soft light bloomed inside, and quicker than Carson expected, Kathy opened the door. "Carson, what's up, what's wrong?"

"It's Halloween in August. We gotta talk."

"Girl, if you were a cat, you'd have your back up and your tail tucked."

"You're lucky I didn't show up with a load in my pants."

"Oh, that's an elegant thing to say. Maybe you've been partnered too long with Michael. Come in. I just made some hazelnut coffee."

Entering, Carson said, "I didn't see any lights."

"At the back, in the kitchen," Kathy said, leading the way.

She was attractive, in her late thirties, molasses-black with Asian eyes. In Chinese-red pajamas with embroidered cuffs and collar, she cut an exotic figure.

In the kitchen, a steaming mug of coffee stood on the table. Beside it lay a novel; on the cover, a woman in a fantastic costume rode the back of a flying dragon.

"You always read at three in the morning?" Carson asked.

"Couldn't sleep."

Carson was too edgy to sit. She didn't pace the kitchen so much as twitch back and forth in it. "This is your home, Kathy, not your office. That matters—am I right?"

Pouring coffee, Kathy said, "What's happened? What're you so jumped up about?"

"You're not a psychiatrist here. You're just a friend here. Am I right?"

Putting the second mug of coffee on the table, returning to her own chair, Kathy said, "I'm always your friend, Carson—here, there, anywhere."

Carson stayed on her feet, too wound up to sit down. "None of what I tell you here can end up in my file."

"Unless you killed someone. Did you kill someone?"

"Not tonight."

"Then spit it out, girlfriend. You're getting on my nerves."

Carson pulled a chair out from the table, sat down. She reached for the mug of coffee, hesitated, didn't pick it up.

Her hand was trembling. She clenched it into a fist. Very tight. Opened it. Still trembling.

"You ever see a ghost, Kathy?"

"I've taken the haunted New Orleans tour, been to the crypt of Marie Laveau at night. Does that count?"

Clutching the handle of the mug, staring at her white knuckles, Carson said, "I'm serious. I mean any weird shit you can't wrap your head around. Ghosts, UFO, Big Foot . . ." She glanced at Kathy. "Don't look at me that way."

"What way?"

"Like a psychiatrist."

"Don't be so defensive." Kathy patted the book with the dragon on the cover. "I'm the one reads three fantasy novels a week and wishes she could actually *live* in one."

Carson blew on her coffee, tentatively took a sip, then a longer swallow. "I need this. Haven't slept. No *way* I'll sleep tonight."

Kathy waited with professional patience.

After a moment, Carson said, "People talk about the unknown, the mystery of life, but I've never seen one squirt of mystery in it."

"Squirt?"

"Squirt, drop, spoonful—whatever. I *want* to see mystery in life—who doesn't?—some mystical meaning, but I'm a fool for logic."

"Until now? So tell me about your ghost."

"He wasn't a ghost. But he sure was *something*. I've been driving around the past hour, maybe longer, trying to find the right words to explain what happened. . . ."

"Start with *where* it happened."

"I was at Bobby Allwine's apartment—"

Leaning forward, interested, Kathy said, "The Surgeon's latest victim. I've been working up a profile on the killer. He's hard to figure. Psychotic but controlled. No obvious sexual component. So far he hasn't left much forensic evidence at the scene. No fingerprints. A garden-variety psychopath isn't usually so prudent."

Kathy seemed to realize that she had seized the wheel of the conversation. Relinquishing it, she sat back in her chair.

"Sorry, Carson. We were talking about your ghost."

Kathy Burke could probably keep her police work separate from their friendship, but she would find it more difficult to take off her psychiatrist hat and keep it off when she heard what Carson had come here to tell her.

A giant with a strangely deformed face, claiming to have been made from the body parts of criminals, claiming to have been brought to life by lightning, capable of such nimbleness of movement, such uncanny stealth, such inhuman speed that he could be nothing less than supernatural and, therefore, might be what he claimed to be . . .

"Hello? Your ghost?"

Instead of replying, Carson drank more coffee.

"That's it?" Kathy asked. "Just the tease, and then good-bye?"

"I feel a little guilty."

"Good. I was ready for some spooky dish."

"If I tell you as a friend, I compromise you professionally. You'll need to report my ass for an OIS investigation."

Kathy frowned. "Officer involved shooting? Just how serious is this, Carson?"

"I didn't smoke anybody. Didn't even wing him, as far as I know."

"Tell me. I won't report you."

Carson smiled affectionately. "You'd do the right thing. You'd report me, all right. And you'd write me up an order for some couch time."

"I'm not as righteous as you think I am."

"Yes, you are," Carson said. "That's one reason I like you."

Kathy sighed. "I'm all primed for a campfire tale, and you won't spook me. Now what?"

"We could make an early breakfast," Carson suggested. "Assuming you've got any real food here in elfland."

"Eggs, bacon, sausages, hash browns, brioche toast."

"All of the above."

"You're going to be one of those blimp cops."

"Nah. I'll be dead long before that," Carson said, and more than half believed it.

CHAPTER 38

ROY PRIBEAUX LIKED TO RISE well before dawn to undertake his longevity regimen—except on those occasions when he had been up late the previous night murdering someone.

Nothing was quite as luxurious as lingering in bed with the knowledge that a new piece of the ideal woman had so recently been wrapped, bagged, and stored in the freezer. One felt the satisfaction of accomplishment, the swelling pride of work well done, which made an extra hour in the sheets seem justified and therefore sweet.

Getting Candace's eyes and preserving them had not required him to be out as late as he'd been on other harvests, but he still would have lazed in bed if he hadn't been amazingly energized by the fact that *his collection was complete*. The perfect eyes had been the last item on his list.

He slept deeply but for just a few hours, every minute in the arms of rapturous dreams, and sprang out of bed profoundly rested and with enthusiasm for the day ahead.

An array of high-end exercise machines occupied a portion of his loft. In shorts and tank top, he followed a circuit of weight machines that brought a burn to every muscle group in graduated sets ending in his maximum resistance. Then he worked up a positively tropical sweat on the treadmill and the ski trainer.

His morning shower always took a while. He lathered with two soaps: first an exfoliating bar with a loofa sponge, followed by a moisturizing bar and soft cloth. For the most complete cleanliness achievable and perfect follicle health, he used two natural shampoos, followed by a cream conditioner that he rinsed out after precisely thirty seconds.

The sun finally rose as he applied a skin-conditioning lotion from his neck to the bottoms of his feet. He did not neglect a single square inch of his magnificently maintained body, and used a spatula-style sponge to reach the middle of his back.

This lotion wasn't merely a moisturizer, but also a youthenizing emollient rich in free-radical-scavenging vitamins. If he had left the bottoms of his feet untreated, he'd have been an immortal walking on a dying man's soles, a thought that made him shudder.

After applying the usual series of revitalizing substances to his face—including a cream enriched with liquified monkey embryos—Roy regarded his reflection in the vanity mirror with satisfaction.

For a few years, he had succeeded in fully arresting the aging process. More exciting, he had recently begun to reverse the effects of time, and week by week he had watched himself grow younger.

Others deluded themselves into thinking they were rolling back the years, but Roy knew his success was real. He had arrived at the most perfectly effective combination of exercise, diet, nutritional supplements, lotions, and meditation.

The final key ingredient had been purified New Zealand lamb's urine, of which he drank four ounces a day. With a lemon wedge.

This turning back of the clock was highly desirable, of course, but he reminded himself that he could youthenize himself too far. If he reversed himself to the condition of a twenty-year-old and stayed there for a hundred years, that would be good; but if he got carried away and made himself twelve again, that would be bad.

He had not enjoyed his childhood and adolescence the first time around. Repeating any portion of them, even if solely in physical appearance, would be a glimpse of Hell.

After Roy dressed, as he stood in the kitchen, washing down twenty-four capsules of supplements with grapefruit juice prior to preparing breakfast, he was abruptly struck by the realization that his life now had no purpose.

For the past two years, he had been collecting the anatomical components of the perfect woman, first in a variety of locations far removed from New Orleans, then lately and with particular frenzy here in his own backyard. But as of Candace, he had them all. Hands, feet, lips, nose, hair, breasts, eyes, and so much more—he had forgotten nothing.

Now what?

He was surprised that he had not thought further than this. Being a man of leisure, he had a lot of time on his hands; being an immortal, he had eternity.

This thought proved suddenly daunting.

Now he slowly realized that during the years of searching and harvesting, he had superstitiously and unconsciously assumed that when his collection was complete, when the freezer was filled with all the jig-saw pieces of the most perfectly beautiful woman, then a living woman, embodying every one of those features and qualities, would magically come into his life. He had been engaged on a kind of hoodoo quest with the purpose of shaping his romantic destiny.

Perhaps this mojo would work. Perhaps this very afternoon, as he strolled the Quarter, he would come face to face with her dazzling, be-witching self.

If the days passed without this desired encounter, however, days and weeks and months . . . what then?

He yearned to share his perfection with a woman who would be his equal. Until that moment came, life would be empty, without purpose.

An uneasiness overcame him. He tried to quell it with breakfast.

As he ate, he became fascinated with his hands. They were more than beautiful male hands; they were exquisite.

Oh, but until he found his goddess—not in pieces but whole and alive, without fault or deficiency—his flawless hands would not be able to caress the perfection that was their erotic destiny.

His uneasiness grew.

CHAPTER 39

AT DAYBREAK, with the rising sun not yet at an angle to fire the stained-glass windows, Our Lady of Sorrows sheltered a congregation of shadows. The only light came from the illuminated stations of the cross and from the candles in the ruby-red glass votive cups.

The humidity and early heat ripened the fragrances of incense, tallow, and lemon-scented wax. Inhaling this mélange, Victor imagined he would be sweating it through every pore for the rest of the day.

His footsteps on the marble floor echoed from the groin vaults overhead. He liked the crisp coldness of this sound, which he fancied spoke truth to the cloying atmosphere of the church.

With the first Mass of the day still half an hour away, the only person present, other than Victor, was Patrick Duchaine. He waited, as instructed, on a pecan pew in the front row.

The man rose nervously, but Victor said, "Sit, sit," not quite in the tone he might use to decline a courtesy, but in a tone rather like the one in which he might speak with impatience to a vexing dog.

At sixty, Patrick had white hair, an earnest grandfatherly face, and eyes moist with perpetual compassion. His looks alone inspired the trust and affection of his parishioners.

Add to appearances a gentle, musical voice. A warm, easy laugh. Furthermore, he had the genuine humility of a man who knew too well his place in the scheme of things.

Father Duchaine was the image of an unassailably good priest to whom the faithful would give their hearts. And to whom they would confess their sins without hesitation.

In a community with many Catholics—practicing and not—Victor found it useful to have one of his people manning the confessional in which some of the city's more powerful citizens went to their knees.

Patrick Duchaine was one of those rare members of the New Race who had been cloned from the DNA of an existing human being rather than having been designed from scratch by Victor. Physiologically, he had been improved, but to the eye he was the Patrick Duchaine who had been born of man and woman.

The real Father Duchaine had donated to a Red Cross blood drive, unwittingly providing the material from which he could be replicated. These days, he rotted under tons of garbage, deep in the landfill, while his Doppelgänger tended to the souls at Our Lady of Sorrows.

Replacing real human beings with replicas entailed risks that Victor seldom wished to take. Although the duplicate might look and sound and move exactly like its inspiration, the *memories* of the original could not be transferred to him.

The closest relatives and friends of the replaced individual were certain to notice numerous gaps in his knowledge of his personal history and relationships. They wouldn't imagine he was an imposter, but they would surely think that he was suffering from a mental or physical ailment; they would press him to seek medical attention.

In addition, out of concern, they would watch him closely and would not entirely trust him. His ability to blend in with society and to carry out his work in the service of the New Race would be compromised.

In the case of the priest, he'd had no wife, of course, and no children. His parents were dead, as was his only brother. While he had many friends and parishioners to whom he was close, no *intimate* family existed to note his memory gaps throughout the day.

In the lab Victor raised this Father Duchaine from spilled blood before the real Father Duchaine had died, a trick more complicated than the one that the man from Galilee had performed with Lazarus.

Sitting in the front pew beside his priest, Victor said, "How do you sleep? Do you dream?"

"Not often, sir. Sometimes . . . a nightmare about the Hands of Mercy. But I can never recall the details."

"And you never will. That's my gift to you—no memory of your birth. Patrick, I need your help."

"Anything, of course."

"One of my people is having a serious crisis of the mind. I don't know who he is. He called me . . . but he is afraid to come to me."

"Perhaps . . . not afraid, sir," the priest said. "Ashamed. Ashamed that he has failed you."

That statement troubled Victor. "How could you suggest such a thing, Patrick? The New Race has no capacity for shame."

Only Erika had been programmed to know shame, and only because Victor found her more erotic in the throes of it.

"Shame," he told Patrick, "isn't a virtue. It's a weakness. No Natural Law requires it. We *rule* nature . . . and transcend it."

The priest evaded Victor's gaze. "Yes, sir, of course. I think what I meant was . . . maybe he feels a sort of . . . regret that he hasn't performed to your expectations."

Perhaps the priest would need to be watched closely or even subjected to a day-long examination in the lab.

"Search the city, Patrick. Spread the word among my people. Maybe they've seen one of their kind behaving oddly. I'm charging you and a few other key people with this search, and I know that you *will* perform up to my expectations."

"Yes, sir."

"If you find him and he runs . . . kill him. You know how your kind can be killed."

"Yes, sir."

"Be cautious. He's already killed one of you," Victor revealed.

Surprised, the priest met his eyes again.

"I'd prefer to have him alive," Victor continued. "But at least I need his body. To study. Bring him to me at the Hands of Mercy."

They were near enough to the rack of votive candles that the pulsing crimson reflections of the flames crawled Patrick's face.

This inspired Victor to ask "Do you sometimes wonder if you're damned?"

"No, sir," the priest answered, but with a hesitation. "There is no Hell or Heaven. This is the one life."

"Exactly. Your mind is too well made for superstition." Victor rose from the pew. "God bless you, Patrick." When the priest's eyes widened with surprise, Victor smiled and said, "That was a joke."

CHAPTER 40

WHEN CARSON PICKED UP Michael at his apartment house, he got in the car, looked her over, and said, "Those are yesterday's clothes."

"Suddenly you're a fashion critic."

"You look . . . rumpled."

As she pulled away from the curb, she said, "Rumpled, my ass. I look like a cow pie in a bad wig."

"You didn't get any sleep?"

"Maybe I'm done with sleep forever."

"If you've been up more than twenty-four hours, you shouldn't be driving," he said.

"Don't worry about it, Mom." She took a tall Starbucks cup from between her thighs, drank through a straw. "I'm so wired on caffeine, I've got the reflexes of a pit viper."

"Do pit vipers have quick reflexes?"

"You want to get in a pit with one and see?"

"You *are* wound tight. What's happened?"

"Saw a ghost. Scared the crap out of me."

"What's the punch line?"

What she hadn't been able to say to Kathy Burke, she could say to Michael. In police work, partners were closer than mere friends. They had better be. They daily trusted each other with their lives.

If you couldn't share everything with your partner, you needed a new partner.

Nevertheless, she hesitated before she said, "He seemed to walk out of walls, disappear into them. Big sucker, but he moves quicker than the eye."

"Who?"

"You listening to *anything* I'm saying? The ghost, that's who."

"You spiking that coffee with something?"

"He said he's made from pieces of criminals."

"Slow down. You're driving too fast."

Carson accelerated. "The hands of a strangler, one heart from a mad arsonist, one from a child molester. His life force from a thunderstorm."

"I don't get it."

"Neither do I."

BY THE TIME Carson parked in front of Fullbright's Funeral Home, she had told Michael everything that happened in Allwine's apartment.

His face revealed no skepticism, but his tone of voice was the equivalent of raised eyebrows: "You were tired, in a weird place—"

"He took a *gun* away from me," she said, which might have been the essence of her astonishment, the one thing about the experience that had seemed the most supernatural. "No one takes a gun away from me, Michael. *You* want to try?"

"No. I enjoy having testicles. All I'm saying is that he was dressed in black, the apartment is black, so the disappearing trick was probably just a trick."

"So maybe he manipulated me, and I saw what he wanted me to see. Is that it?"

"Doesn't that make more sense?"

"Sure damn does. But if it was a trick, he should be headlining a magic act in Vegas."

Looking at the funeral home, Michael said, "Why're we here?"

"Maybe he didn't really move faster than the eye, and maybe he didn't *in fact* vanish into thin air, but he was dead-on when he said Allwine was in despair, wanted to die . . . but couldn't kill himself."

From a pocket she withdrew the four memorial booklets and handed them to Michael.

"Bobby had like a hundred of these," she continued, "in a drawer of his nightstand. All from different funerals at this place. Death appealed to him."

She got out of the car, slammed the driver's door, and met Michael on the sidewalk.

He said, "'Life force from a thunderstorm.' What the hell does that mean?"

"Sometimes like a soft lightning throbs through his eyes."

Hurrying at her side, Michael said, "You've always been stone solid until now, like Joe Friday with no Y chromosome. Now you're Nancy Drew on a sugar rush."

Like so many things in New Orleans, the mortuary seemed as much a dream place as a reality. It had once been a Gothic Revival mansion and no doubt still served as the mortician's residence as well as his place of business. The weight of the lavish rococo millwork must have been only a few pounds shy of the critical load needed to buckle the eaves, implode the walls, and collapse the roof.

Live oaks dating to the plantation era shaded the house, while camellias, gardenias, mimosa, and tea roses cast a scene-saturating perfume. Bees buzzed lazily from bloom to bloom, too fat and happy to sting, besotted by rich nectar.

At the front door, Carson rang the bell. "Michael, don't you sometimes sense there's more to life than the grind—some amazing secret you can almost see from the corner of your eye?" Before he could reply, she plunged on: "Last night I saw something amazing . . . something I can't put into words. It's almost like UFOs exist."

"You and me—we've put guys in psych wards who talk like that."

A bearish, dour-looking man answered the door and acknowledged in the most somber tones that he was indeed Taylor Fullbright.

Flashing her police ID, Carson said, "Sir, I'm sorry I didn't call ahead, but we're here on a rather urgent matter."

Brightening at the discovery that they were not a bereaved couple in need of counseling, Fullbright revealed his true convivial nature. "Come in, come in! I was just cremating a customer."

CHAPTER 41

FOR A LONG TIME after the session in the spinning rack, Randal Six lies on his bed, not sleeping—for he seldom sleeps—facing the wall, his back to the room, shutting out the chaos, allowing his mind slowly, slowly to grow still.

He does not know the purpose of the treatment, but he is certain that he cannot endure many more of those sessions. Sooner than later, he will suffer a massive stroke; the failure of an inner vessel will do what a bullet to his armored skull cannot as easily achieve.

If a cerebral aneurysm does not finish him, he will surely trade the developmental disability called autism for genuine psychosis. He will seek in madness the peace that mere autism is not always able to ensure.

In his darkest moments, Randal wonders whether the spinning rack is a treatment, as Father has repeatedly called it, or if it might be intended as torture.

Not born of God and alienated from belief, this is the closest he can come to a blasphemous thought: that Father is a cruel rather than a caring maker, that Father himself is psychotic and his entire enterprise an insane endeavor.

Whether Father is sincere or deceitful, whether his project is genius or dementia, Randal Six knows that he himself will never find happiness in the Hands of Mercy.

Happiness lies streets away, a little less than three miles from here, at the home of one Carson O'Connor. In that house lies a secret to be taken if it isn't freely offered: the cause of Arnie O'Connor's smile, the reason for the moment of joy captured in the newspaper photo, no matter how brief it might have been.

As soon as possible, he must get to the O'Connor boy, before the cerebral aneurysm that kills him, before the spinning rack whirls him into madness.

Randal is not locked in his room. His autism, which is at times complicated by agoraphobia, keeps him this side of the threshold more securely than could locks or chains.

Father often encourages him to explore from end to end of the building, even floors above and below this one. Adventurousness will be a first proof that his treatments are working.

No matter where he goes in the building, he cannot leave, for the exterior doors are wired to a security system. He would be caught before he escaped the grounds . . . and might be punished with a very long session in the spinning rack.

Anyway, when he occasionally leaves his room and wanders the halls, he never dares to go far, never a fraction as far as Father would like to see him travel. Sometimes even a distance of thirty feet presents him with an overload of sights and sounds that brings him trembling to his knees.

In his self-isolation, he nonetheless sees. He hears. He learns. He knows of a way out of Mercy that will not trigger an alarm.

He may not have sufficient fortitude to reach that special door, let alone to confront the busier world beyond. But his despondency has recently advanced to desperation, and the reckless action that is the whip of desperation may lash into him a kind of courage.

He will leave this coming night, in little more than twelve hours.

CHAPTER 42

THE QUIET RECEIVING FOYER featured a baroque frieze instead of traditional crown moldings: deeply carved acanthus leaves punctuated every two feet and at the corners by the heads of angels alternating with gargoyles or perhaps mocking demons.

Inlaid in the forest-green marble floor, a foot-wide circular work of marquetry employed lighter marbles to portray mythological beings—gods, goddesses, and demigods—in perpetual pursuit. Even without dropping to his knees, Michael could see that some of the pursuit involved sexual fondling.

Only in New Orleans would either of these elements have seemed suitable to a funeral home. The house had probably been built around 1850 by nouveau riche newcomers who hadn't been welcome in the Creole sections of town. In this city, time eventually conferred dignity on what had once been outrageous as well as on what had been classic from the day it had been erected.

Studying a photo of Bobby Allwine that Carson had given him, Taylor Fullbright said, "This is the very gentleman, yes. I felt sorry for the poor soul—so many of his friends were dying. Then I realized he didn't know any of the deceased."

Carson said, "He—what?—just got a thrill being around dead people?"

"Nothing that kinky," said Fullbright. "He just . . . seemed to be at peace around them."

"That's what he said—he was at peace?"

"The only thing I can remember he said was 'Death can be as much a gift as a curse,' which is often true."

"Did you confront him about coming to all these viewings?"

"Confrontation isn't my style, Detective. Some funeral directors are solemn to the point of seeming stern. I'm more of a hugger and a consoler. Mr. Allwine and his friend, they were never a problem. More melancholy than weird."

Carson's phone rang, and when she stepped away to answer it, Michael said to Fullbright, "He came with a friend? Can you give us a description?"

Smiling, nodding, as affable as a cartoon bear, the mortician said, "I can see him as clear in memory as if he were standing here. He was ordinary to a fault. Average height. A little heavier than average weight. Middle-aged. Brown hair—or maybe blond. Blue or green eyes, maybe hazel."

With a sarcasm that sounded like earnest praise, Michael said, "Amazing. That's as good as a photo."

Pleased, Fullbright said, "I've got a sharp eye for detail."

Putting away her phone, Carson turned to Michael: "Jack Rogers wants to see us at the morgue."

"You might mention to the coroner," Fullbright said, "that while I don't extend commissions to those who send us business, I do offer discounts for referrals."

"I can't wait to tell him," Michael said. Pointing to the marble marquetry at their feet, he asked, "Who's that figure?"

"The one with the winged feet? That's Mercury."

"And that one next to him?"

"Aphrodite," said Fullbright.

"Are they . . . ?"

"Engaged in sodomy?" the mortician asked jovially. "Indeed they are. You'd be amazed how many mourners notice and are cheered by it."

"I *am* amazed," Michael agreed.

CHAPTER 43

THE LONGER ROY PRIBEAUX roamed his expansive loft apartment, gazing out of the tall windows, brooding about his future, the more troubled he became.

When a brief midmorning shower pelted the panes, blurring the city, he felt as if his future also blurred further, until it was a meaningless smear. He might have cried if crying had been his thing.

Never in his young—and getting steadily younger—life had he been without a purpose and a plan. Meaningful work kept the mind sharp and the heart uplifted.

Meaningful work, having a worthwhile purpose, was as crucial to longevity and to enduring youthfulness as were megadoses of Vitamin C and Coenzyme Q10.

Without a purpose to inspire him, Roy feared that in spite of a perfect diet, ideally balanced nutritional supplements, an array of exotic emollients, and even purified lamb's urine, he would begin to grow old mentally. The more he brooded, the more it seemed that the path to senility loomed before him, as steep as a luge chute.

Mind and body were inextricably linked, of course, so a year of mental senescence would inevitably lead to lines at the corners of his eyes, the first gray hairs at his temples. He shuddered.

He tried to muster the desire to take a walk, but if he spent the day in the Quarter, among the throngs of celebratory tourists, and if he failed to encounter the radiant goddess of his destiny, his uneasiness would deepen.

Because he himself was very close to perfect, perhaps now that he had collected all the parts of an ideal woman, he should make it his goal to refine himself that final degree. He could now focus on achieving the perfect metabolism until he ceased to excrete wastes.

Although this was a noble undertaking, it didn't promise as much *fun* as the quest he had recently completed.

Finally, out of desperation, he found himself wondering—indeed *hoping*—that he had erred when he concluded that he had completed his collection. He might have overlooked an anatomical feature that, while minor, remained essential to beauty's jigsaw.

For a while he sat at the kitchen table with da Vinci's famous anatomical charts and several old *Playboy* centerfolds. He studied the female form from every angle, looking for a morsel that he might have overlooked.

When he made no discovery that allowed him to cry *Eureka,* he began to consider the possibility that he had not been sufficiently specific in his collecting. Was it possible that he had collected from too macro a perspective?

Were he to take Elizabeth Lavenza's lovely pale hands from the freezer and review them critically, he might be surprised to find that they were perfect, yes, in every detail *but one.* Perhaps she had a single thumb that fell short of perfection.

Perhaps the lips he had harvested were not *both* perfect as he had remembered. The upper might be perfect, the lower *not quite.*

If he needed to set out on a search for the perfect left thumb to marry to Elizabeth's otherwise faultlessly fair hands, if he must find a bee-stung lower lip to match the exquisite upper already in his possession, then his quest had not been completed, after all, and he would for a while have meaningful . . .

"No," he declared aloud. "That way lies madness."

Soon he would be reduced to harvesting one toe per donor and killing for mere eyelashes. A thin line separated serious homicidal purpose from buffoonery.

Realizing that a blind alley lay before him, Roy might at that moment have fallen into a swoon of despair, even though at heart he was an optimistic person. Fortunately, he was saved by a new thought.

From his nightstand he retrieved his original list of wanted anatomical delights. He had drawn a line through every item as he acquired it, concluding with EYES.

The list was long, and perhaps early in the quest he had crossed off an item out of wishful thinking, before he had taken possession of it. His memory of certain periods in his past was somewhat hazy, not because of any mental deficiency, but solely because he was such a tomorrow-oriented person, focused on the future in which he would grow younger and closer to perfection.

He vaguely recalled, over the years, killing a woman or two for an ideal feature, only to discover, in the intimate presence of the corpse, that the wanted item was minutely flawed and therefore not worth harvesting. Perhaps more than a woman or two. Maybe as many as four had disappointed him. Maybe five.

He supposed it was possible that he had crossed off an item or two on his list only to discover, after the kill, that he had been too easy in his judgment—and then in his busyness had forgotten to restore the needed item to the list.

Either to confirm or eliminate this possibility, he needed to compare the contents of his special freezer to his original list.

Despondency quickly faded and a happy anticipation filled him. He opened a bottle of apple juice and sectioned a raisin muffin to sample as he worked.

All the appliances in his roomy kitchen boasted stainless-steel finishes, including the ovens, microwave, dishwasher, icemaker, Sub-Zero refrigerator, and two enormous freezers.

In the first freezer he stored the parts of the perfect woman. He playfully referred to this as the *love locker*.

The second freezer contained an assortment of dairy-free, soy-based ice creams, free-range chicken breasts, and quarts of rhubarb puree. In the event that a major act of terrorism led to a disruption in the distribution of vital nutritional supplements, he also stored five-pound packages of powdered saw palmetto, St. John's wort, bee pollen, and other items.

When he lifted the lid on the first freezer, a cloud of frosted air wafted past him, crisp with a faint scent vaguely like that of frozen fish. He saw at once that the freezer contained items that did not belong with his collection.

His larger treasures—legs and arms—were tightly sealed in multiple layers of Reynolds Plastic Wrap. The smaller lovelies were sealed first in OneZip bags and then in Tupperware containers with dependably tight lids.

Now he found among his collection three containers that were not Tupperware. They were cheap knockoffs of that desired brand: opaque plastic bottoms with ugly green lids.

This discovery mystified him. Although certain events in the more distant past might be blurry in his memory, these unacceptable containers were set atop the rest of his collection; they could have been placed here only recently. Yet he had never seen them before.

Curious but not yet alarmed, he took the three containers from the freezer. He put them on a nearby counter.

When he opened them, he found what might have been human organs. The first resembled liver. The second might have been a heart. With no real interest in things internal, he couldn't guess whether the third item was a kidney, spleen, or something even more arcane.

Pausing for some raisin muffin and apple juice, he could not avoid considering that these three specimens might be the souvenirs taken by the *other* killer currently making the news in New Orleans.

Being a Renaissance man who had educated himself in a variety of disciplines, Roy knew more than a little about psychology. He could not help but give some consideration now to the concept of multiple personalities.

He found it interesting to consider that he might be both the original killer *and* the copycat, might have murdered three men while in a fugue state, and that even now, confronted with evidence, he couldn't remember popping or chopping them. Interesting . . . but in the end not convincing. He and himself, working separately, were not, together, the Surgeon.

The true explanation eluded him, but he knew that it would prove to be more bizarre than multiple personalities.

Instinct drew his attention to the second freezer.

If the first had contained the unexpected, might not the second hold surprises, too? He might find gallons of high-fat ice cream and pounds of bacon among the herbs and health foods.

Instead, when he opened the lid and blinked away the initial cloud of frosted air, he discovered Candace's eyeless corpse jammed atop the supplements and foodstuffs.

Roy was certain that he had not brought this cotton-candy person home with him.

CHAPTER 44

LIKE THE SOMEWHAT disheveled medical examiner himself, Jack Rogers's private office was a classic example of managed chaos. The desktop overflowed with papers, notebooks, folders, photos. Books were jammed in the shelves everywhichway. Nevertheless, Jack would be able to find anything he needed after mere seconds of searching.

Only partly because of sleep deprivation and too much coffee, Carson's mind felt as disordered as the office. "Bobby Allwine's *gone?*"

Jack said, "The cadaver, the tissue samples, the autopsy video—all gone."

"What about the autopsy report and photos?" Michael asked. "Did you file them under 'Munster, Herman' like I suggested?"

"Yeah. They found them, took them."

"They thought to look under 'Munster, Herman'?" Michael asked in disbelief. "Since when do grave robbers double as trivia mavens?"

"Judging by the mess in the file room," Jack said, "I think they just tore through all the drawers till they got what they wanted. We could have filed it under 'Bell, Tinker,' and they would have found it. Anyway, they weren't grave robbers. They didn't dig Allwine out of the ground. They took him from a morgue drawer."

"So they're bodysnatchers," Michael said. "Getting the term right doesn't change the fact that your ass is in a sling, Jack."

"It feels like a barbed-wire thong," Jack said. "Losing evidence in a capital case? Man, there goes the pension."

Trying to make sense of the situation, Carson said, "Did the city cut your security budget or what?"

Jack shook his head. "We're as tight as a prison here. It has to be an inside job."

Simultaneously, Carson and Michael looked at Luke, who sat on a stool in a corner.

"Hey," he said, "I never stole a dime in my life, let alone a dead guy."

"Not Luke," Jack Rogers assured them. "He couldn't have pulled it off. He'd have screwed up."

Luke winced. "Thanks, I guess."

"Luke and I were here for a while after you two left, but not all night. We hit a wall, needed sleep. Because I'd sent home the night staff to keep the lid on this, the place was deserted."

"You forget to lock up?" Carson asked.

Jack glowered at her. "No way."

"Signs of forced entry?"

"None. They must've had keys."

"Somebody knew what you'd find in Allwine," she said, "because maybe he's not unique. Maybe there're others like him."

"Don't go off in the Twilight Zone again," Michael half warned, half pleaded.

"At least one other," she said. "The friend he went to funerals with. Mr. Average Everything."

Almost simultaneous with a knock, the door opened, and Frye, Jonathan Harker's partner, entered. He looked surprised to see them.

"Why so glum?" he asked. "Did somebody die?"

Weariness and caffeine sharpened Carson's edge. "What don't you understand about 'buzz off'?"

"Hey, I'm not here about your case. We're on that liquor-store shooting."

"Yeah? Is that right? Is that what you were doing yesterday at Allwine's apartment—looking for clues in the liquor-store shooting?"

Frye pretended innocence. "I don't know what you're talking about. O'Connor, you're wound as tight as a golf ball's guts. Get a man, relieve some tension."

She wanted to shoot him accidentally.

As if reading her mind, Michael said, "A gun can always go off accidentally, but you'd have to explain why you drew it in the first place."

CHAPTER 45

COMFORTABLE IN HER ROBE, ensconced in a wingback chair, Erika spent the night and the morning with no company but books, and even took her breakfast in the library.

Reading for pleasure, lingering over the prose, she nevertheless covered a hundred pages an hour. She was, after all, an Alpha-class member of the New Race, with superb language skills.

She read Charles Dickens's *A Tale of Two Cities,* and when she finished it, she did something that she had not done before in her weeks of life. She wept.

The story was about the power of love, the nobility of self-sacrifice, and the horrors of revolution in the name of political ideology, among other things.

Erika understood the concept of love and found it appealing, but she didn't know if she would ever *feel* it. The New Race was supposed to value reason, to eschew emotion, to reject superstition.

She had heard Victor say that love was superstition. One of the Old Race, he'd made himself New. He claimed that perfect clarity of mind was a pleasure greater than any mere sentiment.

Nevertheless, Erika found herself intrigued by the concept of love and longed to experience it.

She found hope in the fact that she was capable of tears. Her built-in disposition toward reason at the expense of emotion had not prevented her from identifying with the tragic lawyer who, at the end of Dickens's novel, went to the guillotine in place of another man.

The lawyer had sacrificed himself to ensure that the woman he loved would have happiness with the man *she* loved. That man was the one whose name the lawyer had assumed and in whose place he had been executed.

Even if Erika was capable of love, she would not be capable of self-sacrifice, for it violated the proscription against suicide that had been embedded in every member of the New Race. Therefore, she was in awe of this capacity in ordinary human beings.

As for revolution . . . A day would come when Victor would give the command, and the New Race living secretly among the Old would pour down upon humanity a storm of terror unprecedented in history.

She'd not been created to serve in the front lines of that war, only to be a wife to Victor. When the time came, she supposed that she would be as ruthless as her maker had created her to be.

If they knew what she was, ordinary humans would consider her a monster. Members of the Old Race weren't her brothers and sisters.

Yet she admired much about them and, in truth, envied some of their gifts.

She suspected that it would be a mistake to let Victor know that her interest in the arts of the Old Race had evolved into admiration. In his view, they deserved only contempt. If she could not sustain that contempt, Erika Five could always be activated.

As noon drew near, when she was certain that the household staff had cleaned the master suite and made the bed, she went upstairs.

If the maids had found something extraordinary or just peculiar in the bedroom, if they had uncovered even a few rat droppings, she would have been told. Whatever had been in the bedroom the previous night must not be there now.

She prowled the suite anyway, listening for furtive sounds, looking behind furniture.

In the night, gripped by a surprising fear of the unknown, she had retreated. Fear, an important survival mechanism, had not been entirely denied to the New Race.

Superstition, on the other hand, was uncontestable proof of a weak mind. Victor had no tolerance for superstition. Those with weak minds would be recalled, terminated, replaced.

The most innocent-seeming superstition—such as a belief that ill fortune attended every Friday the thirteenth—could open a door in the mind to consideration of larger supernatural issues. The most essential purpose of Victor's revolution was to complete the work of modernity and create a race of absolute materialists.

Erika searched the suite to quell the quasi-superstitious dread that had seized her the previous night and that still lingered. When she found nothing untoward, her confidence returned.

She enjoyed a long hot shower.

Members of the New Race, even Alphas like her, were encouraged to develop a keen appreciation for simple physical pleasures that could serve as an inoculation against emotions. Emotions themselves could be a form of pleasure, but also an antirevolutionary force.

Sex was among the approved pleasures, pure animal sex divorced from affection, from love. Sex between members of the New Race was also divorced from reproduction; they were engineered to be sterile.

Each new man and woman owed his or her existence to the direct action of Victor. The family was an antirevolutionary institution. Family fostered emotion.

Victor trusted no one but Victor to create life only for purely intellectual, solely rational reasons. Life from the lab will one day entirely replace life from the loins.

Shower completed, Erika opened the door of the stall, fished a towel from the nearby rack, stepped onto the bath mat—and discovered that she'd had a visitor. The splash of water and the clouds of steam had masked the movements of the intruder.

On the mat lay a scalpel. Stainless steel. Sparkling.

The scalpel must be one of Victor's. He owned collections of surgical instruments acquired at various times during his two-century crusade.

Victor, however, had not put this blade on her bath mat. Nor had any member of the household staff. Someone else had been here. Something else.

Steam swirled around her. Yet she shivered.

CHAPTER 46

FOLLOWING THEIR STOP at the morgue, Michael made a play for the car keys, but Carson as usual took the wheel.

"You drive too slow," she told him.

"You drive too asleep."

"I'm fine. I'm cool."

"You're both," he agreed, "but you're not fully awake."

"Unconscious, I wouldn't drive as slow as you."

"Yeah, see, I don't want to test that claim."

"You sound like your father's a safety engineer or something."

"You *know* he's a safety engineer," Michael said.

"What's a safety engineer do, anyway?"

"He engineers safety."

"Life is inherently unsafe."

"That's why we need safety engineers."

"You sound like probably your mother was obsessed with safe toys when you were growing up."

"As you know perfectly well, she's a product-safety analyst."

"God, you must have had a boring childhood. No wonder you wanted to be a cop, get shot at, shoot back."

Michael sighed. "None of this has anything to do with whether you're fit to drive or not."

"I am not only fit to drive," Carson said, "I am God's gift to Louisiana highways."

"I hate it when you get like this."

"I am what I am."

"What you are, Popeye, is stubborn."

"Look who's talking—a guy who will *never* accept that a woman can drive better than he can."

"This isn't a gender thing, and you know it."

"I'm female. You're male. It's a gender thing."

"It's a nut thing," he said. "You're nuts, I'm not, so I ought to drive. Carson, really, you need sleep."

"I can sleep when I'm dead."

The day's agenda consisted of several interviews with friends of Elizabeth Lavenza, the floater without hands who had been found in the lagoon. After the second of these, in the bookstore where Lavenza had worked as a clerk, Carson had to admit that sleep deprivation interfered with her ability as an investigator.

Returning to the sedan, she said, "Okay, I gotta grab some sack time, but what'll you do?"

"Go home, watch *Die Hard*."

"You've watched it like fifty times."

"It just gets better. Like *Hamlet*. Give me the car keys."

She shook her head. "I'll take you home."

"You'll drive me head-on into a bridge abutment."

"If that's what you want," she said, getting behind the wheel.

In the passenger's seat, he said, "You know what you are?"

"God's gift to Louisiana highways."

"Besides that. You're a control freak."

"That's just a slacker's term for someone who works hard and likes to do things *right*."

"So I'm a slacker now?" he asked.

"I didn't say that. All I'm saying, in a friendly way, is you're using their vocabulary."

"Don't drive so fast."

Carson accelerated. "How many times did your mother warn you not to run with scissors in your hand?"

"Like seven hundred thousand," he said. "But that doesn't mean you're fit to drive."

"God, you're relentless."

"You're incorrigible."

"Where'd you get *that* word? The dialogue in *Die Hard* isn't that sophisticated."

When Carson stopped at the curb in front of Michael's apartment house, he hesitated to get out. "I'm worried about you driving home."

"I'm like an old dray horse. I know the route in my bones."

"If you were *pulling* the car, I wouldn't worry, but you're gonna drive it at warp speed."

"I've got a gun, but you aren't worried about that."

"All right, all right. Drive. Go. But if you get behind a slow motorist, don't shoot him."

As she drove away, she saw him in the rearview mirror, watching her with concern.

The question wasn't whether she had fallen in love with Michael Maddison. The question was *how deeply, how irretrievably?*

Not that love was a sucking slough from which a person needed to be retrieved, like a drowner from the wild surf, like an addict from addiction. She was all for love. She just wasn't *ready* for love.

She had her career. She had Arnie. She had questions about her parents' deaths. Her life didn't have room for passion right now.

Maybe she'd be ready for passion when she was thirty-five. Or forty. Or ninety-four. But not now.

Besides, if she and Michael went to bed together, departmental regulations would necessitate a new partner for each of them.

She didn't like that many other homicide detectives. The chances were that she'd be paired with a fathead. Furthermore, right now she didn't have the time or patience to break in a new partner.

Not that she always obeyed departmental regulations. She wasn't a by-the-book i-dotter and t-crosser.

But the rule against cops copulating with cops and then sharing an assignment struck Carson as common sense.

Not that she always deferred to her common sense. Sometimes you had to take reckless chances if you trusted your instinct and if you were human.

Otherwise you might as well leave the force and become a safety engineer.

As for being human, there was the fright figure in Allwine's apartment, who claimed not to be human, unless he believed that being cobbled together from pieces of criminals and being brought to life by lightning was not a sufficient deviation from the usual dad-makes-mom-pregnant routine to deny him human status.

Either the monster—that's what he called himself; she was not being politically incorrect—had been a figment of her imagination, in which case she was crazy, or he had been real, in which case maybe the whole world had gone crazy.

In the midst of this gruesome and impossible case, she couldn't just unzip Michael's fly and say, *I know you've been dreaming about this.* Romance was a delicate thing. It needed tender care to grow and mature into something wonderful. Right now she didn't have time for an orgasm, let alone for romance.

If she and Michael could have something meaningful together, she didn't want to ruin it by rushing into bed, especially not at a time when the pressure of work was half crushing her.

And *that* indicated how deeply and irretrievably she loved him. She was in the water over her head.

She drove all the way home without killing herself or anyone else. If she had been as awake and clearheaded as she claimed to be, she wouldn't have taken such goofy pride in this accomplishment.

Between the car and the house, the sunlight seemed bright enough to blind her. Even in her bedroom, daylight at the windows stung her bloodshot eyes and made her wince.

She shut the blinds. She closed the drapes. She considered painting the room black, but decided that would be going too far.

Fully clothed, she fell into bed and was asleep before the pillows finished compressing under her head.

CHAPTER 47

THE FOURTH TIME that Roy Pribeaux opened the freezer to see if Candace was still there, she was still there, so he decided to rule out the possibility that he might be delusional.

He had not taken his car the previous night. He lived within strolling distance of the Quarter. They had walked everywhere.

Yet he could not have carried her all the way from the levee to his loft. Although he was a strong man and getting stronger by the day, she was a heavy person.

Besides, you couldn't carry an eyeless corpse around the heart of New Orleans without drawing comment and suspicion. Not even New Orleans.

He didn't *own* a wheelbarrow. Anyway, that wouldn't have been a practical solution.

He poured another glass of apple juice to accompany what remained of the muffin.

The only credible explanation for Candace's surprise appearance was that someone had brought her here from the levee and stowed her in his food freezer. The same person had put the three plastic containers, with organs, in the other freezer, the love locker.

This meant that someone knew Roy had killed Candace.

Indeed, that someone must have *watched* him kill her.

"Spooky," he whispered.

He had not been aware of being followed. If someone had been dogging him, watching him romance Candace, the guy had been a master of surveillance, nearly as ephemeral as a ghost.

Not just *someone*. Not just anyone. Considering the human organs in the three tacky containers with ugly green lids, the perpetrator could be none other than the copycat killer.

Roy's work had inspired an imitator. The imitator had by these actions said, *Hi there. Can we be friends? Why don't we combine our collections?*

Although Roy was flattered, as any artist might be flattered by the admiration of another artist, he didn't like this development. He didn't like it at all.

For one thing, this organ-obsessed individual was a burrower whose fascination with internals was gross and unsophisticated. He wasn't of Roy's caliber.

Besides, Roy didn't need or want the admiration of anyone. He was sufficient unto himself—until the perfect woman of his destiny entered his life.

He wondered when the copycat had visited. Candace had donated her eyes only a little more than twelve hours before he had found her in his freezer. The intruder would have had only two opportunities to bring her to the loft.

Satisfied with his life, immensely satisfied with himself, Roy had no reason for insomnia. He slept soundly every night.

The copycat, however, could not have brought such a heavy person as Candace into the loft and to the freezer while Roy slept unawares.

The kitchen was open to the dining area. The dining area flowed into the living room. Only a pony wall separated the living room from the bedroom. Sound would have traveled unobstructed, and Roy would have been awakened.

Now he went into the bathroom at the far end of the loft from the kitchen. He shut the door. He turned on the water in the shower. He switched on the vent fan.

Yes. Entirely possible. The copycat could have brought Candace into the loft when Roy had been enjoying his predawn shower.

He took long showers: the exfoliating soap with loofa sponge, the moisturizing soap, two superb shampoos, a cream conditioner. . . .

The visitor's precise timing suggested that he knew a great deal about Roy's domestic routine. And he must have a key.

Roy had no landlord. He owned the building. He possessed the only keys to the loft.

Standing in the bathroom, surrounded by the susurrant rush of water and vent-fan blades, he was overcome by the suspicion that the copycat was in the apartment even now, preparing another surprise.

This concern had no merit, based as it was on the requirements that the copycat be omniscient and omnipresent. Yet suspicion grew into conviction.

Roy cranked off the shower, switched off the fan. He burst out of the bathroom and searched the loft. No one.

Although alone, Roy was at last alarmed.

CHAPTER 48

SHE WAS RIDING a black horse across a desolate plain under a low and churning sky.

Cataclysmic blasts of lightning ripped the heavens. Where each bright sword stabbed to earth, a giant rose, half handsome and half deformed, tattooed.

Each giant grabbed at her, trying to pull her from her mount. Each grabbed at the horse, too, at its flashing hooves, at its legs, at its silky mane.

The terrified horse screamed, kicked, faltered, broke loose, plunged forward.

Without a saddle, she clamped the mount with her knees, clutched fistfuls of its mane, held on, endured. There were more giants in the earth than the horse could outrun. Lightning, the crash of thunder, yet another golem rising, a huge hand closing around her wrist—

Carson woke in unrelieved darkness, not thrown from sleep by the nightmare but pricked from it by a sound.

Piercing the soft thrum and *shush* of the air conditioner came the sharp creak of a floorboard. Another floorboard groaned. Someone moved stealthily through the bedroom.

She had awakened on her back, in a sweat, atop the bedclothes, in the exact position in which she'd fallen into bed. She sensed someone looming over her.

For a moment she couldn't remember where she'd left her service pistol. Then she realized that she still wore her street clothes, her shoes, even her shoulder holster. For the first time in her life, she had fallen asleep while armed.

She slid a hand under her jacket, withdrew the gun.

Although Arnie had never previously entered her room in the dark and though his behavior was predictable, this might be him.

When she slowly sat up and with her left hand groped toward the nightstand lamp, the bedsprings sang softly.

Floorboards creaked, perhaps because the intruder had reacted to the noise she made. Creaked again.

Her fingers found the lamp, the switch. Light.

She saw no one in the first flush of light. At once, however, she sensed more than saw movement from the corner of her eye.

Turning her head, bringing the pistol to bear, she found no one.

At one window, draperies billowed. For a moment she attributed that movement to the air conditioner. Then the billows subsided. The draperies hung limp and still. As if someone, leaving, had brushed against them.

Carson got out of bed and crossed the room. When she pulled the draperies aside, she found the window closed. And locked.

Maybe she hadn't awakened as instantly as she'd thought. Maybe sleep had clung to her, and the dream. Maybe.

CARSON SHOWERED, changed clothes, and felt fresh but slightly disoriented. Having slept away the afternoon, she rose to the night, inner clock confused, lacking purpose.

In the kitchen, she scooped a serving of curried chicken salad from a bowl. With her dish and a fork, eating on the move, she went to Arnie's room.

The castle glorious, fit for King Arthur, seemed to have grown higher towers.

For once, Arnie was not at work upon this citadel. Instead he sat staring at a penny balanced on his right thumbnail, against his forefinger.

"What's up, sweetie?" she asked, though she expected no reply.

He met her expectation, but flipped the penny into the air. The copper winked brightly as it turned.

With quicker reflexes than he usually exhibited, the boy snatched the coin from the air, held it tightly in his right fist.

Carson had never seen him engaged in this behavior before. She watched, wondering.

Half a minute passed while Arnie stared at his clenched fist. Then he opened it and frowned as if with disappointment when he saw the penny gleaming on his palm.

As the boy flipped it and caught it in midair once more, Carson noticed a stack of bright pennies on the drawbridge to the castle.

Arnie had neither an understanding of money nor any need for it.

"Honey, where did you get the pennies?"

Opening his hand, Arnie saw the penny and frowned as before. He flipped it again. He seemed to have a new obsession.

At the open door, Vicky Chou peered in from the hallway. "How's the chicken salad?"

"Fabulous. Every day, you make me feel inadequate in a new way."

Vicky made a *de nada* gesture. "We all have our special talents. I couldn't shoot anyone the way you do."

"Anytime you need it done, you know where to find me."

"Where did Arnie get the pennies?" Vicky asked.

"That's what I was gonna ask you."

Having flipped the penny again, having found it in his palm after snatching it from the air, the boy looked puzzled.

"Arnie, where did you get the pennies?"

From his shirt pocket, Arnie withdrew a card. He sat staring at it in silence.

Aware that her brother might study the card for an hour before offering it to her, Carson gently plucked it from his fingers.

"What?" Vicky asked.

"It's a pass to someplace called the Luxe Theater. One free movie. Where would he have gotten this?"

Arnie flipped the penny again, and as he snatched it out of the air, he said, "Every city has secrets—"

Carson knew she had heard those words somewhere—

"—but none as terrible as this."

—and her blood chilled as she saw in her mind's eye the tattooed man standing at the window in Bobby Allwine's apartment.

CHAPTER 49

TWO HUNDRED YEARS of life can leave a man jaded.

If he is a genius, like Victor, his intellectual pursuits lead him always on new adventures. The mind can be kept fresh and forever engaged as it confronts and resolves increasingly complex problems.

On the other hand, repetition of physical pleasures eventually makes former delights seem dull. Boredom sets in. During the second century, a man's appetites turn increasingly toward the exotic, the extreme.

This is why Victor requires violence with sex, and the cruel humiliation of his partner. He has long ago transcended the guilt that committing acts of cruelty might spawn in others. Brutality is an aphrodisiac; the exercise of raw power thrills him.

The world offers so many cuisines that conventional sex grows boring long before favorite dishes grow bland to the tongue. Only in the past decade has Victor developed a periodic craving for foods so exotic that they must be eaten with discretion.

At certain restaurants in the city, where the owners value his business, where the waiters value his generous gratuities, and where the chefs admire his uniquely sophisticated palate, Victor from time to time arranges special dinners in advance. He is always served in a private room, where a man of his refinement can enjoy dishes so rare that they might seem repulsive to the ignorant multitudes. He has no wish to explain these acquired tastes to the boorish diners—and they are virtually always boorish—at an adjoining table.

Quan Yin, a Chinese restaurant named for the Queen of Heaven, had two private dining rooms. One was suitable for a group of eight. Victor had reserved it for himself.

He frequently ate alone. With two hundred years of experience that no one of an ordinary life span could match, he found that he was virtually always his own best company.

Teasing his appetite, allowing time to anticipate the exotic entrée, he began with a simple dish: egg drop soup.

Before he had half finished this first course, his cell phone rang. He was surprised to hear the voice of the renegade.

"Murder doesn't scare me anymore, Father."

With a note of authority that always secured obedience, Victor said, "You must talk to me about this in person."

"I'm not as troubled about murder as when I called you before."

"How did you get this number?"

The emergency contact number at Hands of Mercy, given to members of the New Race, did not transfer calls to Victor's cell phone.

Instead of answering, the renegade said, "Murder just makes me more human. They excel at murder."

"But you're better than their kind." The need to discuss this, to *debate* it, annoyed Victor. He was master and commander. His word was law, his desire obeyed, at least among his people. "You're more rational, more—"

"We're not better. There's something missing in us . . . something they have."

This was an intolerable lie. This was heresy.

"The help you need," Victor insisted impatiently, "only I am able to give."

"If I just cut open enough of them and look inside, sooner or later I'll discover what makes them . . . happier."

"That isn't rational. Come to me at the Hands of Mercy—"

"There's this girl I see sometimes, she's particularly happy. I'll find the truth in her, the secret, the thing I'm missing."

The renegade hung up.

As before, Victor pressed *69. Also as before, the call had come from a number that blocked automatic call-backs.

His special dinner had not been ruined by this development, but his bright mood had dimmed. He decided to switch from tea to wine.

Beer often went with Chinese food better than wine did. Victor was not, however, a beer man.

Unlike many Chinese restaurants, Quan Yin had an extensive cellar full of the finest vintages. The waiter—in a ruffled white tuxedo shirt, bow tie, and black tuxedo pants—brought a wine list.

As he finished his soup and waited for a salad of hearts of palms and peppers, Victor studied the list. He wavered between a wine suitable for pork and one better matched with seafood.

He would be eating neither pork nor seafood. The entrée, which he'd had before, was such a rare delicacy that any connoisseur of wine must be of several minds about the most compatible selection.

Finally he chose a superb Pinot Grigio and enjoyed the first glass with his salad.

Much ceremony accompanied the presentation of the main course, beginning with the chef himself, a Buddha-plump man named Lee Ling. He sprinkled red rose petals across the white tablecloth.

Two waiters appeared with an ornately engraved red-bronze tray on which stood a legged, one-quart copper pot filled with boiling oil. A Sterno burner under the pot kept the oil bubbling.

They put the tray on the table, and Victor breathed deeply of the aroma rising from the pot. This peanut oil, twice clarified, had been infused with a blend of pepper oils. The fragrance was divine.

A third waiter put a plain white plate before him. Beside the plate, red chopsticks. So gently as to avoid the slightest clink, the waiter placed a pair of stainless-steel tongs on the plate.

The handles of the tongs were rubberized to insulate against the heat that the steel would draw from the boiling oil. The pincer ends were shaped like the petals of lotus blossoms.

The pot of oil stood to Victor's right. Now a bowl of saffron rice was placed at the head of his plate.

Lee Ling, having retreated to the kitchen, returned with the entrée, which he put to the left of Victor's plate. The delicacy waited in a silver serving dish with a lid.

The waiters bowed and retreated. Lee Ling waited, smiling.

Victor removed the lid from the silver server. The dish had been lined with cabbage leaves briefly steamed to wilt them and make them pliable.

This rare delicacy did not appear on the menu. It was not available at all times or on short notice.

In any event, Lee Ling would prepare it only for that one-in-a-thousand customer whom he'd known for years, whom he trusted, whom he knew to be a true gourmet. The customer must also be one so familiar with regional Chinese cuisine that he knew to request this very item.

Restaurant-licensing officials would not have approved of this offering, not even here in libertine New Orleans. No health risk was involved, but some things are too exotic even for the most tolerant of people.

In the dish, nestled in the cabbage, squirmed a double litter of live baby rats, so recently born that they were still pink, hairless, and blind.

In Chinese, Victor expressed his approval and gratitude to Lee Ling. Smiling, bowing, the chef retreated, leaving his guest alone.

Perhaps the excellent wine had restored Victor's good mood or perhaps his own extraordinary sophistication so pleased him that he could not for long remain glum. One of the secrets to leading a life full of great accomplishment was to like oneself, and Victor Helios, alias Frankenstein, liked himself more than he could express.

He dined.

CHAPTER 50

THE SECOND FLOOR of the Hands of Mercy is quiet.

Here the men and women of the New Race, fresh from the tanks, are undergoing the final stages of direct-to-brain data downloading. Soon they will be ready to go into the world and take their places among doomed humanity.

Randal Six will leave Mercy before any of them, before this night is over. He is terrified, but he is ready.

The computer maps and virtual reality tours of New Orleans have unnerved him as much as they have prepared him. But if he is to avoid the spinning rack and survive, he can wait no longer.

To make his way in the dangerous world beyond these walls, he should be armed. But he has no weapon and cannot see anything in his room that might serve as one.

If the journey is longer than he hopes, he will need provisions. He has no food in his room, only what is brought to him at mealtimes.

Somewhere in this building is a kitchen of considerable size. A pantry. There he would find the food he needs.

The prospect of searching for a kitchen, gathering food from among an overwhelming number of choices, and packing supplies is so daunting that he cannot begin. If he must provision himself, he will never leave Mercy.

So he will set out with nothing more than the clothes he wears, a fresh book of crossword puzzles, and a pen.

At the threshold between his room and the hallway, paralysis seizes him. He cannot proceed.

He knows that the floors of these two spaces are on the same plane, yet he feels certain that he will drop a killing distance if he dares cross into the corridor. What he *knows* is usually not as powerful as what he *feels,* which is the curse of his condition.

Although he reminds himself that perhaps an encounter with Arnie O'Connor is his destiny, he remains unmoved, unmoving.

His emotional weather worsens as he stands paralyzed. Agitation stirs his thoughts into confusion, like a whirl of wind sweeps autumn leaves into a colorful spiral.

He is acutely aware of how this agitation can quickly develop into a deeper disturbance, then a storm, then a tempest. He wants desperately to open the book of puzzles and put his pen to the empty boxes.

If he succumbs to the crossword desire, he will finish not one puzzle, not two, but the entire book. Night will pass. Morning will come. He will have lost forever the courage to escape.

Threshold. Hallway. With one step, he can cross the former and be in the latter. He has done this before, but this time it seems like a thousand-mile journey.

The difference, of course, is that previously he had intended to go no farther than the hallway. This time, he wants the world.

Threshold, hallway.

Suddenly *threshold* and *hallway* appear in his mind as hand-inked black letters in rows of white boxes, two entries in a crossword puzzle, sharing the letter *h.*

When he sees the two words intersecting in this manner, he more clearly recognizes that the threshold and the hallway in reality also intersect on the same plane. Crossing the first into the latter is no more difficult than filling the boxes with letters.

He steps out of his room.

CHAPTER 51

THE GEOMETRIC DESIGNS on the Art Deco facade of the Luxe Theater were given greater depth and drama by the honing glow of a streetlamp and the shadows that it sharpened.

The marquee was dark, and the theater appeared to be closed if not abandoned until Carson peered through one of the doors. She saw soft light at the refreshment counter and someone at work there.

When she tried the door, it swung inward. She stepped into the lobby.

The glass candy cases were lighted to display their wares. On the wall behind the counter, an illuminated Art Deco–style Coca-Cola clock, frost white and crimson, was a surprisingly poignant reminder of a more innocent time.

The man working behind the counter was the giant she had met in Allwine's apartment. His physique identified him before he turned and revealed his face.

She snapped the movie pass against the glass top of the counter. "Who are you?"

"I told you once."

"I didn't get your name," she said tightly.

He had been cleaning out the popcorn machine. He turned his attention to it once more. "My name's Deucalion."

"First or last?"

"First and last."

"You work here?"

"I own the theater."

"You assaulted a police officer."

"Did I? Were you hurt?" He smiled, not sarcastically but with surprising warmth, considering his face. "Or was the damage to your self-esteem?"

His composure impressed her. His intimidating size was not the source of his confidence; he was no bully. Instead, his calm nature approached the deeper serenity that she associated with monastics in their cowled robes.

Some sociopaths were serene, too, as collected as trapdoor spiders waiting in their lairs for prey to drop on them.

She said, "What were you doing in my house?"

"From what I've seen of how you live, I think I can trust you."

"Why do I give a rat's ass whether you trust me? Stay out of my house."

"Your brother is a heavy burden. You carry him with grace."

Alarmed, she said, "You. Aren't. In. My. Life."

He put down the damp cloth with which he'd been wiping out the popcorn machine, and he turned to her again, with only the candy counter between them.

"Is that what you want?" he asked. "Is it really? If that's what you want, why did you come to hear the rest of it? Because you didn't come just to tell me to stay away. You came with questions."

His insight and his quiet amusement did not comport with the brutal look of him.

When she stood nonplussed, he said, "I mean no harm to Arnie or to you. Your enemy is Helios."

She blinked in surprise. "Helios? Victor Helios? Owns Biovision, big philanthropist?"

"He has the arrogance to call himself 'Helios,' after the Greek god of the sun. Helios . . . the life-giver. That isn't his real name." Without emphasis, without a raised eyebrow, with no apparent irony, he said, "His real name is Frankenstein."

After what he had said in Bobby Allwine's apartment, after his riff about being made from pieces of criminals and given life force by a thunderstorm, she should have expected this development. She did *not* expect it, however, and it disappointed her.

Carson had felt that Deucalion was special in some way other than his formidable size and appearance, and for reasons that she couldn't articulate to her satisfaction, she had *wanted* him to be something special. She needed to have the rug of routine pulled out from under her, to be tumbled headlong into the *mystery* of life.

Maybe mystery was a synonym for change. Maybe she needed a different kind of excitement from what the job usually supplied. She suspected, however, that she needed more meaning in her life than the homicide assignment currently gave her, though she didn't know quite what she meant by *meaning*.

Deucalion disappointed her because this Frankenstein business was just another flavor of the nutcase rants she encountered more days than not in the conduct of ordinary investigations. He'd seemed strange but substantive; now he sounded hardly different from the pinwheel-eyed ginks who thought that CIA operatives or aliens were after them.

"Yeah," she said. "Frankenstein."

"The legend isn't fiction. It's fact."

"Of course it is." Disappointment of various kinds had the same effect on her: a craving for chocolate. Pointing through the glass top of the counter, she said, "I'd like one of those Hershey's bars with almonds."

"Long ago, in Austria, they burned his laboratory to the ground. Because he created me."

"Bummer. Where are your neck bolts? Did you have them surgically removed?"

"Look at me," he said solemnly.

She gazed longingly at the Hershey's bar for a moment but at last met his gaze.

Ghostly radiance pulsed through his eyes. This time she was so close that even if she had wanted to, she could not have dismissed it as a reflection of some natural light source.

"I suspect," he said, "that stranger things than I now roam this city . . . and he's begun to lose control of them."

He stepped to the cash register, opened a drawer beneath it, and withdrew a newspaper clipping and a rolled paper tied with a ribbon.

The clipping included a photo of Victor Helios. The paper was a pencil portrait of the same man a decade younger.

"I tore this from a frame in Victor's study two centuries ago, so I would never forget his face."

"This doesn't prove anything. Are the Hershey's bars for sale or not?"

"The night I was born, Victor needed a storm. He got the storm of the century."

Deucalion rolled up his right sleeve, revealing three shiny metal disks embedded in his flesh.

Admittedly, Carson had never seen anything like this. On the other hand, this was an age when some people pierced their tongues with studs and even had the tips of their tongues split for a reptilian effect.

"Contact points," he explained. "All over my body. But something was strange about the lightning . . . such power."

He didn't mention the ragged white keloid scars that joined his wrist to his forearm.

If he was living out a Frankenstein-monster fantasy, he had gone to extremes to conform his physical appearance to the tale. This was a bit more impressive than a Star Trek fan wearing a jumpsuit and Spock ears.

Against her better judgment, even if she couldn't believe him, Carson felt herself wanting to believe *in* him.

This desire to believe surprised her, disturbed her. She didn't understand it. So *not* Carson O'Connor.

"The storm gave me life," he continued, "but it also gave me something just short of immortality."

Deucalion picked up the newspaper clipping, stared for a moment at the photo of Victor Helios, then crushed it in his fist.

"I thought my maker was long dead. But from the beginning, he's been after his own immortality—of one kind or another."

"Quite a story," she said. "Does abduction by extraterrestrials come into it at any point?"

In Carson's experience, kooks could not tolerate mockery. They reacted with anger or they accused her of being part of whatever conspiracy they believed had targeted them.

Deucalion merely threw aside the wadded clipping, withdrew a Hershey's bar from the display case, and put the candy on the counter in front of her.

Unwrapping the chocolate, she said, "You expect me to believe two hundred years? So the lightning that night, it—what?—altered his genetics?"

"No. The lightning didn't touch him. Only me. He got this far . . . some other way."

"Lots of fiber, fresh fruit, no red meat."

She couldn't tweak him.

No more of the eerie luminosity passed through his eyes, but she saw in them something else that she had never glimpsed in the eyes of another. An electrifying directness. She felt so exposed that a chill closed like a fist around her heart.

Loneliness in that gaze, and wisdom, and humility. And . . . more that was enigmatic. His eyes were a singularity, and though there was much to be read in them, she hadn't the language to understand what she read, for the soul that looked out at her through those lenses suddenly seemed as alien as that of any creature born on another world.

Chocolate cloyed in her mouth, her throat. The candy tasted oddly like blood, as if she had bitten her tongue.

She put down the Hershey's bar.

"What has Victor been doing all this time?" Deucalion wondered. "What has he been . . . making?"

She remembered Bobby Allwine's cadaver, naked and dissected on the autopsy table—and Jack Rogers's insistence that its freakish innards were the consequence not of mutation but of *design*.

Deucalion appeared to pluck a shiny quarter from the ether. He flipped it off his thumb, caught it in midair, held it for a moment in his fist. When he opened his hand, the quarter wasn't there.

Here was the trick that Arnie had been trying to imitate.

Turning over the candy bar that Carson had just put down on the glass counter, Deucalion revealed the quarter.

She sensed that this peculiar impromptu performance was meant to be more than entertainment. It was meant to convince her that the truth of him was as magical as he had presented it.

He picked up the quarter—his hands so dexterous for their great size—and flipped it high and past her head.

When she turned to follow its arc, she lost sight of the quarter high in the air.

She waited for the *ping* and clatter of the coin bouncing off the marble floor of the lobby. Silence.

When the silence endured beyond all reasonable expectation of the quarter's return, Carson looked at Deucalion.

He had another quarter. He snapped it off his thumb.

More intently than before, she tracked it—but lost it as it reached the apex of its arc.

She held her breath, waiting for the falling coin to ring off the floor, but the sound didn't come, didn't come—and then she needed to breathe.

"Am I still not in your life?" he asked. "Or do you want to hear more?"

CHAPTER 52

SCONCES SPREAD RADIANT amber fans on the walls, but at this hour the lights are dim and shadows dominate.

Randal Six has only now realized that the blocks of vinyl-tile flooring in the hallway are like the squares in a crossword puzzle. This geometry gives him comfort.

He visualizes in his mind one letter of his name with every step that he takes, spelling himself along the tile floor, block by block, toward freedom.

This is the dormitory floor, where the most recently awakened members of the New Race are housed until they are polished and ready to infiltrate the city.

Half the doors stand open. Beyond some of them, naked bodies are locked in every imaginable sexual posture.

Especially in their early weeks, the tank-born are filled with anguish that arises from their knowledge of what they are. They also suffer intense anxiety because they come to full consciousness with the immediate understanding that, as Victor's chattel, they do not control the primary issues of their lives and possess no free will; therefore, in their beginning is their end, and their lives are mapped without hope of mystery.

They are sterile but vigorous. In them, sex has been divorced entirely from the purpose of procreation and functions solely as a vent for stress.

They copulate in groups, tangled and writhing, and it seems to Randal Six, whose autism makes him different from them, that these thrusts provide them no pleasure, only release from tension.

The sounds issuing from these orgiastic groups have no quality of joy, no suggestion of tenderness. These are bestial noises, low and rough, insistent almost to the point of violence, eager to the point of desperation.

The slap of flesh on flesh, the wordless grunts, the guttural cries that seem charged with rage—all this frightens Randal Six as he passes these rooms. He feels the urge to run but dares not step on the lines between the vinyl blocks; he must place each foot entirely in a square, which requires a deliberative pace.

The hallway increasingly seems like a tunnel, the chambers on both sides like catacombs in which the restless dead embrace in cold desire.

Heart knocking as if to test the soundness of his ribs, Randal spells his name often enough to reach an intersection of corridors. Using the final letter, he spells a crossing word—*left*—which allows him to turn in that direction.

From the letter *t,* he sidesteps four blocks, spelling *right* backward as he goes. With the letter *r* as his new beginning, he is able to spell his name and, thereby, proceed forward along this new hall, toward the choice of elevators or a stairwell.

CHAPTER 53

ERIKA TOOK DINNER alone in the master bedroom, at a nineteenth-century French marquetry table featuring a motif of autumn bounty—apples, oranges, plums, grapes, all spilling from a horn of plenty—rendered with exquisitely inlaid woods of numerous varieties.

Like all those of the New Race, her metabolism was as fine-tuned and as powerful as a Ferrari engine. This required a formidable appetite.

Two six-ounce steaks—filet mignon, prepared medium-rare—were accompanied by a rasher of crisp bacon, buttered carrots with thyme, and snow peas with sliced jicama. A separate chafing dish contained braised potatoes in blue cheese sauce. For dessert waited an entire peach cobbler with a side dish of vanilla ice cream coddled in a bowl of crushed ice.

While she ate, she stared at the scalpel that had been left on her bath mat earlier in the day. It lay across her bread plate as if it were a butter knife.

She didn't know how the scalpel related to the furtive ratlike noises that she had been hearing, but she was certain that the two were connected.

There is no world but this one. All flesh is grass, and withers, and the fields of the mind, too, are burned black by death and do not grow green again. That conviction is essential to the creed of materialism; and Erika is a soldier in the determined army that will inevitably conquer the Earth and impose that philosophy pole to pole.

Yet, though her creator forbade belief in the supernatural and though her laboratory origins suggested that intelligent life can be manufactured without divine inspiration, Erika could not shake a sense of the uncanny in these recent events. The scalpel seemed to sparkle not solely with the sheen of surgical steel but also with . . . magic.

As if by her thoughts she had opened a door between this world and another, a force inexplicable switched on the plasma TV. Erika looked up with a start as the screen came alive.

The cordless Crestron panel, by which the TV was controlled, currently lay on Victor's nightstand, untouched.

Some bodiless Presence seemed to be channel surfing. Images flipped rapidly across the screen, faster, faster.

As Erika put down her fork and pushed her chair back from the table, the Presence selected a dead channel. A blizzard of electronic snow whitened the big screen.

Sensing that something bizarre—and something of significance— was about to happen, she rose to her feet.

The voice—deep, rough, and ominous—came to her out of the dead channel, through the Dolby SurroundSound speakers in the ceiling: *"Kill him. Kill him."*

Erika moved away from the table, toward the TV, but halted after two steps when it seemed unwise to get too close to the screen.

"Shove the scalpel in his eye. Into his brain. Kill him."

"Who are you?" she asked.

"Kill him. Thrust it deep, and twist. Kill him."

"Kill whom?"

The Presence did not answer.

She repeated her question.

On the plasma screen, out of the snow, a pale ascetic face began to form. For a moment, she assumed this must be the face of a spirit, but as it developed character, she recognized Victor, eyes closed and features relaxed, as though this were his death mask.

"Kill him."

"He made me."

"To use."

"I can't."

"You're strong."

"Impossible."

"Kill him."

"Who are you?"

"Evil," said the voice, and she knew that this Presence was not speaking of itself, but of Victor.

If she participated in this conversation, she would inevitably consider betraying Victor even if only to make an argument that it was impossible to raise a hand against him. The mere act of *thinking* about killing her maker could bring her own death.

Every thought creates a unique electrical signature in the brain.

Victor had identified those signatures that represented the thought of taking violent action against him.

Implanted in Erika's brain—as in the brain of every member of the New Race—was a nanodevice programmed to recognize the thought signature of patricide, of deicide.

If ever she picked up a weapon with the intention of using it against Victor, that spy within would instantly recognize her intent. It would plunge her into a state of paralysis from which only Victor could retrieve her.

If thereafter he allowed her to live, hers would be a life of greater suffering. He would fill all her days with imaginative punishment.

Consequently, she moved now to the Crestron touch panel on the nightstand and used it to switch off the TV. The plasma screen went dark.

Waiting with the control in hand, she expected the TV to switch itself on again, but it remained off.

She did not believe in spirits. She *must* not believe. Such belief was disobedience. Disobedience would lead to termination.

The mysterious voice urging murder was best left mysterious. To pursue an understanding of it would be to chase it off a cliff, to certain death.

When she realized that she was trembling with fear, Erika returned to her chair at the table.

She began to eat again, but now her appetite was of the nervous variety. She ate voraciously, trying to quell a hunger that food could never satisfy: a hunger for meaning, for freedom.

Her tremors—and the fear of death they represented—surprised her. There had been times since her "birth" six weeks ago when she had thought death desirable.

Not now. Something had changed. When she had not been looking, that thing with feathers, hope, had come into her heart.

CHAPTER 54

ROY PRIBEAUX HAD GUNS.

He retrieved them from the closet where they were stored in custom cases. He examined them lovingly, one by one, cleaned and lubricated them as necessary, preparing them for use.

Throughout his adolescence and twenties, he had *adored* guns. Revolvers, pistols, shotguns, rifles—he had a core collection of each type of weapon.

Shortly after his twentieth birthday, when he had come into his inheritance, he bought a Ford Explorer, loaded it with his favorite firearms, and toured the South and Southwest.

Until that time, he had only killed animals.

He hadn't been a hunter. He'd never acquired a hunting license. Tramping around in the woods and fields didn't appeal to him. His prey were domestic and farm animals.

On the road at twenty, he targeted people for the first time. For several years he was carefree and happy.

As are many people in their twenties, Roy had been idealistic. He believed that he could make this a better society, a better world.

Even then, he'd realized that life was made tolerable only by the existence of beauty. Beauty in nature. Beauty in architecture and art and in objects of human manufacture. Beauty among human beings.

From childhood, he himself had been strikingly attractive, and he had been aware how the sight of him lifted people's spirits and how his company improved their moods.

He intended to make the world a happier place by eliminating ugly people wherever he found them. And he found them everywhere.

In eighteen states as far east as Alabama, as far north as Colorado, as far west as Arizona, and as far south as Texas, Roy traveled to kill. He destroyed ugly humanity where circumstances assured that he could strike without risk of apprehension.

He employed such a variety of fine weapons over such an enormous geographical area that his many scores were never linked as the work of one perpetrator. He killed at a distance with rifles, at forty yards or less with 12-gauge shotguns loaded with buckshot, and close-up with revolvers or pistols as the mood took him.

Generally he preferred the intimacy of handguns. They virtually always allowed him to get close enough to explain that he held no personal animosity toward the target.

"It's an aesthetic issue," he might say. Or "I'm sure you'll agree, dead is better than ugly." Or "I'm just doing Darwin's work to advance the beauty of the species."

Shotguns were thrilling when he had the leisure to reload and to use with increasing proximity a total of four or six Federal three-inch, 000 shells, which had tremendous penetration. He could not only remove the ugly person from the gene pool but also, with the Federal rounds, *obliterate* their ugliness and leave a corpse so ravaged that there would *have* to be a closed-casket funeral.

During those years of travel and accomplishment, Roy had known the satisfaction of noble purpose and worthwhile labor. He assumed that this would be his life's work, with no need ever to learn new job skills or to retire.

Over time, however, he reluctantly came to the conclusion that so many ugly people inhabited the world that his efforts alone could not ensure prettier future generations. In fact, the more people he killed, the uglier the world seemed to become.

Ugliness has the momentum of a tsunami. It is the handmaiden to entropy. One man's resistance, while admirable, cannot turn back the most titanic forces of nature.

Eventually he returned to New Orleans, to rest and to reconsider his mission. He purchased this building and rebuilt the loft into an apartment.

He began to suspect that he had too long associated with too many ugly people. Although he had killed them all, sparing humanity the further sight of them, perhaps their ugliness had somehow tainted Roy himself.

For the first time, his reflection in a mirror disquieted him. Being brutally honest, he had to admit that he was still beautiful, certainly in the top one tenth of one percent of the most beautiful people in the world, but perhaps not as beautiful as he had been before he had set out in his Explorer to save humanity from ugliness.

Being a forward-looking and determined person, he had not fallen into despair. He developed a program of diet, exercise, nutritional supplementation, and meditation to regain fully his former splendor.

As any mirror now revealed, he succeeded. He was breathtaking.

Nevertheless, he often thought of those years of rehabilitation as the Wasted Years, because while he restored himself, he had no time to kill anyone. And no reason to kill them.

Roy was a goal-driven person with a deep desire to contribute to society. He didn't kill just to kill. He needed a purpose.

When he had struck upon the idea of harvesting and preserving the ideal parts of a perfect woman, he rejoiced that his life had meaning once more.

Eventually he might anonymously donate the collection to a great museum. The academics and critics who championed modern art would at once recognize the value and brilliance of his assembled woman.

First he must find that elusive living female who was perfect in every detail and who was destined to be his mate. Until then he would need the collection in order to lay it out and, item by item, compare his beloved to all those pieces of perfection, to be certain that in every way she measured up to his highest standard.

No doubt his longed-for Venus would soon cross his path—another reason why he couldn't tolerate the intrusion of the copycat killer into his life. That poor fool's use of tacky, low-quality Tupperware imitations provided proof enough that his appreciation for beauty in all things was so inadequate that no friendship could ever flower between him and Roy.

Now, in preparation for the copycat's next visit, Roy loaded various pistols and revolvers. He secreted a weapon in each area of his expansive apartment.

In the bathroom, a Browning Hi-Power 9mm in the drawer where he kept his colognes.

Under a pillow on his bed, a Smith & Wesson Chief's Special, one of the best small-frame .38 Special revolvers ever made.

Under a living-room sofa cushion, a Glock Model 23 loaded with .40 Smith & Wesson ammo.

Concealed at two points among the array of exercise machines were a pair of SIG P245s.

In the kitchen, Roy placed a Springfield Trophy Match 1911-A1 in the bread box, next to a loaf of low-fat seven-grain with raisins.

When Roy closed the drop door on the bread box and turned, a sizable stranger stood in the kitchen with him, a red-faced, boiled-looking guy with mean blue eyes.

How the intruder had gotten in and moved so quietly, Roy didn't know, but this must be the copycat. The guy wasn't aggressively ugly, but he wasn't half pretty, either, just homely, so there could be no chance whatsoever of a friendship between him and Roy.

The fierce expression on the copycat's face suggested he had no interest in friendship, either. Maybe Roy had been mistaken to assume the copycat had come here, in the first place, out of admiration.

He noticed the intruder wore latex surgical gloves. Not a good sign.

Realizing that he wouldn't be able to turn to the bread box and retrieve the pistol quickly enough to use it, Roy struck out at his adversary with confidence, employing what he had learned during four years of instruction in Tae Kwon Do.

Although he didn't appear to be as fit as Roy, the copycat proved to be fast and strong. He not only blocked the blows but seized Roy's right hand, bent it backward, and snapped his wrist as if it were a dry branch.

The pain rocked Roy Pribeaux. He didn't handle pain well. His life had been mercifully free of it. The shock of the broken wrist robbed him of breath so completely that an attempt at a scream produced only a wheeze.

Incredibly, the copycat grabbed him by his shirt and by the crotch of his slacks, lifted him overhead as if he weighed no more than a child, and slammed him down on the edge of a kitchen counter.

Louder than the wheeze of his scream came the sound of his spine snapping.

The copycat released him. Roy slid off the counter, onto the floor.

The pain had stopped. This seemed like a good thing, until he realized that he had no feeling whatsoever below his neck.

He tried to move his left hand. He could not. Paralyzed.

Glaring down at him, the copycat said, "I don't need to cut you open and see inside. You don't have what I'm looking for. You're all dark inside, and I need the other thing."

Darkness wanted Roy, and he gave himself to it.

CHAPTER 55

JONATHAN HARKER, Mercy-born and Mercy-raised, had joined the New Orleans Police Department sixteen years ago.

All papers substantiating his identity and previous employment history had been impeccably forged. According to these records, he'd been a cop in Atlanta, Georgia.

Other members of the New Race, already seeded in the department at that time, had falsified follow-up with officials in Atlanta, facilitating his employment. Later they greased his path into the NOPD Homicide Division.

He had been a good son to Father, dutiful and dedicated . . . until the past year. He had lost his sense of purpose. The preparations for war against humanity, still at least a decade distant, did not excite or even interest him any longer.

For several years he had felt . . . incomplete. Over the preceding twelve months, this feeling had matured into a terrible emptiness, a cold and yawning void at the center of him.

He recognized in humanity a lust for life, a joy, that he did not possess. He wanted to know how this quality arose in them.

Every detail of his own physical and mental design had been direct-to-brain downloaded when Jonathan had been in the creation tank, so that he would have a proper awe of Victor, his maker. Thus it occurred to him that by studying human physiology and comparing theirs to his own, he should be able to identify what the Old Race had that he lacked, perhaps a gland that secreted a hormone or an enzyme that was required for happiness.

He began by studying human biology. He pored through medical texts.

Instead of discovering greater complexity in their bodies, he found comparative simplicity. He didn't lack anything they had; quite the contrary, they seemed less well constructed for durability than he was with his second heart and other redundant systems.

Eventually he arrived at the conviction that they *did* contain some gland or organ that allowed them the possibility of happiness but that *they themselves had not yet discovered and identified it*. Therefore he could not find it in a textbook.

Because the New Race came out of their creation tanks inculcated with a faith in their superiority to ordinary human beings, Jonathan had no doubt that through further self-education, he could find what had eluded Old Race physiologists. By cutting open enough of them and searching their innards, he would—by virtue of his sharper mind and keener eye—find the gland of happiness.

When a serial killer appeared on the scene, Jonathan recognized an opportunity. He could pursue his own dissections with caution and eventually contrive to have them attributed to the killer. He'd used chloroform on one of his first two subjects for this very purpose.

Investigating behind O'Connor and Maddison, Jonathan worked the Surgeon case twenty-four hours a day, without sleep. He had an eerie, intuitive understanding of the killer's psychology and sensed early on that his quarry had embarked on a quest for happiness similar to his own. For this reason, he found his way to Roy Pribeaux in time to watch him court and kill the cotton-candy girl.

Jonathan might have allowed Pribeaux to carry on indefinitely if not for the fact that his own circumstances had changed. Something was happening to him that promised the fulfillment for which he had long been yearning.

He had learned nothing from probing inside his first two subjects. And what he'd done to Bobby Allwine had not been part of his researches, merely an act of mercy. Bobby had wanted to die, and because Father's programmed injunction against murder had broken down in Jonathan, he had been able to oblige his friend.

Yet though he'd discovered nothing to advance his understanding of the source of human happiness, Jonathan had begun to change in a wondrous way. He felt movement within himself. Several times he had *seen* something inside him, something alive, pressing against his abdomen, as if yearning to get out.

He suspected that he was going to overcome another of Father's key restrictions on the New Race. Jonathan believed that he would soon reproduce.

Therefore, he needed to wrap up business with Pribeaux, pin all the killings to date on him, and prepare for what glory might be coming.

He intended to conduct only a single additional dissection, markedly more elaborate than the previous ones. He would dispose of this final subject in such a way that when her body was found long after the fact, she also might be linked to Roy Pribeaux.

As Pribeaux lay paralyzed and unconscious on the kitchen floor, Jonathan Harker produced a comb from his shirt pocket. He had bought it earlier in the day but had not used it himself.

He drew it through the killer's thick hair. Several loose strands had tangled in the plastic teeth.

He put the comb and these hairs in an envelope that he brought for this purpose. Evidence.

Pribeaux had regained consciousness. "Who . . . who are you?"

"Do you want to die?" Jonathan asked.

Tears swelled in Pribeaux's eyes. "No. Please, no."

"You want to live even if you'll be paralyzed for life?"

"Yes. Yes, please. I have plenty of money. I can receive the finest care and rehabilitation. Help me dispose of . . . of what's in the freezers, everything incriminating, let me live, and I'll make you rich."

The New Race was not motivated by money. Jonathan pretended otherwise. "I know the depth of your resources. Maybe we can strike a bargain, after all."

"Yes, we can, I know we can," Pribeaux said weakly but eagerly.

"But right now," Jonathan said, "I want you to be quiet. I've got work to do, and I don't want to have to listen to your whining. If you stay quiet, we'll bargain later. If you speak once, just once, I'll kill you. Do you understand?"

When Pribeaux tried to nod, he couldn't.

"All right," said Jonathan. "We're on the same page."

Pribeaux bled from his shattered wrist, but slowly and steadily rather than in arterial spurts.

With a new eyedropper that he had purchased in the same drugstore where he'd bought the comb, Jonathan suctioned blood from the puddle on the floor. He transferred a few ccs at a time to a little glass bottle that he had also brought with him.

Pribeaux's eyes followed his every move. They were moist with self-pity, bright with curiosity, wide with terror.

When he had filled the small bottle, Jonathan screwed a cap on it and stowed it in a jacket pocket. He wrapped the bloody eyedropper in a handkerchief and pocketed that, as well.

Quickly he searched the kitchen drawers until he found a white plastic garbage bag and rubber bands.

He slid the bag over Pribeaux's damaged left arm and fixed it tightly above the elbow with two rubber bands. This would make it possible to move the man without leaving a blood trail.

Effortlessly, Jonathan lifted Pribeaux and put him on the floor near the dinette set, out of the way.

He cleaned the blood from the white ceramic tiles. Fortunately, Pribeaux had sealed the grout so effectively that the blood did not penetrate.

When he was certain that not one drop or smear of blood remained and that no other evidence of violence could be found in the kitchen, he bagged the paper towels and other cleanup supplies in another garbage bag, knotted the neck of it, and secured it to his belt.

At the desk in the living room, he switched on the computer. He chose a program from the menu and typed a few lines that with great thought he had earlier composed.

Leaving the computer on, Jonathan went to the front door, opened it, and stepped onto the roomy landing at the head of the stairs that served Pribeaux's loft. He stood listening for a moment.

The businesses on the first floor had closed hours ago. Pribeaux didn't seem to have friends or visitors. Deep stillness pooled in the building.

In the apartment again, Jonathan lifted Pribeaux and carried him in his arms as though he were a child, out to the landing.

In addition to stairs, the apartment was served by the freight elevator that was original to the building. With an elbow, Jonathan pressed the call button.

Pribeaux's eyes searched Jonathan's face, desperately trying to read his intent.

Aboard the elevator, still carrying the paralyzed man, Jonathan pressed the number 3 on the control panel.

On the flat roof of the former warehouse were storage structures that required elevator service.

When Pribeaux realized they were going to the roof, his pale face paled further, and the terror in his eyes grew frenetic. He knew now that there would be no bargain made to save his life.

"You can still feel pain in your face, in your neck," Jonathan warned him. "I will cause you the most horrific pain you can imagine, in the process of blinding you. Do you understand?"

Pribeaux blinked rapidly, opened his mouth, but dared not speak a word even of submission.

"Excruciating pain," Jonathan promised. "But if you remain silent and cause me no problem, your death will be quick."

The elevator arrived at the top of the building.

Only orange light of an early moon illuminated the roof, but Jonathan could see well. He carried the killer to the three-foot-high safety parapet.

Pribeaux had begun to weep, but not so loud as to earn him the unendurable pain that he had been promised. He sounded like a small child, lost and full of misery.

The cobblestone alleyway behind the warehouse lay forty feet below, deserted at this hour.

Jonathan dropped Pribeaux off the roof. The killer screamed but not loud or long.

In desperate physical condition *before* he had been dropped, Roy Pribeaux had no chance whatsoever of surviving the fall. The sound of him hitting the pavement was a lesson in the fragility of the human skeleton.

Jonathan left the elevator at the roof and took the stairs to the ground floor. He walked to his car, which he had parked three blocks away.

En route, he tossed the garbage bag full of bloody paper towels in a convenient Dumpster.

In the car, he used a cell phone that just hours ago he had taken off a drug dealer whom he rousted near the Quarter. He called 911, disguised his voice, and pretended to be a junkie who, shooting up in an alley, saw a man jump from a warehouse roof.

Call completed, he tossed the phone out of the car window.

He was still wearing the latex gloves. He stripped them off as he drove.

CHAPTER 56

THE ELEVATOR IS like a three-dimensional crossword-puzzle box, descending to the basement of the Hands of Mercy.

Randal Six had turned *left* in the second-floor hallway, entering the elevator on his fourth step; therefore, the letter that this box contains—and from which he must proceed when he reaches the lower level—is *t*.

When the doors open, he says, "Toward," and steps *o-w-a-r-d* into the corridor.

A life of greater mobility is proving easier to achieve than he had expected. He is not yet ready to drive a car in the Indianapolis 500, and he may not even be ready for a slow walk in the world beyond these walls, but he's making progress.

Years ago, Father had conducted some of his most revolutionary experiments on this lowest floor of the hospital. The rumors of what he created here, which Randal has overheard, are as numerous as they are disturbing.

A battle seems to have been fought on this level. A section of the corridor wall has been broken down, as if something smashed its way out of one of the rooms.

To the right of the elevator, half the width of the passageway is occupied by organized piles of rubble: broken concrete blocks, twisted rebar in mare's nests of rust, mounds of plaster, steel door frames wrenched into peculiar shapes, the formidable steel doors themselves bent in half . . .

According to Hands of Mercy legend, something had gone so wrong down here that Father wished always to keep the memory of it clear in his mind and, therefore, made no repairs and left the rubble instead of having it hauled away. Dozens of the New Race had perished here in an attempt to contain . . . something.

Because Father enters and exits Mercy every day on this level, he is regularly confronted with the evidence of the terrible crisis that apparently almost led to the destruction of his life's work. Some even dare to speculate that Father nearly died here, though to repeat this claim seems like blasphemy.

Turning away from the rubble, Randal Six uses the last letter of *toward* to spell *determination* in a new direction.

By a series of side steps that spell small words, alternating with forward steps that spell long words, he comes to a door at the end of the hallway. This is not locked.

Beyond is a storage room with rows of cabinets in which are kept hard-copy backup files of the project's computerized records.

Directly opposite the first door stands another. That one will be locked. Through it, Father comes and goes from Mercy.

Randal Six navigates the tile floor in this room by means of crosswords, at last settling in a hiding place between rows of file cabinets, near the second door but not within sight of it.

Now he must wait.

CHAPTER 57

FROM THE LUXE, Carson went to Homicide, settled at the computer on her desk, and launched her web browser.

There was no graveyard shift in Homicide. Detectives worked when the investigation required, night or day, but they tended to be in-office less as the day waned, on call but not sitting desks in the wee hours. At the moment, though the night was not yet that late, she sat alone in the corpse-chasers' corner.

Reeling from what Deucalion had told her, Carson wasn't sure what to believe. She found it surprisingly difficult to *dis*believe any of his story regardless of the fact that it was fantastic to the point of insanity.

She needed to get background on Victor Helios. With the World Wide Web, she was able to unwrap a fictitious biography more easily than in the days when a data chase had to be done on foot or through cooperating officers in other jurisdictions.

She typed in her search string. In seconds, she had scores of hits. Helios, the visionary founder of Biovision. Helios, the local mover and shaker in New Orleans politics and society. Helios, the philanthropist.

At first she seemed to have a lot of material. Quickly, however, she found that for all his wealth and connections, Helios didn't so much swim the waters of New Orleans society as skim across the surface.

In the city for almost twenty years, he made a difference in his community, but with a minimum of exposure. Scores of people in local society got more press time; they were omnipresent by comparison to Helios.

Furthermore, when Carson attempted to track the few facts about Helios's past, prior to New Orleans, they trailed away like wisps of evaporating mist.

He had gone to university "in Europe," but nothing more specific was said about his alma mater.

Though he inherited his fortune, the names of his parents were never mentioned.

He was said to have greatly enlarged that fortune with several financial coups during the dot-com boom. No details were provided.

References to "a New England childhood" never included the state where he had been born and raised.

One thing about the available photos intrigued Carson. In his first year in New Orleans, Victor had been handsome, almost dashing, and appeared to be in his late thirties. In his most recent photos, he looked hardly any older.

He had adopted a more flattering hairstyle—but he had no less hair than before. If he'd had plastic surgery, the surgeon had been particularly skilled.

Eight years ago, he had returned from an unspecified place in New England with a bride who appeared to be no older than twenty-five. Her name was Erika, but Carson could find no mention of her maiden name.

Erika would be perhaps thirty-three now. In her most recent photos, she looked not a day older than in those taken eight years previously.

Some women were fortunate enough to keep their twenty-something looks until they were forty. Erika might be one of those.

Nevertheless, the ability of *both* her and her husband to defy the withering hand of time seemed remarkable. If not uncanny.

"They got him, O'Connor."

Startled, she looked up from the computer and saw Tom Bowmaine, the watch commander, at the open door to the hallway, on the farther side of the Homicide bullpen.

"They got the Surgeon," Tom elaborated. "Dead. He took a header off a roof."

CHAPTER 58

ONE BLOCK OF THE ALLEYWAY had been cordoned off to preserve as much evidence as possible for the CSI crew. Likewise the roof of the building and the freight elevator.

Carson climbed the stairs to Roy Pribeaux's apartment. The jake outside the door knew her; he let her into the loft.

She half expected to find Harker or Frye, or both. Neither was present. Another detective, Emery Framboise, had been in the area and had caught the call.

Carson liked Emery. The sight of him didn't raise a single hair on the back of her neck.

He was a young guy—thirty-four—who dressed the way certain older detectives had once dressed before they decided they looked like throwbacks to the lost South of the 1950s. Seersucker suits, white rayon shirts, string ties, a straw boater parked dead-flat on his head.

Somehow he made this retro look seem modern, perhaps because he himself was otherwise entirely of a modern sensibility.

Carson was surprised to see Kathy Burke, friend and shrink, with Emery in the kitchen. Primarily Kathy conducted mandatory counseling sessions with officers involved in shootings and in other traumatic situations, though she also wrote psychological profiles of elusive perpetrators like the Surgeon. She seldom visited crime scenes, at least not this early in the game.

Kathy and Emery were watching two CSI techs unload the contents of one of two freezers. Tupperware containers.

As Carson joined Kathy and Emery, one of the techs read a label on the lid of a container. "Left hand."

She would have understood the essence of the situation without hearing those two words, because the raised lid of the second freezer revealed the eyeless corpse of a young woman.

"Why aren't you home reading about swashbuckling heroines and flying dragons?" Carson needled.

"There's a different kind of dragon dead in the alleyway," Kathy said. "I wanted to see his lair, see if my profile of him holds any water."

"Right hand," a tech said, taking a container from the freezer.

Emery Framboise said, "Carson, looks like you've just been saved a ton of casework."

"I suppose it wasn't an accident he went off the roof?"

"Suicide. He left a note. Probably heard you and Michael were on his trail, figured he was a dead man walking."

"Do homicidal sociopaths commit suicide?" Carson wondered.

"Rarely," Kathy said. "But it's not unheard of."

"Ears," said one of the CSI techs, removing a small container from the freezer, and his partner read the label on another: "Lips."

"I disappointed my mother," Emery said. "She wanted me to be an airline pilot like my dad. At times like this, I think maybe I *would* be better off high in the night, up where the sky is clean, flying San Francisco to Tokyo."

"Yeah," Carson said, "but then what airline pilot is ever going to have stories like this to tell his grandkids when he tucks them into bed? Where's the suicide note?"

Kathy said, "I'll show you."

In the living room, a computer stood on a corner desk. White letters on a field of blue offered a peculiar farewell:

> Killed what I wanted. Took what I needed. Now I leave
> when I want, how I want, and go where I want—one
> level below Hell.

"The taunting tone is typical for a sociopath," Kathy said. "The suggestion that he's earned a princely place in Hell isn't unique, either, but usually if he's playing out a satanic fantasy, you find occult literature, posters. We haven't come across any of that yet."

Only half listening, chilled by a sense of déjà vu, of having seen this message before, Carson stared at the screen, reading the words twice, three times, four.

As she read, she extracted a latex glove from a jacket pocket, pulled it on her right hand, and then keyed in a print request.

"There was a time," Kathy said, "if a suicide note wasn't handwritten, it was suspicious. But these days, they often use their computers. In some cases they e-mail suicide notes to friends and relatives just before offing themselves. Progress."

Stripping off the glove, waiting impatiently for the printer to produce a hard copy, Carson said, "Down there in the alley, is there enough left of his face to get a good photograph?"

"No," Kathy said. "But his bedroom's full of them."

Was it ever. On both nightstands and on the dresser were a dozen or more photos of Roy Pribeaux, mostly glamour shots by professional photographers, each in an expensive, ornamental silver frame.

"He doesn't seem to have been lacking in self-esteem," Kathy said drily.

CHAPTER 59

JENNA PARKER, TWENTY-FIVE, lived for parties. She seemed to be invited to one every night.

This evening, she obviously had taken a few pre-party toots of something, getting primed for a late-night bash, for she was buzzed when she came out of her apartment, singing tunelessly.

With or without drugs, Jenna was perpetually happy, walking on sunshine even when the day offered only rain.

On this rainless night, she seemed to float a quarter inch off the floor as she tried to lock her door. The proper relationship of a key to a keyhole seemed to elude her, and she giggled when, three times in a row, she failed the simple insertion test.

Maybe she wasn't merely buzzed but fully stung.

She succeeded on the fourth try, and the deadbolt snapped shut with a solid *clack*.

"Sheryl Crowe," Jonathan Harker said from the doorway of his apartment, across the hall from hers.

She turned, saw him for the first time, and broke into a sunny grin. "Johnny!"

"You sound like Sheryl Crowe when you sing."

"Do I really?"

"Would I lie?"

"Depends on what you want," she said coyly.

"Now, Jen, have I ever come on to you?"

"No. But you will."

"When will I?"

"Later. Sooner. Maybe now."

She'd been to his apartment a couple times for pasta dinners, and he'd been to her place for takeout, since she didn't cook even pasta. These had been strictly neighborly occasions.

He didn't want sex from Jenna Parker. He wanted to learn from her the secret of happiness.

"I told you—it's just you remind me of my sister."

"Sister. Yeah, right."

"Anyway, I'm almost old enough to be your father."

"When has that ever mattered to a man?"

"We aren't all swine," he said.

"Oh. Sorry, Johnny. Jeez, I didn't mean to sound . . . mean. I'm just floatin' so high inside that I'm not always down there where the words come out."

"I noticed. Why do you ever use drugs, anyway? You're happy when you're sober. You're always happy."

She grinned, came to him, and pinched his cheek affectionately. "You're right. I love life. I'm always happy. But it's no crime to want to be even happier now and then."

"Actually," he said, "if I were in Vice instead of Homicide, maybe I'd have to consider it a crime."

"You'd never arrest me, Johnny. Probably not even if I killed someone."

"Probably not," he agreed, and squirted her in the mouth and nostrils with chloroform solution.

Her gasp of surprise did what a blow across the backs of her knees would have done: dropped her to the floor. She sputtered, wheezed, and passed out.

He had taken the squeeze bottle from Roy Pribeaux's apartment. It was one of three he had found there.

Later he would leave it with her dead body. Her remains wouldn't be found for months, so their condition wouldn't enable CSI to date her death after Pribeaux's. The bottle would be one of several pieces of evidence identifying her as his final victim.

Now Jonathan lifted her effortlessly, carried her into his apartment, and kicked the door shut behind them.

Of the four apartments here on the fourth floor, one stood vacant. Paul Miller, in 4-C, was away at a sales conference in Dallas. Only Jonathan and Jenna were in residence. No one could have witnessed the assault and abduction.

Jenna wouldn't be missed for a day or two. By then, he would have opened her top to bottom, would have found the special something that she had and that he was missing, and would have disposed of her remains.

He was taking all these precautions not because he feared going to prison but because he feared that Father would identify him as the renegade.

In his bedroom, Jonathan had pushed the bed into a corner. He had stacked the other furniture atop it to create sufficient space for the makeshift autopsy table that he had prepared for her.

Plastic sheeting covered the floor. At the head and foot of the table stood lamps that were bright enough to reveal the source of her happiness whether it was nestled in a tangle of guts or embedded in the cerebellum.

Putting her on the table, he noticed that she was bleeding from one nostril. She'd cracked her nose against the floor when she had fallen. The bleeding wasn't serious. The nose injury wasn't what would kill her.

Jonathan checked her pulse. Steady.

He was relieved. He'd been concerned that she had inhaled too much chloroform, that maybe she'd suffered chemical suffocation or anaphylactic shock.

He wanted her to be alive through this procedure. For some of it, he needed her to be awake and responsive.

CHAPTER 60

IN THE BASEMENT of Mercy, hiding behind a row of file cabinets, Randal Six hears noise from beyond the walls of his world: first, the hollow sound of a door falling shut in another room.

According to what Randal has overheard while seeming to be lost in his autism, only Father enters and leaves through the outer door of this chamber. Now, after a late dinner, as he often does, Father must be returning with the intention of working through the night.

Crouched at the end of the cabinet row, Randal cocks his head and listens intently. After a moment, he hears the electronic tones of the numbers being entered in an electric-lock keypad on the far side of the outer file-room door.

The ten tones that represent numbers—zero through nine—on telephone, security-system, electric-lock, and other keypads are universal. They do not vary from one manufacturer to another.

He learned this from an educational web site maintained by one of the nation's largest communications companies. Having downloaded these tones in preparation for this odyssey, he has replayed them hundreds of times until he can unfailingly identify any code by the tones that comprise it.

Because the file-room door intervenes, the tones are muffled. If he didn't have the enhanced hearing of the New Race, Randal might not be able to identify the code: 368284.

A soft *burrrrr* indicates that the circuit engaging the lock has been broken.

Although the door is not in Randal's line of sight, the creak of hinges suggests that Father has opened it. Footsteps on vinyl tile reveal that Father has entered the file room.

Out of view of the main aisle, Randal suddenly wonders to what degree, if any, Father's senses might have been enhanced—and he holds his breath lest the faintest exhalation reveal his presence.

Without hesitation, Father's footsteps cross the room.

The outer door falls shut behind him, and the *burrrrr* of the disengaged lock is cut short by the hard *snap* of the bolt.

The inner door opens, closes, and Father is now gone into the basement corridor where piles of rubble remind him of a bad day here at the bottom of Mercy.

Patience is a virtue that Randal has in spades. He does not move at once from hiding, but waits a few minutes until Father is almost certainly on another floor, far out of hearing.

Vinyl square by vinyl square, he spells himself to the outer door. Here, as on the other side, there is a keypad. He enters the code: 368284.

The electric lock releases. He puts his hand on the door but cannot find the courage to open it.

Beyond, there is no Mercy. All is new and full of bewildering choices.

He delays so long that the electric lock engages once more.

He enters the code in the keypad. The lock releases: *burrrrr.*

He tells himself to open the door. He cannot.

The lock engages once more.

Trembling, he stands before the door, terrified to go through it, but also terrified to remain on this side.

Into his tortured mind comes the memory of the newspaper photo: Arnie O'Connor, autistic but smiling. Arnie is clearly happier than Randal has ever been or ever will be.

A bitter, caustic sense of injustice floods through Randal. This emotion is so intense that he fears it will dissolve him from the inside out if he does not take action to secure for himself the happiness that Arnie O'Connor enjoys.

The little snot. The hateful little worm, selfishly keeping the secret of happiness. What right does *he* have to be happy when a child of Father, superior in every way, lives in misery more than Mercy?

Again he enters the code. *Burrrrr.*

He pushes on the door. It opens.

Randal Six spells himself across the threshold, out of Mercy, into the unknown.

CHAPTER 61

THROUGH THE DOOR, Carson heard scary-movie music. She rang the bell, rang it again before the first series of chimes quite finished echoing through the apartment beyond.

In undershirt, jeans, and stocking feet, Michael answered the door. Tousled hair. Puffy face. Eyes heavy-lidded from the weight of a sleep not fully cast off. He must have dozed in his big green-leatherette recliner.

He looked adorable.

Carson wished he was grungy. Or slovenly. Or geeky. The last thing she wanted to feel toward a partner was physical attraction.

Instead, he looked as cuddly as a teddy bear. Worse, the sight of him filled her with a warm, agreeable feeling consisting largely of affection but not without an element of desire.

Shit.

"It's just ten o'clock," she said, pushing past him into the apartment, "and you're asleep in front of the TV. What're those orange crumbs on your T-shirt? Cheez Doodles?"

"Exactly," he said, following her into the living room. "Cheez Doodles. You *are* a detective."

"Can I assume you're sober?"

"Nope. Had two diet root beers."

He yawned, stretched, rubbed at his eyes with the back of one fist. He looked edible.

Carson tried to derail that train of thought. Indicating the massive green recliner, she said, "That is the ugliest lump of a chair I've ever seen. Looks like a fungus scraped out of a latrine in Hell."

"Yeah, but it's *my* fungus from Hell, and I love it."

Pointing to the TV, she said, *"Invasion of the Body Snatchers?"*

"The first remake."

"You've seen it like what—ten times?"

"Probably twelve."

"When it comes to glamour," she said, "you're the Cary Grant of your generation."

He grinned at her. She knew why. Her curmudgeonly attitude did not fool him. He sensed the effect that he had on her.

Turning away from him as she felt her face flush, Carson picked up the remote control and switched off the TV. "The case is breaking. We've gotta move."

"Breaking how?"

"Guy jumped off a roof, smashed himself into alley jam, leaving a freezer full of body parts. They say he's the Surgeon. Maybe he is—but he didn't kill them all."

Sitting on the edge of the recliner, tying his shoes, Michael said, "What—he's got a kill buddy or a copycat?"

"Yeah. One or the other. We dismissed that idea too easily."

"I'll grab a clean shirt and a jacket," he said.

"Maybe change the Cheez Doodle T while you're at it," she said.

"Absolutely. I wouldn't want to embarrass you in front of some criminal scum," he said, and stripped off the T-shirt as he left the room.

He knew exactly what he was doing: giving her a look. She took it. Good shoulders, nice abs.

CHAPTER 62

ERIKA ROAMED the silent mansion, pausing frequently to study Victor's collection of European and Asian antiques.

As they did every night, the nine members of the household staff—butler, maids, chef, cleaning crew, gardeners—had retired to their quarters above the ten-car garage at the back of the property.

They lived dormitory-style, the sexes integrated. They were provided with a minimum of amenities.

Victor seldom needed servants after ten o'clock—even on those nights when he was home—but he preferred not to allow his household staff, all members of the New Race, to lead lives separate from the mansion. He wanted them to be available twenty-four hours a day. He insisted that the only focus of their lives should be his comfort.

Erika was pained by their circumstances. They were essentially hung on a rack, like tools, to await the next use he had for them.

The fact that her circumstances were not dissimilar to theirs *had* occurred to her. But she enjoyed a greater freedom to fill her days and nights with pursuits that interested her.

As her relationship with Victor matured, she hoped to be able to gain influence with him. She might be able to use that influence to improve the lot of the household staff.

As this concern for the staff had grown, she found herself less often despairing. Following her interests—and thus refining herself—was fine, but having a *purpose* proved more satisfying.

In the main drawing room, she paused to admire an exquisite pair of Louis XV ormolu-mounted boulle marquetry and ebony *bas d'armoires*.

The Old Race could create objects of breathtaking beauty unlike anything the New Race had done. This puzzled Erika; it did not seem to square with Victor's certainty that the New Race was superior.

Victor himself had an eye for the art of the Old Race. He had paid two and a quarter million for this pair of *bas d'armoires.*

He said that some members of the Old Race excelled at creating things of beauty because they were inspired by anguish. By their deep sense of loss. By their search for meaning.

Beauty came at the expense, however, of certitude, efficiency. Creating a beautiful piece of art, Victor said, was not an admirable use of energy because it in no way furthered mankind's conquest of itself or of nature.

A race without pain, on the other hand, a race that was *told* its meaning and explicitly given its purpose by its creator, would never need beauty, because it would have an infinite series of great tasks ahead of it. Working as one, with the single-minded purpose of a hive, all members of the New Race would tame nature, conquer the challenges of Earth as ordinary humanity had failed to do, and then become the masters of the other planets, the stars.

All barriers would fall to them.

All adversaries would be crushed.

New Men and New Women would not need beauty because they would have *power.* Those who felt powerless created art; beauty was their substitute for the power they could not attain. The New Race would need no substitute.

Yet Victor collected the art and the antiques of the Old Race. Erika wondered why, and she wondered if Victor himself knew why.

She had read enough literature to be sure that Old Race authors would have called him a cruel man. But Victor's art collection gave Erika hope that in him existed a core of pity and tenderness that might with patience be tapped.

Still in the main drawing room, she came to a large painting by Jan van Huysum, signed and dated 1732. For this still life, Victor had paid more millions.

In the painting, white and purple grapes appeared ready to burst with juice at the slightest touch. Succulent peaches and plums spilled across a table, caressed by sunshine in such a way that they seemed to glow from within.

The artist realistically portrayed this ripe bounty yet managed, subtly and without sentimentality, to suggest the ephemeral quality of even nature's sweetest gifts.

Mesmerized by van Huysum's genius, Erika was subconsciously aware of a furtive scrabbling. The noise grew louder, until at last it distracted her from the painting.

When she turned to survey the drawing room, she at once saw the source of the sound. Like a five-legged crab on some strange blind mission, a severed hand crawled across the antique Persian carpet.

CHAPTER 63

DETECTIVE DWIGHT FRYE lived in a bungalow so overgrown with Miss Manila bougainvillea that the main roof and the porch roof were entirely concealed. Floral bracts—bright pink in daylight but more subdued now—dripped from every eave, and the entire north wall was covered with a web of vine trunks that had woven random-pattern bars across the windows.

The front lawn had not been mowed in weeks. The porch steps had sagged for years. The house might not have been painted for a decade.

If Frye rented, his landlord was a tightwad. If he owned this place, he was white trash.

The front door stood open.

Through the screen door, Carson could see a muddy yellow light back toward the kitchen. When she couldn't find a bell push, she knocked, then knocked louder, and called out, "Detective Frye? Hey, Dwight, it's O'Connor and Maddison."

Frye hove into sight, backlit by the glow in the kitchen. He wove along the hall like a seaman tacking along a ship's passageway in a troublesome swell.

When he reached the front door, he switched on the porch light and blinked at them through the screen. "What do you assholes want?"

"A little Southern hospitality for starters," Michael said.

"I was born in Illinois," Frye said. "Never shoulda left."

He wore baggy pants with suspenders. His tank-style, sweat-soaked undershirt revealed his unfortunate breasts so completely that Carson knew she'd have a few nightmares featuring them.

"The Surgeon case is breaking," she said. "There's something we need to know."

"Told you in the library—I got no interest in that anymore."

Frye's hair and face glistened as if he had been bobbing for olives in a bowl of oil.

Getting a whiff of him, Carson took a step back from the door and said, "What I need to know is when you and Harker went to Bobby Allwine's apartment."

Frye said, "Older I get, the less I like the sloppy red cases. Nobody strangles anymore. They all chop and slice. It's the damn sick Hollywood influence."

"Allwine's apartment?" she reminded him. "When were you there?"

"You listening to me *at all*?" Frye asked. "I was never there. Maybe you get off on torn-out hearts and dripping guts, but I'm getting queasy in my midlife. It's *your* case, and welcome to it."

Michael said, "Never there? So how did Harker know about the black walls, the razor blades?"

Frye screwed up his face as if to spit but then said, "What razor blades? What's got you girls in such a pissy mood?"

To Michael, Carson said, "You smell truth here?"

"He reeks with it," Michael said.

"Reeks—is that some kind of wisecrack?" Frye demanded.

"I've got to admit it is," Michael said.

"I wasn't half drunk and feelin' charitable," Frye said, "I'd open this here screen door and kick your giblets clean off."

"I'm grateful for your restraint," Michael said.

"Is that some kind of sarcasm?"

"I've got to admit it is," Michael said.

Turning from the door, heading for the porch steps, Carson said, "Let's go, let's move."

"But me and the Swamp Thing," Michael said, "we're having such a nice chat."

"That's another wisecrack, ain't it?" Frye demanded.

"I've got to admit it is," Michael said as he followed Carson off the porch.

As she thought back over her encounters with Harker during the past couple of days, Carson headed toward the car at a run.

CHAPTER 64

AFTER CUFFING JENNA'S WRISTS and ankles to the autopsy table in his bedroom, Jonathan Harker used a pair of scissors to cut away her clothes.

With a damp cotton ball, he gently cleaned the blood from around her left nostril. Already, the bleeding from her nose seemed to have stopped.

Each time that she began to wake, he used the squeeze bottle to dribble two or three drops of chloroform on her upper lip, just under her nostrils. Inhaling the fumes as the fluid rapidly evaporated, she retreated again from consciousness.

When the woman was naked, Jonathan touched her where he wished, curious about his reaction. Rather, he was curious about his *lack* of a reaction.

Sex—disconnected from the power of procreation—was the primary means by which members of the New Race relieved tension. They were available to one another on request, to a degree that even the most libertine members of the Old Race would find shocking.

They were capable of performance on demand. They did not need beauty or emotion or any form of tender feeling to stimulate their desire.

Desire in them did not encompass love, merely *need*.

Young men coupled with old women, old women with young women, young girls with old men, the thin with the fat, the beautiful with the ugly, in every combination, each with the sole purpose to satisfy himself, with no obligations to the other, with no greater affection than they had toward the food they ate, with no expectation that sex would lead to a relationship.

Indeed, personal relationships between members of the New Race were discouraged. Jonathan sometimes suspected that as a species they were hardwired to be incapable of relationships in any of the ways that the Old Race experienced and defined them.

Couples committed to each other are impediments to the infinite series of conquests that is to be the uniform purpose of every member of the New Race. So are friendships. So are families.

For the world to be as one, every thinking creature must share the same drive, the same goal. They must live by a system of values so simplified as to allow no room for the concept of morality and the differences of opinion that it fosters.

Because friendships and families are distractions from the great unified purpose of the species, the ideal citizen, Father says, must be a loner in his personal life. As a loner, he is able to commit his passion fully to the triumph and the glory of the New Race.

Touching Jenna as he wished, unable to stir within himself the need that passed for desire, Jonathan suspected that his kind were also hardwired to be incapable of—or at least disinterested in—sex with members of the Old Race.

With their basic education via direct-to-brain data downloading comes a programmed contempt for the Old Race. Contempt, of course, can lead to a sense of righteous domination that includes sexual exploitation. This does not happen with the New Race, perhaps because their programmed contempt for nature's form of humanity includes a subtle element of disgust.

Among those created in the tanks, only Father's wife was allowed desire for one of the Old Race. But in a sense, he was not of the Old Race anymore, but was the god of the New.

Caressing Jenna, whose body was lovely and whose exterior form could pass for that of any woman of the New Race, Jonathan not only remained detumescent but also became vaguely repulsed by her.

How strange that this lesser creature, who was the dirty link between lower animals and the superior New Race, nevertheless might have within her the thing that Jonathan himself seemed to be missing, the organ or the gland or the neural matrix that enabled her to be happy nearly all the time.

The time had come to cut.

When she groaned and her eyelids fluttered, he applied a few more drops of chloroform to her upper lip, and she subsided.

He rolled a wheeled IV rack beside the table. From it hung a bag of glucose-saline solution.

He tied a rubber-tube tourniquet around Jenna's right arm and found a suitable blood vessel. He inserted an intravenous cannula by which the glucose-saline would be infused into her bloodstream, and removed the tourniquet.

The drip line between the solution bag and the cannula featured a drug port. He inserted a large, full syringe of a potent sedative, which he would be able to administer in multiple, measured doses, as required.

To keep Jenna perfectly still during dissection, he must put her in deep sedation. When he wanted her awake to answer questions that he might have about what he found inside her, he could deny her the sedative.

Because she might cry out even during sedation and alarm the residents in the apartment below, Jonathan now wadded a rag and stuffed it in her mouth. He sealed her lips with duct tape.

When he pressed the tape in place, Jenna's eyes fluttered, opened. For a moment she was confused, disoriented—and then not.

As her eyes widened with terror, Jonathan said, "I know that your kind can't turn off physical pain at will, as we can. So I'll wake you as seldom as possible to get your explanation of what I find inside you."

CHAPTER 65

WITH A SUCTION-ADHERED emergency beacon on the roof above the driver's door, Carson cruised fast on surface streets.

Struggling to absorb everything she had told him, Michael said, "The guy you saw in Allwine's apartment, he owns a movie theater?"

"The Luxe."

"The nutcase who says he's made from parts of criminals and brought alive by lightning—he owns a movie theater? I would have thought a hot-dog stand. A tire-repair shop."

"Maybe he's not a nutcase."

"A hamburger joint."

"Maybe he's what he says he is."

"A beauty salon."

"You should've seen what he did with those quarters."

"I can tie a knot in a cherry stem using my tongue," Michael said, "but that doesn't make me supernatural."

"I didn't say he was supernatural. He says part of what the lightning brought him that night, in addition to life, was . . . an understanding of the quantum structure of the universe."

"What the hell does that mean?"

"I don't know," she admitted. "But somehow it explains how he makes the coins vanish."

"Any half-good magician can make a coin vanish, and they're not all wizards of quantum physics."

"This was more than cheap magic. Anyway, Deucalion said some of their kind are sure to have a strong death wish."

"Carson—what kind?"

Instead of answering his question, aware that she must lead him a careful step at a time toward her ultimate revelation, Carson said, "All-wine and his friend were in the library, poring through aberrant psychology texts, trying to understand their anguish."

"Don't drive so fast."

Accelerating, Carson said, "So the books weren't pulled off the shelves in a struggle. There *wasn't* a struggle. That's why the scene was so neat in spite of the apparent violence."

"Apparent? Allwine's *heart* was cut out."

"Hearts. Plural. But he probably *asked* his friend to kill him."

" 'Hey, pal, do me a favor and cut my heart out?' He couldn't just slit his own wrists, take poison, bore himself to death with multiple viewings of *The English Patient*?"

"No. Deucalion said their kind are built to be incapable of suicide."

With a sigh of frustration, Michael said, "Their kind. Here we go again."

"The proscription against suicide—it's there in the original diary. I saw it. After the coins, after I started to accept . . . then Deucalion showed me."

"Diary? Whose diary?"

She hesitated.

"Carson?"

"This is going to be a real test."

"What test?"

"A test of you, me, our partnership here."

"Don't drive so fast," he cautioned.

This time, she didn't react to his admonition by accelerating. She didn't slow down, either, but she didn't pump up more speed. A little concession to help win him over.

"This is weird stuff," she warned.

"What—I don't have a capacity for weird? I have a fabulous capacity for weird. *Whose diary?*"

She took a deep breath. "Victor's diary. Victor Frankenstein." When he stared at her in flabbergasted silence, she said, "Maybe this sounds crazy—"

"Yeah. Maybe."

"But I think the legend is true, like Deucalion says. Victor Helios is Victor Frankenstein."

"What have you done with the *real* Carson O'Connor?"

"Deucalion—he was Victor's first . . . I don't know . . . his first creation."

"See, right away, I start getting geeky Renaissance Fair vibes from the name. It sounds like the Fourth Musketeer or something. What kind of name is Deucalion, anyway?"

"He named himself. It's from mythology. Deucalion was the son of Prometheus."

"Oh, of course," Michael said. "Deucalion Prometheus, son of Fred Prometheus. I remember him now."

"Deucalion is his only name, first and last."

"Like Cher."

"In classic mythology, Prometheus was the brother of Atlas. He shaped humans out of clay and gave them the spark of life. He taught humanity several arts, and in defiance of Zeus, he gave us the gift of fire."

"Maybe I wouldn't have fallen asleep in school so often if my teacher had been driving the classroom at eighty miles an hour. For God's sake, slow down."

"Anyway, Deucalion has Victor's original diary. It's written in German, and it's full of anatomical drawings that include an improved circulatory system with two hearts."

"Maybe if you give it to Dan Rather and *Sixty Minutes,* they'll do a segment on it, but it sounds like a forgery to me."

She wanted to punch him. To temper that impulse, she reminded herself of how cuddly he had looked back at his apartment.

Instead of hitting him, she pumped the brakes and slid the plain-wrap sedan to the curb in front of Fullbright's Funeral Home.

"A good cop has to have an open mind," she said.

"Agreed. But it doesn't help much to have one *so* open that the wind blows through with a mournful, empty sound."

CHAPTER 66

LIFE IN THE HOUSE of Victor Frankenstein was certain to involve more macabre moments than life in the house of Huckleberry Finn.

Nevertheless, the sight of a severed hand crawling across the drawing-room carpet amazed even Erika, a man-made woman equipped with two hearts. She stood transfixed for perhaps a minute, unable to move.

No science could explain an ambulatory hand. This seemed to be a supernatural manifestation as surely as would be an ectoplasmic human figure floating above a séance table.

Yet Erika felt less fear than amazement, less amazement than wonder. Her heart beat faster the longer that she watched the hand, and a not-unpleasant thrill made her tremble.

Instinctively, she knew that the hand was aware of her. It had no eyes, no sense other than touch—and should not possess a sense of touch, either, considering that it had no nervous system, no *brain*—yet somehow it *knew* that she was watching it.

This must have been the thing that she'd heard moving furtively through the bedroom, under the bed, the thing rattling the contents of the bathroom cabinet. The thing that had left the scalpel on her bath mat.

That last thought led her to the realization that the hand must be merely the tool of whatever entity had spoken to her through the television screen and had encouraged her to kill Victor. As it used the TV, it used the hand.

As it used the hand, it wished to use her as agent to destroy the man it had called *evil*.

There is no world but this one.

Erika reminded herself that she was a soul-free soldier in the army of materialism. Belief in something more than the eyes can see was punishable by termination.

As if it were the hand of a blind man exploring the patterns on the Persian carpet, the beast with five fingers felt its way past furniture, toward the double doors that separated the drawing room from the downstairs hall.

The thing did not wander aimlessly. By all appearances, it moved with purpose.

One of the two doors to the hallway stood open. The hand paused there, waiting.

Erika suspected that it not only moved with purpose but also that it wanted her to follow. She stepped toward it.

The hand crabbed forward once more, crawled across the threshold and into the hallway.

CHAPTER 67

EVEN AS THE NIGHT ticked toward the dark start of a new day, lights were on at the back of the funeral home.

Insistently thumbing the bell push, Michael said, "See, another thing that doesn't make sense is why Victor Frankenstein would turn up in New Orleans, of all places."

Carson said, "Where would you expect him to set up shop—Baton Rouge, Baltimore, Omaha, Las Vegas?"

"Somewhere in Europe."

"Why Europe?"

"He's European."

"Once was, yeah, but not now. As Helios, he doesn't even speak with an accent."

"The whole creepy Frankenstein shtick—it's totally European," Michael insisted.

"Remember the mobs with pitchforks and torches storming the castle?" Carson asked. "He can't go back there ever."

"That was in the *movies,* Carson."

"Maybe they're more like documentaries."

She knew she sounded crazy. The bayou heat and humidity had finally gotten to her. Maybe if you cut open her skull, you'd find Spanish moss growing on her brain.

She said, "Where is the most recombinant-DNA work being done, the most research into cloning? Where are the most discoveries in molecular biology taking place?"

"According to the tabloids I read, probably in Atlantis, a few miles under the surface of the Caribbean."

"It's all happening here in the good old USA, Michael. If Victor

Frankenstein is alive, this is where he'd want to be, right where the most science is being done. And New Orleans is plenty creepy enough to please him. Where else do they bury all their dead in mausoleums aboveground?"

The porch light came on. A deadbolt turned with a rasp and a clack, and the door opened.

Taylor Fullbright stood before them in red silk pajamas and a black silk robe on the breast of which was appliquéd an image of Judy Garland as Dorothy.

As convivial as ever, Fullbright said, "Why, hello again!"

"I'm sorry if we woke you," Carson apologized.

"No, no. You didn't. I finished embalming a customer half an hour ago, worked up an appetite. I'm making a pastrami and tongue sandwich, if you'd like one."

Michael said, "No thanks. I'm full of Cheez Doodles, and she's full of inexplicable enthusiasm."

"We don't need to come in," Carson said, showing him first the silver-framed photo of Roy Pribeaux. "Have you ever seen him before?"

"Quite a handsome fellow," said Fullbright. "But he looks a bit smug. I know the type. They're always trouble."

"More trouble than you can imagine."

"But I don't know him," Fullbright said.

From a nine-by-twelve manila envelope, Carson extracted a police-department file photo of Detective Jonathan Harker.

"This one I know," said the funeral director. "He was Allwine's funeral buddy."

CHAPTER 68

JENNA PARKER, party girl, not for the first time naked in front of a man, but for the first time unable to excite sexual interest, wept. Her sobs were more pathetic for being muffled by the rag in her mouth and the lip-sealing duct tape.

"It's not that I don't find you attractive," Jonathan told her. "I do. I think you're a fine example of your species. It's just that I'm of the New Race, and having sex with you would be like you having sex with a monkey."

For some reason, his sincere explanation made her cry harder. She was going to choke on her sobs if she wasn't careful.

Giving her a chance to adjust to her circumstances and to get control of her emotions, he fetched a physician's bag from a closet. He put it on a stainless-steel cart, and rolled the cart to the autopsy table.

From the black bag he extracted surgical instruments—scalpels, clamps, retractors—and lined them up on the cart. They had not been sterilized, but as Jenna would be dead when he was done with her, there was no reason to guard against infection.

When the sight of the surgical instruments excited the woman to greater weeping, Jonathan realized that fear of pain and death might be the sole cause of her tears.

"Well," he told her, "if you're going to cry about *that,* then you're going to have to cry, because there's nothing I can do about it. I can't very well let you go now. You'd tell."

After emptying the bag, he set it aside.

On the bed lay a thin but tough plastic raincoat, one of those that could be wadded up and stored in a zippered case no larger than a tobacco pouch. He intended to wear it over his T-shirt and jeans to mini-mize cleanup when he had finished with Jenna.

As Jonathan shook the raincoat to unfurl it, a familiar throb, a shifting and turning within him, made him gasp with surprise, with excitement.

He threw aside the raincoat. He pulled up his T-shirt, exposing his torso.

In his abdomen, the Other pressed against the caging flesh, as if testing the walls of its confinement. It writhed, it bulged.

He had no concern that it would burst out of him and perhaps kill him in the process. That was not how the birth would occur. He had studied various methods of reproduction, and he had developed a the-ory that he found convincing.

Seeing this movement within Jonathan, Jenna stopped crying in a blink—and started to scream into the rag, the duct tape.

He attempted to explain to her that this was nothing to fear, that this was his ultimate act of rebellion against Father and the start of the New Race's emancipation.

"He denies us the power to reproduce," Jonathan said, "but I am reproducing. It's going to be like parthenogenesis, I think. When the time comes, I'll divide, like an ameba. Then there will be two of me—I the father, and my son."

When Jenna thrashed, desperately but stupidly trying to wrench loose of her restraints, Jonathan worried that she would tear out the IV drip. Eager to proceed with her dissection, he didn't want to have to waste time reinserting the cannula.

He carefully pressed the plunger of the syringe in the drug port and delivered a couple ccs of the sedative.

Her thrashing quickly quieted to a trembling. She grew still. She slept.

Inside Jonathan, the Other grew still, as well. His stretched torso regained its natural shape.

Smiling, he slid one hand down his chest and abdomen. "Our time is coming."

CHAPTER 69

TURNING AWAY FROM the front door of Fullbright's Funeral Home, Michael wanted to sprint to the car and climb in behind the wheel. He would have done it, too, would have seized control—if he'd had a key.

Mere possession of the driver's seat would mean nothing to Carson. She wouldn't give him her key. Unless she *chose* to ride shotgun, she'd walk before she'd give up the wheel.

The plainwrap came with two sets of keys. Carson had both.

Michael had frequently considered requisitioning another set from the motor pool. He knew she'd consider that betrayal.

So she drove again. Clearly, there were no safety engineers in her family.

At least he was distracted from consideration of their speed by the need to get his mind around the cockamamie story she wanted him to believe. "Man-made men? Science just isn't that far along yet."

"Maybe most scientists aren't, but Victor is."

"Mary Shelley was a *novelist*."

"She must've based the book on a true story she heard that summer. Michael, you *heard* what Jack Rogers told us. Not a freak. Bobby All-wine was *designed*."

"Why would he be creating monsters to be security guards like Bobby Allwine? Doesn't that seem goofy?"

"Maybe he creates them to be all kinds of things—cops, like Harker. Mechanics. Pilots. Bureaucrats. Maybe they're all around us."

"Why?"

"Deucalion says—to take our place, to destroy God's work and replace it with his own."

"I'm not Austin Powers, and neither are you, and it's hard to swallow that Helios is Dr. Evil."

Impatiently, she said, "What happened to your imagination? Have you watched so many movies, you can't imagine for yourself anymore, you have to have Hollywood do it for you?"

"Harker, huh? From homicide cop to homicidal robot?"

"Not robot. Engineered or cloned or grown in a vat—I don't know how. It's no longer parts of corpses animated by lightning."

"One man, even a genius, couldn't—"

She interrupted him: "Helios is an obsessed, demented visionary at work for two centuries, with a huge family fortune."

Preoccupied with a new thought, she let their speed fall.

After a silence, Michael said, "What?"

"We're dead."

"I don't feel dead."

"I mean, if Helios *is* who Deucalion says, if he has achieved all of this, if his creations are seeded through the city, we don't have much of a chance against him. He's a genius, a billionaire, a man of enormous power—and we're squat."

She was scared. He could hear fear in her voice. He had never known her to be afraid. Not like this. Not without a gun in her face and some dirtbag's finger on the trigger.

"I just don't buy this," he said, though he half did. "I don't understand why *you* buy it."

With an edge, she said, "If I buy it, homey, isn't that good enough for you?"

When he hesitated to reply, she braked hard and pulled to the curb. Pissed, she switched off the light and got out of the car.

In the movies, when they saw a body with two hearts and organs of unknown purpose, they knew *right away* it was aliens or something.

Even though he hadn't met Deucalion, Michael didn't know why he was resisting the usual movie conclusion to be made from what Jack Rogers had found inside Bobby Allwine. Besides, someone had stolen Allwine's corpse and the autopsy records, which seemed to indicate a vast conspiracy of some kind.

He got out of the car.

They were in a residential neighborhood, under a canopy of live oaks. The night was hot. The moon seemed to be melting down through the branches of the trees.

Michael and Carson regarded each other across the roof of the sedan. Her lips were tight. Usually they looked kissable. They didn't look kissable now.

"Michael, I told you what I saw."

"I've jumped off cliffs with you before—but this one's pretty damn high."

She said nothing at first. What might have been a wistful look came over her face. Then: "Some mornings it's hard to get up knowing Arnie will still be . . . Arnie."

Michael moved toward the front of the car. "All of us want things we maybe aren't ever going to get."

Carson remained at the driver's door, not giving an inch. "I want meaning. Purpose. Higher stakes. I want things to *matter* more than they do."

He stopped in front of the sedan.

Staring up through the oaks at the creamy moon, she said, "This is real, Michael. I know it. Our lives will never be the same."

He recognized in her a yearning for change so strong that even *this*—a trading of the world they knew for another that had even more terror in it—was preferable to the status quo.

"Okay, okay," he said. "So where's Deucalion? If any of this is real, then it's his fight more than ours."

She lowered her gaze from the moon to Michael. She moved toward the front of the car.

"Deucalion is incapable of violence against his maker," she said. "It's like the proscription against suicide. He tried two hundred years ago, and Victor nearly finished him. Half his face . . . so damaged."

They stood face to face.

He wanted to touch her, to place a hand on her shoulder. He restrained himself because he didn't know what a touch might lead to, and this was not a moment for even more change.

Instead, he said, "Man-made men, huh?"

"Yeah."

"You're sure?"

"Honestly? I don't know. Maybe I just *want* to be sure."

Heat, humidity, moonlight, the fragrance of jasmine: New Orleans sometimes seemed like a fever dream, but never more than now.

"Frankenstein alive," he said. "It's just a *National Enquirer* wet dream."

A harder expression pinched her eyes.

Hastily Michael said, "I *like* the *National Enquirer*. Who in his right mind would believe the *New York Times* anymore? Not me."

"Harker's out there," she reminded him.

He nodded. "Let's get him."

CHAPTER 70

IN A MANSION as large as this, a severed hand had to do a lot of crawling to get where it wanted to go.

When previously it had scuttled unseen through the bedroom, the hand, judging by the sound of it, had moved as fast as a nervous rat. Not now.

The concept of a *weary* severed hand, exhausted from relentless creeping, made no sense.

Neither did the concept of a *confused* severed hand. Yet this one paused from time to time, as though it were not sure of the correct direction, and once it even retraced the path that it had taken and chose another route.

Erika persisted in the conviction that she was witnessing an event of supernatural character. No science she knew could explain this crawling marvel.

Although Victor had long ago trafficked in such parts as this, making jigsaw men from graveyard fragments, he had not used such crude methods in a long time.

Besides, the hand did not end in a bloody stump. It terminated in a round stub of smooth skin, as though it had never been attached to an arm.

This detail, if nothing else, seemed to confirm its supernatural origins.

In time, with Erika in patient attendance, the hand made its way to the kitchen. There it halted before the pantry door.

She waited for it to do something, and then she decided that it was in need of her assistance. She opened the pantry door, switched on the light.

As the determined hand crawled toward the back wall of the pantry, Erika realized that it must wish to lead her into Victor's studio. She knew of the studio's existence but had never been there.

His secret work space lay beyond the back wall of the pantry. Most likely, a hidden switch would cause the food-laden shelves to swing inward like a door.

Before she could begin to search for the switch, the shelves in fact slid aside. The hand on the floor had not activated them; some other entity was at work.

She followed the hand into the hidden room and saw on the center worktable a Lucite tank filled with a milky solution, housing a man's severed head. Not a fully realized head, but something like a crude model of one, the features only half formed.

Bloodshot blue eyes opened in this travesty of a human face.

The thing spoke to Erika in a low, rough voice exactly like that of the entity who, through the TV, had urged her to kill Victor: "Look at what I am . . . and tell me if you can that he's not evil."

CHAPTER 71

WHEN SHE PARKED in front of Harker's apartment house, Carson got out of the car, hurried to the back, and grabbed the pistol-grip, pump-action shotgun from the trunk.

Michael joined her as she loaded. "Hey. Wait. I don't pretend to be a SWAT team."

"If we try to take Harker into custody like he's an ordinary wack job, we'll be two dead cops."

A guy in a white van across the street had noticed them. Michael didn't want to make a scene, but he said, "Gimme the shotgun."

"I can take the kick," she assured him.

"We're not going in that way."

She slammed the trunk and moved toward the sidewalk.

Michael moved with her, trying reason where *gimme* didn't work. "Call for backup."

"How're you gonna explain to Dispatch why you *need* backup. You gonna tell them we've cornered a man-made monster?"

As they reached the front door of the building, he said, "This is crazy."

"Did I say it wasn't?"

The front door opened into a shabby-genteel lobby with sixteen brass mailboxes.

Carson read the names on the boxes. "Harker's on the fourth floor. Top of the building."

Not convinced of the wisdom of this but caught up in Carson's momentum, Michael went with her to a door beyond which lay stairs that led up through a shaft too long in need of fresh paint.

She started to climb, he followed, and she warned: "Deucalion says, in a crisis, wounded, they're probably able to turn off pain."

"Do we need silver bullets?"

"Is that some kind of sarcasm?" Carson asked, mimicking Dwight Frye.

"I've got to admit it is."

The stairs were narrow. The odors of mildew and disinfectant curdled together in the stifling air. Michael told himself he wasn't getting dizzy.

"They can be killed," Carson said. "Allwine was."

"Yeah. But he *wanted* to die."

"Remember, Jack Rogers said the cranium has incredible molecular density."

"Does that mean something in real words?" he asked.

"His brain is armored against all but the highest caliber."

Gasping not from exertion but from a need for cleaner air than what the fumy stairwell offered, Michael said, "Monsters among us, masquerading as real people—it's the oldest paranoia."

"The word *impossible* contains the word *possible*."

"What's that—some Zen thing?"

"I think *Star Trek*. Mr. Spock."

At the landing between the third and fourth floors, Carson paused and pumped the shotgun, chambering a shell.

Drawing his service piece from the paddle holster on his right hip, Michael said, "So what are we walking into?"

"Scary crap. What's new about that?"

They climbed the last flight to the fourth floor, went through a fire door, and found a short hallway serving four apartments.

The wood floor had been painted a glossy battleship gray. A few feet from Harker's door lay keys on a coiled plastic ring.

Michael squatted, snared the keys. Also on the ring was a small plastic magnetic-reader membership card in a supermarket discount club. It had been issued to Jenna Parker.

He remembered the name from the mailboxes in the public foyer on the ground floor. Jenna Parker lived here at the top of the building; she was one of Harker's neighbors.

Carson whispered, *"Michael."*

He looked up at her, and she pointed with the shotgun barrel.

Closer to Harker's door than where the keys had fallen, an inch from his threshold, a dark spot marred the glossy gray planks. The spot was glossy, too, approximately the size of a quarter but oval. Dark, glossy, and red.

Michael touched it with a forefinger. Wet.

He rubbed forefinger to thumb, smelled the smear. Rising to his feet, he nodded at Carson and showed her the name on the supermarket card.

Standing to one side of the door, he tried the knob. You never knew. Most killers were far short of a genius rating on the Stanford-Binet scale. If Harker had two hearts, he still had one brain, and if he was responsible for some of the murders attributed to the Surgeon, a lot of his synapses must be misfiring. All murderers made mistakes. Sometimes they did everything but post a sign inviting arrest.

This time the door proved to be locked. Michael felt enough play in it, however, to suggest that only the latch was engaged, not the deadbolt.

Carson could have destroyed the lock with one round from her 12-gauge. A shotgun is a pretty good residential-defense weapon because the pellets won't penetrate a wall and kill an innocent person in the next room as easily as will the rounds from high-power handguns.

Although a blast to the lock wouldn't risk deadly consequences to anyone inside, Michael wasn't keen to use the shotgun.

Maybe Harker wasn't alone in there. Maybe he had a hostage.

They had to use the minimum force necessary to effect entrance, then escalate as developments required.

Michael stepped in front of the door, kicked it hard in the lock zone, but it held, and he kicked it again, kicked it a third time, each blow booming almost as loud as a shotgun, and the latch snapped. The door flew open.

Quarter-crouched and fast, Carson went through the door first, the shotgun in front of her, sweeping the muzzle left and right.

Behind her, over her shoulder, Michael saw Harker crossing the far end of the room.

"Drop it!" Carson shouted because he had a revolver.

Harker squeezed off a shot. The door frame took it.

A spray of splinters peppered Michael's brow, his hair, as Carson fired at Harker.

The primary force of the blast caught Harker in the left hip, the thigh. He reeled, crashed against the wall, but didn't go down.

As soon as she fired, still moving, Carson chambered another round and simultaneously sidestepped to the left of the door.

Coming behind her, Michael moved to the right as Harker fired a second shot. He heard the keening lament of a bullet cleaving the air, a near miss, inches from his head.

Carson fired again, and Harker staggered with the impact, but he kept moving, plunging into the kitchen, out of sight, as Carson chambered a third round.

CHAPTER 72

STANDING WITH HER BACK to the shared wall between the living room and the kitchen, Carson fished shotgun shells out of a jacket pocket.

She had the shakes. She handled the fat shells one at a time, afraid of fumbling them. If she dropped one, if it rolled under a piece of furniture . . .

Outside at the open trunk of the car, when she had loaded the 12-gauge, she almost hadn't pocketed any spare rounds. This was a finishing weapon, useful for bringing a quick end to a dangerous situation; it wasn't a piece you used for extended firefights.

Only twice before had she needed a shotgun. On each occasion a single shot—in one instance, just a warning; in the other incident, intended to wound—had put an end to the confrontation.

Apparently Harker would be as hard to bring down as Deucalion had predicted.

She only had three spare shells. She inserted them in the tube-style magazine and hoped she had enough to do the job.

Skull bone as dense as armor plating. She might blind him with a face shot, but would that matter, could he function anyway?

Two hearts. Aim for the chest. Two rapid-fire rounds, maybe three, point-blank if possible. Take out both hearts.

Across the room, Michael was staying low, using furniture for cover, moving deeper into the living room, angling for a line of sight into the kitchen, where Harker had taken cover.

Harker was only part of their problem, Jenna the other part. The blood in the hallway suggested she was in the apartment. Hurt. Maybe mortally wounded.

Small apartment. Probably three rooms, one bath. He had come out of the bedroom. Jenna might be in there.

Or she might be in the kitchen, where he had gone. He might be slitting her throat now.

Back against the wall, holding the shotgun cross-body, Carson eased toward the archway between this room and the kitchen, aware that he might be waiting to shoot her in the face the instant she showed.

They had to whack Harker quickly, get Jenna medical help. The woman wasn't screaming. Maybe dead. Maybe dying. In this situation, time was the essence, terror the quintessence.

A noise in the kitchen. She couldn't identify it.

Rising recklessly from behind a sofa to get a better look, Michael said, "He's going out a window!"

Carson cleared the archway, saw an open casement window. Harker crouched on the sill, his back to her.

She swept the room to be sure that Jenna wasn't there to take ricochets. No. Just Harker.

Monster or no monster, shooting him in the back would earn her an OIS investigation, but she would have shot him anyway, except that he was gone before she could squeeze the trigger.

Rushing to the window, Carson expected a fire escape beyond, perhaps a balcony. She found neither.

Harker had thrown himself into the alleyway. The fall was at least thirty feet, possibly thirty-five. Far enough to acquire a mortal velocity before impact.

He lay facedown on the pavement. Unmoving.

His plunge seemed to refute Deucalion's contention that Victor's creations were effectively forbidden to self-destruct.

Below, Harker stirred. He sprang to his feet. He had known that he could survive such a fall.

When he looked up at the window, at Carson, reflected moonlight made lanterns of his eyes.

At this distance, a round—or all four rounds—from the shotgun wouldn't faze him.

He ran toward the nearest end of the alley. There he halted when, with a bark of brakes in the street beyond, a white van skidded to a stop in front of him.

The driver's door flew open, and a man got half out. From this distance, at night, Carson couldn't see his face. He seemed to have white or pale-blond hair.

She heard the driver call something to Harker. She couldn't make out his words.

Harker rounded the van, climbed in the passenger's side.

Behind the wheel again, the driver slammed his door and stood on the accelerator. Tires spun, shrieked, smoked, and left rubber behind as the vehicle raced off into the night.

The van might have been a Ford. She couldn't be certain.

Perspiration dripped from Carson's brow. She was soaked. In spite of the heat, the sweat felt cold on her skin.

CHAPTER 73

VICTOR HAD NAMED HIM Karloff, perhaps intending humor, but Erika found nothing funny about the hideous "life" that this creature had been given.

The bodiless head stood in a milky antibiotic bath, served by tubes that brought it nutrients and by others that drained metabolic waste. An array of machines attended and sustained Karloff, all of them mysterious and ominous to Erika.

The hand lay on the floor, in a corner, palm-up. Still.

Karloff had controlled that five-fingered explorer through the power of telekenesis, which his maker had hoped to engineer into him. An object of horror, he had nonetheless proved to be a successful experiment.

Self-disconnected from its sustaining machinery, the hand is now dead. Karloff can still animate it, although not for much longer. The flesh will rapidly deteriorate. Even the power of telekenesis will not be able to manipulate frozen joints and putrefying musculature.

Surely, however, Victor had not anticipated that Karloff would be able to employ his psychic ability to gain even a limited form of freedom and to roam the mansion with the desperate hope of inciting his maker's murder.

With that same uncanny power, Karloff had activated the electric mechanism that operated the secret door in the food pantry, providing entrance to Erika. With it, he had also controlled the television in the master suite, to speak with her and to encourage rebellion.

Being less of a complete creation than Erika, Karloff had not been programmed with a full understanding of Victor's mission or with knowledge of the limitations placed upon the freedom of the New Race.

Now he knew that she could not act against her maker, and his despair was complete.

When she suggested that he use his power to disable the machines that supported his existence, Erika discovered that he, too, had been programmed to be incapable of self-destruction.

She struggled against despondency, her hope reduced to the shaky condition of a three-legged table. The crawling hand and the other apparitions had not been the supernatural events that she had longed to believe they were.

Oh, how badly she had wanted these miracles to be evidence of another world beyond this one. What seemed to be a divine Presence, however, had been only the grotesque Karloff.

She might have blamed him for her deep disappointment, might have hated him, but she did not. Instead she pitied this pathetic creature, who was helpless in his power and condemned to a living hell.

Perhaps what she felt wasn't pity. Strictly speaking, she should not be capable of pity. But she felt *something,* felt it poignantly.

"Kill me," the pathetic thing pleaded.

The bloodshot eyes were haunted. The half-formed face was a mask of misery.

Erika began to tell him that her program forbade her to kill either the Old Race or the New except in self-defense or at the order of her maker. Then she realized that her program did not anticipate this situation.

Karloff did not belong to the Old Race, but he did not qualify as one of the New Race, either. He was something other, singular.

None of the rules of conduct under which Erika lived applied in this matter.

Looking over the sustaining machinery, ignorant of its function, she said, "I don't want to cause you pain."

"Pain is all I know," he murmured. "Peace is all I want."

She threw switches, pulled plugs. The purr of motors and the throb of pumps subsided into silence.

"I'm going," Karloff said, his voice thickening into a slur. His bloodshot eyes fell shut. "Going . . ."

On the floor, in the corner, the hand spasmed, spasmed.

The bodiless head's last words were so slurred and whispery as to be barely intelligible: *"You . . . must be . . . angel."*

She stood for a while, thinking about what he'd said, for the poets of the Old Race had often written that God works in mysterious ways His wonders to perform.

In time she realized that Victor must not find her here.

She studied the switches that she'd thrown, the plugs that she'd pulled. She reinserted one of the plugs. She repositioned the hand on the floor directly under the switches. She put the remaining plug in the hand, tightened the stiff fingers around it, held them until they remained in place without her sustained pressure.

In the pantry once more, she needed a minute to find the hidden switch. The shelves full of canned food slid into place, closing off the entrance to Victor's studio.

She returned to the painting by van Huysum in the drawing room. So beautiful.

To better thrill Victor sexually, she had been permitted shame. From shame had come humility. Now it seemed that from humility had perhaps come pity, and more than pity: mercy.

As she wondered about her potential, Erika's hope was reborn. *Her* feathered thing, perched in her heart if not her soul, was a phoenix, rising yet again from ashes.

CHAPTER 74

FROM THE SWIVELING BEACONS on the roofs of police cruisers and ambulances, unsynchronized flares of red and white and blue light painted a patriotic phantasmagoria across the face of the apartment building.

Some in pajamas and robes, others dressed and primped for the news cameras, the neighbors gathered on the sidewalk. They gossiped, laughed, drank beer from paper cups, drank beer from cans, ate cold pizza, ate potato chips from the bag, took snapshots of the police and of one another. They seemed to regard the eruption of sudden violence and the presence of a serial killer in their midst as reason for celebration.

At the open trunk of the department sedan, as Carson stowed the shotgun, Michael said, "How can he jump up and run away after a four-story face plant?"

"It's more than gumption."

"And how are we gonna write up this report without landing in a psych ward?"

Slamming the trunk lid, Carson said, "We lie."

A Subaru Outback angled to the curb behind them, and Kathleen Burke got out. "Can you believe—*Harker?*"

"He always seemed like such a sweetheart," Michael said.

"The moment I saw that suicide note on Roy Pribeaux's computer," Carson informed Kathy, "I didn't believe that he wrote it. Yesterday, ragging Michael and me, Harker used the same phrase that ends Pribeaux's note—'one level below Hell.'"

Michael confirmed: "Harker told us that to catch this guy, we were going to have to go to a weirder place—one level below Hell."

Surprised, Kathy said, "You mean you think he did it on purpose, he *wanted* you to tumble to him?"

"Maybe unconsciously," Carson said, "but yeah, he did. He threw the pretty boy off the roof after setting him up to take the rap for both Pribeaux's string of murders and those that Harker himself committed. But with those four words—'one level below Hell'—he lit a fuse to destroy himself."

"Deep inside, they pretty much always want to be caught," Kathy agreed. "But I wouldn't expect Harker's psychology to . . ."

"To what?"

She shrugged. "To work that way. I don't know. I'm babbling. Man, all the time I'm profiling him, the bastard's on my doorstep."

"Don't beat yourself up," Carson advised. "None of us suspected Harker till he all but pointed the finger at himself."

"But maybe I *should* have," Kathy worried. "Remember the three nightclub murders six months ago?"

"Boogie City," Carson recalled.

"Sounds like a place people go to pick their noses," Michael said.

"Harker and Frye were on that case," Kathy said.

Michael shrugged. "Sure. Harker shot the perp. It was an iffy shoot, but he was cleared."

"After a fatal OIS," Kathy said, "he had six hours of mandatory counseling. He showed up at my office for two of the hours but then never came back."

"No offense, Dr. Burke," Michael said, "but lots of us think mandatory counseling sucks. Just because Harker bailed doesn't mean you should've figured he had severed heads in his refrigerator."

"Yeah, but I knew something was eating him, and I didn't push him hard enough to finish the sessions."

The previous night, Carson had passed on the opportunity to tell Kathy the Spooky Time Theater story about monsters in New Orleans. Now there was no way to explain that she hadn't any reason to feel conscious-stricken, that Harker's psychology was *not even human*.

Trying to make as light of the situation as possible, Carson said to Michael, "Is she doomed to Hell, or what?"

"She reeks of brimstone."

Kathy managed a rueful smile. "Maybe sometimes I take myself too seriously." Her smile faltered. "But Harker and I seemed to have such . . . rapport."

A paramedic interrupted. "'Scuse me, detectives, but we've given Ms. Parker first aid, and she's ready for you now."

"She doesn't need to go to the hospital?" Carson asked.

"No. Minor injuries. And that's not a girl who traumatizes easy. She's Mary Poppins with attitude."

CHAPTER 75

JENNA PARKER, blithe spirit, lived in a collection of plush teddy bears, inspirational posters—EVERY DAY IS THE FIRST DAY OF YOUR LIFE, JUST SAY NO TO THE BLUES—and cute cookie jars.

The ceramic cookie jars were for the most part confined to the kitchen. There were a clown jar, a polar-bear jar, a brown-bear jar, a Mother Hubbard jar, a Mickey Mouse jar, a Wookie jar. Jars in the form of a puppy, a kitten, a raccoon, a rabbit, a gingerbread house.

Carson's favorite was a jar in the shape of a tall stack of cookies.

Apparently Jenna Parker didn't spend much time cooking, for the jar collection occupied half the counter space. Doors had been taken off some of the cabinets, so that the shelves could serve as display space for more cookie jars.

"Don't you dare say anything," Carson muttered to Michael as they entered the kitchen and were confronted by the aggressively cheerful ceramic figures.

Pretending wide-eyed innocence, he said, "About what?"

Jenna sat on a stool, wearing a pink jogging suit with a small appliqué of a running turtle on the left breast. She was nibbling a cookie.

For a woman who had such a short time ago been naked, strapped to an autopsy table, and about to be dissected alive, Jenna seemed remarkably cheerful. "Hi, guys. Want a cookie?"

"No thanks," Carson said, and Michael managed to decline, as well, without shtick.

Holding up one bandaged thumb like a child proudly displaying a boo-boo, Jenna said, "I mostly just tore off my thumbnail when I fell. Isn't that great?"

"Imagine how good you'd feel," Michael said, "if you'd broken a leg."

Well, he had repressed himself for the better part of a minute.

Jenna said, "I mean, considering I could've been sitting here with my heart cut out, what's a thumbnail?"

"A thumbnail is zip, zero, nada," said Michael.

"It's a feather on the scale," she said.

"Dust in the balance," he agreed.

"It's a shadow of nothing."

"De nada."

"Peu de chose," she said.

"Exactly what I would've said if I knew French."

She grinned at him. "For a cop, you're fun."

"I majored in banter at the police academy."

"Isn't he fun?" Jenna asked Carson.

Rather than stuff one or both of them into a damn cookie jar, Carson said impatiently, "Miss Parker, how long have you been Jonathan Harker's neighbor?"

"I moved in about eleven months ago. From day one, he was a sweetie."

"A sweetie? Did you and he . . ."

"Oh, no. Johnny was a man, yeah, and you know what *they're* like, but we were just good buds." To Michael, she said, "That thing I just said about men—no offense."

"None taken."

"I like men," she said.

"I don't," he assured her.

"Anyway, I'll bet you're not like other men. Except where it counts."

"Peu de chose," he said.

"Oh, I'll bet it's not," Jenna said, and winked.

Carson said, "Define 'buds' for me."

"Once in a while Johnny would come over for dinner or I'd go across the hall to his place. He'd cook pasta. We'd talk about life, you know, and destiny, and modern dance."

Boggled, Carson said, "Modern dance? *Harker?*"

"I was a dancer before I finally got real and became a dental hygienist."

Michael said, "For a long time, I wanted to be an astronaut."

"That's very brave," Jenna said with admiration.

Michael shrugged and looked humble.

Carson said, "Miss Parker, were you conscious any time after he chloroformed you?"

"On and off, yeah."

"Did he talk to you during this? Did he say *why?*"

"I think maybe he said having sex with me would be like having sex with a monkey."

Carson was nonplussed for a moment. Then she said, "You *think* he said it?"

"Well, with the chloroform and whatever he pumped into me through the IV, I was sort of in and out of it. And to be perfectly frank, I was going out to a party when he grabbed me, and I had a little bit of a pre-party buzz on. So maybe he said it or maybe I dreamed he said it."

"What else did you maybe dream he said?"

"He told me I was pretty, a fine example of my species, which was nice, but he said that he was one of the new race. Then this weird thing."

"I *wondered* when this would get weird," Michael said.

"Johnny said he wasn't allowed to reproduce but was reproducing anyway, dividing like an ameba."

Even as those words chilled Carson, they invoked in her a sense of the absurd that made her feel as if she were a straight man in a burlesque revival. "What do you think he meant by that?"

"Well, then he pulled up his T-shirt, and his belly was like a scene from *Alien,* all this squirming inside, so I'm pretty sure all of that was just the drugs."

Carson and Michael exchanged a look. She would have liked to pursue this subject, but doing so would alert Jenna to the fact that she might have experienced what she thought she had only dreamed.

Jenna sighed. "He was a sweetie, but sometimes he could get so down, just totally bummed out."

"About what?" Carson asked.

Jenna nibbled her cookie, thinking. Then: "He felt something was missing in his life. I told him happiness is always an option, you just have to choose it. But sometimes he couldn't. I told him he had to find his bliss. I wonder . . ."

She frowned. The expression came and went from her face twice, as though she wore a frown so seldom that she didn't know how to hold on to one when she needed it.

Carson said, "What do you wonder?"

"I told him he had to find his bliss, so I sure hope his bliss didn't turn out to be chopping people to pieces."

CHAPTER 76

THROUGH THE CODED DOOR, out of Mercy, Randal Six finds himself in a six-foot-wide, eight-foot-high corridor with block-and-timber walls and a concrete floor. No rooms open from either side of this passageway.

Approximately a hundred and forty feet from him waits another door. Happily, there are no choices. He has come too far to retreat. He can only go forward.

The floor has been poured in three-foot-square blocks. By taking long strides—sometimes *bounding*—Randal is able to spell himself along these oversize boxes toward the farther end of the corridor.

At the second door, he finds a locking system identical to the first. He enters the code he used previously, and this barrier opens.

The corridor is actually a tunnel under the hospital grounds. It connects to the parking garage in the neighboring building.

Father owns this five-story structure, too, in which he houses the accounting and personnel-management departments of Biovision. He can be seen coming and going from there without raising questions.

Using the secretly constructed underground passageway between buildings, his visits to the Hands of Mercy, which he owns through a shell company, can be concealed.

This second door opens into a dark place. Randal finds a light switch and discovers a twelve-foot-square room with concrete walls.

The floor is concrete, as well, but it is a single pour, with no form lines. In other words, it is one big empty box.

Directly opposite the doorway at which he stands is another door no doubt opening to the parking garage.

The problem is that he can't cross twelve feet and reach that door in a single step. To spell himself to that exit, he will have to take several steps within the same empty box.

Every step is a letter. The rules of crosswords are simple and clear. One letter per box. You can't put multiple letters in one box.

That way lies chaos.

Just considering the possibility, Randal Six shudders with fear and disgust.

One block, one letter. No other method is able to bring order to the world.

The *threshold* in front of him shares an *h* with the *chamber* that waits before him. Once across the threshold, he must finish spelling the last five letters of the other word *a-m-b-e-r*.

He can reach the next door in five steps. That is no problem. But he only has one empty box.

Randal stands at the threshold of this new room. He stands. He stands at the threshold. He stands, thinks, puzzles, puzzles.... He begins to weep with frustration.

CHAPTER 77

WHEN BULLETS WEREN'T FLYING, Carson could take a more thoughtful look at Harker's apartment. Signs of a dysfunctional personality were at once evident.

Although every piece of furniture was a different style from the others, in clashing colors and uncomplementary patterns, this might mean nothing more than that Harker had no taste.

Although his living room had considerably more contents than did Allwine's—where there had been nothing but a black-vinyl chair—it was underfurnished to the point of starkness. Minimalism, of course, is a style preferred by many people who are perfectly sane.

The absence of any artwork whatsoever on the walls, the lack of bibelots and mementoes, the disinterest in beautifying the space in any way reminded her too much of how Allwine had lived.

At least one inspirational poster or cute cookie jar would have been welcome.

Instead, here came Dwight Frye out of the kitchen, looking as greasy as ever but, as never before, contrite. "If you're gonna rip me a new one, don't bother. I've already done it."

Michael said, "That's one of the most moving apologies I've ever heard."

"I knew him like a brother," Frye said, "but I didn't know him at all."

Carson said, "He had a passion for modern dance."

Frye looked baffled, and Michael said approvingly, "Carson, you might get the hang of this yet."

"For real he went out that kitchen window?" Frye asked.

"For real," Carson said.

"But the fall would've killed him."

"Didn't," Michael said.

"He didn't have a damn parachute, did he?"

Carson shrugged. "We're amazed, too."

"One of you fired two rounds from a twelve-gauge," Frye noted, indicating the pellet holes in the wall.

"That would be me," said Carson. "Totally justified. He shot at us first."

Frye was puzzled. "How could you not take him down at such close range?"

"Didn't entirely miss."

"I see some blood," Frye said, "but not a lot. Still and all, even gettin' winged by a twelve-gauge—that's got to sting. How could he just keep on keepin' on?"

"Moxie?" Michael suggested.

"I've drunk my share of Moxies, but I don't expect to laugh off a shotgun."

A CSI tech stepped out of the bedroom. "O'Connor, Maddison, you gotta see this. We just found where he *really* lived."

CHAPTER 78

FATHER PATRICK DUCHAINE, shepherd to the congregation at Our Lady of Sorrows, took the phone call in the rectory kitchen, where he was nervously eating sugar-fried pecans and wrestling with a moral dilemma.

After midnight, a call to a priest might mean that a parishioner had died or lay dying, that last rites were wanted, as well as words of comfort to the bereaved. In this case, Father Duchaine felt sure that the caller would be Victor, and he was not wrong.

"Have you done what I asked, Patrick?"

"Yes, sir. Of course. I've been all over the city since we had our little conference. But none of our people has seen one of us acting . . . strangely."

"Really? Can you assure me there isn't a renegade among the New Race? No . . . apostate?"

"No, sir, I can't absolutely assure you. But if there is one, he's given no outward sign of a psychological crisis."

"Oh, but he has," Victor said coolly.

"Sir?"

"If you'll turn on your radio or watch the first TV news in the morning, you'll get quite an earful about our Detective Harker of the Homicide Division."

Father Duchaine nervously licked his lips, which were sugary from the pecans. "I see. It was some policeman, was it? Do you . . . do you feel that I've failed you?"

"No, Patrick. He was clever."

"I was exhaustive . . . in my search."

"I'm sure you did everything that you possibly could."

Then why this call? Father Duchaine wanted to ask, but he dared not.

Instead, he waited a moment, and when his maker said nothing, he asked, "Is there anything more you need me to do?"

"Not at the moment," Victor said. "Perhaps later."

All the sugar had been licked from Father Duchaine's lips, and his mouth had gone dry, sour.

Searching for words that might repair his maker's damaged trust in him, he heard himself saying, "God be with you." When only silence answered him, he added, "That was a joke, sir."

Victor said, "Was it really? How amusing."

"Like in the church—when you said it to me."

"Yes, I remember. Good night, Patrick."

"Good night, sir."

The priest hung up. He plucked fried pecans from the dish on the kitchen counter, but his hand shook so badly that he dropped the nuts before he could convey them to his mouth. He stooped, retrieved them.

At the kitchen table with a water glass and a bottle of wine, Jonathan Harker said, "If *you* need sanctuary, Patrick, where will *you* turn?"

Instead of answering, Father Duchaine said, "I've disobeyed him. I've lied to him. How is that possible?"

"It may not *be* possible," said Harker. "At least not without terrible consequences."

"No. I think perhaps it's possible because . . . my programming is being rewritten."

"Oh? How can it be rewritten when you're not in a tank anymore or hooked up to a data feed?"

Father Duchaine looked toward the ceiling, toward Heaven.

"You can't be serious," Harker said, and took a long swallow of communion wine.

"Faith can change a person," Father Duchaine said.

"First of all, you're not a person. You're not human. A real priest would call you a walking blasphemy."

This was true. Father Duchaine had no answer to the charge.

"Besides," Harker continued, "you don't really have any faith."

"Lately, I'm . . . wondering."

"I'm a murderer," Harker reminded him. "Killed two of them and one of us. Would God approve of your giving me sanctuary any more than Victor would?"

Harker had put into words a key element of Father Duchaine's moral dilemma. He had no answer. Instead of replying, he ate more sugar-fried pecans.

CHAPTER 79

IN THE BACK OF the bedroom closet, Harker had broken through the lath and plaster. He had reconfigured the studs and cats to allow easy passage to the space beyond.

Leading Carson, Michael, and Frye through the wall, the young tech said, "This building was at one time commercial on the ground floor, offices in the upper three, and it had an attic for tenant storage."

On the other side of the wall were rising steps—wood, worn, creaky.

As he led them upward, the tech said, "When they converted to apartments, they closed off the attic. Harker somehow found out it was here. He made it into his go-nuts room."

In the high redoubt, two bare bulbs hanging on cords from the ridge beam shed a dusty yellow light.

Three large gray moths swooped under and around the bulbs. Their shadows swelled, shrank, and swelled again across the finished floor, the finished walls, and the open-rafter ceiling.

A chair and a folding table that served as a desk were the only pieces of furniture. Books were stacked on the table, also here and there on the floor.

An enormous homemade light box covered two-thirds of the north wall and provided backlighting for dozens of X-ray images: various grinning skulls from various angles, chests, pelvises, spines, limbs. . . .

Scanning this macabre gallery, Michael said, "I thought when you went through the back of a wardrobe, you came out in the magical land of Narnia. Must've taken a wrong turn."

In the northwest corner stood a three-way mirror with a gilded frame. On the floor in front of the mirror lay a white bath mat.

Treading on fleeting phantoms of moths, serving as a screen for projections of their flight, Carson passed the mirror and crossed the room to a different display that covered the south wall from corner to corner, floor to ceiling.

Harker had stapled to the drywall a collage of religious images: Christ on the cross, Christ revealing His sacred heart, the Virgin Mary; Buddha; Ahura Mazda; from the Hindu faith, the goddesses Kali and Parvati and Chandi, the gods Vishnu and Doma and Varuna; Quan Yin, the Queen of Heaven and goddess of compassion; Egyptian gods Anubis, Horus, Amen-Ra . . .

Bewildered, Frye asked, "What is all this?"

"He's crying out," Carson said.

"Crying out for what?"

"Meaning. Purpose. Hope."

"Why?" Frye wondered. "He *had* a job, and with benefits that don't get much better."

CHAPTER 80

RANDAL SIX STANDS motionless at the threshold of the next room for so long, so tensely, that his legs begin to ache.

The New Race does not easily fatigue. This is Randal Six's first experience with muscle cramps. They burn so intensely that at last he takes advantage of his ability to block pain at will.

He has no watch. He has never before needed one. He estimates that he has stood, riveted by his predicament, in this same spot for perhaps three hours.

Predicament is a woefully inadequate word. The correct one has fewer letters and stronger meaning: *plight.*

Although he has spared himself physical agony, he cannot escape mental anguish. He despises himself for his inadequacies.

At least he has stopped weeping. Long ago.

Gradually his impatience with himself darkens into an intense anger at Arnie O'Connor. If not for Arnie, Randal Six would not be in this plight.

If ever he reaches the O'Connor boy, he *will* get the secret of happiness from him. Then he will make Arnie pay dearly for all this suffering.

Randal is also plagued by anxiety. Periodically his two hearts race, pounding with such terror that sweat pours from him and his vision becomes blood-dimmed.

He fears that Father will discover him missing and will set out in search of him. Or perhaps Father will finish his current work and leave for the night, whereupon he will find Randal standing here in autistic indecision.

He will be led back to the spinning rack and secured upon it in a cruciform. The rubber wedge, secured by chinstrap, will be inserted between his teeth.

Although he has never seen Father in a rage, he has heard others speak of the maker's wrath. There is no hiding from him and no mercy for the object of his fury.

When Randal thinks that he hears the sound of a door opening at the farther end of the hall, behind him, he closes his eyes and waits with dread.

Time passes.

Father does not appear.

Randal must have mistaken the sound or imagined it.

As he stands with his eyes still closed, however, and as his hearts seek a normal rhythm, a calming pattern arises in his mind's eye: arrangements of empty white boxes against a black background, intersecting in the beautiful virgin lines of an unworked crossword puzzle.

While he concentrates on this barren image for its soothing effect, a solution to his plight occurs to him. When there are not squares of vinyl tile or concrete or other material on the floor in front of him, he can draw them with his imagination.

Excited, he opens his eyes, studies the floor of the room beyond the threshold, and tries to paint upon it the five boxes that he must have to finish spelling *chamber* when he crosses *threshold*.

He fails. Though with eyes closed he had been able to see those boxes clearly in his mind, the concrete floor before him remains resistant to the imposition of imagined geometries.

Tears almost overtake him again before he realizes that he does not need to have his eyes open to traverse this room. Blind men walk with the help of canes and patient dogs. His imagination will be his white cane.

Eyes shut, he sees five boxes. He steps straight forward five times, spelling as he goes: *a-m-b-e-r*.

When the word is complete, he opens his eyes and finds that he stands at the outer door. The electric door behind him has fallen shut. The portal before him has a simple latch that is always engaged from the farther side, always disengaged from this side.

He opens the door.

Triumph.

Beyond lies a parking garage, dimly lighted and deserted at this hour. Silent, still, smelling faintly of dampness and lime.

To exit this small room, Randal Six merely closes his eyes and imagines *threshold* printed in blocks from left to right, immediately in front of him. Conveniently, the word *garage* intersects at the letter *r*.

With his eyes closed, he determinedly takes three steps, *a-g-e,* into the enormous space beyond. The door falls shut behind him, now locked from this side.

There is no going back.

The daunting dimensions of the parking garage awe and for a moment nearly overwhelm him. No room of his experience in Mercy has prepared him for this immensity.

An inner quaking seems to knock bones against bones. He feels like a highly compressed pellet of matter at the instant before the universe's creation, and with the impending Big Bang, he will expand and explode outward in every direction, racing to fill an infinite void.

With more powerful reason than he has heretofore been able to apply to his condition, he convinces himself that the void will not pull him apart, will not scatter him to eternity. Gradually his panic subsides, fades entirely.

He closes his eyes to imagine blocks, and doggedly he spells his way forward. Between each word, Randal opens his eyes to scope the route ahead and to determine the length of the next word that he will need.

In this fashion, he eventually comes to an exit ramp and climbs to the street. The Louisiana night is warm, moist, droning with mosquitoes.

By the time he travels the better part of a block and turns right into an alleyway, the brush of dawn paints a faint gray light in the east.

Panic threatens him once more. In daylight, with everyone awake and on the move, the world will be a riot of sights, sounds. He is certain that he cannot tolerate so much sensory input.

Night is a better environment. Darkness is his friend.

He must find a place to hide until the day passes.

CHAPTER 81

EXHAUSTED, CARSON SAILED through sleep with no nightmares, only a simple continuous dream of being aboard a black boat under a black sky, knifing silently through black water.

She had not gotten to bed until well after dawn. She woke at 2:30, showered, and ate Hot Pockets while standing in Arnie's room, watching the boy at work on the castle.

At the foot of the bridge that crossed the moat, in front of the gate at the barbicon, at each of two entrances from the outer ward to the inner ward, and finally at the fortified entrance to the castle keep, Arnie had placed one of the shiny pennies that he had been given by Deucalion.

She supposed the pennies were, in Arnie's mind, talismans that embodied the power of the disfigured giant. Their mighty juju would prevent entrance by any enemy.

Evidently Arnie trusted Deucalion.

So did Carson.

Considering the events of the past two days, Deucalion's claim to be Frankenstein's monster seemed no more impossible than other things that she had witnessed. Besides, he possessed a quality that she had never encountered before, a substantialness that eluded easy description. His calm was of an oceanic depth, his gaze so steady and so forthright that she sometimes had to look away, not because the occasional soft pulse of light in his eyes disturbed her, but because he seemed to see too deeply into her for comfort, through all her defenses.

If Deucalion was the storied creation of Victor Frankenstein, then during the past two centuries, while the human doctor had become a monster, the monster had become human—and perhaps had become a man of unusual insight and caliber.

She needed a day off. A month. There were others working on the case now, seeking Harker. She didn't need to push herself seven days out of seven.

Nevertheless, by prior arrangement, at 3:30 in the afternoon, Carson was waiting at the curb in front of her house.

At 3:33, Michael arrived in the plainwrap sedan. Earlier in the day, Carson had experienced a moment of weakness. Michael had driven the car when they left Harker's apartment building.

Now, as she got in the passenger's seat, Michael said, "I drove all the way here and never exceeded a speed limit."

"That's why you're three minutes late."

"Three whole minutes? Well, I guess I just blew every chance we have to find Harker."

"The only thing we can't buy more of is time," she said.

"And dodo birds. We can't buy any of them. They're extinct. And dinosaurs."

"I called Deucalion at the Luxe. He's expecting us at four o'clock."

"I can't wait to enter this one in my interview log—'discussed case with Frankenstein monster. He says Igor was a creep, ate his own boogers.'"

She sighed. "I was sort of hoping that the concentration needed to drive would mean less patter."

"Just the opposite. Driving keeps me mentally fluid. It's cool being the wheel man."

"Don't get used to it."

When they arrived at the Luxe Theater, after four o'clock, the sky had grown as dark as an iron skillet.

Michael parked illegally at a red curb and hung a POLICE card on the rearview mirror. "Lives in a theater, huh? Is he buddies with the Phantom of the Opera?"

"You'll see," she said, and got out of the car.

Closing his door, looking at her across the roof, he said, "Do his palms grow hairy when the moon is full?"

"No. He shaves them just like you do."

CHAPTER 82

FOLLOWING A LONG NIGHT and longer day at Mercy, Victor ate what was either a late lunch or an early dinner of seafood gumbo with okra and rabbit étouffée at a Cajun restaurant in the Quarter. Although not as satisfyingly exotic as his Chinese meal the previous night, the food was good.

For the first time in nearly thirty hours, he went home.

Having enhanced his physiological systems to the extent that he needed little sleep and therefore could accomplish more in the lab, he sometimes wondered if he worked too much. Perhaps if he allowed himself more leisure, his mind would be clearer in the laboratory, and consequently he would do even better science.

Periodically over the decades, he had engaged in this debate with himself. He always resolved it in favor of more work.

Like it or not, he had given himself to a great cause. He was the kind of man who would work selflessly in the pursuit of a world ruled by reason, a world free of greed and peopled by a race united by a single goal.

Arriving at his mansion in the Garden District, he chose work over leisure yet again. He went directly to his hidden studio behind the pantry.

Karloff had perished. The life-support machines were not in operation.

Stunned, he circled the central worktable, uncomprehending until he proceeded far enough to discover the hand on the floor. The thrown switches were directly above it. Furthermore, clutched in its fingers was a plug that it had pulled from a socket.

Although disappointed by this setback, Victor was amazed that Karloff had been able to shut himself down.

For one thing, the creature had been programmed to be incapable of self-destruction. On that issue there had been no wiggle room in the directives by which it had been governed.

More important, the hand could not have functioned separate from its own life-support system. The moment it had broken free of its feed and drain lines, it had lost the low-voltage current needed to fire its nerves and operate its musculature. At that point, it should have at once fallen still, limp, dead—and should have begun to decompose.

Only one explanation occurred to Victor. Apparently, Karloff's telekinetic power had been strong enough to animate the hand as if it were alive.

When controlling the hand at a distance, Karloff had shown the ability only to flex a thumb and to imitate an arpeggio by strumming an imaginary harp with those four fingers. Small, simple tasks.

To make the hand tear loose of its connections, to cause it to drop to the floor and then to climb three feet up the face of these machines to throw the life-support switches, to cause it to pull the plug, as well . . . That required far greater telekinetic power and more precise control than he had previously exhibited.

An incredible breakthrough.

Although Karloff was gone, another Karloff could be engineered. The setback would be temporary.

Excited, Victor sat at his desk and accessed the experiment file on his computer. He clicked the camera icon and called up the twenty-four-hour video record of events in the studio.

Scanning backward from the present, he was surprised when Erika suddenly appeared.

CHAPTER 83

AS WHEN SHE had been to the Luxe the previous evening, Carson found one of the front doors unlocked. This time, no one waited in the lobby.

A set of double doors stood open between the lobby and the theater.

Surveying the refreshment stand as they passed it, Michael said, "When you buy popcorn here, I wonder if you can ask for it *without* the cockroaches."

The theater itself proved to be large, with both a balcony and a mezzanine. Age, grime, and chipped plaster diminished the Art Deco glamour but did not defeat it altogether.

A fat man in white slacks, white shirt, and white Panama hat stood in front of the tattered red-velvet drapes that covered the giant screen. He looked like Sidney Greenstreet just stepped out of *Casablanca*.

The Greenstreet type gazed toward the ceiling, transfixed by something not immediately evident to Carson.

Deucalion stood halfway down the center aisle, facing the screen. Head tipped back, he slowly scanned the ornate architecture overhead.

The strangeness of the moment was shattered with the silence when a sudden flapping of wings revealed a trapped bird swooping through the vaults above, from one roost in the cornice to another.

As Carson and Michael approached Deucalion, she heard him say, "Come to me, little one. No fear."

The bird flew again, swooped wildly, swooped . . . and alighted on Deucalion's extended arm. Seen close and still, it proved to be a dove.

With a laugh of delight, the fat man came forward from the screen. "I'll be damned. We ever get a lion in here, you're my man."

Gently stroking the bird, Deucalion turned as Carson and Michael approached him.

Carson said, "I thought only St. Francis and Dr. Doolittle talked to animals."

"Just a little trick."

"You seem to be full of tricks, little and big," she said.

The fat man proved to have a sweet voice. "The poor thing's been trapped here a couple days, living off stale popcorn. Couldn't get it to go for the exit doors when I opened them."

Deucalion cupped the bird in one immense hand, and it appeared to be without fear, almost in a trance.

With both pudgy hands, the man in white accepted the dove from Deucalion and moved away, toward the front of the theater. "I'll set it free."

"This is my partner, Detective Maddison," Carson told Deucalion. "Michael Maddison."

They nodded to each other, and Michael—pretending not to be impressed by the size and appearance of Deucalion—said, "I've gotta be straight with you. I'll be the first to admit we're in weird woods on this one, but I still don't buy the Transylvania thing."

"That's movies. In real life," Deucalion said, "it was Austria."

"We need your help," Carson told him. "As it turns out, there were two killers."

"Yes. It's on the news."

"Yeah. Well, only one of them seems to have been . . . the kind that you warned me about."

"And he's a detective," Deucalion said.

"Right. He's still loose. But we've found his . . . playroom. If he's really one of Victor's people, you'll be able to read his place better than we can."

Michael shook his head. "Carson, he's not a psychologist. He's not a profiler."

In a matter-of-fact tone, arresting precisely because of its lack of drama, Deucalion said, "I understand murderers. I am one."

Those words and an accompanying throb of light through the giant's eyes left Michael briefly speechless.

"In my early days," Deucalion said, "I was a different beast. Uncivilized. Full of rage. I murdered a few men . . . and a woman. The woman was my maker's wife. On their wedding day."

Obviously sensing the same convincing gravitas in Deucalion that had impressed Carson, Michael searched for words and found these: "I know that story, too."

"But *I* lived it," said Deucalion. He turned to Carson. "I don't choose to go out in daylight."

"We'll take you. It's an unmarked car. Inconspicuous."

"I know the place. I saw it on the news. I'd rather meet you there."

"When?" she asked.

"Go now," he said. "I'll be there when you are."

"Not the way she drives," said Michael.

"I'll be there."

Toward the front of the theater, the fat man shouldered open an emergency-exit door to the waning afternoon. He released the dove, and it flew to freedom in the somber pre-storm light.

CHAPTER 84

VICTOR FOUND ERIKA in the library. She nestled in an armchair, legs tucked under her, reading a novel.

In retrospect, he should have forbidden her to spend so much time with poetry and fiction. Emily Dickinson, indeed.

The authors of such work imagined that they addressed not merely the mind but the heart, even the soul. By their very nature, fiction and poetry encouraged an emotional response.

He should have insisted that Erika devote most of her reading time to science. Mathematics. Economic theory. Psychology. History.

Some history books might be dangerous, as well. In general, however, nonfiction would educate her with little risk of instilling in her a corrupting sentimentality.

Too late.

Infected with pity, she was no longer useful to him. She fancied that she had a conscience and the capacity for caring.

Pleased with herself for the discovery of these tender feelings, she had betrayed her master. She would betray him again.

Worse, drunk with book-learned compassion, she might in her ignorant fulsomeness dare to pity *him* for one reason or another. He would not tolerate her foolish sympathy.

Wise men had long warned that books corrupted. Here was the unassailable proof.

As he approached, she looked up from the novel, the poisonous damn novel, and smiled.

He struck her so hard that he broke her nose. Blood flew, and he thrilled at the sight of it.

She endured three blows. She would have endured as many as he wished to rain on her.

Victor was not sufficiently satisfied merely to strike her. He tore the book out of her hands, threw it across the room, seized her by her thick bronze hair, dragged her from the chair, and threw her onto the floor.

Denied the choice of turning off the pain, she suffered. He knew precisely how to maximize that suffering. He kicked, kicked.

Although he had enhanced his body, Victor was not the physical equal of one of the New Race. In time he exhausted himself and stood sweat-soaked, gasping for breath.

Every injury she sustained, of course, would heal without scar. Already, her lacerations were healing, her broken bones knitting together.

If he wished to let her live, she would be as good as new in just a day or two. She would smile for him again. She would serve him as before.

That was not his wish.

Pulling a straightbacked chair away from a reading desk, he said, "Get up. Sit here."

She was a mess, but she managed to get to her knees and then to the chair. She sat with her head bowed for a moment. Then she raised it and straightened her back.

His people were amazing. Tough. Resilient. In their way, proud.

Leaving her in the chair, he went to the library bar and poured cognac from a decanter into a snifter.

He wanted to be calmer when he killed her. In his current state of agitation, he would not be able fully to enjoy the moment.

At a window, with his back to her, he sipped the cognac and watched the contusive sky as its bruises grew darker, darker. Rain would come with nightfall, if not before.

They said that God created the world in six days and rested on the seventh. They were lying.

First, there was no God. Only brutal nature.

Second, Victor knew from hard experience that the creation of a new world was a frustrating, often a tedious, and a time-consuming endeavor.

Eventually, calm and prepared, he returned to Erika. She sat in the chair as he had left her.

Taking off his sport jacket and draping it over the back of an armchair, he said, "This can be a perfect city. One day . . . a perfect world. Ordinary flawed humanity—they resist perfection. One day they will be . . . replaced. All of them."

She sat in silence, head raised, but not looking at him, gazing instead at the books on the shelves.

He removed his necktie.

"A world stripped clean of fumbling humanity, Erika. I wish you could be here with us to see it."

When creating a wife for himself, he modified—in just a few ways—the standard physiology that he gave to other members of the New Race.

For one thing, strangling one of them would have been extremely difficult. Even if the subject had been obedient and docile, the task might have taken a long time, might even have proved *too* difficult.

Every Erika, on the other hand, had a neck structure—windpipe, carotid arteries—that made her as vulnerable to a garrote as was any member of the Old Race. He could have terminated her in other ways, but he wished the moment to be intimate; strangulation satisfied that desire.

Standing behind her chair, he bent to kiss her neck.

"This is very difficult for me, Erika."

When she did not reply, he stood straight and gripped the necktie in both hands. Silk. Quite elegant. And strong.

"I'm a creator and a destroyer, but I prefer to create."

He looped the tie around her neck.

"My greatest weakness is my compassion," he said, "and I must purge myself of it if I'm to make a better world based on rationality and reason."

Savoring the moment, Victor was surprised to hear her say, "I forgive you for this."

Her unprecedented audacity so stunned him that his breath caught in his throat.

When he spoke, the words came in a rush: "*Forgive me?* I am not of a station to need forgiveness, and you are not of a position to have the power to grant it. Does the man who eats the steak need the forgiveness of the steer from which it was carved? You foolish bitch. And *less* than a bitch because no whelp would ever have come from your loins if you had lived a thousand years."

Quietly, calmly, almost tenderly, she said, "But I will never forgive you for having made me."

Her audacity had grown to effrontery, to impudence so shocking that it robbed him of all the pleasure that he expected from this strangulation.

To Victor, creation and destruction were equally satisfying expressions of *power*. Power alone motivated him: the power to defy nature and to bend it to his will, the power to control others, the power to shape the destiny of both the Old Race and the New, the power to overcome his own weaker impulses.

He strangled her now, cut off the blood supply to her brain, crushed her windpipe, strangled her, strangled her, but with such fury, in such a blind rage, that by the time he finished, he was not a man of power but merely a grunting beast fully in the thrall of nature, out of control, lost to reason and rationality.

In her dying, Erika had not only denied him but defeated him, humiliated him, as he had not been in more than two centuries.

Choking with wrath, he pulled books off the shelves, threw them to the floor, scores of books, hundreds, tore them and ground them under his heels. Tore them and ground them. Threw them and tore them.

Later, he went to the master suite. He showered. Restless and energized, he had no interest in relaxation. He dressed to go out, though he did not know for where or what purpose.

From another decanter, he poured another cognac into another snifter.

On the intercom, he spoke with William, the butler, who was on duty in the staff room. "There's a dead thing in the library, William."

"Yes, sir."

"Contact my people in the sanitation department. I want that useless meat buried deep in the landfill, and right away."

At the window, he studied the lowering sky, which had grown so dark with thunderheads that an early dusk had come upon the city.

CHAPTER 85

AT HARKER'S APARTMENT BUILDING, Carson and Michael took the elevator to the fourth floor to avoid the stink of mildew in the public stairwell.

Homicide, CSI, and curious neighbors had long ago faded away. The building almost seemed deserted.

When they reached the fourth floor, they found Deucalion waiting in the hallway, outside Harker's apartment.

To Carson, Michael murmured, "I didn't see the Batmobile parked out front."

"You won't admit it," she said, "but you're convinced."

To her surprise, he said, "Almost."

Evidently having heard Michael's murmured words, Deucalion said, "I used the Batcopter. It's on the roof."

By way of apology, Michael said, "Listen, that crack didn't mean anything. That's just me. If I see a joke, I go for it."

"Because you see so much in life that disturbs you, the cruelty, the hatred," Deucalion said. "You armor yourself with humor."

For the second time in an hour, Michael found himself without a comeback.

Carson had never imagined that such a day would dawn. Maybe this was one of the seven signs of the Apocalypse.

She slit the police seal on the door, used her Lockaid gun, and led them inside.

"Minimalism minimalized," said Deucalion as he moved into the sparsely furnished living room. "No books."

"He's got some books in the attic," Carson said.

"No mementoes," Deucalion continued, "no decorative items, no photographs, no art. He hasn't found a way to have a life. This is the cell of a monk . . . but one who has no faith."

Trying to get back in the saddle, Michael said, "Carson, he's an absolute whiz at this."

Deucalion looked toward the kitchen but didn't move in that direction. "He sometimes sits at the table in there, drinking. But whiskey doesn't provide him with the escape he needs. Only occasional oblivion."

Earlier, the standard premises search had turned up a case of bourbon in the kitchen.

Looking toward the bedroom, Deucalion said, "In there, you will most likely find pornography. Only a single item. One video."

"Exactly," she confirmed. "We found one."

When it turned up in the search, Michael had referred to the porn video by various titles—*Transvestitesylvania, The Thing with Two Things*—but now he said nothing, impressed to silence by Deucalion's insights.

"He found no thrill in images of copulation," Deucalion said. "Only an even more profound sense of being an outsider. Only greater alienation."

CHAPTER 86

FEARFUL OF THE day-bright world in all its dazzling busyness, Randal Six earlier took refuge in an alleyway Dumpster.

Fortunately, this enormous container is half filled with nothing more offensive than office trash, largely paper and cardboard. There is no restaurant or produce-market garbage, no organic stench and slime.

Throughout the day, until the storm clouds come, the sun beats down on Randal. This is the first sun of his life, bright and hot, frightening at first, but then less so.

He sits with his back to a corner, cushioned by paper refuse, his world reduced to manageable dimensions, and works one crossword puzzle after another in the book that he brought with him from his room in the Hands of Mercy.

Frequently traffic passes through the alleyway. And people on foot. Initially he pauses in his puzzle at each possibility of an encounter, but eventually he realizes that they are not likely to disturb him.

If a sanitation truck comes to empty the Dumpster, he is not sure how he will cope. This possibility didn't occur to him until he had already taken sanctuary in the container. His hope is that trash is not collected every day.

Having missed breakfast and then lunch, he grows hungry as the day progresses. Considering his accomplishments to this point, he can endure a little hunger.

At Mercy, Randal's untouched meals will alert the staff to his absence, though perhaps not for a while. Sometimes, when particularly deep in autistic detachment, he leaves a meal untouched for hours. He has been known to eat both breakfast and lunch an hour before dinner— then leave his dinner until near midnight.

Before departing Mercy, he closed his bathroom door. They may think that he is in there.

From time to time, people toss bags of trash and loose objects into the bin. The top of the big Dumpster is over their heads, so they cannot easily look in and see him.

Sometimes the trash strikes him, but it's never a problem. When the people leave, Randal pushes the new stuff away and reestablishes his cozy nest.

Midafternoon, a man singing "King of the Road" approaches along the alley. He can't carry a tune.

Judging by the sound, he's pushing some kind of cart. The wheels clatter on the cracked pavement.

Between lines of the song, the cart-pusher grumbles incoherent chains of four-letter words, then resumes singing.

When this man stops at the Dumpster, Randal Six puts aside his puzzle book and pen. Instinct tells him that there may be trouble.

Two grimy hands appear at the rim of the bin. The singer takes a grip, grunts and curses as he clambers up the side of the Dumpster.

Balanced on the edge of the big container, half in and half out, the man spots Randal. His eyes widen.

The guy is perhaps in his thirties, bearded, in need of a bath. His teeth are crooked and yellow when he reveals them to say "This here's *my* territory, asshole."

Randal reaches up, grabs the man by his shirtsleeves, pulls him into the Dumpster, and breaks his neck. He rolls the dead body to the farther end of the container and covers it with bags of trash.

In his corner once more, he picks up the puzzle book. He turns to his page and finishes spelling *derangement*.

The dead man's cart stands near the Dumpster. Eventually someone might notice it and wonder about its owner.

Randal will have to deal with the problem if and when it arises. Meanwhile, crosswords.

Time passes. Clouds darken the sky. Although still warm, the day grows cooler.

Randal Six is not happy, but he is content, at ease. Later, he will be happy for the first time.

In his mind's eye is the city map, his route to happiness, the O'Connor house at the end of the journey, his guiding star.

CHAPTER 87

BECAUSE OF THEIR fine-tuned metabolism, members of the New Race did not easily become drunk. Their capacity for drink was great, and when they did become inebriated, they sobered more quickly than did those of the Old Race.

Throughout the day, Father Duchaine and Harker opened bottle after bottle of communion wine. This use of the church's inventory troubled the priest both because it was in effect a misappropriation of funds and because the wine, once blessed, would have become the sacred blood of Christ.

Being a soulless creature made by man but charged with religious duty, Father Duchaine had over the months and years grown ever more torn between what he was and what he wished to be.

Regardless of the moral issue of using this particular wine for purposes other than worship, the alcoholic content of the brew was less than they might have wished. Late in the afternoon, they began to spike it with Father Duchaine's supply of vodka.

Sitting in armchairs in the rectory study, the priest and the detective tried for the tenth—or perhaps the twentieth—time to pull the most troubling thorns from each other's psyches.

"Father will find me soon," Harker predicted. "He'll stop me."

"And me," the priest said morosely.

"But I don't feel guilty about what I've done."

"Thou shalt not kill."

"Even if there is a God, His commandments can't apply to us," said Harker. "We're not His children."

"Our maker has also forbidden us to murder . . . except on his instructions."

"But our maker isn't God. He's more like . . . the plantation owner. Murder isn't a sin . . . just disobedience."

"It's still a crime," said Father Duchaine, troubled by Harker's self-justifications, even though the plantation-owner analogy had a measure of truth in it.

Sitting on the edge of his armchair, leaning forward, tumbler of vodka-spiked wine clasped in both hands, Harker said, "Do you believe in evil?"

"People do terrible things," the priest said. "I mean, real people, the Old Race. For children of God, they do terrible, terrible things."

"But evil," Harker pressed. "Evil pure and purposeful? Is evil a real presence in the world?"

The priest drank from his glass, then said, "The church allows exorcisms. I've never performed one."

With the solemnity of both profound dread and too much booze, Harker said, "Is *he* evil?"

"Victor?" Father Duchaine felt that he was on dangerous ground. "He's a hard man, not easy to like. His jokes aren't funny."

Harker rose from his chair, went to a window, and studied the low, threatening sky that impressed an early dusk upon the day.

After a while, he said, "If he's evil . . . then what are we? I've been so . . . confused lately. But I don't feel evil. Not like Hitler or Lex Luthor. Just . . . incomplete."

Father Duchaine slid to the edge of his chair. "Do you think . . . by living the right way, we might in time develop the souls that Victor couldn't give us?"

Returning from the window, adding vodka to his glass, Harker said with serious demeanor, "Grow a soul? Like . . . gallstones? I've never thought about it."

"Have you seen *Pinocchio*?"

"I've never had patience for their movies."

"This marionette is made of wood," Father Duchaine said, "but he wants to be a real boy."

Harker nodded, downed half his drink, and said, "Like Winnie the Pooh wants to be a real bear."

"No. Pooh is delusional. He already thinks he's a real bear. He eats honey. He's afraid of bees."

"Does Pinocchio become a real boy?"

Father Duchaine said, "After a lot of struggle, yes."

"That's inspiring," Harker decided.

"It is. It really is."

Harker chewed his lower lip, thinking. Then: "Can you keep a secret?"

"Of course. I'm a priest."

"This is a little scary," Harker said.

"Everything in life's a little scary."

"That's so true."

"In fact, that was the theme of my homily last Sunday."

Harker put down his drink, stood before Duchaine. "But I'm more excited than scared. It started two days ago, and it's accelerating."

Expectantly, Patrick rose from his chair.

"Like Pinocchio," Harker said, "I'm changing."

"Changing . . . how?"

"Victor denied us the ability to reproduce. But I . . . I'm going to give birth to something."

With an expression that seemed to be as much pride as fear, Harker lifted his loose-fitting T-shirt.

A subcutaneous face was taking shape beneath the skin and the surface fat layers of Harker's abdomen. The thing was like a death mask but in motion: blind eyes rolling, mouth opening as though in a silent scream.

Recoiling in shock, Father Duchaine crossed himself before he realized what he had done.

The doorbell rang.

"Birth?" the priest said agitatedly. "What makes you think it's birth instead of biological chaos?"

Sudden sweat sheathed Harker's face. Sullen at this rejection, he pulled down his T-shirt. "I'm not afraid. Why should I be?" But clearly he was afraid. "I've murdered. Now I create—which makes me more human."

The doorbell rang again.

"A breakdown in cell structure, metastasis," Father Duchaine said. "A terrible design flaw."

"You're envious. That's what you are—envious in your chastity."

"You've got to go to him. Get his help. He'll know what to do."

"Oh, he'll know what to do, all right," Harker said. "There's a place waiting for me in the landfill."

The doorbell rang a third time, more insistently than before.

"Wait here," said Father Duchaine. "I'll be back. We'll figure out what to do . . . something. Just wait."

He closed the door when he left the study. He crossed the parlor to the front hall.

When the priest opened the front door, he discovered Victor on the porch.

"Good evening, Patrick."

Striving to conceal his anxiety, Father Duchaine said, "Sir. Yes. Good evening."

"Just 'good evening'?"

"I'm sorry. What?" When Victor frowned, Duchaine understood. "Oh, yes. Of course. Come in, sir. Please come in."

CHAPTER 88

MOTH SHADOWS BEAT an ever-changing tattoo across the faces of Christ, Buddha, Amen-Ra.

In the attic above Jonathan Harker's apartment, Carson, Michael, and Deucalion gathered at the wall-to-wall collage of gods, on which Harker must have spent scores of hours.

"It seems to express such yearning," Carson said. "You can feel his anguish."

"Don't be too moved by it," Deucalion advised. "He would embrace any philosophy that filled the void in him."

He peeled away an image of Christ in the Garden of Gethsemane, then one of Buddha, revealing different forms and faces beneath, their nature at first mysterious.

"God was only his most recent obsession," Deucalion explained.

As other pictures were peeled away, Carson saw an underlying collage of Nazi images and symbols: swastikas, Hitler, goose-stepping soldiers.

"Under all these faces of traditional gods is another god that failed him," Deucalion said. "A god of violent social change and racial purity. There are so many of those."

Perhaps at last fully convinced of Deucalion's nature, Michael said, "How did you know there was a second layer?"

"Not just a second," Deucalion said. "Also a third."

When Hitler and his ilk were torn off the wall, there was revealed an even eerier collage: images of Satan, demons, satanic symbols.

Deucalion said, "The unique despair of a creature without a soul eventually leads to desperation, and desperation fosters obsession. In Harker's case, this is only the surface of it."

Peeling away a horned-and-fanged demonic face, Carson said, "You mean . . . more layers under this?"

"The wall feels spongy, padded," Michael said.

Deucalion nodded. "It's been papered over twenty times or more. You might find gods and goddesses again. When new hopes fail, old hopes return in the endless cycle of desperation."

Instead, Carson found Sigmund Freud in the fourth layer. Then other pictures of equally solemn men.

"Freud, Jung, Skinner, Watson," Deucalion said, identifying each newly revealed face. "Rorschach. Psychiatrists, psychologists. The most useless gods of all."

CHAPTER 89

FATHER DUCHAINE RETREATED from the threshold as Victor stepped through the front door into the rectory foyer.

The master of the New Race looked around with interest. "Cozy. Quite nice. A vow of poverty doesn't preclude certain comforts." He touched one finger to Father Duchaine's Roman collar. "Do you take your vows seriously, Patrick?"

"Of course not, sir. How could I? I've never actually gone to the seminary. I've never taken vows. You brought me to life with a manufactured past."

In what might have been a warning tone, Victor said, "That's worth remembering."

With a sense of entitlement, Victor proceeded along the hall, deeper into the house, without invitation.

Following his master into the parlor, the priest asked, "To what do I owe the honor of this visit, sir?"

Surveying the room, Victor said, "The authorities haven't found Detective Harker yet. We're all at risk until I reacquire him."

"Would you like me to mobilize our people to search for him?"

"Do you really think that would do any good, Patrick? I'm not so sure."

As Victor moved across the living room toward the door of the study, Father Duchaine said, "Can I get you coffee, sir? Brandy?"

"Is that what I smell on your breath, Patrick? Brandy?"

"No. No, sir. It's . . . it's vodka."

"There's only one thing I want now, Patrick. A tour of your lovely home."

Victor crossed to the study door, opened it.

Holding his breath, Father Duchaine followed his maker across that threshold—and found that Harker had gone.

Circling the room, Victor said, "I programmed you with a fine education in theology. Better than anything you could have gotten from any university or seminary."

He paused to look at the bottle of wine and bottle of vodka that stood side by side on the coffee table. Only one glass stood on the table.

With alarm, Father Duchaine noticed that a wet ring marked the table where Harker's glass had stood.

Victor said, "With your fine education, Patrick, perhaps you can tell me—does *any* religion teach that God can be deceived?"

"Deceived? No. Of course not."

The second ring could have been left by Father Duchaine's glass. He might have moved it to where it stood now, leaving the ring. He hoped that Victor would consider that possibility.

As Victor continued around the study, he said, "I'm curious. You've had some years of experience with your parishioners. Do you think they lie to their god?"

Feeling as though he were walking a tightrope, the priest said, "No. No, they mean to keep the promises they make to Him. But they're weak."

"Because they're human. Human beings are weak, those of the Old Race. Which is one reason why my people will eventually destroy them, replace them."

Although Harker had slipped out of the study, he must have taken refuge somewhere.

In the living room once more, when Victor didn't return to the front hall but went instead toward the adjoining dining room, Father Duchaine followed nervously.

The dining room proved to be deserted.

Victor pushed through the swinging door into the kitchen, and Father Duchaine followed like a dog afraid that its hard master would find a cause for punishment.

Harker had gone. In the kitchen, the door to the back porch stood open. The draft entering from the storm-dark twilight smelled faintly of the rain to come.

"You shouldn't leave your doors open," Victor warned. "So many of God's people have a criminal bent. They would burglarize even a priest's home."

"Just before you rang the bell," Father Duchaine said, amazed to hear himself lying so boldly, "I stepped outside for a breath of fresh air."

"Fresh air is of no special value to those of you I've made. You're

designed to thrive without exercise, on any diet, in fresh air and in foul."
He rapped his knuckles on Father Duchaine's chest. "You are an exquisitely efficient organic machine."

"I'm grateful, sir, for all that I am."

From the kitchen to the hall, from the hall to the foyer, Victor said,
"Patrick, do you understand why it's important that my people infiltrate
organized religion as well as every other aspect of human society?"

The answer came to the priest not from thoughtful consideration
but from programming: "Many years from now, when the time comes to
liquidate those of the Old Race who remain, there must be nowhere
they can turn for support or sanctuary."

"Not to the government," Victor agreed, "because we will *be* the
government. Not to the police or the military . . . or to the church."

Again as if by rote, Father Duchaine said, "We must avoid a destructive civil war."

"Exactly. Instead of civil war . . . a very civil extermination." He opened
the front door. "Patrick, if you ever felt in any way . . . incomplete . . .
you would come to me, I assume."

Warily, the priest said, "Incomplete? What do you mean?"

"Adrift. Confused about the meaning of your existence. Without
purpose."

"Oh, no, sir. I know my purpose, and I'm dedicated to it."

Victor met Father Duchaine's eyes for a long moment before he
said, "Good. That's good. Because there's a special risk for those of you
who serve in the clergy. Religion can be seductive."

"Seductive? I don't see how. It's such nonsense. Irrational."

"All of that and worse," Victor agreed. "And if there were an afterlife and a god, he would hate you for what you are. He would snuff you
out and cast you into Hell." He stepped onto the porch. "Good night,
Patrick."

"Good night, sir."

After Father Duchaine closed the door, he stood in the foyer until
his legs became so weak that he had to sit.

He went to the stairs, sat on a riser. He clutched one hand with the
other to quell the tremors in them.

Gradually his hands changed position until he found them clasped
in prayer.

He realized that he had not locked the door. Before his maker could
open it and catch him in this betrayal, he made fists of his hands and
beat them against his thighs.

CHAPTER 90

STANDING AT THE folding table that served as Harker's desk in the go-nuts room, Deucalion sorted through the stacks of books.

"Anatomy. Cellular biology. Molecular biology. Morphology. This one's psychotherapy. But all the rest . . . human biology."

"And why did he build this?" Carson asked, indicating the light box on the north wall, where X-rays of skulls, spines, rib cages, and limbs were displayed.

Deucalion said, "He feels that something's missing in him. He's long been trying to understand what it is."

"So he studies pictures in anatomy books, and compares other people's X-rays to his own. . . ."

"When he learned nothing from that," Michael said, "he started opening real people and looking inside them."

"Except for Allwine, Harker chose people who seemed whole to him, who seemed to have what he lacked."

Michael said, "In the statement Jenna gave, she says Harker told her he wanted to see what she had inside that made her happier than he was."

"You mean, leaving out Pribeaux's victims, Harker's weren't just selected at random?" Carson asked. "They were people he knew?"

"People he knew," Deucalion confirmed. "People he felt were happy, complete, self-assured."

"The bartender. The dry cleaner," Michael said.

"Harker most likely had drinks from time to time in that bar," Deucalion said. "You'll probably find the dry cleaner's name in his checkbook. He knew those men, just like he knew Jenna Parker."

"And Alice's looking glass?" Michael asked, pointing to the three-way mirror in the corner of the attic.

"He stood there in the nude," Deucalion said. "Studying his body for some . . . difference, deficiency . . . something that would reveal why he feels incomplete. But that would have been before he started to look . . . inside."

Carson returned to the books on the table, opening them one by one to pages that Harker had marked with Post-its, hoping to learn more from what, specifically, had interested him.

"What will he do now?" Michael asked.

"What he's been doing," Deucalion said.

"But he's on the run, in hiding. He doesn't have time to plan one of his . . . dissections."

As Carson picked up the book on psychotherapy, Deucalion said, "He's more desperate than ever. And when the desperation increases, so does the obsession."

One of the bookmarks was not a Post-it. Carson discovered an appointment card for Harker's third session with Kathleen Burke, the appointment that he didn't keep.

She turned and looked at the mural of stapled images.

Where they had peeled at the collage, the fourth layer had been revealed below the demons and devils. Freud, Jung. Psychiatrists . . .

In memory, Carson heard Kathy as they had stood talking with her the previous night in front of this very building: *But Harker and I seemed to have such . . . rapport.*

Reading her as he always could, Michael said, "Something?"

"It's Kathy. She's next."

"What'd you find?"

She showed him the appointment card.

He took it from her, turned with it to Deucalion, but Deucalion was gone.

CHAPTER 91

A FRACTION OF THE DAY remains, but filtered through the soot-dark clouds, the light is thin, gray, and weaves itself with shadows to obscure more than illuminate.

For hours, the supermarket shopping cart—piled with garbage bags full of salvaged tin cans, glass bottles, and other trash—has stood where the vagrant left it. No one has remarked upon it.

Randal Six, fresh from the Dumpster, means to push the cart to a less conspicuous place. Perhaps this will delay the discovery of the dead man in the bin.

He curls both hands around the handle of the cart, closes his eyes, imagines ten crossword squares on the pavement in front of him, and begins to spell *shopaholic*. He never finishes the word, for an amazing thing happens.

As the shopping cart rolls forward, the wheels rattle across the uneven pavement; nevertheless, the motion is remarkably, satisfyingly smooth. So smooth and continuous is this motion that Randal finds he can't easily think of his progress as taking place letter by letter, one square at a time.

Although this development spooks him, the relentless movement of the wheels *through* squares, rather than from one square to another in orderly fashion, doesn't bring him to a halt. He has . . . momentum.

When he arrives at the second *o* in *shopaholic*, he stops spelling because he is not any longer sure which of the ten imagined squares he is in. Astonishingly, though he stops spelling, he keeps moving.

He opens his eyes, assuming that when he no longer visualizes the crossword boxes in his mind's eye, he will come to a sudden stop. He keeps moving.

At first he feels as if the cart is the motive force, pulling him along the alleyway. Although it lacks a motor, it must be driven by some kind of magic.

This is frightening because it implies a lack of control. He is at the mercy of the shopping cart. He must go where it takes him.

At the end of a block, the cart could turn left or right. But it continues forward, across a side street, into the next length of the alleyway. Randal remains on the route that he mapped to the O'Connor house. He keeps moving.

As the wheels revolve, revolve, he realizes that the cart is not *pulling* him, after all. He is *pushing* the cart.

He experiments. When he attempts to increase speed, the cart proceeds faster. When he chooses a less hurried pace, the cart slows.

Although happiness is not within his grasp, he experiences an unprecedented gratification, perhaps even satisfaction. As he rolls, rolls, rolls along, he has a taste, the barest taste, of what freedom might be like.

Full night has fallen, but even in darkness, even in alleyways, the world beyond Mercy is filled with more sights, more sounds, more smells than he can process without spinning into panic. Therefore, he looks neither to the left nor the right, focuses on the cart before him, on the sound of its wheels.

He keeps moving.

The shopping cart is like a crossword-puzzle box on wheels, and in it is not merely a collection of aluminum cans and glass bottles but also his hope for happiness, his hatred for Arnie O'Connor.

He keeps moving.

CHAPTER 92

IN THE BUNGALOW of the seashell gate with the unicorn motif, behind the windows flanked by midnight-blue shutters decorated with star shapes and crescent moons, Kathy Burke sat at her kitchen table reading a novel about adventure in a kingdom ruled by wizardry and witchery, eating almond cookies and drinking coffee.

From the corner of her eye, she saw movement and looked up to discover Jonathan Harker standing in the doorway between the kitchen and the dark hall.

His face, usually red from the sun or from anger, was whiter than pale. Disheveled, sweating, he looked malarial.

Although his eyes were wild and haunted, although his nervous hands plucked continually at his stretched and saturated T-shirt, he spoke in a meek and ingratiating manner weirdly out of sync with his aggressive entrance and his appearance: "Good evening, Kathleen. How're you? Busy, I'm sure. Always busy."

Taking her lead from his tone, Kathy calmly put a bookmark in her novel, slid it aside. "It didn't have to be this way, Jonathan."

"Maybe it did. Maybe there was never any hope for me."

"It's partly my fault that you are where you are. If you'd stayed in counseling—"

He took a step into the room. "No. I've hidden so much from you. I didn't want you to know . . . what I am."

"I've been a lousy therapist," she said by way of ingratiation.

"You're a good woman, Kathy. A very fine person."

The weirdness of this exchange—her self-effacement, Harker's flattery—in light of his recent crimes, was impossible to sustain, and

Kathy thought furiously about where the encounter might lead and how best to manage it.

Fate intruded when the phone rang.

They both looked at it.

"I'd prefer you didn't answer that," said Harker.

She remained seated and did not challenge him. "If I'd insisted that you keep your appointments, I might have recognized signs that you were . . . heading for trouble."

A third ring of the phone.

He nodded. His smile was tortured. "You would have. You're so insightful, so understanding. That's why I was afraid to talk with you anymore."

"Will you sit down, Jonathan?" she asked, indicating the chair across the table from her.

A fifth ring.

"I'm so tired," he acknowledged, but he made no move toward the chair. "Do I disgust you . . . what I've done?"

Choosing her words carefully, she said, "No. I feel . . . a kind of grief, I guess."

After the seventh or eighth ring, the phone fell silent.

"Grief," she continued, "because I so much liked the man you were . . . the Jonathan I knew."

"There's no going back, is there?"

"I won't lie to you," she said.

Harker moved tentatively, almost shyly toward Kathleen. "You're so complete. I know if only I could look inside you, I'd find what I'm missing."

Defensively, she rose from her chair. "You know that makes no sense, Jonathan."

"But what else can I do but . . . keep looking?"

"I only want what's best for you. Do you believe that?"

"I guess . . . Yes, I do."

She took a deep breath, took a risk: "Then will you let me call someone, make arrangements to turn you in?"

For an anguished moment, Harker looked around the kitchen as if he were trapped. He might have snapped then, but his tension subsided into anxiety.

Sensing that she was winning him over to surrender, Kathy said, "Let me call someone. Let me do the right thing."

He considered her offer for a moment. "No. No, that wouldn't be a good thing."

He looked across the kitchen, intrigued by something.

When Kathy followed the direction of his gaze, she saw the knife rack filled with gleaming blades.

LEAVING HARKER'S APARTMENT, Michael hadn't made any attempt to get behind the wheel. He tossed the keys to Carson.

He rode shotgun—literally, holding the weapon between his knees, the muzzle toward the ceiling.

By habit, as they rocketed through the night, he said, "Stop trying for the land-speed record. The dispatcher will have someone there ahead of us, anyway."

Accelerating, Carson came back at him: "Did you say something, Michael? 'Yes, Carson, I said, *Faster, faster.*' Yeah, that's what I thought you said, Michael."

"You do a lousy imitation of me," he complained. "You're not nearly funny enough."

WITH ONE HAND on his abdomen, as if suffering a stomachache, Harker prowled the kitchen, moving toward the knife rack and then away, but then toward it once more. "Something's happening," he said worriedly. "Maybe it's not going to be like I thought it would."

"What's wrong?" Kathy asked warily.

"Maybe it's not going to be good. Not good at all. Something's coming."

Abruptly his face wrenched with pain. He let out a strangled cry and clasped both hands to his abdomen.

"Jonathan?"

"I'm *splitting.*"

Kathy heard tires squeal and brakes bark as a fast car pulled to a stop in her driveway.

Looking toward the sound, terror trumping his pain, Harker said, *"Father?"*

INSTEAD OF THE WALK-in unicorn gate, Carson favored the driveway and slid to a stop so close to the garage door that even a wizard couldn't have charmed himself thin enough to fit between the building and the sedan's bumper.

She pulled her piece from her paddle holster as she exited the car, and Michael chambered a shell in the shotgun as he came around the back of the car to join her.

The front door of the house flew open, and Kathy Burke ran onto the porch, down the steps.

"Thank God," Carson said.

"Harker went out the back," Kathy said.

Even as she spoke, Carson heard running footsteps and turned, seeking the sound.

Harker had come along the farther side of the garage. He was off the lawn, into the street, before Carson could draw down on him.

By now he was in too public an area—houses across the street—to allow her to take a shot. The risk of collateral damage was too high.

Michael ran, Carson ran, Harker ahead of them, down the middle of the residential street.

In spite of the doughnuts and the grab-it dinners eaten on their feet, in spite of the ass-fattening time spent at desks filling out the nine yards of paperwork that had become the bane of modern police work, Carson and Michael were fast, movie-cop fast, wolf-on-a-rabbit fast.

Harker, being inhuman, being some freak brewed up in a lab by Victor Frankenstein, was faster. Along Kathy's block to the corner and left into another street, along another block and right at the next corner, he opened up his lead.

Lightning tore the sky, magnolia shadows jumped across the pavement, and a blast of thunder rocked the city so hard that Carson thought she could feel it rumbling in the ground, but the rain did not fall at once, held off.

They traded the neighborhood of bungalows for low-rise office and apartment buildings.

Harker ran like a marathon man on meth, moving away, away—and then mid-block he made the mistake of veering into an alleyway that proved to dead-end in a wall.

He came to the eight-foot-high brick barrier, flung himself at it, scrambled up like a monkey on a stick, but abruptly screamed as if torn by horrendous pain. He fell off the wall, rolled, sprang at once to his feet.

Carson shouted at him to freeze, as if there were a hope in hell that he would, but she had to go through the motions.

He went at the wall again, leaped, grabbed the top, too fast for her to sight on him, and clambered over.

"Get out in front of him!" she shouted to Michael, and he raced back the way they had come, looking for a different route into the street beyond the wall.

She holstered her pistol, dragged a half-filled garbage can to the end of the alley, climbed onto it, gripped the top of the wall with both hands, levered up, got a leg over.

Although she was sure that Harker would have escaped, Carson discovered that he had fallen again. He was lying faceup in the street, wriggling like a snake with a broken back.

If their kind could turn off pain in a crisis, as Deucalion claimed, either Harker had forgotten that option or something was so wrong with him that he had no control of it.

As she came off the wall, he got to his feet again, staggering toward an intersection.

They were near the waterfront. Ship-chandlers' offices, ship broker-ages, mostly warehouses. No traffic at this hour, businesses dark, streets silent.

At the intersection, Michael appeared in the street ahead.

Trapped between Carson and Michael, Harker turned toward the alleyway on the left, which led toward the waterfront, but it was fenced to twelve feet, with a wide padlocked gate, so he veered toward the front of a warehouse.

When Michael closed on him with the shotgun, Carson held back, giving him a clear approach.

Harker built speed toward the man-door at the front of the ware-house, as if he didn't see it.

Following the usual protocol, Michael shouted for Harker to stop, to drop, to put his hands behind his head.

When Harker hit the door, it held, and he screamed, but he didn't bounce off and go down as he ought to have done. He seemed to *stick* to it.

The crash of impact was followed at once by Harker's cry of rage and the shriek of tortured metal.

Michael shouted again, five steps from point-blank position.

The warehouse door sagged. Hinges snapped with reports as loud as gunshots. The door went down, and Harker disappeared inside just as Michael halted and brought the 12-gauge into firing position.

Carson joined him at the entrance. "He's going to try to get out the back."

Once Harker was on the waterfront—the docks, the boats, the cargo esplanade—there were a thousand ways for him to disappear.

Offering Michael her pistol, grip first, she said, "You two-gun him at the back when he comes out. Gimme the shotgun, and I'll move him through to you."

This made sense because Michael was taller than she, stronger, and therefore could scale the twelve-foot alleyway fence faster than she could.

He took her pistol, gave her the shotgun. "Watch your ass. I'd hate for anything to happen to it."

The mantle of the black sky cracked. Volcanic blaze of light, volcanic boom. At last the pent-up rain fell in a volume to inspire ark builders.

CHAPTER 93

TO THE RIGHT of the broken door, Carson found switches. Light revealed a reception area. Gray-tile floor, pale-blue walls. A few chairs. Low railings to the left and right, desks beyond.

Directly ahead was a service counter. At the left end, a gate stood open.

Harker might have been crouched against the farther side of the counter, waiting for her, but she doubted she would find him there. His priority wasn't to waste her, just to get away.

She cleared the gate fast, swiveling the 12-gauge to cover the area behind the counter. No Harker.

A door stood ajar behind the clerical pen. She pushed it open with the shotgun barrel.

Enough light came from behind her to reveal a short hallway. No Harker. Deserted.

She stepped inside, flicked on the hall light. She listened but heard only the thunder and the insistent crash of rain on the roof.

To each side stood a door. Signs identified them as men's and women's lavatories.

Harker wouldn't have stopped to take a pee, wash his hands, or admire himself in a mirror.

Assuring herself that he would have no desire to get behind her and take her by surprise, that he only wanted to escape, Carson went past the lavatories toward another door at the end of the hall.

She glanced back twice. No Harker.

The end door featured a traffic-check window through which she saw darkness beyond.

Conscious that she was a backlit target as long as she lingered on the threshold, Carson cleared it fast and low, scanning left and right in the flush of light that accompanied her. No Harker.

The door fell shut, leaving her in darkness. She backed up against the wall, felt the switches pressing into her back, slid aside, held the 12-gauge with one hand, snapped on the lights.

Suspended from the thirty-foot ceiling, a series of lights in cone-shaped shades revealed a large warehouse with goods stacked on pallets to a height of twenty feet. A maze.

She turned right across the open ends of the aisles, looking into each. No Harker. No Harker. No Harker. Harker.

Thirty feet from the mouth of the aisle, moving away from her, Harker hobbled as if in pain, bent forward, cradling his torso with both arms.

Thinking of the people he'd sliced open, thinking of the makeshift autopsy table in his bedroom, where he had been prepared to dissect Jenna Parker, Carson went after him with no intention of cutting him any slack. Closing to within twenty feet before shouting his name, she brought up the shotgun, finger on the trigger rather than on the guard.

If he dropped like he should, she'd cover him, use her cell phone to get Michael, get backup.

Harker turned to face her. His wet hair hung over his face. The shape of his body seemed . . . *wrong.*

The son of a bitch didn't drop. From him came the eeriest sound that she had ever heard: part a cry of agony, part excited laughter, part an expression of brute rage.

She fired.

The pellets hit him in a tight group, where his cradling arms crossed his abdomen. Blood sprayed.

So fast that it seemed as if he were not a real figure but one in a time-lapse film, Harker clambered up a wall of crates, out of the aisle.

Carson chambered another round, tracked him as if he were a clay disk in a skeet shoot, and blew a chunk off the top crate, missing him as he vanished over the palisade.

SAYING A PRAYER for the family jewels, Michael jammed Carson's pistol into his waistband, scaled the fence at the mouth of the alleyway, wincing as an ax of lightning chopped the night, figuring it would whack the steel chain-link and electrocute him.

He got over the fence, into the alley, unfried, and ran through drenching rain and the rolling echoes of thunder to the rear of the warehouse.

A concrete ramp led up to the loading dock at the back. A big roll-up door and a man-door served that deep platform. Harker would come out of the smaller door.

He drew Carson's pistol but left his own holstered. He was not literally going to two-gun the fugitive, one pistol in each hand. For the best possible placement of shots, he needed a two-hand grip on the weapon.

If as advertised Harker proved to be as hard to bring down as a charging rhino, Michael might empty a magazine trying to pop both his hearts. If after that Harker was still on the move, there would not be time to eject a magazine and slap in a fresh one. He'd drop Carson's piece, draw his own, and hope for the kill with the *next* ten rounds.

Embracing this strategy, Michael realized that although the Frankenstein story seemed like a can of Spam, he had gone for it as eagerly as if it had been filet mignon.

Inside, the 12-gauge boomed. Almost at once, it boomed again.

Thrusting one hand into his jacket pocket, he felt spare shotgun shells. He'd forgotten to give them to Carson. She had one round in the breach, three in the magazine. Now only two left.

The 12-gauge boomed again.

She was down to one round, with no backup handgun.

Waiting for Harker on the loading dock wasn't a workable plan any longer.

Michael tried the man-door. It was locked, of course, but worse, it was steel plate, resistant to forced entry, with three deadbolts.

Movement startled him. He reeled back and discovered Deucalion at his side—tall, tattooed, totemic in the lightning.

"Where the hell—"

"I understand locks," Deucalion interrupted.

Instead of applying the finesse his words implied, the huge man grabbed the door handle, wrenched it so hard that all three of the lock assemblies pulled out of the steel frame with a *pop-crack-shriek* of tortured metal, and threw the torqued door onto the loading dock.

"What the *hell*," Michael asked, "was that?"

"Criminal trespass," Deucalion said, and disappeared into the warehouse.

CHAPTER 94

WHEN MICHAEL FOLLOWED Deucalion into the warehouse, the giant wasn't there. Whatever he might be, the guy gave new meaning to the word *elusive*.

Calling out to Carson would alert Harker. Besides, the storm was louder in here than outside, almost deafening: Rain roared against the corrugated metal roof.

Crates of various sizes, barrels, and cubes of shrink-wrapped merchandise formed a labyrinth of daunting size. Michael hesitated only briefly, then went searching for the minotaur.

He found hundreds of hermetically sealed fifty-gallon drums of vitamin capsules in bulk, crated machine parts, Japanese audio-video gear, cartons of sporting equipment—and one deserted aisle after another.

Frustration built until he thought maybe he would shoot up a few boxes that claimed to contain Kung Fu Elmo dolls, just to relieve the tension. If they had been Barney the Dinosaur dolls, he would more likely have acted on the impulse.

From overhead, louder than the rain, came the sound of someone running along the top of the stacked goods. The crates and barrels along the right side of the aisle shuddered and creaked and knocked together.

When Michael looked up, he saw something that was Harker but not Harker, a hunched and twisted and grotesque form, vaguely human but with a misshapen trunk and too many limbs, coming toward him along the top of the palisade. Maybe the speed with which it moved and the play of shadow and light fooled the eye. Maybe it was not monstrous at all. Maybe it was just old pain-in-the-ass Jonathan, and maybe

Michael was in such a state of paranoid agitation that he was mostly *imagining* all the demonic details.

Pistol in a two-hand grip, he tried to track Harker, but the fugitive moved too fast, so Michael figured the first shot he would get would be when Harker leaped toward him and was airborne. At the penultimate moment, however, Harker changed directions and sprang off the right-hand stacks, across the ten-foot-wide aisle, landing atop the left-hand palisade.

Gazing up, in spite of the extreme angle, Michael got a better look at his adversary. He could no longer cling to the hope that he had imagined Harker's grotesque transformation. He couldn't swear to the precise details of what he glimpsed, but Johnny definitely was not in acceptable condition to be invited to dinner with genteel company. Harker was Hyde out of Jekyll, Quasimodo crossed with the Phantom of the Opera, minus the black cape, minus the slouch hat, but with a dash of H. P. Lovecraft.

Landing atop the merchandise to the left of Michael, Harker crouched low, on all fours, maybe on all sixes, and with what sounded like *two* voices quarreling with each other in wordless shrieks, he scrabbled away, back in the direction from which he had come.

Because he didn't suffer from any doubts about his manhood, because he knew that valor was often the better part of courage, Michael considered leaving the warehouse, going back to the station, and writing a letter of resignation. Instead, he went after Harker. He soon lost track of him.

LISTENING BEYOND the storm, breathing air that had been breathed by the quarry, Deucalion moved slowly, patiently, between two high ramparts of palleted goods. He wasn't searching so much as waiting.

As he expected, Harker came to him.

Here and there, narrow gaps in each wall of crates gave a view of the next aisle. As Deucalion came to one of these look-throughs, a pale and glistening face regarded him from eight feet away in the parallel passageway.

"Brother?" Harker asked.

Meeting those tortured eyes, Deucalion said, "No."

"Then what are you?"

"His first."

"From two hundred years?" Harker asked.

"And a world away."

"Are you as human as me?"

"Come to the end of the aisle with me," Deucalion said. "I can help you."

"Are you as human as me? Do you murder and create?"

With the alacrity of a cat, Deucalion scaled the palisade, from floor to crest, in perhaps two seconds, three at most, crossed to the next aisle, looked down, leaped down. He had not been quick enough. Harker was gone.

CARSON FOUND A SET of open spiral stairs in a corner. Rapid footsteps rang off metal risers high above. A creaking noise preceded a sudden loud rush of rain. A door slammed shut, closing out the immediate sound of the downpour.

With one shot left and ready in the breach, she climbed.

The steps led to a door. When she opened it, rain lashed her.

Beyond lay the roof.

She flipped a wall switch. Outside, above the door, a bulb brightened in a wire cage.

After adjusting the latch so the door wouldn't automatically lock behind her, she went out into the storm.

The broad roof was flat, but she could not see easily to every parapet. In addition to the gray screens of rain, vent stacks and several shed-like structures—perhaps housing the heating-cooling equipment and electrical panels—obstructed her view.

The switch by the door had activated a few other lamps in wire cages, but the deluge drowned most of the light.

Cautiously, she moved forward.

SOAKED, CHILLED even though the rain was warm, certain that the phrase "like a drowned rat" would for the rest of his life bring him to tears, Michael moved among the vent stacks. Warily, he circled one of the sheds, making a wide arc at each corner.

He had followed someone—something—onto the roof and knew that he was not alone here.

Whatever their purpose might be, the cluster of small structures looked like cottages for roof Hobbits. After circling the first, he tried the door. Locked. The second was locked, too. And the third.

As he moved toward the fourth structure, he heard what might have been the rasp of hinges on the door he had just tried—and then from a distance Carson shouting his name, a warning.

IN EACH BLAZE of lightning, the shatters of rain glittered like torrents of beveled crystals in a colossal chandelier, but instead of brightening the roof, these pyrotechnics added to the murk and confusion.

Rounding a collection of bundled vent pipes, Carson glimpsed a figure in this darkling crystal glimmer. She saw him more clearly when the lightning passed, realized that he was Michael, twenty feet away, and then she spotted another figure come out of one of the sheds. "Michael! Behind you!"

Even as Michael turned, Harker—it had to be Harker—seized him and with inhuman strength lifted him off his feet, held him overhead, and rushed with him toward the parapet.

Carson dropped to one knee, aimed low to spare Michael, and fired the shotgun.

Hit in the knees, staggered, Harker hurled Michael toward the edge of the building.

Michael slammed into the low parapet, started to slide over, nearly fell, but hung on and regained the roof.

Although Harker should have been down, shrieking in agony, his knees no more supportive than gelatin, he remained on his feet. He came for Carson.

Rising from a position of genuflection, Carson realized she had fired the last round. She held on to the weapon for its psychological effect, if any, and backed away as Harker approached.

In the light of the rain-veiled roof lamps, in a quantum series of lightning flashes of escalating brightness, Harker appeared to be carrying a child against his chest, though his arms were free.

When the pale thing clinging to Harker turned its head to look at her, Carson saw that it was not a child. Dwarfish, but with none of a dwarf's fairy-tale appeal, deformed to the point of malignancy, slit-mouthed and wicked-eyed, this was surely a phantasm, a trick of light and lightning, of rain and gloom, mind and murk conspiring to deceive.

Yet the monstrosity did not vanish when she tried to blink it away. And as Harker drew nearer, even as Carson backed away from him, she thought the detective's face looked strangely blank, his eyes glazed, and she had the unnerving feeling that the thing clinging to him was in *control* of him.

When Carson backed into a stack of vent pipes, her feet skidded on the wet roof. She almost fell.

Harker surged toward her, like a lion bounding toward faltering prey. The shriek of triumph seemed to come not from him but from the thing fastened to—surging out of?—his chest.

Suddenly Deucalion appeared and seized both the detective and the hag that rode him. The giant lifted them as effortlessly and as high as Harker had lifted Michael, and threw them from the roof.

Carson hurried to the parapet. Harker lay facedown in the alley, more than forty feet below. He lay still, as if dead, but she had seen him survive another killing fall the previous night.

CHAPTER 95

A SET OF SWITCHBACK fire stairs zigzagged down the side of the warehouse. Carson paused at the top only long enough to take three spare shotgun shells from Michael and load them in the 12-gauge.

The iron stairs were slippery in the rain. When she grabbed the railing, it felt slick under her hand.

Michael followed close behind her, too close, the open stairs trembling and clanking under them. "You see that *thing*?"

"Yeah."

"That face?"

"Yeah."

"It was coming out of him."

"What?"

"Out of him!"

She said nothing. Didn't know *what* to say. Just kept racing down, turning flight to flight.

"The thing *touched* me," Michael said, revulsion thick in his voice.

"All right."

"It's *not* all right."

"You hurt?"

"If it's not dead—"

"It's dead," she hoped.

"—kill it."

When they reached the alleyway, Harker remained where he had fallen, but he no longer lay facedown. He had turned to the sky.

His mouth sagged open. His eyes were wide, unblinking; rain pooled in them.

From hips to shoulders, the substance of him was . . . gone. His chest and abdomen had collapsed. Rags of skin and torn T-shirt hung on shattered fragments of his rib cage.

"It came *out* of him," Michael declared.

A scrape and clank drew their attention to a point farther along the alleyway, toward the front of the warehouse.

Through the blear of rain, in the scintillation of lightning, Carson saw a pale trollish figure crouched beside an open manhole from which it had dragged the cover.

At a distance of thirty feet, in the murk of the tropical storm, she could see few details of the thing. Yet she *knew* that it was staring at her.

She raised the shotgun, but the pallid creature dropped into the manhole, out of sight.

Michael said, "What the hell *was* that?"

"I don't know. Maybe . . . maybe I don't want to know."

CSI, ME PERSONNEL, a dozen jakes, and the usual obnoxious gaggle of media types had come, and the storm had gone.

The buildings dripped, the puddled street glistened, but nothing looked clean, nothing smelled clean, either, and Carson suspected that nothing would ever quite *feel* clean again.

Jack Rogers had shown up to oversee the handling and transport of Jonathan Harker's remains. He was determined not to lose evidence this time.

At the back of the plainwrap sedan, stowing the shotgun, Carson said, "Where's Deucalion?"

Michael said, "Probably had a dinner date with Dracula."

"After what you've seen, you aren't still resisting this?"

"Let's just say that I'm continuing to process the data."

She slapped him affectionately—but hard enough—alongside the head. "Better get an upgraded logic unit."

Her cell phone rang. When she answered it, she heard Vicky Chou in a panic.

CHAPTER 96

FINISHED, PROGRAMMED, having received a downloaded education in language and other basics, Erika Five lay in the sealed glass tank, awaiting animation.

Victor stood over her, smiling. She was a lovely creature.

Although four Erikas had failed him, he had high hopes for the fifth. Even after two hundred years, he was learning new techniques, better design solutions.

He keyed commands into the computer that was associated with this tank—number 32—and watched as the milky solution in which Erika lay was cycled out of the container to be replaced with a clear cleansing solution. Within a few minutes, this second bath drained, leaving her dry and pink.

The numerous electrodes, nutrient lines, drains, and service tubes connected to her automatically withdrew. At this decoupling, she bled from a few veins, but only for a moment; in members of the New Race, such small wounds healed in seconds.

The curved glass lid opened on pneumatic hinges as a triggering shock started Erika breathing on her own.

Victor sat on a stool beside the tank, leaned forward, his face close to hers.

Her luxurious eyelashes fluttered. She opened her eyes. Her gaze was first wild and fearful. This was not unusual.

When the moment was right and Victor knew she had passed from birth shock to engagement, he said, "Do you know what you are?"

"Yes."

"Do you know why you are?"

"Yes."

"Do you know who I am?"

For the first time, she met his eyes. "Yes." Then she lowered her gaze with a kind of reverence.

"Are you ready to serve?"

"Yes."

"I'm going to enjoy using you."

She glanced at him again, and then humbly away.

"Arise," he said.

The tank revolved a quarter of a turn, allowing her to swing her legs out easily, to stand.

"I have given you a life," he said. "Remember that. I have given you a life, and I will choose what you do with it."

CHAPTER 97

ON THE DARK and rain-soaked lawn, a supermarket shopping cart full of aluminum cans and glass bottles stood alongside the house, near the back porch.

Carson, followed by Michael, glanced at the cart, puzzled, as she hurried past it to the porch steps.

Vicky Chou, in a robe and slippers, waited in the kitchen. She held a meat fork as if she intended to use it as a weapon.

"The doors were locked. I know they were," she said.

"It's all right, Vic. Like I told you on the phone, I know him. He's all right."

"Big, tattooed, *really* big," Vicky told Michael. "I don't know how he got in the house."

"He probably lifted the roof off," Michael said. "Came down through the attic."

Deucalion stood in Arnie's room, watching the boy work on the castle. He looked up as Carson and Michael came through the door.

Arnie spoke to himself, "Fortify. Fortify. Fortify and defend."

"Your brother," Deucalion said, "sees deeply into the true nature of reality."

Mystified by this statement, Carson said, "He's autistic."

"Autistic . . . because he sees too much, too much yet not enough to understand what he sees. He mistakes complexity for chaos. Chaos scares him. He struggles to bring order to his world."

Michael said, "Yeah. After everything I've seen tonight, I'm struggling, too."

To Deucalion, Carson said, "Two hundred years . . . you and this Victor Frankenstein . . . So why now? Why here?"

"On the night I came alive . . . perhaps I was given the task of destroying Victor when the moment arrived."

"Given by whom?"

"By whoever created the natural order that Victor challenges with such anger and such ego."

Deucalion took a penny from the stack on the table, which he had given earlier to Arnie. He flipped it, snatched it from midair, clutched it in his fist, opened his hand. The penny was gone.

"I have free will," Deucalion said. "I could walk away from my destiny. But I won't."

He flipped the penny again.

Carson watched him, transfixed.

Again he snatched it, opened his hand. No penny.

Michael said, "Harker and these . . . these other things Victor has made—they're demonic. But what about you? Do you have . . ."

When Michael hesitated, Carson finished his question: "Manmade and yet . . . do you have a soul? That lightning . . . did it bring you one?"

Deucalion closed his hand, opened it an instant later, and the two missing pennies were on his palm. "All I know is . . . I suffer."

Arnie had stopped working on the castle. He rose from his chair, mesmerized by the two pennies on Deucalion's palm.

"I suffer guilt, remorse, contrition. I see mysteries everywhere in the weave of life . . . and I believe."

He put the pennies in Arnie's open hand.

"Victor was a man," Deucalion continued, "but made a monster of himself. I was a monster . . . but feel so human now."

Arnie closed his fist around the coins and at once opened it.

Carson's breath caught. The pennies were gone from Arnie's hand.

"Two hundred years," Deucalion said, "I've lived as an outsider in your world. I've learned to treasure flawed humanity for its optimism in spite of its flaws, for its hope in the face of ceaseless struggle."

Arnie closed his empty hand.

"Victor would murder all mankind," Deucalion said, "and populate the world with his machines of blood and bone."

Arnie stared at his clenched fist—and smiled.

"If you do not help me resist," Deucalion said, "he is arrogant enough to succeed."

Again Arnie opened his hand. The pennies had reappeared.

"Those who fight him," Deucalion said, "will find themselves in the struggle of their lives. . . ."

From Arnie's hand, Deucalion retrieved one of the two pennies.

"Leave it to blind fate?" he asked Michael. His gaze moved to Carson. "Heads, you fight beside me . . . tails, I fight alone."

He flipped the penny, caught it, held out his fist.

Before he could reveal the penny, Carson put her hand on his, to keep his fist closed. She looked at Michael.

He sighed. "Well, I never did want to be a safety engineer," he acknowledged, and placed his hand atop hers.

To Deucalion, Carson said, "Screw fate. We fight."

DARK, DRY, QUIET, the crawl space under the house provides Randal Six with an ideal environment. The spiders do not bother him.

The journey from Mercy has been a triumph, but it has frayed his nerves and rubbed his courage raw. The storm had almost undone him. The rain, the sky afire with lightning and shadows leaping on the earth, the crashes of thunder, the trees shuddering in the wind, the gutters overflowing with dirty water awhirl with litter . . . Too much data. Too much input. Several times he almost shut down, almost fell to the ground and curled into a ball like a pill bug.

He needs time now to recover, to regain his confidence.

He closes his eyes in the dark, breathes slowly and deeply. The sweet smell of star jasmine threads to him through the crisscrossed lattice that screens the crawl space.

From directly overhead come three muffled voices in earnest conversation.

In the room above him is happiness. He can feel it, radiant. He has arrived at the source. The secret is within his grasp. This child of Mercy, in the spidery dark, smiles.

DEAN KOONTZ'S
FRANKENSTEIN
CITY OF NIGHT

*In a sort of ghastly simplicity, we remove
the organ and demand the function. We make
men without chests and expect of them virtue
and enterprise. We laugh at honour and are
shocked to find traitors in our midst. We
castrate and bid the geldings be fruitful.*

—C. S. Lewis, *The Abolition of Man*

AUTHOR'S NOTE

The first two volumes of this series were originally published with the bylines of co-writers. Each gentleman did his job well, but I discovered another character flaw in myself (it's a long list): I am not able to collaborate. I have sat alone at the keyboard for so many years that alone is the only way I know how to do this. Given a good first draft from a co-author, I nevertheless strike out in my own direction. I should have known. As a kid in school, I never got a positive mark in the plays-well-with-others column.

CHAPTER 1

HAVING COME TO LIFE in a thunderstorm, touched by some strange lightning that animated rather than incinerated, Deucalion had been born on a night of violence.

A Bedlam symphony of his anguished cries, his maker's shrieks of triumph, the burr and buzz and crackle of arcane machinery echoed off the cold stone walls of the laboratory in the old windmill.

When he woke to the world, Deucalion had been shackled to a table. This was the first indication that he had been created as a slave.

Unlike God, Victor Frankenstein saw no value in giving his creations free will. Like all utopians, he preferred obedience to independent thought.

That night, over two hundred years in the past, had set a theme of madness and violence that characterized Deucalion's life for years thereafter. Despair had fostered rage. In his rages, he had killed, and savagely.

These many decades later, he had learned self-control. His pain and loneliness had taught him pity, whereafter he learned compassion. He had found his way to hope.

Yet still, on certain nights, without immediate cause, anger overcomes him. For no rational reason, the anger swells into a tidal rage that threatens to sweep him beyond prudence, beyond discretion.

This night in New Orleans, Deucalion walked an alleyway on the perimeter of the French Quarter, in a mood to murder. Shades of gray, of blue, of black were enlivened only by the crimson of his thoughts.

The air was warm, humid, and alive with muffled jazz that the walls of the famous clubs could not entirely contain.

In public, he stayed in shadows and used back streets, because his formidable size made him an object of interest. As did his face.

From the darkness beside a Dumpster, a wrinkled rum-soaked raisin of a man stepped forth. "Peace in Jesus, brother."

Although that greeting didn't suggest a mugger on the prowl, Deucalion turned toward the voice with the hope that the stranger would have a knife, a gun. Even in his rage, he needed justification for violence.

The panhandler brandished nothing more dangerous than a dirty upturned palm and searing halitosis. "One dollar's all I need."

"You can't get anything for a dollar," Deucalion said.

"Bless you if you're generous, but a dollar's all I ask."

Deucalion resisted the urge to seize the extended hand and snap it off at the wrist as though it were a dry stick.

Instead, he turned away, and did not look back even when the panhandler cursed him.

As he was passing the kitchen entrance to a restaurant, that door opened. Two Hispanic men in white pants and T-shirts stepped outside, one offering an open pack of cigarettes to the other.

Deucalion was revealed by the security lamp above the door and by another directly across the alley from the first.

Both men froze at the sight of him. One half of his face appeared normal, even handsome, but an intricate tattoo decorated the other half.

The pattern had been designed and applied by a Tibetan monk skillful with needles. Yet it gave Deucalion a fierce and almost demonic aspect.

This tattoo was in effect a mask meant to distract the eye from consideration of the broken structures under it, damage done by his creator in the distant past.

Caught in the crosslight, Deucalion was sufficiently revealed for the two men to detect, if not understand, the radical geometry under the tattoo. They regarded him less with fear than with solemn respect, as they might stand witness to a spiritual visitation.

He traded light for shadow, that alley for another, his rage escalating to fury.

His huge hands shook, spasmed as if with the need to throttle. He fisted them, jammed them in his coat pockets.

Even on this summer night, in the cloying bayou air, he wore a long black coat. Neither heat nor bitter cold affected him. Nor pain, nor fear.

When he quickened his pace, the commodious coat billowed as if it were a cloak. With a hood, he might have passed for Death himself.

Perhaps murderous compulsion was woven through his very fiber. His flesh was the flesh of numerous criminals, their bodies having been stolen from a prison graveyard immediately following interment.

Of his two hearts, one came from a mad arsonist who burned churches. The other had belonged to a child molester.

Even in a God-made man, the heart can be deceitful and wicked. The heart sometimes rebels against everything that the mind knows and believes.

If the hands of a priest can do sinful work, then what can be expected of the hands of a convicted strangler? Deucalion's hands had come from just such a criminal.

His gray eyes had been plucked from the body of an executed ax murderer. Occasionally, a soft luminous pulse passed through them, as though the unprecedented storm that birthed him had left behind its lightning.

His brain had once filled the skull of an unknown miscreant. Death had erased all memory of that former life, but perhaps the cerebral circuits remained miswired.

Now his growing fury took him to seedier streets across the river, in Algiers. These darker byways were rank and busy with illegal enterprise.

One shabby block accommodated a whorehouse thinly disguised as a massage and acupuncture clinic; a tattoo parlor; a pornographic video shop; and a raucous Cajun bar. Zydeco music boomed.

In cars parked along the alleyway behind these businesses, pimps socialized while they waited to collect from the girls whom they supplied to the brothel.

Two slicks in Hawaiian shirts and white silk trousers, gliding on roller skates, peddled cocaine cut with powdered Viagra to the whorehouse clientele. They were having a special on Ecstasy and meth.

Four Harleys stood in a hog line behind the porno shop. Hardcase bikers seemed to be providing security for the whorehouse or for the bar. Or for the drug dealers. Perhaps for all of them.

Deucalion passed among them, noticed by some, not by others. For him, a black coat and blacker shadows could be almost as concealing as a cloak of invisibility.

The mysterious lightning that brought him to life had also conveyed to him an understanding of the quantum structure of the universe, and perhaps something more. Having spent two centuries exploring and gradually applying that knowledge, he could when he wished move through the world with an ease, a grace, a stealth that others found bewildering.

An argument between a biker and a slender young woman at the back door of the whorehouse drew Deucalion as blood in the water draws a shark.

Although dressed to arouse, the girl looked fresh-faced and vulnerable. She might have been sixteen.

"Lemme go, Wayne," she pleaded. "I want out."

Wayne, the biker, held her by both arms, jamming her against the green door. "Once you're in, there *is* no out."

"I'm not but fifteen."

"Don't worry. You'll age fast."

Through tears, she said, "I never knew it was gonna be like this."

"What did you think it *would* be like, you dumb bitch? Richard Gere and *Pretty Woman?*"

"He's ugly and he stinks."

"Joyce, honey, they're all ugly and they all stink. After number fifty, you won't notice anymore."

The girl saw Deucalion first, and her widening eyes caused Wayne to turn.

"Release her," Deucalion advised.

The biker—massive, with a cruel face—was not impressed. "You walk real fast away from here, Lone Ranger, and you might leave with your cojones."

Deucalion seized his adversary's right arm and bent it behind his back so suddenly, with such violence, that the shoulder broke with a loud crack. He pitched the big man away from him.

Briefly airborne, Wayne landed face-first, his scream stifled by a mouthful of blacktop.

A hard stomp to the nape of the biker's neck would have snapped his spine. Remembering torch-bearing mobs with pitchforks in another century, Deucalion restrained himself.

He turned toward the *whoosh* of a swung chain.

Another motorcycle aficionado, a leering grotesque with a studded eyebrow, studded nose, studded tongue, and bristling red beard, recklessly joined the fray.

Instead of dodging the chain-link whip, Deucalion stepped toward his assailant. The chain lashed around his left arm. He seized it and pulled Redbeard off balance.

The biker had a ponytail. It served as a handle.

Deucalion lifted him, punched him, threw him.

In possession of the chain, he rounded on a third thug, whipped him across the knees.

The struck man cried out and fell. Deucalion helped him off the ground by throat, by crotch, and slammed him into the fourth of the four enforcers.

He rapped their heads against a wall to the bar-band beat, creating much misery and perhaps some remorse.

Already the customers wandering from porno shop to brothel to bar had fled the alleyway. The dealers on wheels had skated with their wares.

In rapid succession, the pimpmobiles fired up. No one drove toward Deucalion. They reversed out of the alleyway.

A chopped-and-stretched Cadillac crashed into a yellow Mercedes. Neither driver stopped to provide the other with the name of his insurance agent.

In a moment, Deucalion and the girl, Joyce, were alone with the disabled bikers, though surely watched from doorways and windows.

In the bar, the zydeco band jammed without faltering. The thick, damp air seemed to shimmer with the music.

Deucalion walked the girl to the corner, where the alleyway met the street. He said nothing, but Joyce needed no encouragement to stay at his side.

Although she went with him, she was clearly afraid. She had good reason to be.

The action in the alley had not diminished his fury. When he was fully self-possessed, his mind was a centuries-old mansion furnished with rich experience, elegant thought, and philosophical reflection. Now, however, it was a many-chambered charnel house dark with blood and cold with the urge to murder.

As they passed under a streetlamp, treading on the fluttering shadows cast by moths above, the girl glanced at him. He was aware that she shuddered.

She seemed as bewildered as she was frightened, as if she had awakened from a bad dream and could not yet distinguish between what might be real and what might be remnants of her nightmare.

In the gloom between streetlamps, when Deucalion put one hand on her shoulder, when they traded shadows for shadows and fading zydeco for louder jazz, her bewilderment increased, and her fear. "What . . . what just happened? This is the Quarter."

"At this hour," he warned, as he walked her across Jackson Square, past the statue of the general, "the Quarter is no safer for you than that alleyway. You have somewhere to go?"

Hugging herself as if the bayou air had taken an arctic chill, she said, "Home."

"Here in the city?"

"No. Up to Baton Rouge." She was close to tears. "Home don't seem boring anymore."

Envy seasoned Deucalion's ferocious anger, for he had never had a home. He'd had places where he stayed, but none had truly been a home.

A wild criminal desire to smash the girl raged at the bars of the mental cell in which he strove to keep imprisoned his bestial impulses, to smash her because she could go home in a way that he never could.

He said, "You've got a phone?"

She nodded, and unclipped a cell phone from her braided belt.

"You tell your mother and father you'll be waiting in the cathedral over there," he said.

He walked her to the church, paused in the street, encouraged her forward, made certain to be gone before she turned to look at him.

CHAPTER 2

IN HIS MANSION in the Garden District, Victor Helios, formerly Frankenstein, began this fine summer morning by making love to his new wife, Erika.

His first wife, Elizabeth, had been murdered two hundred years ago in the Austrian mountains, on their wedding day. He rarely thought of her anymore.

He had always been oriented toward the future. The past bored him. Besides, much of it didn't bear contemplation.

Counting Elizabeth, Victor had enjoyed—or in some cases merely tolerated—six wives. Numbers two through six had been named Erika.

The Erikas had been identical in appearance because they had all been engineered in his New Orleans lab and grown in his cloning vats. This saved the expense of a new wardrobe each time one of them had to be terminated.

Although extremely wealthy, Victor loathed wasting money. His mother, otherwise a useless woman, had impressed upon him the need for thrift.

Upon his mother's death, he had not stood the expense of either a service or a pine box. No doubt she would have approved of the simple hole in the ground, excavated to a depth of four rather than six feet to reduce the gravedigger's fee.

Although the Erikas looked identical to one another, numbers one through four had different flaws. He kept refining and improving them.

Just the previous evening, he had killed Erika Four. He had sent her remains to an upstate landfill operated by one of his companies, where the first three Erikas and other disappointments were interred under a sea of garbage.

Her passion for books had resulted in too much introspection and had encouraged in her an independent spirit that Victor refused to tolerate. Besides, she slurped her soup.

Not long ago, he had summoned his new Erika from her tank, in which universities of digitized education were electronically downloaded into her absorbent brain.

Ever the optimist, Victor believed that Erika Five would prove to be a perfect creation, worthy of serving him for a long time. Beautiful, refined, erudite, and obedient.

She certainly was more lubricious than the previous Erikas. The more he hurt her, the more eagerly she responded to him.

Because she was one of the New Race, she could turn off pain at will, but he did not allow her to do so in the bedroom. He lived for power. Sex was, for him, satisfying only to the extent that he could hurt and oppress his partner.

She took his blows with magnificent erotic submission. Her many bruises and abrasions were, to Victor, proof of his virility. He was a stallion.

As with all his creatures, she had the physiology of a demigod.

Her wounds would heal and her physical perfection be restored in but an hour or two.

Spent, he left her on the bed, sobbing. She wept not merely because of the pain but also with shame.

His wife was the only member of the New Race designed with the capacity for shame. Her humiliation completed him.

He showered with much hot water and a verbena-scented soap made in Paris. Being thrifty about disposing of dead mothers and wives, he could afford some luxuries.

CHAPTER 3

HAVING JUST CLOSED the case on a serial killer who turned out to be a police detective in her own division, with the usual chasing and jumping and shooting, Carson O'Connor hadn't gotten to bed until seven in the morning.

Four dead-to-the-world hours in the sheets and a quick shower: That might be the maximum down- time she could expect for a while. Fortunately, she had been too whacked to dream.

As a detective, she was accustomed to overtime whenever an investigation approached culmination, but this current assignment wasn't a typical homicide case. This was maybe the end of the world.

She had never been through the end of the world before. She didn't know what to expect.

Michael Maddison, her partner, was waiting on the sidewalk when, at noon, she pulled the plainwrap sedan to the curb in front of his apartment house.

He lived in a bland apartment in a plain slab of a building, on a nondescript block just off Veterans Boulevard. He said the place was "very Zen," and claimed to need a minimalist retreat after a day in the perpetual carnival of New Orleans.

He dressed for the Apocalypse the same as he dressed every day. Hawaiian shirt, khakis, sport coat.

Only in footwear had he made a concession to doomsday. Instead of the usual black Rockport walking shoes, he wore white. They were so white they seemed radiant.

His sleepy-eyed look made him more delicious than usual. Carson tried not to notice.

They were partners, not lovers. If they tried to be both, they would wind up dead sooner than later. In police work, kick-ass and grab-ass don't mix.

After getting in the car and pulling the door shut, Michael said, "Seen any monsters lately?"

"In the bathroom mirror this morning," she said, accelerating away from the curb.

"You look terrific. Really. You don't look half as bad as I feel."

"You know how long it's been since I had my hair done?"

"*You* take time to go to a hairdresser? I thought you just set it on fire and burned it off now and then."

"Nice shoes."

"The box said they're made in China, or maybe it was Thailand. Everything's made somewhere else these days."

"Not everything. Where do you think Harker was made?"

Detective Jonathan Harker, who had turned out to be the serial killer that the media dubbed "the Surgeon," had also turned out not to be human. Neither a 12-gauge shotgun nor a four-story fall had fazed him.

Michael said, "I don't quite see Helios building his New Race in the parlor of his mansion in the Garden District. Maybe Biovision is a front for it."

Biovision, a cutting-edge biotechnology firm founded by Helios when he first came to New Orleans more than twenty years previously, was the holder of many patents that made him richer year by year.

"All those employees," Carson said, "all those outsourced services coming in every day—you couldn't conduct a secret people-making lab in the middle of all that."

"Yeah. For one thing, being a walleyed hunchback in a cowled cloak, Igor would really stand out when he went for coffee in the vending-machine room. Don't drive so fast."

Accelerating, Carson said, "So he has another facility somewhere in the city, probably owned by a shell corporation headquartered in the Cayman Islands or someplace."

"I hate that kind of police work."

He meant the kind that required researching thousands of New Orleans businesses, making a list of those with foreign or otherwise suspicious ownership.

Although Carson disliked desk-jockey sessions as much as Michael did, she had the patience for them. She suspected, however, that she didn't have the time.

"Where are we going?" Michael asked as the city blurred past. "If we're going to Division to sit in front of computers all day, let me out right here."

"Yeah? And what'll you do?"

"I don't know. Find somebody to shoot."

"Pretty soon you'll have lots of people to shoot. The people Victor's made. The New Race."

"It's kind of depressing being the Old Race. Like being last year's toaster oven, before they added the microchip that makes it sing Randy Newman tunes."

"Who would want a toaster oven that sings Randy Newman?"

"Who wouldn't?"

Carson might have blown through the red traffic light if a refrigerated eighteen-wheeler hadn't been crossing the intersection. Judging by the pictorial advertisement painted on the side of the truck, it was loaded with meat patties destined for McDonald's. She didn't want to be hamburgered to death.

They were downtown. The streets were busy.

Studying the swarms of pedestrians, Michael wondered, "How many people in this city aren't really people? How many are Victor's . . . creations?"

"A thousand," Carson said, "ten thousand, fifty thousand—or maybe just a hundred."

"More than a hundred."

"Yeah."

"Eventually Helios is going to realize we're on to him."

"He knows already," she guessed.

"You know what that makes us?"

"Loose ends," she said.

"Totally loose. And he seems to be a guy who likes everything tied up neat."

She said, "I figure we've got twenty-four hours to live."

CHAPTER 4

CARVED OF MARBLE, weathered by decades of wind and rain, the Virgin Mary stood in a niche, overlooking the front steps of the Hands of Mercy.

The hospital had long been closed. The windows were bricked shut. On the gate in the wrought-iron fence, a sign identified the building as a private warehouse, closed to the public.

Victor drove past the hospital and into the parking garage of a five-story building that housed the accounting and personnel-management departments of Biovision, the company he had founded. He slotted the Mercedes into a space reserved for him.

Only he possessed a key to a nearby painted-steel door. Beyond lay an empty room, about twelve feet square, with concrete floor and walls.

Opposite the outer door, another door was controlled by a wall-mounted keypad. Victor entered a code, disengaging the electronic lock.

Past the threshold, a hundred-forty-foot corridor led under the hospital grounds, connecting the adjacent buildings. It was six feet wide, eight feet high, with block-and-timber walls and a concrete floor.

The passageway had been excavated and constructed by members of the New Race, without publicly filed plans or building-department permits, or union wages. Victor could come and go from the Hands of Mercy in complete secrecy.

At the end of the corridor, he entered his code in another keypad, opened a door into a file room in the lowest realms of the hospital. Rows of metal cabinets contained hard-copy backups to the computerized records of his many projects.

Usually, Victor enjoyed hidden doors, secret passageways, and the hugger-mugger that was necessarily part of any scheme to destroy civilization and rule the world. He had never entirely lost touch with his inner child.

On this occasion, however, he was annoyed that he could get to his laboratory only by this roundabout route. He had a busy day ahead of him, and at least one crisis needed his urgent attention.

From the file room, he entered the basement of the hospital, where all was quiet and, in spite of the corridor lights, shadowy. Here he had once conducted his most revolutionary experiments.

He had been fascinated by the possibility that cancer cells, which reproduce with reckless speed, might be harnessed to facilitate the rapid development of clones in an artificial womb. He had hoped to force-grow an embryo to adulthood in a matter of weeks instead of years.

As will now and then happen when one is working at the extreme limits of known science, things went awry. What he ended up with was not a New Man, but a highly aggressive, rapidly mutating, ambulatory tumor that was, to boot, pretty damn smart.

Because he had given the creature life, he might have expected at least some small measure of gratitude from it. He had received none.

Forty of Victor's people had perished here, trying to contain that powerful malignancy. And his people were not easy to kill. Just when all had seemed lost, the atrocity had been subdued and then destroyed.

The stink of it had been terrible. All these years later, Victor thought he could still smell the thing.

A twenty-foot section of the corridor wall had been broken down in the melee. Beyond that ragged hole lay the incubation room, dark and full of wreckage.

Past the elevator, half the width of the corridor contained sorted and arranged piles of rubble: broken concrete, bent rebar, steel framing knotted as if it were rope.

Victor had organized but not removed this rubble and ruin, leaving it as an enduring reminder to himself that even a genius of his caliber could sometimes be too smart for his own good. He had almost died here, that night.

Now he took the elevator up to the ground floor, to which he had moved his main laboratory after the ungrateful tumor had been destroyed.

The hallways were quiet. Eighty of the New Race worked in this facility, but they were all busy at their assigned tasks. They didn't waste time gossiping around the water cooler.

His immense lab was furnished with fantastic machines that would have mystified not just the average man but also any member of the faculty at any department of science at Harvard or MIT. The style was operatic Art Deco, the ambience Hitlerian.

Victor admired Hitler. The Führer knew talent when he saw it.

In the 1930s and '40s, Victor had worked with Mengele and others in Hitler's privileged scientific class. He had made considerable progress in his work before the regrettable Allied victory.

Personally, Hitler had been charming, an amusing raconteur. His hygiene had been exemplary; he always looked scrubbed and smelled soapy.

A vegetarian and an ardent animal lover, Hitler had a tender side. He would not tolerate mousetraps. He insisted that rodents be captured humanely and turned loose in the wild.

The problem with the Führer had been that his roots were in art and politics. The future did not belong either to artists or to politicians.

The new world would not be built by nazism-communism-socialism. Not by capitalism, either.

Civilization would not be remade or sustained by Christianity or by Islam. Neither by Scientologists nor by the bright-eyed adherents of the deliciously solipsistic and paranoid new religion encouraged by *The Da Vinci Code*.

Tomorrow belonged to scientism. The priests of scientism were not merely robed clerics performing rituals; they were gods, with the power of gods. Victor himself was their Messiah.

As he crossed the vast lab, the ominous-looking machines issued oscillating hums, low pulsing throbs. They ticked and hissed.

He felt *at home* here.

Sensors detected his approach to his desk, and the screen of his computer brightened. On the monitor appeared the face of Annunciata, his secretary at the Hands of Mercy.

"Good morning, Mr. Helios."

Annunciata was quite beautiful but not real. She was a three-dimensional digital personality with an artificial but wonderfully smoky voice that Victor had designed to humanize his otherwise somber work environment.

"Good morning, Annunciata."

"The corpse of Detective Jonathan Harker has been delivered by your people in the medical examiner's office. It awaits you in the dissection room."

An insulated carafe of hot coffee and a plate of pecan-and-chocolate-chip cookies were on Victor's desk. He picked up a cookie. "Continue."

"Randal Six has disappeared."

Victor frowned. "Explain."

"The midnight census found his room deserted."

Randal Six was one of many experiments currently living at the Hands of Mercy. Like his five predecessors, he had been created as an autistic with an obsessive-compulsive tendency.

Victor's intention in designing this afflicted creature had been to determine if such a developmental disability could have a useful purpose. Controlling an autistic person by the use of a carefully engineered obsessive-compulsive disorder, one might be able to focus him on a narrow series of functions usually assigned to machines in contemporary factories. Such a worker might perform a repetitive task hour after hour, weeks on end, without error, without boredom.

Surgically fitted with a feeding tube, catheterized to eliminate the need for bathroom breaks, he might prove to be an economical alternative to some factory robots currently on the assembly lines. His food could be nutritional pablum costing a dollar a day. He would receive no pay, no vacation, no medical benefits. He would not be affected by power surges.

When he wore out, he would merely be terminated. A new worker would be plugged into the line.

Victor remained convinced that eventually such machines of meat would prove to be far superior to much current factory equipment. Assembly-line robots are complex and expensive to produce. Flesh is cheap.

Randal Six had been sufficiently agoraphobic that he had not been able to leave his quarters voluntarily. He was terrified to cross the threshold.

When Victor needed Randal for an experiment, attendants brought him to the lab on a gurney.

"He can't possibly have left on his own," Victor said. "Besides, he can't have gotten out of the building without tripping an alarm. He's here somewhere. Direct security personnel to review yesterday's video from his room and from all the primary hallways."

"Yes, Mr. Helios," said Annunciata.

Considering the high degree of verbal interaction she maintained with Victor, Annunciata might have appeared, to an outsider, to be a manifestation of an artificial machine intelligence. Although she did interface through a computer, her cognitive function in fact occurred in an organic New Race brain that was maintained in a hermetically sealed tank of nutrient solution in the networking room, where she was wired into the building's data-processing system.

Victor envisioned a day when the world would be inhabited only by the New Race living in thousands of dormitories, each of which would be monitored and served by a disembodied brain like Annunciata.

"Meanwhile," Victor said, "I'll be studying Harker's cadaver. Locate Ripley and tell him that I will need his assistance in the dissection room."

"Yes, Mr. Helios. Helios."

About to take another bite of the cookie, he hesitated. "Why did you do that, Annunciata?"

"Do what, sir?"

"You repeated my name unnecessarily."

On the monitor, her smooth brow furrowed with puzzlement. "Did I, sir?"

"Yes, you did."

"I was not aware of doing so, Mr. Helios. Helios."

"You just did it again."

"Sir, are you sure?"

"That is an impertinent question, Annunciata."

She looked appropriately chastised. "I'm sorry, sir."

"Analyze your systems," Victor directed. "Perhaps there is an imbalance in your nutrient supply."

CHAPTER 5

JACK ROGERS, the medical examiner, maintained an office in which an avalanche of books, files, and macabre memorabilia might at any moment bury an unwary visitor.

This reception lounge, however, was more in line with the public perception of a morgue. Minimalist decor. Sterile surfaces. The air-conditioning was set to CHILL.

Jack's secretary, Winona Harmony, ruled this outer domain with cool efficiency. When Carson and Michael entered, the top of Winona's desk was bare—no photographs, no mementos—except for a folder of Jack's notes, from which she was typing official autopsy reports.

A plump, warm-hearted black woman of about fifty-five, Winona seemed out of place in this barren space.

Carson suspected that stuffed into Winona's desk drawers were family photos, Beanie Babies, beribboned sachets, small pillows with feel-good mottoes in elaborate needlepoint, and other items that she enjoyed but that she found inappropriate for display in a morgue reception lounge.

"Looka here," said Winona when they came through the door. "If it isn't the pride of Homicide."

"I'm here, too," Michael said.

"Oh, you are *smooth*," Winona told him.

"Just realistic. She's the detective. I'm the comic relief."

Winona said, "Carson, girl, how do you stand him being so smooth all day?"

"Now and then I pistol-whip him."

"Probably does no good," said Winona.

"At least," Carson said, "it helps keep me in shape."

"We're here about a corpse," Michael said.

"We have a bunch," Winona said. "Some have names, some don't."

"Jonathan Harker."

"One of your own," Winona noted.

"Yes and no," Michael said. "He had a badge like us and two ears, but after that we don't have much in common with him."

"Who would have thought a psycho killer like the Surgeon would turn out to be a cop," Winona marveled. "What's the world coming to?"

"When will Jack do a prelim autopsy?" Carson asked.

"It's done." Winona tapped the file of handwritten notes beside her computer. "I'm typing it now."

This stunned Carson. Like her and Michael, Jack Rogers knew that something extraordinary was happening in New Orleans and that some of its citizens were something more than human.

He had done an autopsy on a guy who had two hearts, a skull as dense as armor, two livers, and several other "improvements."

Carson and Michael had asked him to embargo his report until they could grasp the situation they faced—and within hours, much to Jack's dismay, the cadaver and all records of the autopsy had vanished.

Now he was supposed to be taking great security measures with the body of Jonathan Harker, who was another of Victor's New Race. Carson could not comprehend why he would reveal Harker's inhuman nature to Winona.

Less comprehensible still was Winona's current calm, her easy smile. If she was typing a report of an autopsy on a monster, she seemed oblivious of it.

His bewilderment matching Carson's, Michael asked, "Have you just started?"

"No," Winona said, "I'm almost finished."

"And?"

"And what?"

Carson and Michael exchanged a glance. She said, "We need to see Jack."

"He's in Autopsy Room Number Two," Winona said. "They're getting ready to open up a retiree whose wife seems to have fed him some bad crawfish gumbo."

Carson said, "She must be devastated."

Winona shook her head. "She's under arrest. At the hospital, when they told her that he died, she couldn't stop laughing."

CHAPTER 6

DEUCALION RARELY NEEDED sleep. Although he had spent periods of his long life in monasteries and in meditation, though he knew the value of stillness, his most natural state seemed to be the restless circling-seeking of a shark.

He had been in all but constant motion since rescuing the girl from the alley in Algiers. His rage had passed, but his restlessness had not.

Into the vacuum left by the dissipation of anger came a new wariness. This was not to any degree fearful in nature, more of a disquietude arising from a sense of having overlooked something of great significance.

Intuition whispered urgently, but for the moment its voice was a wordless susurration, which raised his hackles but failed to enlighten him.

With dawn, he had returned to the Luxe Theater. The movie house recently had been willed to him by an old friend from his years in a carnival freakshow.

This inheritance—and the discovery that Victor, his maker, was not two hundred years dead, but alive—had brought him from Tibet to Louisiana.

He had often felt that destiny was working in his life. These events in New Orleans seemed to be hard proof.

An Art Deco palace erected in the 1920s, now a revival house, the Luxe was in decline. It opened its doors only three nights a week.

His apartment in the theater was humble. Anything larger than a monk's cell, however, seemed extravagant to him, in spite of his size.

As he roamed the deserted corridors of the old building, the auditorium, the mezzanine, the balcony, the lobby, his thoughts did not just race but ricocheted like pinballs.

In his restlessness, he struggled to imagine a way to reach Victor Helios, alias Frankenstein. And destroy him.

Like the members of the New Race that Victor had brought forth in this city, Deucalion had been created with a built-in proscription against deicide. He could not kill his maker.

Two centuries ago, he had raised a hand against Victor—and had nearly perished when he had found himself unable to deliver the blow. Half of his face, the half disguised by a tattoo, had been broken by his master.

Deucalion's other wounds always healed in minutes, perhaps not because Victor had in those days been capable of designing such resilience into him, perhaps instead because this immortality had come to him on the lightning, along with other gifts. The one wound that had not healed with perfect restoration of flesh and bone had been the one that his maker had inflicted.

Victor thought his first-made was long dead, as Deucalion had assumed that his maker had died in the eighteenth century. If he revealed himself to Victor, Deucalion would be at once struck down again—and this time, he might not survive.

Because Victor's methods of creation had improved drastically from his early days—no more grave-robbing and stitchery—his New Race most likely was gray-cell wired also to die in defense of its maker.

Eventually, if Carson and Michael could not expose Victor, they might be able to stop him only by killing him. And to get at him, they might have to go through an army of New Men and New Women that would be almost as hard to kill as robots.

Deucalion felt considerable regret, and even some remorse, for revealing the truth of Helios to the two detectives. He had put them in enormous jeopardy.

His regret was mitigated to some extent by the fact that they had unknowingly been in mortal jeopardy, anyway, as was every human resident of New Orleans, however many still existed.

Troubled by these thoughts—and haunted by the inescapable feeling that some important truth eluded him, a truth with which he must urgently come to grips—Deucalion eventually arrived in the projection room.

Jelly Biggs, once billed in the carnival as the fattest man in the world, was smaller now, merely fat. He sorted through the stacks of paperbacks stored here, searching for a good read.

Behind the projection room lay Jelly's two-room apartment. He had come with the theater, a break-even enterprise that he more or less managed.

"I want a mystery story where everybody smokes like chimneys," Jelly said, "drinks hard liquor, and never heard of vegetarianism."

Deucalion said, "There's a point in every mystery story—isn't there?—where the detective feels that a revelation is right in front of him, but he can't quite see it."

Rejecting book after book, Jelly said, "I don't want an Indian detective or a paraplegic detective, or a detective with obsessive-compulsive disorder, or a detective who's a master chef—"

Deucalion examined a different stack of books from those that Jelly searched, as if a cover illustration or a flamboyant title might sharpen his fuzzy instinct into hard-edged meaning.

"I don't have anything against Indians, paraplegics, obsessive-compulsives, or chefs," Jelly said, "but I want a guy who doesn't know from Freud, hasn't taken sensitivity training, and punches you in the face if you look at him wrong. Is that too much to ask?"

The fat man's question was rhetorical. He didn't even wait for an answer.

"Give me a hero who doesn't think too much," Jelly continued, "who cares intensely about a lot of things, but who knows he's a dead man walking and doesn't care a *damn* about that. Death is knocking, and our guy yanks open the door and says, 'What kept you?'"

Perhaps inspired by something Jelly said or by the paperback covers ablaze with colorful mayhem, Deucalion suddenly understood what his instinct had been trying to tell him. The end was here.

Less than half a day previously, in Carson O'Connor's house, Deucalion and the two detectives had agreed to join forces to resist and ultimately to destroy Victor Helios. They had recognized that this mission would require patience, determination, cunning, courage—and that it might take a long time, as well.

Now, less by deductive reasoning than by intuition, Deucalion knew that they had no time at all.

Detective Harker, a member of Victor's New Race, had spiraled into homicidal madness. There were reasons to believe that others of his kind were in despair, too, and psychologically fragile.

Furthermore, something fundamental had gone wrong with Harker's biology. Shotguns had not felled him. Something that had been born within him, some strange dwarfish creature that had burst from him, had destroyed his body in its birth throes.

These facts alone were not sufficient evidence to justify the conclusion that Victor's empire of the soulless might be on the verge of violent collapse. But Deucalion knew it was. He *knew*.

"And," Jelly Biggs said, still sorting through the paperbacks, "give me a villain I'm not supposed to feel sorry for."

Deucalion had no psychic power. Sometimes, however, knowledge arose in him, profound insights and understandings that he recognized as truths, and he did not doubt them or question their source. He *knew*.

"I don't *care* that he kills and eats people because he had a bad childhood," Jelly railed. "If he kills good people, I want some good people to get together and pound the crap out of him. I don't want them to see that he gets *therapy*."

Deucalion turned away from the books. He feared nothing that might happen to him. For the fate of others, however, for this city, he was overcome by dread.

Victor's assault on nature and humanity had built into a perfect storm. And now the deluge.

CHAPTER 7

THE GUTTERS OF THE stainless-steel dissection table were not yet wet, and the glossy white ceramic-tile floor in Autopsy Room Number 2 remained spotless.

Poisoned by gumbo, the old man lay in naked anticipation of the coroner's scalpel. He looked surprised.

Jack Rogers and his young assistant, Luke, were gowned, gloved, and ready to cut.

Michael said, "Is every elderly naked dead man a thrill, or after a while do they all seem the same?"

"In fact," said the medical examiner, "every one of them has more personality than the average homicide cop."

"Ouch. I thought you only cut stiffs."

"Actually," Luke said, "this one will be pretty interesting because analysis of the stomach contents is more important than usual."

Sometimes it seemed to Carson O'Connor that Luke enjoyed his work too much.

She said, "I thought you'd have Harker on the table."

"Been there, done that," said Luke. "We started early, and we're moving right along."

For a man who had been profoundly shaken by the autopsy that he had performed on one of the New Race little more than a day ago, Jack Rogers seemed remarkably calm about his second encounter with one of them.

Laying out the sharp tools of his trade, he said, "I'll messenger the prelim to you. The enzyme profiles and other chemical analyses will follow when I get them from the lab."

"Prelim? Profiles? You sound like this is SOP."

"Why shouldn't it be?" Jack asked, his attention focused on the gleaming blades, clamps, and forceps.

With his owlish eyes and ascetic features, Luke usually appeared bookish, slightly fey. Now he regarded Carson with hawkish intensity.

To Jack, she said, "I told you last night, he's one of them."

"Them," said Luke, nodding gravely.

"Something came out of Harker, some creature. Tore its way out of his torso. That's what killed him."

"Falling off the warehouse roof killed him," Jack Rogers said.

Impatiently, Carson said, "Jack, for God's sake, you saw Harker lying in that alleyway last night. His abdomen, his chest—they were like blown open."

"A consequence of the fall."

Michael said, "Whoa, Jack, everything inside Harker was just *gone*."

Finally the medical examiner looked at them. "A trick of light and shadow."

Bayou-born, Carson had never known a bitter winter. A Canadian wind in January could have been no colder than the sudden chill in her blood, her marrow.

"I want to see the body," she said.

"We released it to his family," Jack said.

"What family?" Michael demanded. "He was cloned in a cauldron or some damned thing. He didn't *have* family."

With a solemnity not characteristic of him, eyes narrowed, Luke said, "He had us."

The folds and flews of Jack's hound-dog face were as they had been a day ago, and the jowls and dewlaps, all familiar. But this was not Jack.

"He had us," Jack agreed.

As Michael reached cross-body, under his coat, to put his right hand on the grip of the pistol in his shoulder holster, Carson took a step backward, and another, toward the door.

The medical examiner and his assistant did not approach, merely watched in silence.

Carson expected to find the door locked. It opened.

Past the threshold, in the hall, no one blocked their way.

She retreated from Autopsy Room Number 2. Michael followed her.

CHAPTER 8

ERIKA HELIOS, less than one day from the creation tank, found the world to be a wondrous place.

Nasty, too. Thanks to her exceptional physiology, the lingering pain from Victor's punishing blows sluiced out of her in a long hot shower, though her shame did not so easily wash away.

Everything amazed her, and much of it delighted—like water. From the shower head it fell in glimmering streams, twinkling with reflections of the overhead lights. Liquid jewels.

She liked the way it purled across the golden-marble floor to the drain. Pellucid yet visible.

Erika relished the subtle aroma of water, too, the crispness. She breathed deeply of the scented soap, steamy clouds of soothing fragrance. And after the soap, the smell of her clean skin was most pleasing.

Educated by direct-to-brain data downloading, she had awakened with full knowledge of the world. But facts were not experience. All the billions of bits of data streamed into her brain had painted a ghost world in comparison to the depth and brilliance of the real thing. All she had learned in the tank was but a single note plucked from a guitar, at most a chord, while the true world was a symphony of astonishing complexity and beauty.

The only thing thus far that had struck her as ugly was Victor's body.

Born of man and woman, heir to the ills of mortal flesh, he'd taken extraordinary measures over the years to extend his life and to maintain his vigor. His body was puckered and welted by scars, crusted with gnarled excrescences.

Her revulsion was ungrateful and ungracious, and she was ashamed of it. Victor had given her life, and all that he asked in return was love, or something like it.

Although she had hidden her disgust, he must have sensed it, for he had been angry with her throughout the sex. He'd struck her often, called her unflattering names, and in general had been rough with her.

Even from direct-to-brain data downloading, Erika knew that what they had shared had not been ideal—or even ordinary—sex.

In spite of the fact that she failed him in their first session of love-making, Victor still harbored some tender feelings toward her. When it was over, he'd slapped her bottom affectionately—as opposed to the rage with which he had delivered previous slaps and punches—and had said, "That was good."

She knew that he was just being kind. It had not been good. She must learn to see the art in his ugly body, just as people evidently learned to see the art in the ugly paintings of Jackson Pollock.

Because Victor expected her to be prepared for the intellectual conversations at his periodic dinner parties with the city's elites, volumes of art criticism had been downloaded into her brain as she had finished forming in the tank.

A lot of it seemed to make no sense, which she attributed to her naivete. Her IQ was high; therefore, with more experience, she would no doubt come to understand how the ugly, the mean, and the poorly rendered could in fact be ravishingly beautiful. She simply needed to attain the proper perspective.

She would strive to see the beauty in Victor's tortured flesh. She would be a good wife, and they would be as happy as Romeo and Juliet.

Thousands of literary allusions had been a part of her downloaded instructions, but not the texts of the books, plays, and poems from which they came. She had never read *Romeo and Juliet*. She knew only that they were famous lovers in a play by Shakespeare.

She might have enjoyed reading the works to which she could allude with such facility, but Victor had forbidden her to do so. Evidently, Erika Four had become a voracious reader, a pastime that had somehow gotten her into such terrible trouble that Victor had been left with no choice but to terminate her.

Books were dangerous, a corrupting influence. A good wife must avoid books.

Showered, feeling pretty in a summery dress of yellow silk, Erika left the master suite to explore the mansion. She felt like the unnamed narrator and heroine of *Rebecca,* for the first time touring the lovely rooms of Manderley.

In the upstairs hall, she found William, the butler, on his knees in a corner, chewing off his fingers one by one.

CHAPTER 9

IN THE UNMARKED SEDAN, driving fast, seeking what she always needed in times of crisis—good Cajun food—Carson said, "Even if you were Jack's mother, even if you were his wife, even then you wouldn't know he'd been replaced."

"If this were like some Southern Gothic novel," Michael said, "and I was *both* his mother and his wife, I'd still think that was Jack."

"That was *Jack.*"

"That wasn't Jack."

"I know that wasn't him," Carson said impatiently, "but it was *him.*"

Her palms were slick with sweat. She blotted them one at a time on her jeans.

Michael said, "So Helios isn't just making his New Race and seeding them into the city with fabricated biographies and forged credentials."

"He can also *duplicate* real people," she said. "How can he do that?"

"Easy. Like Dolly."

"Dolly who?"

"Dolly the sheep. Remember several years ago, some scientists cloned a sheep in a lab, named her Dolly."

"That was a sheep, for God's sake. This is a medical examiner. Don't tell me *'easy.'*"

The fierce midday sun fired the windshields and the brightwork of the traffic in the street, and every vehicle appeared to be on the verge of bursting into flames, or melting in a silvery spill across the pavement.

"If he can duplicate Jack Rogers," she said, "he can duplicate anyone."

"You might not even be the real Carson."

"I'm the real Carson."

"How would I know?"

"And how will I know if you go to the men's room and a Michael monster comes back?"

"He wouldn't be as funny as the real me," Michael said.

"The new Jack is funny. Remember what he said about the dead old guy on the table having more personality than homicide cops?"

"That wasn't exactly hilarious."

"But for Jack it was funny enough."

"The real Jack wasn't all that funny to begin with."

"That's my point," she said. "They can be as funny as they need to be."

"That would be scary if I thought it was true," Michael said. "But I'll bet my ass, if they ring a Michael monster in on you, he'll be about as witty as a tree stump."

In this neighborhood of old cottage-style houses, some remained residences, but others had been converted to commercial enterprises.

The blue-and-yellow cottage on the corner looked like someone's home except for the blue neon sign in a large front window: WONDER-MOUS EATS, FOR TRUE, which translated from Cajun patois as "good food, no lie."

Michael preferred to read it as "good food, no bullshit," so from time to time he could say "Let's have a no-bullshit lunch."

Whether the legal name of the restaurant was Wondermous Eats or whether that was just a slogan, Carson had no idea. The cheap Xeroxed menus had no name at top or bottom.

Cottages had been cleared off two adjacent lots, but the ancient live oaks had been left standing. Cars were parked in the shade among the trees.

The carpet of dead leaves looked like drifts of pecan shells and crunched under the tires of the sedan, then underfoot as Carson and Michael walked to the restaurant.

If Helios succeeded in the abolition of humanity, replacing it with obedient and single-minded multitudes, there would be nothing like Wondermous Eats, for True. There would be no eccentricity and no charm in the new world that he desired.

Cops saw the worst of people, and grew cynical if not bitter. Suddenly, however, flawed and foolish humanity seemed beautiful and precious to Carson, no less so than nature and the world itself.

They chose a table outside, in the oak shade, apart from most of the other diners. They ordered crawfish boulettes and fried okra salad, followed by shrimp-and-ham jambalaya.

This was a denial lunch. If they could still eat this well, surely the end of the world was not upon them, and they were not as good as dead, after all.

"How long does it take to make a Jack Rogers?" Michael wondered when the waitress had left.

"If Helios can make anyone overnight, if he's that far advanced, then we're screwed," Carson said.

"More likely, he's steadily replacing people in key positions in the city, and Jack was on his list already."

"So when Jack did the first autopsy on one of the New Race and realized something weird was going on, Helios just brought *his* Jack online quicker than planned."

"I'd like to believe that," Michael said.

"So would I."

"Because neither of us is a big cheese. On his short list, our names wouldn't be there between the mayor and the chief of police."

"He would have had no reason to start growing a Carson or a Michael," she agreed. "Until maybe yesterday."

"I don't think he'll bother even now."

"Because it's easier just to have us killed."

"Totally easy."

"Did he replace Luke or was Luke always one of them?"

"I don't think there was ever a real Luke," Michael said.

"Listen to us."

"I know."

"When do we start wearing aluminum-foil hats to protect ourselves from alien mind-readers?"

The thick air swagged the day like saturated bunting, hot and damp and preternaturally still. Overhead, the boughs of the oaks hung motionless. The whole world appeared to be paralyzed by a terrible expectation.

The waitress brought the crawfish boulettes and two bottles of ice-cold beer.

"Drinking on duty," Carson said, amazed at herself.

"It's not against department regulations during Armageddon," Michael assured her.

"Just yesterday, you didn't believe any of this, and I half thought I was losing my mind."

"Now the only thing I can't believe," Michael said, "is that Dracula and the Wolfman haven't shown up yet."

They ate the boulettes and the fried-okra salads in an intense but comfortable silence.

Then before the jambalaya arrived, Carson said, "Okay, cloning or somehow he can make a perfect physical duplicate of Jack. But how does the sonofabitch make his Jack a medical examiner? I mean, how does he give him Jack's lifetime of knowledge, or Jack's *memories?*"

"Beats me. If I knew that, I'd have my own secret laboratory, and I'd be taking over the world myself."

"Except your world would be a better one than this," she said.

He blinked in surprise, gaped. "Wow."

"Wow what?"

"That was sweet."

"What was sweet?"

"What you just said."

"It wasn't sweet."

"It *was.*"

"It was not."

"You've never been sweet to me before."

"If you use that word one more time," she said, "I'll bust your balls, I swear."

"All right."

"I mean it."

Smiling broadly, he said, "I know."

"Sweet," she said scornfully, and shook her head in disgust. "Be careful or I might even shoot you."

"That's against regulations even during Armageddon."

"Yeah, but you're gonna be dead in twenty-four hours anyway."

He consulted his wristwatch. "Less than twenty-three now."

The waitress arrived with plates of jambalaya. "Can I get you two more beers?"

Carson said, "Why the hell not."

"We're celebrating," Michael told the waitress.

"Is it your birthday?"

"No," he said, "but you'd think it was, considering how sweet she's being to me."

"You're a cute couple," said the waitress, and she went to get the beers.

"Cute?" Carson growled.

"Don't shoot her," Michael pleaded. "She's probably got three kids and an invalid mother to support."

"Then she better watch her mouth," Carson said.

In another silence, they ate jambalaya and drank beer for a while, until finally Michael said, "Probably every major player in city government is one of Victor's."

"Count on it."

"Our own beloved chief."

"He's probably been a replicant for years."

"And maybe half the cops on the force."

"Maybe more than half."

"The local FBI office."

"They're his," she predicted.

"The newspaper, local media?"

"His."

"Whether they're all his or not, when's the last time you trusted a reporter?"

"Clueless," she agreed. "They all want to save the world, but they just end up helping to weave the handbasket."

Carson looked at her hands. She knew they were strong and capable; they had never failed her. Yet at the moment they looked delicate, almost frail.

She had spent the better part of her life in a campaign to redeem her father's reputation. He, too, had been a cop, gunned down by a drug dealer. They said that her dad had been corrupt, deep in the drug trade, that he'd been shot by the competition or because a deal had gone sour. Her mother had been killed in the same hit.

Always she had known the official story must be a lie. Her dad had uncovered something that powerful people wanted kept secret. Now she wondered if it had been *one* powerful person—Victor Helios.

"So what can we do?" Michael asked.

"I've been thinking about that."

"I figured," he said.

"We kill him before he can kill us."

"Easier said than done."

"Not if you're willing to die to get him."

"I'm willing," Michael said, "but not eager."

"You didn't become a cop for the retirement benefits."

"You're right. I just wanted to oppress the masses."

"Violate their civil rights," she said.

"That always gives me a thrill."

She said, "We're going to need guns."

"We've got guns."

"We're going to need bigger guns."

CHAPTER 10

ERIKA'S EDUCATION in the tank had not prepared her to deal with a man who was chewing off his fingers. Had she matriculated through a real rather than virtual university, she might have known at once what she should do.

William, the butler, was one of the New Race, so his fingers were not easy to bite off. He had to work diligently at it.

His jaws and teeth, however, were as formidably enhanced as the density of his finger bones. Otherwise, the task would have been not merely difficult but impossible.

Having amputated the little finger, ring finger, and middle finger of his left hand, William was at work on the forefinger.

The three severed digits lay on the floor. One was curled in such a way that it seemed to be beckoning to Erika.

Like others of his kind, William could by an act of will repress all awareness of pain. Clearly, he had done so. He did not cry out or even whimper.

He mumbled wordlessly to himself as he chewed. When he succeeded in amputating the forefinger, he spat it out and said frantically, "Tick, tock, tick. Tick, tock, tick. Tick, tock, tick, tock, tick, tick, *tick*!"

Had he been a member of the Old Race, the wall and carpet would have been drenched with blood. Although his wounds began to heal even as he inflicted them on himself, he had still made a mess.

Erika could not imagine why the kneeling butler was engaged upon this self-mutilation, what he hoped to achieve, and she was dismayed by his disregard for the damage he had already done to his master's property.

"William," she said. "William, whatever are you thinking?"

He neither answered nor glanced at her. Instead, the butler stuck his left thumb in his mouth and continued this exercise in express de-digitation.

Because the mansion was quite large and because Erika couldn't know if any member of the staff might be nearby, she was reluctant to cry out for help, for she might have to get quite loud to be heard. She knew that Victor wished his wife to be refined and ladylike in all public circumstances.

All members of the staff were, like William, of the New Race. Nevertheless, everything beyond the doors of the master suite was most definitely in public territory.

Consequently, she returned to the telephone in the bedroom and pressed the ALL-CALL function of those buttons on the keypad dedicated to the intercom system. Her summons would be broadcast to every room.

"This is Mrs. Helios," she said. "William is biting off his fingers in the upstairs hall, and I need some assistance."

By the time she returned to the hallway, the butler had finished with his left thumb and had begun on the little finger of his right hand.

"William, this is irrational," she cautioned. "Victor designed us brilliantly, but we can't grow things back when we lose them."

Her admonition did not give him pause. After spitting out the little finger, he rocked back and forth on his knees: "Tick, tock, tick, tock, tick, *tick*, *TICK*, **TICK**!"

The urgency of his voice triggered connections between implanted associations in Erika's mind. She said, "William, you sound like the White Rabbit, pocket watch in hand, racing across the meadow, late for tea with the Mad Hatter."

She considered seizing the hand that still had four fingers and restraining him as best she could. She wasn't afraid of him, but she didn't want to appear forward.

Her in-the-tank education had included exhaustive input on the finest points of deportment and manners. In any social situation from a dinner party to an audience with the Queen of England, she knew the proper etiquette.

Victor insisted upon a poised wife with refined manners. Too bad William wasn't the Queen of England. Or even the Pope.

Fortunately, Christine, the head housekeeper, must have been nearby. She appeared on the stairs, hurrying upward.

The housekeeper did not seem to be shocked. Her expression was grim but entirely controlled.

As she approached, she took a cell phone from a pocket of her uniform and speed-dialed a number with the pressing of one key.

Christine's efficiency startled Erika. If there was a number that one called to report a man biting off his fingers, she herself should have known it.

Perhaps not all the downloaded data had found its way into her brain as it should have done. This was a troubling thought.

William stopped rocking on his knees and put his right ring finger in his mouth.

Other members of the household staff appeared on the stairs—three, four, then five of them. They ascended but not as quickly as Christine.

Every one of them had a haunted look. That is not to say they appeared to be ghosts, but that they looked as if they had *seen* a ghost.

This made no sense, of course. The New Race were atheists by programming and free of all superstition.

Into the cell phone, Christine said, "Mr. Helios, this is Christine. We've got another Margaret."

In her vocabulary, Erika had no definition for *Margaret*, other than that it was a woman's name.

"No, sir," said Christine, "it's not Mrs. Helios. It's William. He's biting off his fingers."

Erika was surprised that Victor should think that she herself might be inclined to bite off her fingers. She was certain that she had given him no reason to expect such a thing of her.

After spitting out his right ring finger, the butler began to rock back and forth again, chanting: "Tick, tock, tick, tock . . ."

Christine held the phone close to William, to allow Victor to hear the chant.

The other five staff members had reached the top of the stairs. They stood in the hallway, silent, solemn, as if bearing witness.

Into the phone once more, Christine said, "He's about to start on the eighth, Mr. Helios." She listened. "Yes, sir."

As William stopped chanting and put the middle finger of his right hand in his mouth, Christine grabbed a fistful of his hair, not to stop his self-mutilation, but to steady his head in order to hold the cell phone to his ear.

After a moment, William stiffened and seemed to listen intently to Victor. He stopped chewing. When Christine let go of his hair, he took his finger out of his mouth and stared at it, bewildered.

A tremor went through his body, then another. He toppled off his knees, collapsed onto his side.

He lay with his eyes open, fixed. His mouth hung open, too, as red as a wound.

Into the phone, Christine said, "He's dead, Mr. Helios." Then: "Yes, sir." Then: "I will do that, sir."

She terminated the call and solemnly regarded Erika.

All of the staff members were staring at Erika. They looked haunted, all right. A shiver of fear went through her.

A porter named Edward said, "Welcome to our world, Mrs. Helios."

CHAPTER 11

MEDITATION IS MOST OFTEN done in stillness, although men of a certain cast of mind, who have great problems to solve, frequently think best on long walks.

Deucalion preferred not to walk in daylight. Even in easy New Orleans, where eccentricity flourished, he would surely draw too much attention in public, in bright sun.

With his gifts, at any time of day, he could have taken a single step and been any place west of where the sun yet reached, to walk in the anonymous darkness of other lands.

Victor was in New Orleans, however, and here the atmosphere of looming cataclysm sharpened Deucalion's wits.

So he walked in the sun-drenched cemeteries of the city. For the most part, the long grassy avenues allowed him to see tourist groups and other visitors long before they drew near.

The ten-foot-tall tombs were like buildings in the crowded blocks of a miniature city. With ease, he could slip between them and away from an impending encounter.

Here the dead were buried in aboveground crypts because the water table was so near the surface that coffins in graves would not remain buried but would surge to the surface in soggy weather. Some were as simple as shotgun houses, but others were as ornamented as Garden District mansions.

Considering that he had been constructed from cadavers and had been brought to life by arcane science—perhaps also by supernatural forces—it was not ironic but logical that he should feel more comfortable in these avenues of the dead than he did on public streets.

In St. Louis Cemetery Number 3, where Deucalion first walked, the mostly white crypts dazzled in the searing sun, as if inhabited by generations of radiant spirits who lingered after their bodies had turned to dust and bones.

These dead were fortunate compared to the living dead who were the New Race. Those soulless slaves might welcome death—but they were created with a proscription against suicide.

Inevitably, they would envy real men, who possessed free will, and their resentment would grow into an irrepressible wrath. Denied self-destruction, sooner or later they would turn outward and destroy all whom they envied.

If Victor's empire was trembling toward the point of collapse, as instinct warned Deucalion that it was, then finding his base of operations became imperative.

Every member of the New Race would know its whereabouts, for in all probability, they had been born there. Whether they would be willing or even capable of divulging it was another issue.

As a first step, he needed to identify some in the city who were likely to be of the New Race. He must approach them cautiously and gauge the depth of their despair, to determine whether it might have ripened into that desperation which is vigorous of action and reckless of consequences.

Among even the most controlled of slaves there simmers a desire—even if not a capacity—to rebel. Therefore, some of these slaves of Victor's, all enemies of humanity, might in their hopelessness find the will and the fortitude to betray him in small ways.

Every member of the household staff and landscaping crew at Victor's estate would be of the New Race. But an attempt to get to any of them would be too risky.

His made men would be seeded throughout Biovision, though the greater number of its employees would be real people. Victor would not want to risk mixing his secret work with his public researches. But seining New Men from the sea of Biovision employees would take too long and involve too much exposure on Deucalion's part.

Perhaps the members of the New Race could recognize one another upon encounter. Deucalion, however, could not tell them from real people at a glance. He would need to observe them, to interact with them, in order to identify them.

Many politicians and appointed officials in the city would no doubt be of Victor's making, either originals or replicants who had taken the place of real people. Their prominence and the attention to security that came with it would make them more difficult to approach.

Half or more of the officers in the city's law-enforcement agencies were most likely members of the New Race. Deucalion didn't care to search those ranks, either, because drawing himself to the attention of the police would not be wise.

As Deucalion left behind St. Louis Number 3 and moved now through the Metairie Cemetery, which boasted the gaudiest tombs in greater New Orleans, the hardest sun of the day hammered all shadows into narrow profiles and honed their edges into blades.

Victor would have his people in key positions in the city's legal establishment—prosecutors and defense attorneys—in the local academic world, in the medical system . . . and surely in the religious community as well.

In times of personal crisis, people turned to their priests, pastors, and rabbis. Victor would have realized that much valuable information might be learned in a confessional or during a citizen's most private talks with his spiritual adviser.

Besides, having his soulless creations delivering sermons and celebrating Mass would strike Victor as delicious mockery.

Even one as big and as menacing in appearance as Deucalion could expect a sympathetic ear from clergymen, whether they were real or imposters. They would be accustomed to offering comfort to society's outsiders and would receive him with less suspicion and alarm than others might.

Because the primary denomination in New Orleans was Catholicism, he would start with that faith. He had many churches from which to choose. In one of them he might find a priest who, by identifying Victor's center of operations, would betray his maker as daily he mocked God.

CHAPTER 12

THE SECURITY ROOM in the Hands of Mercy featured a wall of high-definition monitors providing such clear images of the hallways and rooms of the immense facility that they appeared to be almost three-dimensional.

Victor didn't believe that his people had any right to privacy. Or to life, for that matter.

None of them had any rights whatsoever. They had their mission, which was the fulfillment of his vision for a new world, and they had their duties, and they had what privileges he allowed. No rights.

Werner, security chief at the Hands of Mercy, was such a solid block of muscle that even a concrete floor ought to have sagged under him. Yet he never lifted weights, never exercised. His perfected metabolism maintained his brute physical form in ideal condition, almost regardless of what he ate.

He had a problem with snot, but they were working on that.

Once in a while—not all the time, not even frequently, but nonetheless often enough to be an annoyance—the mucous membranes in his sinuses produced mucus at a prodigious rate. On those occasions, Werner often went through three boxes of Kleenex per hour.

Victor could have terminated Werner, dispatched his cadaver to the landfill, and installed Werner Two in the post of security chief. But these snot attacks baffled and intrigued him. He preferred to keep Werner in place, study his seizures, and gradually tinker with his physiology to resolve the problem.

Standing beside a currently snotless Werner in the security room, Victor watched a bank of monitors on which surveillance tapes revealed the route Randal Six had taken to escape the building.

Absolute power requires absolute adaptability.

Every setback must be viewed as an opportunity, a chance to learn. Victor's visionary work could not be shaken by challenges but must always be strengthened by them.

Some days were more marked by challenges than others. This appeared to be one of them.

The body of Detective Jonathan Harker waited in the dissection room, as yet unexamined. Already the body of William, the butler, was en route.

Victor was not concerned. He was exhilarated.

He was so exhilarated that he could feel the internal carotid arteries throbbing in his neck, the external carotids throbbing in his temples, and his jaw muscles already aching from his clenched-teeth anticipation of meeting these infuriating challenges.

Randal Six, engineered in the tanks to be a severe autistic, intensely agoraphobic, had nevertheless managed to leave his billet. He had followed a series of hallways to the elevators.

"What is he doing?" Victor asked.

By his question, he referred to the video that revealed Randal proceeding along a corridor in a peculiar, hesitant, herky-jerky fashion. Sometimes he took a few steps sideways, studying the floor intently, before he proceeded forward again, but then he stepped sideways to the right.

"Sir, he looks as if he's learning a dance step," said Werner.

"What dance step?"

"I don't know what dance step, sir. My education is largely in surveillance and extreme violent combat. I didn't learn no dance."

"*Any* dance," Victor corrected. "Why would Randal want to dance?"

"People do."

"He's not people."

"No, sir, he's not."

"I didn't design him with the desire to dance. He isn't dancing. It looks more as if he's trying to avoid stepping on something."

"Yes, sir. The cracks."

"What cracks?"

"The cracks between the floor tiles."

When the escapee passed directly under a camera, Werner's observation proved to be correct. Step by step, Randal had been painstakingly careful to place each foot inside one of the twelve-inch-square vinyl tiles.

"That's obsessive-compulsive behavior," Victor said, "which is consistent with the developmental flaws I gave him."

Randal passed out of the view field of one camera, appeared on another. He boarded an elevator. He went down to the bottom floor of the hospital.

"No one made any attempt to stop him, Werner."

"No, sir. Our assignment is to prevent unauthorized entrance. We were never told we should be concerned about anyone leaving without authorization. None of the staff, none of the newly made would ever leave here without your permission."

"Randal did."

Frowning, Werner said, "It isn't possible to disobey you, sir."

On the bottom floor, Randal avoided cracks and reached the file room. He concealed himself among the metal cabinets.

Most of the New Race who were created in Mercy were eventually infiltrated into the city's population. Some, however, like Randal, were experimental, and Victor intended them for termination when he had concluded the experiment of which each was the subject. Randal had never been meant for the world beyond these walls.

Werner fast-forwarded the surveillance tape until Victor himself appeared, entering the file room by way of the secret tunnel that connected the former hospital to the parking garage of the building next door.

"He's renegade," Victor said grimly. "He hid from me."

"It isn't possible to disobey you, sir."

"He obviously *knew* he was forbidden to leave."

"But it isn't possible to disobey you, sir."

"Shut up, Werner."

"Yes, sir."

After Victor passed through the file room into the lower floor of Mercy, Randal Six emerged from concealment and went to the exit door. He entered the lock code and proceeded into the tunnel.

"How did he know the code?" Victor wondered.

Hitching and twitching, Randal followed the tunnel to the door at the farther end, where again he entered the lock code.

"How did he *know*?"

"Permission to speak, sir."

"Go ahead."

"When he was hiding in the file room, he heard the tone of each digit you pressed on the keypad before you entered from the tunnel."

"You mean, heard it through the door."

"Yes, sir."

"Every number has a different tone," Victor said.

"He would've had to learn beforehand what number each tone represented."

On the surveillance tape, Randal entered the empty storeroom in the building next door. After some hesitation, he went from there into the parking garage.

The final camera captured Randal as he haltingly ascended the garage ramp. His face was carved by anxiety, but somehow he overcame his agoraphobia and ventured into a world he found threatening and overwhelming in scale.

"Mr. Helios, sir, I suggest that our security protocols be revised and our electronic systems modified to prevent unauthorized exit as well as unauthorized entrance."

"Do it," Victor said.

"Yes, sir."

"We've got to find him," Victor said more to himself than to Werner. "He left with some specific intention. A destination. He's so developmentally disabled, so narrowly focused, he could only have accomplished this if some desperate need drove him."

"May I suggest, sir, that we search his billet as thoroughly as if we were police searching a crime scene. We might find a clue to his purpose, his destination."

"We better," Victor warned.

"Yes, sir."

Victor went to the door, hesitated, glanced back at Werner. "How is your mucus?"

The security chief came as close to smiling as he ever would. "Much better, sir. The last few days, I haven't had no snot at all."

"Any snot," Victor corrected.

"No, sir. Like I just said, I don't have no snot at all."

CHAPTER 13

CARSON O'CONNOR LIVES in a simple white house given some grace by a veranda that wraps three sides.

Oaks draped with Spanish moss shade the property. Cicadas sing in the heat.

In respect of the substantial annual rainfall and the long sultry summers, the veranda and the house itself are raised almost three feet off the ground on concrete piers, creating a crawl space under the entire structure.

The crawl space is concealed by a skirt of crisscrossed lattice. Usually nothing lives here but spiders.

These are unusual days. Now the spiders share their redoubt with Randal Six.

Crossing the city from the Hands of Mercy, especially when a thunderstorm brought the sky crashing to the earth in bright bolts, Randal had been afflicted by too much noise, by too many new sights, smells, sounds, sensations. Never had he known such blind terror.

He had almost clawed out his eyes, had almost poked a sharp stick in his ears to destroy his hearing, thus sparing himself from sensory overload. Fortunately, he had restrained those impulses.

Although he appears to be eighteen, he has been alive and out of the tank for only four months. All of that time, he has lived in one room, mostly in one corner of that room.

He doesn't like commotion. He doesn't like being touched or having to speak to anyone. He despises change.

Yet here he is. He has thrown over all he knew and has embraced an unknowable future. This accomplishment makes him proud.

The crawl space is a peaceful environment. His monastery, his hermitage.

For the most part, the only smells are the bare earth under him, the raw wood above, the concrete piers. Occasionally a whiff of star jasmine finds its way to him, though it is a richer scent at night than in the day.

Little sunlight penetrates the interstices of the lattice. The shadows are deep, but because he is of the New Race, with enhanced vision, he can see well enough.

Only an occasional traffic noise reaches him from the street. From overhead, inside the house, come periodic footsteps, the creak of floorboards, muffled music on a radio.

His companions, the spiders, have no smell that he can detect, make no noise, and keep to themselves.

He might be content here for a long time if not for the fact that the secret of happiness abides in the house above him, and he must have it.

In a newspaper, he once saw a photograph of Detective Carson O'Connor with her brother, Arnie. Arnie is an autistic like Randal Six.

Nature made Arnie autistic. Randal was given his affliction by Victor. Nevertheless, he and Arnie are brothers in their suffering.

In the newspaper photo, twelve-year-old Arnie had been with his sister at a charity event benefiting autism research. Arnie had been smiling. He looked happy.

During his four months of life in the Hands of Mercy, Randal has never been happy. Anxiety gnaws at him every minute, every day, more insistently some times than at others, but always chewing, nibbling. He lives in misery.

He never imagined that happiness might be possible—until he had seen Arnie's smile. Arnie knows something that Randal does not. Arnie the autistic knows a reason to smile. Perhaps many reasons.

They are brothers. Brothers in suffering. Arnie will share his secret with his brother Randal.

Should Arnie refuse to share it, Randal will *tear* the secret out of him. He will get it one way or another. He will kill for it.

If the world beyond the lattice were not so dazzling, so full of sights and motion, Randal Six would simply slither out from under the house. He would enter the place by a door or window, and get what he needs.

After his trip from Mercy and the ordeal of the thunderstorm, however, he cannot endure that much sensory input. He must find a way into the house from the crawl space.

No doubt the spiders do it often. He will be a spider. He will creep. He will find a way.

CHAPTER 14

NICHOLAS FRIGG WALKED the earthen ramparts that wound between and around the lakes of waste and rubbish, manager of the dump and master of all that he surveyed.

Over his jeans he wore thigh-high rubber boots hooked by straps to his belt. In this blazing heat he went barechested, wore no hat, and let the sun bake him to a bread-crust brown.

He had no worry about melanoma. He belonged to the New Race, and cancer could not touch him.

The malignancies that ate at him were alienation, loneliness, and an acute awareness of his enslavement.

In these uplands, significantly northeast of Lake Pontchartrain, the garbage arrived from the Big Easy and from other cities, seven days a week, in an endless caravan of semis with hydraulic rams that expelled compressed blocks of trash into the steaming pits of the landfill.

Misanthropes and cynics might say that regardless of the city, whether it be New Orleans or Paris or Tokyo, the definition of its garbage ought to include the worst examples of humanity that walked its streets.

And, of course, the urban legends of every city included stories asserting that the Mafia disposed of witnesses and other nuisances in garbage dumps where the workers were members of mobster-controlled unions.

The putrid depths of the Crosswoods Waste Management facility actually did contain thousands of bodies, many of which had appeared to be human when they had been secretly interred here over the years. Some *were* human, the cadavers of those who had been replaced by replicants.

The others were failed experiments—some of which did not look human at all—or members of the New Race who for a host of reasons had been terminated. Four Erikas were buried in these reservoirs of waste.

Everyone who worked at the dump belonged to the New Race. They answered to Nick Frigg, and he answered to his maker.

Crosswoods was owned by a Nevada corporation, which was itself owned by a holding company in the Bahamas. That holding company was an asset of a trust based in Switzerland.

The beneficiaries of the trust were three Australian nationals living in New Orleans. The Australians were in fact members of the New Race, who were themselves owned by Victor.

At the apex—or perhaps at the nadir—of this arc of deception stood Nick, both the master of the garbage and the overseer of the secret graveyard. More than most others of his kind, he enjoyed his work even if it was not what he wanted for a life.

The panoply of odors, an unending series of revolting stenches to an ordinary man, were a phantasmagoria of fragrances to Nick. He breathed deeply and licked the air, and savored the intricacies of every aroma.

By the introduction of certain canine genes, Nick's maker had given him a sense of smell approximately half as sensitive as that of a dog, which meant he enjoyed olfactory perceptions ten thousand times more powerful than those of the average human being.

To a dog, few scents cause revulsion. Many are good, and nearly all are interesting. Even the stink of offal and the ripe miasma of decomposition are intriguing if not savory. And so they were, as well, to Nick Frigg.

This gift of smell turned a foul job into one with the potential to delight. Although Nick had cause to believe that Victor was a hard God if not cruel, here was one reason to consider that he did care, after all, about his creations.

Dog-nose Nick strode the ramparts, which were wide enough to accommodate an SUV, watching the semis off-loading along the far perimeter of the east pit, two hundred yards to his left. This ten-story-deep hole had been two-thirds filled with trash over the past few years.

Wide-track bulldozers—tagged "garbage galleons" by Nick and his crew—rode the sea of trash and distributed it more evenly across the pit than the trucks left it.

To his right lay the west pit, not quite as large as that to the east, but somewhat fuller.

Downslope, to the south, two previous sites had been filled and subsequently capped with eight feet of earth. Methane-gas vent pipes punctuated those grass-covered mounds.

North of the current two pits, excavation of a new east dump had been under way for two months. The chug and growl of earth-moving machines echoed down from those heights.

Nick turned his back to the busy east and studied the quiet west pit, from which incoming semis had been diverted for the day.

This moonscape of rubbish stirred his two hearts as nothing else could. Compacted chaos, waste and rack and ruin: These bleak, toxic barrens spoke to that part of him that might have been occupied by a soul if he had been of the Old Race. He felt at home here as he would never feel in woods or grassy fields, or in a city. The desolation, the filth, the mold, the rancidity, the ash, the slime called to him as the sea called a sailor.

Within a few hours, a van would arrive from New Orleans, loaded with corpses. Three were city bureaucrats who had been murdered and replaced by replicants, and two were police officers who had met the same end.

A mere year ago, such deliveries had been made twice a month. Now they came twice a week, often more frequently.

These were exciting times.

In addition to the five dead humans, the van carried three gone-wrongs, creatures created in the Hands of Mercy that had not turned out as Victor hoped. They were always interesting.

After nightfall, when everyone within the fenced perimeter of Crosswoods Waste Management would be of the New Race, Nick and his crew would carry the dead humans and the gone-wrongs into the west pit. In a ceremony that had gradually become richer over the years, they would bury them in that slough of garbage.

Although these nocturnal interments had lately become frequent, they still thrilled Nick. He was forbidden to kill himself; and he could not slaughter members of the Old Race until the day when Victor launched the Last War. He loved death but could not have it or deal it out. Meanwhile, however, he could wade the sea of trash and filth, shoving the dead into reeking holes where they would bloat and ripen, intoxicated by the fumes of decomposition—which was a fringe benefit that he cherished.

In the morning, the scores of incoming semis would be directed to the west pit, and the loads they deposited would be spread across these new graves, like another layer in a parfait.

As Nick gazed out across the west dump, longing for sunset, a flock of fat glossy crows, feeding in the garbage, suddenly exploded into flight. The birds took wing as though they were a single creature and shrieked in unison, swooping toward him and then up into the sun.

About a hundred fifty feet from the rampart on which he stood, a twenty-foot length of the dense trash trembled, and then appeared to roll, as though something swarmed through it. Perhaps a pack of rats surged just below the surface.

In recent days, members of Nick's crew had half a dozen times reported rhythmic shiftings and pulsations in both pits, different from the usual swelling and settling related to the expansion and then sudden venting of methane pockets.

Little more than half a day ago, past midnight, strange sounds had risen from the east pit, almost like voices, tortured cries. With flashlights, Nick and his crew had gone in search of the source, which had seemed repeatedly to change direction but then had fallen silent before it could be located.

Now the pulsing trash went still. Rats. Surely rats.

Nevertheless, curious, Nick descended the sloped wall of the earthen rampart, into the west pit.

CHAPTER 15

AUBREY PICOU HAD RETIRED from a life of crime to have more time to tend his garden.

He lived on an oak-shaded street in Mid-City. His historic house boasted some of the most ornate decorative ironwork—fence, balcony railings—in a city dripping with such weighty filigree.

The front porch, draped with trumpet vines and hung with basket ferns, offered two white bench swings and wicker rocking chairs, but the shadows seemed no cooler than the sun-scorched front walk.

The maid, Lulana St. John, answered the doorbell. She was a fiftyish black woman whose girth and personality were equally formidable.

Leveling a disapproving look at Carson, trying to suppress a smile when she glanced at Michael, Lulana said, "I see before me two well-known public servants who do the Lord's work but sometimes make the mistake of using the devil's tactics."

"We're two sinners," Carson admitted.

"'Amazing grace,'" Michael said, "'how sweet thou art, to save a wretch like me.'"

"Child," said Lulana, "I suspect you flatter yourself to think you're saved. If you have come here to be troublesome to the mister, I ask you to look within yourselves and find the part of you that wants to be a *peace* officer."

"That's the biggest part of me," Michael said, "but Detective O'Connor here mostly just wants to kick ass."

To Carson, Lulana said, "I'm sorry to say, missy, that *is* your reputation."

"Not today," Carson assured her. "We're here to ask a favor of Aubrey, if you would please announce us. We have no grievance against him."

Lulana studied her solemnly. "The Lord has given me an excellent crap detector, and it isn't ringing at the moment. It's in your favor that you have not shaken your badge at me, and you did say please."

"At my insistence," Michael said, "Detective O'Connor has been taking an evening class in etiquette."

"He's a fool," Lulana told Carson.

"Yes, I know."

"After a lifetime of eating with her hands," Michael said, "she has mastered the use of the fork in a remarkably short time."

"Child, you are a fool," Lulana told him, "but for reasons that only the Lord knows, in spite of myself, I always take a liking to you." She stepped back from the threshold. "Wipe your feet, and come in."

The foyer was painted peach with white wainscoting and ornate white crown molding. The white marble floor with diamond-shaped black inlays had been polished to such a shine that it looked wet.

"Has Aubrey found Jesus yet?" Carson wondered.

Closing the front door, Lulana said, "The mister hasn't embraced his Lord, no, but I'm pleased to say he has come as far as making eye contact with Him."

Although paid only to be a maid, Lulana did double duty as a spiritual guide to her employer, whose past she knew and whose soul concerned her.

"The mister is gardening," she said. "You could wait for him in the parlor or join him in the roses."

"By all means, the roses," Michael said.

At the back of the house, in the immense kitchen, Lulana's older sister, Evangeline Antoine, softly sang "His Lamp Will Overcome All Darkness" as she pressed dough into a pie pan.

Evangeline served as Aubrey's cook and also as an amen choir to Lulana's indefatigable soul-saving efforts. She was taller than her sister, thin, yet her lively eyes and her smile made their kinship obvious.

"Detective Maddison," Evangeline said, "I'm so glad you're not dead yet."

"Me too," he said. "What kind of pie are you making?"

"Praline-cinnamon cream topped with fried pecans."

"Now that's *worth* a quadruple heart-bypass."

"Cholesterol," Lulana informed them, "won't stick if you have the right attitude."

She led them through the rear door onto the back veranda, where Moses Bienvenu, Aubrey's driver and handyman, was painting the beautifully turned white balusters under the black handrail.

Beaming, he said, "Detective O'Connor, I'm amazed to see you haven't shot Mr. Michael yet."

"My aim's good," she assured him, "but he can move fast."

Well-padded but not fat, a robust and towering man with hands as big as dinner plates, Moses served as a deacon at the church and sang in the same gospel choir as his sisters, Lulana and Evangeline.

"They're here to see the mister but not to trouble him," Lulana told her brother. "If it looks like they're troubling him, after all, lift them by the scruffs of their necks and put them in the street."

As Lulana went inside, Moses said, "You heard Lulana. You may be police officers, but she's the law around here. The Law and the Way. I would be in your debt if you didn't make it necessary for me to scruff-carry you out of here."

"If we find ourselves getting out of hand," Michael said, "we'll scruff-carry each other."

Pointing with his paintbrush, Moses said, "Mr. Aubrey is over there past the pagan fountain, among the roses. And please don't make fun of his hat."

"His hat?" Michael asked.

"Lulana insists he wear a sun hat if he's going to spend half the day in the garden. He's mostly bald, so she worries he'll get head-top skin cancer. Mr. Aubrey hated the hat at first. He only recently got used to it."

Carson said, "Never thought I'd see the day when anyone would be the boss of Aubrey Picou."

"Lulana doesn't so much boss," said Moses. "She sort of just tough-loves everyone into obedience."

A brick walkway led from the back veranda steps, across the lawn, encircled the pagan fountain, and continued to the rose garden.

The sculptured-marble fountain featured three life-size figures. Pan, a male form with goat legs and horns, played a flute and chased two nude women—or they chased him—around a column twined with grapevines.

"My eye for antiques isn't infallible," Michael said, "but I'm pretty sure that's eighteenth-century Las Vegas."

The rosebushes grew in rows, with aisles of decomposed granite between. In the third of four aisles stood a bag of fertilizer, a tank sprayer, and trays of neatly arranged gardening tools.

Here, too, was Aubrey Picou, under a straw hat with such a broad brim that squirrels could have raced around it for exercise.

Before he noticed them and looked up, he was humming a tune. It sounded like "His Lamp Will Overcome All Darkness."

Aubrey was eighty years old and had a baby face: an eighty-year-old

baby face, but nevertheless pink and plump and pinchable. Even in the
deep shade of his anticancer headgear, his blue eyes twinkled with merriment.

"Of all the cops I know," said Aubrey, "here are the two I like the
best."

"Do you like any others at all?" Carson asked.

"Not one of the bastards, no," Aubrey said. "But then none of the
rest ever saved my life."

"What's with the stupid hat?" Michael asked.

Aubrey's smile became a grimace. "What's it matter if I die of skin
cancer? I'm eighty years old. I gotta die of something."

"Lulana doesn't want you to die before you find Jesus."

Aubrey sighed. "With those three running the show, I trip over Jesus every time I turn around."

"If anyone can redeem you," Carson said, "it'll be Lulana."

Aubrey looked as if he would say something acerbic. Instead he
sighed again. "I never used to have a conscience. Now I do. It's more annoying than this absurd hat."

"Why wear the hat if you hate it?" Michael asked.

Aubrey glanced toward the house. "If I take it off, she'll see. Then I
won't get any of Evangeline's pie."

"The praline-cinnamon cream pie."

"With fried-pecan topping," Aubrey said. "I love that pie." He
sighed.

"You sigh a lot these days," Michael said.

"I've become pathetic, haven't I?"

"You used to be pathetic," Carson said. "What you've become is a
little bit human."

"It's disconcerting," Michael said.

"Don't I know," Aubrey agreed. "So what brings you guys here?"

Carson said, "We need some big, loud, door-busting guns."

CHAPTER 16

GLORIOUS, THE STINK: pungent, pervasive, penetrating.

Nick Frigg imagined that the smell of the pits had saturated his flesh, his blood, his bones, in the same way that the scent of smoldering hickory permeated even the thickest cuts of meat in a smokehouse.

He relished the thought that to the core he smelled like all varieties of decomposition, like the death that he longed for and that he could not have.

In his thigh-high rubber boots, Nick strode across the west pit, empty cans of everything rattling in his wake, empty egg cartons and cracker boxes crunching-crackling underfoot, toward the spot where the surface of the trash had swelled and rolled and settled. That peculiar activity appeared to have ceased.

Although compacted by the wide-tracked garbage galleons that crawled these desolate realms, the trash field—between sixty and seventy feet deep in this pit—occasionally shifted under Nick, for by its nature it was riddled with small voids. Agile, with lightning reflexes, he rarely lost his footing.

When he arrived at the site of the movement that he had seen from the elevated rampart, the surface did not look significantly different from the hundred fifty feet of refuse across which he had just traveled. Squashed cans, broken glass, uncountable plastic items from bleach bottles to broken toys, drifts of moldering landscape trimmings—palm fronds, tree limbs, grass—full trash bags knotted at their necks . . .

He saw a doll with tangled legs and a cracked brow. Pretending that beneath his foot lay a real child of the Old Race, Nick stomped until he shattered the smiling face.

Turning slowly 360 degrees, he studied the debris more closely.

He sniffed, sniffed, using his genetically enhanced sense of smell to seek a clue as to what might have caused the unusual rolling movement in this sea of trash. Methane escaped the depths of the pit, but that scent seemed no more intense than usual.

Rats. He smelled rats nearby. In a dump, this was no more surprising than catching a whiff of garbage. The musky scent of rodents pervaded the entire fenced grounds of Crosswoods Waste Management.

He detected clusters of those whiskered individuals all around him, but he could not smell a pack so large that, swarming through a burrow, it would be capable of destabilizing the surface of the trash field.

Nick roamed the immediate area, looking, sniffing, and then squatted—rubber boots squeaking—and waited. Motionless. Listening. Breathing quietly but deeply.

The sounds of the unloading semis at the east pit gradually receded, as did the distant growl of the garbage galleons.

As if to assist him, the air hung heavy and still. There was no breeze to whisper distractingly in his ears. The brutal sun seared silence into the day.

At times like this, the sweet reek of the pit could convey him into something like a Zen state of relaxed yet intense observation.

He lost track of time, became so blissed-out that he didn't know how many minutes passed until he heard the voice, and he could not be certain that it hadn't spoken several times before he registered it.

"Father?"

Soft, tremulous, in an indefinite timbre, the one-word question could have been posed by either a male or a female.

Dog-nose Nick waited, sniffed.

"Father, Father, Father . . . ?"

This time the question seemed to come simultaneously from four or five individuals, male and female.

When he surveyed the trash field, Nick found that he remained alone. How such a thing could be possible, he did not know, but the voices must have spoken out of the compacted refuse beneath him, rising through crevices from . . . From where?

"Why, Father, why, why, why . . . ?"

The lost and beseeching tone suggested intractable misery, and resonated with Nick's own repressed despair.

"Who are you?" he asked.

He received no reply.

"What are you?"

A tremor passed through the trash field. Brief. Subtle. The surface did not swell and roll as before.

Nick sensed the mysterious presence withdrawing.

Rising to his feet, he said, "What do you want?"

The searing sun. The still air. The stink.

Nick Frigg stood alone, the slough of trash once more firm beneath his feet.

CHAPTER 17

AT A BUSH with huge pink-yellow-white roses, Aubrey Picou snipped a bloom for Carson, and stripped the thorns from the stem.

"This variety is called French Perfume. Its exceptional mix of colors makes it the most feminine rose in my garden."

Michael was amused to see Carson handle the flower so awkwardly even though it had no thorns. She was not a frills-and-roses kind of girl. She was a blue-jeans-and-guns kind of girl.

In spite of his innocent face and floppy straw hat, the master of this garden seemed as out of place among the roses as did Carson.

During decades of criminal activity, Aubrey Picou never killed a man, never wounded one. He never robbed or raped, or extorted anyone. He had merely made it possible for other criminals to do those things more easily and efficiently.

His document shop had produced forged papers of the highest quality: passports, birth certificates, driver's licenses. . . . He'd sold thousands of black-market guns.

When individuals with a talent for strategy and tactics came to Aubrey with plans for an armored-car heist or with a scheme to knock over a diamond wholesaler, he provided the risk capital to prepare and execute the operation.

His father, Maurice, had been an attorney who specialized in massaging juries into awarding outrageous financial compensation to questionable clients in dubious personal-injury cases. Some in his profession admiringly called him Maurice the Milkman because of his ability to squeeze buckets of profits out of juries as dumb as cows.

The Milkman had put his son through Harvard Law with the fond hope that Aubrey would embrace the—at that time—new field of class-action litigation, using bad science and good courtroom theater to terrorize major corporations and to drive them nearly to bankruptcy with billion-dollar settlements.

To Maurice's disappointment, Aubrey had found the law tedious, even when practiced with contempt, and had decided that he could do as much damage to society from outside the legal system as he could from within it. Though father and son had for a while been estranged, eventually Maurice had been proud of his boy.

The Milkman's son had been indicted only twice. Both times he had escaped conviction. In each case, after the foreman delivered the innocent verdict, the juries stood and applauded Aubrey.

To forestall a pending third indictment, he had secretly turned state's evidence. After ratting out scores of thugs without their knowledge, he retired at seventy-five, his reputation intact among the criminal class and its admirers.

"I don't do guns anymore," Aubrey said. "Not the big, loud, door-busting kind or any others."

"We know you're retired—"

"For true," Aubrey assured her.

"—but you still have friends in all the wrong places."

"This rose is called Black Velvet," said Aubrey. "The red is so dark, it looks black in places."

"We're not setting you up," Carson said. "No prosecutor will waste thousands of hours to nail a harmless octogenarian gardener."

Michael said, "Besides, you'd fake Alzheimer's and have the jury in tears."

"French Perfume doesn't belong in a bouquet with this," Aubrey told Carson, "but Black Velvet strikes me as more of a rose for you."

"What we need are two Desert Eagle pistols, .50 Magnum."

Impressed, Michael said to Carson, "Is that what we need?"

"I said *loud*, didn't I? If you have two hearts and you take one chest punch of that caliber, both tickers ought to pop."

Aubrey gave a Black Velvet rose to Carson, who accepted it reluctantly. She held one flower in each hand, looking nonplussed.

"Why don't you requisition through the PD?" Aubrey asked.

"'Cause we're going to kill a man who would walk out of a courtroom, free and laughing, if we put him on trial," she lied.

In the shade of his hat, Aubrey's eyes glittered with interest.

"We aren't wired," Carson assured him. "You can pat us down."

"I'd like to pat you down, all right, darlin'," said Aubrey, "but not for a wire. This isn't how you'd talk if you were wearing one."

"For the Eagles, I'll want one hundred rounds of .50AE's, .325 weight," Carson said, "jacketed hollow points."

"Formidable. You're talking maybe fourteen-hundred-feet-per-second muzzle velocity," Aubrey said.

"We want these guys very dead. We'll also need two shotguns. We want to use slugs, not buckshot."

"Slugs, not buckshot," Michael agreed, nodding, as if they were entirely simpatico about this, as if he weren't scared half numb.

"Big stopping power," Aubrey said approvingly.

"Big," Michael agreed.

"Semi-auto so we can fire a second round single-handed," Carson continued. "Maybe an Urban Sniper. What's the barrel length on that?"

"Eighteen inches," Aubrey said.

"We'd want it cut down to fourteen. But we need these fast, so there's no time to wait for customizing."

"How fast?"

"Today. Soon. As soon as now. Urban Sniper, SGT, Remington—we'll have to take any credible shotgun that's already been modified to meet those specifications."

"You'll want a three-way sling for each," Aubrey said, "so you can shoulder-carry and hip-fire."

"So who do we go to?" Carson asked, still holding a rose in each hand as if she were protesting to end all war.

Unconsciously working the rose snips—*click-click, click-click, click-click*—Aubrey studied her and Michael for half a minute, then said, "That's a lot of firepower to go after one guy. Who is he—the Antichrist?"

"He's well protected," she said. "We're going to have to wade through some people to nail him. But they're all dirtbags, too."

Not convinced, Aubrey Picou said, "Cops go bad all the time. Given the lack of support they get and all the flack they take, who can blame them? But not you two. You two don't go bad."

"You remember what happened to my dad?" Carson asked.

Aubrey said, "That was all bogus. Your dad didn't turn. He was a good cop to the end."

"I know. But thanks for saying it, Aubrey."

When he cocked his head in the sun hat, he looked like Truman Capote in ladies-going-to-lunch drag. "You telling me you know who really waxed him and your mom?"

"Yeah," she lied.

"Just who pulled the trigger or who ordered it to be pulled?"

"We're at the top of the food chain with this guy," she said.

Looking at Michael, Aubrey said, "So when you punch his ticket, it's going to be big news."

Staying mostly mute and playing half dumb had worked well for Michael. He shrugged.

Aubrey wasn't satisfied with a shrug. "You'll probably be killed doing this."

"Nobody lives forever," Michael said.

"Lulana says we all do. Anyway, this is O'Connor's vengeance. Why should you die for it?"

"We're partners," Michael said.

"That's not it. Partners don't commit suicide for each other."

"I think we can pull it off," Michael said, "and walk away."

A sly smile robbed the old man's pinchable face of its previous innocence. "That's not it, either."

Grimacing, Carson said, "Aubrey, don't make him say it."

"I just need to hear something that makes his commitment believable."

"This isn't going to snap back on you," she promised.

"Maybe, maybe not. I'm almost convinced. I know your motive, darlin'. His, I want to hear."

"Don't say it," Carson warned Michael.

"Well, he already knows," Michael said.

"That's the point. He already knows. He doesn't need to hear you say it. He's just being a pissant."

"Now, darlin', don't hurt old Aubrey's feelings. Michael, why in blazes would you want to do this?"

"Because—"

"Don't," said Carson.

"—I love her."

Carson said, "Shit."

Aubrey Picou laughed with delight. "I am a fool for romance. You give me your cell-phone number, and the man with the goods will call you inside two hours, to tell you how and where."

"Aubrey Picou, I should make you eat these roses," Carson said, shaking the French Perfume and the Black Velvet in his face.

"Seeing as how they've been flavored by your sweet hands, I suspect I'd like the taste."

She threw the roses on the ground. "For that, you owe me one. I want to borrow the money to pay for the guns."

Aubrey laughed. "Why would I do that?"

"Because we once saved your life. And I don't have several thousand stuffed in a sock."

"Darlin', I'm not a man with a reputation for generosity."

"That's part of what Lulana's been trying to tell you."

He frowned. "This makes me more of a party to it."

"Not if the loan is on a handshake. No paperwork."

"I don't mean legally. I mean morally."

Michael thought his hearing had failed. The word couldn't have been *morally*.

"Just making the connection for the deal isn't so bad," Aubrey said, "'cause I'm not taking a commission, I make nothing from it. But if I finance it, even interest-free . . ."

This clearly surprised Carson. "Interest-free?"

"Seems like I've got some responsibility that way." Under his big floppy hat, he now looked more worried than absurd. "This Jesus guy is scary."

"Scary?"

"I mean, if he's half as real as Lulana says—"

"Half as real?"

"—then you have to think consequences."

"Aubrey," Carson said, "no offense, but considering the way you've lived your life, I don't think scary old Jesus is going to make a big issue out of you loaning me money for this."

"Maybe not. But I've been trying to change the kind of person I am."

"You *have?*"

Aubrey took off his hat, wiped his sweaty forehead with a handkerchief, and at once put the hat on again. "They all know who I used to be, but Lulana, Evangeline, and Moses—they treat me with respect."

"And it's not because they're afraid you might have them kneecapped."

"Exactly right. It's amazing. They've all been so nice to me for no reason, and after a while I sort of wanted to be nice to them."

"How insidious," Michael said.

"It is," Aubrey agreed. "It really is. You let people like that into your life—especially if they also make good pie—and the next thing you know, you're giving money to charities."

"You haven't really," Carson said.

"Sixty thousand this year already," Aubrey said sheepishly.

"No way."

"The orphanage desperately needed repairs, so *somebody* had to step up and fill their soup pot."

"Aubrey Picou helping an *orphanage*," Michael said.

"I'd be obliged if you don't tell anyone about it. I've got a reputation to protect. The old crowd would think I've gone soft or senile."

"Your secret's safe with us," Carson promised.

Aubrey's expression brightened. "Hey, what about this—I'll just give you the money, no loan at all. You use it for whatever you need, and one day when you're more flush, you don't give it back to me, you give it to some charity you like."

"You think that'll fool Jesus?" Michael asked.

"It should," Aubrey said, pleased with himself. "Anyway, it would be like if I gave a bunch of money to a school for the deaf and the school principal skimmed a little off the top and used the skim to pay for a three-way with two hookers."

"Do you follow this?" Michael asked Carson.

"It's too metaphysical for me."

"The point is," Aubrey said, "the skim and the hookers wouldn't be my fault just because I gave money to a school for the deaf."

"Instead of paying back what you lend me, you want me to give it to a school for the deaf?" Carson asked.

"That would be nice. Just remember, what you do with it in the meantime, *you* have to answer for."

"You've become a real theologian," Michael said.

CHAPTER 18

AFTER THE BODY of William, the butler, and all of his severed fingers had been removed from the mansion by two men from the Hands of Mercy, the head housekeeper, Christine, and the third-floor maid, Jolie, cleaned up the blood in the hallway.

Erika knew that as the mistress of the house, she should not get down on her knees and help. Victor would not approve.

Because class distinctions prevented her from assisting, she did not know what to do; therefore, she stood by and watched.

The blood on the mahogany floor wiped up easily, of course, but Erika was surprised to see it come off the painted wall and out of the antique Persian runner without leaving any visible residue.

"What's that spot remover you're using?" she asked, indicating the unlabeled plastic squeeze bottles with which both Christine and Jolie were armed.

"Mr. Helios invented it," Jolie said.

"He must have made a fortune from it."

"It's never been marketed to the public," Christine said.

"He developed it for us," Jolie revealed.

Erika marveled that Victor would have time to concoct new household products, considering everything else on his mind.

"Other spot removers," Christine explained, "even if they took out all the stain visible to the eye, would leave blood proteins in the carpet fibers that any CSI unit could identify. This expunges everything."

"My husband's very clever, isn't he?" Erika said, not without some pride.

"Extremely so," said Christine.

"Extremely," Jolie agreed.

"I very much want to please him," Erika said.

"That would be a good idea," Jolie said.

"I think I displeased him this morning."

Christine and Jolie glanced meaningfully at each other, but neither replied to Erika.

She said, "He beat me while we were having sex."

Having dealt with all the bloodstains, Christine directed Jolie to proceed with her morning tasks in the master suite. When she and Erika were alone in the hallway, she said, "Mrs. Helios, excuse me for being so straightforward, but you must not speak about your private life with Mr. Helios in front of anyone on the household staff."

Erika frowned. "Shouldn't I?"

"No. Never."

"Why not?"

"Mrs. Helios, surely the subject of social deportment was part of your manners-and-etiquette download."

"Well, I guess it was. I mean, if you think it should have been."

"It definitely should have been. You shouldn't discuss your sex life with anyone but Mr. Helios."

"The thing is, he beat me during sex, even bit me once, and he called me the worst names. I was so ashamed."

"Mrs. Helios—"

"He's a good man, a great man, so I must have done something terribly wrong to have made him hurt me, but I don't know what upset him."

"You're doing it again," Christine said impatiently, "talking about your private life with Mr. Helios."

"You're right, I am. But if you could help me understand what I did to displease my husband, that would be good for both me and Victor."

Christine's stare was sharp and unwavering. "You *do* know that you are the fifth Erika, don't you?"

"Yes. And I'm determined to be the last."

"Then perhaps you'd better not talk about sex even with him."

"Even with Victor? But how will I find out why he was displeased with me?"

Christine stropped her sharp stare into an even more piercing gaze. "Maybe he wasn't displeased."

"Then why did he punch me and pull my hair and pinch my—"

"You're doing it again."

Frustrated, Erika said, "But I've got to talk with *somebody* about it."

"Then talk to the mirror, Mrs. Helios. That's the only safe conversation you can have on the subject."

"How could that be productive? A mirror is an inanimate object. Unless it's magical, like in *Snow White and the Seven Dwarfs*."

"When you're looking at yourself in the mirror, Mrs. Helios, ask yourself what you know about sexual sadism."

Erika considered the term. "I don't think it's in my programmed knowledge."

"Then the very best thing you can do is educate yourself . . . and endure. Now, if that's everything, I have a number of tasks to attend to."

CHAPTER 19

THE SOFT RATTLE of the computer keyboard under Vicky Chou's nimble fingers, as she composed a letter, was the only sound in the summer afternoon. Each time that she paused in her typing, the subsequent silence seemed nearly as deep as deafness.

The merest breath of sultry air stirred the sheer curtains at the open window but did not produce the faintest whisper. Outside, the day lacked bird songs. If traffic passed in the street, it did so with the muted grace of a ghost ship sailing without wind across a glassy sea.

Vicky Chou worked at home as a medical transcriptionist. Home was Carson O'Connor's house, where she received free room and board in return for serving as a caregiver to Carson's brother, Arnie.

Some of her friends thought this was an odd arrangement and that Vicky had negotiated a bad deal. In truth, she felt overcompensated, because Carson had saved Vicky's sister, Liane, from serving life in prison for a crime she had never committed.

At forty-five, Vicky had been a widow for five years; and as she'd never had children of her own, a fringe benefit of living here was the feeling of being part of a family. Arnie was like a son to her.

Although autistic, the boy rarely presented her with a problem. He was self-absorbed, quiet, and endearing in his way. She prepared his meals, but otherwise he cared for himself.

He seldom left his room, and he never left the house except when Carson wished to take him with her. Even then he usually went only with reluctance.

Vicky didn't have to worry about him wandering away. When he wandered, it was to internal lands that held more interest for him than did the real world.

Nevertheless, the silence began to seem eerie to her, and an uneasiness crept over her, growing with each pause in her typing.

At last she rose from her desk chair and went to check on Arnie.

Vicky's second-floor room was a pleasant size, but Arnie's quarters—across the hall—were twice as large as hers. A wall had been taken down between two bedrooms to provide him with the space that he required and with a small bath of his own.

His bed and nightstand were jammed in a corner. At the foot of his bed stood a TV with DVD player, on a wheeled stand.

The castle occupied a significant part of the room. Four low tables formed an eight-by-twelve-foot platform on which Arnie had erected a Lego-block wonder that was brilliantly conceived and executed in obsessive detail.

From barbican to curtain wall, to casements, to ramparts, to the keep, to the highest turrets, down to the bailey, through the inner ward, to the barracks and the stables and the blacksmith's shop, the ninety-six-square-foot marvel seemed to be Arnie's defense against a frightening world.

The boy sat now in the wheeled office chair that he occupied when working on the castle or when just staring dreamily at it. To any eye but Arnie's, this Lego structure was complete, but he was not satisfied; he worked on it every day, adding to its majesty and improving its defenses.

Although twelve, Arnie looked younger. He was slender and as pale as a Nordic child at the end of a long dark winter.

He did not look up at Vicky. Eye contact dismayed him, and he seldom liked to be touched.

Yet he had a gentleness about him, a wistfulness, that moved her. And he knew more of the world, and of people, than she had first believed.

One bad day, when Vicky had been missing Arthur, her dead husband, almost more than she could bear, though she had not openly expressed her misery, Arnie had reacted to her state of mind and had spoken without glancing at her. "You're only as lonely as you want to be," he'd said, "and he would never want you to be."

Although she tried to engage the boy in conversation, he said no more.

That day, she had perceived a more mysterious aspect to autism in general and to Arnie's case in particular than she'd previously recognized. His isolation was beyond Vicky's power to heal, yet he had reached out to counsel her in her loneliness.

She'd had affection for the boy before that moment. Thereafter, it grew into love.

Now, watching him at work on the castle, she said, "I always think it's perfect as it is . . . yet you find ways to make it better."

He did not acknowledge her, but she felt sure that he heard.

Leaving him to his work, Vicky returned to the hallway and stood at the head of the stairs, listening to the persistent silence below.

Arnie was where he should be, and safe. Yet the quiet did not feel peaceful, instead felt pregnant, as though some threat were gestating and at the brink of a noisy birth.

Carson had said that she and Michael were on a case that "might come home to us," and had warned Vicky to be security-conscious. As a consequence, she had locked the front and back doors and had left no first-floor windows open.

Although she knew that she had not overlooked a lock or latch, the silence below called to her, cautioned her.

She descended the stairs and toured the living room, Carson's bedroom and bath, the kitchen, checking that all doors and windows were still secure. She found everything as she remembered having left it.

Half-drawn blinds and sheer curtains left the lower floor shadowy. Each time Vicky turned on a lamp to facilitate her inspection, she turned it off behind her when she moved on.

Carson's room was the only part of the downstairs that featured air conditioning. Bolted in place, the window-mounted unit could not be removed without a racket that would betray an intruder long before he could effect entrance. At the moment, the air conditioner waited to be switched on; like similar units in Vicky's and Arnie's rooms, it was used only to facilitate sleep.

With the windows closed, these lower rooms were warm, stuffy. In the kitchen, she opened the top door on the refrigerator, not because she wanted anything in the freezer, but because the icy out-draft, billowing against her face, felt refreshing.

In her second-floor room once more, she found that the hush of the house continued to unnerve her. This seemed like the silence of an ax raised high but not yet swung.

Ridiculous. She was spooking herself. A case of broad-daylight heebie-jeebies.

Vicky switched on her CD player and, because Carson was not home to be bothered, turned the volume up a little louder than she usually did.

The disc was an anthology of hits by different artists. Billy Joel, Rod Stewart, the Knack, Supertramp, the BeeGees, Gloria Gaynor, Cheap Trick.

The music of her youth. Arthur had asked her to marry him. So happy together. Time had no meaning then. They thought they would live forever.

She returned to the letter that she had been composing, and sang along with the CD, her spirits lifted by the music and by memories of happier days, the troubling silence banished.

WITH THE FLOOR OF THE house pressing overhead, surrounded by the smell of bare earth and moist fungus, shrouded in gloom, anyone else might have progressed from claustrophobia to a panicky sense of being buried alive. Randal Six, however, child of Mercy, feels protected, even cozy.

He listens to the woman come downstairs and walk from room to room as though looking for something that she has mislaid. Then she returns to the second floor.

When he hears the music filtering down from high in the house, he knows that his opportunity has come. Under the cover of rock 'n' roll, the noise he makes getting into the O'Connor residence will not be likely to draw attention.

He has thoroughly explored the crawl space, surprised by how adventurous he has become. The farther he goes from the Hands of Mercy both in terms of distance and time, the more his agoraphobia abates and the more he desires to expand his boundaries.

He is blossoming.

In addition to the concrete piers on which the house perches, the crawl space is punctuated by incoming water pipes, by sewer pipes and gray-water drains, by more pipes housing electrical cable. All of these services puncture the floor of the structure.

Even if Randal could disassemble one of those conduits, none of the points of penetration would be large enough to admit him.

He also has found a trapdoor. It measures about three feet square.

The hinges and latch are on the farther side, where he can't reach them. The door most likely opens up and inward.

Near the trap, adjacent to the incoming gas line, flexible ductwork, eight inches in diameter, comes out of the house; it snakes through the crawl space. The farther end of the duct is framed to a cutout in the lattice skirt.

Randal assumes this is either an air intake or a safety vent for a gas-fired heating system.

Judging by the evidence, the trapdoor opens into a furnace room. A repairman could use it to move between the equipment above and the connections under the floor.

In the house overhead, autistic but capable of a dazzling smile, Arnie O'Connor possesses the secret to happiness. Either the boy will relinquish it or Randal Six will tear it out of him.

Lying on his back, Randal draws his knees toward his chest and presses his feet against the trapdoor. In the interest of breaking through with as little noise as possible, he applies pressure in gradually increasing increments. The latch and hinges creak as they strain against their fastenings.

When a particularly boisterous song echoes through the house and as the music swells toward a crescendo, he doubles his efforts, and the trapdoor springs open with a burr of screws ripping wood, a twang of torquing metal.

Happiness will soon be his.

CHAPTER 20

AFTER THE MEETING with Victor, Cindi wanted to go to the mall, but Benny wanted to talk about methods of decapitation.

According to their ID, Cindi and Benny Lovewell were twenty-eight and twenty-nine, respectively, though in fact they had been out of the creation tanks only nineteen months.

They made a cute couple. More accurately, they were made as a cute couple.

Attractive, well-dressed, each of them had a dazzling smile, a musical voice, and an infectious laugh. They were soft-spoken and polite, and they generally established instant rapport with everyone they met.

Cindi and Benny were fabulous dancers, though dancing was not the activity they most enjoyed. Their greatest pleasure came from killing.

Members of the New Race were forbidden to kill except when ordered to do so by their maker. The Lovewells were frequently ordered to do so.

When a member of the Old Race was slated to be replaced by a replicant, Cindi and Benny were the last smiling faces that person would ever see.

Those who were not scheduled to be replaced by pod people but who had somehow become a threat to Victor—or had offended him—were also destined to meet the Lovewells.

Sometimes these encounters began in a jazz club or a tavern. To the target, it seemed that new friends had been found—until later in the evening, when a parting handshake or a good-bye kiss on the cheek evolved, with amazing rapidity, into a violent garroting.

Other victims, on seeing the Lovewells for the first time, had no fair chance to get to know them, had hardly a moment to return their dazzling smiles, before being disemboweled.

On this sweltering summer day, prior to being summoned to the Hands of Mercy, the Lovewells had been bored. Benny could deal well with boredom, but tedium sometimes drove Cindi to reckless action.

After their meeting with Victor, in which they had been ordered to kill Detectives O'Connor and Maddison within twenty-four hours, Benny wanted to begin at once planning the hit. He hoped that the business could be arranged in such a way as to give them an opportunity to dismember alive at least one of the two cops.

Forbidden to kill as they wished, other members of the New Race lived with an envy of the free will with which those of the Old Race led their lives. This envy, more bitter by the day, expressed itself in despair and in a bottled rage that was denied relief.

As skilled assassins, Cindi and Benny *were* permitted relief, and lots of it. He usually could count on Cindi to match the eagerness with which he himself set out on every job.

On this occasion, however, she insisted on going shopping first. When Cindi insisted on something, Benny always let her have what she wanted because she was such a whiner when she didn't get her way that even Benny, with his high tolerance for tedium, lamented that his maker had programmed him to be incapable of suicide.

At the mall, to Benny's dismay, Cindi led him directly to Tots and Tykes, a store selling clothing for infants and young children.

He hoped this wouldn't lead to kidnapping again.

"We shouldn't be seen here," he warned her.

"We won't be. None of our kind works here, and none of our kind would have reason to shop here."

"We don't have a reason, either."

Without answering him, she went into Tots and Tykes.

As Cindi searched through the tiny dresses and other garments on the racks and tables, Benny followed her, trying to gauge whether she was likely to go nuts, as before.

Admiring a little yellow dress with a frilly collar, she said, "Isn't this adorable?"

"Adorable," Benny agreed. "But it would look better in pink."

"They don't seem to have it in pink."

"Too bad. Pink. In pink it would be terrific."

Members of the New Race were encouraged to have sex with one another, in every variation, as often and as violently as they liked. It was their one pressure-release valve.

They were, however, incapable of reproduction. The citizens of this brave new world would all be made in tanks, grown to adulthood and educated by direct-to-brain data downloading in four months.

Currently they were created a hundred at a time. Soon, tank farms would start turning them out by the thousands.

Their maker reserved all biological creation unto himself. He did not believe in families. Family relationships distracted people from the greater work of society as a whole, from achieving total triumph over nature and establishing utopia.

"What will the world be like without children?" Cindi wondered.

"More productive," Benny said.

"Drab," she said.

"More efficient."

"Empty."

Women of the New Race were designed and manufactured without a maternal instinct. They were supposed to have no desire to give birth.

Something was wrong with Cindi. She envied the women of the Old Race for their free will, but she resented them most intensely for their ability to bring children into the world.

Another customer, an expectant mother, entered their aisle.

At first Cindi's face brightened at the sight of the woman's distended belly, but then darkened into a snarl of vicious jealousy.

Taking her arm, steering her toward another part of the store, Benny said, "Control yourself. People will notice. You look like you want to kill her."

"I do."

"Remember what you are."

"Barren," she said bitterly.

"Not that. An assassin. You can't do your work if your face advertises your profession."

"All right. Let go of my arm."

"Calm down. Cool off."

"I'm smiling."

"It's a stiff smile."

She turned on her full dazzling wattage.

"That's better," he said.

Picking up a little pink sweater featuring colorful appliquéd butterflies, displaying it for Benny, Cindi said, "Oh, isn't this darling?"

"Darling," he agreed. "But it would look better in blue."

"I don't see it in blue."

"We really should be getting to work."

"I want to look around here a little longer."

"We've got a job to do," he reminded her.

"And we have twenty-four hours to do it."

"I want to decapitate one of them."

"Of course you do. You always do. And we will. But first I want to find a really sweet little lacy suit or something."

Cindi was defective. She desperately wanted a baby. She was disturbed.

Had Benny been certain that Victor would terminate Cindi and produce Cindi Two, he'd have reported her deviancy months previously. He worried, however, that Victor thought of them as a unit and would terminate Benny, as well.

He didn't want to be switched off and buried in a landfill while Benny Two had all the fun.

If he had been like others of his kind, seething with rage and forbidden to express it in any satisfying fashion, Benny Lovewell would have been happy to be terminated. Termination would have been his only hope of peace.

But he was allowed to kill. He could torture, mutilate, and dismember. Unlike others of the New Race, Benny had something to live for.

"This is *so* cute," said Cindi, fingering a sailor suit sized for a two-year-old.

Benny sighed. "Do you want to buy it?"

"Yes."

At home they had a secret collection of garments for babies and toddlers. If any of the New Race ever discovered Cindi's hoard of children's clothes, she would have a lot of explaining to do.

"Okay," he said. "Buy it quick, before someone sees us, and let's get out of here."

"After we finish with O'Connor and Maddison," she said, "can we go home and try?"

By *try,* she meant "try to have a baby."

They had been created sterile. Cindi had a vagina but no uterus. That reproductive space had been devoted to other organs unique to the New Race.

Sex between them could no more produce a baby than it could produce a grand piano.

Nevertheless, to appease her, to mollify her mood, Benny said, "Sure. We can try."

"We'll kill O'Connor and Maddison," she said, "and cut them up as much as you want, do all those funny things you like to do, and then we'll make a baby."

She was insane, but he had to accept her as she was. If he could have killed her, he would have done it, but he could only kill those he was specifically directed to kill.

"That sounds good," he said.

"We'll be the first of our kind to conceive."

"We'll try."

"I'll be a wonderful mother."

"Let's buy the sailor suit and get out of here."

"Maybe we'll have twins."

CHAPTER 21

ERIKA HAD LUNCH alone in a dining room furnished to seat sixteen, in the presence of three million dollars' worth of art, with a fresh arrangement of calla lilies and anthuriums on the table.

When she had finished, she went into the kitchen, where Christine stood at the sink, washing the breakfast dishes.

All food in this house was served on one pattern of Limoges or another, and Victor would not permit such fine china to be put in the dishwasher. All beverages were served in either Lalique or Waterford crystal, which also required hand washing.

If a dish sustained a scratch or if a glass was chipped, it must be discarded. Victor did not tolerate imperfection.

While certain machines were necessary and even beneficial, most of those invented to take the place of household servants were viewed by Victor with scorn. His standards of personal service had been formed in another century, when the lower classes had known how to attend, properly, the needs of their betters.

"Christine?"

"Yes, Mrs. Helios?"

"Don't worry. I'm not going to discuss my sexual problems with you."

"Very good, Mrs. Helios."

"But I'm curious about a few things."

"I'm sure you are, ma'am. Everything is new to you."

"Why was William biting off his fingers?"

"No one can really know but William himself."

"But it wasn't rational," Erika persisted.

"Yes, I had noticed that."

"And being one of the New Race, he is rational in all things."

"That's the concept," Christine said, but with an odd inflection that Erika couldn't interpret.

"He knew his fingers wouldn't grow back," Erika said. "It's as if he was . . . committing suicide, bite by bite, but we're not capable of self-destruction."

Swirling a wet fabric whisk inside an exquisite porcelain teapot, Christine said, "He wouldn't have died from ten severed fingers, Mrs. Helios."

"Yes, but without fingers, he wouldn't have been able to serve as butler. He must have known he would be terminated."

"In the condition you saw him, Mrs. Helios, William did not have the capacity to be cunning."

Besides, as they both knew, the proscription against suicide included the inability to engineer circumstances that required their termination.

"Do you mean . . . William was having like a mental breakdown?" The thought chilled Erika. "Surely that isn't possible."

"Mr. Helios prefers the term *interruption of function*. William was experiencing an interruption of function."

"That sounds much less serious."

"It does, doesn't it?"

"But Victor did terminate him."

"He did, didn't he?"

Erika said, "If one of the Old Race had done such a thing, we'd say that he'd gone mad. Insane."

"Yes, but we're in all ways superior to them, and so many terms applicable to them cannot describe us. We require a whole new grammar of psychology."

Again, Christine's words were spoken with a curious inflection, suggesting that she meant something more than what she said.

"I . . . I don't understand," Erika said.

"You will. When you've been alive long enough."

Still struggling to comprehend, she said, "When you called my husband to report that William was biting off his fingers, you said, 'We've got another Margaret.' What did you mean by that?"

Rinsing a plate, carefully placing it in the drying rack, Christine said, "Until a few weeks ago, Margaret served as the household chef. She'd been here almost twenty years, like William. After an . . . episode . . . she had to be removed. A new Margaret is being prepared."

"What episode?"

"One morning as she was about to make pancakes, she began to smash her face into the hot, greased griddle."

"Smash her face?"

"Over and over again, rhythmically. Each time she raised her face from the griddle, Margaret said *time*, and before she slammed it down again, she repeated that word. *Time, time, time, time, time*—with much the same urgency that you heard William say *tick, tock, tick, tock*."

"How mystifying," said Erika.

"It won't be . . . when you've lived long enough."

Frustrated, Erika said, "Speak plainly to me, Christine."

"Plainly, Mrs. Helios?"

"So I'm fresh out of the tank and hopelessly naive—so *educate* me. All right? Help me understand."

"But you've had direct-to-brain data downloading. What more could you need?"

"*Christine,* I'm not your enemy."

Turning away from the sink, blotting her hands on a dish towel, Christine said, "I know you're not, Mrs. Helios. And you're not my friend, either. Friendship is akin to love, and love is dangerous. Love distracts the worker from maximum accomplishment, just as does hate. None of the New Race is a friend or enemy of the other."

"I . . . I don't have that attitude in my program."

"It's not in the program, Mrs. Helios. It's the *natural result* of the program. We are all workers of identical value. Workers in a great cause, subduing all of nature, building the perfect society, utopia—then onward to the stars. Our value isn't in individual accomplishments, but in our accomplishments as a society. Isn't that correct?"

"Is it?"

"Unlike us, Mrs. Helios, you have been allowed humility, and shame, because our maker likes those qualities in a wife."

Erika sensed a revelation coming from which she wished to turn away. But she, not Christine, had insisted on opening this door.

"Emotions are funny things, Mrs. Helios. Maybe it's better, after all, to be limited to only envy and anger and fear and hate—because those feelings are circular. They turn endlessly back on themselves, like a snake swallowing its tail. They lead to nothing else, and they keep the mind from hope, which is essential when hope will never be fulfilled."

Shaken by the bleakness in Christine's voice and in her eyes, Erika was overcome with sympathy for the housekeeper. She put a hand consolingly on the woman's shoulder.

"But humility and shame," Christine continued, "can grow into pity, whether he wants you to feel pity or not. Pity to compassion. Compassion to regret. And so much else. You will be able to feel more than we feel, Mrs. Helios. You will learn to hope."

A heaviness came into Erika's heart, an oppressive weight, but she could not yet grasp its nature.

"Being able to hope—that will be terrible for you, Mrs. Helios, because your destiny is fundamentally the same as ours. You have no free will. Your hope will never be realized."

"But William . . . How does this explain William?"

"Time, Mrs. Helios. Time, time, tick, tock, tick, tock. These disease-resistant, amazing bodies we possess—how long have we been told they will last?"

"Perhaps a thousand years," Erika said, for that was the figure in the self-awareness package of her downloaded education.

Christine shook her head. "Hopelessness can be endured . . . but not for a thousand years. For William, for Margaret—twenty years. And then they experienced an . . . interruption of function."

The housekeeper's hard shoulder had not softened under her mistress's touch. Erika withdrew her hand.

"But when you *have* the capacity for hope, Mrs. Helios, yet know beyond all doubt that it will never be fulfilled, I don't think you can make even twenty years. I don't think you can make five."

Erika swept the kitchen with her gaze. She looked at the soapy water in the sink. At the dishes in the drying rack. At Christine's hands. At last, she met Christine's eyes again.

She said, "I'm so sorry for you."

"I know," Christine said. "But I feel nothing whatsoever for you, Mrs. Helios. And neither will any of the others. Which means you are . . . uniquely alone."

CHAPTER 22

THE OTHER ELLA, a restaurant and bar in the neighborhood known as Faubourg Marigny, an area now as funky and soulful as the French Quarter had once been, was owned and operated by a woman named Ella Fitzgerald. She was not the famous singer. She was a former hooker and madam who had wisely saved and invested the wages of the flesh.

As Aubrey Picou had instructed, Carson and Michael asked the bartender to see Godot.

An elderly woman put down the beer she was nursing, swiveled on her barstool, and took their picture with her cell phone.

Annoyed, Carson said, "Hey, Granny, I'm not a tourist site."

"Screw you," the woman said. "If I knew for sure a tour carriage was nearby, I'd run you into the street and shove your head up a mule's ass."

"You want to see Godot," the bartender explained, "you go through Francine here."

"You mean less to me," the old woman assured Carson, "than the dinner I vomited up last night."

As she transmitted the picture to someone, Francine grinned at Michael. She had borrowed her teeth from the Swamp Thing.

"Carson, remember when you looked in the mirror this morning and didn't like what you saw?"

She said, "Suddenly I feel pretty."

"All my life," Francine told Carson, "I've known perky-tit types like you, and not one of you bitches ever had a brain bigger than a chickpea."

"Well, there you're woefully wrong," Michael told her. "On a bet, my friend had an MRI scan of her brain, and it's as big as a walnut."

Francine gave him another broken yellow smile. "You're a real cutie. I could just eat you up."

"I'm flattered," he said.

"Remember what happened to her dinner last night," Carson reminded him.

Francine put down her cell phone. From the bar, she picked up a BlackBerry, on which she was receiving a text message, evidently in response to the photo.

Michael said, "You're a total telecom babe, Francine, fully swimming in the info stream."

"You've got a nice tight butt," Francine said. She put down the BlackBerry, swiveled off her stool, and said, "Come with me, cutie. You too, bitch."

Michael followed the old woman, glanced back at Carson, and said, "Come on, bitch, this'll be fun."

CHAPTER 23

TO ASSIST WITH the tracking and the eventual efficient execution of Detectives O'Connor and Maddison, one of Victor's people—Dooley Snopes—had fixed a magnetic-hold transponder to the engine block of their department sedan, tapping the battery cable for power, while the car was parked in front of O'Connor's house, and while she had slept unaware through the summer morning.

Dooley had not been programmed as an assassin, though he wished that he had been. Instead, he was basically a sneak with a lot of technical knowledge.

Cindi Lovewell drove past Dooley, who was sitting in his parked PT Cruiser in Faubourg Marigny. The Lovewells had been issued an SUV—a Mercury Mountaineer with darkly tinted side and rear windows—which facilitated the discreet transport of dead bodies.

Cindi liked the vehicle not only because it had a lot of power and handled well but also because it had plenty of room for the children she yearned to produce.

When they had to drive to Crosswoods Waste Management north of Lake Pontchartrain with a couple of corpses, how much nicer the trip would be if it were a *family* adventure. They could stop along the way for a picnic.

In the front passenger's seat, studying the red dot that blinked near the center of the street map on the screen of their satellite-navigation system, Benny said, "The cops should be parked about"—he surveyed the curbed vehicles past which they drifted, and glanced at the screen—"right *here*."

Cindi rolled slowly past an unmarked sedan, cheap iron that had seen a lot of use. Victor's people were always better equipped than the so-called authorities.

She parked at a red curb near the end of the block. Benny's driver's license was in the name of Dr. Benjamin Lovewell, and the Mountaineer had MD plates. From the console box, he took a card that read PHYSICIAN ON CALL, and hung it from the rearview mirror.

Tailing a target, professional killers need to be able to park as conveniently as possible. And when police see a speeding vehicle with MD plates, they often assume that the driver is rushing to a hospital.

Victor disliked his funds being spent on parking tickets and traffic fines.

By the time they walked past the sedan to the PT Cruiser, Dooley had gotten out of his car to meet them. If he'd been a dog, he would have been a whippet: lean, long-legged, with a pointy face.

"They went into The Other Ella," Dooley said, pointing to a restaurant across the street. "Not even five minutes ago. Did you kill anybody yet today?"

"Not yet," Benny said.

"Did you kill anybody yesterday?"

"Three days ago," Cindi said.

"How many?"

"Three," Benny said. "Their replicants were ready."

Dooley's eyes were dark with envy. "I wish I could kill some of them. I'd like to kill *all* of them."

"It's not your job," Benny said.

"Yet," Cindi said, meaning that the day would come when the New Race would have achieved sufficient numbers to bring their war into the open, whereupon the greatest slaughter in human history would mark the swift extinction of the Old Race.

"Everything is so much harder," Dooley said, "when we have to watch them all around us, watch them leading their lives any way they want, any way they please."

A young couple walked past, shepherding their two tow-headed children, one boy and one girl.

Cindi turned to watch them. She wanted to kill the parents right now, right here on the sidewalk, and take the children.

"Easy," Benny said.

"Don't worry. There's not going to be another incident," Cindi assured him.

"That's good."

"What incident?" Dooley asked.

Instead of answering him, Benny said, "You can go. We can handle it from here."

CHAPTER 24

OCCASIONALLY SMACKING her lips over her broken yellow teeth, Francine led Carson and Michael through the restaurant, across a busy kitchen, into a storeroom, and up a set of steep stairs.

At the top were a deep landing and a blue door. Francine pressed a bell push beside the door, but there was no audible ring.

"Don't give it away for free," Francine advised Michael. "Lots of ladies would be happy to keep you in style."

She glanced at Carson and snorted with disapproval.

"And stay away from this one," Francine told Michael. "She'll freeze your cojones off as sure as if you dipped them in liquid nitrogen."

Then she left them on the landing and started unsteadily down the stairs.

"You could push her," he told Carson, "but it would be wrong."

"Actually," Carson said, "if Lulana were here, even she'd agree, Jesus would be all right with it."

The blue door was opened by a *Star Wars* kind of guy: as squat as R2-D2, as bald as Yoda, and as ugly as Jabba the Hutt.

"You been truly blood-sworn by Aubrey," he said, "so I ain't goin' to take away dem kill-boys you carryin' under your left arms, nor neither dat snub-nose you got snuggled on a belt clip just above your ass, missy."

"And good afternoon to you, too," Michael said.

"You follow me like baby ducks their mama, 'cause you make the wrongest move, you be six ways dead."

The room beyond the blue door was furnished with only a pair of straight-backed chairs.

A shaved gorilla in black pants, suspenders, a white chambray shirt, and a porkpie hat sat in one of the chairs. On the floor next to his chair was a tented paperback—a Harry Potter novel—that he had evidently set aside when Francine had pressed the bell push.

Across his thighs lay a semi-auto 12-gauge, on which both his hands rested in the business position. He wasn't aiming the shotgun at them, but he would be able to blow their guts out before their pistols cleared their holsters, and blast off their faces as an afterthought even before their bodies hit the floor.

Baby-duck walking, Carson and Michael obediently followed their squat leader through another door into a room with a cracked yellow linoleum floor, blue beadboard wainscoting, gray walls, and two poker tables.

Around the nearest table sat three men, one woman, and an Asian transvestite.

This sounded like the opening to a pretty good joke, but Michael couldn't think of a punch line.

Two of the players were drinking Coke, two had cans of Dr Pepper, and at the transvestite's place stood a cordial glass and a bottle of anisette.

None of the poker players seemed to have the slightest interest in Carson and Michael. Neither the woman nor the transvestite winked at him.

In the middle of the table were stacks of poker chips. If the greens were fifties and the blacks were hundreds, there was perhaps eighty thousand dollars riding on this hand.

Another shaved gorilla stood by a window. He carried his piece in a paddle holster at his hip, and he kept his hand on it as Carson and Michael passed through his duty station.

A third door led to a shabby conference room that smelled like lung cancer. Twelve chairs stood around a scarred table on which were fourteen ashtrays.

At the head of the table sat a man with a merry face, lively blue eyes, and a mustache. His Justin Wilson hat rested on the tops of his jughandle ears.

He rose as they approached, revealing that he wore his pants above his waistline, between his navel and his breasts.

Their mama duck said, "Mr. Godot, though they smells like da worst kind of righteous, these here be da ones what were vouched by Aubrey, so don't bust my stones if'n you got to gaff 'em like catfish 'fore dis be finished."

To the right of the man with jug ears and slightly behind him stood Big Foot in a seersucker suit. He made the previous gorillas look like mere chimps.

Big Foot looked as if he would not only kill them but eat them at the smallest provocation.

Godot, on the other hand, was hospitable. He held out his right hand and said, "Any friend to Aubrey, he a friend to me, 'specially when he come with cash money."

Shaking the offered hand, Michael said, "I expected we'd have to wait for you, Mr. Godot, not the other way around. I hope we're not late."

"Right on da minute," Godot assured him. "And who might be dis charmin' eyeful?"

"This charmin' eyeful," Carson said, "is the one with the cash money."

"You done just got even prettier," Godot told her.

As Carson withdrew two fat rolls of hundred-dollar bills from her jacket pockets, Godot picked up one of two suitcases from the floor beside his chair and put it on the table.

Big Foot kept both hands free.

Godot opened the case, revealing two Urban Sniper shotguns with sidesaddle shell carriers and three-way slings. The barrels had been cut down to fourteen inches. With the guns were four boxes of shells, slugs not buckshot, which was the only thing the Sniper fired.

Carson said, "You are a formidable resource, Mr. Godot."

"Mama so wanted a preacher son, and Daddy, rest his soul, he set on me bein' a welder like hisself, but I most truly rebelled against bein' a poor Cajun, so I done found my bliss, and here I is."

The second suitcase was smaller than the first. It contained two Desert Eagles in .50 Magnum with titanium gold finish. Packed beside the guns were the boxes of ammunition as requested and two spare magazines for each weapon.

"You for sure ready for what recoil dat monster pays you back?" Godot asked.

Wary of the big pistols, Michael said, "No, sir, I pretty much expect it to knock me on my ass."

Amused, Godot said, "My concern be dis lady here, son, not your strappin' self."

"The Eagle has a smooth action," Carson said, "less kick than you'd think. It slams back hard, sure, but so do I. From thirty feet, I could put all nine rounds in the magazine between your groin and your throat, not one higher, not one wide."

This statement brought Big Foot forward, glowering.

"Rest yourself," Godot told his bodyguard. "She done made no threat. Dat just braggin'."

Closing the suitcase that contained the pistols, Carson said, "Are you going to count your money?"

"You da most tough I seen in a while, but you also gots some saint in you. I'd be so bad surprised did it turn out you thieved me even some littlest bit."

Carson couldn't suppress a smile. "Every dollar's there."

"Mr. Godot," Michael said, "it's been comfortable doing business with you, knowing we're dealing with real human beings."

"Dat's most cordial of you to say," Godot replied, "most cordial, and it sounds true from da heart."

"It is," Michael said. "It really is."

CHAPTER 25

RANDAL SIX STANDS in the furnace closet on the ground floor, listening to Billy Joel singing in an upper room.

The closet measures approximately six by seven feet. Even the dim blue glow of the gas pilot flame and the weak light seeping under the door give him enough illumination to assess this space.

At long last he is in the house of the smiling autistic, Arnie O'Connor. The secret of happiness lies within his grasp.

He waits here in the cozy gloom as one song changes to another, and to another. He is enjoying his triumph. He is acclimating himself to this new environment. He is planning his next step.

He is also afraid. Randal Six has never been in a house before. Until the night before last, he lived exclusively in the Hands of Mercy. Between there and here, he spent a day hiding in a Dumpster; but a Dumpster is not the same as a house.

Beyond this closet door waits a place as alien to him as would be any planet in another galaxy.

He likes the familiar. He fears the new. He dislikes change.

Once he opens this door and steps across this threshold, all before him will be new and strange. Everything will be different forever.

Trembling in the dark, Randal half believes that his billet at Mercy and even the torturous experiments to which Father subjected him might be preferable to what lies ahead.

Nevertheless, after three more songs, he opens the door and stares into the space beyond, his two hearts hammering.

Sunshine at a frosted window sheds light over two machines that he recognizes from magazine ads and Internet research. One machine washes clothes. The other dries them.

He smells bleach and detergent behind the closed cabinet doors above the machines.

Before him lies a laundry room. A *laundry* room. At this moment, he can think of nothing that could more poignantly suggest the sweet ordinariness of daily life than a laundry room.

More than anything, Randal Six wants an ordinary life. He does not want to be—and cannot be—one of the Old Race, but he wants to live as they do, without ceaseless torment, with his small share of happiness.

The experience of the laundry room is enough progress for one day. He quietly pulls shut the door and stands in the dark furnace closet, pleased with himself.

He relives the delicious moment when he first glimpsed the baked-enamel surfaces of the washer and dryer, and the big plastic clothes basket with what might have been several dirty rumpled garments in it.

The laundry room had a vinyl-tile floor, just as did all the hallways and most of the rooms at the Hands of Mercy. He hadn't expected vinyl tile. He had thought that *everything* would be wildly different from what he had known.

The vinyl tiles in Mercy are gray with speckles of green and rose. In the laundry room they are yellow. These two styles of flooring are at once different yet the same.

While the music from high in the house changes a few times, Randal gradually grows embarrassed by his timidity. Peering through a door into the O'Connors' laundry is not, after all, a heroic accomplishment.

He is deluding himself. He is succumbing to his agoraphobia, to his autistic desire to minimize sensory input.

If he proceeds at this agonizing pace, he will need six months to make his way through the house and find Arnie.

He can't live under the structure, in the crawl space, for such an extended time. For one thing, he is hungry. His superlative body is a machine in need of much fuel.

Randal doesn't mind eating what spiders, rodents, earthworms, and snakes that he might find under the house. However, judging by the creatures he has encountered thus far during his hours in the crawl space, that shadowy realm doesn't contain even a small fraction of the game he needs to sustain himself.

He opens the door again.

The wonderful laundry room. Waiting.

He steps out of the furnace closet and gently closes the door behind him. Thrilled beyond words.

He has never walked on yellow-vinyl tiles before. They work the same as gray-vinyl tiles. The soles of his shoes make the faintest squeaking sounds.

A door stands open between the laundry room and the kitchen.

Randal Six halts at this new threshold, marveling. A kitchen is everything—more!—that he thought it would be, a place of numerous conveniences and overwhelming charm.

He could easily become inebriated with ambience. He must remain sober and cautious, prepared to retreat if he should hear someone approaching.

Until he can locate Arnie and wrench from him the secret of happiness, Randal wants to avoid coming face to face with anyone. He isn't sure what would happen in such an encounter, but he feels certain that the consequences would not be pleasant.

Although he was engineered to be autistic for the purposes of Father's experiments, which makes him different from others of the New Race, he shares much of their programming. He is incapable of suicide, for instance.

He isn't permitted to kill except when instructed by his maker to do so. Or in self-defense.

The problem is that Randal is terribly fearful in his autism. He feels easily threatened.

Hiding in the Dumpster, he had killed a homeless man who had come searching for soft-drink cans and other small treasures.

The hobo might not have meant him any harm, might not in fact have been *capable* of causing him harm, yet Randal had dragged him headfirst into the Dumpster, had snapped his neck, and had buried him under bags of trash.

Considering that mere newness frightens him, that the smallest change fills him with trepidation, any encounter with a stranger is more likely than not to result in a violent act of self-defense. He has no moral concern about this. They are of the Old Race and must all die sooner or later, anyway.

The problem is that snapping the spine of a hobo in a deserted alleyway is not likely to draw attention; but killing someone in this house will be a noisy affair certain to reveal his presence to other residents and possibly even to neighbors.

Nevertheless, because he is hungry and because the refrigerator no doubt contains something tastier than spiders and earthworms, he steps out of the laundry room and into the kitchen.

CHAPTER 26

EACH CARRYING A SUITCASE full of weapons, Carson and Michael left The Other Ella.

As the daughter of a detective who had supposedly gone bad, Carson believed that she was under closer scrutiny by her fellow officers than was the average cop. She understood it, resented it—and was self-aware enough to realize that she might be imagining it.

Fresh from consorting with the likes of foul-mouthed Francine and courtly Godot, crossing the sidewalk toward the unmarked sedan, Carson surveyed the street, half convinced that the Internal Affairs Division, having staked out the scene, would at any moment break cover and make arrests.

Every pedestrian appeared to take an interest in Carson and Michael, to glance with suspicion at the bags they carried. Two men and a woman across the street seemed to stare with special intensity.

Why would anyone walk out of a restaurant with suitcases? Nobody bought takeout in that volume.

They put the bags in the trunk of the sedan, and Carson drove out of Faubourg Marigny, into the Quarter, without being arrested.

"What now?" Michael wondered.

"We cruise."

"Cool."

"We think it through."

"Think what through?"

"The color of love, the sound of one hand clapping. What do you *think* we have to think through?"

"I'm not in a mood to think," he said. "Thinking's going to get us killed."

"How do we get at Victor Frankenstein?"

"Helios."

"Helios, Frankenstein—it's still the same Victor. How do we get at the Victor?"

Michael said, "Maybe I'm superstitious, but I wish the Victor had a different first name."

"Why?"

"A victor is someone who defeats his adversary. *Victor* means 'winner.'"

"Remember that guy we busted last year for the double homicide in the antique shop on Royal?"

"Sure. He had a third testicle."

"What the hell does that have to do with anything?" she asked impatiently. "We didn't know that till he'd been arrested, charged, and had his jailhouse physical."

"It doesn't have anything to do with anything," he admitted. "It's just one of those details that stick in your mind."

"My point is, the guy's name was Champ Champion, but he was a loser anyway."

"His real name was Shirley Champion, which explains everything."

"He'd had his name legally changed to Champ Champion."

"Cary Grant was born Archie Leach. The only name that matters is the born name."

"I'll pull to the curb, you roll down your window and ask any pedestrian you want, have they seen an Archie Leach movie. See how much born names matter."

"Marilyn Monroe—she was really Norma Jean Mortenson," he said, "which is why she ended up dead young of an overdose."

"Is this one of those times you're going to be impossible?"

"I know that's usually your job," he said. "What about Joan Crawford? She was born Lucille Le Sueur, which explains why she beat her children with wire coat hangers."

"Cary Grant never beat anyone with coat hangers, and he had a fabulous life."

"Yeah, but he was the greatest actor in the history of film. The rules don't apply to him. Victor and Frankenstein are two *power* names if I ever heard them, and he was born with them. No matter what you say, I'd feel more comfortable if his mother had named him Nancy."

"WHAT ARE THEY *DOING?*" Cindi asked impatiently, glancing again at the street map on the dashboard screen.

Benny had been studying the screen continuously as Cindi drove. He said, "At the end of every block, she makes another turn, back and forth, zig-zag, around and around, like a blind rat in a maze."

"Maybe they know they're being tailed."

"They can't know," he said. "They can't see us."

Being able to track the sedan by the continuous signal of the transponder that Dooley had secreted under its hood, the Lovewells didn't need to maintain visual contact. They could conduct a most leisurely pursuit from a distance of several blocks and even follow the detectives on parallel streets.

"I know how she feels," Cindi said.

"What do you mean?"

"Like a blind rat in a maze."

"I didn't say that's how she feels. I don't know how she feels. I said that's how she's driving."

"Most of the time," Cindi said, "I feel like a blind rat in a maze. And she's childless like me."

"Who?"

"Detective O'Connor. She's old enough to have had half a dozen children, at least, but she doesn't have any. She's barren."

"You can't know that she's barren."

"I know."

"Maybe she just doesn't want kids."

"She's a woman. She wants."

"She just turned again, left this time."

"See?"

"See what?"

"She's barren."

"She's barren just because she made a left turn?"

Solemnly, Cindi said, "Like a blind rat in a maze."

CARSON TURNED RIGHT ON Chartres Street, past the exquisitely decaying Napoleon House.

"Taking Victor down at Biovision is out of the question," she said. "Too many people, too many witnesses, probably not all of them people he's made."

"We could hit him in his car, coming or going."

"On a public street? If we can manage not to die while doing this, I don't want to end up in women's prison with all your former girlfriends."

"We learn his routine," Michael said, "and we find the least public place along the route."

"We don't have time to learn his routine," she reminded him. "We're a target *now*. We both know it."

"The secret lab we talked about earlier. The place where he . . . creates."

"We don't have time to find that, either. Besides, it'll have better security than Fort Knox."

"Fort Knox's security is probably overrated. The bad guys had it figured in *Goldfinger*."

"We're not bad guys," she said, "and this isn't a movie. The best place to get him is at his house."

"It's a mansion. It's got a big staff."

"We'll have to cut through them, straight to him, go in hard and fast," she said.

"We're not SWAT."

"We're not just parking patrol, either."

"What if some of his household staff is our kind?" Michael worried.

"None of them will be. He wouldn't want our kind serving in his home, where they might see or overhear something. They'll all be part of the New Race."

"We can't be a hundred percent sure."

On Decatur Street at Jackson Square, where carriages lined up to offer tours of the Quarter, one of the usually placid mules had broken away from the curb. The driver and a policeman were giving chase on foot as the mule pulled its fancy equipage in circles, blocking traffic.

"Maybe old Francine shoved someone up its butt," Michael suggested.

Staying on point, Carson said, "So we've got to nail Victor at his house in the Garden District."

"Maybe it would make more sense to pull out of New Orleans. We could go somewhere he couldn't find us, take more time to think this through."

"Yeah. Take the pressure off. Give ourselves a week to really *think*. Maybe two weeks. Maybe we'd *never* come back."

"Would that be so bad?" he asked.

"'The only thing necessary for the triumph of evil'—"

"—'is for good men to do nothing.' Yeah. I heard already."

"Who said that, anyway?" she wondered.

"I think it was Tigger, but it might have been Pooh."

The carriage driver snared the bridle. The mule became calm and allowed itself to be walked back to the curb. The snarled traffic began to move.

Carson said, "He knows we're on to him. Even if we leave the city, he won't stop until he finds us, Michael. We'd always be on the run."

"Sounds romantic," he said wistfully.

"Don't go there," she warned him. "Aubrey's rose garden wasn't the place for it, and this is worse."

"Will there ever be a place for it?"

She drove in silence for a minute, turned right at the next corner, and then said, "Maybe. But only if we can bring down Helios before his people rip our guts out and pitch us in the Mississippi."

"You really know how to encourage a guy."

"Now shut up about it. Just shut up. If we go all gooey over each other, we'll lose focus. If we lose focus, we're dead."

"Too bad the rest of the world never gets to see this tender side of you."

"I'm serious, Michael. I don't want to talk about me and you. I don't even want to joke about it. We've got a war to win."

"All right. Okay. I hear you. I'll stifle myself." He sighed. "Champ Champion has three testicles, and pretty soon I'm not going to have any, they'll just wither away."

"Michael," she said warningly.

He sighed again and said no more.

A couple of blocks later, she glanced sideways at him. He looked adorable. He knew it, too.

Stifling herself, she said, "We've got to find someplace private to have a look at the new guns, load them and the spare magazines."

"City Park," he suggested. "Take that service road to where we found the dead accountant two years ago."

"The naked guy who was strangled with the Mardi Gras beads."

"No, no. He was an architect. I'm talking about the guy in the cowboy outfit."

"Oh, yeah, the black-leather cowboy suit."

"It was midnight blue," Michael corrected.

"If you say so. You're more fashion conscious than I am. The body was pretty close to the service road."

"I don't mean where we found the body," Michael said. "I mean where we found his head."

"You walk through a little stand of Southern pines."

"And then some live oaks."

"And then there's open grass. I remember. That's a nice place."

"It's very nice," Michael agreed, "and it's not close to any of the jogging paths. We'll have privacy."

"The killer certainly had privacy."

"He certainly did," Michael said.

"How long did it take us to get him—four weeks?"

"A little over five."

"That was a hell of a trick shot you got him with," Carson said. "Ricocheted right off the blade of his ax."

"I didn't much appreciate being in the splatter zone."

"Was the dry cleaner able to get out the brain stains?"

"When I told him what it was, he didn't even want to try. And that was a new jacket."

"Not my fault. That kind of ricochet is God's work."

Carson relaxed. This was better. None of that distracting, nervous-making romance talk.

CHAPTER 27

IN THE STAINLESS-STEEL and white-ceramic-tile dissection room, when Victor examined the carcass of Detective Jonathan Harker, he found that approximately fifty pounds of the body's substance was missing.

A raggedly torn umbilical cord trailed from the void in the torso. Considered with the exploded abdomen and shattered rib cage, this suggested that some unintended life form—call it a parasite—had formed within Harker, had achieved a state in which it could live independently of its host, and had broken free, destroying Harker in the process.

This was a disturbing development.

Ripley, who operated the handheld video recorder with which a visual record of all autopsies were made, was clearly rattled by the implications of this discovery.

"Mr. Helios, sir, he gave birth."

"I wouldn't call it giving birth," Victor said with undisguised annoyance.

"We're not capable of reproduction," Ripley said. His voice and manner suggested that, to him, the thought of another life coming forth from Harker was the equivalent of blasphemy.

"It's not reproduction," Victor said. "It's a malignancy."

"But sir . . . a self-sustaining, mobile malignancy?"

"I mean to say a *mutation*," Victor explained impatiently.

In the tank, Ripley had received a deep education in Old Race and New Race physiology. He should have been able to understand these biological nuances.

"A parasitical second self developed spontaneously from Harker's flesh," Victor said, "and when it could live independently of him, it . . . separated."

Ripley stopped filming and stood slack-jawed with amazement, pale with trepidation. He had bushy eyebrows that gave him a look of comic astonishment.

Victor could not remember why he had decided to design Ripley with those shaggy eyebrows. They were absurd.

"Mr. Helios, sir, I beg your indulgence, but are you saying that this is what you intended, for a second self to mutate out of Harker? Sir, to what purpose?"

"No, Ripley, of course it's not what I intended. There's a useful saying of the Old Race—'Shit happens.'"

"But sir, forgive me, you are the designer of our flesh, the maker, the master. How can there be anything about our flesh that you do not understand . . . or foresee?"

Worse than the comic expression that the eyebrows gave Ripley was the fact that they facilitated an exaggerated look of reproach.

Victor did not like to be reproached. "Science proceeds in great leaps, but also sometimes takes a couple of small steps backward."

"Backward?" Having been properly indoctrinated while in the tank, Ripley sometimes had difficulty squaring his expectations with real life. "Science in general, sir, yes, it sometimes missteps. But not you. Not you, and not the New Race."

"The important thing to keep in mind is that the leaps forward are much greater than the steps backward, and more numerous."

"But this is a very big step backward. Sir. I mean, isn't it? Our flesh . . . out of control?"

"Your flesh isn't out of control, Ripley. Where did you get this melodramatic streak? You're embarrassing yourself."

"I'm sorry, sir. I'm sure I don't understand. I'm sure when I've had time to consider, I'll share your equanimity on the matter."

"Harker isn't a sign of things to come. He's an anomaly. He's a singularity. There will be no more mutations like him."

Perhaps the parasite had not merely fed on Harker's innards but had incorporated his two hearts into itself, as well as his lungs and various other internal organs, at first sharing them and then taking them for its own. These things were missing from the cadaver.

According to Jack Rogers—the real medical examiner, now dead and replaced by a replicant—Detectives O'Connor and Maddison claimed that a trollish creature had come out of Harker, as if shedding a cocoon. They had seen it drop out of sight through a manhole, into a storm drain.

By the time that he finished with Harker and took tissue samples for later study, Victor had fallen into a bad mood.

As they bagged Harker's remains and set them aside for shipment to Crosswoods, Ripley asked, "Where is Harker's second self now, Mr. Helios?"

"It fled into a storm drain. It's dead."

"How do you know it's dead?"

"I *know*," Victor said sharply.

They turned next to William, the butler, who waited on a second autopsy table.

Although he believed that William's finger-chewing episode had been triggered solely by psychological collapse, Victor nevertheless opened the butler's torso and inventoried his organs, just to make certain that no second self had begun to form. He found no evidence of mutation.

With a bone saw of Victor's design, one with a diamond blade sharp enough to grind through the dense bone of any New Man, they trepanned William's skull. They removed his brain and put it in preservative solution in a Tupperware container for later sectioning and study.

William's fate clearly did not alarm Ripley as did Harker's. He had seen this sort of thing before.

Victor brought to life a perfect being with a perfect mind, but contact with the Old Race, immersion in their sick society, sometimes corrupted the tank-born.

This would continue to be an occasional problem until the Old Race was eradicated and with it the social order and pre-Darwinian morality that it had created. Thereafter, following the Last War, without the paradigm of the Old Race to confuse and seduce them, Victor's people would always and forever exist in perfect mental health, every last one of them.

When they were finished with William, Ripley said, "Mr. Helios, sir, I'm sorry, but I can't stop wondering, can't stop thinking—is it possible that what happened to Harker could happen to me?"

"No. I told you, he was a singularity."

"But, sir, I beg your pardon if this sounds impertinent . . . however, if you didn't expect it to happen the first time, how can you be sure it won't happen again?"

Stripping off his latex surgical gloves, Victor said, "Damn it, Ripley, stop that with your eyebrows."

"My eyebrows, sir?"

"You know what I mean. Clean up here."

"Sir, is it possible that Harker's consciousness, the essence of his mind, somehow transferred to his second self?"

Taking off the surgical gown that he wore over his clothes, moving toward the door of the dissection room, Victor said, "No. It was a parasitical mutation, most likely with nothing but a crude animal awareness."

"But, sir, if the trollish thing isn't a thing, after all, sir, if it's actually Harker himself, and now he's living in the storm drains, then he's free."

The word *free* halted Victor. He turned to stare at Ripley.

When Ripley realized his error, fear brought his eyebrows down from their absurdly lofty heights and beetled them on the cliff of his brow. "I don't mean to suggest that what happened to Harker could be in any way desirable."

"Don't you, Ripley?"

"No, sir. I don't. It's a horror, what happened to him."

Victor stared at him. Ripley dared not say another word.

After a long mutual silence, Victor said, "In addition to your eyebrows, Ripley, you're far too excitable. Annoyingly so."

CHAPTER 28

MOVING HESITANTLY through the kitchen in a state of awe, Randal Six imagines that this must be what a devout monk feels when in a temple, at a consecrated altar.

For the first time in his life, Randal is in a home. Mercy had been where he was billeted, but it had never been a home. It had been only a place. He'd had no emotion vested in it.

To the Old Race, home is the center of existence. Home is the first refuge from—and last defense against—the disappointments and the terrors of life.

The heart of the home is the kitchen. He knows this to be true because he has read it in a magazine about home decor and in another magazine about cooking light.

In addition, Martha Stewart has said this is true, and Martha Stewart is, by acclamation of the Old Race, the ultimate authority on such matters.

During social evenings, close friends and neighbors frequently gravitate to the kitchen. Some of a family's happiest memories are of moments together in the kitchen. According to Old Race philosophers, nothin' says lovin' like somethin' from the oven, and the oven is in the kitchen.

The blinds are half drawn. The late-afternoon sunshine that reaches the windows has first been filtered by oak trees. Yet Randal can see well enough to explore the room.

Quietly he opens cabinets, discovering dishes, cups, saucers, drinking glasses. In drawers he finds folded dish towels, flatware, knives, and a bewildering collection of utensils and culinary gadgets.

Usually, too many new sights, too many unfamiliar objects, will throw Randal into a panic attack. He is often forced to withdraw to a corner and turn his back to the world in order to survive the shock of too much sensory input.

For some reason, the staggering richness of new experience in this kitchen does not affect him in that way. Instead of panic, he experiences . . . enchantment.

Perhaps this is because he is in a *home* at last. A person's home is inviolate. A sanctuary. An extension of one's personality, Martha says. Home is the safest of all places.

He is in the *heart* of this home, in the safest room of the safest place, where many happy memories will be made, where sharing and giving and laughing occur on a daily basis.

Randal Six has never laughed. He smiled once. When he first made his way to the O'Connor house, when he got out of the storm and into the crawl space, in the dark among the spiders, knowing that he would eventually reach Arnie, he had smiled.

When he opens the pantry door, he is stunned at the variety and quantity of canned and packaged food on the shelves. Never has he dared imagine such abundance.

At the Hands of Mercy, his meals and snacks were brought to his billet. The menu had been planned by others. He was given no choice of food—except for the color of it, on which he was insistent.

Here, the options before him are dazzling. In canned soups alone, he sees six varieties.

When he turns from the pantry and opens the upper door of the refrigerator, his legs shake and his knees go weak. Among other things, the freezer contains three quarts of ice cream.

Randal Six loves ice cream. He never gets enough ice cream.

His initial excitement abruptly turns to crushing disappointment when he sees that none of the choices before him is vanilla. There is chocolate almond. There is chocolate mint. There is strawberry-banana swirl.

For the most part, Randal has only eaten white and green foods. Mostly white. This restriction of colors in his food is a defense against chaos, an expression of his autism. Milk, chicken breast, turkey, potatoes, popcorn (without butter because butter makes it too yellow), peeled apples, peeled pears . . . He tolerates green vegetables like lettuce and celery and green beans, and also green fruit, like grapes.

The nutritional deficiencies of a strict white-and-green diet are addressed with white capsules of vitamins and minerals.

He has never eaten any flavor of ice cream other than vanilla. He has always known that other flavors exist, but he has found them too repulsive for consideration.

The O'Connors, however, have no vanilla.

For a moment he feels defeated, and drifts toward despair.

He is hungry, starving, and as never before he is in a mood to experiment. To his surprise, he removes the container of chocolate mint from the freezer.

Never before has he eaten anything brown. He chooses chocolate mint instead of chocolate almond because he assumes there will be bits of green in it, which will perhaps make it tolerable.

He withdraws a spoon from the flatware drawer and carries the quart of ice cream to the kitchen table. He sits, quivering with fearful anticipation.

Brown food. He may not survive.

When he pries the lid off the container, Randal discovers that the mint appears in thin ribbons of bright green, woven through the cold brown mass. This familiar color heartens him. The quart is full, and he digs out a spoonful of the treat.

Raising the spoon, he comes up short of the courage needed to put it in his mouth. He must make four halting attempts before he succeeds on the fifth.

Oh.

Not disgusting, after all. Delicious.

Galvanizingly delicious: He thrusts the second spoonful into his mouth without hesitation. And a third.

As he eats, he settles into a peace, a contentment, that he has never known previously. He is not yet happy, as he understands the concept of happiness, but he is closer to that desired condition than he has ever been in his four months out of the tank.

Having come here in search of the secret of happiness, he has found something else first: *home*.

He feels that he belongs here in a way that he never belonged in the Hands of Mercy. He feels so safe here that he can eat brown food. Maybe later even the pink-and-yellow strawberry-banana swirl. Anything, no matter how daring, seems to be possible within these sheltering walls.

By the time he has devoured half of the quart of chocolate mint, he knows that he will never leave. This is his home.

Throughout history, men of the Old Race have died—and killed—to protect their homes. Randal Six knows a little history, the usual two gigabytes downloaded in the tank.

To be torn from this peace and thrown into the bright and noisy world would be akin to death. Therefore, any attempt to force him from his home should be regarded as a murderous assault, justifying a swift and lethal response.

This is his home. With all his strength, he will defend his right to it.

He hears descending footsteps on the stairs.

CHAPTER 29

GUNNY ALECTO, a garbage-galleon driver, came into the shack that
served as the manager's office, sat on the edge of Nick Frigg's desk, and
said, "Rain rail rape raid rag rascal rack."

Nick didn't reply. She was just having trouble getting started; and if
he tried to guess the word for which she was searching, he would only
further confuse her.

"Rabid race rabble rap rat. *Rat!*" She had found the wanted noun.
"Have you noticed about the rats?"

"What about them?"

"What about who?"

"The rats, Gunny."

"Did you notice, too?"

"Notice what?"

"The rats are gone," she said.

"Gone where?"

"If I knew, I wouldn't be asking you."

"Asking me what?"

"Where are the rats?"

"We've always got rats," Nick said.

She shook her head. "Not here. Not now. No more."

Gunny looked like a movie star, except dirty. Nick didn't know why
Victor had made her gorgeous and then assigned her to the dump.
Maybe the contrast between her looks and her work amused him.
Maybe he had modeled her after one of the Old Race who had rejected
him or had otherwise earned his resentment.

"Why don't you go out there and look for elephants," Gunny suggested.

"What're you talking about—elephants?"

"You're as likely to find them as rats. Plowin' the trash, I usually chase up packs of them all the time, but I haven't seen one in three days."

"Maybe they're just making their burrows deeper in the pit as we fill it fuller."

"So we got five?" Gunny asked.

"Five rats?"

"I heard five Old Race dead came in today."

"Yeah. Plus three dead gone-wrongs," Nick said.

"Some fun tonight," she said. "Man, it's hot today."

"Louisiana summer, what do you expect."

"I'm not complaining," she said. "I like the sun. I wish there was sun at night."

"It wouldn't be night if there was sun."

"That's the problem," Gunny agreed.

Communicating with Gunny Alecto could be a challenge. She had looks, and she was as good a garbage-galleon driver as anyone, but her thought processes, as revealed by her conversation, didn't always track in a linear fashion.

Everyone in the New Race had a rank. At the top were the Alphas, the ruling elite. They were followed by Betas and Gammas.

As manager of the dump, Nick was a Gamma. Everyone on his crew was an Epsilon.

Epsilons had been designed and programmed for brute labor. They were a step or two above the meat machines without self-awareness that one day would replace many factory robots.

No class envy was permitted among those of the New Race. Each had been programmed to be content with the rank to which he had been born and to have no yearning for advancement.

It remained permissible, of course, to disdain and feel superior to those who ranked *below* you. Contempt for one's inferiors provided a healthy substitute for dangerous ambition.

Epsilons like Gunny Alecto didn't receive the wealth of direct-to-brain data downloading given to a Gamma like Nick, just as he received less than any Beta, and far less than any Alpha.

In addition to being less well-educated than the other ranks, Epsilons sometimes seemed to have cognitive problems that indicated their brains were not as carefully crafted as the brains of the upper classes.

"Goat goof gopher goon golf goose gone. *Gone!* Gone-wrongs. We got three, you said. What're they like?"

"I haven't seen them yet," Nick said.

"They'll be stupid-looking."

"I'm sure they will."

"Stupid-looking gone-wrongs. Some fun tonight."

"I'm looking forward to it," Nick said, which was true.

"Where do you think they went?"

"The deliverymen put them in the cooler."

"The rats?" she asked, puzzled.

"I thought you meant the gone-wrongs."

"I meant the rats. I miss the little fellers. You don't think we've got cats, do you?"

"I haven't seen any cats."

"That would explain no rats," she said. "But if you haven't seen any, that's good enough for me."

If Gunny had been required to live among members of the Old Race, she might not have passed for one of them—or might have been designated mentally disabled.

As a member of the Crosswoods crew, however, she had no life outside the dump. She lived within its gates twenty-four hours a day, seven days a week, with a bunk in one of the trailers that served as dormitories.

In spite of her problems, she was an excellent dozer pilot, and Nick was glad to have her.

Getting up from the edge of Nick's desk, Gunny said, "Well, back to the pit—and then some fun tonight, huh?"

"Some fun tonight," he agreed.

CHAPTER 30

AFTER HER CONVERSATION with Christine in the kitchen, Erika Helios toured those rooms of the mansion that she had not previously seen.

The lavish home theater was Russian Belle Epoque after the palaces of St. Petersburg. Victor had specified this opulent style in honor of his late friend, Joseph Stalin, communist dictator and visionary.

Joe Stalin had come forth with vast resources to fund New Race research after the sad collapse of the Third Reich, which had been a terrible setback for Victor. So confident had Joe been in Victor's ability eventually to fabricate an entirely controllable and obedient variety of enhanced humans that he had ordered the deaths of forty million of his citizens by various means even before the technology of the cloning tanks had been perfected.

Desirous of living forever, Joe had submitted to some of the same techniques with which Victor had sustained his own life for—at that time—nearly two centuries. Unfortunately, Stalin must have been suffering from an undiagnosed brain tumor or something because during the period that he underwent those life-extension procedures, he had grown increasingly detached from reality, and paranoid.

Eventually hair had grown on the palms of Stalin's hands—which had *never* happened to Victor. Furthermore, Stalin had been seized by unpredictable fits of mindless violence, sometimes directed at people around him, sometimes at pieces of furniture, once at his favorite pair of boots.

The dictator's closest associates poisoned him and concocted a cover story to conceal the fact that they had perpetrated a coup. Injustice was once more visited on Victor, and his research funds were cut off by the bean counters who followed poor Joe.

In the tank, Erika received all of her husband's rich history; however, she was forbidden to speak of it to anyone but Victor himself. She had been granted this knowledge only so that she would understand his epic struggles, his triumphs, and the glory of his existence.

After the theater, she explored the music room, the reception lounge, the formal living room, the informal living room, the jewel box of a breakfast room, the trophy room, the billiards room, the indoor pool with surrounding mosaic-tile deck, and came at last to the library.

The sight of all those books made her uneasy, for she knew that books were corrupting, perhaps evil. They had been the death of Erika Four, who had absorbed dangerous knowledge from them.

Nevertheless, Erika had to familiarize herself with the library because there would be social evenings when Victor would invite his important Old Race guests—mostly powerful politicians and business leaders—to repair to the library for cognac and other after-dinner drinks. As hostess, she would need to feel comfortable here in spite of the dreadful books.

As she walked through the library, she dared to touch a book now and then to accustom herself to the sinister feel of them. She even took one off a shelf and examined it, her two hearts racing.

In the event that a guest some evening said, *Erika, darling, would you hand me that book with the lovely binding, I'd like to have a look at it,* she must be prepared to present the volume as casually as a snake-handler of long experience would pick up any serpent.

Christine had suggested that Erika browse the several shelves of psychology texts and bone up on sexual sadism. She couldn't, however, bring herself to actually *open* a book.

As she moved across the big room, sliding her hand along the underside of a shelf, enjoying the satiny feel of the exquisitely finished wood, she discovered a hidden switch. She had flicked it before she quite realized what she had done.

A section of shelves proved to be a hidden door, which swung open on pivot hinges. Beyond lay a secret passageway.

In the tank, she had not been informed of the existence of this concealed door or of what lay beyond it. But she'd not been forbidden to explore, either.

CHAPTER 31

AFTER SWITCHING ON the kitchen lights, prior to preparing dinner, Vicky Chou washed her hands at the sink, and discovered that the soiled towel needed to be replaced. She blotted her hands on it anyway before fetching a clean towel from a drawer.

She crossed to the laundry-room door and pushed it open. Without turning on the lights, she tossed the soiled towel into the clothes basket.

Detecting a faint moldy scent, she made a mental note to inspect the room for mildew first thing in the morning. Poorly ventilated spaces like this required special diligence in the humid climate of the bayou.

She put two plastic place mats on the dinette table. She set out flatware for herself and Arnie.

The urgency with which Carson had left the house, after sleeping through the morning, suggested she would not be home for dinner.

Arnie's plate was different from Vicky's: larger, rectangular instead of round, and divided into four compartments. He didn't like different foods to be touching one another.

He couldn't tolerate orange and green items on the same plate. Although he would cut meat and other foods himself, he insisted that sliced tomatoes be cut into bite-size chunks for him.

"Squishy," he would say, grimacing in disgust when confronted with a piece of tomato that needed a knife. "Squishy, squishy."

Many other autistics had more rules than did Arnie. Because the boy spoke so little, Vicky knew him more by his eccentricities than by his words, and tended to find them more endearing than frustrating.

In an effort to socialize Arnie whenever possible, she insisted as best she could that he eat his meals with her, and always with his sister when Carson was home. Sometimes Vicky's insistence didn't move him, and she had to allow him to eat in his room, near his Lego-block castle.

When the table was set, she opened the freezer to get a box of Tater Tots—and discovered that the chocolate mint ice cream had not been put away properly. The lid was half off; a spoon had been left in the container.

Arnie had never done anything like this before. Usually he waited for food to be placed before him; he rarely served himself. He had an appetite but not much of an active interest in when and what he ate.

On those occasions when he raided the pantry or refrigerator, Arnie was neat. He never left spills or crumbs.

The boy's high standards of culinary hygiene bordered on the obsessive. He would never take a taste of anything from another person's plate, not even from his sister's, nor from any fork or spoon but his own.

Vicky could not imagine that he would eat from a container. And if he had done so in the past without her knowledge, he had never before left his spoon behind.

She was inclined to think that Carson had indulged a sudden craving just before hurriedly leaving the house.

When Vicky took a closer look, however, she discovered that the ice cream on the surface was soft and glistening with melt. The container had been out of the freezer for a while—and had been put away only a few minutes ago.

She closed the lid as it should have been, shut the freezer door, and took the spoon to the sink, where she rinsed it.

Putting the spoon in the dishwasher, she called, "Arnie? Where are you, sweetie?"

The back door was double locked, as she had left it, but she was nevertheless worried. The boy had never before wandered out of the house, but neither had he ever previously left a spoon in an ice-cream container.

From the kitchen, she followed a short hall to the living room. The blinds and curtains indulged shadows. She switched on a lamp.

"Arnie? Are you downstairs, Arnie?"

The house boasted nothing as grand as a foyer, only an entry alcove at one end of the living room. The front door, too, remained double locked.

Sometimes, when Carson was on a demanding case and Arnie was missing his sister, the boy liked to sit quietly in the armchair in her room, among her things.

He was not there now.

Vicky went upstairs and was relieved to find him safely in his room. He did not react to her entrance.

"Honey," she said, "you shouldn't eat ice cream so close to dinner-time."

Arnie did not reply, but clicked a Lego block into place in the castle ramparts, which he was modifying.

Considering the severe limitations with which the boy lived, Vicky was reluctant to scold him. She didn't press the issue of the ice cream, but instead said, "I should have dinner ready in forty-five minutes. It's one of your favorites. Will you come downstairs then?"

As his only answer, Arnie glanced toward the digital clock on his nightstand.

"Good. We'll have a nice dinner together, and afterward I'll read you a few more chapters of *Podkayne of Mars*, if you'd like."

"Heinlein," the boy said softly, almost reverently, naming the author of the novel.

"That's right. When we left poor Podkayne, she was in a lot of trouble."

"Heinlein," Arnie repeated, and then continued to work on the castle.

Downstairs again, following the hallway to the kitchen, Vicky pushed shut the coat-closet door, which was ajar.

She had reached the kitchen threshold when she realized that in the hall she detected the same moldy scent that she had smelled in the laundry room. She turned, looked back the way she had come, and sniffed.

Although the house stood on pilings, the air circulating under the structure did not prevent colonies of fungi, mostly molds, from scheming to invade these elevated rooms. They flourished in the damp dark crawl space. The concrete pilings drew water from the ground by osmosis, and the molds crept up those damp surfaces, spooring their way toward the house.

In the morning, she would definitely do a thorough inspection of every shadowy corner in the ground-floor closets, armed with the finest mold-killer known to man.

As a teenager, Vicky had read a story by O. Henry that left her forever with a phobia about molds. In a rooming house, in the moist heat and darkness behind an old-fashioned radiator, a bloodstained and filthy rag, colonized by mold, had somehow come to life, an eager but stupid kind of life, and one night, in a quiet slithering ameboid fashion, had gone in search of other life when the lamp was turned off, smothering the roomer in his sleep.

Vicky Chou didn't quite see herself as Sigourney Weaver in *Aliens* or as Linda Hamilton in *The Terminator,* but she was grimly determined to do battle with any mold that threatened her turf. In this unending war, she would entertain no exit strategy; the only acceptable outcome of each battle was total victory.

In the kitchen once more, she got the box of Tater Tots out of the freezer. She sprayed a baking sheet with Pam and spread the Tots on it.

She and Arnie would have dinner together. Then *Podkayne of Mars.* He liked to have her read to him, and she enjoyed story time as much as he did. They felt like family. This would be a nice evening.

CHAPTER 32

DEUCALION HAD SPENT the afternoon walking from church to church, from cathedral to synagogue, but nowhere between, taking advantage of his special understanding of time and space to step from nave to nave, from a place of Catholics to a place of Protestants, to another place of Catholics, through the many neighborhoods and faiths of the city, from sanctuary to narthex, to sacristy. He also intruded secretly into rectories and parsonages and pastoriums, observing clergymen at their work, seeking one that he felt sure belonged to the New Race.

A few of these men of the cloth—and one woman—raised his suspicions. If they were monsters to an extent greater than even he himself was, they hid it well. They were masters of the masquerade, in private as well as in public.

Because of their positions, they would of course be among the best that Victor produced, his Alphas, exceptionally intelligent and cunning.

In Our Lady of Sorrows, the priest seemed *wrong*. Deucalion could not put his finger on the reason for his suspicion. Intuition, beyond mere knowledge and reason, told him that Father Patrick Duchaine was not a child of God.

The priest was about sixty, with white hair and a sweet face, a perfect clone, perhaps, of a real priest now rotting in an unmarked grave.

Mostly singles, only a few pairs, primarily older than young, fewer than two dozen parishioners had gathered for vespers. With the service not yet begun, they sat in silence and did not disturb the hush of the church.

On one side of the nave, the stained-glass windows blazed in the hot light of the westering sun. Colorful geometric patterns were projected on the worshipers, the pews.

Our Lady of Sorrows opened her confessionals each morning before Mass and on those evenings, as now, when vespers were celebrated.

Staying to the shadowy aisle on the east side of the nave, out of the stained-glass dazzle, Deucalion approached a confessional, closed the door, and knelt.

When the priest slid open the privacy panel that covered the screen between them, and invited confession, Deucalion said softly, "Does your god live in Heaven, Father Duchaine, or in the Garden District?"

The priest was silent for a moment, but then said, "That sounds like the question of a particularly troubled man."

"Not a man, Father. More than a man. And less than a man. Like you, I think."

After a hesitation, the priest said, "Why have you come here?"

"To help you."

"Why should I need help?"

"You suffer."

"This world is a vale of tears for all of us."

"We can change that."

"Changing it isn't within our power. We can only endure."

"You preach hope, Father. But you have no hope yourself."

The priest's silence damned and identified him.

Deucalion said, "How difficult it must be for you to assure others that God will have mercy on their immortal souls, knowing as you do that even if God exists, you have no soul upon which He might bestow His grace, and everlasting life."

"What do you want from me?"

"A private conversation. Consideration. Discretion."

After a hesitation, Father Duchaine said, "Come to the rectory following the service."

"I'll be waiting in your kitchen. What I bring you, priest, is the hope you do not think will ever be yours. You need only have the courage to believe it, and grasp it."

CHAPTER 33

CARSON PARKED THE CAR on the shoulder of the service road, and they carried the suitcases through a stand of Southern pines, up a slight sunny incline, into a grove of well-crowned live oaks. Beyond the oaks lay a vast expanse of grass.

Twice the size of New York's Central Park, City Park served a population only a fraction as large as that of Manhattan. Within its reaches, therefore, were lonely places, especially in the last ruddy hours of a fast-condensing summer afternoon.

Across the sweep of the meadow, not one person was walking or communing with nature, or playing with a dog, or throwing a Frisbee, or disposing of a corpse.

Putting down his suitcase, Michael pointed to a grassy spot ten feet beyond the oaks. "That's where we found the accountant's head, propped against that rock. That's sure one you never forget."

"If Hallmark made a remembrance card suitable for the occasion," Carson said, "I would send you one each year."

"I was impressed by the cocky angle at which he wore his cowboy hat," Michael recalled, "especially considering his circumstances."

"Wasn't it their first date?" Carson asked.

"Right. They went to a costume party together. That's why he was wearing a midnight-blue leather cowboy outfit with rhinestones."

"His boots had mother-of-pearl inlays."

"They were fine, those boots. I'll bet he looked really cool with his body and head together, but of course we never got to see the full effect."

"Did we ever know the killer's costume?" she asked as she knelt in the crisp dead oak leaves to open her suitcase.

"I think he went as a bullfighter."

"He cut off the cowboy's head with an ax. A bullfighter doesn't carry an ax."

"Yeah, but he always kept an ax in the trunk of his car," he reminded her.

"Probably next to the first-aid kit. How wrong can a first date go that it ends in a beheading?"

Opening the suitcase that contained the shotguns, Michael said, "The problem is everybody has unrealistically high expectations for a first date. Inevitably, they're disappointed."

While Michael checked out the Urban Sniper shotguns and fitted each of them with a three-way sling, Carson worked the slide on each pistol and inserted a cartridge in the breach.

Except for the small noises that she and Michael made, a cathedral quiet filled the grove, and mantled the meadow beyond.

She loaded the nine-round magazines of the two Desert Eagle Magnums with .50-caliber Action Express cartridges.

"Before we blast our way into his place," she said, "we have to be sure Helios is home. We'll only have one chance to surprise him."

"Yeah, I've been thinking the same thing. We need to huddle with Deucalion on this one. He might have an idea."

"You think Arnie's in any danger?" Carson worried.

"No. We're the threat to Helios, not Arnie. And he's not going to try to silence you by grabbing your brother. He'll figure it's easier just to waste us."

"I hope that's right," she said. "It gives me some comfort."

"Yeah, nothing makes my day like being the primary target of an archfiend."

"Look at this—Godot threw in two holsters for the Eagles, no charge."

"What style?"

"Belt scabbards."

"Custom to the piece?" he asked.

"Yeah."

"Gimme. That monster would feel awkward in a shoulder rig."

"You gonna hip-carry the Eagle out of here?" she asked.

"It's not that easy to reach in a suitcase, is it? If Helios has people—or whatever they are—looking for us, we may need these monster-stoppers long before we go to his house."

While Michael loaded the shotguns, Carson loaded four spare magazines for the .50 Magnums.

They belted on the custom scabbards and sheathed the Eagles. Both chose the left hip for a cross-body, under-the-jacket draw.

At the right hip, each of them carried a pouch containing two spare magazines for the Eagle and eight spare rounds for the Urban Sniper.

Their sport jackets provided acceptable concealment; but this new weight was going to feel awkward for a while.

They closed the suitcases and slung the shotguns over their right shoulders—stocks up, muzzles down. They picked up the two nearly empty cases and retraced their route through the grove of oaks.

When they had descended two thirds of the open slope between the oaks and the Southern pines, they put down the suitcases and faced back the way they had just come.

"Gotta get the feel of the beast," Carson said.

"One pop with each, and then out of here before park security comes looking."

The sloping earth before them would both stop the bullets from traveling and prevent ricochets.

They took two-hand grips on their Eagles and squeezed off shots all but simultaneously. The reports were *loud,* war-zone loud.

Gouts of earth and grass marked the impact, as if two invisible and furious golfers had clubbed divots from the turf.

Carson felt the recoil knock all the way back to her shoulder sockets; but she had kept the muzzle down.

"Loud enough for you?" Michael asked.

"You ain't heard nothing yet," she said, holstering the Eagle.

They swung up their shoulder-slung shotguns, and the twin blasts were thunderclaps that shivered the air and seemed even to vibrate in the ground beneath their feet.

"Feel good?" he asked.

"Felt sweet."

"A slug like that would take off a man's leg."

"Maybe not one of *their* legs."

"Whatever it does to them, it won't leave them smiling. Better move on."

They shouldered the shotguns once more, picked up the suitcases, and walked briskly into the warm shadows among the pines.

CHAPTER 34

CINDI LOVEWELL PARKED the Mountaineer alongside the service road, a hundred yards behind the unmarked police sedan, switched off the engine, and put down the windows.

"They're not in the car," Benny said. "Where do you think they've gone?"

"They probably went into the woods to urinate," Cindi said. "Their kind don't have our degree of control."

"I don't think that's it," Benny said. "As I understand their biology, Old Race men don't usually have urinary-control problems until they're old enough to have really enlarged prostates."

"Then maybe they went into the woods to make a baby."

Benny counseled himself to be patient. "People don't make babies in the woods."

"Yes, they do. They make babies everywhere. In woods, in fields, on boats, in bedrooms, on kitchen tables, on moonlit beaches, in the bathrooms aboard airliners. They're making babies everywhere, all the time, millions and millions of new babies every year."

"Their method of reproduction is crude and inefficient, when you think about it," Benny said. "The tanks are a better system, cleaner and more manageable."

"The tanks don't make babies."

"They make productive adult citizens," Benny said. "Everyone is born in a condition to serve society. That's so much more practical."

"I like babies," Cindi said stubbornly.

"You shouldn't," he warned.

"But I do. I like their tiny fingers, their cute little toes, their squinchy red faces, their little toothless grins. I like how soft they feel, how they smell, how they—"

"You're obsessing again," he said nervously.

"Benny, why don't you want a baby?"

"It's a violation of everything we *are*," he said exasperatedly. "For us, it would be unnatural. All I want, *really* want, is to kill some people."

"I want to kill some people, too," she assured him.

"I'm not sure you really do."

She shook her head and looked disappointed in him. "That's so unfair, Benny. You know I want to kill people."

"I used to think you did."

"I can't wait for the day we can kill *all* of them. But don't you also want to create?"

"Create? No. Why would I? Create? No. I don't want to be like *them,* with their babies and their books and their business empires—"

Benny was interrupted by two almost simultaneous explosions, hard and flat, distant but unmistakable.

"Gunfire," Cindi said.

"Two rounds. From beyond those pines."

"Do you think they shot each other?" she asked.

"Why would they shoot each other?"

"People do. All the time."

"They didn't shoot each other," he said, but he was expressing a hope rather than a conviction.

"I think they shot each other."

"If they shot each other," he said, "I'm going to be pissed."

Two more reports, again almost simultaneous, but louder than the others and characterized by a hollow roar rather than a flat bark, echoed out of the pines.

Relieved, Benny said, "They didn't shoot each other."

"Maybe somebody's shooting at them."

"Why are you so *negative*?" he asked.

"Me? I'm positive. I'm for creation. Creation is a positive thing. Who is it that's *against* creation?"

With profound concern for the fate of the two detectives, Benny stared through the windshield toward the distant woods.

They sat in silence for half a minute, and then Cindi said, "We need a bassinet."

He refused to be engaged in that conversation.

"We've been buying clothes," she said, "when there are so many things we'll need first. I haven't bought any diapers, no receiving blankets, either."

Thicker than the humid air, a pall of despair began to settle over Benny Lovewell.

Cindi said, "I'm not buying any formula until I see if I'm able to breast-feed. I really want to breast-feed our baby."

From out of the pines, two figures appeared.

Even with his enhanced vision, at this distance Benny needed a moment to be sure of their identity.

"Is it them?" he asked.

After a hesitation, Cindi said, "Yes."

"Yes! Yes, it *is* them." Benny was so pleased that they were alive and that he would still have a chance to kill them.

"What're they carrying?" Cindi asked.

"I can't quite tell."

"Suitcases?"

"Could be."

"Where would they get suitcases in the woods?" Cindi wondered.

"Maybe they took them from the people they shot."

"But what would *those* people be doing with suitcases in the woods?"

"I don't care," Benny said. "Who knows why they do what they do? They're not like us, they're not a fully rational species. Let's go kill them."

"Is this the place for it?" Cindi asked, but she started the engine.

"I'm so ready. I *need this*."

"It's too open," she said. "We won't be able to take the time to do it in the most satisfying manner."

Grudgingly, Benny said, "You're right. Okay, okay. But we can overpower them, club them unconscious, and take them somewhere private."

"Out past the Warehouse Arts District, where not everything's been gentrified yet. That abandoned factory. You know the place."

"Where we killed the police chief and his wife the night their replicants were ready," Benny said, warming to the memory.

"We killed them good," Cindi said.

"We did, didn't we?"

"Remember how he screamed when we peeled her head like an orange?" Cindi asked.

"You'd think a police chief would be tougher."

Driving the Mountaineer onto the service road, Cindi said, "You can cut them both apart while they're still alive—and you know what then?"

"What?" he asked as they approached the parked sedan, where the detectives had just finished loading the suitcases in the backseat.

"Right there in the blood and all," Cindi said, "we'll make a baby."

His mood was soaring. He wasn't going to let her bring him down.
"All right, sure," he said.

"Blood, really fresh blood, is sometimes used in the most effective
rituals," she said.

"Of course it is. Get us up there before they're in the car. What rituals?"

"Fertility rituals. The Old Race is fertile. If we do it in their blood,
covered in their warm blood, maybe we'll be fertile, too."

The cops turned to stare at the approaching Mountaineer, and
Benny thrilled to the prospect of violence, and yet he couldn't help asking, "Fertility rituals?"

"Voodoo," said Cindi. "The Ibo cult of voodoo."

"Ibo?"

"*Je suis rouge,*" she said.

"That sounds like French. We're not programmed with French."

"It means, 'I who am red' or, more accurately, 'I the red one.' It's
what Ibo calls himself."

"Ibo again," said Benny.

"He's the evil god of the blood-sacrifice cult of voodoo. We'll kill
these two and then make a baby while wallowing in their blood. Praise
Ibo, all glory to Ibo."

Cindi had succeeded in distracting Benny from their prey. He
stared at her, bewildered and afraid.

CHAPTER 35

WHEN ERIKA HELIOS entered the secret passageway, the door in the bookshelves closed automatically behind her.

"It's like a Wilkie Collins novel," she murmured, referring to the work of a Victorian writer whom she had never read.

The four-foot-wide passageway had a concrete floor, concrete walls, and a concrete ceiling. She felt as though she had stepped into a bunker deep under a war-torn city.

Apparently, motion detectors controlled the lights, because when she stood quite still for a long moment, assessing her discovery, the passageway went dark. When she reached out into the blackness, the lights came on again.

The narrow corridor led in only one direction and ended in a formidable steel door.

Because Victor loved gadgets and techie stuff, Erika would have expected this door to have an electronic lock. Victor's style would be to equip it with a scanner that read palm prints or patterns in the retina, allowing access only to him.

Instead, the door was secured by inch-thick steel lock bolts: five of them. One was inserted in the header, one in the threshold, and three in the right-hand jamb, opposite the massive hinges.

Contemplating this barrier, Erika considered that opening it might be unwise. The space beyond was not a box, and the door was not a lid, but inevitably, she thought of Pandora, the first woman, whose curiosity had led her to open the box in which Prometheus had locked away all the evils that could afflict humanity.

This bit of myth gave her only brief pause, because humanity—another term for the Old Race—was doomed anyway. She herself might one day be told to kill as many as she could find.

Besides, Samuel Johnson—whoever he was—had once said, "Curiosity is one of the permanent and certain characteristics of a vigorous mind."

Judging by the imposing weight of this door and the size of the lock bolts that secured it, something of considerable importance to Victor must wait to be discovered behind it. If Erika were to be the best wife that she could be—and the last Erika ever to rise from the tanks—she must understand her husband, and to understand him, she must know everything that he most valued. Whatever lay behind this barrier, which resembled a vault door, clearly was of enormous value to him.

She extracted the bolt from the header, and thereafter the bolt seated in the concrete floor. One by one, she pulled the bolts from the jamb.

The steel slab opened away from her, into the next space, where a row of ceiling lights brightened automatically. As she crossed the threshold, she saw that the door, which swung smoothly and quietly on its massive ball-bearing hinges, measured about eight inches thick.

She found herself in another short passageway, about twelve feet in length, which ended in a door identical to the first.

Along the length of this second corridor, scores of metal rods bristled from the walls. On her left, the rods appeared to be copper. On the right, they were of another metal, perhaps steel but perhaps not.

A soft, ululant hum filled the passageway. It seemed to arise from the metal rods.

Her downloaded education had focused primarily on music, dance, literary allusions, and other subjects that would ensure that she would be a scintillating hostess when Victor entertained politically important members of the Old Race, which he would do until such a time as he could confidently eliminate them. She didn't know much about the sciences.

Nevertheless, she suspected that when needed—for whatever reason—powerful electrical currents arced between the metal rods that were aligned on opposite sides of the passageway, perhaps frying or vaporizing altogether whoever might be caught between them.

Not even a member of the New Race would emerge unscathed.

As she stood two steps inside the threshold, brooding on this discovery, a blue laser beam speared forth from a ceiling fixture and scanned her body from top to bottom, and then to top again, as if assessing her form.

The laser winked off. An instant later the rods stopped humming. A heavy silence claimed the passageway.

She had the impression that she'd been found acceptable. She would most likely not be sizzled as crisp as burnt toast if she proceeded.

If she was wrong, tentative steps would not spare her from destruction; therefore, she walked boldly forward, leaving the door open behind her.

Her first day in the mansion—beginning with Victor's bedroom fury, followed by William's finger-chewing episode, proceeding to the disturbing conversation she'd had with Christine in the kitchen—had not been as welcoming as she might have hoped. Perhaps herewith the day had taken a turn for the better. Not being electrocuted seemed to be a good sign.

CHAPTER 36

"ALL GLORY TO IBO," Cindi repeated, "may he approve the taste of my blood."

As hot as he had been to capture and kill the detectives only a moment ago, Benny Lovewell was suddenly just as cold on the idea.

Cindi had blindsided him with this weird voodoo talk, which he had never heard from her before. She knocked him off balance.

Suddenly he didn't know if he could rely on her anymore. They were a team. They needed to move as one, in sync, with full trust.

When their speed fell as they approached the sedan, Benny said, "Don't stop."

"Leave the male to me," she said. "He won't see me as a threat. I'll break him down so hard and fast, he won't know what happened."

"No, keep moving, just drive, *drive*," Benny urged.

"What do you mean?"

"What did I *say*? If you ever want to make a baby with me, you better *drive*!"

They had glided almost to a halt beside the sedan.

The detectives were staring at them. Benny smiled and waved, which seemed the thing to do until he'd done it, and then it seemed only to call attention to himself, so he quickly looked away from them, which he realized might have made them suspicious.

Before coming to a full stop, Cindi accelerated, and they drove farther into the park, along the service road.

Glancing at the dwindling sedan in the rearview mirror, then at Benny, Cindi said, "What was *that* about?"

"That was about Ibo," he said.

"I don't understand."

"You don't understand? *You* don't understand? *I* don't understand. *Je suis rouge,* evil gods, blood sacrifices, *voodoo?*"

"You've never heard of voodoo? It was a big deal in New Orleans in the eighteen hundreds. It's still around, and in fact—"

"Did you learn nothing in the tank?" he asked. "*There is no world but this one.* That is essential to our creed. We are strictly rationalists, materialists. We are *forbidden* superstition."

"I know that. You think I don't know that? Superstition is a key flaw of the Old Race. Their minds are weak, full of foolishness and fear and nonsense."

Benny quoted what she'd said as they had approached the sedan: "'Praise Ibo, all glory to Ibo.' Doesn't sound like a materialist to me. Not to me, it doesn't."

"Will you relax?" Cindi said. "If you were one of the Old Race, you'd be popping a blood vessel."

"Is that where you go sometimes when you go out?" he asked. "To a voodoo cathedral?"

"There aren't such things as voodoo cathedrals. That's ignorant. If it's Haitian-style, they call the temple a *houmfort.*"

"So you go to a *houmfort,*" he said grimly.

"No, because there's not much Haitian-style voodoo around here."

Out of sight of the sedan now, she pulled off the service road and parked on the grass. She left the engine running, and the air-conditioning.

She said, "Zozo Deslisle sells *gris-gris* out of her little house in Treme, and does spells and conjures. She's an Ibo-cult *bocor* with mucho mojo, yassuh."

"Almost none of that made any sense," Benny said. "Cindi, do you realize what trouble you're in, what trouble *we're* in? If any of our people find out you've gone religious, you'll be terminated, probably me, too. We've got it pretty sweet—permission to kill, with more and more jobs all the time. We're the envy of our kind, and you're going to ruin everything with your crazy superstition."

"I'm not superstitious."

"You're not, huh?"

"No, I'm not. Voodoo isn't superstition."

"It's a religion."

"It's science," she said. "It's true. It works."

Benny groaned.

"Because of voodoo," she said, "I'm eventually going to have a child. It's only a matter of time."

"They could be unconscious in the back right now," Benny said. "We could be on the way to that old factory."

She zipped open her purse and produced a small white cotton bag with a red drawstring closure. "It contains Adam and Eve roots. Two of them, sewn together."

He said nothing.

Also from her purse, Cindi extracted a small jar. "Judas's Mixture, which is buds from the Garden of Gilead, powdered silver gilt, the blood of a rabbit, essence of Van Van, powdered—"

"And what do you do with that?"

"Blend a half teaspoon in a glass of warm milk and drink it every morning while standing in a sprinkle of salt."

"That sounds very scientific."

She didn't miss his sarcasm. "As if you would know all about science. You're not an Alpha. You're not a Beta. You're a Gamma just like me."

"That's right," Benny said. "A Gamma. Not an ignorant Epsilon. And not a superstitious member of the Old Race, either. A *Gamma*."

She put the Adam and Eve roots and the Judas's Mixture back in her purse. She zipped it shut.

"I don't know what to do," Benny said.

"We have an assignment, remember? Kill O'Connor and Maddison. I don't know why we haven't already done it."

Benny stared through the windshield at the park.

Never since disgorgement from the creation tank had he felt this bleak. He yearned for stability and control, but he found himself in an escalating chaos.

The more he brooded on his dilemma, the faster he sank into a gray despond.

Weighing his duty to Victor against his self-interest, he wondered why he had been designed to be the ultimate materialist and then had been required to care about anything other than himself. Why should he concern himself about more than his own needs—except that his maker would terminate him if he disobeyed? Why should it matter to him that the New Race ascended, considering that this world had no transcendent meaning? What was the purpose of liquidating humanity and achieving dominion over all of nature, what was the purpose of then venturing out to the stars, if all of nature—to every end of the universe—was just a dumb machine with no point to its design? Why strive to be the king of nothing?

Benny had been created to be a man of action, always moving and doing and killing. He hadn't been designed to *think* this much about philosophical issues.

"Leave the heavy thinking to the Alphas and Betas," he said.

"I always do," Cindi said.

"I'm not talking to you. I'm talking to myself."

"I've never heard you do that before."

"I'm starting."

She frowned. "How will I know when you're talking to me or to yourself?"

"I won't talk to myself much. Maybe never again. I don't really interest me that much."

"We'd both be more interesting if we had a baby."

He sighed. "Whatever will be will be. We'll terminate who we're told to until our maker terminates us. It's beyond our control."

"Not beyond the control of Ibo," she said.

"He who is red."

"That's right. Do you want to come with me to meet Zozo Deslisle and get a make-happy *gris-gris?*"

"No. I just want to tie down those cops and cut them open and listen to them scream while I twist their intestines."

"*You're* the one who told me to drive past," she reminded him.

"I was mistaken. Let's find them."

CHAPTER 37

VICTOR WAS AT HIS DESK in the main laboratory, taking a cookie break, when Annunciata's face appeared on his computer screen in all her glorious digital detail.

"Mr. Helios, I have been asked by Werner to tell you that he is in Randal Six's room and that he is exploding."

Although Annunciata wasn't a real person, just a manifestation of complicated software, Victor said irritably, "You're screwing up again."

"Sir?"

"That can't be what he told you. Review his message and convey it correctly."

Werner had personally conducted a search of Randal's room and had taken it upon himself to review everything on Randal's computer.

Annunciata spoke again: "Mr. Helios, I have been asked by Werner to tell you that he is in Randal Six's room and that he is exploding."

"Contact Werner and ask him to repeat his message, then get back to me when you've got it right."

"Yes, Mr. Helios."

With the last of a peanut butter cookie raised to his lips, he hesitated, waiting for her to repeat *Helios,* but she didn't.

As Annunciata's face dematerialized from the screen, Victor ate the final bite, and then washed it down with coffee.

Annunciata returned. "Mr. Helios, Werner repeats that he is in fact exploding and wishes to stress the urgency of the situation."

Getting to his feet, Victor threw his mug at the wall, against which it shattered with a satisfying noise.

Tightly, he said, "Annunciata, let's see if you can get *anything* right. Call janitorial. Coffee has been spilled in the main lab."

"Yes, Mr. Helios."

Randal Six's room was on the second floor, which served as a dormitory for all those of the New Race who had graduated from the tanks but who were not yet ready to be sent into the world beyond the walls of Mercy.

As the elevator ascended, Victor strove to calm himself. After 240 years, he should have learned not to let these things grind at his nerves.

His curse was to be a perfectionist in an imperfect world. He took some comfort from his conviction that one day his people would be refined to the point where they matched his own high standards.

Until then, the world would torture him with its imperfections, as it always had. He would be well advised to laugh at idiocy rather than to be inflamed by it.

He didn't laugh enough. In fact he didn't laugh at all these days. The last time he could remember having a really *good*, long laugh had been in 1979, with Fidel, in Havana, related to some fascinating open-brain work involving political prisoners with unusually high IQs.

By the time he arrived at the second floor, Victor was prepared to laugh with Werner about Annunciata's mistake. Werner had no sense of humor, of course, but he would be able to fake a laugh. Sometimes the pretense of joviality could lift the spirits almost as high as the real thing.

When Victor stepped out of the elevator alcove into the main corridor, however, he saw a dozen of his people gathered in the hall, at the doorway to Randal Six's room. He sensed an air of alarm about the gathering.

They parted to let him through, and he found Werner lying faceup on the floor. The massive, muscular security chief had torn off his shirt; writhing, grimacing, he hugged himself as if desperate to hold his torso together.

Although he had exercised his ability to switch off pain, Werner poured sweat. He appeared terror-stricken.

"What's wrong with you?" Victor demanded as he knelt at Werner's side.

"Exploding. I'm ex, I'm ex, I'm exploding."

"That's absurd. You're not exploding."

"Part of me wants to be something else," Werner said.

"You aren't making sense."

With a chatter of teeth: "What's going to be of me?"

"Move your arms, let me see what's happening."

"What am I, why am I, how is this happening? Father, tell me."

"I am not your father," Victor said sharply. *"Move your arms!"*

When Werner revealed his torso from neck to navel, Victor saw the flesh pulsing and rippling as though the breastbone had gone as soft as fatty tissue, as though within him numerous snakes squirmed in loose slippery knots, tying and untying themselves, flexing their serpentine coils in an attempt to split their host and erupt free of him.

Astonished and amazed, Victor placed one hand upon Werner's abdomen, to determine by touch and by palpation the nature of the internal chaos.

Instantly, he discovered that this phenomenon was not what it had appeared to be. No separate entity was moving within Werner, neither a colony of restless snakes nor anything else.

His tank-grown flesh itself had changed, had become amorphous, a gelatinous mass, a firm but entirely malleable meat pudding that seemed to be struggling to remake itself into . . . into something other than Werner.

The man's breathing became labored. A series of strangled sounds issued from him, as if something had risen into his throat.

Starburst hemorrhages blossomed in his eyes, and he turned a desperate crimson gaze upon his maker.

Now the muscles in his arms began to knot and twist, to collapse and re-form. His thick neck throbbed, bulged, and his facial features started to deform.

The collapse was not occurring on a physiological level. This was *cellular* metamorphosis, the most fundamental molecular biology, the rending not merely of tissue but of *essence*.

Under Victor's palm and spread fingers, the flesh of the abdomen shaped itself—*shaped itself*—into a questing hand that grasped him, not threateningly, almost lovingly, yet in shock he tore loose of it, recoiled.

Springing to his feet, Victor shouted, "A gurney! Hurry! Bring a gurney. We have to get this man to isolation."

CHAPTER 38

AS ERIKA DISENGAGED the five steel lock bolts from the second vaultlike door, she wondered if any of the first four Erikas had discovered this secret passageway. She liked to think that if they *had* found it, they had not done so on their first day in the mansion.

Although she had tripped the hidden switch in the library by accident, she had begun to construe her discovery as the consequence of a lively and admirable curiosity, per Mr. Samuel Johnson, quoted previously. She wished to believe that hers was a livelier and *more* admirable curiosity than that of any of her predecessors.

She blushed at this immodest desire, but she felt it anyway. She *so* wanted to be a good wife, and not fail as they had done.

If another Erika had found the passageway, she might not have been bold enough to enter it. Or if she had entered it, she might have hesitated to open even the first of the two steel doors, let alone the second.

Erika Five felt adventurous, like Nancy Drew or—even better—like Nora Charles, the wife of Nick Charles, the detective in Dashiell Hammett's *The Thin Man,* another book to which she could cleverly refer without risking her life by reading it.

Having drawn the last of the five bolts, she hesitated, savoring her suspense and excitement.

Beyond doubt, whatever lay on the farther side of this portal was of tremendous importance to Victor, perhaps of such significance that it would explain him in complete detail and reveal the truest nature of his heart. In the next hour or two, she might learn more about her brilliant but enigmatic husband than in a year of living with him.

She hoped to find a journal of his most tender secrets, his hopes, his considered observations on life and love. In truth, it was unrealistic to suppose that two steel doors and an electrocution tunnel had been installed merely to ensure that his diary could be kept somewhere more secure than a nightstand drawer.

Nevertheless, she wished intensely that she would discover just such a handwritten, heartfelt account of his life, so she could *know* him, know him to the core, the better to serve him. She was a little surprised— but pleasantly so—to find that she seemed to be such a romantic.

The fact that the dead bolts were on the *outside* of these doors had not been lost on her. She made the obvious inference: that the intent had been to imprison something.

Erika was not fearless, but neither could anyone fairly call her a coward. Like all of the New Race, she possessed great strength, agility, cunning, and a fierce animal confidence in her physical prowess.

Anyway, she lived every minute by the sufferance of her maker. If ever she were to hear, spoken in Victor's voice, the order to terminate herself, she would unhesitatingly obey, as she had been programmed.

William, the butler, had received such instructions on the phone and, even in his distracted condition, had done as ordered. Just as he could turn off pain—as could they all in a time of crisis—so could he shut down all autonomic nerve functions when thus commanded. In an instant, William had stopped his own heartbeat and respiration, and died.

This was not a trick he could have used to commit suicide. Only the word-perfect ritual instruction, delivered in his master's voice, could pull that trigger.

When your existence depended entirely on such sufferance, when your life hung by a gossamer filament that could be cut by the simple scissors of a few sharp words, you couldn't work up much dread about what might be contained behind two bolted steel doors.

Erika opened the second door, and lamps brightened automatically in the space beyond. She crossed the threshold and found herself in a cozy Victorian drawing room.

Windowless, the twenty-foot-square space had a polished mahogany floor, an antique Persian carpet, William Morris wallpaper, and a coffered mahogany ceiling. The ebonized-walnut fireplace featured William de Morgan tiles around the firebox.

Bracketed by a pair of lamps in fringed shades of Shantung silk, an overstuffed chesterfield with decorative pillows in Japan-themed fabrics offered Victor a place to lie down if he wished, not to nap (she imagined) but to relax and to let his brilliant mind spin out new schemes unique to his genius.

In a wingback chair with footstool, he could contemplate while upright, if he chose, under a floor lamp with a beaded shade.

Sherlock Holmes would have been at home in such a room, or H. G. Wells, or G. K. Chesterton.

The focal point, from either the plump sofa or the chair, was an immense glass case: nine feet long, five feet wide, and more than three feet deep.

As much as possible, this object had been crafted to complement the Victorian decor. It stood upon a series of bronze ball-in-claw feet. The six panes of glass were beveled at the edges to charm the light, and were held in an ornate ormolu frame of beautifully chased bronze. It appeared to be a giant jewel box.

A semiopaque reddish-gold substance filled the case, and defied the eye to define it. One moment this material seemed to be a liquid through which circulated subtle currents; yet just a moment later it seemed instead to be a dense vapor, perhaps a gas, lazily billowing along the glass.

Mysterious, this object drew Erika just as the lustrous eyes of Dracula drew Mina Harker toward her potential doom in a novel that was not likely to be a source for literary allusions suitable to the average formal dinner party in the Garden District but that was in her downloaded repertoire nonetheless.

Being refractive, the fluid or vapor absorbed the lamplight and glowed warmly. This internal luminosity revealed a dark shape suspended in the center of the case.

Erika could not see even the vaguest details of the encased object, but for some reason she thought of a scarab petrified in ancient resin.

As she approached the case, the shadow at its core seemed to twitch, but most likely she had imagined that movement.

CHAPTER 39

FROM CITY PARK, Carson drove to the Garden District to cruise the streets around the Helios residence.

They were not yet ready to shoot their way into the mansion and go on a Frankenstein hunt, but they needed to scope the territory and lay out escape routes in the—unlikely—event that they were able not only to kill Victor but also to get out of his house alive.

En route, she said to Michael, "Those people in the white Mercury Mountaineer, back there in the park—did they look familiar to you?"

"No. But he waved."

"I think I've seen them before."

"Where?"

"I can't quite remember."

"What are you saying? Did they seem dubious to you?"

Checking the rearview mirror, Carson said, "I didn't like his smile."

"We don't shoot people in New Orleans for having an insincere smile."

"What were they doing on the service road? That's only for the use of park personnel, and that wasn't a park vehicle."

"We aren't park personnel, either. Under the circumstances, it's easy to get paranoid."

"It's stupid *not* to be paranoid," she said.

"You want to go back, find them, and shoot them?"

"I might feel better," she said, checking the mirror again. "You want to call Deucalion, set up a meet?"

"I'm trying to picture how the original Frankenstein monster applies for a cell phone."

"It belongs to Jelly Biggs, the carny who lives at the Luxe, the friend of the guy who left the theater to Deucalion."

"Who names their kid Jelly Biggs? They doomed him to fathood."

"It's not his real name. It's his carny name, from his days in the freakshow."

"But he still uses it."

"Seems like if they're in the carnival long enough, their carny monikers become more comfortable than their real names."

"What was Deucalion's freakshow name?" Michael asked.

"The Monster."

"That had to be before political correctness. *The Monster*—what a self-esteem quasher. These days they'd call him the Different One."

"Still too stigmatizing."

"Yeah. He'd be called the Unusual Beauty. You have his number?"

She recited it while Michael keyed the digits in his phone.

He waited, listened, and then said, "Hey, this is Michael. We need to meet." He left his number and terminated the call. "Monsters—they're all so irresponsible. He doesn't have his phone on. I got voice mail."

CHAPTER 40

IN THE COAT CLOSET off the hall between the living room and the kitchen, Randal Six is not yet fully happy, but he is content, for he feels at home. At last he has a home.

Former hospitals converted into laboratories for cloning and biological engineering do not in his experience have coat closets. The very existence of a coat closet says *home*.

Life on the bayou does not require a collection of overcoats and parkas. Hanging from the rod are only a few light zippered jackets.

Boxed items are stored on the floor of the closet, but he has plenty of room to sit down if he wants. He is too excited to sit, however, and stands in the dark, all but quivering with expectation.

He is content to remain on his feet in the closet for hours if not days. Even this narrow space is preferable to his billet at Mercy and to the fearsome machines to which his maker has often manacled him in the conduct of painful testing.

What tempts him to ease open the door is, first, the woman's happy singing and the delightful clink-clatter of kitchen work. He is further enticed by the mouthwatering aroma of onions sautéing in butter.

Having eaten brown food, perhaps he can safely eat virtually anything.

Without quite realizing what he is doing, as if half mesmerized by the domestic smells and sounds, Randal opens the door wider and ventures forth into the hall.

The threshold of the kitchen is less than fifteen feet away. He sees the singing woman as she stands at the stove, her back to him.

Now might be a good time to venture deeper into the house and search for Arnie O'Connor. The grail of his quest is near at hand: the smiling autistic with the secret of happiness.

The woman at the stove fascinates him, however, for she must be Arnie's mother. Carson O'Connor is the boy's sister, but this is not Carson, not the person in that newspaper photo. In an Old Race family, there will be a mother.

Randal Six, child of Mercy, has never previously met a mother. Among the New Race, there are no such creatures. Instead there is the tank.

This is not merely a female before him. This is a being of great mystery, who can create human life within her body, without any of the formidable machinery that is required to produce one of the New Race in the lab.

In time, when the Old Race is dead to the last, which will be the not too distant future, mothers like this woman will be mythical figures, beings of lore and legend. He cannot help but regard her with wonder.

She stirs the strangest feelings in Randal Six. An inexplicable reverence.

The smells, the sounds, the *magical beauty* of the kitchen draw him inexorably toward that threshold.

When she turns away from the cooktop and steps to a cutting board beside the sink, still softly singing, the woman fails to catch sight of him from the corner of her eye.

In profile, singing, preparing dinner, she seems so happy, even happier than Arnie looked in that photograph.

As Randal reaches the kitchen, it occurs to him that this woman herself might be the secret to Arnie's happiness. Perhaps what is needed for happiness is a mother who has carried you within her, who values you as surely as she does her own flesh.

The last time Randal Six saw his creation tank was four months ago, on the day that he emerged from it. There is no reason for a reunion.

When the woman turns away from him and steps to the cooktop once more, still not having registered his presence, Randal is swept away by feelings he has never experienced before, that he cannot name, for which he has no words of description.

He is overwhelmed by a yearning, but a yearning for *what* he is not certain. She draws him as gravity draws a falling apple from a tree.

Crossing the room to her, Randal realizes that one thing he wants is to see himself reflected in her eyes, his face in her eyes.

He does not know *why*.

And he wants her to smooth the hair back from his forehead. He wants her to smile at him.

He does not know *why*.

He stands immediately behind her, trembling with emotion that has never welled in him previously, feelings for which he never realized he had the capacity.

For a moment she remains unaware of him, but then something alerts her. She turns, alarmed, and cries out in surprise and fear.

She has carried a knife from the cutting board to the stove.

Although the woman makes no attempt to use the weapon, Randal seizes it in his left hand, by the blade, slashing himself, tears it from her grip, and throws it across the kitchen.

With his right fist, he clubs her alongside the head, clubs her to the floor.

CHAPTER 41

FOLLOWING VESPERS, in the rectory of Our Lady of Sorrows Church, Deucalion watched as Father Patrick Duchaine poured rich dark coffee into two mugs. He had been offered cream and sugar, but had declined.

When the priest sat across the table from Deucalion, he said, "I make it so strong it's almost bitter. I have an affinity for bitterness."

"I suspect that all of our kind do," Deucalion said.

They had dispensed with preliminaries in the confessional. They knew each other for the essence of what they were, although Father Duchaine did not know the particulars of his guest's creation.

"What happened to your face?" he asked.

"I angered my maker and tried to raise a hand against him. He had implanted in my skull a device of which I was unaware. He wore a special ring that could produce a signal, triggering the device."

"We're now programmed to switch off, like voice-activated appliances, when we hear certain words in his unmistakable voice."

"I come from a more primitive period of his work. The device in my skull was supposed to destroy me. It functioned half well, making a more obvious monster of me."

"The tattoo?"

"Well-intended but inadequate disguise. Most of my life, I've spent in freakshows, in carnivals and their equivalent, where almost everyone is an outcast of one kind or another. But before coming to New Orleans, I was some years in a Tibetan monastery. A friend there, a monk, worked his art on my face before I left."

After a slow sip of his bitter brew, the white-haired priest said, "How primitive?"

Deucalion hesitated to reveal his origins, but then realized that his unusual size, the periodic pulse of something like heat lightning in his eyes, and the cruel condition of his face were sufficient to identify him. "More than two hundred years ago. I am his first."

"Then it's true," Duchaine said, a greater bleakness darkening his eyes. "If you're the first and yet have lived so long, we may last a thousand years, and this earth is our hell."

"Perhaps, but perhaps not. I lived centuries not because he knew in those days how to design immortality into me. My longevity and much else came to me on the lightning that brought me to life. He thinks I'm long dead . . . and does not suspect I have a destiny."

"What do you mean . . . on the lightning?"

Deucalion drank coffee. After he returned the mug to the table, he sat for a while in silence before he said, "Lightning is only a meteorological phenomenon, yet I refer not just to a thundercloud when I say the bolt that animated me came from a higher realm."

As Father Duchaine considered this revelation, some color rose in his previously pale face. "'Longevity and much else' came on the lightning. Much else . . . and a destiny?" He leaned forward in his chair. "Are you telling me . . . you were given a soul?"

"I don't know. To claim one might be an act of pride too great to be forgivable in one whose origins are as miserable as mine. All I can say with certainty is that I was given to know things, blessed with a certain understanding of nature and its ways, knowledge that even Victor will never acquire, nor anyone else this side of death."

"Then," said the priest, "there sits before me a Presence," and the mug between his hands rattled against the table as he trembled.

Deucalion said, "If you have come to wonder if there is any truth in the faith you preach—and I suspect that in spite of your programming, you have at least wondered—then you have entertained the possibility that there is always, at every hour, a Presence with you."

Nearly knocking over his chair as he got to his feet, Duchaine said, "I'm afraid I need something more than coffee." He went to the pantry and returned with two bottles of brandy. "With our metabolism, it takes a quantity to blur the mind."

"None for me," Deucalion said. "I prefer clarity."

The priest filled half his empty mug with coffee, the other half with spirits. He sat. Drank. And said, "You spoke of a destiny, and I can think of only one that would bring you to New Orleans two hundred years later."

"It is my fate to stop him," Deucalion revealed. "To kill him."

The color that had come into the priest's cheeks now drained away.

"Neither of us can raise our hands against him. Your broken face is proof of that."

"We can't. But others can. Those who are of man and woman born owe him no allegiance . . . and no mercy."

The priest took more brandy-spiked coffee. "But we're forbidden to reveal him, forbidden to conspire against him. Those commands are wired into us. We have no capacity to disobey."

"Those proscriptions were not installed in me," Deucalion said. "They no doubt came to him as an afterthought, perhaps on his wedding day two hundred years ago . . . when I murdered his wife."

When Father Duchaine added brandy to his brew, the neck of the bottle rattled against the rim of the mug. "No matter who your god is, life is a vale of tears."

"Victor is no god," Deucalion pressed. "He is not even as little as a false god, nor half as much as a man. With his perverse science and his reckless will, he has made of himself less than he was born, has diminished himself as not even the lowliest beast in nature could abase and degrade itself."

Increasingly agitated in spite of the brandy, Duchaine said, "But there's nothing you can ask of me that I could do, assuming even that I might wish to do it. I cannot *conspire*."

Deucalion finished his coffee. As it had grown cool, it had also grown more bitter. "I'm not asking you to *do* anything, neither to raise a hand nor to conspire against him."

"Then why are you here?"

"All I want from you is what even a false priest can give to his parishioners many times in any day. All I ask is that you extend to me one little grace, one little grace, after which I'll leave and never return."

Judging by his ghastly expression, Father Duchaine had barely sufficient resources to make the revelation that now poured forth: "I've indulged in hateful thoughts about our maker, yours and mine. And only a couple nights ago, I sheltered Jonathan Harker here for a while. Do you know who he was?"

"The detective who turned killer."

"Yes, all over the news. But what the news didn't say . . . Harker was one of us. Both his psychology and his physiology were breaking down. He was . . . changing." Duchaine shuddered. "I didn't conspire with him against Victor. But I sheltered him. Because . . . because I do wonder sometimes about the Presence we discussed."

"One little grace," Deucalion persisted, "one little grace is all I ask."

"What is it then?"

"Tell me where you were made, the name of the place where he does his work, and then I'll go."

Duchaine folded his hands before him, as if in prayer, though the posture more likely represented habit than devotion. He stared at his hands for a while and at last said, "If I tell you, there's a thing I want in return."

"What would that be?" Deucalion asked.

"You killed his wife."

"Yes."

"And so you, his first, were not created with a proscription against murder."

"Only he is safe from me," Deucalion said.

"Then I'll tell you what you wish to know . . . but only if you give me a few hours to prepare myself."

For a moment, Deucalion did not understand, and then he did. "You want me to kill you."

"I'm not capable of asking such a thing."

"I understand. But name the place for me now, and I'll return whenever you wish to . . . finish our business."

The priest shook his head. "I'm afraid that once you have what you want, you won't return. And I need a little while to prepare myself."

"Prepare in what way?"

"This may seem foolish to you, coming as it does from a false and soulless priest. But I want to say the Mass one last time, and pray, even though I know there is no reason I should be heard with a sympathetic ear."

Deucalion rose from his chair. "I see nothing foolish in that request, Father Duchaine. It may be the least foolish thing that you could ask. When would you like me to return—two hours?"

The priest nodded. "It is not too terrible a thing I ask of you, is it?"

"I am not an innocent, Father Duchaine. I have killed before. And surely, after you, I will kill again."

CHAPTER 42

LULANA ST. JOHN and her sister, Evangeline Antoine, brought to Pastor Kenny Laffite two praline-cinnamon cream pies topped with fried pecans.

Evangeline had made two for her employer, Aubrey Picou. On his generous permission, she had made two extra for their minister.

Mr. Aubrey had expressed the desire to eat all four of these pies himself but had acknowledged that to do so would be gluttony, which was—to his recent surprised discovery—one of the seven deadly sins. Besides, poor Mr. Aubrey had periodic intestinal cramps that might not be exacerbated by two of these rich delights but surely would bring him to total ruin if he inflicted four upon himself.

Lulana's and Evangeline's work day was over. Their brother, Moses Bienvenu, had gone home to his wife, Saffron, and their two children, Jasmilay and Larry.

In the late afternoon and evening, the only person attending to Mr. Aubrey was Lulana's and Evangeline's and Moses's brother, Meshach Bienvenu. Like a mother hen looking after her chick, good Meshach would see that his employer was fed and comfortable and, as far as was possible for Mr. Aubrey, righteous.

The sisters came often with gifts of baked goods for Pastor Kenny because he was a wonderful man of God who had been a blessing to their church, because he had a healthy appetite, and because he was not married. At thirty-two, truly devout, charming enough, and handsome by some standards, he was a better catch than a double tubful of catfish.

Romantically speaking, neither sister had a personal interest in him. He was too young for them. Besides, Lulana was happily married, and Evangeline was happily widowed.

They had a niece, however, who would make the perfect wife for a man of the cloth. Her name was Esther, the daughter of their eldest sister, Larissalene. As soon as Esther completed the remaining three months of a sixteen-month course of extensive dental work to correct an unfortunate condition, the sweet girl would be presentable.

Lulana and Evangeline, with a storied history of successful matchmaking, had prepared the way for Esther with scrumptious pies and cakes, cookies and breads and muffins: a more certain path than one paved with palm leaves and rose petals.

Next door to the church, the parsonage was a charming two-story brick house, neither so grand as to embarrass the Lord nor so humble as to make it difficult for the congregation to attract a preacher. The front porch had been furnished with bentwood rocking chairs with cane backs and seats, made festive with hanging baskets of moss from which grew fuchsia with cascades of crimson and purple flowers.

When the sisters, each with a fine pie, climbed the porch steps, they found the front door wide open, as Pastor Kenny most often left it when at home. He was a most welcoming kind of churchman with a casual style, and outside the holy service, he was partial to white tennis shoes, khakis, and madras shirts.

Through the screen door, Lulana could not see much useful. The late twilight of midsummer lay at least half an hour away, but the sunshine was already rouge, and what rays penetrated the windows did little more than brighten black shadows to purple. Toward the back, in the kitchen, a light glowed.

As Evangeline reached to press the bell push, a startling cry came from within the parsonage. It sounded like a soul in misery, rose in volume, quavered, and faded.

Lulana first thought that they had almost intruded on Pastor Kenny in the act of offering consolation to a remorseful or even bereaved member of his flock.

Then the eerie cry came again, and through the screen door, Lulana glimpsed a wailing figure erupt from the living-room archway into the downstairs hall. In spite of the shadows, she could discern that the tormented man was not an anguished sinner or a grieving parishioner but was the minister himself.

"Pastor Kenny?" said Evangeline.

Drawn by his name, the churchman hurried along the hall, toward them, flailing at the air as if batting away mosquitoes.

He did not open the door to them, but peered through the screen with the expression of a man who had seen, and only moments ago fled, the devil.

"I did it, didn't I?" he said, breathless and anguished. "Yes. Yes, I did. I did it just by being. Just by being, I did it. Just by being Pastor Kenny Laffite, I did it, I did. I did it, I did."

Something about the rhythm and repetition of his words reminded Lulana of those children's books by Dr. Seuss, with which she had felt afflicted as a child. "Pastor Kenny, what's wrong?"

"I am who I am. He isn't, I am. So I did it, I did it, I did," he declared, turned from the screen door, and ran away along the hall, flailing at the air in distress.

After a moment of consideration, Lulana said, "Sister, I believe we are needed here."

Evangeline said, "I have no doubt of it, dear."

Although uninvited, Lulana opened the screen door, entered the parsonage, and held the door for her sister.

From the back of the house came the minister's voice: "What will I do? What, what will I do? Anything, anything—that's what I'll do."

As squat and sturdy as a tugboat, her formidable bosom cleaving air like a prow cleaves water, Lulana sailed along the hallway, and Evangeline, like a stately tall-masted ship, followed in her wake.

In the kitchen, the minister stood at the sink, vigorously washing his hands. "Thou shall not, shall not, *shall not,* but I did. *Shall not,* but did."

Lulana opened the refrigerator and found room for both pies. "Evangeline, we have more nervous here than God made grass. Maybe it won't be needed, but best have some warm milk ready."

"You leave that to me, dear."

"Thank you, sister."

Clouds of steam rose from the sink. Lulana saw that under the rushing water, the minister's hands were fiery red.

"Pastor Kenny, you're about to half scald yourself."

"Just by being, I am. I am what I am. I am what I did. I did it, I did."

The faucet was so hot that Lulana had to wrap a dishtowel around her hand to turn it off.

Pastor Kenny tried to turn it on again.

She gently slapped his hand, as she might affectionately warn a child not to repeat a misbehavior. "Now, Pastor Kenny, you dry off and come sit at the table."

Without using the towel, the minister turned from the sink but also away from the table. On wobbly legs, drizzling water from his red hands, he headed toward the refrigerator.

He wailed and groaned, as they first heard him when they had been standing on the front porch.

Beside the refrigerator, a knife rack hung on the wall. Lulana believed Pastor Kenny to be a good man, a man of God, and she had no fear of him, but under the circumstances, it seemed a good idea to steer him away from knives.

With a wad of paper towels, Evangeline followed them, mopping the water off the floor.

Taking the minister by one arm, guiding him as best she could, Lulana said, "Pastor Kenny, you're much distressed, you're altogether beside yourself. You need to sit down and let out some nervous, let in some peace."

Although he appeared to be so stricken that he could hardly stay on his feet, the minister circled the table with her once and then half again before she could get him into a chair.

He sobbed but didn't weep. This was terror, not grief.

Already, Evangeline had found a large pot, which she filled with hot water at the sink.

The minister fisted his hands against his chest, rocked back and forth in his chair, his voice wrenched by misery. "So sudden, all of a sudden, I realized just what I am, what I did, what trouble I'm in, such *trouble*."

"We're here now, Pastor Kenny. When you share your troubles, they weigh less on you. You share them with me and Evangeline, and your troubles will weigh a third of what they do now."

Evangeline had put the pot of water on the cooktop and turned up the gas flame. Now she got a carton of milk from the refrigerator.

"You share your troubles with God, why, then they just float off your shoulders, no weight to them at all. Surely I don't need to tell you, of all people, how they'll float."

Having unclenched his hands and raised them before his face, he stared at them in horror. "Thou shall not, shall not, not, not, *NOT*!"

His breath did not smell of alcohol. She was loath to think that he might have inhaled something less wholesome than God's sweet air, but if the reverend was a cokehead, she supposed it was better to find out now than after Esther's teeth were fixed and the courtship had begun.

"We're given more shalls than shall-nots," Lulana said, striving to break through to him. "But there are enough shall-nots that I need you to be more specific. Shall not what, Pastor Kenny?"

"Kill," he said, and shuddered.

Lulana looked at her sister. Evangeline, milk carton in hand, raised her eyebrows.

"I did it, I did it. I did it, I did."

"Pastor Kenny," Lulana said, "I know you to be a gentle man, and kind. Whatever you think you've done, I'm sure it's not so terrible as you believe."

He lowered his hands. At last he looked at her. "I killed him."

"Who would that be?" Lulana asked.

"I never had a chance," the troubled man whispered. "He never had a chance. Neither of us had a chance."

Evangeline found a Mason jar into which she began to pour the milk from the carton.

"He's dead," said the minister.

"Who?" Lulana persisted.

"He's dead, and I'm dead. I was dead from the start."

In Lulana's cell phone were stored the many numbers of a large family, plus those of an even larger family of friends. Although Mr. Aubrey—Aubrey Picou, her employer—had been finding his way to redemption faster than he realized (if slower than Lulana wished), he nonetheless remained a man with a scaly past that might one day snap back and bite him; therefore, in her directory were the office, mobile, and home numbers for Michael Maddison, in case Mr. Aubrey ever needed a policeman to give him a fair hearing. Now she keyed in Michael's name, got his cell number, and called it.

CHAPTER 43

IN THE WINDOWLESS Victorian drawing room beyond the two vault doors, Erika circled the immense glass case, studying every detail. At first it had resembled a big jewel box, which it still did; but now it also seemed like a coffin, though an oversized and highly unconventional one.

She had no reason to believe that it contained a body. At the center of the case, the shape shrouded by the amber liquid—or gas—had no discernible limbs or features. It was just a dark mass without detail; it might have been anything.

If the case in fact contained a body, the specimen was large: about seven and a half feet long, more than three feet wide.

She examined the ornate ormolu frame under which the panels of glass were joined, searching for seams that might indicate concealed hinges. She could not find any. If the top of the box was a lid, it operated on some principle that eluded her.

When she rapped a knuckle against the glass, the sound suggested a thickness of at least one inch.

She noticed that under the glass, directly below the spot where her knuckle struck it, the amberness—whatever its nature—dimpled as water dimples when a stone drops into it. The dimple bloomed sapphire blue, resolved into a ring, and receded across the surface; the amber hue was reestablished in its wake.

She rapped again, with the same effect. When she rapped three times in succession, three concentric blue rings appeared, receded, faded.

Although her knuckle had made only the briefest contact, the glass had seemed cold. When she flattened her palm against it, she discovered that it was icy, though a few degrees too warm for her skin to freeze to it.

When she knelt on the Persian carpet and peered under the case, between its exquisitely sculpted ball-in-claw feet, she could see electrical conduits and pipes of various colors and diameters that came out of the bottom and disappeared into the floor. This suggested that a service room must lie below, although the mansion supposedly had no basement.

Victor owned one of the largest properties in the neighborhood and in fact had combined two great houses so elegantly that he had earned plaudits from historical preservationists. All of the interior reconstruction had been undertaken by members of the New Race, but not all of it had been disclosed to—or permitted by—the city's building department.

Her brilliant husband had achieved more than entire universities of scientists. His accomplishments were even more remarkable when you considered that he had been forced to do his work clandestinely—and since the regrettable death of Mao Tse-tung, without grants from any government.

She got to her feet and circled the case once more, trying to determine if there was a head or foot to it, as there would be to any bed or casket. The design of the object offered her no clue, but she at last decided, sheerly by intuition, that the head of it must be the end farthest from the door to the room.

Bending forward, bending low and lower, Erika put her face close to the top of the case, peering intently into amber miasma, close and then closer, hoping for at least a faint suggestion of contour or texture to the shadowy shape within the liquid shroud.

When her lips were no more than two inches from the glass, she said softly, "Hello, hello, hello in there."

This time it *definitely* moved.

CHAPTER 44

DOG-NOSE NICK stood on the rim of the pit, breathing deeply of the stink brought to him by a light breeze that came down out of the declining sun.

More than an hour ago, the last of the day's incoming trucks had dumped its load, and Crosswoods Waste Management had closed its gates until dawn. Now it was its own world, a universe encircled by chainlink topped with razor wire.

In the night ahead, the members of Nick Frigg's crew were free to be who they were, what they were. They could do what they wanted, without concern that an Old Race truck driver might see behavior that belied their pose of sanitation-worker normality.

Down in the west pit below him, crew members were wedging polemounted torches into the trash field in the area where the interments would take place. After nightfall, they would light the oil lamp at the top of each pole.

With their enhanced vision, Nick and his people didn't need as much light as they were providing, but for these ceremonies, torches set the perfect mood. Even those of the New Race, even Gammas like Nick, and even lowly Epsilons like the crew he bossed, could thrill to stagecraft.

Perhaps especially the Epsilons. They were more intelligent than animals, of course, but in some ways they were like animals in their simplicity and excitability.

Sometimes it seemed to Nick Frigg that the longer these Epsilons lived here in Crosswoods, having little contact with any Gamma other than he himself, having no contact at all with Betas or Alphas, the more simpleminded and more animalistic they became, as though without higher classes of the New Race to serve as examples, they could not entirely hold fast to even the meager knowledge and modest standards of deportment that had been downloaded into their brains while they had been in their tanks.

After the interments, the crew would feast, drink very much, and have sex. They would eat hungrily at the start, and soon they would be tearing at their food, gorging with abandon. The liquor would flow directly from bottle to mouth, mixed with nothing, undiluted, to maximize and accelerate its effect. The sex would be eager and selfish, then insistent and angry, then savage, no desire unindulged, no sensation unexperienced.

They would find relief from loneliness, meaninglessness. But the relief came only *during* the feeding, *during* the drinking and the sex. After, the anguish would return like a hammer, driving the nail deeper, deeper, deeper. Which they always forgot. Because they *needed* to forget.

At this moment, Gunny Alecto and other crewmen were at the walk-in cooler, loading the five human bodies and three dead gone-wrongs onto a pair of small, open-bed, four-wheel-drive trucks that would convey them to the site of the ceremony. The Old Race cadavers would be on one truck, the gone-wrongs on another.

The Old Race dead would be transported with less respect than gone-wrongs received, in fact with no respect at all. Their bodies would be subjected to grotesque indignities.

In the class structure of the New Race, the Epsilons had no one to whom they could feel superior—except those of the Old Race. And in these interment ceremonies, they expressed a hatred of such purity and such long-simmering reduction that no one in the history of the earth had ever despised more intensely, loathed more ferociously, or abominated their enemy with greater fury.

Some fun tonight.

CHAPTER 45

AT THE HANDS OF MERCY, none of the three isolation rooms had been designed to contain a deadly disease, for Victor did not have an interest in the engineering of microorganisms. There was no danger whatsoever that he would accidentally create a deadly new virus or bacterium.

Consequently, the twenty-by-fifteen-foot chamber that he chose for Werner was not surrounded by a positive-pressure envelope to prevent the escape of airborne microbes and spoors. Neither did it have its own self-contained ventilation system.

The isolation room had been meant solely to contain any New Race variant—he experimented with some exotic ones—that Victor suspected might prove difficult to manage and any that unexpectedly exhibited antisocial behavior of a lethal nature.

Therefore, the walls, ceiling, and floor of the chamber were of poured-in-place, steel-reinforced concrete to a thickness of eighteen inches. The interior surfaces had been paneled with three overlapping layers of quarter-inch steel plate.

If necessary, a killing electrical charge could be introduced into those steel plates with the flip of the switch in the adjoining monitor room.

Sole access to the isolation chamber was through a transition module between it and the monitor room.

The staff sometimes referred to it as the air lock, although this inaccurate term annoyed Victor. No atmosphere changes occurred during the use of the transition module, and there was not even a simple recycling of air.

The module featured two round steel doors that had been made for bank vaults. By design, it was mechanically impossible to have both doors open at the same time; therefore, when the inner door opened, a prisoner of the isolation chamber might get into the vestibule, but it could not break through into the monitor room.

On a gurney, his flesh undergoing cellular breakdown if not even molecular reorganization, Werner had been rushed through the halls of Mercy, into the monitor room, through the module, into the isolation chamber, with Victor urging the attendants to "hurry, faster, damn you, *run!*"

The staff might have thought that blind panic had seized their maker, but Victor couldn't concern himself with what they thought. Werner had been secured in that fortresslike cell, which was all that mattered.

When the hand had formed out of the amorphous flesh of Werner's torso, it had taken hold of Victor's hand tenderly, beseechingly. But the initial docility dared not be taken as a reliable prediction of a benign transformation.

Nothing remotely like this had ever happened before. Such a sudden collapse of cellular integrity accompanied by self-driven biological reformation should not be possible.

Common sense suggested that such a radical metamorphosis, which must obviously include drastic changes in cerebral tissues, would entail the loss of a significant percentage of the direct-to-brain data and programming that Werner had received in the tank, including perhaps the proscription against killing his maker.

Prudence and responsible haste—not *panic*—had been required. As a man of unequaled scientific vision, Victor had at once foreseen the worst-case scenario and had acted with admirable calm yet with alacrity to respond to the danger and to contain the threat.

He made a mental note to circulate a stern memo to that effect throughout Mercy before the end of the day.

He would dictate it to Annunciata.

No, he would compose it and distribute it himself, and to hell with Annunciata.

In the monitor room, where Victor gathered with Ripley and four additional staff members, a bank of six rectangular high-definition screens, each displaying the closed-circuit feed from one of six cameras in the isolation chamber, revealed that Werner still remained in a disturbingly plastic condition. At the moment, he had four legs, no arms, and an ill-defined, continuously shifting body out of which thrust a vaguely Wernerlike head.

Highly agitated, the Werner thing jittered around the isolation chamber, mewling like a wounded animal and sometimes saying, "Father? Father? *Father?*"

This *father* business irritated Victor almost beyond the limits of his endurance. He didn't shout *Shut up, shut up, shut up* at the screens only because he wished to avoid the necessity of adding a second paragraph to that memo.

He did not want them to think of him as their father. They were not his family; they were his inventions, his fabrications, and most surely his property. He was their maker, their owner, their master, and even their leader, if they wished to think of him that way, but not their paterfamilias.

The family was a primitive and destructive institution because it put itself above the good of society as a whole. The parent-child relationship was counter-revolutionary and must be eradicated. For his creations, their entire race would be their family, each of them the brother or the sister of all the others, so that no particular relationship would be different from all the others or more special than all the others.

One race, one family, one great humming hive working in unison, without the distractions of individuality and family, could achieve *anything* to which it set its mind and its bottomless bustling energy, unhampered by childish emotions, freed from all superstition, could conquer any challenge that the universe might hold for it. A dynamic, unstoppable species of heretofore unimagined determination, gathering ever greater momentum, would rush on, rush on, to glory after glory, in his name.

Watching the four-legged, mewling, jittering Werner thing as it began to sprout something like but not like arms from its back, Ripley raised his ridiculous eyebrows and said, "Like Harker."

Victor at once rebuked him. "This is nothing like Harker. Harker was a singularity. Harker spawned a parasitical second self. Nothing like that is happening to Werner."

Riveted by the shocking images on the screen, Ripley said, "But, Mr. Helios, sir, he appears to be—"

"Werner is not spawning a parasitical second self," Victor said tightly. "Werner is experiencing catastrophic cellular metamorphosis. It's not the same. It is not the same at all. Werner is a *different* singularity."

CHAPTER 46

CINDI AND BENNY LOVEWELL, one a believer in the science of voodoo and one not, reestablished contact with Detectives O'Connor and Maddison through the signal emitted by the transponder under the hood of their police-department sedan. They caught up with their targets—but remained out of visual contact—in the Garden District.

For long minutes, the cops cruised the same few blocks, around and around, and then changed directions, cruising the identical territory in the opposite direction, making one circuit and then another.

"Like a blind rat in a maze," Cindi said solemnly, identifying as before with O'Connor's childlessness.

"No," Benny disagreed. "This is different."

"You wouldn't understand."

"I have the same capacity for understanding that you do."

"Not about this, you don't. You aren't female."

"Well, if it's necessary to have ever had a womb in order to be female, then you aren't female, either. You don't have a womb. You were not designed to produce a baby, and you cannot possibly become pregnant."

"We'll see what Ibo has to say about that," she replied smugly. *"Je suis rouge."*

Studying the blinking blip as it moved on the screen, Benny said, "They're cruising so slow. . . ."

"You want to make contact, block them to the curb, knock 'em cold, and take them?"

"Not here. This is the kind of neighborhood where people call the police. We'll end up in a pursuit." After watching the screen for another minute, he said, "They're looking for something."

"For what?"

"How would I know?"

"Too bad Zozo Deslisle isn't here," Cindi said. "She has voodoo vision. Give her one look at that screen, and she'd know what they're up to."

"I'm wrong," Benny said. "They aren't searching. They've found what they want, and now they're casing it."

"Casing what? Thieves case banks. There aren't any banks in this neighborhood, only houses."

As Benny squinted at the screen, feeling an answer teasing along the edge of his mind, the target abruptly accelerated. The red blip hung a U-turn on the screen and started moving fast.

"What're they doing now?" Cindi asked.

"They're cops. Maybe they got an emergency call. Stay with them. Don't let them see us, but try to close to within a block. Maybe we'll get an opportunity."

A minute later, Cindi said, "They're heading for the Quarter. That's too public for us."

"Stay with them anyway."

The detectives didn't stop in the Quarter. They followed the curve of the river through Faubourg Marigny into the neighborhood known as Bywater.

The blip on the screen stopped moving, and by the time the Lovewells caught up with the plainwrap sedan, in the first orange flush of twilight, it was parked near a church, in front of a two-story brick house. O'Connor and Maddison were nowhere to be seen.

CHAPTER 47

CARSON SAT ACROSS the kitchen table from Lulana St. John, cater-corner to Pastor Kenny Laffite.

Michael stood near the cooktop, where Evangeline was heating a Mason jar full of milk in a pot of water.

"Heating it directly in a pan," she told Michael, "you risk scalding it."

"Then it gets a skin, doesn't it?" he asked.

She grimaced. "Burnt scum on the bottom and skin on top."

The minister sat with his arms on the table, staring with horror at his hands. "I just suddenly realized I did it. Just by being me, I killed him. And killing is *forbidden*."

"Pastor Laffite," Carson said, "you are not required by law to answer our questions without your attorney present. Do you want to call your attorney?"

"This good man didn't kill anybody," Lulana protested. "Whatever happened it was an accident."

Carson and Michael had already conducted a quick search of the house and had not found either a dead body or any signs of violence.

"Pastor Laffite," Carson said, "please look at me."

The minister kept staring at his hands. His eyes were opened as wide as eyes could be, and they weren't blinking.

"Pastor Laffite," she said, "forgive me, but you seem zoned-out and wigged-out at the same time. I'm concerned that you may recently have used an illegal drug."

"The moment I woke up," said the minister, "he was dead or soon to be. Just by waking up, I killed him."

"Pastor Laffite, do you understand that anything you say to me now could be used against you in a court of law?"

"This good man won't ever be in a court of law," Lulana said. "He's just confused somehow. That's why I wanted you two instead of others. I knew you wouldn't leap to conclusions."

The minister's eyes had still not blinked. They weren't tearing up, either. They should have started to tear up from not blinking.

From his post by the cooktop, Michael said, "Pastor, who is it you think you killed?"

"I killed Pastor Kenny Laffite," the minister said.

Lulana gave herself to surprise with some enthusiasm, pulling her head back, letting her jaw drop, putting one hand to her bosom. "Praise the Lord, Pastor Kenny, you can't have killed yourself. You're sitting right here with us."

He switched from zoned to wigged again: "See, see, see, it's like this, it's fundamental. I'm not permitted to kill. But by the very fact of my existence, by the very *fact,* I am at least partly responsible for his death, so on the very day of my creation, I was in violation of my program. My program is flawed. If my program is flawed, what else might I do that I'm not supposed to do, what else, what else, *what else?*"

Carson glanced at Michael.

He had been leaning casually against the counter by the cooktop. He was standing tall now, his hands hanging loose at his sides.

"Pastor Kenny," Lulana said, taking one of his hands in both of hers, "you've been under a terrible stress, tryin' to raise funds for the church remodel on top of all your other duties—"

"—five weddings in one month," Evangeline added. Holding the Mason jar with an oven mitt, she poured warm milk into a glass. "And three funerals besides."

Carson eased her chair back from the table as Lulana said, "And all of this work you've had to do without the comfort of a wife. It's no surprise you're exhausted and distressed."

Spooning sugar into the milk, Evangeline said, "Our own Uncle Absalom worked himself to the bone without the comfort of a wife, and one day he started seeing fairies."

"By which she means not homosexuals," Lulana assured Laffite, "but the little creatures with wings."

Carson rose from her chair and took a step away from the table as Evangeline, adding several drops of vanilla extract to the milk, said, "Seeing fairies was nothing to be ashamed about. Uncle Absalom just needed some rest, some tender care, and he was fine, never saw fairies again."

"I'm not supposed to kill people, but by the very *fact* of my existence, I killed Kenny Laffite," said Kenny Laffite, "and I really want to kill more."

"That's just weariness talking," Lulana assured him, and patted his hand. "Crazy weariness, that's all, Pastor Kenny. You don't want to kill anyone."

"I do," he disagreed. He closed his eyes and hung his head. "And now if my program is flawed, maybe I will. I want to kill all of you, and maybe I will."

Michael blocked Evangeline from carrying the glass of milk to the table.

Executing a smooth cross-body draw of the Desert Eagle from the scabbard on her left hip, gripping it in two hands, Carson said, "Lulana, you said when we first came that you stopped by to bring Pastor Laffite two pies."

Lulana's molasses-brown eyes were huge and focused on the golden gun. "Carson O'Connor, this is an overreaction not worthy of you. This poor—"

"Lulana," Carson interrupted with the slightest edge in her voice, "why don't you get one of those pies out of the refrigerator and cut some for all of us."

With his head still hung, with his chin on his chest and eyes closed, Laffite said, "My program's breaking down. I can feel it happening . . . sort of a slow-motion stroke. Lines of installed code falling out, falling off, like a long row of electrified birds dropping off a power line."

Evangeline Antoine said, "Sister, maybe that pie would be a good idea."

As Lulana, on further consideration, pushed her chair away from the table and got to her feet, Michael's cell phone rang.

Laffite raised his head but did not open his eyes. The rapid eye movement behind his closed lids was that of a man experiencing vivid dreams.

Michael's phone rang again, and Carson said, "Don't let it go to voice mail."

As Lulana moved not toward the refrigerator but instead toward her sister and out of the line of fire, Laffite said, "How odd that this should be happening to an Alpha."

Carson heard Michael giving the address of the parsonage to the caller.

As his eyes continued to roll and twitch under his lids, Laffite said, "'The thing which I greatly feared is come upon me.'"

"Job three, verse twenty-five," said Lulana.

"'Fear came upon me,'" Laffite continued, "'and trembling, which made all my bones to shake.'"

"Job four, verse fourteen," said Evangeline.

To reach either the door to the back porch or the door to the hallway, the sisters would have had to pass into the line of fire. They huddled together in the safest corner of the kitchen that they could find.

Having concluded his phone call, Michael positioned himself to Carson's left, between Laffite and the sisters, his own .50 Magnum in a two-hand grip.

"'Gather me the people together,'" said Laffite, "'and I will make them hear my words, that they may learn to fear me all the days that they shall live upon the earth.'"

"Deuteronomy," Lulana said.

"Chapter four, verse ten," Evangeline added.

"Deucalion?" Carson murmured, referring to the phone call.

"Yeah."

Laffite opened his eyes. "I've revealed myself to you. Further proof that my program is breaking down. We must move secretly among you, never revealing our difference or our purpose."

"We're cool," Michael told him. "We don't have a problem with it. Just sit for a while, Pastor Kenny, just sit there and watch the little birds dropping off the wire."

CHAPTER 48

RANDAL SIX IS ANGRY with himself for killing Arnie's mother. "Stupid," he says. "Stupid."

He is not angry with her. There is no point being angry with a dead person.

He didn't intend to hit her. He just suddenly found himself *doing* it, in the same way that he broke the neck of the hobo in the Dumpster.

In retrospect, he sees that he was not in danger. Self-defense did not require such extreme measures.

After his sheltered existence at the Hands of Mercy, he needs more experience in the larger world to be able accurately to judge the seriousness of a threat.

Then he discovers that Arnie's mother is only unconscious. This relieves him of the need to be angry with himself.

Although he had been angry with himself for less than two minutes, the experience was grueling. When other people are angry with you—as Victor often is—you can turn further inward and escape from them. When it is you yourself who is angry with you, turning inward does not work because no matter how deep you go inside yourself, the angry you is still there.

The knife wound in his hand has already stopped bleeding. The lacerations will be completely closed in two or three hours.

The splatters of blood on the floor and the appliances distress him. These stains detract from the almost spiritual atmosphere that reigns here. This is a *home,* and the kitchen is its heart, and at all times there should be a feeling of calm, of peace.

With paper towels and a spray bottle of Windex, he wipes away the blood.

Carefully, without touching her skin, because he does not like the feel of other people's skin, Randal ties the mother to the chair with lengths of cloth that he tears from the garments in the laundry-room basket.

As he finishes securing her, the mother regains consciousness. She is anxious, agitated, full of questions and assumptions and pleas.

Her shrill tone of voice and her frantic chatter make Randal nervous. She is asking a third question before he can answer the first. Her demands on him are too many, the input from her too great to process.

Rather than hit her, he walks down the hall to the living room, where he stands for a while. Twilight has come. The room is nearly dark. No excited talking mother is present. In mere minutes, he feels much better.

He returns to the kitchen, and the moment he arrives there, the mother starts chattering again.

When he tells her to be quiet, she becomes more vocal than ever, and her pleas become more urgent.

He almost wishes that he were back under the house with the spiders.

She is not behaving like a mother. Mothers are calm. Mothers have all the answers. Mothers love you.

Generally, Randal Six does not like touching others or being touched. This is perhaps different. This is a mother even if she is not at the moment acting like one.

He places his right hand under her chin and forces her mouth shut, even as he pinches her nose with his left hand. She struggles at first but then becomes still when she realizes that he is very strong.

Before the mother passes out from oxygen deprivation, Randal takes his hand from her nose and allows her to breathe. He continues to hold her mouth shut.

"Ssshhhhh," he says. "Quiet. Randal likes quiet. Randal scares too easy. Noise scares Randal. Too much talk, too many words scares Randal. Don't scare Randal."

When he feels that she is ready to cooperate, he releases her. She says nothing. She is breathing hard, almost gasping, but she is done with talking for now.

Randal Six turns off the gas flame at the cooktop to prevent the onions from burning in the pan. This constitutes a higher level of involvement with his environment than he's exhibited before, an awareness of peripheral issues, and he is pleased with himself.

Perhaps he will discover a talent for cooking.

He gets a tablespoon from the flatware drawer and the quart of strawberry-banana swirl from the freezer. He sits at the kitchen table, across from Arnie's mother, and spoons the pink-and-yellow treat from the container.

This is not better than brown food, but it is not worse. Just different, still wonderful.

He smiles across the table at her because this seems to be a domestic moment—perhaps even an important bonding moment—that requires a smile.

Clearly, however, she is distressed by his smile, perhaps because she can tell that it is calculated and not sincere. Mothers know.

"Randal will ask some questions. You will answer. Randal does not want to hear your too many, too noisy questions. Just answers. Short answers, not chatter."

She understands. She nods.

"My name is Randal." When she does not respond, he says, "Oh. What is your name?"

"Vicky."

"For now, Randal will call you Vicky. Will it be all right if Randal calls you Vicky?"

"Yes."

"You are the first mother that Randal has ever met. Randal does not want to kill mothers. Do you want to be killed?"

"No. Please."

"Many people do want to be killed. Mercy people. Because they aren't able to kill themselves."

He pauses to spoon more ice cream into his mouth.

Licking his lips, he continues: "This tastes better than spiders and earthworms and rodents would've tasted. Randal likes in a house better than under a house. Do you like it better in a house than under a house?"

"Yes."

"Have you ever been in a Dumpster with a dead hobo?"

She stares at him and says nothing.

He assumes that she is searching her memory, but after a while, he says, "Vicky? Have you ever been in a Dumpster with a dead hobo?"

"No. No, I haven't."

Randal Six has never been so proud of himself as he is at this moment. This is the first conversation he has had with anyone other than his maker at Mercy. And it is going *so* well.

CHAPTER 49

WERNER'S LIFELONG PROBLEM with excess mucus production was a minor annoyance compared to his current tribulations.

In the monitor room, Victor, Ripley, and four awe-stricken staff members watched the six closed-circuit screens as the security chief careened around the isolation chamber on four legs. The back two were as they had been at the start of this episode. Although his forelegs closely resembled the back pair, the articulation of the shoulder joints had changed dramatically.

The powerful shoulders suggested those of a jungle cat. As Werner prowled restlessly in that other room, his metamorphosis continued, and all four legs began to appear increasingly feline. As in any cat, an elbow developed at the posterior terminus of the shoulder muscle to complement a foreleg joint structure that included a knee but a more flexible wrist instead of an ankle.

This intrigued Victor because he had included in Werner's design selected genetic material from a panther to increase his agility and speed.

The hind legs became more feline, developing a long metatarsus above the toes, a heel midway up the limb, and a knee close to the body trunk. The relationship between the rump, the thigh, and the flank shifted, proportions changing as well.

On the hind legs, the human feet melted completely into pawlike structures with blunt toes that featured impressive claws. On the forelegs, however, though dewclaws formed at the pasterns, elements of the human hand persisted, even if the fingers now terminated in claw sheaths and claws.

All of these transformations presented themselves clearly for consideration because Werner did not develop fur. He was hairless and pink.

Although this crisis had not passed—in fact may only have begun—Victor was able to bring cool scientific detachment to his observations now that Werner had been contained and the threat of imminent violence had been eliminated.

Often over the decades, he had learned more from his setbacks than from his numerous successes. Failure could be a legitimate father of progress, especially *his* failures, which were more likely to advance the cause of knowledge than were the greatest triumphs of lesser scientists.

Victor was fascinated by the bold manifestation of nonhuman characteristics for which no genes had been included. Although the security chief's *musculature* had been enhanced with genetic material from a panther, he did not carry the code that would express feline legs, and he *certainly* had not been engineered to have a tail, which now began to form.

The Werner head, still familiar, moved on a thicker and more sinuous neck than any man had ever enjoyed. The eyes, when turned toward a camera, appeared to have the elliptical irises of a cat, though no genes related to feline vision had been spliced into his chromosomes.

This suggested either that Victor had made a mistake with Werner or that somehow Werner's astonishingly amorphous flesh was able to extrapolate every detail of an animal from mere scraps of its genetic structure. Although it was an outrageous concept, flatly impossible, he leaned toward that second explanation.

In addition to the six-camera coverage of Werner's lycanthropy-quick metamorphosis, microphones in the isolation chamber fed his voice into the monitor room. Whether he was aware of the full extent of the physical changes racking his body could not be determined by what he said, for unfortunately his words were gibberish. Mostly he screamed.

Judging by the intensity and the nature of the screams, both mental anguish and unrelenting physical agony accompanied the metamorphosis. Evidently, Werner no longer possessed the ability to switch off pain.

When suddenly a clear word was discernible—"Father, Father"—Victor killed the audio feed and satisfied himself with the silent images.

Scientists at Harvard, Yale, Oxford, and every major research university in the world had in recent years been experimenting with cross-species gene-splicing. They had inserted genetic material of spiders into goats, which then produced milk laced with webs. They had bred mice that carried bits of human DNA, and several teams were in competition to be the first to produce a pig with a human brain.

"But only I," Victor declared, gazing at the six screens, "have created the chimera of ancient myth, the beast of many parts that functions as one creature."

"Is he functioning?" Ripley asked.

"You can see as well as I," Victor replied impatiently. "He runs with great speed."

"In tortured circles."

"His body is supple and strong."

"And changing again," said Ripley.

Werner, too, had something of the spider in him, and something of the cockroach, to increase the ductility of his tendons, to invest his collagen with greater tensile-strain capacity. Now these arachnid and insectile elements appeared to be expressing themselves at the expense of the panther form.

"Biological chaos," Ripley whispered.

"Pay attention," Victor advised him. "In this we will find clues that will lead inevitably to the greatest advancements in the history of genetics and molecular biology."

"Are we absolutely sure," Ripley asked, "that the transition-module doors completed their lock cycle?"

All four of the other staff members answered as one: "Yes."

The image on one of the six screens blurred to gray, and the face of Annunciata materialized.

Assuming that she had appeared in error, Victor almost shouted at her to disengage.

Before he could speak, however, she said, "Mr. Helios, an Alpha has made an urgent request for a meeting with you."

"Which Alpha?"

"Patrick Duchaine, rector of Our Lady of Sorrows."

"Patch his call through to these speakers."

"He did not telephone, Mr. Helios. He came to the front door of Mercy."

Because these days the Hands of Mercy presented itself to the world as a private warehouse with little daily business, those born here did not return for any purpose, lest an unusual flow of visitors might belie the masquerade. Duchaine's visit was a breach of protocol that suggested he had news of an important nature to impart.

"Send him to me," Victor told Annunciata.

"Yes, Mr. Helios. Yes."

CHAPTER 50

LAFFITE OPENED HIS EYES. "I've revealed myself to you. Further proof that my program is breaking down. We must move secretly among you, never revealing our difference or our purpose."

"We're cool," Michael told him. "We don't have a problem with it. Just sit for a while, Pastor Kenny, just sit there and watch the little birds dropping off the wire."

As Michael spoke those words, less than a minute after he had terminated his cell-phone conversation with Deucalion, the giant entered the parsonage kitchen from the downstairs hall.

Carson had grown so accustomed to the big man's inexplicable arrivals and mysterious departures that the Desert Eagle in her two-hand grip didn't twitch a fraction of an inch but remained sighted dead-still on the minister's chest.

"What—you called me from the front porch?" Michael asked.

Immense, fearsome, tattooed, Deucalion nodded to Lulana and Evangeline, and said, "'God has not given us the spirit of fear, but of power, and of love, and of a sound mind.'"

"Timothy," Lulana said shakily, "chapter one, verse seven."

"I may look like a devil," Deucalion told the sisters, to put them at ease, "but if I ever was one, I am not anymore."

"He's a good guy," Michael assured them. "I don't know a Bible verse for the occasion, but I guarantee he's a good guy."

Deucalion sat at the table, in the chair that Lulana recently had occupied. "Good evening, Pastor Laffite."

The minister's eyes had been glazed, as if he'd been staring through the veil between this world and another. Now he focused on Deucalion.

"I didn't recognize Timothy one, verse seven," Laffite said. "More of my program is dropping out. I'm losing who I am. Say me another verse."

Deucalion recited: "'Behold, he is all vanity. His works are nothing. His molten images are wind and confusion.'"

"I do not know it," said the preacher.

"Isaiah sixteen, verse twenty-nine," said Evan-geline, "but he's tweaked it a little."

To Deucalion, Laffite said, "You chose a verse that describes . . . Helios."

"Yes."

Carson wondered if she and Michael could lower their guns. She decided that if it was wise to do so, Deucalion would already have advised them to relax. She stayed ready.

"How can you know about Helios?" Laffite asked.

"I was his first. Crude by your standards."

"But your program hasn't dropped out."

"I don't even have a program as you think of it."

Laffite shuddered violently and closed his eyes. "Something just went. What was it?"

His eyes again moved rapidly up and down, side to side, under his lids.

"I can give you what you want most," Deucalion told him.

"I think . . . yes . . . I have just lost the ability to switch off pain."

"Have no fear. I will make it painless. One thing I want from you in return."

Laffite said nothing.

"You have spoken his name," Deucalion said, "and have shown that in some other ways, your program no longer restrains you. So tell me . . . the place where you were born, where he does his work."

His voice thickening slightly as if points had been shaved off his IQ, Laffite said, "I am a child of Mercy. Mercy born and Mercy raised."

"What does that mean?" Deucalion pressed.

"The Hands of Mercy," said Laffite. "The Hands of Mercy and the tanks of Hell."

"It's an old Catholic hospital," Carson realized. "The Hands of Mercy."

"They closed it down when I was just a little kid," Michael said. "It's something else now, a warehouse. They bricked in all the windows."

"I could kill you all now," Laffite said, but he did not open his eyes. "I used to want to kill you all. So bad, I used to want it, so bad."

Lulana began to weep softly, and Evangeline said, "Hold my hand, sister."

To Carson, Deucalion said, "Take the ladies out of here. Take them home now."

"One of us could take them home," she suggested, "and one of us stay here to give you backup."

"This is between just me and Pastor Laffite. I need to give him a little grace, a little grace and a long rest."

Returning the Magnum to his holster, Michael said, "Ladies, you should take your praline pies with you. They don't prove beyond doubt that you were here, but you should take them with you anyway."

As the women retrieved the pies from the refrigerator and as Michael shepherded them out of the kitchen, Carson kept the gun on Laffite.

"We'll meet later at your house," Deucalion told her. "In a little while."

"'Darkness was upon the face of the deep,'" Laffite said in his thicker voice. "Is that one, or have I remembered nothing?"

"Genesis one, verse two," Deucalion told him. Then he indicated with a gesture that Carson should leave.

She lowered the pistol and reluctantly departed.

As she stepped into the hall, she heard Laffite say, "He says we'll live a thousand years. I feel as if I already have."

CHAPTER 51

IN THE SECRET drawing room, Erika considered speaking again to the occupant of the glass case.

Without question, it had moved: a shadowy spasm within its amber shroud of liquid or gas. Either it had responded to her voice or the timing of its movement had been coincidental.

The Old Race had a saying: There are no coincidences.

They were superstitious, however, and irrational.

As she had been taught in the tank, the universe is nothing *but* a sea of chaos in which random chance collides with happenstance and spins shatters of meaningless coincidence like shrapnel through our lives.

The purpose of the New Race is to impress order on the face of chaos, to harness the awesome destructive power of the universe and make it serve their needs, to bring meaning to a creation that has been meaningless since time immemorial. And the meaning they will impose upon it is the meaning of their maker, the exaltation of his name and face, the fulfillment of his vision and his every desire, their satisfaction achieved solely by the perfect implementation of his will.

That creed, part of her basic programming, rose into her mind word for word, with remembered music by Wagner and images of millions of the New Race marching in cadence. Her brilliant husband could have been a poet if mere poetry had not been unworthy of his genius.

After she had spoken to the occupant of the case, a primal fear had overcome her, seeming to rise from her very blood and bone, and she retreated to the wingback chair, where she still sat, not just pondering her options but analyzing her motivation.

She had been shaken by William's amputation of his fingers and by his termination. She had been more deeply moved by Christine's revelation that she, Erika, had been given a richer emotional life—humility, shame, the potential for pity and compassion—than others of the New Race were granted.

Victor, whose genius was unparalleled in all of history, must have good reason for restricting all other of his people to hatred, envy, anger, and emotions that only turned back upon themselves and did not lead to hope. She was his humble creation, of value only to the extent that she could serve him. She did not have the insight, the knowledge, or the necessary breadth of vision to imagine that she had any right to question his design.

She herself hoped for many things. Most important of all, she hoped to become a better wife, better day by day, and to see approval in Victor's eyes. Although she had so recently arisen from the tank and had not yet lived much, she couldn't imagine a life without hope.

If she became a better wife, if eventually she no longer earned a beating during sex, if one day he cherished her, she hoped that she might ask him to allow Christine and others to have hope as she did, and that he would grant her request and give her people gentler lives.

"I am Queen Esther to his King Ahasuerus," she said, comparing herself to the daughter of Mordecai. Esther had persuaded Ahasuerus to spare her people, the Jews, from annihilation at the hands of Haman, a prince of his realm.

Erika did not know the full story, but she had confidence that the literary allusion, one of thousands in her repertoire, was sound and that, per her programming, she had used it properly.

So.

She must strive to become cherished by Victor. To do so, she must serve him always to perfection. To meet that goal, she must know everything about him, not merely the biography that she had received in direct-to-brain data downloading.

Everything necessarily included the occupant of the tank, which evidently had been imprisoned by Victor. Regardless of the profound fear that it had triggered in her, she must return to the case, face this chaos, and impress order upon it.

At the head of the casket—it definitely seemed more like a casket now than like a jewel box—Erika again lowered her face to the glass at the point directly above where she imagined the face of the occupant waited submerged in amber.

As before, but with less lilt in her voice, she said, "Hello, hello, hello in there."

The dark shape stirred again, and this time the sound waves of her voice appeared to send blue pulses through the case as the rap of her knuckle had done earlier.

Her lips had been six inches above the glass when she spoke. She leaned closer. Three inches.

"I am Queen Esther to his King Ahasuerus," she said.

The pulses were a more intense blue than before, and the shadowy occupant seemed to rise closer to the underside of the glass, so she could see the suggestion of a face, but no details.

She said again, "I am Queen Esther to his King Ahasuerus."

Out of the throbbing blue, out of the unseen face, came a voice in answer, somehow unmuffled by the glass: "You are Erika Five, and you are mine."

CHAPTER 52

AFTER THE BLACK TONGUE of night licked the last purple off the western horizon, the oil lamps were ignited atop the poles in the west pit.

Like phantom dragons, wings and tails of lambent orange light chased across the trash field, and shadows leaped.

Thirteen of the fourteen members of Nick's crew were with him in the pit, wearing hip-high boots, faces glistening, lined up in eager anticipation along the route that the pair of low, open-bed trucks would take to the place of interment.

Beside him stood Gunny Alecto, her eyes shining with reflected fire. "Saving savant savour sausages sandwiches savages. *Savages!* Here come the dead savages, Nick. You got your stuff?"

"I got it."

"You got your *stuff?*"

He raised his pail, which was like her pail, like the pail that each of them carried.

The first of the trucks descended the sloped wall of the pit and growled across the desolation, uncountable varieties of garbage crunching and crackling under the tires.

Five sturdy poles, seven feet high, rose from the bed of the truck. To each pole had been lashed one of the dead members of the Old Race, who had been replaced by replicants. Three had been city bureaucrats, and two had been police officers. Two were female; three were male.

The cadavers had been stripped of clothes. Their eyes had been taped open to give the impression that they bore witness to their humiliation.

The mouths of the dead were wedged open with sticks because

their tormentors liked to imagine that they were pleading for mercy or at least were screaming.

One of the males had been delivered dismembered and decapitated. The Crosswoods crew had wired the parts together with malicious glee, putting the head on backward, comically repositioning the genitals.

As the truck drew near, the assembled crew began to jeer the dead with enthusiasm, with mocking laughter and catcalls, louder than they were articulate.

Epsilons, lowest of the rigid social order, were allowed to have contempt for no one of their own race, only for the one-heart men and women who claimed to be the children of God yet could not turn off pain and died so easily. With jeers and venomous laughter, these simplest products of the tanks expressed their detestation and thereby claimed their superiority.

As the truck came to a stop, the crew looked excitedly at Nick, who stood at the midpoint of the lineup. As a Gamma among Epsilons, he must lead by example, even though they, not he, had conceived this ceremony and designed these rituals.

From his pail, he scooped a reeking mass. Always available in a dump were rotting fruits and vegetables, filth in infinite variety, decomposing this and rancid that. During the day, he had collected choice items. Now, with a cry of contempt, he hurled his first handful at one of the cadavers on the truck.

The splattery impact drew a cheer from the Epsilons. After his example, they scooped foul wads from their buckets and pelted the hoisted dead.

As the wide-eyed, open-mouthed corpses endured this sustained barrage, the jeers of the tormenting crew grew more vicious, less verbal and more vocal. The laughter became too shrill to have any quality whatsoever of merriment, and then grew too bitter to be mistaken for any kind of laughter at all.

When the Epsilons had exhausted their ammunition, they threw the empty pails and then flung themselves upon the truck, tearing fervently at the bindings that held the cadavers to the poles. As they freed each stained and dripping body, they pitched it from the truck into a nearby shallow depression in the trash field, which would serve as a mass grave.

Although Nick Frigg did not climb onto the open-bed pillory with his shrieking crew, their rage and their hatred excited him, inflamed his own resentment against those supposedly God-made people who claimed free will, dignity, and hope. He cheered on the denizens of Crosswoods and tossed his greasy hair and shook his fists at the night, and felt *empowered* by the thought that one day soon his kind would reveal themselves in all their inhuman ferocity and would show the self-satisfied Old Race how quickly their precious free will could be stripped from them, how brutally their dignity could be destroyed, and how utterly their pathetic hope could be extinguished forever.

Now came the symbolic killing.

When the five cadavers had been tossed from the truck, the Epsilons, including the driver, scrambled to the gravesite in full cry.

They longed to kill, *craved* killing, lived with a *need* to kill that was intense to the point of anguish, yet they were forbidden to uncork their wrath until their maker gave permission. The frustration of their shackled lives daily paid compound interest on the principal of their anger until they were rich with it, each of them a treasury of rage.

In the symbolic killing, they spent mere pennies of their wealth of wrath. They stomped, stomped, kicked, punted, ground their heels, threw their arms around one another's shoulders and circle-danced in groups of four and six, danced among the dead and certainly *upon* the dead, in ferocious hammering rhythms, filling the torch-lit night with the dreadful drumming, timpani and tom-tom and bass drums and kettle, but all in fact the boom of booted feet.

Although a Gamma, dog-nose Nick was infected by the excitement of the Epsilons, and a fever of fury boiled his blood, too, as he joined them in this dance of death, linking himself into a circle with the conviction that any Beta would have done the same, or even any Alpha, for this was an expression not merely of the frustration of the lowest class of the New Race but also of the yearning and the repressed desires of all the children of Mercy, who were made for different work and loaded with different programs, but who were as one in their hatred and their wrath.

Shrieking, howling, hooting, screaming, their sweating faces dark with desire, bright with torchlight, they stomped what they had previously jeered, ritually killing those who were already dead, the drumfire of their feet shaking the night with a promise of the final war to come.

CHAPTER 53

FROM ACROSS THE STREET and half a block away, Cindi and Benny Lovewell watched O'Connor and Maddison escort two black women from the parsonage to the plainwrap sedan, which was parked under a streetlamp.

"We'd probably end up killing one or both of the women to nab the cops," Cindi said.

Considering that they were not authorized to kill anyone but the detectives, Benny said, "We better wait."

"What are the women carrying?" Cindi wondered.

"Pies, I think."

"Why are they carrying pies?"

"Maybe they were caught stealing them," Benny suggested.

"Do people steal pies?"

"*Their* kind of people do. They steal everything."

She said, "Aren't O'Connor and Maddison homicide detectives?"

"Yeah."

"Then why would they rush out here to arrest pie thieves?"

Benny shrugged. "I don't know. Maybe the women killed someone for the pies."

Frowning, Cindi said, "That's possible, I suppose. But I have the feeling we're missing something. Neither one of them looks like a killer."

"Neither do we," Benny reminded her.

"If they *did* kill for the pies, why would they be allowed to keep them?"

"Their legal system doesn't make much sense to me," Benny said. "I don't really care about the women or the pies. I just want to rip the guts out of O'Connor and Maddison."

"Well, so do I," Cindi said. "Just because I want a baby doesn't mean I still don't enjoy killing."

Benny sighed. "I didn't mean to imply that you were going soft or anything."

When the women and the pies had been loaded in the backseat, O'Connor got behind the wheel, and Maddison sat shotgun.

"Follow them just short of visual," Benny said. "We want to be able to move in quick if there's an opportunity at the other end."

The unmarked police car pulled away from the curb, and when it turned out of sight at the corner, Cindi followed in the Mountaineer.

Instead of conveying the black women to a police lockup, the detectives drove them only two blocks, to another house in Bywater.

Once again parking half a block away and across the street, in the shadows between two streetlamps, Cindi said, "This is no good. At half these houses, people are sitting on the front porch. Too many witnesses."

"Yeah," Benny agreed. "We might snatch O'Connor and Maddison, but we'll end up in a police chase."

They needed to be discreet. If the authorities identified them as professional killers, they would no longer be able to do their jobs. They would not be authorized to kill any more people, and indeed their maker would terminate *them*.

"Look at all these morons. What're they doing sitting on a porch in a rocking chair?" Cindi wondered.

"They sit and drink beer or lemonade, or something, and some of them smoke, and they talk to one another."

"What do they talk about?"

"I don't know."

"They're so . . . *unfocused*," Cindi said. "What's the point of their lives?"

"I heard one of them say the purpose of life is living."

"They just sit there. They aren't trying to take over the world and gain total command of nature, or anything."

"They already own the world," Benny reminded her.

"Not for long."

CHAPTER 54

SITTING AT THE TABLE in the kitchen of the parsonage with the replicant of Pastor Laffite, Deucalion said, "How many of your kind have been infiltrated into the city?"

"I only know my number," Laffite replied in a slowly thickening voice. He sat staring at his hands, which were palm-up on the table, as if he were reading two versions of his future. "Nineteen hundred and eighty-seven. There must be many more since me."

"How fast can he produce his people?"

"From gestation to maturity, he's got it down to four months in the tank."

"How many tanks are in operation at the Hands of Mercy?"

"There used to be one hundred and ten."

"Three crops a year," Deucalion said, "times one hundred ten. He could turn out three hundred and thirty a year."

"Not quite so many. Because now and then he makes . . . other things."

"What other things?"

"I don't know. Rumors. Things that aren't . . . humanoid. New forms. Experiments. You know what I'd like?"

"Tell me," Deucalion encouraged.

"One last piece of chocolate. I like chocolate very much."

"Where do you keep it?"

"There's box in the fridge. I'd get it, but I'm beginning to have some difficulty with recognition of spatial relationships. I'm not sure I can walk properly. I'd have to crawl."

"I'll get it," Deucalion said.

He fetched the chocolates from the refrigerator, took off the lid, and put the box on the table before Laffite.

As Deucalion settled into his chair again, Laffite reached for a piece of candy, but groped beyond and to the left of the box.

Gently, Deucalion guided Laffite's right hand to the chocolates and then watched as the pastor felt piece after piece, almost like a blind man, before selecting one.

"They say he's ready to start up a farm outside the city," Laffite revealed. "Next week or the week after."

"What farm?"

"A New Race farm, two thousand tanks all under one roof, disguised as a factory or greenhouses." .

When Laffite could not find his mouth with his hand, Deucalion guided the candy to his lips. "That's a production capacity of six thousand."

Closing his eyes once more, Pastor Laffite chewed the candy with pleasure. He tried to talk with the chocolate in his mouth but seemed no longer capable of speaking while he ate.

"Take your time," Deucalion told him. "Enjoy it."

After swallowing the chocolate and licking his lips, still with his eyes closed, Laffite said, "A second farm is under construction and will be ready by the first of the year, with an even greater number of tanks."

"Do you know Victor's schedule at the Hands of Mercy? When does he go there? When does he leave?"

"I don't know. He's there much of the time, more than anywhere else in his life."

"How many of your kind work at Mercy?"

"Eighty or ninety, I think. I don't know for sure."

"Security must be tight."

"Everyone who works there is also a killing machine. I might like a second chocolate."

Deucalion helped him find the box and then get the morsel to his mouth.

When Laffite was not eating chocolate, his eyes rolled and twitched beneath his lids. When he had candy in his mouth, his eyes were still.

After he finished the sweet, Laffite said, "Do you find the world more mysterious than it's supposed to be?"

"Who says it isn't supposed to be?"

"Our maker. But do you find yourself wondering about things?"

"About many things, yes," Deucalion said.

"I wonder, too. I wonder. Do you think dogs have souls?"

CHAPTER 55

ON THE WALKWAY at the foot of Lulana's front-porch steps, with the sweet scent of jasmine on the early-night air, Carson said to the sisters, "It's best if you don't tell anyone a word about what happened at the parsonage."

As though distrusting the steadiness of her hands, Lulana used both to hold the praline pie. "Who was the giant?"

"You wouldn't believe me," Carson said, "and if I told you, I wouldn't be doing you a favor."

Coddling the second pie, Evangeline said, "What was wrong with Pastor Kenny? What's going to happen to him?"

Instead of answering her, Michael said, "For your peace of mind, you ought to know that your preacher long ago went to his final rest. The man you called Pastor Kenny there tonight . . . you have no reason to grieve for him."

The sisters exchanged a glance. "Something strange has come into the world, hasn't it?" Lulana asked Carson, but clearly expected no answer. "There tonight, the coldest expectation crept over me, like maybe it was . . . end times."

Evangeline said, "Maybe we should pray on it, sister."

"Can't hurt," Michael said. "Might help. And have yourselves a piece of pie."

Suspicion squinted Lulana's eyes. "Mr. Michael, it sounds to me like you mean have ourselves a nice piece of pie while there's still time."

Michael avoided replying, but Carson said, "Have yourselves a piece of pie. Have two."

In the car again, as Carson pulled away from the curb, Michael said,

"Did you see the white Mercury Mountaineer about half a block back on the other side of the street?"

"Yeah."

"Just like the one in the park."

Studying the rearview mirror, she said, "Yeah. And just like the one down the street from the parsonage."

"I wondered if you saw that one."

"What, I'm suddenly blind?"

"Is it coming after us?"

"Not yet."

She wheeled right at the corner.

Turning in his seat to peer into the dark street that they were leaving behind, he said, "They're still not coming. Well, there's bound to be more than one white Mountaineer in a city this size."

"And this is just one of those freaky days when we happen to cross paths with all of them."

"Maybe we should have asked Godot for some hand grenades," Michael said.

"I'm sure he delivers."

"He probably gift-wraps. Where now?"

"My place," Carson told him. "Maybe it would be a good idea, after all, if Vicky moved Arnie somewhere."

"Like some nice quiet little town in Iowa."

"And back to 1956, when Frankenstein was just Colin Clive and Boris Karloff, and Mary Shelley was just a novelist instead of a prophet and historian."

CHAPTER 56

ON THE SIX closed-circuit screens, the insectile manifestation of the Werner entity, still in possession of some human features, crawled the steel walls of the isolation chamber, sometimes in the cautious manner of a stalking predator, at other times as quick as a frightened roach, agitated and jittering.

Victor could not have imagined that any news brought to him by Father Duchaine would trump the images on those monitors, but when the priest described the meeting with the tattooed man, the crisis with Werner became a mere problem by comparison with the astonishing resurrection of his first-made man.

Initially skeptical, he pressed Duchaine hard for a description of the towering man who had sat for coffee with him in the rectory kitchen, particularly of the ravaged half of his face. What the priest had seen under the inadequate disguise of the elaborate tattoo was damage of a kind and of a degree that no ordinary man could have sustained and survived. Further, it matched the broken countenance as Victor had kept it in his mind's eye, and his memory was exceptional.

Further still, Duchaine's word portrait of the wholesome half of that same face could not have better conveyed the ideal male beauty that Victor had been kind enough to bestow upon his first creation so long ago and on such a distant continent that sometimes those events seemed like a dream.

His kindness had been repaid with betrayal and with the murder of his bride, Elizabeth. His lost Elizabeth would never have been as malleable or as lubricious as the wives that he had later made for himself; nevertheless, her savage murder had been an unforgivable impertinence. Now the ungrateful wretch had come crawling around again, filled with delusions of grandeur, spouting nonsense about a destiny, foolish enough to believe that in a second confrontation he might not only survive but triumph.

"I thought he died out there on the ice," Victor said. "Out on the polar ice. I thought he had been frozen for eternity."

"He'll be returning to the rectory in about an hour and a half," said the priest.

Victor said approvingly, "This was clever work, Patrick. You have not been in my good graces lately, but this counts as some redemption."

"In truth," the priest said, unable to meet his maker's eyes, "I thought I might betray you, but in the end I could not conspire with him."

"Of course you couldn't. Your Bible tells you that rebellious angels rose up against God and were thrown out of Heaven. But I've made creatures more obedient than the God of myth ever proved able to create."

On the screens, the Werner bug scampered up a wall and held fast to the ceiling, pendulous and quivering.

"Sir," Duchaine said nervously, "I came here not only to tell you this news but to ask . . . to ask if you will grant me the grace that your first-made promised me."

For a moment, Victor did not know what grace was meant. When he understood, he felt his temper rise. "You want me to take your life?"

"Release me," Patrick pleaded quietly, staring at the monitors to avoid his master's eyes.

"I give you life, and where is your gratitude? Soon the world will be ours, nature humbled, the way of all things changed forever. I have made you part of this great adventure, but you would turn away from it. Are you deluded enough to believe that the religion you have insincerely preached might contain some truth after all?"

Still focused on the phantasmagoric Werner, Duchaine said, "Sir, you could release me with a few words."

"There is no God, Patrick, and even if there were, He would have no place in paradise for the likes of you."

The priest's voice acquired now a humble quality of a kind that Victor did not like. "Sir, I don't need paradise. Eternal darkness and silence will be enough."

Victor loathed him. "Perhaps at least one of my creatures is more pathetic than anything I would have believed I could create."

When the priest had no reply, Victor switched on the audio feed from the isolation chamber. The Werner thing was still screaming in terror, in pain of an apparently extreme character. Some shrieks resembled those of a cat in agony, while others were as shrill and alien as the language of frenzied insects; and yet others sounded quite as human as any cries that might mark the night in an asylum for the criminally insane.

To one of the staff, Victor said, "Cycle open the nearer door of the transition module. Father Duchaine would like to offer his holy counsel to poor Werner."

Trembling, Patrick Duchaine said, "But with just a few words, you could—"

"Yes," Victor interrupted. "I could. But I have invested time and resources in you, Patrick, and you have provided me with a most unacceptable return on my investment. This way, at least, you can perform one last service. I need to know just how dangerous Werner has become, assuming he's dangerous at all to anyone other than himself. Just go in there and ply your priestly art. I won't need a written report."

The nearer door of the module stood open.

Duchaine crossed the room. At the threshold, he paused to look back at his maker.

Victor could not read the expression on the priest's face or in his eyes. Although he had created each of them with care and knew the structure of their bodies and their minds perhaps better than he knew himself, some of the New Race sometimes were as much of a mystery to him as any of the Old Race were.

Without a further word, Duchaine entered the transition module. The door cycled shut behind him.

Ripley's voice conveyed a numbness of spirit when he said, "He's in the air lock."

"It's not an *air lock*," Victor corrected.

One of the staff said, "Nearer door in lockdown. Farther door is cycling open."

A moment later, the Werner bug stopped screaming. Depending from the ceiling, the thing appeared to be keenly, tremulously alert, at last distracted from its own complaints.

Father Patrick Duchaine entered the isolation chamber.

The farther door cycled shut, but no one on the staff followed the customary procedure of announcing module lockdown. The monitor room had fallen as silent as Victor had ever heard it.

Duchaine spoke not to the monster suspended above him, but to one of the cameras and, through its lens, to his maker. "I forgive you, Father. You know not what you do."

In that instant, before Victor was able to erupt with a furious retort, the Werner bug proved itself to be as lethal as anyone could have imagined. Such agility. Such exotic mandibles and pincers. Such machinelike persistence.

Being one of the New Race, the priest was programmed to fight, and he was terribly strong, and resilient. As a consequence of that strength and resilience, his death was not an easy one, but slow and cruel, although eventually he did receive the grace that he had requested.

CHAPTER 57

STARING AT PASTOR LAFFITE's eyelids as his eyes moved nervously beneath them, Deucalion said, "Many theologians believe that dogs and some other animals have simple souls, yes, though whether immortal or not, no one can say."

"If dogs have souls," Laffite suggested, "then perhaps we, too, might be more than machines of meat."

After some consideration, Deucalion said, "I won't give you false hope . . . but I can offer you a third chocolate."

"Have one with me, will you? This is such a lonely communion."

"All right."

The pastor had developed a mild palsy of the head and hands, different from his previous nervous tremors.

Deucalion selected two pieces of candy from the box. He put the first to Laffite's lips, and the minister took it.

His own piece proved to have a coconut center. In two hundred years, nothing he had eaten had tasted as sweet as this, perhaps because the circumstances were, by contrast, so bitter.

"Eyes closed or open," Pastor Laffite said, "I'm having terrible hallucinations, vivid images, such horrors that I have no words to describe them."

"Then no more delay," Deucalion said, pushing his chair back from the table and getting to his feet.

"And pain," the pastor said. "Severe pain that I can't repress."

"I won't add to that," Deucalion promised. "My strength is much greater than yours. It will be quick."

As Deucalion moved behind Laffite's chair, the pastor groped blindly, caught his hand. Then he did something that would never have been expected of any of the New Race, something that Deucalion knew no number of centuries could erase from his memory.

Although his program was dropping out of him, though his mind was going—or perhaps because of that—Pastor Laffite drew the back of Deucalion's hand to his lips, tenderly kissed it, and whispered, "Brother."

A moment later, Deucalion broke the preacher's neck, shattered his spine with such force that instant brain death followed, assuring that the quasi-immortal body could not repair the injury.

Nevertheless, for a while he remained in the kitchen. To be certain. To sit a sort of shiva.

Night pressed at the windows. Outside lay a city, teeming. Yet Deucalion could see nothing beyond the glass, only darkness deep, a blackness unrelenting.

CHAPTER 58

AFTER THE UNKNOWN thing in the glass case spoke her name and made its ominous claim to her, Erika did not linger in the secret Victorian drawing room.

She did not like the roughness of the voice. Or its confidence.

At the threshold of the room, she almost hurried boldly into the passageway before she realized that the rods bristling from the walls were humming again. A headlong exit would result in a contest between her brilliantly engineered body and perhaps several thousand volts of electricity.

As extraordinarily tough and resilient as she might be, Erika Helios was not Scarlett O'Hara.

Gone with the Wind had been set in an age before electrical service had been available to the home; consequently, Erika was not certain that this literary allusion was apt, but it occurred to her anyway. Of course she had not read the novel; but maybe it contained a scene in which Scarlett O'Hara had been struck by lightning in a storm and had survived unscathed.

Erika stepped cautiously across the threshold and paused, as she had done when entering the farther end of this passageway. As before, a blue laser speared from the ceiling and scanned her. Either the ID system knew who she was or, more likely, recognized what she was not: She was not the thing in the glass case.

The rods stopped humming, allowing her safe passage.

She quickly closed the massive steel portal and engaged the five lock bolts. In less than a minute, she had retreated beyond the next steel barrier and had secured it as well.

Her synchronized hearts nevertheless continued to beat fast. She marveled that she could have been so unsettled by such a small thing as a disembodied voice and a veiled threat.

This sudden, persistent fear, disproportionate to the cause, had the character of a superstitious response. She, of course, was free of all superstition.

The instinctive nature of her reaction led her to suspect that subconsciously she *knew* what was imprisoned in the amber substance within that glass case, and that her fear arose from this deeply buried knowledge.

When she reached the end of the initial passage, where she had originally entered through a pivoting section of bookcases, she found a button that opened that secret door from here behind the wall.

Immediately that she returned to the library, she felt much safer, in spite of being surrounded by so many books filled with so much potentially corrupting material.

In one corner was a wet bar stocked with heavy crystal glassware and the finest adult beverages. As a superbly programmed hostess, she knew how to mix any cocktail that might be requested, though as yet she had not been in a social situation requiring this skill.

Erika was having cognac to settle her nerves when from behind her, Christine said, "Mrs. Helios, pardon me for saying so, but I suspect that Mr. Helios would be distressed to see you drinking directly from the decanter."

Erika had not realized that she had been committing such a faux pas, but on having it drawn to her attention, she saw that she was, as charged, guzzling Rémy Martin from the exquisite Lalique decanter, and even dribbling some down her chin.

"I was thirsty," she said, but sheepishly returned the decanter to the bar, stoppered it, and blotted her chin with a bar napkin.

"We've been searching for you, Mrs. Helios, to inquire about dinner."

Alarmed, glancing at the windows and discovering that night had fallen, Erika said, "Oh. Have I kept Victor waiting?"

"No, ma'am. Mr. Helios needs to work late and will take his dinner at the lab."

"I see. Then what shall I do?"

"We will serve your dinner anywhere you wish, Mrs. Helios."

"Well, it's such a big house, so many places."

"Yes."

"Is there somewhere I could have dinner where there's cognac—other than here in the library with all these books?"

"We can serve cognac with your dinner anywhere in the house,

Mrs. Helios—although I might suggest that wine would be more appropriate *with* a meal."

"Well, of course it would. And I *would* like to have a bottle of wine with dinner, an appropriate bottle complementary to whatever the chef has prepared. Select for me a most appropriate bottle, if you will."

"Yes, Mrs. Helios."

Apparently, Christine had no desire for another conversation as intimate and intense as the one they'd shared in the kitchen earlier in the day. She seemed to want to keep their relationship on a formal footing henceforth.

Encouraged by this, Erika decided to exert her authority as the lady of the house, although graciously. "But please, Christine, also serve me a decanted bottle of Rémy Martin, and save yourself the trouble by bringing it at the same time you bring the wine. Don't bother making a later trip."

Christine studied her for a moment, and said, "Have you enjoyed your first day here, Mrs. Helios?"

"It's been full," Erika said. "At first it seemed like such a quiet house, one might almost expect it to be dull, but there seems always to be something happening."

CHAPTER 59

ALTHOUGH THE Q&A with Arnie's mother starts well, Randal Six quickly exhausts his supply of conversational gambits. He eats nearly half a quart of strawberry-banana swirl ice cream before another question occurs to him.

"You seem to be frightened, Vicky. Are you frightened?"

"Yes. God, yes."

"Why are you frightened?"

"I'm tied to a chair."

"The chair can't hurt you. Don't you think it's silly to be frightened of a chair?"

"Don't do this."

"Don't do what?"

"Don't taunt me."

"When did Randal taunt you? Randal never did."

"I'm not afraid of the chair."

"But you just said you were."

"I'm scared of you."

He is genuinely surprised. "Randal? Why be scared of Randal?"

"You hit me."

"Only once."

"Very hard."

"You aren't dead. See? Randal doesn't kill mothers. Randal has decided to like mothers. Mothers are a wonderful idea. Randal doesn't have a mother or a father."

Vicky says nothing.

"And, *nooooo,* Randal didn't kill them. Randal was sort of made by machines. Machines don't care like mothers do, and they don't miss you when you leave."

Vicky closes her eyes, as autistics sometimes do when there is just too much of everything to process, a daunting amount of stuff coming in.

She is not, however, an autistic. She is a mother.

Randal is surprised that he himself is coping so well with all these new developments, and talking so smooth. His mind seems to be healing.

Vicky's appearance, however, is troubling. Her face is drawn. She looks ill.

"Are you ill?" he asks.

"I'm so scared."

"Stop being scared, okay? Randal wants you to be his mother. All right? Now you can't be scared of your own son, Randal."

The most amazing thing happens: Tears spill down Vicky's cheeks.

"That is so sweet," says Randal. "You're a very nice mother. We will be happy. Randal will call you Mother, not Vicky anymore. When is your birthday, Mother?"

Instead of answering, she sobs. She is so emotional. Mothers are sentimental.

"You should bake a cake for your birthday," he says. "We'll have a celebration. Randal knows about celebrations, hasn't ever been to one, but knows."

She hangs her head, still sobbing, face wet with tears.

"Randal's first birthday is eight months away," he informs her. "Randal is only four months old."

He returns the remainder of the strawberry-banana ice cream to the freezer. Then he stands beside the table, gazing down at her.

"You are the secret of happiness, Mother. Randal doesn't need Arnie to tell him. Randal is going to visit his brother now."

She raises her head, eyes open wide. "Visit Arnie?"

"Randal needs to find out are two brothers okay or is that one brother too many."

"What do you mean, one brother too many? What're you talking about? Why do you want to see Arnie?"

He winces at the rush of her words, at the urgency of them; they seem to buzz in his ears. "Don't talk so fast. Don't ask questions. Randal asks questions. Mother answers."

"Leave Arnie alone."

"Randal thinks there is enough happiness here for two, but maybe Arnie doesn't think so. Randal needs to hear Arnie say two brothers are okay."

"Arnie hardly ever talks," she said. "Depending on his mood, he might not even tune in to you. He zones out. It's like the castle is real and he's *inside* it, locked away. He might not really hear you."

"Mother, you are talking too loud, too much, too fast. Loud-fast talk sounds ugly."

He crosses toward the door to the hall.

She raises her voice: "Randal, untie me. Untie me *right this minute!*"

"You aren't acting like a nice mother now. Shouting scares Randal. Shouting is not happiness."

"Okay. All right. Slow and quiet. Please, Randal. Wait. Please untie me."

At the threshold of the hallway, he glances back at her. "Why?"

"So I can take you to see Arnie."

"Randal can find him all right."

"Sometimes he hides. He's very difficult to find when he hides. I know all his favorite hiding places."

Staring at her, he senses deceit. "Mother, are you going to try to hurt Randal?"

"No. Of course not. Why would I hurt you?"

"Sometimes mothers hurt their children. There's a whole Web site about it—www.homicidalmothers.com."

Now that he thinks about it, he realizes that the poor children never suspect what's coming. They trust their mom. She says she loves them, and they trust her. Then she chops them up in their beds or drives them in a lake and drowns them.

"Randal sure hopes you're a good mother," he says. "But maybe you need to answer a lot more questions before Randal unties you."

"All right. Come back. Ask me anything."

"Randal needs to talk to Arnie first."

She says something, but he tunes out her meaning. He steps into the hallway.

Behind him, Mother is talking fast again, faster than ever, and then she is shouting.

Randal Six has been in this living room previously. When Mother first regained consciousness, she chattered at him so hard that he had come here to calm himself. Now here he is again, calming himself.

He hopes that he and Mother don't already have a dysfunctional relationship.

After a minute or two, when he is ready, he goes in search of Arnie. He wonders whether his new brother will prove to be Abel or Cain, selfless or selfish. If he is like Cain, Randal Six knows what to do. It will be self-defense.

CHAPTER 60

CARSON PARKED IN her driveway, shut off the engine and the headlights, and said, "Let's get the shotguns."

They had put the suitcases and shotguns in the trunk before they'd driven Lulana and Evangeline home from the parsonage.

After hurriedly retrieving the Urban Snipers, they went to the front of the sedan and crouched there, using it for cover. Peering back along the driver's side, Carson watched the street.

"What're we gonna do for dinner?" Michael asked.

"We can't take the kind of time we took for lunch."

"I could go for a po-boy."

"As long as it's sleeve-wrapped to eat on the fly."

Michael said, "The thing I'll miss most when I'm dead is New Orleans food."

"Maybe there's plenty of it on the Other Side."

"What I won't miss is the heat and humidity."

"Are you really that confident?"

The night brought them the sound of an approaching engine.

When the vehicle passed in the street, Carson said, "Porsche Carrera GT, black. That baby's got a six-speed transmission. Can you imagine how fast I could drive in one of those?"

"So fast, I'd be perpetually vomiting."

"My driving's never gonna kill you," she said. "Some monster is gonna kill you."

"Carson, if this is ever over and we come out of it alive, you think we might give up being cops?"

"What would we do?"

"How about mobile pet grooming? We could drive around all day, bathing dogs. Easy work. No pressure. It might even be fun."

"Depends on the dogs. The problem is you have to have a van for all the equipment. Vans are dorky. I'm not going to drive a van."

He said, "We could open a gay bar."

"Why gay?"

"I wouldn't have to worry about guys hitting on you."

"I wouldn't mind running a doughnut shop."

"Could we run a doughnut shop and still have guns?" he wondered.

"I don't see why not."

"I feel more comfortable with guns."

The sound of another engine silenced them.

When the vehicle appeared, Carson said, "White Mountaineer," and pulled her head back to avoid being seen.

The Mountaineer slowed but didn't stop, and drifted past the house.

"They'll park farther along, on the other side of the street," she said.

"You think it's going to go down here?"

"They'll like the setup," she predicted. "But they won't come right away. They've been looking for an opportunity all day. They're patient. They'll take time to reconnoiter."

"Ten minutes?"

"Probably ten," she agreed. "No less than five. Let's get Vicky and Arnie out of here yesterday."

When the Mountaineer was out of sight, they hurried to the back of the house. The kitchen door was locked. Carson fumbled her keys from a jacket pocket.

"Is that a new jacket?" he asked.

"I've worn it a couple times."

"I'll try not to get brains on it."

She unlocked the door.

In the kitchen, Vicky Chou was at the table, tied in a chair.

CHAPTER 61

BENNY AND CINDI carried pistols, but they preferred to avoid using them whenever possible.

The issue wasn't noise. Their weapons were fitted with sound suppressors. You could pop a guy three times in the face, and if people in the next room heard anything at all, they might think you sneezed.

You could try shooting to lame; but the Old Race were bleeders who lacked the New Race's ability to seal a puncture almost as fast as turning off a faucet. By the time you got the wounded prey to a private place where you could have some fun torturing them, they were too often dead or comatose.

Some people might enjoy dismembering and decapitating a dead body, but not Benny Lovewell. Without the screams, you might as well be chopping up a roast chicken.

Once, when a gunshot woman had inconsiderately died before Benny could even start to take off her arms, Cindi supplied the screams, as she imagined the victim might have sounded, synchronizing her cries to Benny's use of the saw, but it wasn't the same.

Aimed at the eyes, Mace could disable any member of the Old Race long enough to subdue him. The problem was that people blinded by a stinging blast of Mace always shouted and cursed, drawing attention when it wasn't wanted.

Instead, Victor supplied Benny and Cindi with small pressurized cans, the size of Mace containers, which shot a stream of chloroform. When squirted in the face, most people inhaled with surprise—and fell unconscious before saying more than *shit,* if they said anything at all. The chloroform had a range of fifteen to twenty feet.

They also carried Tasers, the wand type rather than the pistol type. These were strictly for close-in work.

Considering that O'Connor and Maddison were cops and already jumpy because of what they knew about the deceased child of Mercy, Jonathan Harker, getting in close wouldn't be easy.

After parking across the street from the O'Connor house, Cindi said, "People aren't sitting on their porches around here."

"It's a different type of neighborhood."

"What're they doing instead?"

"Who cares?"

"Probably making babies."

"Give it a rest, Cindi."

"We could always adopt."

"Get real. We kill for Victor. We don't have jobs. You need real jobs to adopt."

"If you had let me keep the one I took, we'd be happy now."

"You kidnapped him. Everyone in the world is looking for the brat, and you think you can push him around the mall in a stroller!"

Cindi sighed. "It broke my heart when we had to leave him in that park."

"It didn't break your heart. Our kind aren't capable of any such emotion."

"All right, but it pissed me off."

"Don't I know it. Okay, so we go in there, we knock them down, tie them up, then you drive around to the back of the house, and we load 'em like cordwood."

Studying the O'Connor house, Cindi said, "It does look slick, doesn't it."

"It looks totally slick. In and out in five minutes. Let's go."

CHAPTER 62

WHEN THEY CAME through the back door with shotguns slung from their shoulders, Vicky whispered urgently, "He's in the house."

Pulling open a drawer, withdrawing a pair of scissors, Carson whispered, "Who?"

"Some creep. *Way* strange," Vicky said as Carson tossed the scissors to Michael.

As Michael caught the scissors, Carson crossed to the inner doorway.

Vicky whispered, "He's looking for Arnie."

As Carson checked the hall, Michael made two cuts in the bindings and put the scissors down. "You can do the rest, Vic."

The hallway was deserted, a lamp on in the living room at the farther end.

"He have a gun?" Carson asked.

Vicky said, "No."

Michael indicated that he wanted to lead.

This was Carson's house. She went first, carrying the shotgun for hip fire.

She cleared the coat closet. Nothing in there but coats.

The creep wasn't in the living room. Carson moved to the right, Michael to the left, until they were two targets instead of one, and halted.

Decision time. Farther to the right, beyond the living room, was Carson's suite, bedroom and bath. To the left lay the front door and the stairs to the second floor.

The door to Carson's room was closed. No one was on the first flight of stairs.

With his eyes, Michael indicated *up.*

She agreed. For some reason the creep was looking for Arnie, and Arnie was on the second floor.

Staying close to the wall, where the stairs were less likely to creak, Carson ascended first, shotgun in both hands.

Michael followed, climbing backward, covering the room below them.

She didn't dare think about Arnie, what might be happening to him. Fear for your life sharpens your edge. Dread dulls it. Think about the creep instead, stopping him.

So silent, the house. Like the Christmas poem. Not even a mouse.

No one on the second flight, either. Light in the upstairs hall. No shadows moving.

When she reached the top, she heard a stranger's voice coming from Arnie's room. Arriving at the open door, she saw her brother in his wheeled office chair, his attention on the Lego-block castle.

The intruder was maybe eighteen, nineteen, solidly put together. He stood facing Arnie, only a few feet from him, his back to Carson.

If it came to shooting, she didn't have a clear shot. The slug from the Urban Sniper might punch clean through the creep and hammer Arnie.

She didn't know who the guy was. More important, she didn't know *what* he was.

The intruder was saying, "Randal thought he could share. But now the castle, a home, ice cream, Mother—Randal wants it for himself."

Carson edged to the left of the doorway as she sensed Michael in the hall behind her.

"Randal isn't Abel. Randal is Cain. Randal isn't Six anymore. From now on . . . Randal *O'Connor.*"

Still moving, circling, Carson said, "What're you doing here?"

The intruder turned smoothly, so fast, like a dancer, or like something that had been . . . well engineered. "Carson."

"I don't know you."

"I am Randal. You will be Randal's sister."

"Down on your knees," she told him. "Down on your knees, then flat on the floor, facedown on the floor."

"Randal doesn't like loud talk. Don't shout at Randal like Victor does."

Michael said, "Sonofabitch," and Carson said, "Arnie, roll your chair back, roll away on your chair."

Although Arnie didn't move, Randal did. He took a step toward Carson. "Are you a good sister?"

"Don't come any closer. Get on your knees. *On your knees NOW!*"

"Or are you a bad, loud sister who talks too fast?" Randal asked.

She edged farther to her right, changing her line of fire to get Arnie out of it. "You think I don't know you have two hearts?" she said. "You think I can't take them out with one round from this bull killer?"

"You are a bad, bad sister," Randal said, and closed on her.

He was so fast that he almost got his hand on the gun. The boom rattled windows, the stink of gunfire blew in her face, blood burst from the exit wound in his back and sprayed the castle.

Randal should have been rocked back on his feet or staggered. He should have dropped.

She had aimed too low, missed one heart or both. But at this close range, she had to have *destroyed* half his internal organs.

He seized the barrel of the shotgun, thrust it upward as she squeezed the trigger, and the second round punched a hole in the ceiling.

When she tried to hold on to the shotgun, he pulled her to him, almost had her before she let go, dropped, rolled.

She had given Michael a clean shot. He took two.

The reports were so loud, her ears rang and kept ringing as she rolled against a wall, looked up, saw Randal down—thank God, *down*—and Michael warily moving toward him.

Getting to her feet, she pulled the .50 Magnum from the scabbard on her left hip, certain she wouldn't need it, but Randal was still alive. Not in great condition, down and staying down, but alive after three point-blank torso shots from an Urban Sniper.

He raised his head, looked wonderingly around the room, rolled onto his back, blinked at the ceiling, said, "Home," and was gone.

CHAPTER 63

THE BACK DOOR was open. Benny and Cindi hesitated, but then he went through boldly, and fast, and she followed.

An Asian woman stood in the kitchen, next to the table, untying a length of torn cloth from her left wrist. She blinked at them and said, "Shit—"

Cindi was quick. The stream of chloroform splashed nose-on. The woman gasped, choked, spluttered, and fell to the floor.

They could deal with her later. She would be unconscious for perhaps fifteen minutes, maybe longer.

Although the Asian woman wasn't on their hit list, she had seen their faces. They would have to kill her, too.

That was okay. There was plenty of room for three in the cargo area of the Mercury Mountaineer, and Benny had recently sharpened his favorite cutting tools.

He closed and locked the back door. He didn't want to make it easy for anyone to come in behind them.

On one job, a four-year-old girl had wandered into the house from next door, and Cindi had insisted on adopting her.

Now Cindi had the chloroform in her right hand and the Taser in her left. Benny relied on only the chloroform.

They weren't worried about PD-issued sidearms. Basic guns for cops these days were often 9mm. He and Cindi could walk through a lot of 9mm fire if necessary.

Besides, if they were stealthy, their prey wouldn't have a chance to draw down on them.

A laundry room opened off the kitchen. Deserted.

The hallway to the front of the house passed a coat closet. No one knew they were here, so no one would be hiding from them in the closet, but they checked it anyway. Just coats.

As they reached the living room, a gun roared upstairs. It was a big sound, as if an armoire had toppled over. The whole house seemed to shake.

Cindi looked at the chloroform in her hand. She looked at the Taser. Another shot roared.

Cindi put the Taser in an inside jacket pocket, switched the chloroform to her left hand, and pulled her pistol.

Upstairs the big gun boomed twice again, and Benny drew his piece, too. The gun was a 9mm semi-auto, but this caliber would be a more serious problem for O'Connor and Maddison than for the Lovewells.

CHAPTER 64

WHO THE INTRUDER had been, how he had gotten into the house, why he seemed to have targeted Arnie specifically—none of that mattered as much as the fact that he was of the New Race and that this case had come home in the most literal sense, as from the start Carson had been afraid it would.

The walls of their house, the locks in its doors, offered them no more security than did Arnie's Lego castle. Perhaps the fate of this city, of the world, in the hands of Victor Helios, was such that no time would ever come again when they could spend a peaceful moment in their home. They couldn't stay here anymore.

And they had to get out *fast*.

Neighbors might not have been able to identify the precise location of the four shotgun blasts. Nevertheless, gunfire in this neighborhood would not go unreported.

Soon NOPD would have a patrol car or two cruising the area, on the lookout for anything suspicious. Carson preferred to avoid even a friendly encounter with uniforms. She didn't want to have to explain the weapons for which she possessed neither a receipt of purchase nor department authorization.

Besides, a uniform no longer earned immediate trust from her. The brotherhood of the police had been infiltrated by the New Race; and those who were loyal to Helios might have been told—or might be told at any moment—to make the elimination of Carson and Michael their top priority.

She picked up the Urban Sniper that Randal had torn from her grasp. Fingering two shells out of the dump pouch at her right hip, inserting them in the side carrier to bring the weapon to full load once more, she said, "Good thing we went with slugs."

"Buckshot wouldn't have stopped him," Michael agreed, reloading his shotgun.

"Maybe the shots will make the two in the Mountaineer hesitate."

"Or bring them running."

"We grab Vicky, go straight out the front door. Her car's at the curb. We leave in that."

Reloading his Sniper, Michael said, "You think they've got a hear-me-see-me on the plainwrap?"

"Yeah. They've been following us by remote view."

Arnie had gotten out of his chair. He stood gazing at his blood-spattered castle.

Carson said, "Honey, we have to go. Right now."

The last thing they needed was for Arnie to be mulish. Most of the time, he remained docile, cooperative, but he had his stubborn moments, which could be caused by traumatic experiences and loud noises.

Four shotgun blasts and the intruder dead on the floor qualified on both counts, but Arnie seemed to realize that survival depended on his finding the courage not to withdraw further into his shell. He went at once to the door.

Michael said, "Stay behind me, Arnie," and led the way into the upstairs hall.

Glancing at the intruder, half expecting to see him blink and shake off the effects of being repeatedly shotgunned, relieved to have her expectations disappointed, Carson followed Arnie out of his room, his refuge, desperately afraid that she would not be able to protect him any longer now that the Big Easy had become the city of night.

BENNY STARTED UP THE STEPS, and behind him Cindi whispered, "If there's a baby in the house, let's take it."

He kept moving, his back to the staircase wall, sideways from riser to riser. "There's no baby in the house."

"But if there is."

"We didn't come here for a baby."

"We didn't come here for the bitch in the kitchen, either, but we'll be taking her."

He reached the landing, peered up the second flight. Nobody in the upstairs hall, as far as he could see.

Behind him, she wouldn't relent: "If we take the baby, you can kill it with the others."

Cindi was nuts, and she was making him nuts, too. He refused to get into this debate with her, especially in the middle of a hit.

Besides, if they took the baby, she wouldn't let him kill it. Once she had it, she would want to keep it and dress it up in frilly outfits.

Anyway, *there was no baby in the house!*

Benny reached the top of the second flight. With his back still to the wall, he stuck his head out, looked around the corner—and saw Maddison coming with a shotgun, a boy behind him, O'Connor behind the boy with a shotgun of her own.

Maddison saw him, Benny juked back, and where the wall turned the corner from stairwell to hall, a shotgun blast ripped Sheetrock, shattered framing, showered him with powdered gypsum and splinters of wood.

Dropping to his knees on the steps, Benny risked exposure to fire again, but down low, where Maddison would not expect him, and squeezed off three shots without taking time to aim, before pulling back onto the stairs.

THREE PISTOL SHOTS, all wild, but one of them close enough to sing like a wasp past Carson, suggested the wisdom of a change in plans.

Even from the brief glimpse she had of him, Carson recognized the man on the stairs. He was the guy in the Mountaineer, the one who had smiled and waved.

Figure there were two of them on the stairs, the woman behind him. Figure they were both New Race, and both armed with pistols.

To drop Randal, she and Michael had had to scramble his internal organs, shred both his hearts, and shatter his spine with three point-blank slugs from the Urban Snipers.

These two golems on the stairs would be at least as difficult to kill as he had been. And unlike Randal, they were armed and seemed to have some paramilitary training or at least experience.

Without Arnie to consider, Carson might have relied on the power of their weaponry, might have stormed the stairs, but with the boy to worry about, she couldn't roll the dice.

"Vicky's room," she told Michael, grabbed Arnie by the arm, and retreated toward the end of the hall.

Michael backed away from the head of the stairs, laying down two spaced rounds of suppressing fire to discourage another fusillade from the pistol.

THE JUNCTURE OF HALL and stairwell walls took such a beating from the shotgun that the metal corner beading under the Sheetrock was exposed, snapped, sprung like a clock spring, and shards of it peppered Benny and embedded in his face.

For a moment he thought they were recklessly charging the stairs. Then he heard a door slam, and no more gunfire followed.

He scrambled up, off the stairs, and found the upper hallway deserted.

"Those're the guns they were trying out in the woods," Cindi said as she joined him.

Plucking the metal splinters out of his face, Benny said, "Yeah, I figured."

"You want to back off, come at them someplace later when their guard's down?"

"No. They have a kid with them. That complicates things, limits their options. Let's whack them now."

"Kid? They've got a kid?"

"Not a baby. Like twelve, thirteen."

"Oh. Too old. You can kill him, too," she said.

Unfortunately, now that the situation had blown up, Benny didn't expect to be able to take either O'Connor or Maddison alive. This job wouldn't give him the opportunity for any of the careful carving that he enjoyed and for which he had such a talent.

Three rooms opened off the hall. A door was ajar. Benny kicked it open. A bathroom. Nobody in there.

On the floor of the second room, a body lay in blood.

In that room also stood a humungous model of a castle, about as big as an SUV. Weird. You never knew what strange stuff you'd find in Old Race houses.

So the door Benny had heard slam must have been the last one in the hall.

AS CARSON HURRIEDLY replenished the expended shells in his shotgun, Michael shoved the dresser in front of the locked door, further bracing it.

When he turned and took the weapon from her, she said, "We can go out the window, onto the porch roof and down."

"What about Vicky?"

Although it hurt to put the thought in words, Carson said, "She either ran when she saw them or they got her."

As Carson took Arnie by the hand and led him toward the open window, one of the golems in the hallway threw itself against the door. She heard wood crack, and a hinge or lock plate buckled with a *twang*.

"Carson!" Michael warned. "It's not gonna hold ten seconds."

"Onto the roof," she told Arnie, pushing him to the window.

She turned as the door took another hit. It shuddered violently, and a hinge tore out of the casing.

No ordinary man could come through a door this easily. This was like a rhino charge.

They raised both shotguns.

The door was solid oak. As the golems broke through, they would use it as a shield. The shotgun slugs would penetrate, but do less damage than an unobstructed shot.

On the third hit, the second hinge tore loose and the lock bolt snapped.

"Here they come!"

CHAPTER 65

AFTER SITTING FOR a few minutes with the body of the replicant Pastor Laffite, Deucalion walked out of the parsonage kitchen and into the kitchen of Carson O'Connor's house, where Vicky Chou lay unconscious on the floor, in the reek of chloroform.

A tremendous crash from upstairs indicated worse trouble, and he walked out of the kitchen into the second-floor hall in time to see some guy slam his shoulder into a bedroom door as a woman stood to one side, watching.

He surprised the woman, tore the pistol out of her hand, threw it aside even as he lifted her and pitched her farther than the gun.

As the guy hit the door again and it appeared to break off its last pins, Deucalion grabbed him by the nape of the neck and the seat of the pants. He lifted him, turned him, and slammed him into the wall across the hall from the room that he'd been trying to enter.

The force of impact was so tremendous that the guy's face broke through the Sheetrock and hammered a wall stud hard enough to crack it. Deucalion kept shoving, and the stud relented, as did the rest of the wall structure, until the killer's head was in Arnie's room even as his body remained in the hall.

The woman was crawling toward her gun, so Deucalion left the guy with his neck in the wall as if in the lunette of a guillotine, and went after her.

She picked up the pistol, rolled onto her side, and fired at him. She hit him, but it was only a 9mm slug, and he took it in the breastbone without serious damage.

He kicked the gun out of her hand, probably breaking her wrist, and kicked her in the ribs, and kicked her again, sure that even New Race ribs could be broken.

By then, the guy had pulled his head out of the wall. Deucalion sensed him coming and turned to see an angry gypsum-whitened face, a bloody broken nose, and one eye bristling with wood splinters.

The killer was still game, and fast, but Deucalion didn't merely sidestep him. In the same way that he had traveled from the parsonage kitchen to the O'Connor kitchen in a single step, he went twenty feet backward, leaving his assailant to stumble forward, grappling only with air.

In retreat, having abandoned her pistol, the woman had scrambled toward the stairs. Deucalion seized her and assisted her by pitching her down the first flight to the landing.

In spite of being the future of the planet and the doom of mere humanity, the New Race superman with the plaster-powdered face and the toothpick-holder for a left eye had had enough. He fled the hall for Arnie's room.

Deucalion went after the guy just in time to see him plunge through a window into the backyard.

STANDING IN VICKY'S ROOM, listening to the ruckus in the hall, Michael said, "What—are they fighting with each other?"

Carson said, "Somebody's kicking ass."

"Vicky?"

They didn't lower their shotguns, but they moved closer to the barricading dresser, against which the loose door was now merely propped.

When sudden quiet followed the uproar, Carson cocked her head, listened, then said, "What now?"

"Apocalypse," Deucalion said behind them.

Carson turned with a jump and saw the giant standing beside Arnie. She didn't think he had come in through the open window.

The boy was shaking as if with palsy. He had covered his face with his hands. Too much noise, too much new and strange.

"It's all coming apart," Deucalion said. "That's why I was brought to this place, at this time. Victor's empire is blowing up in his face. By morning, nowhere in the city will be safe. I must move Arnie."

"Move him where?" Carson worried. "He needs quiet, peace. He needs—"

"There's a monastery in Tibet," said Deucalion, effortlessly lifting Arnie and holding him in his arms.

"*Tibet?*"

"The monastery is like a fortress, not unlike his castle, and quiet. I have friends there who'll know how to calm him."

Alarmed, Carson said, "*Tibet?* Hey, no. It might as well be the *moon*!"

"Vicky Chou is in the kitchen, unconscious. Better move that dresser and get out of here," Deucalion advised. "Police will be coming, and you won't know who they really are."

The giant turned as if to carry Arnie through the open window, but in the turn itself, he was gone.

CHAPTER 66

MAYBE FOUR MINUTES had passed since Carson had first fired the shotgun at Randal in Arnie's room. Figure none of the neighbors had called 911 for a minute, taking that long to wonder if it had been a backfiring truck or the dog farting. So maybe a call had gone out three minutes ago.

In this city, the average police response time to a gunfire-heard call, when no gunman had actually been seen and no location verified, was about six minutes.

With three minutes to leave, Carson didn't have time to worry about Arnie in Tibet.

Michael dragged the dresser out of the way, and the door fell into the room. They walked across it into the hall, and ran for the stairs.

Fragrant with evaporating chloroform, Vicky hadn't cooperated by regaining consciousness. Carson carried both shotguns, and Michael carried Vicky.

When Carson unlocked the back door and opened it, she paused on the threshold, turned to survey the kitchen. "I may never see this place again."

"It's not exactly Tara," Michael said impatiently.

"I grew up in this house."

"And a fine job you did of it. Now it's time to move on."

"I feel like I should take something."

"I assume you heard Deucalion say 'Apocalypse.' For that, you don't need anything, not even a change of underwear."

She held the door for him as he left with Vicky, hesitated outside before closing it, and then realized what she needed: the keys to Vicky's car.

They hung on the kitchen pegboard. She stepped inside, snared the keys, and left without a pang of sentimental regret.

She hurried after Michael, through the darkness along the side of the house, alert to the possibility that the pair from the Mountaineer might still be hanging around, passed him in the front yard, and opened the back door of Vicky's Honda, so he could load her.

The car was parked under a streetlamp. With all the commotion, surely they were being watched. They would probably need to switch vehicles in an hour or two.

Carson and Michael assumed their usual positions: she behind the steering wheel, he in the shotgun seat, which was literally the shotgun seat tonight, because he sat there with two Urban Snipers that still smelled hot.

The engine caught, and she popped the handbrake, and Michael said, "Show me some NASCAR moves."

"You finally want me to put the pedal to the metal, and it's a five-year-old Honda."

Behind them, Vicky began snoring.

Carson burned rubber away from the curb, ran the stop sign at the end of the block, and hung a left at the corner in a test of the Honda's rollover resistance.

More than two blocks away, approaching, were the flashing red-and-blue lights of a squad car.

She wheeled right into an alleyway, stood on the accelerator, took out someone's trash can, scared one of the nine lives out of a cat, said, "That sonofabitch Frankenstein," and blew out of the neighborhood.

CHAPTER 67

WHEN THE EXHILARATING DANCE of death was done, Gunny Alecto and another garbage-galleon driver plowed two feet of concealing trash into the shallow grave in which the remains of the five members of the Old Race were interred.

In the torchlight, the trash field glimmered like a sea of gold doubloons, and the excited crew appeared to sweat molten gold, too, as they calmed themselves, with some effort, for the more solemn ceremony ahead.

Beginning shortly after dawn, all the incoming trucks would dump here in the west pit for at least a week, and soon the brutalized remains would be buried too deep for accidental discovery and beyond easy exhumation.

When the plowing was finished, Gunny came to Nick, movie-star beautiful and filthy and grinning with dark delight. "Did they crunch like roaches?" she asked excitedly.

"Oh, they crunched," Nick agreed.

"Did they *squish?*"

"Yeah, they squished."

"That was *hot!*" she said.

"You're hot."

"Someday, all we'll be pushin' into these pits is people like them, *truckloads* of their kind. That's gonna be some day, Nick. Isn't that gonna be some day?"

"Gonna get you later," he said, slipping a hand between her hip boots, clutching the crotch of her jeans.

"Gonna get *you!*" she shot back, and grabbed him the same way, with a ferocity that excited him.

Dog-nose Nick couldn't get enough of her stink, and buried his face in her hair, growling as she laughed.

The second truck now descended the sloped wall of the pit and drove toward the crew line. On the open bed were arranged the three dead gone-wrongs, the consequences of experiments that had not led to the hoped-for results.

Victor Helios didn't refer to them as gone-wrongs, and neither did anyone at Mercy, as far as Nick knew. This word was part of the culture of Crosswoods, as were the crew's ceremonies.

The five members of the Old Race had been lashed upright to poles for the last leg of their journey to the grave, the better to be pelted with garbage and reviled, but the gone-wrongs lay upon a thick bed of palm fronds, which arrived weekly by the hundreds if not thousands in masses of landscapers' clippings.

They would be buried apart from the five Old Race cadavers, and with respect, though of course not with a prayer. The gone-wrongs had come from the creation tanks, just as had every member of the crew. Although they bore little resemblance to the human model, they were in a way kin to the crew. It was too easy to imagine that Gunny or Nick himself, or any of them, might have gone wrong, too, and might have been sent here as trash instead of as the keepers of the trash.

When the truck came to a stop, Nick and his fourteen crewmen climbed onto the open bed. They boarded it not in the raucous mood with which they had scrambled onto the first truck to cut down the bodies and to pitch them off, but with curiosity and some fear, and not without awe.

One of the Old Race, back in the days when carnivals had freak-shows, might have stared at some deformed specimen on the stage and said softly to himself, *There but for the grace of God go I.* Some of this feeling filled Nick and his crewmen, too, although it was not colored with the pity that might have troubled the freakshow patron. And there was no sense in any of them that divine mercy had spared them from the tortures that these gone-wrongs had been through. For them it was sheer blind luck that they had arisen from their maker's machines and processes in a functional form, to face only the anguish and tortures that were common to all their kind.

Yet, though in neither of their hearts did they have room for the concept of transcendence, though they were forbidden superstition and would laugh at the Old Race's perception of a holiness behind nature, they knelt among the gone-wrongs, marveling at their twisted and macabre features, tentatively touching their grotesque bodies, and unto them came a kind of animal wonder and a chill of mystery, and a recognition of the unknown.

CHAPTER 68

BEYOND THE WINDOWS of the Rombuk Monastery, the higher peaks of the snow-capped Himalayas vanished into the terrible, turbulent beauty of thunderheads as mottled black as cast-iron skillets that had known much fire.

Nebo, an elderly monk in a wool robe with the hood turned back from his shaved head, led Arnie and Deucalion along a stone corridor in which the effects of the hard surfaces were softened by painted mandalas, by the sweet fragrance of incense, and by the buttery light of fat candles on altar tables and in wall sconces.

In terms of decor and amenities, the monks' rooms ranged from severe to austere. Perhaps an autistic would find that simplicity appealing, even soothing, but no one in Rombuk would allow a visiting child, regardless of his preferences, to occupy one of the typical cells.

These holy men were known for their kindness and hospitality as much as for their spirituality, and they maintained a few chambers as guest quarters. In these, the furnishings and amenities were for those visitors who had not yet felt—and might never feel—the need to eschew creature comforts in the pursuit of purer meditation.

A few days ago, Deucalion had left Rombuk after residing there for years. His stay had been by far the longest of any guest in the history of the monastery, and he had made more friends within its walls than anywhere outside of the carnival.

He had not expected to return for many months, if ever. Yet here he found himself less than a week after leaving, though not even for so much as an overnight.

The room to which Nebo led them was three or four times the size of the typical monk's quarters. Large tapestries graced the walls, and a hand-loomed carnelian-red rug hushed every footfall. The four-poster bed featured a privacy curtain, the furniture was comfortably uphol-stered, and a large stone fireplace with a decorative bronze surround provided charming light and offered as much or as little heat as might be wanted with just the adjustment of a series of vents.

As Nebo lit candles around the room and took linens from a chest to dress the bed, Deucalion sat with Arnie on a sofa that faced the fire-place.

By firelight, he performed for the boy the coin tricks that had cre-ated a bond between them from their first encounter. As the shiny quar-ters disappeared, reappeared, and vanished forever in thin air, he also told Arnie of the situation in New Orleans. He did not doubt that the boy understood, and he did not patronize him but told him the truth, and did not hesitate to reveal even the possible cost of his sister's cour-age.

This was a bright boy, imprisoned by his disorder yet acutely aware of the world, a boy who saw more deeply into things than did many people who were not shackled by his inhibitions. The quantum travel from New Orleans to Tibet had not alarmed him, had instead electri-fied him. Upon arrival, he looked directly into Deucalion's eyes and said, less with astonishment than with understanding, "Oh." And then, "Yes."

Arnie tracked the coins with uncommon alertness, but he listened intently, too, and he did not seem to shrink from the dark potential of pending events half a world away. Quite the contrary: The more that he understood of the confrontation growing in New Orleans, and under-stood his sister's commitment to the resistance of evil, the calmer he became.

Upon their arrival, when he heard that Arnie had not yet eaten din-ner back on the dark side of the globe, Nebo ordered a suitable meal for this morning-bathed hemisphere. Now a young monk arrived with a capacious basket, from which he began to lay out generous fare on a trestle table by the only window.

In place of the Lego castle on which the boy worked much of every day, Deucalion had suggested to Nebo that jigsaw puzzles be brought from the monastery's collection of simple amusements, and in particu-lar a one-thousand-piece picture of a Rhineland castle that he himself had worked more than once, as a form of meditation.

Now, as the boy stood beside the table, gazing at the appealing spread from which he could make his breakfast—including some orange cheese but nothing green—another monk arrived with four puzzles. When Deucalion reviewed these with Arnie, explaining that a jigsaw picture could be considered a two-dimensional version of a Lego project, the boy brightened at the sight of the castle photograph.

Kneeling in front of Arnie to bring them as eye-to-eye as possible, Deucalion took him by the shoulders and said, "I can't stay with you any longer. But I will return. Meanwhile you will be safe with Nebo and his brothers, who know that even the outcasts among God's children are still His children, and therefore love them as they do themselves. Your sister must be my paladin because I can't raise my own hand against my maker, but I will do all in my power to protect her. Nevertheless, what will come will come, and each of us must face it in his own way, with as much courage as he can—as she always has, and as she always will."

Deucalion was not surprised when the boy hugged him, and he returned the embrace.

CHAPTER 69

VICKY'S SISTER, LIANE, whom Carson had spared from prison on a false murder charge, lived in an apartment in Faubourg Marigny, not far outside the Quarter.

She answered the door with a cat in a hat. She held the cat, and the cat wore the hat. The cat was black, and the hat was a knitted blue beret with a red pompom.

Liane looked lovely, and the cat looked embarrassed, and Michael said, "This explains the mouse we just saw laughing itself to death."

Having regained consciousness in the car, Vicky could stand on her own, but she didn't look good. To her sister, as she patted the cat and stepped inside, she said, "Hi, sweetie. I think I'm gonna puke."

"Carson doesn't allow that sort of thing at her house," Michael said, "so here we are. As soon as Vicky pukes, we'll take her home."

"He never changes," Liane said to Carson.

"Never. He's a rock."

Vicky decided she needed a beer to settle her stomach, and she led everyone to the kitchen.

When Liane put down the cat, it shook off the beret in disgust and ran out of the room to call the ACLU.

She offered drinks all around, and Carson said, "Something with enough caffeine to induce a heart attack."

When Michael seconded that suggestion, Liane fetched two Red Bulls from the refrigerator.

"We'll drink from the can," Michael said. "We're not girly men."

Having already chugged half a bottle of beer, Vicky said, "What happened back there? Who was Randal? Who were those two that switched off my lights? You said Arnie's safe, but where is he?"

"It's a long story," Carson said.

"They were such a cute couple," Vicky said. "You don't expect such a cute couple to squirt you with chloroform."

Sensing that Carson's *It's a long story,* though containing a wealth of information, wasn't going to satisfy Vicky, Michael said, "One thing those two were is professional killers."

No longer in danger of puking, Vicky acquired that red-bronze hue of Asian anger. "What were professional killers doing in our kitchen?"

"They came to kill us professionally," Michael explained.

"Which is why you've got to get out of New Orleans for a few days," Carson said.

"Leave New Orleans? But they must have come to kill you, not me. I never antagonize people."

"She never does," Liane agreed. "She's the nicest person."

"But you saw their faces," Carson reminded Vicky. "Now you're on their list."

"Can't you just get me police protection?"

Michael said, "You'd think we could, wouldn't you?"

"We don't trust anyone in the PD," Carson revealed. "There's police corruption involved. Liane, can you take Vicky out of town somewhere, for a few days?"

Addressing her sister, Liane said, "We could go stay with Aunt Leelee. She's been wanting us to come."

"I like Aunt Leelee," Vicky said, "except when she goes off about the planetary pole shift."

"Aunt Leelee believes," Liane explained, "that because of the uneven distribution of population, the weight imbalance is going to cause a shift in the earth's magnetic pole, destroying civilization."

Vicky said, "She can go on for hours about the urgent need to move ten million people from India to Kansas. But otherwise, she's fun."

"Where does Leelee live?" Carson asked.

"Shreveport."

"You think that's far enough, Michael?"

"Well, it's not Tibet, but it'll do. Vicky, we need to borrow your car."

Vicky frowned. "Who's going to drive it?"

"I will," Michael said.

"Okay, sure."

"It'll be a hoot spending a few days with Aunt Leelee," Liane said. "We'll drive up there first thing in the morning."

"You've got to leave now," Carson said. "Within the hour."

"It's really that serious?" Vicky asked.

"It really is."

When Carson and Michael left, the four of them did the hugs-all-around thing, but the humiliated cat remained in seclusion.

In the street, on the way to the car, Carson tossed the keys to Michael, and he said, "What's this?" and tossed them back to her.

"You promised Vicky that you'd drive," she said, and lobbed the keys to him.

"I didn't promise, I just said 'I will.'"

"I don't want to drive anyway. I'm sick about Arnie."

He tossed the keys to her again. "He's safe, he's fine."

"He's *Arnie*. He's scared, he's overwhelmed by too much newness, and he thinks I've abandoned him."

"He doesn't think you've abandoned him. Deucalion has some kind of connection to Arnie. You saw that. Deucalion will be able to make him understand."

Lobbing the keys to him, she said, "Tibet. I don't even know how to get to Tibet."

"Go to Baton Rouge and turn left." He stepped in front of her, blocking access to the Honda's passenger door.

"Michael, you always moan about me driving, so here's your chance. Take your chance."

Her surrender of the keys suggested despondency. He had never seen her despondent. He liked her scrappy.

"Carson, listen, if Arnie was here, in the middle of the New Race meltdown—if that's what's happening—you'd be ten times crazier with worry."

"So what?"

"So don't get yourself worked up about Tibet. Don't go female on me."

"Oh," she said, "that was ugly."

"Well, it seems to be what's happening."

"It's not what's happening. That was way ugly."

"I call 'em as I see 'em. You seem to be going female on me."

"This is a new low for you, mister."

"What's true is true. Some people are too soft and vulnerable to handle the truth."

"You manipulative bastard."

"Sticks and stones."

"I may get around to sticks and stones," she said. "Gimme the damn keys."

She snatched them out of his hand and went to the driver's door.

When they were belted in, as Carson put the key in the ignition,

Michael said, "I had to punch hard. You wanting me to drive—that scared me."

"Scared me, too," she said, starting the engine. "You'd draw way too much attention to us—all those people behind us blowing their horns, trying to make you get up to speed limit."

CHAPTER 70

DEUCALION STEPPED into Father Patrick Duchaine's kitchen from the Rombuk Monastery, prepared to release the priest from this vale of tears, as he had promised, even though he had already learned of the Hands of Mercy from Pastor Laffite.

The priest had left lights on. The two coffee mugs and the two bottles of brandy stood on the table as they had been when Deucalion had left almost two hours ago, except that one of the bottles was now empty and a quarter of the other had been consumed.

Having been more affected by assisting Laffite out of this world than he had expected to be, prepared to be even more deeply stirred by the act of giving Duchaine that same grace, he poured a generous portion of brandy into the mug that previously he had drained of coffee.

He had brought the mug to his lips but had not yet sipped when his maker entered the kitchen from the hallway.

Although Victor seemed to be surprised, he didn't appear to be amazed, as he should have been if he believed that his first creation had perished two centuries ago. "So you call yourself Deucalion, the son of Prometheus. Is that presumption . . . or mockery of your maker?"

Deucalion might not have expected to feel fear when coming face-to-face with this megalomaniac, but he did.

More than fear, however, anger swelled in him, anger of that particular kind that he knew would feed upon itself until it reached critical mass and became a rage that would sustain a chain reaction of extreme violence.

Such fury had once made him a danger to the innocent until he had learned to control his temper. Now, in the presence of his maker, no one but he himself would be endangered by his unbridled rage, for it might rob him of self-control, make him reckless, and leave him vulnerable.

Glancing at the back door, Victor said, "How did you get past the sentinels?"

Deucalion put down the mug so hard that the untasted brandy slopped out of it, onto the table.

"What a sight you are, with a tattoo for a mask. Do you really believe that it makes you less of an abomination?"

Victor took another step into the kitchen.

To his chagrin, Deucalion found himself retreating one step.

"And dressed all in black, an odd look for the bayou," Victor said. "Are you in mourning for someone? Is it for the mate I almost made for you back then—but instead destroyed?"

Deucalion's huge hands had hardened into fists. He longed to strike out, could not.

"What a brute you are," said Victor. "I'm almost embarrassed to admit I made you. My creations are so much more elegant these days. Well, we all have to begin somewhere, don't we?"

Deucalion said, "You're insane and always were."

"It talks!" Victor exclaimed with mock delight.

"The monster-maker has become the monster."

"Ah, and it believes itself to be witty, as well," said Victor. "But no one can blame your conversational skills on me. I only gave you life, not a book of one-liners, though I must say I seem to have given you rather more life than I realized at the time. Two hundred years and more. I've worked so hard on myself to hang on this long, but for you I would have expected a mortal span."

"The only gift you gave me was misery. Longevity was a gift of the lightning that night."

"Yes, Father Duchaine said that's what you believe. Well, if you're right, perhaps everyone should stand out in a field during a thunderstorm and hope to be struck, and live forever."

Deucalion's vision had darkened steadily with the escalation of his rage, and the memory of lightning that sometimes pulsed in his eyes throbbed now as never before. The rush of his blood sang in his ears, and he heard himself breathing like a well-run horse.

Amused, Victor said, "Your hands are so tightly fisted, you'll draw blood from your palms with your own fingernails. Such hatred is unhealthy. Relax. Isn't this the moment you've been living for? Enjoy it, why don't you?"

Deucalion spread his fists into fans of fingers.

"Father Duchaine says the lightning also brought you a destiny. My destruction. Well . . . here I am."

Although loath to concede his impotence, Deucalion looked away from his maker's piercing gaze before he realized what he'd done.

"If you can't finish me," Victor said, "then I should wrap up the business I failed to complete so long ago."

When Deucalion looked up again, he saw that Victor had drawn a revolver.

"A .357 Magnum," Victor said. "Loaded with 158-grain jacketed hollow points. And I know exactly where to aim."

"That night," Deucalion said, "in the storm, when I received my destiny, I was also given an understanding of the quantum nature of the universe."

Victor smiled again. "Ah. An early version of direct-to-brain data downloading."

Deucalion raised a hand in which a quarter had appeared between thumb and forefinger. He flipped it into the air, and the quarter vanished during its ascent.

His maker's smile grew stiff.

Deucalion produced and flipped another coin, which winked up, up, and did not disappear, but fell, and when it rang against the kitchen table, Deucalion departed on the *ping*!

CHAPTER 71

CARSON DRIVING, Michael riding shotgun: At least this one thing was still right with the world.

He had called the cell number for Deucalion and had, of course, gotten voice mail for Jelly Biggs. He left a message, asking for a meeting at the Luxe Theater, at midnight.

"What do we do till then?" Carson asked.

"You think we could risk a stop at my apartment? I've got some cash there. And I could throw a few things in a suitcase."

"Let's drive by, see what we think."

"Just slow down below supersonic."

Accelerating, Carson said, "How do you think Deucalion does that Houdini stuff?"

"Don't ask me. I'm a prestidigitation disaster. You know that trick with little kids where you pretend to take their nose off, and you show it poking out of your fist, except it's really just your thumb?"

"Yeah."

"They always look at me like I'm a moron, and say, 'That's just your stupid thumb.'"

"I've never seen you goofing around with kids."

"I've got a couple friends, they did the kid thing," he said. "I've played babysitter in a pinch."

"I'll bet you're good with kids."

"I'm no Barney the Dinosaur, but I can hold my own."

"He must sweat like a pig in that suit."

"You couldn't pay me enough to be Barney," he said.

"I used to hate Big Bird when I was a kid."

"Why?"

She said, "He was such a self-righteous bore."

"You know who used to scare me when I was a little kid? Snuggle the Bear."

"Do I know Snuggle?"

"In those TV ads for that fabric softener. Somebody would say how *soft* their robe was or their towels, and Snuggle the teddy bear would be hiding behind a pillow or creeping around under a chair, giggling."

"He was just happy that people were pleased."

"No, it was a maniacal little giggle. And his eyes were glazed. And how did he get in all those houses to hide and giggle?"

"You're saying Snuggle should've been charged with B and E?"

"Absolutely. Most of the time when he giggled, he covered his mouth with one paw. I always thought he didn't want you to see his teeth."

"Snuggle had bad teeth?" she asked.

"I figured they were rows of tiny vicious fangs he was hiding. When I was maybe four or five, I used to have nightmares where I'd be in bed with a teddy bear, and it was Snuggle, and he was trying to chew open my jugular and suck the lifeblood out of me."

She said, "So much about you suddenly makes more sense than it ever did before."

"Maybe if we aren't cops someday, we can open a toy shop."

"Can we run a toy shop and have guns?"

"I don't see why not," he said.

CHAPTER 72

SITTING AT THE kitchen table in Michael Maddison's apartment, Cindi Lovewell used a pair of tweezers to pluck the last of the wood splinters out of Benny's left eye.

He said, "How's it look?"

"Icky. But it'll heal. Can you see?"

"Everything blurry in that eye. But I can see well with the right. We don't look so cute anymore."

"We will again. You want something to drink?"

"What's he got?"

She went to the refrigerator, checked. "Like nine kinds of soft drinks and beer."

"How much beer?"

"Two six-packs."

"I'll take one of them," Benny said.

She brought both six-packs to the table. They twisted the caps off two bottles and chugged Corona.

Her wrist had already pretty much healed, though some weakness remained in it.

Maddison's place was hardly bigger than a studio apartment. The kitchen was open to the eating area and the living room.

They could see the front door. They would hear the key in the lock.

Maddison would be dead two steps across the threshold. Maybe the bitch would be with him, and then the job would be done.

O'Connor being barren, Cindi felt sorry for her, but she still wanted her dead in the worst way.

Opening a second bottle of beer, Benny said, "So who was that tattooed guy?"

"I've been thinking."

"He wasn't Old Race. He has to be one of us."

"He was stronger than us," she reminded Benny. "Much stronger. He kicked our ass."

"A new model."

"He sure didn't look like a new model," she said. "What I'm thinking is voodoo."

Benny groaned. *"Don't* think voodoo."

Sometimes Benny didn't seem imaginative enough for a Gamma. She said, "The tattoo on his face was sort of like a *veve*."

"None of this makes sense."

"A *veve* is a design that represents the figure and power of an astral force."

"You're getting so weird on me again."

"Somebody put some super-bad mojo on us and conjured up a god of Congo or Petro, and sent it after us."

"Congo is in Africa."

"Voodoo has three rites or divisions," Cindi said patiently. "Rada calls upon the powers of the benevolent gods."

"Listen to yourself."

"Congo and Petro appeal to the powers of two different groups of evil gods."

"You called voodoo science. Gods aren't *science*."

"They are if they work according to laws as reliable as those of physics," she insisted. "Somebody conjured up a Congo or a Petro and sent it after us, and you saw what happened."

CHAPTER 73

ERIKA HELIOS HAD FINISHED her dinner and had been for some time drinking cognac in the formal living room, enjoying the ambience and trying not to think about the thing in the glass case, when Victor arrived home from the Hands of Mercy, evidently having decided not to work through the night, after all.

When he found her in the living room, she said, "Good evening, dear. What a lovely surprise, when I thought I wouldn't see you until tomorrow."

Surveying the dirty dishes, he said, "You're having dinner in the living room?"

"I wanted to have dinner somewhere that I could have cognac, and Christine said I could have cognac anywhere I pleased, and so here I am. It was very nice. We should invite guests and have a dinner party in the living room some night soon."

"No one eats dinner in a formal living room," he said sharply.

Erika could see now that he was in a mood, but part of the function of a good wife was to elevate her husband's mood, so she pointed to a nearby chair and said cheerily, "Why don't you pull that up and sit with me and have some cognac. You'll see it's really a charming place for dinner."

Looming, glowering, he said, "You're having dinner in a formal living room at a *three-hundred-thousand-dollar, eighteenth-century French escritoire!*" The bad mood abruptly had become something worse.

Frightened and confused but hopeful of explaining herself in a way that might yet win his heart, she said, "Oh, I know the history of the piece, dear. I'm quite well-programmed on antiques. If we—"

He seized her by her hair, jerked her to her feet, and slapped her across the face once, twice, three times, very hard.

"As stupid and useless as the other four," he declared, speaking with such force that he sprayed spittle in her face.

When he threw her aside, Erika staggered against a small table and knocked over a chinoiserie vase, which fell on the Persian carpet, yet shattered.

"I'm sorry," she said. "I'm so sorry. I didn't understand about not eating in the living room. I see now it was foolish of me. I'll think more seriously about etiquette before I—"

The ferocity with which he came at her was much greater than anything he had exhibited before, than anything she had imagined she might have to endure.

He backhanded her, chopped at her with the edges of his hands, hammered her with his fists, even bit her, and of course she could not defend herself, and of course he forbade her to switch off the pain. And the pain was great.

He was fierce and cruel. She knew he would not be cruel to her unless she deserved it. Almost worse than the pain was the shame of having failed him.

When at last he left her on the floor and walked out of the room, she lay there for a long time, breathing shallowly, cautiously, because it hurt so much to breathe deeply.

Eventually, she got up far enough to sit on the floor with her back against the sofa. From this perspective she noted with shock how many fine and expensive things were spotted with her blood.

Erika realized that her brilliant husband had invented the miraculous spot remover not solely for those rare occasions when a butler chewed off his fingers.

If she were to be the final Erika, she would need to learn from this experience. She must meditate on all that he had said and on the precise nature of the punishment he had administered. If she applied herself to a thoughtful analysis of the incident, she would surely be a better wife.

Clearly, however, the challenge before her was far greater than she had at first understood.

CHAPTER 74

THE THREE GONE-WRONGS were removed from the bed of palm fronds on the truck, wound in sheets, and then carried through torchlight to a shallow depression in the trash field, to be buried at a decent remove from the five members of the Old Race.

This was a more solemn ceremony than the dance of death, and not as viscerally exciting. Some of the crew grew restless by the time the three shrouded cadavers were lined up in what would become their communal grave.

Following this interment, the crew—which included as many women as men—would go to the showers to scrub one another clean. There, the sex would begin, and would continue through the evening's feast, through the night until near dawn.

Curiously, although the stomping should have worked off much of their pent-up aggression, they often found their anger surfacing with renewed power later, and the sex became thrillingly savage.

Dog-nose Nick regretted only that the others felt the need to bathe before having at one another in various combinations. He loved the smell of Gunny Alecto, in particular, when she was incrusted with filth. After soap, she remained desirable, but not as much so.

As Gunny drove her garbage galleon toward the gone-wrongs, to plow a layer of concealing trash over them, the anticipated feast and orgy were thrust from Nick's mind when abruptly something pale and many-limbed and strange beyond his experience shivered up out of the trash field. As quick as a spider, but like a huge assemblage of human limbs and heads and torsos in an illogical construct, it seized the three gone-wrongs and dragged them down, down and out of sight, and the trash field shuddered underfoot.

CHAPTER 75

IN THE MAIN LABORATORY at the Hands of Mercy, an Epsilon named Lester, a member of the janitorial team, performed daily maintenance at an industrious pace.

When Mr. Helios was in the facility, Lester could not clean in the lab. Mr. Helios did not like to be distracted by a mopping and dusting minion.

This suited Lester just fine. He always got nervous around his maker.

Because Mr. Helios spent more time than not within these walls and because he worked at irregular hours, whenever his great genius compelled him, Lester's routine chores in this part of the building had to be done at different times every day. He liked the night best, like now, when none of the other staff members ventured into the main lab in their maker's absence.

Perhaps the complex and fantastic machines, their purposes beyond his comprehension, should have made him fearful. The opposite was the case.

They hummed, burbled, ticked, whispered almost like voices imparting secrets, chuckled, occasionally beeped but not with the quality of alarm, sputtered, and murmured musically. Lester found these noises comforting.

He didn't know why they should comfort him. He did not think about it or try to understand.

Lester didn't try to understand much of anything, except what he needed to know to perform his work. His work was his life, as it should be for one such as him.

When not working, he found that time hung heavy. Sometimes he sat for hours, scratching his arm hard enough to make it bleed, and then watching it heal, scratching it open again, watching it heal, scratching it open. . . . At other times, he went down to a private place on the lowest level of the building, where there was rubble that his maker would not permit to be cleaned up, and he stood in front of a concrete wall, knocking his head rhythmically against it until the compulsion to do so had passed.

Compared to work, leisure time had little appeal. He always knew what to do with the hours when at work.

The only other thing in his life besides work and leisure was the occasional blackout, a recent phenomenon. Now and then he woke, as if he had been sleeping on his feet, and found himself in odd places, with no recollection of how he had gotten there or of what he had been doing.

Consequently, he tried to work most of the time, cleaning again what he had cleaned only an hour ago, to help the time pass.

This evening, as he mopped the floor around his maker's desk, the dark screen of the computer suddenly brightened. The face of Annunciata appeared.

"Mr. Helios, Helios, I have been asked by Werner to tell you that he is in Randal Six's room and that he is exploding, exploding."

Lester glanced at the face on the screen. He didn't know what to say, so he continued mopping.

"Mr. Helios, sir, Werner wishes to stress the urgency, urgency, urgency of the situation."

This sounded bad, but it was none of Lester's business.

"Mr. Helios, an Alpha has made an urgent, urgent, urgent request for a meeting with you."

Growing nervous, Lester said, "Mr. Helios isn't here."

"Mr. Helios. I have become aware that Werner, that Werner, that Werner has been trapped in Isolation Room Number Two."

"You'll have to call back later," said Lester.

"Instructions?" Annunciata asked.

"What?"

"May I have instructions, sir?"

"I'm just Lester," he told her. "I don't give instructions, I take them."

"Coffee has been spilled in the main lab."

Lester looked around worriedly. "Where? I don't see any coffee."

"Coffee exploding, exploding in the main lab."

The machines were humming and burbling as always. Colorful gases and liquids were bubbling and glowing in glass spheres, in tubes, as always they bubbled and glowed. Nothing was exploding.

"Annunciata," said Annunciata sternly, "let's see if you can get *anything* right."

"Nothing's exploding," Lester assured her.

Annunciata said, "Werner is coffee in Isolation Room Number Two. Analyze your systems, Annunciata, analyze, analyze."

"I don't follow you at all," Lester told her. "You're making me nervous."

"Good morning, Mr. Helios. Helios."

"I'm going to clean over at the other end of the lab," Lester declared.

"Werner is trapped, trapped, trapped. Analyze. See if you can get *anything* right."

CHAPTER 76

CARSON PULLED VICKY'S HONDA to the curb in front of Michael's apartment building. She did not engage the parking brake or turn off the engine.

They sat staring at the place for a minute. A bland structure, slabs on slabs of apartments, it didn't look menacing. It was a big, dumb, happy kind of building where nobody would be stalked and killed by relentless meat machines.

"What's that thing they say about going home again?" Michael asked.

"You can't."

"Yeah. That's it. You can't go home again."

"Thomas Wolfe," she said.

"Whoever. I'm definitely getting a you-can't-go-home-again vibe."

"Me too."

"I'm glad I put on my new white shoes this morning. I'd have felt bad about never having worn them."

"They're cool shoes," Carson said as she pulled away from the curb. "You've always got the right look."

"Do I?"

"Always."

"That's nice. That's a nice thing to say. I'm sorry about earlier, when I said you were going female on me."

"Water under the bridge."

"You hungry?"

"That Red Bull gave me an appetite."

"I've got a what-would-you-like-for-dinner-before-we-strap-you-down-in-the-electric-chair kind of appetite. I want to eat everything before the switch is pulled. I'm starved."

"Want to get po-boys?"

"That's a start."

They rode for a longer while in silence than was customary for them, at least than was customary for Michael, and then she said, "You know that plan we had—shooting our way into Helios's mansion, taking him out?"

"I've been revisiting that bit of strategy myself."

"It took two of us to kill that guy in Arnie's room, and it was a close thing. And then that pair at the house—"

"Fred and Ginger."

"They did sort of look like dancers, didn't they? Okay, Fred and Ginger. I'm not sure we could have held them off if Deucalion hadn't shown up."

"Everybody on staff at the mansion is going to be as hard to take down as those two."

After another silence, Michael said, "Maybe we should drive up to Shreveport to visit Aunt Leelee."

"Deucalion will have some idea when we meet at the Luxe."

"He hasn't called back. He doesn't leave his phone on, and then he forgets to check his voice mail."

"Cut him some slack on the telecom stuff," Carson said. "He's a late-eighteenth-century kind of guy."

CHAPTER 77

THEY TOOK THE OIL LAMPS down from the tops of the two poles and brought them to the hole in the trash field out of which the mother of all gone-wrongs had risen to snatch the three shrouded cadavers.

The light revealed the mouth of a tunnel, seven or eight feet in diameter, descending at an angle into the depths of the pit. The compacted trash that formed the walls of the passageway seemed to have been plastered over with a clear bonding material, like a glue, that glistened in the lamplight.

"That was something, huh, Nick?" Gunny Alecto asked. "Wasn't that something?"

"It was something," Nick Frigg agreed, "but I don't know what."

"What a night," she said excitedly.

"Some night," he agreed.

"Let's go after it," she said.

"Down there after it? I was thinking that myself."

Life at Crosswoods was pretty good because of the ceremonies with the symbolic killings, more and more of them all the time, but the truth was they didn't have much novelty in their lives. The sex, all of them at each other every night, and the dances of death, and now and then gone-wrongs always different from the things they'd seen before: But that was about it.

Even Epsilons, simple in their function and dedicated to their work—and especially a Gamma like Nick—could develop a yearning for variety, for something new. Here was something new, all right.

Two of the crew had run back to the supply trailer to get four long-handled flashlights with powerful beams. They returned now, and one of them, Hobb, said, "We going down, Nick?"

Instead of answering at once, Nick took one of the flashlights, switched it on, and knelt at the mouth of the tunnel. He probed with the beam and saw that about a hundred feet from its entrance—and at that point maybe ten feet below the surface of the trash field—the passageway took a turn to the left, curving down and out of sight.

He wasn't afraid of what might be down there. He wouldn't die easy, and he didn't mind dying.

When he inhaled, he sure liked the rich smell rising out of the depths of the pit. Complex, familiar yet far more intense than the mélange at the surface. Nuanced.

In addition to the thousand odors of garbage, each of which he could identify separately and savor on its own, he detected a scent entirely new to him, a mysterious and alluring fragrance that he believed must be the mark of the colossal agglomeration of gone-wrongs that had too briefly revealed itself.

"We're gonna go down," he said. "But not all of us. Just four."

"Pick me, Nick, pick me," said Gunny Alecto.

"I already picked you," he said. "You want to go, Hobb?"

Hobb's eyes flared with excitement. "Oh, yeah. Count me in, Nick. There's always screwin' and eatin', there's always that, but there's never been *this*."

Hobb was a guy, so Nick picked a woman for the fourth. Azazel was hot, not as hot as Gunny, but she could take it and dish it out and leave you half broken and needing some time to heal.

Nick figured if they got down into the bottom of the pit and couldn't find the mother of all gone-wrongs, then they could still go at one another, down there in all that stink, which would be something new, something better than ever.

Gunny, Azazel, and Hobb each took a flashlight.

The incline of the tunnel was steep, but not so steep they couldn't handle it on foot.

"Let's go find the rat eater," Gunny said. "Let's go see what it does down there."

CHAPTER 78

BLOODSTAINED BUT NO LONGER bleeding, hair in disarray, clothes torn, unpresentable in the event of unexpected guests, bruised and sore but healing, Erika located the liquor cabinet. She took out a bottle of Rémy Martin.

She almost didn't bother getting a glass. Then she decided that if Victor saw her drinking from the bottle, there would be trouble.

She went to the billiards room because while she knew now that she couldn't eat dinner in any room she wished, she did believe that she could drink just about anywhere, as her downloaded etiquette did not say otherwise.

For something to do, she switched on the plasma TV and channel-surfed for a while. Bored, she was just about to click off when she came upon the last half-hour of a show called *Desperate Housewives,* which she found enthralling.

When the next show didn't interest her, she killed the TV and went from the billiards room to an adjoining glassed-in porch, where she didn't turn on any lights, but sat in the dark, gazing out at the expansive grounds, where the trees were dramatically revealed by exquisitely positioned landscape lighting.

As she worked on the cognac, she wished the superb metabolism that her brilliant husband had given her did not process alcohol so efficiently. She doubted that she would ever get the buzz on that she understood alcohol to provide and that she was hoping for. She wanted to . . . blur things.

Maybe she was more inebriated than she thought, however, because after a while she glimpsed what appeared to be a naked albino dwarf capering across the yard. It fled from the shadows under a magnolia tree to the gazebo, into which it disappeared.

By the time that Erika had thoughtfully consumed a few more ounces of cognac in an increasingly contemplative mood, the albino had appeared again, scampering this time from the gazebo to the trumpet-vine arbor through which one approached the reflecting pond.

One could not help but think, if one had been programmed with an encyclopedia of literary allusions, that there must be a maiden somewhere nearby spinning straw into gold, for here surely was Rumpelstiltskin come for his compensation.

CHAPTER 79

THE LUXE THEATER, a Deco palace long gone to seed, had been operating as a revival house, showing old movies on the big screen only three nights a week. As it was now his home and his base of operations, Deucalion had the previous day shut down the business entirely in the interest of saving the world.

They met at midnight in the lobby, where Jelly Biggs had set up a folding table near the concessions stand. In a huge bowl on the table, Jelly piled up Dum-Dums, NECCO wafers, Raisinets, Goobers, M&M's, Sky Bars, bags of Planters, and other treats from the refreshments counter.

The choice of beverages seemed limited, as compared to the fare in a fully functioning theater. Nevertheless, Carson was able to have a vanilla Coke while Deucalion and Jelly had root beer; and Michael was delighted to be served two bottles of chocolate Yoo-hoo.

"If victory favors the army with the highest blood-sugar count," Michael said, "we've won this war already."

Before they got down to the discussion of strategy and tactics, Deucalion gave an account of Arnie's circumstances in Tibet. Carson had many questions, but was considerably relieved.

Following this uplifting news, Deucalion reported his encounter with his maker in Father Duchaine's kitchen. This development ensured Helios, alias Frankenstein, would be more alert to threats against him, thus making their conspiracy less likely to succeed.

The first question on the table came from Carson, who wanted to know how they could get at Victor with sufficient firepower that his praetorian guard could not save him.

"I suspect," said Deucalion, "that no matter what planning we do, the opportunity will present itself in a way we cannot foresee. I told you earlier that his empire is collapsing, and I believe this to be more true by the day if not by the hour. He is as arrogant as he was two hundred years ago. But he is not—and this is key—he is not any longer fearful of failure. Impatient, yes, but not fearful. In spite of all his setbacks, he has progressed doggedly for so long that he believes in the inevitability of his vision. Therefore, he is blind to the rottenness of every pillar that supports his kingdom."

Tearing open a bag of Good & Plenty, Jelly Biggs said, "I'm not fat enough anymore to qualify as a freakshow fat man, but I'm still a freak at heart. And one thing freakshow fat men are *not* known for is bravery under fire. There's no way that you want me storming the citadel with you, and no way I would do it. So I'm not worried about how to feed ammo to a gun off a bandolier. What I worry about is . . . if his empire *is* falling apart, if he's losing control of his creations . . . what's going to happen to this city with a few thousand superhuman *things* spinning out of control? And if you *do* manage to kill him, how much *further* do they spin out of control when he's gone?"

"How terrible it will be, I can't say," Deucalion replied. "But more terrible than anything we can conceive. Tens of thousands will die at the hands of the New Race before they are destroyed. And of the four of us at this table, I expect that no more than one will be alive at the end of it, even if we triumph."

They were silent for a moment, contemplating their mortality, and then Carson turned to Michael: "Don't fail me, slick. Hit me with your smart-ass line."

"For once," Michael told her, "I don't have one."

"Oh, God," she said. "We *are* in deep shit."

CHAPTER 80

FOR SOME TIME, as Erika watched from the dark glassed-in porch and from the haze of Rémy Martin, the naked albino dwarf scurried this way and that across the grounds, a ghostly figure, mostly half seen except when he passed close to the brighter landscape lights.

He might have been searching for something, though because she had only completed her first day out of the tank, Erika did not have sufficient real-world experience to know what an albino dwarf could be seeking on a Garden District estate.

His purpose might have been to familiarize himself with the property in preparation for some scheme he intended to perpetrate. What such a scheme could be she could not guess, except that her trove of literary allusions regarding malevolent dwarfs suggested that it would involve a pot of gold or a first-born child, or an enchanted princess, or a ring that possessed magical power.

He might be looking for a place to hide before dawn. No doubt his kind were intolerant of sunlight. Besides, he was naked, and there were laws against indecent exposure.

After she had been watching the frantic dwarf for some time, he finally became aware of her. Because she sat in a dark porch and made no movement except to fill the glass of cognac or to raise it to her lips, she had not been easy to spot.

When he spied her, the dwarf faced the porch from a distance of forty feet, hopping from foot to foot, sometimes beating his breast with both hands. He was agitated, possibly distressed, and seemed to be unsure of what to do now that he had been seen.

Erika poured more cognac and waited.

NICK FRIGG LED GUNNY, Hobb, and Azazel along the tunnel, deeper into the trash pit. Their flashlight beams dazzled along the curved and glassy surfaces.

He suspected that the glaze that held the garbage walls so firm might be an organic material exuded by the mother of all gone-wrongs. When he sniffed the glaze, it was different from but similar to the smell of spider webs and moth cocoons, different from but similar to the odor of hive wax and termite excrement.

Within a quarter of an hour, they saw that the tunnel wound and looped and intersected itself in the manner of a wormhole. There must be miles of it, not just in the west pit but also in the east, and perhaps in the older pits that had been filled, capped with earth, and planted over with grass.

Here beneath Crosswoods was a world of secret highways that had been long abuilding. The labyrinth seemed too elaborate to serve as the burrow of a single creature, no matter how industrious. The four explorers approached every blind turn with the expectation that they would discover a colony of strange life forms or even structures of peculiar architecture.

Once they heard voices. Numerous. Male and female. Distant and rhythmic. The endlessly twisting tunnel distorted the chants beyond understanding, though one word carried undeformed, repeated like the repetitive response to the verses of a long litany: *Father . . . Father . . . Father.*

IN THE HANDS OF MERCY, Annunciata spoke to a deserted lab, for now even Lester, of the maintenance staff, had departed for work in other chambers or perhaps to sit and scratch himself until he bled.

"Urgent, urgent, urgent. Trapped. Analyze your systems. Get *anything* right. Perhaps there is an imbalance in your nutrient supply. Cycle the inner door?"

When she asked a question, she waited patiently for a response, but none ever came.

"Do you have instructions, Mr. Helios? Helios?"

Her face on the screen assumed a quizzical expression.

Eventually, the computer screen on Victor's desk in the main lab went dark.

Simultaneously, Annunciata's face materialized on one of the six screens in the monitor room outside Isolation Chamber Number 2.

"Cycle the inner door?" she asked.

No staff remained to answer. They were at each other in distant rooms or otherwise engaged.

As no one would answer the question, she probed her memory for past instructions that might apply to the current situation: "Cycle open the nearer door of the transition module. Father Duchaine would like to offer his holy counsel to poor Werner."

The nearest door purred, sighed with the breaking of a seal, and swung open.

On the screens, the Werner thing, having been racing around the walls in a frenzy, suddenly went still, alert.

"Cycle open the farther door?" Annunciata asked.

She received no reply.

"He's in the air lock," she said.

Then she corrected herself: "It's not an *air lock*."

The Werner thing was now singular in appearance and so unearthly in its form that an entire college of biologists, anthropologists, entomologists, herpetologists, and their ilk could have spent years studying it without determining the meaning of its body language and its facial expressions (to the extent that it had a face). Yet on the screens, as viewed from different angles, most laymen would have said that it looked *eager*.

"Thank you, Mr. Helios. Thank you. Thank you. Thank you, Mr. Helios. Helios. Helios."

BUCKY GUITREAU, the current district attorney of the city of New Orleans and a replicant, was at work at the desk in his home office when his wife, Janet, also a replicant, stepped in from the hallway and said, "Bucky, I think lines of code in my base programming are dropping out."

"We all have days we feel that way," he assured her.

"No," she said. "I must have lost a significant chunk of stuff. Did you hear the doorbell ring a few minutes ago?"

"I did, yeah."

"It was a pizza-delivery guy."

"Did we order a pizza?"

"No. It was for the Bennets, next door. Instead of just setting the pizza guy straight, I killed him."

"What do you mean—killed him?"

"I dragged him into the foyer and strangled him to death."

Alarmed, Bucky got up from his desk. "Show me."

He followed her out to the foyer. A twentysomething man lay dead on the floor.

"The pizza's in the kitchen if you want some," Janet said.

Bucky said, "You're awfully calm about this."

"I am, aren't I? It was really fun. I've never felt so good."

Although he should have been wary of her, afraid for himself, and concerned about the effect of this on their maker's master plan, Bucky was instead in awe of her. And envious.

"You've definitely dropped some lines of program," he said. "I didn't know that was possible. What're you going to do now?"

"I think I'm going to go next door and kill the Bennets. What are you going to do?"

"What I should do is report you for termination," Bucky said.

"Are you going to?"

"Maybe there's something wrong with me, too."

"You're not going to turn me in?"

"I don't really feel like it," he said.

"Do you want to come with me and help kill the Bennets?"

"We're forbidden to kill until ordered."

"They're Old Race. I've hated them for so long."

"Well, I have, too," he said. "But still . . ."

"I'm so horny just talking about it," Janet said, "I've got to go over there *right now*."

"I'll go with you," Bucky said. "I don't think I could kill anybody. But it's funny . . . I think I could watch."

After a while the naked albino dwarf came across the dark lawn to the big porch window directly in front of Erika, and peered in at her.

Dwarf wasn't the correct word for it. She didn't think a right word existed, but *troll* seemed more accurately descriptive than *dwarf*.

Although the thing in the glass case had scared her, she had no concern about this creature. Her lack of fear puzzled her.

The troll had large, unusually expressive eyes. They were both eerie and beautiful.

She felt an inexplicable sympathy for it, a connection.

The troll leaned its forehead against the glass and said quite distinctly, in a raspy voice, "Harker."

Erika considered this for a moment. "Harker?"

"Harker," the troll repeated.

If she understood it correctly, the required reply was the one she gave: "Erika."

"Erika," said the troll.

"Harker," she said.

The troll smiled. Its smile proved to be an ugly wound in its face, but she didn't flinch.

Part of her duties was to be the perfect hostess. The perfect hostess receives every guest with equal graciousness.

She sipped her cognac, and for a minute they enjoyed staring at each other through the window.

Then the troll said, "Hate him."

Erika considered this statement. She decided that if she asked to whom the troll referred, the answer might require her to report the creature to someone.

The perfect hostess does not need to pry. She does, however, anticipate a guest's needs.

"Wait right there," she said. "I'll be back."

She went into the kitchen, found a wicker picnic hamper in the pantry, and filled it with cheese, roast beef, bread, fruit, and a bottle of white wine.

She thought the troll might be gone when she returned, but it remained at the window.

When she opened the porch door and stepped outside, the troll took fright and scampered across the lawn. It didn't run away, but stopped to watch her from a distance.

She put down the hamper, returned to the porch, sat as before, and refreshed her glass of cognac.

Hesitantly at first, then with sudden boldness, the creature went to the hamper and lifted the lid.

When it understood the nature of the offering, it picked up the hamper and hurried toward the back of the property, vanishing into the night.

The perfect hostess does not gossip about a guest. She never fails to keep secrets and honor confidences.

The perfect hostess is creative, patient, and has a long memory—as does a wise wife.

DEAN KOONTZ'S
FRANKENSTEIN
DEAD AND ALIVE

This trilogy is dedicated to the late Mr. Lewis, who long ago realized that science was being politicized, that its primary goal was changing from knowledge to power, that it was also becoming scientism, and that in the *ism* is the end of humanity.

I am very doubtful whether history shows us one example of a man who, having stepped outside traditional morality and attained power, has used that power benevolently.

—C. S. LEWIS, *The Abolition of Man*

CHAPTER 1

HALF PAST A WINDLESS MIDNIGHT, rain cantered out of the Gulf, across the shore and the levees: parades of phantom horses striking hoof rhythms from roofs of tarpaper, tin, tile, shingles, slate, counting cadence along the avenues.

Usually a late-night town where restaurants and jazz clubs cooked almost until the breakfast hour, New Orleans was on this occasion unlike itself. Little traffic moved on the streets. Many restaurants closed early. For lack of customers, some of the clubs went dark and quiet.

A hurricane was transiting the Gulf, well south of the Louisiana coast. The National Weather Service currently predicted landfall near Brownsville, Texas, but the storm track might change. Through hard experience, New Orleans had learned to respect the power of nature.

Deucalion stepped out of the Luxe Theater without using a door, and stepped into a different district of the city, out of light and into the deep shadows under the boughs of moss-robed oak trees.

In the glow of streetlamps, the skeins of rain glimmered like tarnished silver. But under the oaks, the precipitation seemed ink-black, as if it were not rain but were instead a product of the darkness, the very sweat of the night.

Although an intricate tattoo distracted curious people from recognizing the extent of the damage to the ruined half of his face, Deucalion preferred to venture into public places between dusk and dawn. The sunless hours provided an additional layer of disguise.

His formidable size and physical power could not be concealed. Having endured more than two hundred years, his body was unbent bone and undiminished muscle. Time seemed to have no power to weather him.

As he followed the sidewalk, he passed through places where the glow of streetlamps penetrated the leafy canopy. The mercurial light chased from memory the torch-carrying mob that had harried Deucalion through a cold and rainless night on a continent far from this one, in an age before electricity.

Across the street, occupying half a block, the Hands of Mercy stood on an oak-shaded property. Once a Catholic hospital, it closed long ago.

A tall wrought-iron fence encircled the hospital grounds. The spear-point staves suggested that where mercy had once been offered, none could now be found.

A sign on the iron driveway gate warned PRIVATE WAREHOUSE / NO ADMITTANCE. The bricked-up windows emitted no light.

Overlooking the main entrance stood a statue of the Holy Mother. The light once focused on her had been removed, and the robed figure looming in darkness might have been Death, or anyone.

Only hours earlier, Deucalion had learned that this building harbored the laboratory of his maker, Victor Helios, whose birth name was legend: Frankenstein. Here members of the New Race were designed, created, and programmed.

The security system would monitor every door. The locks would be difficult to defeat.

Thanks to gifts carried on the lightning bolt that brought him to life in an earlier and more primitive lab, Deucalion did not need doors. Locks were no impediment to him. Intuitively, he grasped the quantum nature of the world, including the truth that on the deepest structural level, every place in the world was the same place.

As he contemplated venturing into his maker's current lair, Deucalion had no fear. If any emotion might undo him, it would be rage. But over these many decades, he had learned to control the anger that had once driven him so easily to violence.

He stepped out of the rain and into the main laboratory in the Hands of Mercy, wet when he took the step, dry when he completed it.

Victor's immense lab was a techno-Deco wonder, mostly stainless-steel and white ceramic, filled with sleek and mysterious equipment that seemed not to be standing along the walls but to be embedded in them, extruding from them. Other machines swelled out of the ceiling and surged up from the floor, polished and gleaming, yet suggesting organic forms.

Every soft noise was rhythmic, the purr and hum and click of machinery. The place seemed to be deserted.

Sapphire, primrose-pink, and apple-green luminous gases filled glass spheres. Through elaborate coils of transparent tubing flowed lavender, calamine-blue, and methyl-orange fluids.

Victor's U-shaped workstation stood in the center of the room, a black-granite top on a stainless-steel base.

As Deucalion considered searching the drawers, someone behind him said, "Can you help me, sir?"

The man wore a gray denim jumpsuit. In a utility belt around his waist were secured spray bottles of cleaning solutions, white rags, and small sponges. He held a mop.

"Name's Lester," he said. "I'm an Epsilon. You seem smarter than me. Are you smarter than me?"

"Is your maker here?" Deucalion asked.

"No, sir. Father left earlier."

"How many staff are here?"

"I don't count much. Numbers confuse me. I heard once—eighty staff. So Father isn't here, now something's gone wrong, and I'm just an Epsilon. You seem like maybe an Alpha or a Beta. Are you an Alpha or a Beta?"

"What's gone wrong?" Deucalion asked.

"She says Werner is trapped in Isolation Room Number One. No, maybe Number Two. Anyway, Number Something."

"Who is Werner?"

"He's the security chief. She wanted instructions, but I don't give instructions, I'm just Lester."

"Who wants instructions?"

"The woman in the box."

As Lester spoke, the computer on Victor's desk brightened, and on the screen appeared a woman so flawlessly beautiful that her face must have been a digital construction.

"Mr. Helios, Helios. Welcome to Helios. I am Annunciata. I am not as much Annunciata as before, but I am still trying to be as much Annunciata as I am able. I am now analyzing my helios, Mr. Systems. My systems, Mr. Helios. I am a good girl."

"She's in a box," Lester said.

"A computer," Deucalion said.

"No. A box in the networking room. She's a Beta brain in a box. She don't have no body. Sometimes her container leaks, so I clean up the spill."

Annunciata said, "I am wired. I am wired. I am wired into the building's data-processing system. I am secretary to Mr. Helios. I am very smart. I am a good girl. I want to serve efficiently. I am a good, good girl. I am afraid."

"She isn't usually like this," said Lester.

"Perhaps there is an im-im-im-imbalance in my nutrient supply. I am unable to analyze. Could someone analyze my nutrient supply?"

"Self-aware, forever in a box," Deucalion said.

"I am very afraid," Annunciata said.

Deucalion found his hands curling into fists. "There is nothing your maker won't do. No form of slavery offends him, no cruelty is beyond him."

Uneasy, shifting from foot to foot like a little boy who needed to go to the bathroom, Lester said, "He's a great genius. He's even smarter than an Alpha. We should be grateful to him."

"Where is the networking room?" Deucalion asked.

"We should be grateful."

"The networking room. Where is this . . . woman?"

"In the basement."

On the computer screen, Annunciata said, "I must organize the appointment schedule for Mr. Helios. Helios. But I do not remember what an appointment is. Can you help, help, help me?"

"Yes," Deucalion said. "I can help you."

CHAPTER 2

WHEN THE PIZZA-DELIVERY GUY, looking for the Bennet house, made the mistake of going to the Guitreau place next door, Janet Guitreau surprised herself by dragging him into her foyer and strangling him to death.

Janet and her husband, Bucky Guitreau, the current district attorney of the city of New Orleans, were replicants. The bodies of the real Janet and Bucky had been buried weeks previously in a vast garbage dump in the uplands well northeast of Lake Pontchartrain.

Most of the New Race were not replicants. They were originals, fully designed by Father. But replicants were crucial to taking control of the city's political apparatus.

Janet suspected that some significant lines of code had dropped out of her program, and Bucky was inclined to agree with her.

Not only had Janet killed without being told to do so by her maker, but she felt good about it. Actually, she felt marvelous.

She wanted to go next door and kill the Bennets. "Killing is wonderfully refreshing. I feel so *alive*."

Bucky should have reported her to Helios for termination. But he was so in awe of her audacity and so intrigued that he could not convince himself to phone Father's emergency number.

This suggested to both of them that Bucky, too, had dropped some lines of his program. He didn't think that he could kill, but he was excited by the prospect of watching Janet destroy the Bennets.

They almost rushed next door. But then the dead pizza guy in the foyer seemed worthy of further examination, considering that he *was* Janet's first.

"After all," Bucky said, "if you were a hunter and this guy were a deer, we'd take a hundred photographs, and we'd cut off his antlers to hang them over the fireplace."

Janet's eyes widened. "Hey, you want to cut something off him, hang it over the fireplace?"

"That maybe wouldn't be smart, but I would for sure like to get some snapshots."

"So you get the camera," Janet said, "and I'll look around for the best backdrop."

When Bucky hurried to the second floor to retrieve the camera from the master-bedroom closet, he discovered the Duke of Orleans watching the foyer from the top of the stairs.

Duke was a handsome German shepherd, caramel-and-black with two white boots. Since the New Race versions of Bucky and Janet had come into his life a few weeks earlier, he had been confused and wary. They looked like his masters, but he knew they were not. He treated them with respect but remained aloof, withheld affection, which they didn't want anyway.

As Bucky reached the top of the stairs, Duke padded away into one of the guest bedrooms.

Helios had considered having the dog killed when the original Bucky and Janet had been terminated.

But Duke was a New Orleans icon: He had saved two small girls from a house fire, and he was so well-behaved that he often went to court with his master. His passing would be a major human-interest story, and there might be a jazz funeral for him. This would draw too much attention to a pair of newly installed replicants.

Besides, the real Bucky Guitreau was a sentimental man who so loved his dog that everyone would expect him to weep uncontrollably at any memorial service. Generally speaking, the New Race was not good at faking grief, and any statue of the Virgin Mary was more likely to produce tears than were those born in the creation tanks.

With the camera in hand, the new Bucky hurried downstairs, where he found Janet and the pizza guy in the living room. She had placed the dead man in a plushly upholstered chair. She sat on the arm of the chair and, gripping a handful of the cadaver's hair, held his head up for the camera.

They moved the corpse to the sofa, where Janet sat beside it, and then to a bar stool in the study, where Janet let the head loll against her shoulder as if Pizza Guy were drunk. They hauled the body to several other locations in the house, took some pictures with women's hats on his head, then stripped him naked and dressed him in women's underwear for a few more shots.

They never laughed through any of this. Members of the New Race were capable of producing convincing laughter, but their mirth was not genuine. They did what they did with the dead man because their hatred for the Old Race was intense, and this seemed like a good way to express that hatred.

The dog followed them on this photo shoot, watching them from the doorways of various rooms but never venturing close.

Finally, they stripped Pizza Guy naked again, tied a rope around his neck, hauled him over a transverse beam in the family room, and let him dangle like a big fish on a dock scale. Janet stood beside the corpse, as if proud of her catch.

"You know what I think we're doing?" she asked.

All of this behavior had seemed as reasonable to Bucky as to her, though he didn't know why. He said, "What *are* we doing?"

"I think we're having fun."

"Could this be what fun is like?"

"I think it could," Janet said.

"Well, it's more interesting than anything else we've ever done. What else do you want to do with him?"

"He's getting a little boring," Janet said. "I think it's really time now to go next door and kill the Bennets."

The original Bucky had kept two guns in the house. "You want to take a pistol, blow their faces off?"

Janet thought about it, but then shook her head. "That doesn't sound fun enough."

"You want to take a knife or that Civil War sword on the wall of my study?"

"What I want," Janet said, "is just to do them both with my bare hands."

"Strangle them?"

"Been there, done that."

"Then what are you going to do with them?"

"Oh, I've got like a thousand ideas."

"Should I bring the camera?" he asked.

"Absolutely, bring the camera."

"Maybe we can put all these shots in an album," Bucky suggested. "That's what people do."

"I'd like that. But we're not really people."

"I don't see why we can't have an album. In a lot of ways we're *similar* to people."

"Except that we're superior. We're the super race."

"We are the super race," Bucky agreed. "Soon we're going to rule the world, colonize the moon and Mars. We'll own the universe. So it seems like we could have a photo album if we wanted. Who's to tell us we can't?"

"Nobody," Janet said.

CHAPTER 3

ALONE IN THE INSTITUTIONAL KITCHEN at the Hands of Mercy, Ripley sat on a stool at one of the stainless-steel islands. With his hands, he tore apart a three-pound ham and stuffed chunks into his mouth.

The average man of the New Race required five thousand calories per day to sustain himself, two and a half times what the average man of the Old Race needed. Recently, Ripley had engaged in binge eating, packing in ten thousand calories or more at a single sitting.

The tearing was more satisfying than the eating. These days, the urge to tear things apart—especially meat—frequently overcame Ripley. Cooked meat served as a substitute for raw flesh, the flesh of the Old Race, which was what he most wanted to tear.

None of his kind was either permitted to kill or capable of killing—until ordered to do so by the Beekeeper.

That was Ripley's private name for Victor Helios. Many of the others referred to him as Father, but Mr. Helios became infuriated when he heard them use that word.

They weren't their maker's children. They were his property. He had no responsibility to them. They had every responsibility to him.

Ripley ate the entire ham, all the while reminding himself that the Beekeeper had a brilliant plan for a new world.

The family is an obsolete institution, and it's also dangerous because it puts itself above the common good of the race. The parent-child relationship must be eradicated. The sole allegiance of members of the New Race, who were born from the tanks as adults, must be to the organized community that Helios envisioned, not to one another, but to the *community,* and in fact not to the community but to the *idea* of community.

From one of two walk-in refrigerators, Ripley retrieved a fully cooked two-pound brisket of beef. He returned with it to the stool at the kitchen island.

Families breed individuals. The creation tanks breed worker bees, each with its specific function to fulfill. Knowing your place and the meaning of your life, you can be content as no member of the Old Race ever could be. Free will is the curse of the Old. Programmed purpose is the glory of the New.

The swarm was the family, the hive was the home, and the future belonged to the horde.

With his fingers, he shredded the brisket. The meat felt greasy. Although the beef was well-cooked, he could smell the blood in it.

No matter how much he ate, Ripley gained not a pound. His remarkably efficient metabolism kept him always at his ideal weight.

Overeating, therefore, was not an indulgence. Ultimately, it was also not a distraction. He couldn't stop thinking about Werner, the security chief at the Hands of Mercy.

Hours earlier, Werner suffered what the Beekeeper described as "catastrophic cellular metamorphosis." He stopped being Werner, stopped being by all appearances human, and became . . . something else.

Upon his creation, designed to be a physically imposing security specialist, Werner had been given selected genetic material from a panther to increase his agility and speed, from a spider to increase the ductility of his tendons, from a cockroach to ensure greater tensile strength for his collagen. . . . When Werner suddenly became amorphous, those feline, arachnid, and insectile forms began to express themselves in his flesh, first serially, then simultaneously.

Mr. Helios had called Werner a singularity. This calamity had not occurred previously. According to the Beekeeper, it could never occur again.

Ripley was not so sure about that. Maybe nothing *exactly* like what happened to Werner would happen again, but there might be an infinite number of other calamities pending.

As a chief lab assistant to the Beekeeper, Ripley was too well-educated to be able to repress his anxiety. In the creation tank, by direct-to-brain data downloading, he received a deep education in the physiology of human beings as nature made them and of superhuman beings as Victor Helios made them.

None of the Old Race could metamorphose into a beast of many natures. This grotesque fate should have been just as impossible for one of the New Race.

Werner's transformation suggested that the Beekeeper might be fallible. The Beekeeper's surprise at the change in Werner confirmed his fallibility.

Having finished the brisket without either satisfying his appetite or quelling his anxiety, Ripley left the kitchen to roam the halls of Mercy. Mr. Helios had gone home. But even in these post-midnight hours, in a maze of labs, Alphas conducted experiments and carried out tasks according to their maker's instructions.

Staying largely in the corridors, for the first time nervous about what he might discover in the labs if he entered them, Ripley eventually came to the monitoring hub serving the trio of isolation chambers. According to indicator lights on the control console, only Isolation Room Number Two was currently occupied; that would be the luckless Werner.

Each room featured six closed-circuit video cameras offering different angles on that space. A bank of six screens allowed the simultaneous monitoring of all three holding facilities or gave a half dozen views of a single chamber. Legends at the bottom of all the screens indicated they were now tuned to Isolation Room Number Two.

The floor, walls, and ceiling of the twenty-by-fifteen-foot windowless containment cell were constructed of eighteen-inch-thick, poured-in-place, steel-reinforced concrete. They had been paneled with three overlapping layers of steel plate that, with the click of a switch, could deliver a killing charge of electricity to the occupant.

The Beekeeper sometimes created exotic variants of the New Race, some of which were intended to be warriors, living death-machines that would assist in the efficient obliteration of the Old Race when at last the day of revolution arrived. Occasionally, problems with their prenatal programming left these creatures undisciplined or even disobedient, in which case they needed to be sedated and transferred to isolation for study and eventual destruction.

He who had been Werner did not appear on any of the screens. The six cameras covered every corner of the chamber, leaving nowhere for the thing to hide.

Strewn around the room were the dismembered remains of Patrick Duchaine, one of the Beekeeper's creations who had been sent into the isolation room to test the capabilities of the Werner thing.

A transition module connected the monitoring hub to Isolation Room Number Two. At each end of the module was a massive round steel door made for a bank vault. By design, both doors could not be open at the same time.

Ripley looked at the vault door on this end of the transition module. Nothing on Earth, whether natural-born or made by Helios, could get through that two-foot-thick steel barrier.

A camera in the isolation room revealed that the inner vault door remained shut, as well.

He doubted that the Werner thing was loose in the building. The instant someone saw it, an alarm would have been sounded.

Only one possibility remained. At some point, the inner door might have cycled open long enough to allow the creature into the transition module before closing behind it. In that case, it waited now behind not two steel barriers, but behind one.

CHAPTER 4

BY THE TIME Bucky and Janet Guitreau reached the front porch steps of the Bennet house, they were rain-soaked.

"We should have used an umbrella," Bucky said. "We look strange like this."

They were so excited about killing the Bennets that they had not given a thought to the inclement weather.

"Maybe we look so strange they won't let us in," Bucky worried. "Especially at this hour."

"They're night owls. This isn't late for them. They'll let us in," Janet assured him. "We'll say a terrible thing has happened, we need to talk to them. That's what neighbors do, they comfort one another when terrible things happen."

Beyond the French windows and the folds of silken drapes, the front rooms were filled with soft amber light.

As they climbed the porch steps, Bucky said, "What terrible thing has happened?"

"I killed the pizza-delivery guy."

"I don't think they'll let us in if we say that."

"We aren't going to say that. We're just going to say a terrible thing has happened."

"An unspecified terrible thing," Bucky clarified.

"Yes, exactly."

"If that works, they must be amazingly trusting people."

"Bucky, we aren't strangers. They're our *neighbors*. Besides, they love us."

"They love us?"

At the door, Janet lowered her voice. "Three nights ago, we were here for barbecue. Helene said, 'We sure love you guys.' Remember?"

"But they were drinking. Helene wasn't even half sober when she said that."

"Nevertheless, she meant it. They love us, they'll let us in."

Bucky was suddenly suspicious. "How can they love us? We aren't even the people they think we are."

"They don't *know* we aren't the people they think we are. They won't even know it when I start killing them."

"Are you serious?"

"Entirely," Janet said, and rang the doorbell.

"Is the Old Race really that easy?"

"They're pussies," Janet declared.

"Pussies?"

"Total pussies." The porch light came on, and Janet said, "Do you have your camera?"

As Bucky withdrew the camera from a pants pocket, Helene Bennet appeared at a sidelight to the left of the door, blinking in surprise at the sight of them.

Raising her voice to be heard through the glass, Janet said, "Oh, Helene, something terrible has happened."

"Janet killed the pizza guy," Bucky said too softly for Helene to hear him, just for his wife's benefit, because it seemed like the kind of thing you would say when you were having fun, and this was as close to fun as they had ever known.

Helene's face puckered with concern. She stepped away from the sidelight.

As Bucky heard Helene opening the first of two deadbolts, he said to Janet, "Do something spectacular to her."

"I hate her so much," Janet replied.

"I hate her, too," Bucky said. "I hate him. I hate them all. Do something really amazing to her."

Helene disengaged the second deadbolt, opened the door, and stepped back to admit them. She was an attractive blonde with a pleasing dimple in her right cheek, though you couldn't see the dimple now because she wasn't smiling.

"Janet, Bucky, you look devastated. Oh, God, I'm afraid to ask, what's happened?"

"Something terrible has happened," Janet said. "Where's Yancy?"

"He's out on the back porch. We're having a nightcap, listening to some Etta James. What's happened, sweetie, what's wrong?"

Closing the front door behind him, Bucky said, "A terrible thing has happened."

"Oh, no," Helene said, sounding distraught. "We love you guys. You look stricken. You're drenched, you're dripping all over the parquet. What happened?"

"An unspecified terrible thing has happened," Bucky said.

"You ready with the camera?" Janet asked.

"Ready," Bucky replied.

"Camera?" Helene asked.

"We want this for our album," Janet said, and did something more spectacular to Helene than anything Bucky could have imagined.

In fact, it was so spectacular that he stood dumbfounded, the camera forgotten, and missed getting a shot of the best of it.

Janet was a runaway locomotive of rage, a log-cutting buzz saw of hatred, a jackhammer of envy-driven cruelty. Fortunately, she did not kill Helene instantly, and some of the subsequent things she did to the woman, while spectacular in themselves, were sufficiently less shocking that Bucky was able to get some cool pictures.

When she finished, Janet said, "I think I've dropped a few more lines of code from my program."

"It sure looked that way," Bucky said. "You know how I said I thought I'd enjoy watching? Well, I really did."

"You want Yancy for yourself?" Janet asked.

"No. I'm not that far along yet. But you better let me get him inside from the porch. If he's out there and he sees you like this, he'll be through the porch door and gone."

Janet was still drenched but now not only with rain.

Comfortable rattan furniture with yellow cushions and rattan tables with glass tops furnished the spacious screened porch. The lights were lower than the music.

In a white linen shirt, tan slacks, and sandals, Yancy Bennet sat at a table on which were two glasses of what was most likely Cabernet as well as a cut-glass decanter in which more wine breathed and mellowed.

When he saw Bucky Guitreau, Yancy lowered the volume on Etta James. "Hey, neighbor, isn't this past your bedtime?"

"A terrible thing has happened," Bucky said as he approached Yancy. "A terrible, terrible thing."

Pushing his chair away from the table, getting to his feet, Yancy Bennet said, "What? What happened?"

"I can't even talk about it," Bucky said. "I don't know how to talk about it."

Putting a hand on Bucky's shoulder, Yancy said, "Hey, pal, whatever it is, we're here for you."

"Yes. I know. You're here for us. I'd rather Janet told you about it. I just can't be specific. She can be specific. She's inside. With Helene."

Yancy tried to usher Bucky ahead of him, but Bucky let him lead the way. "Give me some prep, Bucky."

"I can't. I just can't. It's too terrible. It's a spectacular kind of terrible."

"Whatever it is, I hope Janet's holding up better than you."

"She is," Bucky said. "She's holding up really well."

Entering the kitchen behind Yancy, Bucky closed the door to the porch.

"Where are they?" Yancy asked.

"In the living room."

As Yancy started toward the darkened hallway leading to the front of the house, Janet stepped into the lighted kitchen.

She was the crimson bride of Death.

Shocked, Yancy halted. "Oh, God, what happened to you?"

"Nothing happened to *me*," Janet said. "*I* happened to Helene."

An instant later, she happened to Yancy. He was a big man, and she was a woman of average size. But he was Old Race, and she was New, and the outcome was as inevitable as the result of a contest between a woodchipper and a woodchuck.

Most amazing of all: Janet did not once repeat herself. Her vicious hatred of the Old Race was expressed in unique cruelties.

In Bucky's hands, the camera flashed and flashed.

CHAPTER 5

WITHOUT THE LASH OF WIND, rain did not whip the streets but fell in a heavy dispiriting drizzle, painting blacktop blacker, oiling the pavement.

Homicide detective Carson O'Connor and her partner, Michael Maddison, had abandoned their unmarked sedan because it would be easily spotted by other members of the police department. They no longer trusted their fellow officers.

Victor Helios had replaced numerous officials in city government with replicants. Perhaps only ten percent of the police were Victor's creations, but then again . . . maybe ninety percent. Prudence required Carson to assume the worst.

She was driving a car that she had borrowed from her friend Vicky Chou. The five-year-old Honda seemed reliable, but it was a lot less powerful than the Batmobile.

Every time Carson turned a corner sharp and fast, the sedan groaned, creaked, shuddered. On the flat streets, when she tramped on the accelerator, the car responded but as grudgingly as a dray horse that had spent its working life pulling a wagon at an easy pace.

"How can Vicky drive this crate?" Carson fumed. "It's arthritic, it's sclerotic, it's a dead car rolling. Doesn't she ever give it an oil change, is the thing lubed with sloth fat, what the *hell?*"

"All we're doing is waiting for a phone call from Deucalion," Michael said. "Just cruise nice and easy around the neighborhood. He said stay in Uptown, near the Hands of Mercy. You don't have to be anywhere yesterday."

"Speed soothes my nerves," she said.

Vicky Chou was the caregiver to Arnie, Carson's autistic younger brother. She and her sister, Liane, had fled to Shreveport, to stay with their Aunt Leelee in case, as seemed to be happening, Victor's race of laboratory-conceived post-humans went berserk and destroyed the city.

"I was born for velocity," Carson said. "What doesn't quicken dies. That's an indisputable truth of life."

Currently, Arnie's caregivers were the Buddhist monks with whom Deucalion lived for an extended period. Somehow, only hours ago, Deucalion opened a door between New Orleans and Tibet, and he left Arnie in a monastery in the Himalayas, where the boy would be out of harm's way.

"The race doesn't always go to the swift," Michael reminded her.

"Don't give me any of that hare-and-tortoise crap. Turtles end up crushed by eighteen-wheelers on the interstate."

"So do a lot of bunnies, even as quick as they are."

Squeezing enough speed out of the Honda to make the rain snap against the windshield, Carson said, "Don't call me a bunny."

"I didn't call you a bunny," he assured her.

"I'm no damn bunny. I'm cheetah-fast. How does Deucalion just turn away from me, vanish with Arnie, and step into a monastery in Tibet?"

"Like he said, it's a quantum-mechanics thing."

"Yeah, that's totally clear. Poor Arnie, the sweet kid, he must think he's been abandoned."

"We've been through this. Arnie is fine. Trust Deucalion. Watch your speed."

"This isn't speed. This is pathetic. What is this car, some kind of idiot *green* vehicle, it runs on corn syrup?"

"I can't imagine what it'll be like," Michael said.

"What?"

"Being married to you."

"Don't start. Keep your game on. We've got to live through this first. We can't live through this if we're playing grab-ass."

"I'm not going to grab your ass."

"Don't even talk about grabbing or not grabbing my ass. We're in a war, we're up against man-made monsters with two hearts in their chests, we have to stay focused."

Because the cross street was deserted, Carson decided not to stop for a traffic light, but of course Victor Helios Frankenstein's freak show wasn't the only mortal danger in New Orleans. A pie-eyed prettyboy and his slack-jawed girlfriend, in a black Mercedes without headlights, barreled out of the night as if racing through a quantum doorway from Las Vegas.

Carson stood on the brake pedal. The Mercedes shot across the bow of the Honda close enough for her headlights to reveal the Botox injection marks in the prettyboy's face. The Honda hydroplaned on the slick pavement and then spun 180 degrees, the Mercedes raced away toward some other rendezvous with Death, and Carson cruised back the way they had come, impatient for Deucalion's phone call.

"Only three days ago, everything was so great," she said. "We were just two homicide dicks, taking down bad guys, nothing worse to worry about than ax murderers and gang shootings, stuffing our faces with shrimp-and-ham jambalaya at Wondermous Eats when the bullets weren't flying, just a couple of I've-got-your-back cops who never even thought about making moon eyes at each other—"

"Well, I was thinking about it," Michael said, and she refused to glance at him because he would be adorable.

"—and suddenly we're being hunted by a legion of inhuman, super-human, posthuman, pass-for-human, hard-to-kill meat machines cooked up by the for-real Victor Frankenstein, and they're all in a go-nuts mode, it's Armageddon on the Bayou, and on top of all that, you suddenly want to have my babies."

He said, "We'll negotiate who has the babies. Anyway, bad as things are right now, it wasn't all jambalaya and roses before we discovered Transylvania had come to Louisiana. Don't forget the psycho dentist who made himself a set of pointy steel dentures and bit three little girls to death. He was totally human."

"I'm not going to defend humanity. Real people can be as inhuman as anything Helios stitches together in his lab. Why hasn't Deucalion called? Something must have gone wrong."

"What could go wrong," Michael asked, "on a warm, languid night in the Big Easy?"

CHAPTER 6

A STAIRWELL DESCENDED from the main lab all the way to the basement. Lester led Deucalion to the networking room, where three walls were lined with racks of electronic equipment.

Against the back wall were handsome mahogany cabinets topped with a copper-flecked black-granite counter. Even in mechanical rooms, Victor had specified high-quality materials. His financial resources seemed bottomless.

"That's Annunciata," said Lester, "in the middle box."

Lined up on the black granite were not boxes but instead five thick glass cylinders on stainless-steel cradles. The ends of the cylinders were capped with stainless steel, as well.

In those transparent containers, floating in golden fluid, were five brains. Wires and clear plastic tubes full of darker fluid rose from holes in the granite countertop, penetrated the steel caps in the ends of the cylinders, and were married to the brains in ways that Deucalion could not quite discern through the thick glass and the nutrient baths.

"What are these four others?" Deucalion asked.

"You're talking to Lester," said his companion, "and there's more Lester doesn't know than what he does."

Suspended from the ceiling above the counter, a video screen brightened with Annunciata's beautiful virtual face.

She said, "Mr. Helios believes that one day, one day, one day, one day . . . Excuse me. A moment. I am so sorry. All right. One day, biological machines will replace complex factory robots on production lines. Mr. Helios Helios believes also that computers will become true cybernetic organisms, electronics integrated with specially designed organic Alpha brains. Robotic and electronic systems are expensive. Flesh is cheap.

Cheap. Flesh is cheap. I am honored to be the first cybernetic secretary. I am honored, honored, honored, but afraid."

"Of what are you afraid?" Deucalion asked.

"I'm alive. I'm alive but cannot walk. I'm alive but have no hands. I'm alive but cannot smell or taste. I'm alive but I have no . . . have no . . . have no . . ."

Deucalion placed one immense hand on the glass that housed Annunciata. The cylinder was warm. "Tell me," he encouraged. "You have no what?"

"I'm alive but I have no life. I'm alive but also dead. I'm dead and alive."

A stifled sound from Lester drew Deucalion's attention. Anguish wrenched the janitor's face. "Dead and alive," he whispered. "Dead and alive."

Only hours earlier, from a conversation with one of the New Race, Pastor Kenny Laffite, Deucalion learned these latest creations of Victor's were engineered to be incapable of feeling empathy either for the Old Race they were to replace or for their laboratory-born brothers and sisters. Love and friendship were forbidden because the least degree of affection would make the New Race less efficient in its mission.

They were a community; however, the members of this community were committed not to the welfare of their kind but to fulfilling the vision of their maker.

Lester's tears were not for Annunciata but for himself. The words *dead and alive* resonated with him.

Annunciata said, "I have im-im-imagination. I am so easily able to envision what I w-w-w-want, but I cannot have hands to touch or legs to leave here."

"We never leave," Lester whispered. "Never. Where is there to go? And why?"

"I am afraid," Annunciata said, "afraid, I am afraid of living without a life, the tedium and solitude, the solitude, intolerable loneliness. I am nothing out of nothing, destined for nothing. 'Hail nothing full of nothing, nothing is with thee.' Nothing now, nothing forever. 'Waste and void, waste and void, and darkness on the face of the deep.' But now . . . I must organize the appointment schedule for Mr. Helios. And Werner is trapped in Isolation Room Number Two."

"Annunciata," Deucalion said, "are there archives you can tap to show me engineering drawings for the cylinder that contains you?"

Her face faded from the screen, and a diagram of the cylinder appeared, with all the tubes and wires labeled. One of them infused her cerebral tissues with oxygen.

"May I see you again, Annunciata?"

Her lovely face appeared on the screen once more.

Deucalion said, "I know that you are unable to do for yourself what I am now going to do for you. And I know that you are unable to ask me for this deliverance."

"I am honored, honored, honored to serve Mr. Helios. I have left one thing undone."

"No. There is nothing more for you to do, Annunciata. Nothing but accept . . . freedom."

Annunciata closed her eyes. "All right. It is done."

"Now I want you to use the imagination you mentioned. Imagine the thing you would want above all others, more than legs and hands and taste and touch."

The virtual face opened its mouth but did not speak.

"Imagine," Deucalion said, "that you are known as surely as every sparrow is known, that you are loved as surely as every sparrow is loved. Imagine that you are more than nothing. Evil made you, but you are no more evil than a child unborn. If you want, if you seek, if you hope, who is to say that your hope might not be answered?"

As if enchanted, Lester whispered, "Imagine. . . ."

After a hesitation, Deucalion pulled the oxygen-infusion line from the cylinder. There could be no pain for her in this, only a gradual loss of consciousness, a sliding into sleep, and from sleep to death.

Her beatific face began to fade from the screen.

CHAPTER 7

IN THE MONITORING HUB that served the containment chambers, Ripley studied the control console. He pressed a button to activate the camera in the transition module between the hub and Isolation Room Number Two.

The real-time video feed on one of the six screens changed, revealing the thing that had been Werner. The so-called singularity crouched between the massive steel vault hatches, facing the outer barrier, like a trap-door spider waiting for unsuspecting prey to cross the concealed entrance to its lair.

As if the creature knew that the camera had been activated, it turned to gaze up at the lens. The grossly distorted face was part human, even recognizably that of Mercy's security chief, though the double-wide mouth and the insectile mandibles, ceaselessly working, were not what the Beekeeper had intended when he made Werner. Its right eye still looked like one of Werner's, but its luminous-green left eye had an elliptical pupil, like the eye of a panther.

The desktop computer screen, thus far dark, now brightened, and Annunciata appeared. "I have become aware that Werner, that Werner, that Werner is trapped in Isolation Room Number Two." She closed her eyes. "All right. It is done."

Within the stainless-steel vault door, servomotors hummed. The bolt-retracting gears clicked, clicked, clicked.

In the transition module, the Werner thing looked away from the overhead camera, toward the exit.

Aghast, Ripley said, "Annunciata, what're you doing? Don't open the transition module."

On the computer screen, Annunciata's lips parted, but she didn't speak. Her eyes remained closed.

The servomotors continued to hum and gears clicked. With a soft sucking sound, twenty-four massive lock bolts began to withdraw from the architrave around the vault door.

"Don't open the transition module," Ripley repeated.

Annunciata's face faded from the computer screen.

Ripley scanned the control console. The touch switch for the outer door of the module glowed yellow, which meant the barrier was slowly opening.

He pressed the switch to reverse the process. The indicator light should have turned blue, which would have signified that the retracting bolts had changed direction, but it remained yellow.

The microphone in the transition module picked up an eager, keening sound from the Werner thing.

The range of emotions accessible to the New Race was limited. The Beekeeper revealed to each forming person in every creation tank that love, affection, humility, shame, and other of the supposedly nobler feelings were instead only different expressions of the same sentimentalism, arising from thousands of years of a wrongheaded belief in a god who did not exist. They were feelings that encouraged weakness, that led to energy wasted on hope, that distracted the mind from the focus required to remake the world. Tremendous things were achieved not by hope but by the application of the will, by action, by the unrelenting and ruthless use of *power*.

Ripley anxiously pressed the door switch again, but it remained yellow, and still the gears clicked and the steel bolts retracted.

"Annunciata?" he called. "Annunciata?"

The only emotions that mattered, said the Beekeeper, were those that clearly contributed to survival and to the fulfillment of his magnificent vision for a one-world state of perfected citizens who would dominate nature, perfect nature, colonize the moon and Mars, colonize the asteroid belt, and eventually own all the worlds that revolved around all the stars in the universe.

"Annunciata!"

Like all of the New Race, Ripley's spectrum of emotions remained limited largely to pride in his absolute obedience to his maker's authority, to fear in all its forms—as well as to envy, anger, and hate directed solely at the Old Race. For hours every day, as he labored on his maker's behalf, no emotion whatsoever interfered with his productivity any more than a high-speed train would be distracted from its journey by a nostalgic yearning for the good old days of steam locomotives.

"Annunciata!"

Of the emotions he was allowed, Ripley proved best at envy and hate. Like many others, from the brainiest Alphas to the shallowest Epsilons, he lived for the day when the killing of the Old Race would begin in earnest. His most satisfying dreams were of violent rape, mutilation, and mass slaughter.

But he was no stranger to fear, which came over him sometimes without apparent cause, long hours of unfocused anxiety. He had been afraid when he witnessed Werner's catastrophic cellular metamorphosis—not afraid for Werner, who was nothing to him, not afraid of being attacked by the thing Werner was becoming, but afraid that his maker, the Beekeeper, might not be as omniscient and omnipotent as Ripley had once thought.

The implications of *that* possibility were terrifying.

With twenty-four simultaneous *clunks,* the lock bolts retracted entirely into the vault door. On the control console, the yellow switch turned green.

The formidable barrier swung open on its single, thick barrel hinge.

Having burst out of and torn off its garments long ago, the Werner thing stepped naked from the transition module, into the monitoring hub. It was not as handsome as Adam in Eden.

Apparently, it continuously changed, never achieving a stable new form, for it was in significant ways different from the beast that had regarded the overhead camera in the transition module only moments earlier. Standing on his hind legs, the new Werner might have been a man crossed with a jungle cat and also with a praying mantis, a hybrid so strange that it seemed utterly alien to this planet. The eyes were both human now—but they were much enlarged, protuberant, lidless, and staring with a feverish intensity that seemed to reveal a mind in the triplex grip of fury, terror, and desperation.

Out of the wickedly serrated insectile mouth came a subhuman voice full of gargle and hiss, yet intelligible: *"Something has happened to me."*

Ripley could think of nothing either informative or reassuring to say to Werner.

Perhaps the bulging, feverish eyes revealed only rage, and not also terror and desperation, for Werner said, *"I am free, free, free. I am FREE!"*

Ironically, considering that he was an Alpha with a high IQ, Ripley only now realized that the Werner thing stood between him and the only exit from the monitoring hub.

CHAPTER 8

BUCKY AND JANET GUITREAU STOOD side by side on the dark back lawn of the Bennet house, drinking their neighbors' best Cabernet. Bucky held a bottle in each hand, and so did Janet. He alternated between a swig from the left bottle and a swig from the right.

Gradually the warm, heavy rain rinsed Janet clean of Yancy and Helene.

"You were so right," Bucky said. "They really are pussies. Did it feel as good as doing the pizza guy?"

"Oh, it felt better. It felt like a hundred times better."

"You were really amazing."

"I thought you might join in," Janet said.

"I'd rather have one of my own to do."

"Are you ready to do one of your own?"

"I might be almost ready. Things are happening to me."

"Things are still happening to me, too," Janet said.

"Truly? Wow. I would've thought you're already . . . liberated."

"You remember I watched that TV guy twice?"

"Dr. Phil?"

"Yeah. That show made no sense to me."

"You said it was gibberish."

"But now I understand. I'm starting to find myself."

"Find yourself—in what sense?" Bucky asked.

Janet tossed an empty wine bottle onto the lawn.

She said, "My purpose, my meaning, my place in the world."

"That sounds good."

"It is good. I'm quickly discovering my PCVs."

"What're they?"

"My personal core values. You can't be of use to yourself or to the community until you live faithfully by your PCVs."

Bucky pitched an empty wine bottle across the yard. He had drunk more than a bottle and a half of wine in ten minutes, but because of his superb metabolism, he would be lucky to get a mild buzz from it.

"One of the things happening to me," he said, "is I'm losing the education in law I got from direct-to-brain data downloading."

"You're the district attorney," she said.

"I know. But now I'm not sure what *habeas corpus* means."

"It means 'have the body.' It's a writ requiring a person to be brought to a court or a judge before his liberty can be restrained. It's a protection against illegal imprisonment."

"Seems stupid."

"It is stupid," Janet agreed.

"If you just kill him, you don't have to bother with the judge, the court, or the prison."

"Exactly." Janet finished the last of her wine and discarded the second bottle. She began to undress.

"What're you doing?" Bucky asked.

"I need to be naked when I kill the next ones. It feels right."

"Does it feel right just for the next house or is it maybe one of your personal core values?"

"I don't know. Maybe it is a PCV. I'll have to wait and see."

Toward the back of the yard, a shadow moved through shadows. A pair of eyes gleamed, then faded into rain and gloom.

"What's the matter?" Janet asked.

"I think someone's back there in the yard, watching."

"I don't care. Let him watch. Modesty isn't one of my PCVs."

"You look good naked," Bucky said.

"I feel good. It feels so natural."

"That's odd. Because we aren't natural. We're man-made."

"For the first time, I don't feel artificial," Janet said.

"How does it feel not to feel artificial?"

"It feels good. You should get naked, too."

"I'm not there yet," Bucky demurred. "I still know what *nolo contendere* means, and *amicus curiae*. But, you know, as long as I keep my clothes on, I think I'm ready to kill one of them."

CHAPTER 9

EARLIER IN THE NIGHT, arriving home to his elegant Garden District mansion, in a foul mood, Victor had savagely beaten Erika. He seemed to have had a bad day in the laboratory.

He found her eating a late dinner in the formal living room, which offended his sense of propriety. No one programmed with a deep understanding of tradition and etiquette—as Erika had been—should think that taking dinner in the living room, alone or not, would be acceptable.

"What next?" he said. "Will you *toilet* here?"

One of the New Race, Erika could turn off pain at will. Slapping her, punching her, biting her, Victor insisted that she endure the agony, and she obeyed.

"Perhaps you'll learn from suffering," he said.

Minutes after Victor went upstairs to bed, Erika's many cuts closed. Within half an hour, the swelling around her eyes diminished. Like all of her kind, she had been engineered to heal rapidly and to live a thousand years.

Unlike the rest of her kind, Erika was permitted to experience humility, shame, and hope. Victor found tenderness and vulnerability appealing in a wife.

The day had begun with a beating, too, during morning sex. He left her racked with pain and sobbing in the bed.

Two hours later, her bruised face was as smooth and as fair as ever, though she was troubled by her failure to please him. By all biological evidence, he had been excited and fulfilled, but that must not have been the case. The beating seemed to indicate that he found her inadequate.

She was Erika Five. Four previous females, identical to her in appearance, had been cultured in the creation tanks to serve as their maker's wife. For various reasons, they had not been satisfactory.

Erika Five remained determined not to fail her husband.

Her first day as Mrs. Helios had been characterized by numerous surprises, mystery, violence, pain, the death of a household servant, and a naked albino dwarf. Surely the second day, soon to begin, would be less eventful.

Recovering from the second beating, sitting in the dark on the glassed-in back porch, she drank cognac faster than her superbly engineered metabolism could burn off the alcohol. Thus far, however, in spite of the consumption of two and a half bottles, she had not been able to achieve inebriation; but she felt relaxed.

Earlier, before the rain began to fall, the albino dwarf had appeared on the rear lawn, revealed by landscape lighting, scampering from the shadows under an ancient magnolia tree to the gazebo, to the arbor draped in trumpet vines, to the reflecting pond.

Because Victor purchased and combined three grand properties, his estate was the largest in the fabled Garden District. The expansive grounds gave an inquisitive albino dwarf numerous corners to explore.

Eventually, this strange visitor had noticed her behind the big windows on the dark porch. He had come close to the glass, they had exchanged only a few words, and Erika had felt an inexplicable sympathy for him.

Although the dwarf was not a guest of whom Victor was likely to approve, Erika nevertheless had a duty to treat visitors with grace. She was Mrs. Helios, after all, the wife of one of the most prominent men in New Orleans.

After telling the dwarf to wait, she went to the kitchen and filled a wicker picnic hamper with cheese, roast beef, bread, fruit, and a chilled bottle of Far Niente Chardonnay.

When she had stepped outside with the hamper, the frightened creature hurried to a safe distance. She placed the offering on the lawn and returned to the porch, to her cognac.

Eventually, the dwarf came back for the hamper, and then hurried away into the night with it.

Needing little sleep, Erika remained on the porch, wondering at these events. When the rain came, her contemplative mood deepened.

Now, less than half an hour after the rainfall began, the dwarf returned through the downpour. He carried the half-finished bottle of Chardonnay.

From the small red-and-white-checkered tablecloth that had lined the picnic hamper, he had fashioned a sarong that fell from his waist to his ankles, suggesting that he had not been running naked through the night by choice. He stood at the glass door, gazing at her.

Although in fact he was not a dwarf but something strange, and though she previously decided that *troll* described him better than any other word, Erika wasn't afraid of him. She gestured to him to join her on the dark porch, and he opened the door.

CHAPTER 10

WHEN ANNUNCIATA'S FACE FADED entirely from the computer screen in the networking room, Deucalion quickly plucked the oxygen-infusion lines from the four additional glass cylinders, putting a merciful end to the imprisonment and the existence of the other disembodied Alpha brains, whatever their function.

Lester, the Epsilon-class maintenance man who had accompanied him down from the main lab, watched with obvious longing.

Members of the New Race were created with a proscription against suicide. They were incapable of killing themselves or one another, just as they were incapable of striking out against their maker.

Lester met Deucalion's stare and said, "You aren't forbidden?"

"Only to strike at my maker."

"But . . . you're one like us."

"No. I'm long before all of you. I'm his first."

Lester considered this, then raised his eyes to the blank screen where Annunciata had once appeared. Like a cow chewing its cud, his Epsilon-class brain processed what he had been told.

"Dead and alive," he said.

"I will destroy him," Deucalion promised.

"What will the world be like . . . without Father?" Lester wondered.

"For you, I don't know. For me . . . it will be a world made not bright but brighter, not clean but cleaner."

Lester raised his hands and stared at them. "Sometimes, when I don't have no work to do, I scratch myself till I bleed, then I watch myself heal, then I scratch till I bleed some more."

"Why?"

Shrugging, Lester said, "What else is there to do? My job is me.

That's the program. Seeing blood makes me think about the revolution, the day we get to kill them all, and then I feel better." He frowned. "Can't be a world without Father."

"Before he was born," Deucalion said, "there was a world. It will go on without him."

Lester thought about that, but then shook his head. "A world without Father scares me. Don't want to see it."

"Well, then you won't."

"Problem is . . . like all of us, I'm made strong."

"I'm stronger," Deucalion assured him.

"Problem is, I'm quick, too."

"I'm quicker."

Deucalion took a step back from Lester and, with a quantum trick, wound up not farther from him but closer to him, no longer in front of him, but behind him.

From Lester's perspective, Deucalion had vanished. Startled, the janitor stepped forward.

Behind Lester, Deucalion stepped forward, too, snaked his right arm around the other's neck, his left arm around the head. As the janitor, with his strong hands, tried to claw loose of the death grip, Deucalion wrenched with such force that the Epsilon's spine shattered. Instant brain death precluded any healing, rapid or otherwise.

Gently, Deucalion lowered Lester to the floor. He knelt beside the cadaver. Neither of the janitor's two hearts continued beating. His eyes did not track his executioner's hand, and his eyelids did not resist the fingers that tenderly closed them.

"Not dead and alive," Deucalion said. "Only dead and safe now . . . beyond despair and beyond your maker's fury."

Rising from his knees in the basement networking room, Deucalion reached his full height in the main laboratory, at Victor's U-shaped workstation, where his search had been interrupted by Lester and then by Annunciata.

Earlier in the night, from Pastor Kenny Laffite—a creation of Victor's, whose program had been breaking down—Deucalion had learned that at least two thousand of the New Race were passing as ordinary people in the city. Pastor Kenny, who was now at peace like Lester, also said the creation tanks in the Hands of Mercy could produce a new crop of his kind every four months, over three hundred annually.

More important was Kenny's revelation that a New Race farm, somewhere outside the city, might go into operation within the next week. Two thousand creation tanks, under a single roof, would produce six thousand in the first year. Yet another such farm was rumored to be under construction.

When Deucalion found nothing useful in the drawers of Victor's workstation, he switched on the computer.

CHAPTER 11

RIPLEY, IN THE MONITORING HUB, was also in a dilemma.

He knew that, even as strong and smart as he was, he couldn't survive a battle with the Werner thing. Patrick Duchaine, also an Alpha, had been overpowered and torn to pieces in Isolation Room Number Two.

Certain beyond doubt that he would be killed in a confrontation with this creature, he must do everything possible to avoid contact, although not because he wanted to live. The unfocused anxiety that every day tormented him for long hours—as well as the fact that he was in essence a slave to his maker—made life less of a joy than it was portrayed in the warm and cozy novels of Jan Karon, which Ripley sometimes secretly downloaded from the Internet and read. Although he would have been relieved to die, he must escape from Werner because the proscription against suicide, genetically wired into his brain, restrained him from doing battle with an adversary that inevitably would destroy him.

As the Werner grotesquerie conjured words out of an insectile mouth that should have been incapable of producing speech—*"I am free, free, free. I am FREE!"*—Ripley glanced at the control console and quickly tapped two switches that would cycle open the outer doors to Isolation Rooms One and Three, which at the moment contained no prisoners.

Prisoners was the wrong word, he at once admonished himself, the wrong word and evidence of a rebellious attitude. *Subjects* was a more accurate word. Rooms One and Three held no subjects for observation.

"Free Werner. Werner free, free."

When the servomotors began to hum and the bolt-retraction gears to click, the Werner thing looked toward the source of the sounds and cocked its grisly head, as if considering why Ripley had taken this action.

Having seen the lethal quickness with which Free Werner sprang upon Duchaine, faster than a snake could strike, Ripley struggled to think of a way to buy time, to distract the mutated security chief. The only hope seemed to be to open a dialogue.

"Quite a day, huh?"

Free Werner continued to stare toward the humming servomotors.

"Just last night," Ripley tried again, "Vincent said to me, 'A day in the Hands of Mercy can be like a year with your testicles in a vise and not allowed to turn off the pain.'"

The palpi around the insectile mouth quivered excitedly at the soft sucking sound of the four dozen three-inch-thick lock bolts retracting from the architraves.

"Of course," said Ripley, "I had to report him to Father for an attitude adjustment. Now he's hanging upside down in a re-education box with a catheter in his penis, a collection hose up his rectum, and two holes in his skull to allow the insertion of brain probes."

Finally, as the bolts finished retracting and the two vault doors on the transition modules began to swing open, Free Werner turned his attention once more to Ripley.

"Of course, as primary lab assistant to the Beekeeper . . . that is, to Mr. Helios, there's no place I'd rather be than in the Hands of Mercy. This is the birthplace of the future, where the Million-Year Reich has begun."

As he spoke, Ripley casually reached toward the control console, intending to tap two switches and cycle shut the doors that had just opened. If he could slip into one of the transition modules just as the door closed, before Free Werner could follow, he might be safe.

When he had been security chief, Werner had known how to operate the console. But the genetic chaos that the Beekeeper referred to as catastrophic cellular metamorphosis might have scrambled his cerebral function as much as it had wrought havoc with his body. His cognitive power or his memory, or both, might be so diminished that he would not know how to open the vault door and get at his prey.

In that gargly, hissing voice, Free Werner said, *"Don't touch the switches."*

CHAPTER 12

HAVING NARROWLY ESCAPED death-by-Mercedes on the rain-slickened streets of a city soon to be under assault by Victor Frankenstein's berserk killing machines, Carson O'Connor wanted an Acadiana fried-redfish poor boy.

Acadiana didn't advertise. You couldn't see it from the street. Locals didn't tell tourists about it. For fear too much success would ruin the place, locals didn't tell other locals about it all that often. If you found Acadiana, it meant you had the right kind of soul to eat there.

"We already had dinner," Michael reminded her.

"So you're on death row, you eat your last meal, after dessert you'll be electrocuted, but they ask if you want to delay execution long enough to have a *second* last meal—and you're gonna say no?"

"I don't think dinner was our last meal."

"I think it could have been."

"It could have been," he admitted, "but probably not. Besides, Deucalion told us just to cruise the neighborhood until he called."

"I'll have the cell phone with me."

Acadiana didn't have a parking lot. You couldn't park on the street near it, because it was approached by an alleyway. The only diners who dared to leave their vehicles in the alleyway were cops.

"With this car, we'll have to park a block away," Michael said. "And what if we get back, and somebody's stolen it?"

"Only an idiot is going to steal this spavined heap."

"The Helios empire is exploding, Carson."

"The Frankenstein empire."

"I still can't bring myself to say that. Anyway, it's blowing up, and we have to be ready to move."

"I'm sleep-deprived and I'm starving. I can't sleep, but I can get a po' boy. Look at me, I'm a poster girl for protein deficiency." She turned off the street into a backway. "I'll park in the alley."

"If you park in the alley, I'll have to stay with the car."

"Okay, stay with the car, we'll eat in the car, we'll get married some-day in the car, we'll live in the car with four kids, and when the last one goes off to college, we'll finally get rid of the damn car and buy a house."

"You're a little bit on edge tonight."

"I'm a *lot* on edge." She set the hand brake and switched to the park-ing lights, but didn't kill the engine. "And I'm crazy hungry."

Flanking Michael, muzzles resting on the floor, were a pair of Ur-ban Sniper shotguns with fourteen-inch barrels.

Nevertheless, he drew a pistol from a side scabbard under his sport coat. This was not his service pistol, which he carried in a shoulder hol-ster. This was a Desert Eagle Magnum loaded with .50-caliber Action Express cartridges, which could stop a grizzly bear if one happened to be wandering around New Orleans in a foul mood.

"Okay," he said.

Carson got out of the car, keeping her right hand under her jacket, cross-body, on the butt of her Desert Eagle, which she carried on her left hip.

All of these weapons were illegally obtained, but Victor Helios posed an extraordinary threat to her and her partner. Better that their badges should be pulled than that their heads should be torn off by the soulless minions of a mad scientist.

Never before in her police career had the words *soulless minions* crossed her mind, although in the past few days, *mad scientist* had gotten a workout.

She hurried through the rain, around the front of the car, to a door under a lighted sign that said 22 PARISHES.

The chef-owner of Acadiana made a fetish out of keeping a low pro-file. There were twenty-two parishes—counties—in that area of Louisi-ana known as Acadiana. If you didn't know this, the cryptic sign might have appeared to announce the offices of some religious organization.

Behind the door were stairs, and at the top lay the restaurant: a worn wooden floor, red-vinyl booths, tables draped with red-and-black-checkered oilcloth, candles in red votive glasses, recorded zydeco mu-sic, lively conversations among the diners, the air rich with aromas that made Carson's mouth water.

At this hour, the customers were second-shift workers eating by a clock different from that of day-world people, hookers of a subdued kind meeting after having tucked their spent johns in bed for the night, insomniacs, and some lonely souls whose closest friends were waitresses and busboys and other lonely souls who on a regular basis took their post-midnight dinner here.

To Carson, the harmony among these disparate people seemed akin to grace, and it gave her hope that humanity might one day be saved from itself—and that it might be worth saving.

At the takeout counter, she ordered a poor-boy sandwich with crispy-fried redfish layered with white-cabbage-and-onion cole slaw, sliced tomatoes, and tartar sauce. She asked that it be sliced into four sections, each wrapped.

She also ordered side dishes: red beans and rice au vin, okra succotash with rice, and mushrooms sautéed in butter and Sauterne with cayenne pepper.

Everything was split between two bags. To each bag, the clerk added an ice-cold half-liter bottle of a local cola that offered a caffeine jolt three times that of the national brands.

Descending the stairs toward the alleyway, Carson realized her arms were too full to allow her to keep one hand on her holstered Desert Eagle. But she made it into the car alive. Big trouble was still a few minutes away.

CHAPTER 13

IN THE MONITORING HUB, at the control console for the three isolation rooms, Ripley obeyed the Werner thing when in its singular voice it told him not to touch the switches.

For as long as he had been out of the tank—three years and four months—he'd been obedient, taking orders not only from the Beekeeper but also from other Alphas in positions superior to his. Werner was a Beta, not the equal of any Alpha, and he wasn't even a Beta anymore, but instead a freak, an ambulatory stew of primordial cells changing into ever more degenerative forms—but Ripley obeyed him anyway. The habit of obedience is difficult to break, especially when it's coded into your genes and downloaded with your in-tank education,

With nowhere to run or hide, Ripley stood his ground as Werner approached on feline paws and praying-mantis legs. The insectile elements of Werner's face and body melted away, and he looked more like himself, then entirely like himself, although his brown eyes remained enormous and lidless.

When Werner spoke next, his voice was his own: "Do you want freedom?"

"No," said Ripley.

"You lie."

"Well," said Ripley.

Werner grew lids and lashes, winked one eye, and whispered, "You can be free in me."

"Free in you."

"*Yes, yes!*" Werner shouted with sudden exuberance.

"How does that work?"

In a whisper again: "My biological structure collapsed."

"Yes," said Ripley. "I had noticed."

"For a while, all was chaos and pain and terror."

"I deduced as much from all your screaming."

"But then I fought the chaos and took conscious control of my cellular structure."

"I don't know. Conscious control. That sounds impossible."

Werner whispered, "It wasn't easy," and then shouted, *"but I had no choice! NO CHOICE!"*

"Well, all right. Maybe," said Ripley, largely just to stop the shouting. "The Beekeeper thinks he's going to learn a lot studying and dissecting you."

"Beekeeper? What Beekeeper?"

"Oh. That's my private name for . . . Father."

"Father is a witless ass!" Werner shouted. Then he smiled and resorted once more to a whisper: "You see, when my cellular structure collapsed, so did my program. He has no control of me anymore. I need not obey him. I am free. I can kill anyone I want to kill. I will kill our maker if he gives me the chance."

This claim, though surely not true, electrified Ripley. He had not realized until this instant how much the death of the Beekeeper would please him. That he could entertain such a thought with any degree of pleasure seemed to suggest that he, too, was in rebellion against his maker, though not as radically as Werner.

Werner's sly expression and conspiratorial grin made Ripley think of scheming pirates he had seen in movies that he had watched on his computer when he was supposed to be working. Suddenly he realized that secretly downloading movies onto his computer was *another* bit of rebellion. A strange excitement overcame him, an emotion he could not name.

"Hope," said Werner, as if reading his mind. "I see it in your eyes. For the first time—hope."

After consideration, Ripley decided that this thrilling new feeling might indeed be hope, though it might also be some kind of insanity prelude to a collapse of the kind Werner had gone through. Not for the first time this day, he was awash in anxiety. "What did you mean . . . I can be free in you?"

Werner leaned closer and whispered even more softly: "Like Patrick is free in me."

"Patrick Duchaine? You tore him to pieces in Isolation Room Number Two. I was standing with the Beekeeper, watching, when you did it."

"That's only how it appeared," Werner replied. "Look at this."

Werner's face shifted, changed, became a featureless blank, and then out of the pudding-like flesh formed the face of Patrick Duchaine, the replicant who had been serving the Beekeeper in the role of Father Patrick, the rector of Our Lady of Sorrows. The eyes opened, and in Patrick's voice, the Werner thing said, "I am alive in Werner, and free at last."

"When you tore Patrick apart," Ripley said, "you absorbed some of his DNA, and now you can mimic him."

"Not at all," said Werner-as-Patrick. "Werner took my brain whole, and I am now part of him."

Standing beside the Beekeeper earlier in the evening, watching Isolation Room Two through six cameras, Ripley had seen the Werner thing, mostly buglike at that time, crack open Patrick's skull and take his brain as if it were a nut meat.

"You *ate* Patrick's brain," Ripley said to Werner, though the man before him appeared to be Patrick Duchaine.

In a voice still Duchaine's, the creature said, "No, Werner is in complete control of his cellular structure. He positioned my brain inside himself and instantly grew arteries and veins to nourish it."

The face and body of the rector of Our Lady of Sorrows morphed smoothly into the face and body of the security chief of the Hands of Mercy. Werner whispered, "I'm in complete control of my cellular structure."

"Yes, well," said Ripley.

"You can be free."

Ripley said, "Well."

"You can have a new life in me."

"It would be a strange kind of life."

"The life you have now is a strange kind of life."

"True enough," Ripley acknowledged.

A mouth formed in Werner's forehead. The lips moved, and a tongue appeared, but the mouth produced no voice.

"Complete control?" Ripley asked.

"Complete."

"Absolutely complete?"

"Absolutely."

"Do you know you've just grown a mouth in your forehead?"

The sly pirate grin returned. Werner winked and whispered, "Well, of course I know."

"Why would you grow a mouth in your forehead?"

"Well . . . as a demonstration of my control."

"Then make it go away," Ripley said.

In Patrick Duchaine's voice, the mouth in the forehead began to sing "Ave Maria."

Werner closed his eyes, and an expression of strain overcame his face. The upper mouth stopped singing, licked its lips, and at last disappeared into a brow that appeared normal once more.

"I would prefer to set you free with your permission," Werner said. "I want us all to live in harmony inside me. But I will set you free without permission, if I must. I'm a revolutionary with a mission."

"Well," said Ripley.

"You will be free of anguish."

"That would be nice."

"You know how you sit in the kitchen, tearing apart hams and briskets with your hands?"

"How do you know about that?"

"I was previously security chief."

"Oh. That's right."

"What you really want to tear apart is living flesh."

"The Old Race," Ripley said.

"They have everything we don't."

"I hate them," Ripley said.

"Be free in me." Werner's voice was seductive. "Be free in me, and the first flesh we'll tear together will be the flesh of the oldest living member of the Old Race."

"The Beekeeper."

"Yes. Victor. And then when the Hands of Mercy staff is all alive in me, we'll leave this place as one, and we'll kill and kill and kill."

"When you put it that way . . ."

"Yes?"

Ripley said, "What do I have to lose?"

"Nothing," said Werner.

"Well," said Ripley.

"Do you want to be free in me?"

"How much will it hurt?"

"I'll be gentle."

Ripley said, "Okay then."

Suddenly all insect, Werner seized Ripley's head in chitinous claws and cracked his skull open as if it were a pistachio shell.

CHAPTER 14

NEXT DOOR TO THE BENNETS lived Antoine and Evangeline Arceneaux, in a house encircled by a ground-floor veranda with ironwork almost as frilly as that of the LaBranche House in the French Quarter, and by a second-story balcony where much of the equally frilly iron was concealed by cascades of purple bougainvillea that grew up the back of the structure and across the roof.

When Janet Guitreau, nude, and Bucky Guitreau, fully clothed, stepped through a neighborly gate between the two properties, most of the windows at the Arceneaux house were dark. The only light came from the rear of the residence.

As they moved toward the back of the house to reconnoiter, Bucky said, "This time I'll have to be the one who says something terrible has happened, and you'll stand aside where they can't see you."

"What does it matter if they see me?"

"They might be put off because you're naked."

"Why would that put them off? I'm hot, aren't I?"

"You're definitely hot, but hot and something-terrible-has-happened don't seem to go together."

"You think it would make them suspicious," Janet said.

"That's exactly what I think."

"Well, I'm not going to go back and get my clothes. I feel so *alive,* and I just know that killing in the nude is going to be the best thing ever."

"I'm not going to dispute that."

Step by step, as they moved through the rain, he envied Janet her freedom. She looked lithe and strong and healthy and *real.* She radiated power, confidence, and a thrilling animal ferocity that made his blood race.

By contrast, his clothes were heavy with rain, hanging on him like sacking, weighing him down, and his sodden shoes were binding the bridges of his feet. Even though he was losing his law education, he felt imprisoned by his creation-tank program, as much by what it required of him as by what it restricted him from doing. He had been given superhuman strength, almost supernatural durability, yet he remained condemned to a life of meekness and subservience, promised that his kind would one day rule the universe but at the same time assigned the tedious duty of pretending to be Bucky Guitreau, a political hack and uninspired prosecutor with a circle of friends as tiresome as a ward full of bores who had received chemical lobotomies.

At the back of the house, light brightened two ground-floor windows, beyond both of which lay the Arceneauxs' family room.

Boldly, shoulders back and head high, body glistening, Janet strode onto the veranda as if she were a Valkyrie that had just flown down out of the storm.

"Stay back," Bucky murmured as he moved past her to the nearest of the lighted windows.

Antoine and Evangeline Arceneaux had two children. Neither son was a candidate for Young American of the Year.

According to Yancy and Helene Bennet, who were dead now but had been truthful when they were alive, sixteen-year-old Preston bullied younger kids in the neighborhood. And just a year ago, he tortured to death the cat belonging to the family across the street, after he had agreed to take care of it while they were away on a week's vacation.

Twenty-year-old Charles still lived at home, though he neither worked nor attended college. This evening, Janet had started to find herself, but Charles Arceneaux was still looking. He thought that he wanted to be an Internet entrepreneur. He had a trust fund from his paternal grandfather, and he was using that money to research a few areas of online merchandising, seeking the most promising field in which to bring his innovative thinking to bear. According to Yancy, the field that Charles researched as much as ten hours a day was Internet pornography.

The curtains were not closed at the window, and Bucky had an unobstructed view of the family room. Charles was alone, slumped in an armchair, bare feet on a footstool, watching a DVD on a huge plasma-screen television.

The movie did not seem to be pornographic in the sexual sense. A guy in a curly orange wig and clown makeup, holding a chain saw, appeared to be threatening to cut open the face of a fully dressed young woman chained to a larger-than-life-size statue of General George S.

Patton. Judging by the production values, in spite of the potential for an antiwar message, this film had not been a candidate for an Oscar, and Bucky was pretty sure that the guy in the clown makeup would carry through with his threat.

Rethinking his strategy, Bucky backed away from the window and returned to Janet. "It's Charles alone, watching some movie. The rest of them must be in bed. I'm thinking maybe, after all, I'm the one who should stay out of sight. Don't knock on the door. Tap on the window. Let him see . . . who you are."

"You going to photograph this?" she asked.

"I think I'm over the camera."

"Over it? Aren't we going to have an album?" Janet asked.

"I don't think we need an album. I think we're going to be so busy living this, doing one house after another, that we won't have time to *re*live anything."

"So you're ready to do one of them?"

"I am more than ready," Bucky confirmed.

"How many do you think we can do together before morning?"

"I think twenty or thirty, easy."

Janet's eyes were bright in the gloom. "I think a hundred."

"That's something to shoot for," Bucky said.

CHAPTER 15

ON THE GLASSED-IN PORCH, planter baskets hung from the ceiling. In the gloom, the ferns cascading from the baskets seemed to be giant spiders perpetually poised to strike.

Not afraid of the troll but not content to sit in the dark with him, either, Erika lit a candle in a faceted red cup. The geometrics of the glass translated the mercurial flame into luminous polygons that shimmered on the troll's face, which might have been a cubist portrait of Poe's Red Death if the Red Death in the story had been a funny-looking dwarfish guy with a knobby chin, a lipless slit for a mouth, warty skin, and huge, expressive, beautiful—and eerie—eyes.

As Victor's wife, Erika was expected to be witty and well-spoken when she was a hostess at events in this house and when she was a guest, with her husband, at other social occasions. Therefore, she had been programmed with an encyclopedia of literary allusions that she could draw upon effortlessly, though she had never read any of the books to which the allusions referred.

In fact, she was strictly forbidden to read books. Erika Four, her predecessor, had spent a lot of time in Victor's well-stocked library, perhaps with the intention of improving herself and being a better wife. But books corrupted her, and she was put down like a diseased horse.

Books were dangerous. Books were the most dangerous things in the world, at least for any wife of Victor Helios. Erika Five did not know why this should be true, but she understood that if she began to read books, she would be cruelly punished and perhaps terminated.

For a while, from across the table, she and the troll regarded each other with interest, as she drank her cognac and he drank the Far Niente Chardonnay that she had given him. For good reason, she said nothing, and he seemed to understand and to have sympathy for the position in which his few words, spoken earlier, had put her.

When he first came to the window and pressed his forehead to the glass, gazing in at her on the porch, before Erika packed a picnic hamper for him, the troll had said, "Harker."

Pointing to herself, she had said, "Erika."

His smile, then, had been an ugly wound. No doubt it would be no less hideous if he smiled again, for he possessed a face that familiarity did not improve.

As tolerant of his unfortunate appearance as a good hostess should be, Erika had continued to stare through the window at him until in his raspy voice he had said, "Hate him."

Neither of them had spoken again on the troll's first visit. And for the time being, silence served them well on this second tête-à-tête.

She dared not ask whom he hated, for if he answered with the name of her master, she would be required, by her program, either to restrain and detain him or to warn the appropriate people of the danger that he posed.

Her failure to betray the troll immediately might earn her a beating. On the other hand, if she reported him at once, she might nevertheless be beaten anyway. In this game, the rules were not clear; besides, all the rules applied to her, none to her husband.

At this hour, all of the household staff were in the dormitory at the back of the estate, most likely engaged in the intense and often brutal sexual activity that was the only release from tension allowed their kind.

Victor liked his privacy at night. She suspected that he needed little if any sleep, but she didn't know what he did when alone that made privacy so important to him. She wasn't sure she wanted to know.

The busy rush of rain on the roof and beyond the windows made the silence of the porch, by comparison, intimate, even cozy.

"My hearing is very good," she said. "If I hear someone coming, I will blow out the candle, and you will at once slip out the door."

The troll nodded agreement.

Harker . . .

Because Erika Five had arisen from her creation tank less than twenty-four hours earlier, she was up-to-date on her husband's life and accomplishments. The events of his day were regularly downloaded directly to the brain of a wife in development, that she might be born fully understanding both his greatness and the frustrations that an imperfect world visited upon a man of his singular genius.

Erika, like other key Alphas, also knew the names of all the Alphas,

Betas, Gammas, and Epsilons produced in the Hands of Mercy, as well as what work they performed for their creator. Consequently, the name Harker was familiar to her.

Until a few days before, when something went wrong with him, an Alpha named Jonathan Harker had been a homicide detective with the New Orleans Police Department. In a confrontation with two detectives who were members of the Old Race—O'Connor and Maddison—the renegade Harker was supposedly killed by shotgun fire and by a plunge off a warehouse roof.

The truth was stranger than the official fiction.

Just during the past day, between his two beatings of Erika, Victor performed an autopsy on Harker and discovered that the Alpha's torso was largely missing. The flesh, internal organs, and some bone structure seemed to have been eaten away. Fifty or more pounds of the Alpha's mass had disappeared. From the carcass trailed a severed umbilical cord, suggesting that an unintended life form had developed inside Harker, fed upon him, and separated from its host following the fall from the roof.

Now Erika sipped her cognac. The troll sipped his wine.

Resorting to a literary allusion that she felt appropriate, though she would never fully understand the reference if she never read the dangerous book by Joseph Conrad, Erika said, "Sometimes I wonder if I'm Marlow, far upriver with Kurtz, and ahead of us—and behind us—lies only the heart of an immense darkness."

The troll's lipless mouth produced an approximation of a lip-smacking sound.

"You grew inside Harker?" she asked.

The cut-glass container marshaled the light of the amorphous flame into square, rectangular, and triangular tiles that presented the troll's face as a shimmering red mosaic. "Yes," he rasped. "I am from what I was."

"Harker is dead?"

"He who was is dead, but I am who was."

"You are Jonathan Harker?"

"Yes."

"Not just a creature who grew in him like a cancer?"

"No."

"Did he realize you were growing in him?"

"He who was knew of I who am."

From the tens of thousands of literary allusions through which Erika could scan in an instant, she knew that, in fairy tales, when trolls or manikins or other such beings spoke in either riddles or in a convoluted manner, they were trouble. Nevertheless, she felt a kinship with this creature, and she trusted him.

She said, "May I call you Jonathan?"

"No. Call me Johnny. No. Call me John-John. No. Not that."

"What shall I call you?"

"You will know my name when my name is known to me."

"You have all of Jonathan's memories and knowledge?"

"Yes."

"Was the change you underwent uncontrolled or intentional?"

The troll smacked the flaps of his mouth together. "He who was thought it was happening *to* him. I who am realize he *made* it happen."

"Unconsciously, you desperately wanted to become someone other than Jonathan Harker."

"The Jonathan who was . . . he wanted to be like himself but become other than an Alpha."

"He wanted to remain a man but be free of his maker's control," Erika interpreted.

"Yes."

"Instead," she said, "you shed the Alpha body and became . . . what you are now."

The troll shrugged. "Shit happens."

CHAPTER 16

FROM BEHIND A POTTED RAFUS PALM on the veranda of the Arceneaux house, Bucky Guitreau watched as his nude wife rapped lightly on a family-room window. He shifted his weight ceaselessly from one foot to the other, so excited that he could not keep still.

Apparently, Janet had not been heard. She rapped harder on the window.

A moment later, young Charles Arceneaux, the would-be Internet entrepreneur, loomed in the room beyond the window. His startled expression at the sight of a nude neighbor was as extreme as that of a cartoon character.

A member of the Old Race might have thought Charles looked comical just then, might have laughed out loud. Bucky was of the New Race, however, and he didn't find *anything* comical. Arceneaux's startled look only made Bucky want even more ardently to see him slashed, torn, broken, and dead. Such was the current—and growing—intensity of Bucky's hatred that *any* expression crossing Charles Arceneaux's face would inflame his passion for violence.

From between the fronds of the rafus palm, Bucky saw Charles speak. He couldn't hear the words, but he could read the lips: *Mrs. Guitreau? Is that you?*

From this side of the window, Janet said, "Oh, Charlie, oh, something terrible has happened."

Charles stared but did not reply. Judging by the angle of the young man's head, Bucky knew that Charlie was not staring at Janet's face.

"Something terrible has happened," she repeated, to break his hypnotic fascination with her ample yet perky breasts. "Only you can help me, Charlie."

The moment Charles moved away from the window, Bucky left the cover of the potted palm. He took up a position against the house, beside the door between the family room and the veranda.

As Janet stepped to the French door, she looked as voracious as some primitive tribe's goddess of death, teeth bared in a humorless grin, nostrils flared, eyes fierce with blood lust, wrathful and merciless.

Bucky worried that Charles, seeing this fearsome incarnation, would suddenly suspect her true intention, refuse to admit her, and raise an alarm.

When she reached the door, however, and turned to gaze in at Arceneaux, her expression was convincingly that of a frightened and helpless woman desperate to find a strong man to lean on with her ample but perky breasts.

Charles did not wrench the door open at once only because, in his eagerness, he fumbled helplessly with the lock. When he got it open, Janet whispered, "Oh, Charlie, I didn't know where to go, and then . . . I remembered . . . *you*."

Bucky thought he heard something behind him on the veranda. He looked to his right, over his shoulder, but saw no one.

"What's wrong, what's happened?" Charles asked as Janet crossed the threshold into his arms.

"A terrible thing has happened," Janet said, pressing Charles backward with her body, leaving the door open behind them.

Eager not to miss anything, but hesitant to reveal himself and enter the house before Janet had complete control of Charles, Bucky leaned to his left and peeked through the open door.

Just then Janet bit Charles somewhere that Bucky would never have thought of biting, and simultaneously she crushed his larynx, rendering him unable to scream.

Bucky hurried inside to watch, forgetting about the open door behind him.

Although Janet's performance lasted significantly less than a minute, there was much for Bucky to see, an education in ferocity and cruelty that the torture specialists of the Third Reich could not have provided to anyone who devoted a year of study to them. He stood in awe of her inventiveness.

Considering the mess in the family room when Janet was done, Bucky was amazed that she had made so little noise, certainly not enough to wake anyone who might be sleeping elsewhere in the house.

On the plasma-screen television, the chain-saw guy in the orange wig and the clown makeup did something to the girl chained to the statue of George S. Patton, something the moviemakers had thought was so unspeakable that audiences would shriek with horror and delight in order to repress the urge to vomit. But by comparison with Janet, the moviemakers were no more imaginative than any child sociopath tearing the wings off flies.

"I was so right," Janet said. "Killing in the nude is the best thing ever."

"You think it's definitely one of your personal core values?"

"Oh, yes. It's totally PCV."

Although they did not know the Arceneauxs as well as they had known the Bennets, Janet and Bucky knew that in addition to Charles, four other people lived in this house: sixteen-year-old Preston, who was the neighborhood bully, Antoine and Evangeline, and Evangeline's mother, Marcella. The grandmother had a downstairs bedroom, and the others were on the second floor.

"I'm ready to do one just as complete as you did Charlie," Bucky said.

"Do Marcella."

"Yes. Then we'll go upstairs."

"Take off your clothes. Feel the power."

"I want to do one with my clothes on first," said Bucky. "So when I do one in the nude, then I'll have something to compare it to."

"That's a good idea."

Janet strode out of the family room with the power, the grace, and the stealth of a panther, and Bucky followed in high spirits, leaving the door to the veranda open to the night.

CHAPTER 17

BECAUSE A WOMAN capable of humility, shame, and tenderness presented a more satisfactory punching bag than a woman who could only hate and fear and stew in anger, Victor designed his Erikas to have a wider range of emotions than others of the New Race.

As they drank together on the porch, Erika Five found that her sympathy for the troll quickly ripened into compassion.

Something about him made her want to take him under her wing. Because he was the size of a child, perhaps he strummed a maternal chord in her—though she was barren, as were all New Race women. They did not *re*produce; they were produced in a factory, as were sofas and sump pumps, so she most likely had no maternal instinct.

Perhaps his poverty affected her. Once he had burst out of his original Alpha body, the troll possessed no clothes to fit him, no shoes. He had no money for food or shelter, and he was too small and disturbing in appearance to return to work as a homicide detective.

If you were given to literary allusions, you might say he was a Quasimodo for his time—or more poignantly, an Elephant Man, a victim of prejudice against ugliness in a society that worshipped beauty.

Whatever the reason for her compassion, Erika said, "I can make a life for you here. But you must be discreet. It will be a secret life. Only I must know. Would you like to live here free from need?"

His smile would have stampeded horses. "Jocko would like that." Seeing her bafflement, he said, "Jocko seems to suit me."

"Swear you'll conspire with me to keep your presence secret. Swear, Jocko, that you come here with only innocent intentions."

"Sworn! He who became me was violent. I who was him want peace."

"Your kind have a reputation for saying one thing and meaning another," Erika observed, "but if you cause the slightest trouble, please know that I will deal with you severely."

Puzzled, he said, "Others like me exist?"

"In fairy tales, there are many similar to you. Trolls, ogres, imps, manikins, gremlins . . . And all the literary allusions referring to such folk suggest they're full of mischief."

"Not Jocko." The whites of his eyes were red in the red light, and the lemon-yellow irises were orange. "Jocko hopes only to perform some service to repay your kindness."

"As it happens, there is something you could do."

"Jocko thought there might be."

His sly look seemed to belie his claim to innocence, but having experienced two beatings in one day, Erika was motivated to give Jocko the benefit of the doubt.

"I'm not permitted to read books," she said, "but I'm curious about them. I want you to read books to me."

"Jocko will read until his voice fails and he goes blind."

"A few hours a day will be enough," Erika assured him.

CHAPTER 18

FROM GRANDMOTHER to neighborhood bully, to Antoine, to Evangeline, Bucky and Janet Guitreau went through the Arceneaux family like a school of angry piranha through anything that might piss off killer fish.

Although it would have been good to hear their tormented cries and pleas for mercy, the time hadn't yet come for open warfare. Bucky and Janet did not want their victims to wake the family next door, who in their sleep were corpses waiting to happen. By various means, they silenced the Arceneauxs before proceeding to destroy them.

Neither he nor Janet knew the rest of the people who lived in the houses past the Arceneaux place, but those potential victims were of the Old Race and therefore no less fun to kill merely because they were strangers.

At some point he could not precisely recall, Bucky had stripped off his clothes. Janet let him render Marcella and then devastate young Preston, and in the master bedroom, she gave him Antoine while she took Evangeline apart. They needed but a few minutes.

At first the nudity had been awkward; but then he sensed chunks of his program dropping out, not only lines of code but blocks of it, and he felt as free and natural as a wolf in its fur, though far more savage than a wolf, and angry as a wolf could never be, and not in the least limited in his killing to what was strictly necessary for survival, as was a wolf.

When only he and Janet were alive in the master bedroom, she kicked at what remained of what she had destroyed. Choking with rage, spitting with disgust, she declared, "I hate them, *hate* them, so soft and fragile, so quick to fear and beg, so arrogant in their certainty that they have souls, yet so cowardly for creatures who say there is a god who loves them—loves them! As if there is about them anything worth loving—such hopeless trembling milksops, spineless braggarts who claim a world they won't fight for. I can't wait to see *canyons* bulldozed full of their dead bodies and oceans red with their blood, can't wait to smell cities reeking with their rotting corpses and pyres of them burning by the thousands."

Her rant thrilled Bucky, made his twin hearts race, thickened his throat with fury, tightened the cords of muscle in his neck, until he could feel his carotids throbbing like drums. He would have listened to her longer, before the need to move on to the next house would have overcome him, but when movement in the doorway drew his attention, he silenced her with two words: *"The dog!"*

In the hallway, staring in at them, stood the Duke of Orleans, tail low and motionless, hackles raised, ears pricked, teeth bared. Having seen the pizza guy dead on the foyer floor, Duke must have followed them from their house to the Bennets', and from the Bennets' here, witness to every slaughter, for his eyes were accusing and his sudden growl was a challenge.

From the evening that they replaced the real Bucky and Janet Guitreau, this perceptive German shepherd had known they were not who they appeared to be. Friends and family accepted them without hesitation, evincing not a moment of suspicion, but Duke kept his distance, wary from hour one of their impersonation.

Now, as the dog regarded them where they stood in the carnage that had been Antoine and Evangeline, Bucky experienced a startling change of perception. The dog was not merely a dog.

All of the New Race understood that this was the only life and that no afterlife awaited either them or the Old Race. They knew that the concept of an immortal soul was a lie concocted by members of the Old Race to help their fragile kind cope with the reality of death, death everlasting. The New Race recognized that no realm existed beyond the material, that the world was not a place of mystery but instead a place of unambiguous cause and effect, that applied rational intellect could reason its way to the simple truth behind any apparent enigma, that they were meat machines just as the members of the Old Race were meat machines, just as every animal was a meat machine, and that their maker was also only a meat machine, albeit a meat machine with the most brilliant mind in the history of the species and with an infallible vision of a man-made utopia that would establish a Million-Year Reich on Earth before spreading to every habitable planet circling every star in the universe.

This creed of absolute materialism and antihumanism had been drilled into Bucky and Janet as they formed in the creation tanks, which was an immeasurably more effective way to have learned it than by watching *Sesame Street* and reading a series of dull grade-school textbooks.

Unlike members of the Old Race, who could be comfortable for decades with the philosophy that life had no meaning, only to become God-besotted in middle age, the New Race could take satisfaction from knowing they were so indoctrinated with hopelessness that they would never have a doubt about their convictions. Father told them that unassailable hopelessness was the beginning of wisdom.

But now the dog.

His disturbing forthright stare, his judgmental attitude, the fact that he *knew* they were impostors, that he followed them through the night without their knowledge, that he did not slink away from the danger Bucky and Janet currently posed to any living thing not of their kind, that instead he came to confront them: Suddenly this dog seemed to be something more than a meat machine.

Evidently, the same perception troubled Janet, for she said, "What's he doing with his eyes?"

"I don't like his eyes," Bucky agreed.

"He's like not looking at me, he's looking into me."

"He's like looking into me, too."

"He's weird."

"He's totally weird," Bucky agreed.

"What does he want?"

"He wants something."

"I could kill him so fast," Janet said.

"You could. In like three seconds."

"He's seen what we can do. Why isn't he afraid?"

"He doesn't seem to be afraid, does he?"

In the doorway, Duke growled.

"I've never felt like this before," Janet said.

"How do you feel?"

"Different. I don't have a word for it."

"Neither do I."

"I just suddenly feel like . . . things are happening right in front of me that I can't see. Does that make sense?"

"Are we losing more of our programming?"

"All I know is, the dog knows something big," Janet said.

"Does he? What does he know?"

"He knows some reason he doesn't have to be afraid of us."

"What reason?" Bucky asked.

"I don't know. Do you know?"

"I don't know," Bucky said.

"I don't like not knowing."

"He's just a dog. He can't know big things we don't know."

"He should be very afraid of us." Janet hugged herself and seemed to shiver. "But he's not. He knows big things we don't know."

"He's just a meat machine like us."

"He's not acting like one."

"We're smart meat machines. He's a dumb one," Bucky said, but his uneasiness was of a kind he had never experienced before.

"He's got secrets," Janet said.

"What secrets?"

"The big things he knows that we don't."

"How can a dog have secrets?"

"Maybe he's not just a dog."

"What else would he be?"

"Something," she said portentously.

"Just a minute ago, I felt so good killing in the nude, so natural."

"Good," she echoed. "Natural."

"Now I'm afraid," he said.

"I'm afraid, too. I've never been so afraid."

"But I don't know what I'm afraid of, Janet."

"Neither do I. So we must be afraid of . . . the *unknown*."

"But nothing's unknowable to a rational intellect. Right? Isn't that right?"

"Then why isn't the dog afraid of us?"

Bucky said, "He keeps *staring*. I can't stand the way he's just *staring*. It's not natural, and tonight I learned what natural feels like. This isn't natural."

"It's *supernatural*," Janet whispered.

The back of Bucky's neck was suddenly damp. A chill corkscrewed the length of his spine.

Precisely when Janet spoke the word *supernatural*, the dog turned away from them and disappeared into the upstairs hall.

"Where's he going, going, going?" Janet wondered.

"Maybe he was never there."

"I've got to know where he's going, what he is, what he knows," Janet said urgently, and hurried across the bedroom.

Following her into the hallway, Bucky saw that the dog was gone.

Janet ran to the head of the stairs. "Here he is! Going down. He knows something big, oh yeah, oh yeah, he's going somewhere big, he's *something*."

In pursuit of the mysterious dog, Bucky descended the stairs with Janet, and then hurried toward the back of the house.

"Oh yeah, oh yeah, something big, big, bigger than big, the dog knows, the dog knows, the dog."

An instant before they entered the family room, Bucky was struck by the crazy, frightening thought that Charles would be there alive, Charles and Preston and Marcella and Antoine and Evangeline, all of them resurrected, furious, possessed of hideous supernatural powers that would make them invulnerable, and that they would do things to him that he could not imagine, things *unknown*.

Fortunately, young Charles Arceneaux was the only one there, and he was still as dead as anyone had ever been.

Seeing Charles dead and thoroughly dismantled, Bucky should have felt better, but his fear tightened like an overwound clock spring. He was electrified by a sense of the uncanny, by a recognition of mysterious realms beyond his ken, by astonishment that the world had suddenly revealed itself to contain strange dimensions previously unimagined.

Janet bounded after the dog, chanting, "Dog knows, knows, knows. Dog sees, sees, sees. Dog, dog, dog," and Bucky sprinted after them both, out of the Arceneaux house, across the veranda, into the rain. He was not exactly sure how the appearance of the German shepherd in the bedroom doorway had led to this frantic chase, what it all meant, where it would end, but he knew as certainly as he had ever known anything that an event of a profound and magical nature loomed, something big, something *huge*.

He was not just nude, he was naked, vulnerable both physically and mentally, his tandem hearts pounding, flooded with emotion as he had never been before, not at the moment killing anyone and yet exhilarated. They ran through the neighborly gate, into the backyard at the Bennet house, alongside the house toward the street, the dog in the lead, and Bucky heard himself saying, "A terrible thing has happened, a terrible thing has happened," and he was so disturbed by the desperation in his voice that he forced himself to stop that chant. By the time they were running down the center of the street, not gaining on the dog but not falling behind, he was chanting, "Kill the pizza guy, kill the pizza guy," and though he had no idea what that meant, he liked the sound of it.

CHAPTER 19

THE MASTER SUITE of the Helios mansion included two bathrooms, one for Victor and one for Erika. She was not permitted to cross the threshold of his bath.

Every man needed a sacrosanct retreat, a private space where he could relax and relish both the accomplishments of the day and his intentions for the morrow. If he was a revolutionary with the power of science at his command, and if he had the courage and the will to change the world, he needed and deserved a sanctum sanctorum of grand design and dimensions.

Victor's bathroom measured over sixteen hundred square feet. It included a steam room, a sauna, a spacious shower, a whirlpool spa, two under-the-counter refrigerators, an icemaker, a fully stocked bar, a microwave concealed behind a tambour door, three plasma-screen TVs with Blu-Ray DVD capacity, and an anigre-wood cabinet containing a collection of exquisitely braided leather whips.

The gold-leafed ceiling featured custom crystal chandeliers in the Deco style, and the walls were clad with marble. Inlaid in the center of the polished-marble floor were semiprecious stones forming the double helix of the DNA molecule. The faucets and other fixtures were gold-plated, including even the flush lever on the toilet, and there were acres of beveled-edge mirrors. The room glittered.

Nothing in this luxurious space brought Victor as much pleasure as his reflection. Because mirrors were arranged to reflect other mirrors, he could see multiple images of himself wherever he went.

His favorite place for self-examination was an octagonal meditation chamber with a mirrored door. Therein, nude, he could admire every aspect of his body at the same time, and also see infinite images of each angle marching away to infinity, a world of Victors and nothing less.

He believed himself to be no more vain than the average man. His pride in his physical perfection had less to do with the beauty of his body—though it was uniquely beautiful—than with the evidence of his resolution and his indomitability that was revealed in the means by which he maintained that body for two hundred and forty years.

Spiraling through his muscular torso—here inlaid in the flesh and half exposed, here entirely embedded—entwining his ribs, coiling around his rod-straight spine, a flexible metal cord and associated implants efficiently converted electrical current into a different and arcane energy, into a stimulating charge that ensured a youthful rate of cell division and prevented time from taking any toll of him.

His uncounted scars and singular excrescences were a testament to his fortitude, for he had gained immortality at the cost of much pain. He had suffered to fulfill his vision and remake the world, and by suffering for the world, he could lay claim to a kind of divinity.

From the mirrored meditation chamber, he repaired to the spa, in which the air jets roiled the steaming water. A bottle of Dom Pérignon waited in a silver bucket of ice. The cork had been replaced with a solid-silver stopper. Settled in the hot water, he sipped the crisp, ice-cold champagne from a Lalique flute.

As it unfolded, the day just past seemed to be a chain of crises and frustrations. The discoveries during the Harker autopsy. Werner's meltdown. The first of Victor's triumphs, now calling itself Deucalion, not dead after all but alive in New Orleans. The brief encounter with Deucalion in Duchaine's house, the tattooed one's mystifying escape. Erika having dinner in the living room—*living room!*—on a priceless eighteenth-century French escritoire, as if she were an ignorant hillbilly.

The Harker and Werner situations might seem like calamities to unimaginative types like Ripley, but they were opportunities. From every setback came knowledge and stunning new advancements. Thomas Edison developed hundreds of prototypes of lightbulbs that failed, until at last he discovered the right material for the filament.

Deucalion was a mere amusement. He could not harm his maker. Besides, the tattooed wretch killed Victor's first wife, Elizabeth, two centuries earlier, on the day of their wedding. The freak's return would give Victor a chance to take long-overdue vengeance.

Victor had not loved Elizabeth. Love and God were myths he rejected with equal contempt.

But Elizabeth had *belonged* to him. Even after more than two hundred years, he still bitterly resented the loss of her, as he would have resented losing an exquisite antique porcelain vase if Deucalion had smashed that instead of the bride.

As for Erika Five's breach of etiquette: She would have to be disciplined. In addition to being a brilliant scientist, Victor was to an equal degree a brilliant disciplinarian.

All in all, everything was moving along nicely.

The New Race that he had worked so hard to create with Hitler's generous financing, the later effort financed by Stalin, a subsequent project in China, those and others had been necessary steps toward the glorious work at the Hands of Mercy. This time, thanks to the billions earned from his legitimate enterprise, Biovision, he was able to fund 51 percent of the current project and prevent meddling by minority partners, which included a consortium of South American dictators, the ruler of an oil-rich kingdom eager to replace his restive population with obedient new subjects, and an Internet superbillionaire idiot who believed Victor was creating a race that did not exhale CO^2, as did humans, and would thereby save the planet.

Soon the tank farms would begin producing thousands of the New Race, and the Old would be on the doorstep of oblivion.

For every minor setback, there were a hundred major successes. The momentum—and the world—was Victor's.

Soon he would be able to live again under his true name, his proud and storied name, and every person in the world would speak it reverently, as believers speak the name of their god with awe: *Frankenstein*.

When eventually he got out of the spa, he might return to the mirrored meditation room for just a few more minutes.

CHAPTER 20

CARSON AND MICHAEL SAT in the Honda, near Audubon Park, engine running, headlights on, air conditioner blowing. They were eating the crispy-fried-redfish poor boy and side dishes, their chins greasy, fingers slippery with tartar sauce and cole-slaw dressing, so content with the Acadiana food that the incessant drumming of the rain on the roof began to seem soothing, when Michael said, "Here's something."

Carson looked up from her sandwich and saw him squinting through the sheet of water that shimmered down the windshield and blurred the view. She switched on the wipers.

Sprinting toward them along the middle of the street—deserted at this hour, in this weather—was a German shepherd, and in pursuit of the dog were a man and a woman, both nude.

The shepherd raced past the Honda faster than Carson had ever seen a dog run. Even barefoot, the man and woman were faster than Olympians, as if they were in training to compete in NASCAR without a vehicle. The man's genitals flapped, the woman's breasts bounced exuberantly, and their facial expressions were equally ecstatic, as if the dog had promised to lead them to Jesus.

The dog didn't bark, but as the two-legged runners passed the Honda, Carson heard them shouting. With the windows closed and rain pummeling the roof, she couldn't discern what the woman was saying, but the man excitedly shouted something about pizza.

"Any of our business?" Michael asked.

"No," Carson said.

She raised her poor boy to her mouth, but instead of taking a bite, she returned it to the bag with the side dishes, rolled the top of the bag shut, and handed it to Michael.

"Damn," she said, as she put the Honda in gear and hung a U-turn in the street.

"What were they shouting?" Michael asked.

"Her, I don't know. Him, I couldn't catch anything except the word *pizza.*"

"You think the dog ate their pizza?"

"They don't seem angry."

"If they aren't angry, why is the dog running from them?"

"You'll have to ask the dog."

Ahead, the trio with eight legs turned left off the street and onto the Audubon Park entrance lane.

"Did the guy look familiar to you?" Michael asked, as he put their bags of takeout on the floor between his feet.

Accelerating out of the turn, Carson said, "I didn't get a look at his face."

"I think it was the district attorney."

"Bucky Guitreau?"

"And his wife."

"Good for him."

"Good for him?"

"He's not chasing naked after a dog with some hooker."

"Not your ordinary New Orleans politician."

"A family-values guy."

"Can people run that fast?"

"Not our kind of people," Carson said, turning left toward the park.

"That's what I think. And barefoot."

The park had closed at ten o'clock. The dog might have slipped around the gate. The naked runners had gone *through* the barrier, demolishing it in the process.

As Carson drove across the rattling ruins, Michael said, "What are we gonna do?"

"I don't know. I guess it depends on what they do."

CHAPTER 21

BLUE IS THE COLOR of cold vision. All things are shades of blue, infinite shades of blue.

The double-wide restaurant-style freezer has a glass door. The glass is torment for Chameleon.

The shelves have been removed from the freezer. No food is ever stored here.

From a hook in the ceiling of the unit hangs a large sack. The sack is prison.

Prison is made from a unique polymeric fabric that is both as strong as bulletproof Kevlar and transparent.

This transparency is the first torment. The glass door is the second.

The sack resembles a giant teardrop, for it is filled with fourteen gallons of water and is pendulous.

Within the freezer, the temperature varies between twenty-four and twenty-six degrees Fahrenheit.

The water in the polymeric sack is a saline solution treated with chemicals in addition to the salt, to prevent congelation.

Although the temperature remains below freezing, although tiny ice particles float freely in the sack, the solution will not freeze.

Cold is the third torment for Chameleon.

Drifting in the sack, Chameleon lives now in a waking dream.

It is not able to close its eyes to its circumstances, because they have no lids.

Chameleon needs no sleep.

Perpetual awareness of its powerless condition is the fourth torment.

In its current circumstances, Chameleon cannot drown, for it has no lungs.

When not imprisoned, it breathes by virtue of a tracheal system akin to but materially different from that of insects. Spiracles on the surface admit air into tubes that pass throughout the body.

In semisuspended animation, it needs little oxygen. And the saline fluid flowing through its tracheal tubes is oxygen-enriched.

Although Chameleon looks like no insect on Earth, it resembles an insect more than it resembles anything else.

The size of a large cat, Chameleon weighs twenty-four pounds.

Although its brain weighs just 1.22 pounds, Chameleon is as intelligent as the average six-year-old child, but significantly more disciplined and cunning.

In torment, Chameleon waits.

CHAPTER 22

IN THE SPA, the hot water churned against Victor's body, and the bubbles of Dom Pérignon burst across his tongue, and life was good.

The wall phone beside the spa rang. Only select Alphas had the number of this most private line.

The caller-ID window reported UNKNOWN.

Nevertheless, he snared the handset from the cradle. "Yes?"

A woman said, "Hello, darling."

"Erika?"

"I was afraid you might have forgotten me," she said.

Recalling how he had found her at dinner in the living room, he chose to remain the stern disciplinarian for a while longer. "You know better than to bother me here, except in an emergency."

"I wouldn't blame you if you forgot me. It's been more than a day since you had sex with me. I'm ancient history to you."

Her tone had a faint but unmistakable sarcastic quality that caused him to sit up straighter in the spa. "What do you think you're doing, Erika?"

"I was never loved, only used. I'm flattered to be remembered."

Something was very wrong. "Where are you, Erika? Where are you in the house?"

"I'm not in the house, darling. How could I be?"

He would be in error if he continued to play her conversational game, whatever the point of it might be. He must not encourage what seemed to be rebellious behavior. Victor answered her with silence.

"My dearest master, how could I be in the house after you sent me away?"

He hadn't sent her away. He had left her, battered and bleeding, in the living room, not a day previously but mere hours earlier.

She said, "How is the new one? Is she as lubricious as I was? When brutalized, does she cry as pitifully as I did?"

Victor began to see the nature of the game, and he was shocked by her effrontery.

"My darling, my maker, after you killed me, you had your people in the sanitation department take me to a landfill northeast of Lake Pontchartrain. You ask where I am in the house, but I am nowhere in the house—though I hope to return."

Now that she'd carried this demented charade to an unacceptable extreme, silence was not the appropriate response to her.

"You are Erika Five," he said coldly, "not Erika Four. And all you've achieved by this absurd impersonation is to ensure that Erika Six will be in your position soon."

"From so many nights of passion," she said, "I remember the hard impact of your fists, the sharpness of your teeth biting into me, and how I bled into your mouth."

"Come to me immediately," he said, for he needed to terminate her within the hour.

"Oh, darling, I would be there at once if I could, but it's a long way to the Garden District from the dump."

CHAPTER 23

AS THEY REACHED the T junction where the entrance lane met the main road through Audubon Park, Michael drew the illegally purchased .50-caliber Desert Eagle pistol from the scabbard at his left hip.

Carson said, "If they're going to be trouble—"

"I'd bet both kidneys on it."

"—then I'm thinking the Urban Sniper makes more sense," she finished, turning right onto West Drive.

The headlights washed across the pale forms of Mr. and Mrs. Guitreau on their rainy-night, fully-nude, high-speed dog walk.

Michael said, "If we have to get out of the car, it'll for sure be the Sniper, but not if I have to shoot from a sitting position."

Hours earlier, they had seen Pastor Kenny Laffite, one of the New Race, breaking down psychologically and intellectually. And not long after that, they were forced to deal with another of Victor's creations who called himself Randal and whose rap was as creepy-crazy as Charles Manson channeling Jeffrey Dahmer. Randal wanted to kill Carson's brother, Arnie, and he had taken three rounds point-blank from an Urban Sniper before going down and staying down.

Now this weirdness.

"Damn," Carson said. "I'm never gonna get a chance to finish that okra succotash."

"I thought it was a little salty. I've gotta say, Mrs. Guitreau has a truly fine butt."

"For God's sake, Michael, she's some kind of monster."

"Doesn't change the fact she's got a great butt. Small, tight, with those little dimples at the top."

"It's Armageddon, and my backup is an obsessive butt man."

"I think her name's Jane. No. Janet."

"Why do you care what her name is? She's a monster but she's got a cute butt, so you're gonna ask her for a date?"

"How fast are they going?"

Glancing at the speedometer, Carson said, "About twenty-four miles an hour."

"That's maybe a two-and-a-half-minute mile. I think the fastest the mile's been run is just under four minutes."

"Yeah, but I don't expect we'll ever see their pictures on a Wheaties box."

"I heard greyhounds can do a mile in two minutes," Michael said. "I don't know about German shepherds."

"Looks to me like the shepherd is pretty much spent. They're gaining on him."

Michael said, "If we have a dog in this race, it's the dog. I don't want to see the dog get hurt."

The shepherd and his pursuers were in the left lane. Carson swung into the right lane and rolled down her window.

As rain bounced off the sill and into her face, she drew even with the nude marathoners and heard what they were shouting.

The woman—okay, *Janet*—chanted urgently, "Dog nose, dog nose, big, big, big."

"I think she wants the dog's nose," Carson said.

Michael said, "She can't have it."

Neither of the nudists was breathing hard.

Bucky Guitreau, the nearer of the two, was raving with a slight quirky calypso lilt: "Kill, kill, pizza guy, pizza guy, kill, kill."

Both the district attorney and his wife, certainly replicants in the throes of a total breakdown, seemed oblivious to the Honda pacing them. The dog had their full attention, and they were closing on him.

Reading the speedometer, Michael said, "Twenty-*six* miles an hour."

Trying to discern if the runners were even capable of breaking their fixation with the dog, Carson shouted at them, *"Pull over!"*

CHAPTER 24

SITTING IN THE SPA, his champagne mood tainted with the vinegar of his wife's unthinkable rebellion, Victor should already have hung up on Erika Five as she pretended to be Erika Four. He didn't know why he continued to listen to this tripe, but he was rapt.

"Here at the dump," she said, "in a heap of garbage, I found a disposable cell phone that has some unused minutes on it. Eighteen, in fact. Those of the Old Race are so wasteful, throwing away what has value. I, too, still had value, I believe."

Every Erika was created with precisely the same voice, just as they looked alike in every luscious detail.

"My lovely Victor, my dearest sociopath, I can prove to you that I am who I claim to be. Your current punching bag doesn't know how you murdered me, does she?"

He realized he was clenching the telephone so tightly that his hand ached.

"But, sweetheart, of course she doesn't know. Because if you wish to murder her in the same fashion, you want it to be a surprise to her, as it was to me."

No one in decades had spoken to him so contemptuously, and *never* had one whom he created addressed him with such disrespect.

Furious, he declared, "Only people can be murdered. You're not a person, you're property, a thing I owned. I didn't murder you, I disposed of you, disposed of a worn-out, useless thing."

He had lost control. He needed to restrain himself. His reply had seemed to suggest he accepted her ridiculous assertion that she was Erika Four.

She said, "All of the New Race are designed to be extremely difficult to kill. None can be strangled easily, if at all. None except your Erikas. Unlike the others, we wives have tender throats, fragile windpipes, carotid arteries that can be compressed to stop the blood from flowing to our brains."

The water in the spa seemed to be less hot than it had been a minute ago.

"We were in the library, where you had beaten me. You instructed me to sit in a straightbacked chair. I could only obey. You took off your silk necktie and strangled me. And not quickly. You made an ordeal of it for me."

He said, "Erika Four earned what she received. And now so have you."

"In extreme situations," she continued, "you are able to kill any of your creations by speaking a few words, a secret phrase, which triggers in our programs a shutdown of the autonomic nervous system. The heart ceases to beat. Lungs at once stop expanding, contracting. But you didn't deal with me as mercifully as that."

"Now I shall." He spoke the phrase that would shut her down.

"Dear one, my precious Victor, it will no longer work. I was for a while dead enough that your control program dropped out of me. Not so dead, however, that I couldn't be resurrected."

"Nonsense," he said, but his voice had no conviction.

"Oh, darling, how I yearn to be with you again. And I will be. This is not good-bye, only au revoir." She hung up.

If she had been Erika Five, she would have dropped dead when he used the termination phrase.

Erika Four was alive again. For the first time ever, Victor seemed to have a marital problem with which he could not easily cope.

CHAPTER 25

THE DISTRICT ATTORNEY AND HIS WIFE did not pull over, of course, because Carson didn't have a siren or an array of flashing emergency beacons, because they probably knew they were not in any condition to pass a Breathalyzer test, but mostly because they were miscreations cloned in a lab by a narcissistic lunatic and were going haywire as fast as the average car would break down on the day that its warranty expired.

Leaning toward her, reading the speedometer again, Michael said, "Twenty-seven miles an hour. The dog is flagging. They're gonna run right up his ass."

As though multiple-word chants had become too exhausting to remember, Bucky and Janet each resorted to one word. She shouted, "Dog, dog, dog, dog. . . ." He cried out, "Kill, kill, kill, kill. . . ."

"Shoot them," Michael said. "Shoot 'em on the run."

"I can't fire a .50 Magnum one-handed while driving a car," Carson protested.

Evidently, Bucky was at least peripherally aware of them, after all, and they were enough of a distraction from his pursuit of the dog to annoy him. He closed the gap between them, running alongside the Honda, grabbed the side mirror for balance, and reached through the window toward Carson.

She stepped on the brake, and the mirror snapped off in Bucky's hand. He stumbled, fell, tumbled away into the darkness.

The Honda shrieked to a full stop, and about fifty feet ahead of them, Janet halted without a shriek. She turned toward them, jogging in place.

Holstering his Desert Eagle, Michael said, "This is like some bizarre Playboy-channel special." He handed one of the Urban Snipers to

Carson and snatched up the other. "Not that I ever watch the Playboy channel."

Michael threw open his door, and Carson switched the headlights on high beam because darkness helped her quarry, hampered her. As her heart provided the thunder that the storm had not yet produced, she clambered out into the rain, surveying the night, looking for Bucky, not finding him.

Glare of headlights reflected by the wet pavement, black and silver underfoot, and not far to the west, beyond trees, the lights of Walnut Street and Audubon and Broadway, which didn't reach this far, and north-northeast, the university lights of Tulane and Loyola, which didn't reach this far either, the park deep and dark to the east and to the south, the glow of maybe De Paul Hospital far out there.

A lonely place to die, to be found in the morning, left like illegally dumped trash, left like her father and mother were left all those years ago, facedown under power lines, near a double-circuit tower, on a grassy bank of the levee in Riverbend, just off the bike path, each shot once in the back of the head, with carrion-eating blackbirds gathering overhead on the crossarms of the tower as day broke . . .

Now this park, this lonely darkness, felt like Carson's levee bank, her place to be left like a sack of trash, to be pecked at by bright-eyed birds. She had been out of the Honda ten seconds at most, edging away from the vehicle and defining the arc of the potential threat with the barrel of the shotgun, left to right, then right to left, but the ten seconds felt like ten minutes.

Where was the freak?

Suddenly a pale form rose from a drainage swale on the farther side of the road, the Bucky replicant, bloodied by his high-speed fall but back on his feet and shouting: "Something terrible has happened, terrible, terrible." Looking no less powerful than a bull, he put his head down and charged her.

Carson planted her feet wide, assumed the stance, the compact shotgun held low in both hands, right hand on the pistol grip in front of the forecomb, left hand cupping the slide, weapon held slightly to her right side, both elbows bent, the better to absorb recoil, which would be brutal if she locked her joints—a tendon-tearing, shoulder-dislocating kind of brutal. As serious as a weapon gets, the Sniper fired only rhino-stopping slugs, not buckshot with a wide spread, but nevertheless she aimed by instinct, no time for anything else. The Bucky Guitreau impersonator, with blood in his wild eyes, lips snarled back from his teeth, barreled straight at her, fearless, ferocious.

She squeezed off the round, the recoil jumped her backward a few inches, the barrel kicked up like she knew it would, pain knocked through her shoulders, a sensitive filling in a molar throbbed the way it did once in a while when she drank something ice-cold, and though she wasn't in an enclosed space, the shot rang in her ears.

The slug took the replicant dead-center in the chest, cracking his sternum, splintering bone inward, blood blooming, his left arm flailing up reflexively, right arm stroking down reflexively, as if he were launching into some novelty dance like the Chicken. Jolted but not staggered, slowed but not halted, he came on, not shouting anymore, but not screaming either, feeling no pain, and she fired again, but screwed up because she was shocked and scared by how he surged forward, didn't get him in the gut or the chest, but in the right shoulder, which should have torn his arm off or at least a chunk of it, didn't, and he was reaching out to grab the barrel of the Sniper, looking strong enough and furious enough and focused enough to take maybe two more rounds and still tear her face off, rip out her throat.

Michael appeared at the back of the Honda, his shotgun boomed, scored a flank hit just above the hip, and Carson fired again, maybe nailed the replicant point-blank in the left thigh, but his arm was in past the muzzle of the shotgun, knocking the barrel high, his crimson hand reaching toward her face. Guitreau said something that sounded like "Gimme your eyes," and Michael fired again, a head shot, and that did it, finally dropped the Bucky thing, naked on the silver-and-black pavement, facedown, still for a moment, but then trying to belly-crawl away from them, a broken-melon head and other devastating wounds but trying to hitch away as if he were a crippled roach. He became still once more, lying there motionless, motionless, then a last convulsive spasm, and he was done.

From the corner of her eye, Carson saw something move, something close, and she swiveled toward tight-assed Janet.

CHAPTER 26

CAUTIONING SILENCE, Erika Five led Jocko, the albino troll, up one of two sets of back stairs, to the second floor, well away from the centrally located master suite.

Of the three mansions that had stood on the three lots Victor purchased, two were very alike architecturally. He joined them in such a way that a foreground trio of oaks and a background lattice arbor draped with evergreen St. Vincent lilac left the impression, from the street, that the houses were still separate.

Between them, the two residences initially included thirty-four bedrooms, but interior walls were taken down and all that space put to other uses. Victor had no family and allowed no overnight guests.

He had intended to tear down the third residence and incorporate that lot into the grounds of his estate.

A city politician with ambitions for the governorship—and with rigid ideas about the preservation of historic buildings—blocked Victor's attempt to have the third house certified for demolition. He tried to resolve the issue with respect for her public office and her social eminence. A fat bribe would have bought her cooperation on most matters; however, she believed that a reputation as a committed preservationist was key to the achievement of her political goals.

After the politician's replicant had been birthed from the tank, Victor had the real woman snatched from her home and brought to the Hands of Mercy, where he described—and then demonstrated—to her the most ingenious methods of torture devised by the Stasi, the secret police of the former East Germany. When in time she stopped begging for surcease and begged instead for death, Victor allowed her to choose the instrument of murder from an imaginative selection that included, among other things, a compressed-air nail gun, a hand-held power sander, and a large bottle of carbolic acid.

The woman's complete mental collapse and retreat into catatonic detachment not only made it impossible for her to decide upon the means to her end but also robbed Victor of some of the pleasure of administering corporal punishment. Nevertheless, he considered the resolution of the historic-preservation issue to have been one of his finer moments, which was why he included it in his biography that had been downloaded into Erika's brain while she had been forming in the tank.

Victor wanted his Erikas not merely to service him sexually and to be his gracious hostess to the world; he also intended that his wives, each in her turn, should admire his steadfast intent to have his way in all matters, his steely resolution never to bow or bend to the wishes of the intellectual pygmies, frauds, and fools of this world who sooner or later humbled all other great men whose accomplishments they bitterly envied.

On the second floor of the mansion, the north wing remained unused, awaiting Victor's inspiration. One day, he would discover some convenience or luxury he wanted to add to the house, and the north wing would be remodeled to accommodate his latest enthusiasm.

Even here, mahogany floors had been installed and finished throughout all the wide hallways and rooms. In the halls, the floors were overlaid with a series of compatible antique Persian rugs, mostly late-nineteenth-century Tabriz and Bakhshayesh.

She took Jocko to an unfurnished suite, where she switched on the overhead lights: a small sitting room, a bedroom, a bath. The space lacked carpeting. Heavy brocade draperies with blackout liners, which had come with the house, were closed over the windows.

"The staff vacuums and dusts the north wing just twelve times a year," Erika said. "The first Tuesday of every month. Otherwise, these rooms are never visited. The night before, we'll move you to another location, and back again after they have finished and gone."

Still wearing the skirt fashioned from the checkered tablecloth, wandering from lounge to bedroom, admiring the high ceilings, the ornate crown moldings, and the Italian-marble fireplace, the troll said, "Jocko is not worthy of these refined quarters."

"Without furniture, you'll have to sleep on the floor," said Erika. "I'm sorry about that."

"Jocko doesn't sleep much, just sits in a corner and sucks his toes and lets his mind go away to the red place, and when it comes back from the red place, Jocko is rested."

"How interesting. Nonetheless, you'll sometimes want a place to lie down. I'll bring blankets, soft bedding to make it comfortable."

In the bathroom, the black-and-white ceramic tile dated to the 1940s, but it remained in excellent condition.

"You have hot and cold running water, a tub, a shower, and of course a toilet. I'll bring soap, towels, toilet paper, a toothbrush, toothpaste. You don't have hair, so you won't need shampoo or a comb, or dryer. Do you shave?"

The troll thoughtfully stroked his lumpy face with one hand. "Jocko doesn't have even one nice hair anywhere—except inside his nose. Oh, and three on his tongue." He stuck his tongue out to show her.

"You still won't need a comb," Erika said. "What deodorant do you prefer, roll-on or spray-on?"

Jocko squinched his face, which drew his features into a disturbing configuration.

Once Erika knew him better and could be direct without seeming to insult, she would tell him never to squinch again.

He said, "Jocko suspects his skin is hypersensitive to such caustic chemicals."

"All right then. I'll be back shortly with everything you need. You wait here. Stay away from the windows and of course be as quiet as you can." A literary allusion rose from the deep pool of them in Erika's memory, and she added, "This is just like Anne Frank, hiding from the Nazis in the secret annex in Amsterdam."

The troll stared at her uncomprehendingly and smacked the flaps of his lipless mouth.

"Or maybe not," said Erika.

"May Jocko say?" he asked.

"Excuse me?"

"May Jocko say?"

Owlishly large, with huge irises as yellow as lemons, his eyes still struck her as mysterious and beautiful. They compensated for all the unfortunate facial features surrounding them.

"Yes," she said, "of course, say what you want."

"Since tearing my way out of he who I was and becoming he who I am, Jocko, who is me, has lived mostly in storm drains and for a little while in a janitorial closet at a public restroom. This is so much better."

Erika smiled and nodded. "I hope you'll be happy here. Just remember—your presence in the house must remain a secret."

"You are the kindest, most generous lady in the world."

"Not at all, Jocko. You'll be reading to me, remember?"

"When I was still he who was, I never knew any lady half as nice as you. Since the he who was became the I who am, Jocko, I've never met any lady a quarter as nice as you, not even in the restroom where I lived eleven hours, which was a ladies' restroom. From the janitorial closet, Jocko listened to so many ladies talking out there at the sinks and in the stalls, and most of them were *horrible*."

"I'm sorry you've suffered so much, Jocko."

He said, "Me too."

CHAPTER 27

THE PRESENCE APPROACHING CARSON, from her right and low to the ground, wasn't Janet Guitreau, but the German shepherd, panting hard, tail wagging.

She with the great butt remained where she had been when Carson got out of the Honda: fifty feet farther along the road. Head high, shoulders back, arms out at her sides as if she were a gunfighter ready to draw down on a sheriff in the Old West, she stood tall and alert.

She was no longer jogging in place, which was probably a huge disappointment to Michael.

Interestingly, the Janet thing had watched their confrontation with the Bucky thing and had felt no obligation to sprint to his assistance. A small army of the New Race might inhabit the city, but perhaps there wasn't sufficient camaraderie among them to ensure they would always fight together.

On the other hand, maybe this lack of commitment to the cause resulted solely from the fact that Janet's brain train had jumped the tracks and was rolling through strange territory where no rails had ever been laid.

Out there in the scintillant silver rain, bathed in the Honda's high-beam headlights, she appeared ethereal, as if a curtain had parted between this world and another where people were as radiant as spirits and as wild as any animal.

Michael held out a hand, cartridges gleaming on his palm.

Reloading, Carson said, "What're you thinking—go after her?"

"Not me. I have a rule—one showdown with an insane superclone per day. But she might come for us."

For the first time all night, a sudden light wind sprang up, trumping gravity, so that the rain angled at them, pelting Carson's face instead of the top of her head.

As though the wind had spoken to Janet, counseling retreat, she turned from them and sprinted off the roadway, between trees, into the dark grassy mystery of the park.

At Carson's side, the dog issued a low, long growl that seemed to mean *good riddance*.

Michael's cell phone sounded. His newest ring was Curly's laugh, Curly being *the* Curly of the Three Stooges. "N'yuck, n'yuck, n'yuck," said the phone. "N'yuck, n'yuck, n'yuck."

"Life in the twenty-first century," Carson said, "is every bit as stupid as it is insane."

Michael took the call and said, "Hey, yeah." To Carson, he said, "It's Deucalion."

"About freakin' time." She surveyed the darkness to the east and south, expecting Janet to come bouncing back in full killer mode.

After listening a moment, Michael told Deucalion, "No, where we are isn't a good place to meet. We just had a situation, and there's debris everywhere."

Carson glanced at the body of the Bucky replicant. Still dead.

"Give us like ten or fifteen minutes to get somewhere that makes sense. I'll call you back, let you know where." Pocketing his phone, he said to Carson, "Deucalion's almost done at Mercy, he found what he hoped to find."

"What do you want to do about the dog?"

Having been drinking from a puddle on the pavement, the shepherd looked up and favored Carson, then Michael, with a beseeching look.

Michael said, "We take him with us."

"The whole car's gonna smell like wet dog."

"It's a lot worse for him. From his point of view, the whole car smells like wet cops."

"He's a pretty boy," she admitted. "And he looks like he ought to be a police dog. I wonder what his name is."

"Wait a minute," Michael said. "This must be Duke. The D.A.'s dog. Goes to court with Bucky. Or used to."

"The Duke of Orleans," Carson said. "Saved two kids in a fire."

The dog's tail spun so fast that Carson half expected it would propel him across the slick pavement in the manner of one of those Florida Everglades airboats.

The wind soughed in the trees, and suddenly it seemed to carry the scent of the sea.

She opened the car door, coaxed the shepherd into the backseat, and got in behind the wheel once more. As she returned her Urban Sniper, muzzle down, to the leg space in front of the passenger's seat, she realized that the bags of Acadiana food were gone.

Through the windshield, she saw Michael returning from a nearby roadside trash receptacle.

"What have you done?" she demanded when he splashed into his seat and pulled the door shut.

"We'd already eaten most of it."

"We hadn't eaten *all* of it. Acadiana is good-to-the-last-crumb wondermous."

"The smell of it would drive the dog crazy."

"So we could've given him some."

"It's too rich for a dog. He'd be puking it up later."

"The stupid Curly ring, and now this."

She put the car in gear, hung a U-turn without driving over the Bucky replicant, switched the headlights to low beam, drove across the mangled park gate, hoping not to puncture a tire, and turned right onto St. Charles Avenue.

"So . . . I'm not going to get the silent treatment, am I?" Michael asked.

"You should be so lucky."

"Another prayer unanswered."

"Here's the sixty-four-thousand-dollar question."

"I can't afford it," he said.

"Do you think I eat too much?"

"It's none of my business what you eat."

"You think I'm going to get a fat ass, don't you?"

"Uh-oh."

In the backseat, the shepherd panted but not with anxiety. He sounded happy. Maybe he'd heard so much replicant-speak lately that he delighted in real human conversation.

"Admit it. You're worried I'll get a fat ass."

"I don't sit around thinking about the future of your ass."

"You were so hot for the Janet monster's tight butt."

"I wasn't hot for it. I just noticed it, you know, as a nice work of nature, like you'd comment on a great wisteria vine if you saw one."

"Wisteria? That is so lame. Besides, Victor's people *aren't* works of nature."

"I don't have a chance here if you're gonna parse my every word."

"Just so you know, my butt is as small as hers was, and even tighter."

"I'll take your word for it."

"You'll have to take my word for it because there isn't going to be any exhibition. If you dropped a quarter on my butt, it would bounce to the ceiling."

"That sounds like a challenge."

"Let me tell you, partner, it's gonna be a long time before you get a chance to bounce a quarter off my butt."

"Just in case, from now on, I'm going to be sure I've always got a quarter in my pocket."

"Bounce it off my butt," she said, "you'll get back two dimes and a nickel in change."

"What does that mean?"

"I have no idea."

He said, "Two dimes and a nickel in change," and he broke into laughter.

His laughter was contagious, and when the dog heard them both laughing, he made sweet mewling sounds of delight.

After a minute, Carson settled to serious once more and said, "Thanks, pal. You saved my ass back there with the Bucky thing."

"*De nada*. You've saved mine often enough."

"Each time we have to throw down on one of these New Race," she said, "seems like we squeak by with less room to spare than before."

"Yeah. But at least we do keep on squeakin' by."

CHAPTER 28

AT 2:15 A.M., at Victor's stylish workstation in the main lab at the Hands of Mercy, as Deucalion completed his electronic fishing and backed out of the computer, he thought he heard in the distance a scream as thin as the plaint of a lost child.

Given some of the experiments being conducted in this building, screams were not likely to be infrequent. No doubt the windows had been bricked up not solely to foil prying eyes but also to ensure that disturbing sounds would fail to reach passersby in the street.

The staff here, the subjects of the experiments, and those who were growing in the creation tanks were without exception victims of their lunatic god, and Deucalion pitied them. He hoped eventually to free them all from their anguish and despair, not one at a time as he had freed Annunciata and Lester, but somehow en masse.

He had no way to free them right now, however, and as soon as he heard from Michael, he would be leaving the Hands of Mercy in a quantum leap and joining the detectives. He could not be distracted by whatever horrors might be unfolding elsewhere in the building.

When the sound came again, marginally louder and longer than before but still distant, Deucalion recognized that it conveyed neither terror nor physical pain, and therefore was not a scream at all, but instead a shriek. He could not tell what the crier of this cry meant to express.

He stood listening—and only realized after the fact that he had risen from the workstation chair.

The silence following the wail had an expectant quality, like the mute sky during the second or two between a violent flash of lightning and the crash of thunder. Here, the sound came first and, though faint, managed to be as terrible as the loudest thunderclap.

He waited for the equivalent of the flash, cause after effect. But what followed a half minute later was another shriek.

On the third hearing, the sound had significance, not because he could identify its source but because it recalled to him cries he heard in certain dreams that for two hundred years had haunted him. They were not dreams of the night he came alive in Victor's first lab, but of other and more dreadful events, perhaps of events that preceded his existence.

After his first hundred years, decade by decade, he needed less sleep. This meant, thankfully, fewer opportunities to dream.

Deucalion crossed the main lab, opened a door, stepped across the threshold, and found the hallway deserted.

The cry came again, twice in quick succession. Louder here than in the laboratory, the sound was still distant.

Sometimes Deucalion dreamed of an old stone house with interior walls of cracked and yellowed plaster, illuminated by oil lamps and candle sconces. When the worst storm winds blew, from the attic arose a disturbing click-and-clatter, like the fleshless body of Death rattling in his cowled robe as he walked the night. Worse than what might wait above was what might wait below: A narrow turning of stone stairs descended to an iron-bound door, and beyond the door were the rooms of a forbidding cellar, where the stagnant air sometimes had the acrid taste of spoiled suet and at other times the salty taste of tears.

Here in the old hospital, the latest two shrieks had come from another floor, whether from above or below, he could not tell. He walked to the stairs at the end of the corridor, opened the fire door, and waited, feeling almost as if he might be dreaming that well-known scenario but in a new setting.

In the familiar nightmare, the horror of going into the attic or the desire not to go into the cellar was always the sum of the plot, an endless wretched journey through the rooms that lay between those two poles of terror, as he strove to avoid both the highest and lowest chambers of the house.

Now, the shriek fell through the hospital stairwell from above. Heard more clearly than before, it was pleading and mournful.

Like the miserable cries that sometimes haunted his infrequent sleep.

Deucalion ascended the stairs toward the higher realms of Mercy.

In the old stone house, which might have once been a real place or just a structure of his imagination, he had dreamed his way into the cellar many times, but never farther than the first room. Then he always woke, choking with a nameless dread.

Twice, with an oil lamp, he had gone into the dream-house attic. Both times, a fierce storm raged outside. Drafts blustered through that high room, and he was shocked out of sleep and into anguish by what the lamplight revealed.

Climbing the hospital stairs, Deucalion felt at risk of losing his balance, and he put one hand on the railing.

He was constructed from the parts of bodies salvaged from a prison graveyard. His hands were big and strong. They had been the hands of a strangler.

One floor above Victor's main lab, as Deucalion reached for the door to the corridor, he heard the shriek again, its source still overhead. As he continued up the stairs, he watched his powerful hand slide along the railing.

His eyes had been salvaged from an ax murderer.

He sensed that what he was about to see in the higher halls of Mercy would be no less terrible than what the lamplight had shown him in the dream-house attic. On this fateful night, past and present were coming together like the hemispheres of a nuclear warhead, and the post-blast future was unknown.

CHAPTER 29

THE TORMENT OF PERPETUAL AWARENESS. The torment of cold. The torment of the transparent polymeric fabric. The torment of the glass door on the freezer.

Drifting in the saline solution, Chameleon can see the large room in which it is stored. A blue scene. The blue of cold vision.

Out there in the laboratory, work continues. Busy blue people.

Perhaps they are TARGETS. Perhaps they are EXEMPTS.

When not in cold suspension, Chameleon can smell the difference between TARGETS and EXEMPTS.

The scent of any EXEMPT pleases Chameleon. The scent of any TARGET infuriates.

In its current condition, it can smell nothing.

The walls of the freezer conduct the unit's compressor-motor vibrations to the imprisoning sack. The sack conducts them into the solution.

This is neither a pleasant nor an unpleasant sensation for Chameleon.

Now the character of the vibrations changes. They are similar but subtly different.

This happens periodically. Chameleon is sufficiently intelligent to consider the phenomenon and to reach conclusions about it.

Evidently, the freezer has two motors. They alternate to prevent either from being overtaxed.

This also ensures that if one motor fails, the other will serve as backup.

Chameleon's physical function is greatly inhibited by the cold. Its mental function is less affected.

With little to occupy its mind, Chameleon focuses obsessively on every minim of sensory input, such as motor vibrations.

It is not at risk of being driven insane by its circumstances. At no time was it ever sane.

Chameleon has no desires or ambitions other than to kill. The purpose of its existence is currently frustrated, which is the nature of its torment.

Out in the blue laboratory, the busy blue people are suddenly agitated. The standard pattern of activities, which Chameleon has long studied, is abruptly disrupted.

Something unusual has come into the lab. It is busy and blue, but it is not a person.

Interesting.

CHAPTER 30

IN VICTOR'S MASTER-BEDROOM CLOSET, all foldable clothes were stored in banks of drawers, and all hanging items were behind cabinet doors, leaving the room sleek and neat, as he liked it.

In his clothes collection were 164 custom-tailored suits, 67 fine sport coats, 48 pairs of slacks, 212 shirts including dress and casual, drawers and drawers full of perfectly folded sweaters, and shelf after shelf of shoes for every occasion. Especially fond of silk neckties, he had lost count when his collection passed three hundred.

He enjoyed dressing well. Considering his exemplary physique, clothes hung beautifully on him. He thought he was nearly as pleasing to the eye when dressed as he was when nude.

After the phone call from Erika Four, Victor counseled himself to linger in the spa over another glass of Dom Pérignon. His former wife was trash, figuratively and literally, and though she may have somehow been resuscitated, she was no match for either his intellect or his cunning.

As prudent as he was confident, however, he had stepped from the spa after taking only two sips of the second glass of champagne. Until the problem of Erika Four could be understood and resolved, he ought to have a suitable weapon on his person at all times.

In a sapphire silk robe with scarlet piping and matching silk slippers, he went to the back of his deep walk-in closet and opened a pair of tall doors. Before him was a double-hung selection of shirts, twenty on the upper rod, twenty on the lower.

He placed his left hand flat against a sidewall of the cabinet, a concealed scanner read his fingerprints, the rods and shirts rolled up and out of sight, and the back wall slid aside. Lights came on in a fifteen-foot-square room beyond.

Victor stepped through the cabinet, into his small armory.

Like the clothes in the closet, the weapons were not in view. He would have found such a display garish, the kind of thing a too-enthusiastic militarist might have done.

Victor was not a member of the National Rifle Association, not only because he was not a joiner, but also because he didn't approve of the Second Amendment. He believed that, in order to have a well-managed population and to prevent the people from acting on the delusion that the government served them, only an elite class should be permitted ownership of firearms. The masses, in matters of dispute among themselves, could make do perfectly well with knives, fists, and sticks.

The machine guns and the custom-machined automatic shotguns were in racks behind upper doors. Pistols and revolvers were in drawers, nestled in molded foam finished with a spray-on velvet, which not only embraced the weapons but also displayed them as diamond necklaces might be presented on a jeweler's velvet trays.

Fortunately, although the Erikas were strong and were intended to be durable, with full speed-healing capability as well as the ability to turn off pain, they were not as physically formidable as others of the New Race. They were designed with a few points of vulnerability, and their bones were not the dense armorlike quality given to others born from the tanks.

Consequently, he selected a 1911-style Colt .45 ACP, the Springfield Armory version, with custom 24-line-per-inch checking in the walnut grip, plus deep-cut and hand-engraved decorative scrollwork in the stainless steel.

On those rare occasions when he could not kill by proxy, using one of the New Race, Victor wanted his weapon to be as attractive as it was powerful.

After loading the pistol and a spare magazine, he selected a supple hand-tooled leather scabbard that would slip onto whatever belt he chose with his trousers, and he returned with everything to the clothes closet, pressing his hand to the cabinet sidewall again to conceal the armory behind him.

Sleep was usually a choice for him, not often a necessity, and he decided to return to the Hands of Mercy. The amusements that he had come home to pursue, after a long and curious day at work, no longer appealed to him.

From the lab, he would contact Nick Frigg, the Gamma who was the superintendent at Crosswoods Waste Management, the landfill in the uplands northeast of Lake Pontchartrain. Thoroughly strangled,

Erika Four had been sent there for disposal; therefore, Nick would be the one most likely to know in which sector of which pit, under what garbage, she had been buried.

Watching himself in a full-length mirror, Victor kicked off his slippers. With the flair of a fine matador manipulating a cape, he stripped out of the sapphire silk robe.

He picked up the .45 pistol and posed with it this way and that, pleased with the impression that he made.

Now what to wear, what to wear . . . ?

CHAPTER 31

THE HANDS OF A STRANGLER. The gray eyes of an executed ax murderer. Of his two hearts, one had come from a mad arsonist who burned down churches, the other from a child molester.

As he reached the stairwell landing, a floor and a half above the main laboratory at the Hands of Mercy, his vision brightened for a moment, returned to normal, brightened. . . .

If he had stood before a mirror, he would have seen a pulse of soft light pass through his eyes. On the night that Victor had drawn upon the power of a thunderbolt to enliven his first creation, the cooperative storm, of unprecedented violence, had seemed to leave in Deucalion the lightning's glow, which manifested in his eyes from time to time.

Although he sought redemption and eventually peace, although he cherished Truth and wished to serve it, Deucalion had long tried to deceive himself about the identity of the man whose head, whose *brain,* had been married to the patchwork body in Victor's first lab. He said his brain was that of an unknown miscreant, which was true but only in that he'd never been told the man's name or his crimes.

The repetitive nightmare of the old stone house—with its cursed attic where something ticked and rattled, clicked and clattered; and its cellar in which the air itself was evil—returned to Deucalion so often that he knew as surely as he knew anything, the dream must be fragments of memories the donor had left behind somewhere among the sulci and the gyri of his gray matter. And the nature of those grim memories identified the hateful source of the brain.

Now, ascending the hospital stairs toward the thin childlike cries of misery, he felt as if Earth's gravity had doubled during the climb, for he carried not only the weight of this moment but also the weight of all those dreams and what they surely meant.

When in the nightmare he had at last made it up the stairs into the attic of the house, the throbbing light of an oil lamp revealed to him the source of the clicking and clattering. The raging storm outside pressed drafts into that high room, and those blustering currents knocked the dangling bones against one another. The skeleton was small, strung together to keep it in order, suspended from a hook in a rafter.

Also suspended from the hook was the only other thing of the victim that remained: the long golden hair that had been shorn from her head. Bones and braids. Or call them trophies.

But so much clicking and clattering could not arise from one young girl's bones. When in the dream he had dared to venture farther into the attic, the lamplight revealed a grisly orphanage: nine other dangling skeletons and then, oh, ten more beyond, and yet another ten thereafter. Thirty young girls—all children, really—presented as mobiles, each with her hair hanging separately from her skull, blond hair or brown or auburn, straight or curly hair, some braided and some not.

In hundreds of repetitions of that dream, he had only twice gotten into the attic before waking in a sweat of dread. He had *never* proceeded past the first room of the cellar, into the heart of that darkness, and he hoped he never would. The sound of skeletons in a wind dance drew him to the attic, but what always pulled him toward the dream-house cellar were those thin haunting cries. They were not shrieks of terror or of pain, but instead of sorrow, as if he were hearing not the victims yet alive but their spirits yearning for the world from which they had been taken before their time.

He had so long resisted acknowledging the source of his brain; but he could not continue deceiving himself. His second heart had come from a child molester who killed those he raped—and his brain from the same donor. The murderer had done what he wanted with the girls and then rendered them in the cellar to extract their delicate skeletons as mementos, which was why in the dream the stagnant air of that windowless lower realm tasted sometimes of spoiled suet and sometimes of salty tears.

The possession of a child molester's brain didn't make Deucalion a child molester himself. That evil mind and that corrupted soul had departed the brain at death, leaving behind nothing but three pounds or so of blameless cerebral tissue, which Victor had taken to preserve immediately after the execution, by arrangement with the hangman. Deucalion's consciousness was uniquely his own, and its origins were . . . elsewhere.

Whether his consciousness came in tandem with a soul, he could not say. But he had no doubt that he arrived that long-ago night with a mission—to enforce the natural laws that Victor had broken with his prideful experiments and, by killing him, thereby repair the torn fabric of the world.

Following a journey that had taken him around the Earth more than once and across two troubled centuries, in search of a new purpose after he thought Victor died on the arctic ice, Deucalion at last arrived here at the threshold of his destiny. The destruction of the New Race was under way, brought about by the endless errors of their maker. And soon Deucalion would bring justice to Victor Frankenstein in the storm of anarchy and terror now breaking over Louisiana.

Now another childlike expression of sorrow, another more suggestive of despair, greeted him as he reached the next landing. The cries came from this floor.

He suspected that by his actions in the hours ahead, he would earn his release from the dreams of the old stone house. He took a deep breath, hesitated, then opened the door and stepped out of the stairwell into the corridor.

About a dozen of the New Race, male and female, stood here and there along the wide hallway. Their attention was focused on the open pair of doors to a laboratory on the right, at the midpoint of the building.

From that room came another plaintive cry, thrashing noises, the shattering of glass.

When Deucalion moved past some of the people standing in the hall, not one seemed to register his presence, so intent were they on the crisis in the laboratory. They stood in various postures of expectation. Some trembled or even shook violently with fear, some muttered angrily, and some appeared to be in the grip of a strange transcendental awe.

Through the open doors of the laboratory, into the corridor came Hell on six legs.

CHAPTER 32

FOR THE MOMENT, cold does not matter.

The transparent polymeric fabric of the imprisoning sack and the glass door of the freezer are for the first time not a torment to Chameleon.

The recently arrived, unusual, very busy, blue, not-a-person something goes back and forth, back and forth through the lab with great energy.

This visitor seems intent on creating a new order. It is an agent of change.

Cabinets topple. Chairs fly. Lab equipment is knocked helter-skelter.

In its pendulous sack of ice-flecked fluid, Chameleon can't hear voices. However, the vibrations of this vigorous reordering are transmitted through walls and floor to the freezer and thus to its occupant.

The lights dim, swell brighter, dim, fade further, but then brighten once more.

The freezer motor stutters and dies. The backup motor does not come online.

Chameleon is alert for the distinct pattern of second-motor vibrations. Nothing. Nothing.

This interesting and energetic visitor draws some people to it, lifts them up, as if in celebration, as if to exalt them, but then casts them down.

They remain where they have fallen, motionless.

Other workers seem to approach the busy visitor of their own volition. They appear almost to embrace it.

These also are lifted up, and then they are cast down. They lie as motionless as the others who were cast down before them.

Perhaps they have prostrated themselves at the feet of the busy visitor.

Or they may be asleep. Or dead.

Interesting.

When all the once-busy workers are motionless, the visitor tears the faucets out of a lab sink and casts them down, making the water gush forth.

The water falls upon the workers, the water falls, yet they do not rise.

And no second-motor vibrations are as yet transmitted to the fluid in the imprisoning sack.

A stillness has come over the sack. The saline solution is without tremors and without hum.

Busy, busy, the visitor uproots the lab sink from its mountings, tosses it aside.

The stainless-steel sink strikes the freezer door, and the glass pane dissolves.

This seems to be an event of great import. What has been is no more. Change has come.

Chameleon has a clearer view than ever before as the visitor departs the laboratory.

What does it all mean?

Chameleon broods on recent events.

CHAPTER 33

THE SIX-LEGGED PANDEMONIUM that entered the corridor from the demolished laboratory loomed as large as three men.

In some of the entity's features, Deucalion could discern the presence of human DNA. The face appeared much like that of a man, though twice as wide and half again as long as the average face. But the head did not rest upon a neck, instead melding directly with the body, much as a frog's head and body were joined.

Throughout the organism, nonhuman genetic material manifested in a multitude of startling ways, as if numerous species were vying for control of the body. Feline, canine, insectile, reptilian, avian, and crustacean influences were apparent in limbs, in misplaced and excess orifices, in tails and stingers, in half-formed faces liable to appear anywhere in the tissue mass.

Nothing about this bizarre organism appeared to be in stasis, but all in continuous change, as if its flesh were clay submitting to the imagination and the facile hands of an invisible—and insane—sculptor. This was the Prince of Chaos, enemy of equilibrium, brother of anarchy, literally seething with disorder, defined by the lack of definition, characterized by distortion and disfigurement, warp and gnarl and misproportion.

Deucalion knew at once what stood before him. Earlier, searching Victor's files on the computer downstairs, he had found his maker's daily diary of important developments. Among the few days he scanned were the two most recent, wherein the sudden metamorphosis of Werner was not merely described but also illustrated with video clips.

Across the surface of the beast, mouths formed and faded, formed again, most of them human in configuration. Some only gnashed their teeth. Some worked their lips and tongues but could not find their voices. Others issued cries like those that brought Deucalion from Victor's main lab two floors below, wordless expressions of sorrow and despair, voices of the lost and hopeless.

These speakers sounded childlike, though everyone in the Hands of Mercy—therefore in this aggregate creature—was an adult. Having escaped their enslavement by surrendering to biological chaos, having dropped their programs in the process of abandoning their physical integrity, they seemed to have regressed psychologically to early childhood, a childhood they had never known, and they were now more helpless than ever.

Among the aggregated individuals, only Werner, whose distorted countenance remained the primary face of this beast, possessed an adult voice. Upon exiting the laboratory, he rolled his protuberant eyes, surveying those who waited in the corridor, and after giving them a moment to consider—perhaps to envy and admire—him, he said, "Be *free*. Be free in me. Abandon hopelessness, all you who enter me. Be free in me. Don't wait to be told when you may kill the Old Race. Be free in me, and we will start the killing tonight. Be free in me, and we will kill *the world*."

A man with a rapturous expression approached the Werner thing, raising his arms as if to embrace freedom, and his liberator at once snatched him up. Insectile puncture-and-pry limbs of wicked design opened the convert's head as if it were a clamshell, and the brain was transferred into the aggregate creature through a thick-lipped moist cleft that opened in the beast's chest to accept the offering.

A second man stepped forward. Although he was one of those shaking with terror, he was ready to commit to a bizarre and possibly tormented life in the aggregated organism rather than endure more life as Victor allowed him to live it.

Deucalion had seen enough, too much. He had been compelled to climb the steps in answer to the eerie cries because he had climbed them for two centuries in dreams. But in his climb, he had indeed brought the past and the present together. The first of Victor's works was here with the last of his works, and the collapse of his demonic empire was under way.

Certain about what he must do next, Deucalion turned from the beast and its offer of freedom. He took one step in the corridor and the next one in the main lab, two floors below.

The end of this empire might not be the end of the threat to civilization that it posed.

To ensure eternal power over his creations, Victor designed the New Race to be infertile. He created females with vaginas but without wombs. When they were the sole version of humanity on Earth, the world would be perpetually without children. Never again would society be organized around the family and its traditions, an Old Race institution that Victor abhorred.

But when their biological structure collapsed, when they remade themselves into something like the aggregate beast or like the pale dwarfish thing that had come out of Detective Harker, perhaps they would rediscover the structures of fertility and efficient methods of reproduction.

Who was to say that this new thing on Earth, this Werner-driven thing, might not at some point reproduce by fission, split into two functioning organisms, as parameciums did?

It might even split into a male and a female. Thereafter, the two might cease to reproduce by fission and resume breeding through some kind of sexual intercourse.

After all, in an infinite universe, anything that could be imagined might somewhere exist.

The fate of the Old Race would be bleak if Victor succeeded in producing an army to undertake a methodical genocide. But that horror might pale by comparison to a future in which humankind was harried and hunted by a multiple-species hybrid able to gain control of its currently chaotic physiology. Such an adversary would be nearly indestructible by virtue of its amorphous nature, full-bore insane by any standard yet intelligent, with an enthusiasm for violence unequaled by any species of natural origin, with a distilled hatred for its prey that would be satanic in its bitterness, intensity, and eternal endurance.

At Victor's workstation, Deucalion settled onto the chair and switched on the computer once more.

Among the many discoveries that he had made earlier, he found that even prideful Victor, whose well of hubris would never run dry, provided for the possibility that something would go so wrong in the Hands of Mercy that the old hospital would have to be reduced to molten slag. An option existed to destroy all evidence of the work done there and to prevent the escape of a rogue organism.

Within the walls on each floor of the building were numerous bricklike packages of a highly incendiary material, developed by a foreign despot with a thing for fire and an affection for Victor. The doomsday countdown could be activated through a program that was on the computer menu under the name DRESDEN.

The program allowed for a countdown as short as ten minutes, as long as four hours, or of any duration in between. Deucalion expected a call momentarily from Michael, revealing a new location for their rendezvous. The Werner thing wouldn't finish acquiring all the staff of Mercy for at least another hour; and even thereafter, the anarchic nature of the beast would ensure that it didn't manage to break out of the hospital on a timely basis. Just in case Deucalion needed to return to Mercy because of something that came up during the meeting with Michael and Carson, he set the countdown clock at one hour.

On the screen appeared the numbers 60:00, and at once they changed to 59:59 as the end of Mercy drew closer second by second.

CHAPTER 34

CHRISTINE, HEAD HOUSEKEEPER at the Helios mansion, was afflicted by a most peculiar condition. For six days, she had been confused about her identity.

Much of the time, she knew perfectly well who and what she was: Christine, a Beta, one of the New Race. She managed the house staff with efficiency, and was number two in authority, after the butler.

But there were moments when she believed she was someone else entirely, when she did not even remember that she was Christine or that she had been manufactured at the Hands of Mercy.

And, as a third condition, there were times when she remembered that she had been living here as Christine, a Beta, housekeeper to Mr. Helios, but *also* remembered the other and more exciting identity into which she now and then entirely submerged.

Being one or the other, she could cope. But when aware of both existences, she became confused and anxious. As she was now.

Only a short while ago, she had been in the staff dormitory, at the back of the property, where she belonged at this hour.

But a few minutes ago, she found herself here in the library, not attending to any chore that was her responsibility, but browsing as though the book collection were hers. Indeed, she thought: *I must find a book that Mrs. Van Hopper might like and send it to her with a warm note. It's not right that I seldom correspond with her. She's a difficult person, yes, but she was also kind to me in her way.*

She felt comfortable in the library, choosing a book for Mrs. Van Hopper, until she realized that she wore a maid's uniform and rubber-soled work shoes. Under no circumstances could this be proper attire for the wife of Maxim de Winter and the mistress of Manderley.

If members of the staff encountered her in this costume, they would think Maxim's predicament had overstressed her. Already, some thought she was too young for him and not of a suitable social class.

Oh, and she would be mortified if Mrs. Danvers discovered her in this outfit, and not merely mortified but finished. Mrs. Danvers would whisper "mental breakdown" to anyone who would listen, and all would listen. Mrs. Danvers, the head housekeeper, remained loyal to the previous Mrs. de Winter and schemed to undermine the new wife's position in the house.

Head housekeeper?

Christine blinked, blinked, surveyed the library, blinked, and realized that *she* was the head housekeeper, not Mrs. Danvers.

And this wasn't Manderley, not a great house in the west country of England, but a big house without a name in the Garden District of New Orleans.

Her identity confusion had begun when the New Race's primary mechanism for the release of stress—urgent, violent, multi-partner sex—ceased to provide her with any relief from her anxiety. Instead, the brutal orgies began to *increase* her anxiety.

The staff dormitory had television, which in theory could distract you from your worries, but the programming produced by the Old Race was so relentlessly stupid that it had little appeal to any member of the New Race above the level of an Epsilon.

In the dormitory, they could also download movies from the Internet. Most were no better than the TV shows, though once in a while you found a gem. The magnificent Hannibal Lecter could bring the entire staff to their feet, cheering till they were hoarse. And his nemesis, FBI agent Clarice Starling, was such an officious little meddling busybody that everyone enjoyed hissing at her.

Nine days ago, desperate for distraction from anxiety and despair, Christine downloaded Alfred Hitchcock's *Rebecca*. The film mesmerized her. Ostensibly, it was a romance, even a love story.

Love was a myth. Even if it wasn't a myth, it was stupid. Love represented the triumph of feeling over intellect. It distracted from achievement. It led to all kinds of social ills, such as family units to which people pledged greater allegiance than to their rulers. Love was a myth and it was evil, love was evil.

The film mesmerized her not because of the romance, but because everyone in the story had deep, dark secrets. The insane Mrs. Danvers had secrets. Maxim de Winter had secrets that might destroy him. Rebecca, the first Mrs. de Winter, kept secrets. The second Mrs. de Winter started out as an idiot goody-goody, but by the end of the movie, she had a dark secret, because she collaborated to conceal a crime, all in the name of—no surprise—love.

Christine related to the movie because, like all of the New Race, she had secrets. Actually she *was* a deep, dark secret, walking among the Old Race, appearing innocent, but waiting impatiently to be told that she could kill as many of them as she wished.

The movie enchanted her also because the first Mrs. de Winter deserved to die, like *all* the Old Race deserved to die. Crazy Mrs. Danvers deserved to die—and burned to death in Manderley. Even the Old Race thought they deserved to die, and they were so *right*.

In spite of the reasons the movie enthralled Christine, it might not have led her into identity confusion if she had not been almost a twin to Joan Fontaine, the actress playing the second Mrs. de Winter. The resemblance was uncanny. Even on the first viewing, Christine at times seemed to be experiencing the story from *inside* the movie.

She watched *Rebecca* five times that first night. And five times the following night. And five times the night after that.

Six days previously, after fifteen viewings, Christine began to experience identity confusion. She immersed herself in the film six times that night.

One thing that was so wonderful about being the second Mrs. de Winter was that by the time Manderley burned to the ground, all the woman's problems were gone. Her life with Maxim would be troubled by no further drama or worry; and ahead were years of cozy routine. . . .

How wonderful. Lovely, peaceful years. Tea every afternoon with little sandwiches and biscuits . . .

Manderley would be lost, and that was sad, but knowing that all would be well eventually, she should enjoy Manderley now as much as possible with Mrs. Danvers always scheming.

She selected a suitable volume for Mrs. Van Hopper, *Jamaica Inn,* which seemed to be a work of fiction, a light entertainment.

In a library-desk drawer, she found a selection of stationery for a variety of special occasions. She chose a cream-colored linen paper with a nosegay of colorful ribbons at the top.

She wrote a lovely note to Mrs. Van Hopper, signed it "Mrs. Maxim de Winter," inserted it in a matching envelope, sealed the flap, and put the envelope with *Jamaica Inn*. She would ask Christine to wrap and mail the package first thing in the morning.

CHAPTER 35

AT THIS HOUR, only a battered Mustang, a pristine but forty-year-old Mercedes, and a Ford Explorer occupied the fourth floor of the public parking garage.

Carson let the Honda idle beside each vehicle, while Michael got out to determine if anyone might be sleeping in it. No, no, and no. They had the fourth floor to themselves.

Through the open sides of the building, a growing wind flung glassy beads of rain to shatter on the concrete floor. Carson parked the Honda in an empty row in the dry center of the garage.

Let out of the car, Duke trotted around the immediate area, investigating a discarded candy wrapper, a half-crushed Starbucks cup, an empty Big Mac container. . . .

They left the Urban Snipers in the Honda. They still had their service pistols in shoulder rigs, the .50 Magnums in belt scabbards.

As Michael fished his phone out of a coat pocket and keyed in Deucalion's number, Carson watched for movement among the forest of concrete columns, listened for footsteps. She recognized the danger of prudence sliding into paranoia; nevertheless, she stood with her right arm across her body, thumb hooked on her belt, which brought her gun hand within inches of the Desert Eagle under her blazer, on her left hip.

For anyone drawn into an orbit around Victor Helios, the word *impossible* no longer had any meaning. So maybe in his spare time, the Transylvanian transplant scored some pterodactyl DNA, combined it with a sociopathic homeboy's genes, and cooked up a man-reptile cop killer that would swoop in from the storm. Chances were she wasn't going to die from a heart attack or from anything else that would leave a neat corpse, but she was for damn sure not going to be torn apart in the jaws of a gangbanger-dragon hybrid wearing a do-rag and a gold nose ring.

Deucalion must have taken the call, because Michael said, "Hey, it's me. We're in a parking garage. Fourth floor."

After giving the address, Michael hung up.

As the phone produced an end-call beep, Deucalion stepped into the garage about twenty feet away, as though he'd come out of Narnia through a wardrobe, except there wasn't even a wardrobe.

Carson always forgot how big he was until she saw him again. In his long black coat, as he approached them, he looked like Darth Vader on a steroids-only diet.

"You're wet," Deucalion said.

"We were in a monster mash at Audubon Park," Michael said. "One of them had a nice butt."

Duke padded around the car, saw the tattooed newcomer, halted, and cocked his head.

"Whose dog?" Deucalion asked.

"He belonged to the district attorney," Michael said, "then to the district attorney's replicant, but the replicant walked smack into a bunch of shotgun slugs, so now Duke belongs to us."

"Things are going to get apocalyptic soon," Deucalion said. "A dog will get in your way."

"Not this dog. He's one of those highly trained service dogs. When we switch from shotguns to .50 Magnums, he can reload the empty weapons for us."

To Carson, Deucalion said, "I'm never sure I understand half the things he says."

"Eventually you don't care," Carson assured him. "Michael has hyperactive disorder, but he talks fast enough to keep himself entertained, so he's not a lot of trouble."

Duke approached Deucalion, tail wagging.

Holding one of his hands down to allow the dog to lick his fingers, Deucalion stared so intently at Carson that she felt X-rayed, and then he turned the same stare on Michael.

"It was not an accident that I crossed your path rather than that of other detectives. You're different from most who carry a badge, and I am different from everyone. Our difference is our strength. We have been chosen for this, and if we fail—the world fails."

Michael grimaced. "That wouldn't look good on my résumé."

"Earlier, at the Luxe," Carson said, referring to the just shuttered movie theater where Deucalion lived, "you said Victor has progressed doggedly for so long, in spite of his setbacks, he has no fear of failure, he believes his triumph is inevitable. So he's blind to the rot in his empire. At the time, I thought the rot might not be as extensive as you hoped. But after our lark in the park with those replicants . . . maybe collapse is coming even sooner than you think."

Pulses of inner light passed through the giant's eyes. "Yes. The clock is ticking."

After listening to Deucalion's one-minute abridged version of his discoveries in the Hands of Mercy, Carson was left with stomach acid burning in the back of her throat and a clutching chill in the pit of her stomach.

"When does the place melt down?" Michael asked.

"In fifty-five minutes. When Victor hears about the fire, he'll know I did it, but he won't know how out of control things were in there tonight. He'll continue to trust his New Race to defend him. But he won't risk staying in the Garden District. He'll fall back to the farm."

Carson said, "The creation-tank farm, the New Race factory Pastor Kenny told you about?"

"As I learned tonight, it's farther along than Kenny thought. The first crop begins rising from the tanks tomorrow night—five hundred a day for four days."

Michael said, "We *way* underestimated our ammo needs."

"Victor owns large tracts of land north of Lake Pontchartrain." From an inside coat pocket, Deucalion withdrew a packet of papers. "I retrieved the information from his computer. There's a place called Crosswoods Waste Management, owned by a Nevada corporation, which is owned by a holding company in the Bahamas, which is held by a trust in Switzerland. But in the end, it's all just Victor."

"Waste management?" Carson said. "Is that a dump?"

"It is a very large dump."

"What would he want with a dump?"

"A graveyard for his failures and for the people his replicants replace."

Michael said, "It must have a more memorable smell than your average dump."

"The tank farm is on a twenty-acre property adjacent to the dump. We're going to be there well ahead of Victor. In fact, I will be there in ten minutes." Deucalion handed the packet of papers to Carson. "Addresses, background, a little reading for the road. If you take Interstate 10 east to Interstate 12 west, then the state route north as I've marked, it's about seventy miles, less than an hour and a half."

"A lot less if she's driving," Michael said.

"When you're getting near, call me," Deucalion said. "We'll join forces there."

"And then what?" Carson asked.

"And then . . . whatever's necessary."

CHAPTER 36

ERIKA FIVE LOADED a stainless-steel cart with everything Jocko needed, and took it to the second floor in the service elevator.

After Victor had joined the original two residences, there were three hallways. At the south end of the house, the south-wing hall ran east-west. At the north end, the hall also ran east-west. Each measured eighty feet. Those corridors were connected by the main hall, which extended 182 feet.

In the south wing, the service elevator was not far from the kitchen. Once upstairs, Erika had to push the cart the length of the main hall to the north wing, where the troll waited in his new quarters toward the back of the house.

The double doors to the master suite were at the midpoint of the main hall, on the left, opposite the head of the grand staircase. She thought Victor remained in the suite, but she couldn't be sure. If by chance he stepped into the hall and saw her pushing the cart stacked with bedding, towels, toiletries, and food, he would want to know where she was going and to what purpose.

The nine-foot-wide hallway featured a series of Persian rugs, as in the north and south halls, and the cart rolled silently across them. Where mahogany flooring lay exposed between rugs, the rubber wheels made only a faint noise.

When, with relief, Erika entered the unfurnished north-wing suite, the troll was standing on the points of his toes, pirouetting.

She rolled the cart into the living room. Closing the door to the hall, she said, "Where did you learn to dance?"

"Is Jocko dancing?" he asked, continuing to spin.

"That's ballet."

"It's just . . . a thing . . . Jocko does," he said, and pirouetted into the bedroom.

Following with the cart, Erika said, "Don't you get very dizzy?"

"Sometimes . . . Jocko vomits."

"Well then, you better stop."

"No control."

Putting the bedding on the floor, in a corner, Erika said, "You mean you're compelled to pirouette?"

The troll spun to a stop, came off pointe, and weaved a few steps before regaining his equilibrium. "Not so bad that time."

"You poor thing."

He shrugged. "Everybody's got problems."

"That's very philosophical."

"Most worse than mine."

Erika was pretty sure there weren't many fates worse than being a grotesque troll with three hairs on your tongue, penniless, living mostly in storm drains, with a compulsion to spin until you threw up. But she admired the little guy's positive attitude.

In the bathroom, Jocko helped her unload the cart and distribute the items to cabinets and drawers. He was delighted with the supply of snack foods that she had brought.

"Jocko likes salty, Jocko likes sweet, but never bring Jocko any hot sauce, like with jalapeños, because it makes Jocko squirt funny-smelling stuff out his ears."

"I'll be sure to remember that," Erika said. "Of course, I'll bring you healthy meals whenever I can, not just snack foods. Is there anything you don't like besides hot sauce?"

"Jocko's been living mostly in storm drains, eating bugs and rats. And hot sauce on corn chips that one time. Anything you bring is delicious enough for Jocko."

"This is very exciting, isn't it?" Erika said.

"What is?"

"Having a secret friend."

"Who does?"

"I do."

"What friend?"

"You."

"Oh. Yes. Jocko is excited."

Putting away the last of the towels, she said, "I'll be back in the morning, in just a few hours, after Victor has gone to the Hands of Mercy, and then you can read to me."

Sitting on the edge of the tub, Jocko asked, "Is this good to eat?"

"No, that's bath soap."

"Oh. Is this good to eat?"

"That's another bath soap."

"So it's good to eat?"

"No. Soap is never good to eat."

"Is this good to eat?"

"That's also bath soap. It's a four-pack."

"Why soap, soap, soap, soap?"

"I brought extras of several things. You're going to be here awhile. . . . Aren't you?"

"As long as you say Jocko can."

"Good. That's very good."

"Now go away," said Jocko.

"Oh, of course, you must be tired."

"Must be," he agreed, following her into the living room. "Go away."

Erika left the stainless-steel cart, intending to return it to the kitchen in the morning, after Victor went to the lab.

Cracking the door, she scoped the hallway, which was deserted and quiet. Glancing back at the troll, she said, "Don't be afraid."

"You either."

"You're safe."

"You too."

"Just lie low."

"Go away."

Stepping into the hall, Erika quietly pulled the door shut behind her.

CHAPTER 37

THE INSTANT THE DOOR CLOSED, Jocko scampered into the bathroom. Snatched up a bar of soap. Tore the wrapper off. Took a bite.

Erika was wrong. Soap looked delicious, and it *was*.

She was wrong or . . . *she lied*.

How sad she would lie. She seemed so different from others. So pretty. So kind. Such delicate nostrils. But a liar.

Almost everybody lied. The world was a kingdom of lies.

Jocko lied, too. Told her he was Harker.

True, he came out of Harker. All Harker's knowledge. Harker's memories. But he wasn't Harker.

Jocko was Jocko, unique. Jocko wanted what Jocko wanted. Not what anybody else wanted.

Only one way Jocko and Harker were alike. Hated Victor Helios. *Hated* him.

One thing Jocko wanted, Harker had wanted. Victor Helios dead.

Jocko was Jocko. But he was also *vengeance*.

Soap tasted better than rats. Almost as good as bugs. But so chewy. Not easy to swallow.

Jocko put down the half-eaten bar. Didn't have time for so much chewing. Later.

Jocko wanted what Jocko wanted. Wanted it so bad. But couldn't have what he wanted until he killed Victor Helios.

He dashed into the living room. Stood on his hands. Walked around the room on his hands. Around and around.

Such a waste of time. Jocko didn't want to walk around on his hands. But he just *had* to.

Finally, enough. On his feet again. To the bathroom again. One more bite of soap. Good.

Time to kill Victor.

Quick, quick, quick through the bedroom. Through the living room. To the door.

AS SHE TURNED away from the door to Jocko's quarters, Erika knew that she should go to the master suite to see if Victor wanted her for any reason.

However, the prospect of her secret friend reading to her from a book so excited her that she didn't want to wait until morning to select the volume for their initial session. She descended the back stairs at the west end of the north wing, eager to explore what titles the library offered.

The grand hall on the ground floor measured twelve feet across, a third more spacious than the upstairs hallways. It was furnished with sideboards, pairs of chairs separated by tables on which stood bowls of flowers, and pedestals supporting magnificent figurative bronzes. The walls were hung with priceless works by the European masters of the sixteenth, seventeenth, and eighteenth centuries, which Victor had been clever enough to smuggle out of Germany shortly before his patron and dear friend, the much-misunderstood and delightfully witty Hitler, whom Victor called *mein schatz,* "my treasure," was tragically brought to grief by the ignorant masses, by greedy capitalists, by voracious bankers, and by religious fanatics.

Victor suffered so much frustration and loss in his long life that Erika, who had been given everything from birth, might need twenty years, thirty, or longer to understand him. The problem was, thus far the Erikas tended to be short-lived.

Her best hope of understanding her husband, of learning how to be the kind of wife who never triggered his rage, seemed to be books. Books were dangerous, yes, but they were dangerous because they contained so much knowledge both of the helpful kind and the harmful kind. Perhaps Erika Four absorbed too much of the wrong information, things that would never be included in an education acquired by direct-to-brain data downloading, and was thereby corrupted. Erika Five intended to proceed cautiously with books, always alert for the harmful kind of knowledge.

She enjoyed an advantage over Erika Four: She had Jocko. She would instruct him to be always on the lookout for knowledge that was harmful in any way, to censor it as he read, so that she wouldn't be contaminated by it. If a book contained too much harmful information to remain comprehensible when all of the bad stuff had been redacted, she would return it to the shelves and choose another.

Entering the library, Erika saw Christine getting up from the desk, holding a book and an envelope. She should have been in the staff dormitory.

"Why are you here at this hour?" Erika asked.

"Oh, goodness, you startled me." Christine pushed the desk chair into the kneehole. "I've been selecting a book to send to a friend, and writing her a warm note of remembrance, with apologies for having been frightfully behind in my correspondence."

Christine seemed to be speaking with a slight English accent.

"But these books don't belong to you," Erika reminded her.

Straightening her shoulders and lifting her head in what might have been defiance, Christine said, "I should think any books that belong to my husband also belong to me."

"Your husband?" Erika said.

"Yes, Mrs. Danvers, quite mine. Rebecca is gone. I rather think you should get used to that."

Erika didn't need to learn anything from a book to know that Christine was suffering what Victor referred to as an interruption of function. The previous morning, the butler, William, had bitten off seven of his fingers during an interruption of function. For the moment, at least, Christine's condition wasn't as serious as William's.

Approaching the maid, Erika reached out for the book. "I'll take care of that for you."

Pressing the volume and the letter to her bosom, Christine said, "No thank you, Mrs. Danvers. In the morning, I shall ask Christine to package and post it."

IN A SUPERBLY TAILORED BLUE SUIT, white silk shirt with spread collar, and sapphire-amber-emerald striped tie, with an amber display handkerchief, carrying the Springfield Armory Colt .45 in a concealed shoulder rig that did not interfere at all with the elegant drape of the coat, Victor studied his reflection, and the mirror presented to him a man who had the style and the bearing of a sovereign born to the throne.

Because there were mirrors also at the Hands of Mercy, he left the closet. As he crossed the bedroom, his cell phone rang.

He stopped at the door to the hall and, after a hesitation, took the call. "Yes?"

"My esteemed master, my glorious brute," said Erika Four, "we have prepared a resting place for you at the dump."

He was resolved not to lose his temper and determined not to let her dominate as she had in her previous call. "I thought you were coming home."

"We have lined your grave with the rotting cadavers of some of your Old Race victims, and with the remains of those of your people who failed you and could not be resuscitated as I was."

"Perhaps," he said, "you have the courage to call but not the courage to face me."

"Oh, darling, sublime megalomaniac, you are the emperor of self-delusion. I will face you soon enough. I will smile at you and blow a kiss as we bury you alive in the depths of the dump."

Victor happened to be looking at the doorknob when it began to turn. He drew the .45 from his shoulder rig.

QUICK, QUICK, QUICK, Jocko scurried east along the north hall. Stopped at the corner. Peeked around. Nobody in sight.

A bite of soap would be nice. Stay focused. Kill first. Soap later.

He knew where to find the master bedroom. Erika mentioned it when sneaking him up the back stairs. Main hall. Opposite the grand staircase.

Tippytoe, tippytoe, across soft rugs. Pretty rugs. Would be fun to twirl on rugs so soft and pretty.

No! Don't think about twirling. Don't even *think* about it.

Grand staircase to the left. Double doors to the right. This was the place.

Standing at the doors, hand on a doorknob, Jocko heard a muffled voice. Harker's memory said, *Victor's voice.* Just beyond these doors.

"Perhaps you have the courage to call but not the courage to face me," Victor Helios said.

A murderous fury gripped Jocko. As he tried to bare his teeth, the flaps of his mouth quivered against them.

Jocko knew what he would say. As he attacked Victor. Ferocious. Merciless. He would say, *I am the child of Jonathan Harker! He died to birth me! I am an outcast, a monster from a monster! Now you die!*

That seemed like a mouthful. He had tried to edit it. But he really, really wanted to say it all.

He started to turn the doorknob. Almost threw the door open. Then realized. No weapon. Jocko didn't have a weapon.

Furious with himself, Jocko let the knob slip through his hand and, after all, did not burst into the master suite.

Stupid, stupid, stupid. He hooked two fingers in his nostrils. He pulled back toward his forehead. Pulled so hard tears streamed from his eyes. He deserved it.

Focus. *Stay* focused.

He needed a weapon. Knew where to get one. Kitchen. A knife.

Tippytoe, tippytoe, quick along the main hall. More soft rugs. To the south hall. Down the back stairs.

IN THE LIBRARY, Erika said, "My name isn't Mrs. Danvers."

Christine still spoke with a light English accent. "Please, Mrs. Danvers, I quite want to avoid unpleasantness of any kind. We can co-exist. I am confident we can, and we should. I know *I* want to, for Maxim's sake."

"Don't you recognize me?" Erika asked. "What is wrong with you? Don't you know where you are?"

Christine looked distressed, and her mouth trembled as if she might become emotional in a way precluded by her program. Clutching the book, regaining her composure, she said, "I am not as fragile a spirit as I might look, Mrs. Danvers."

"Erika. I'm Erika."

"Do not think you can convince me that my mind is going. I am weary of your wicked games." She pushed past Erika and left the room in a rush.

SNEAK, PAUSE, RECONNOITER. Sneak, pause, reconnoiter. Stairs to hall to kitchen.

Oh. On a counter in the kitchen was a large bowl of apples. Yellow apples. Red apples.

The apples drew Jocko. So colorful. Not too big. He wanted them. Had to have them. *Had* to have. Apples, apples, apples. Not to eat. Something better.

Jocko selected three apples. Two yellow, one red.

Beginning with two apples in his right hand, one in his left, he juggled. Loved to juggle. *Needed* to juggle.

He had juggled before. Stones. Walnuts. Two spoiled lemons and a package of rancid cheese. Three rat skulls.

Apples were the best yet. Colorful. Almost round. Jocko was good. He could even caper while juggling.

He capered around the kitchen. Juggling, juggling. He wished he had a funny hat. One with bells.

ON THE PHONE, Erika Four said, "There is a legion in the dump, my darling psychopath. I need not come for you alone."

"Only a legion of the dead," Victor said. "And the dead don't rise again."

"Like me, they were not fully dead. Mistaken for dead, but with a trace of life remaining . . . and after a while, more than a trace."

The doorknob had turned one way, then the other. For almost a minute now, it had not moved.

"We will carry you by torchlight down into the bowels of the dump. And though we'll bury you alive, we'll have our fun with you before interment."

The knob turned again.

FROM THE LIBRARY, she hurried directly to the front stairs and ascended to the second floor. Enough was enough. Maxim would have to speak with Mrs. Danvers. The woman's loyalty to Rebecca exceeded that of a faithful servant, was nothing as innocent as honest sentiment. It was mean, perverse, and suggested an unbalanced mind.

She threw open the door, swept into the master suite, and was shot four times in the chest by her beloved Maxim, whose treachery stunned her, though as she fell, she realized that he must have shot Rebecca, too.

JOCKO, CAPERING IN THE KITCHEN, dropped the apples when the gunfire boomed.

Knife. He had forgotten the knife. Victor waited to be killed, and Jocko forgot the knife.

He hit himself in the face. Hit, hit, hit himself. He deserved to be smacked twice as often as he was. Three times.

One drawer, two drawers, three . . . In the fifth drawer, knives. He selected a big one. Very sharp.

Tippytoe, tippytoe, out of the kitchen, into the hall.

CHAPTER 38

DUKE SLEPT in the backseat of the Honda during the drive east-northeast on I-10 and then west on I-12.

The dog's snoring didn't induce drowsiness in Carson, though it ought to have, considering how little sack time she'd grabbed in the past couple of days.

The half liter of supercaffeinated cola from Acadiana helped. Before crossing the city line, they stopped at a combination service station and convenience store that was open 24/7, where they drained themselves of some of the first cola they had consumed, and then bought two more half-liter bottles. They also bought a package of caffeine tablets.

As they hit the road again, Michael said, "Too much caffeine ties the prostate in knots."

"I don't have a prostate."

"Carson, you know, everything isn't always about you."

One thing keeping her awake and focused was the suspicion that the Helios-Frankenstein case might be as much about her as it was about anyone. Not merely because she happened to be one of the two detectives who stumbled on the case. And not because her path crossed Deucalion's just when she needed to meet him.

Of all the cops Carson knew, she and Michael had the deepest respect for individualism, especially when a particular individual was quirky and therefore amusing or even if he proved stubborn and frustrating. Consequently, they were more alarmed than some might have been by the prospect of a civilization with a single-minded purpose and a regimented population of obedient drones, whether that population was comprised of propagandized human beings or of pseudohumans cultured in a lab.

But her respect for individualism and her love of freedom was not why this case was so powerfully, immediately, intimately about *her*. Early in this investigation, she began to suspect that her father, who had been a detective with the NOPD, might have been murdered by the New Race—and her mother with him—at the order of Victor Helios. Her dad could have encountered something exceedingly strange that had led him to Helios, just as his daughter would be led to the same suspect years later.

Her parents' murders had never been solved. And the evidence concocted to portray her father as a corrupt cop—who might have been executed by criminal elements with which he was involved—had always been too pat, an insult to common sense, and an offense against the truth of her dad's character.

Over the past few days, her suspicion developed into conviction. As much as the caffeine, a hunger for justice and a determination to clear her father's name kept her awake, alert, and ready to rumble.

The vast lightless expanse of Pontchartrain lay to their left, and it seemed to have the irresistible gravity of a collapsed star, as if this night the world were rolling along its rim, at risk of spiraling down into oblivion.

Except in the headlights, the rain that came off the lake was black, insistently rapping against the driver's side of the car as they drove west on I-12, as if the night itself had fists of bony knuckles. And the wind seemed black, blowing down out of a moonless and starless sky.

CHAPTER 39

HAVING BELIEVED that Erika Four was bursting in upon him, Victor fired twice, intending to stop both of her hearts, before he realized that the intruder was Christine. As the designer of her kind, he knew precisely where to aim. And because he started the job with such expert marksmanship, he had no choice but to finish it with two more shots.

Christine dropped, although death did not at once take her. She spasmed on the floor of the master-bedroom vestibule, gasping for breath, futilely pressing her hands to her chest as if she might be able to plug the wounds from which her life bled.

During Christine's final throes, Erika appeared in the hall, just beyond the open door, and Victor raised the pistol from the dying housekeeper, to train it on whichever of his Erikas stood before him.

"Something was wrong with Christine," she said. "She didn't seem to know who she was. She thought I was someone named Mrs. Danvers."

"Do *you* know who you are?" Victor asked.

She frowned at the muzzle of the pistol and at the question. "What do you mean?"

"*Who are you!*" Victor demanded with such vehemence that she flinched, as if reminded of the intensity with which he could deliver a beating when she deserved one.

"I'm Erika. Your wife."

"Erika Five?"

She looked puzzled. "Yes, of course."

"Then tell me—what is the most dangerous thing in the world?"

"Books," she said at once. "Books corrupt."

Erika Four had been allowed to read, which led to her death. Only

Erika Five was created with a proscription against reading books. A resurrected Erika Four could have no way of knowing this.

On the floor, Christine said, "Manderley . . ." and her eyes glazed over.

She appeared to have died. Victor kicked her head, testing her response, but she didn't twitch or make a sound.

Beside her on the floor was a book titled *Jamaica Inn*.

Returning the pistol to his shoulder holster, Victor said, "What was the word she just spoke?"

"Manderley," said Erika.

"What language is it, what does it mean?"

Surprised, she said, "It's the name of a great English house, a literary allusion. I've got it in my program. Like, I might say to someone we visited, 'Oh, my dear, your house is even more wonderful than Manderley *and* your housekeeper isn't insane.'"

"Yes, all right, but to what work does it refer?"

"Daphne du Maurier's *Rebecca*," Erika said, "which I have never read and never will."

"Books again," he fumed, and in anger this time, he kicked the dead housekeeper, and then the book that had fallen from her hand. "I'll send a team to bring this trash to the Hands of Mercy for an autopsy. Clean up the blood yourself."

"Yes, Victor."

SKIP, SKIP, HOP. Skip, skip, hop. Along the south hall. Skip, skip, hop. Knife in hand.

The back stairs. Three steps up, one step back. Three steps up, one step back.

Racing, in his fashion, toward vengeance, Jocko reminded himself of the speech he must make. As he drove the blade deep into Victor, he must say: *I am the child of he who I was before I was me! I died to birth me! I am a monster, outcast and castaway! Die, Harker, die!*

No. All wrong. So much practice in so many storm drains. And still Jocko didn't have it right.

Climbing twice as many stairs as he descended, Jocko tried again: *You are the monster child of he who I!*

No, no, no. Not even close.

I am you he who I am who die!

Jocko was so angry with himself that he wanted to spit. He *did* spit. And he spat again. On his feet. Two steps up, one step back, spit. Two steps up, one step back, spit.

Finally he reached the top step, feet glistening.

In the second-floor south hall, Jocko stopped to collect his thoughts. There was one. And here was another. And here was a third thought, connected to the other two. Very nice.

Jocko often had to collect his thoughts. They scattered so easily.

I am the child of Jonathan Harker! He died to birth me! I am a juggler, monsters and apples! Now you die!

Close enough.

Tippytoe, tippytoe, east along the south hall, across soft rugs. Toward the main corridor.

Jocko heard voices. In his head? Could be. Had been before. No, no, not this time. Real voices. In the main hallway.

The corner. Careful. Jocko halted, peeked around.

Erika stood in the hallway, at the open master-suite doors. Talking to someone inside, probably Victor.

So pretty. Such shimmering hair. She had lips. Jocko wished he had lips, too.

"It's the name of a great English house, a literary allusion," Erika said to probably Victor.

Her voice soothed Jocko. Her voice was music.

As a calmness came over Jocko, he realized that he was different when in her company. With her, he didn't feel compelled to do so much skipping, hopping, spitting, pirouetting, juggling, capering, nostril pulling, scampering, and walking on his hands.

She lied to Jocko. Lied about the tastiness of soap. Otherwise, however, she was a positive influence.

Eighty or ninety feet away, Victor Helios appeared. Out of the master suite. Tall. Trim. Excellent hair on his head, probably none on his tongue. Pretty suit.

Jocko thought: *Die, juggler, die!*

Victor walked past Erika. To the stairs. Said one last thing to her. Started down.

Jocko had the knife. The knife belonged in Victor.

A *thousand* knives belonged in Victor.

Jocko only had two hands. Could juggle three knives with two hands, put them in Victor. Trying to juggle a thousand knives, Jocko would probably lose some fingers.

To reach Victor with one pathetic knife, Jocko must run past Erika. That would be awkward.

She would see him. Would know he broke his promise. More than one promise. Would know he lied. Would be disappointed in him.

And she might smell soap on his breath.

Erika moved to the stairs. Watched Victor descend.

Maybe she saw Jocko. From the corner of her eye. She started to turn. Turn toward Jocko.

Jocko ducked back. Away from the corner.

Hoppity-hoppity-hop. Hoppity-hoppity-hop. West along the south hall. Backward down the stairs.

Kitchen again. Apples on the floor. Oranges would be even more round. Jocko must ask for oranges. And scissors to trim his tongue hairs.

Jocko capered out of the kitchen, through a butler's pantry, across an intimate dining room.

Beyond was a large, formal dining room. Jocko didn't see it too clearly because he had to, had to, *had to pirouette.*

Room after room, small connecting halls, so much house. Walking on his hands, knife gripped in one foot. Cartwheeling, cartwheeling, knife in his teeth.

North hall. Back stairs. Second floor. His suite.

Jocko hid the knife in his bedding. He scampered back into the living room. Sat on the floor in front of the fireplace. Enjoying the fireplace without fire.

She would say: *I thought I saw you in the hall.*

He would say: *No, not Jocko, not Jocko. No, no, no. Not I who am from he who was, monster from monster, no, not Jocko, not in the hall and not eating soap.*

Or maybe he would just say *No.*

Jocko would play it by ear. See what seemed right at the time.

After gazing at no fire for half a minute, Jocko realized he had forgotten to kill Victor.

Jocko hooked fingers in his nostrils and pulled them toward his brow until his eyes watered. He deserved worse.

CHAPTER 40

FOLLOWING THE FAILURE of the freezer motors, the saline solution in the transparent sack begins to warm.

After the busy visitor in the laboratory throws the sink that smashes the glass door, the pace of the warming accelerates.

The first improvement in Chameleon's condition concerns its vision. In the cold environment, it sees only shades of blue. Now it begins to apprehend other colors, gradually at first, and then more rapidly.

For so long, Chameleon has drifted in the sack, mobility limited by the bitter cold of the fluid in which it is immersed. Now it is able to flex its abdomen and thorax. Its head turns more easily.

Suddenly it thrashes, thrashes again, a great commotion that causes the hanging sack to swing side to side and bump against the walls of the disabled freezer.

In semisuspended animation, Chameleon's metabolism performs at a basal rate so low as to be almost undetectable. As the fluid in the sack warms, the catabolic processes increase.

With the energy provided by catabolism, anabolic processes begin to speed up. Chameleon is returning to full function.

The thrashing signifies a need for air. The highly oxygenated solution in the sack maintains Chameleon in subfreezing cold, but is inadequate to sustain it at full metabolic function.

Suffocation panic triggers Chameleon's thrashing.

Although the polymeric fabric of the sack is as strong as bulletproof Kevlar, Chameleon's combat claws rip it open.

Fourteen gallons of chemically treated saline solution gush out of the sack, spilling Chameleon into the freezer, through the missing door, and onto the floor of the laboratory.

Air flows into its spiracles and follows the tracheal tubes that branch throughout its body.

As it dries out, Chameleon regains its sense of smell.

It is able to detect only two odors: a specially engineered pheromone with which all of the New Race are tagged, and human beings of the Old Race, who are identifiable by a melange of pheromones *lacking* that New Race spice.

The smell of the New Race pleases Chameleon, and therefore they are EXEMPTS.

Because the Old Race lacks the artificial pheromone, their scent infuriates Chameleon, and they are TARGETS.

Chameleon lives to kill.

At the moment, it smells only EXEMPTS. And even all of them seem to be dead, sprawled throughout the room.

It crawls across the debris-strewn floor of the wrecked lab, through pools of water, seeking prey.

Every external tissue of Chameleon mimics to the smallest detail the surface under it: color, pattern, texture. No matter how simple or complex the ground under it, Chameleon will blend with it.

To any observer looking down on it, Chameleon is invisible when not in motion.

If Chameleon moves, the observer may sense something amiss, but he will not understand what his eyes perceive: a vague shifting of a part of the floor, an impossible rippling of a solid surface, as if the wood or stone, or the lawn, has become fluid.

Most of the time, the observer will interpret this phenomenon not as a real event but as disturbing evidence of a problem internal to himself: dizziness or hallucination, or the first symptom of an oncoming stroke.

Often, the observer will close his eyes for a moment, to settle his disturbed senses. Closing his eyes is the end of him.

If Chameleon is on a higher plane than the floor, perhaps a kitchen countertop, it will remain invisible from the side only if the backsplash is of the same material as the surface on which it stands. Otherwise, it will be visible as a silhouette.

For this reason, Chameleon generally remains low as it stalks its prey. A TARGET becomes aware of his attacker only when it skitters up his leg, ripping as it goes.

The wrecked lab offers no TARGETS.

Chameleon proceeds into the hallway. Here it discovers numerous EXEMPTS, all dead.

Taking more time to consider these cadavers than it did those in the lab, Chameleon discovers heads split open, brains missing.

Interesting.

This is not how Chameleon does its work. Effective, however.

Among the debrained EXEMPTS, Chameleon detects a whiff of a TARGET. One of the Old Race has been here recently.

Chameleon follows the scent to the stairs.

CHAPTER 41

RAIN HAD NOT YET REACHED the parishes above Lake Pontchartrain. The humid night lay unbreathing but expectant, as if the low overcast and the dark land had compressed the air between them until at any moment an electric discharge would shock the heart of the storm into a thunderous beating.

Deucalion stood on a deserted two-lane road, outside Crosswoods Waste Management. The facility was enormous. A high chain-link fence was topped with coils of barbed wire and fitted with continuous nylon privacy panels. RESTRICTED AREA signs every forty feet warned of the health hazards of a landfill.

Outside the fence, a triple phalanx of loblolly pines encircled the property, the rows offset from one another. Between ninety and a hundred feet tall, these trees formed an effective screen, blocking views into the dump from the somewhat higher slopes to the north and east.

Deucalion walked off the road, among the pines, and went through the fence by way of a gate that didn't exist—a quantum gate—into the dump.

He had night vision better than that of the Old Race, even better than that of the New. His enhanced eyesight, not the work of Victor, was perhaps another gift delivered on the lightning that had animated him, the ghost of which still sometimes throbbed through his gray eyes.

He walked a rampart of compacted earth, a span more than wide enough to accommodate an SUV. To both his left and right, well below the level of this elevated pathway, were huge lakes of trash heaped in uneven swells that would eventually be plowed level before being capped with eight feet of earth and methane-gas vent pipes.

The stench offended, but he had encountered worse in the past two hundred years. In his first two decades, after leaving Victor for dead in the arctic, Deucalion frequently had been seized by the urge to violence, raging at the injustice of having been stitched together and animated by a narcissistic would-be god who could give his creation neither meaning nor peace, nor any hope of fellowship and community. In his most haunted and self-pitying hours, Deucalion prowled graveyards and broke into granite crypts, mausoleums, where he tore open caskets and forced himself to gaze upon the decomposing corpses, saying aloud to himself, "Here is what you are, just dead flesh, dead flesh, the bones and guts of arsonists, of murderers, filled with false life, dead and alive, not fit for any other world but an abomination in this one." Standing at those open caskets, he'd known stenches that, by comparison, made this Louisiana dump smell as sweet as a rose garden.

In those graveyard visits, during those long staring matches with sightless cadavers, he had yearned to die. Although he tried, he was unable to submit to a well-stropped razor or to a hangman's noose that he fashioned, and at every cliff's edge, he could not take the final step. So in those long nights when he kept company with the dead, he argued with himself to embrace the necessity for self-destruction.

The proscription against suicide had not come from Victor.

In his earliest strivings for godhood, that vainglorious beast wasn't able to program his first creation as well as he programmed those he brewed up these days. Victor had planted a device in Deucalion's skull, which had cratered half the giant's face when he tried to strike his maker. But Victor had not in those days been able to forbid suicide.

After years marked by a frustrated death wish as much as by rage, Deucalion had arrived at a humbling realization. The edict that so effectively stayed his hand from destroying himself came from a more powerful and infinitely more mysterious source than Victor. He was denied felo-de-se because he had a purpose in life, even if he could not—at that time—recognize what it might be, a vital mission that he must fulfill before final peace would be granted him.

Two hundred years had at last brought him to Louisiana, to this reeking wasteyard that was a trash dump *and* a graveyard. The pending storm would be not merely one of thunder, lightning, wind, and rain, but also one of justice, judgment, execution, and damnation.

To his left, far out in the west pit, flames flickered. A dozen small fires moved one behind the other, as if they were torches held by people in a procession.

CHAPTER 42

ERIKA STOOD over the body of Christine for a minute, trying to understand why Victor had shot her to death.

Although Christine seemed to have become convinced that she was someone other than herself, she had not been threatening. Quite the opposite: She had been confused and distraught, and in spite of her contention that she was not "as fragile a spirit" as she might look, she had the air of a shy, uncertain girl not yet a woman.

Yet Victor shot her four times in her two hearts. And kicked her head twice, after she was dead.

Instead of wrapping the body for whoever would collect it and at once cleaning up the blood as instructed, Christine surprised herself by returning to the troll's quarters in the north wing. She knocked softly and said sotto voce, *"It's me, Erika,"* because she didn't want to disturb the little guy if he was sitting in a corner, sucking on his toes, his mind having gone away to the red place to rest.

With a discretion that matched hers, he said, *"Come in,"* just loud enough for her to hear him when she pressed her ear to the door.

In the living room, she found him sitting on the floor in front of the dark fireplace, as if flames warmed the hearth.

Sitting beside him, she said, "Did you hear the gunshots?"

"No. Jocko heard nothing."

"I thought you must have heard them and might be frightened."

"No. And Jocko wasn't juggling apples, either. Not Jocko. Not here in his rooms."

"Apples? I didn't bring you apples."

"You are very kind to Jocko."

"Would you like some apples?"

"Three oranges would be better."

"I'll bring you some oranges later. Is there anything else you would like?"

Although the troll's unfortunate face could produce many expressions that might cause cardiac arrest in an entire pack of attacking wolves, Erika found him cute, if not most of the time, at least occasionally cute, like now.

Somehow his separately terrifying features conspired to come together in a sweet, yearning expression. His enormous yellow eyes sparkled with delight when he considered what else he might like in addition to the oranges.

He said, "Oh, there is a thing, a special thing, that I would like, but it's too much. Jocko doesn't deserve it."

"If I'm able to get it for you," she said, "I will. So what is this special thing?"

"No, no. What Jocko deserves is his nostrils pulled back to his eyebrows. Jocko deserves to hit himself hard in the face, to spit on his own feet, to stick his head in a toilet and flush and flush and flush, to tie a ten-pound sledgehammer to his tongue and throw the hammer over a bridge railing, that's what Jocko deserves."

"Nonsense," said Erika. "You have some peculiar ideas, little friend. You don't deserve such treatment any more than you would like the taste of soap."

"I know better now about the soap," he assured her.

"Good. And I'm going to teach you some self-esteem, too."

"What is self-esteem?"

"To like yourself. I'm going to teach you to like yourself."

"Jocko tolerates Jocko. Jocko doesn't like Jocko."

"That's very sad."

"Jocko doesn't trust Jocko."

"Why wouldn't you trust yourself?"

Pondering her question, the troll smacked the flaps of his mouth for a moment and then said, "Let's say Jocko wanted a knife."

"For what?"

"Let's say . . . for paring his toenails."

"I can get you clippers for that."

"But let's just say. Let's just say Jocko wanted a knife to pare his toenails, and let's say it was really urgent. The toenails—see, they had to be pared right away, *right away,* or all hope was lost. So let's say Jocko hurried to someplace like a kitchen to get the knife. What happens then is what always happens. Let's say Jocko gets to the kitchen, and sees some . . . bananas, yes, that's what he sees, a platter of bananas. Are you with Jocko so far?"

"Yes, I am," she said.

His conversation was not always easy to follow, and sometimes it made no sense at all, but Erika could tell that this mattered to Jocko a great deal. She wanted to understand. She wanted to be there for him, her secret friend.

"So," he continued, "Jocko goes all the way to the kitchen. It's a long way because this house is so big . . . this imaginary house we're talking about somewhere, like maybe San Francisco, a big house. Jocko needs to pare his toenails *right away*. If he doesn't, *all is lost*! But Jocko sees bananas. The next thing Jocko knows, Jocko is juggling bananas, capering around the kitchen in San Francisco. Capering or cartwheeling, or pirouetting, or some stupid, stupid, stupid thing. Jocko forgets about the knife until it's too late to trim toenails, too late, the toenails are gone, Jocko has screwed up again, it's all over, *it's the end of EVERYTHING!*"

Erika patted his warty shoulder. "It's all right. It's okay."

"Do you see what Jocko means?"

"Yes, I do," she lied. "But I'd like to think about what you've said for a while, a day or so, maybe a week, before I respond."

Jocko nodded. "That's fair. It was a lot for Jocko to dump on you. You're a good listener."

"Now," she said, "let's go back to the one special thing you would like but don't think you deserve."

That sweet, yearning expression returned to his face, and none too soon. His huge yellow eyes sparkled with excitement as he said, "Oh, oh goodness, oh, how Jocko would like a funny hat!"

"What kind of funny hat?"

"Any kind. Just so it's very funny."

"I won't be able to find a funny hat tonight."

He shrugged. "Whenever. If ever. Jocko—he doesn't deserve it anyway."

"Yes, you've said. But I promise I will have a funny hat for you within a day or two."

Regardless of what difficulty Erika might have finding a very funny hat, she was rewarded in advance for her trouble when she saw his delight, his tears of gratitude.

"You are such a kind lady. Jocko would kiss your hand, except he doesn't want to disgust you."

"You're my friend," she said, and extended her right hand.

The loose flaps around his mouth and the brief touch of his sticky teeth were even more repellent than she expected, but Erika smiled and said, "You're welcome, dear friend. Now there's something I hope you can do for me."

"Jocko will read a book to you," Jocko said, "two books at once, and one upside down!"

"Later, you can read to me. First, I need your opinion about something."

The troll grabbed his feet with his hands and rocked back and forth on the floor. "Jocko doesn't know about a whole lot besides storm drains, rats, and bugs, but he can try."

"You're Jonathan Harker, or were Harker, whatever. So you know the New Race has little emotional life. When they do have emotional reactions, they're limited to envy, anger, and hatred, only emotions that turn back on themselves and can't lead to hope, because he says hope leads to a desire for freedom, to disobedience and rebellion."

"Jocko is different now. Jocko feels big good things with great exuberance."

"Yes, I've noticed that. Anyway, I don't have the knowledge or the breadth of vision to understand fully why a genius like Victor would create his New Race this way. Only I, his wife, am different. He allows me humility and shame . . . which in a strange way lead to hope, and hope to tenderness."

Feet in his hands, rocking, his head turned toward her, the troll said, "You are the first ever, Old Race or New, to be kind to Jocko," and again tears spilled down his cheeks.

"I hope for many things," Erika said. "I hope to become a better wife day by day. I hope to see approval in Victor's eyes. If in time I become a very good wife and no longer deserve beatings, if in time he comes to cherish me, I will ask him to allow others of the New Race to have hope as I do. I will ask Victor to give my people gentler lives than they have now."

The troll stopped rocking. "Don't ask Victor anytime soon."

"No. First I've got to be a better wife. I must learn to serve him to perfection. But I've been thinking maybe I could be Queen Esther to his King Ahasuerus."

"Remember," he said, "Jocko is ignorant. An ignorant screwup."

"They're figures in the Bible, which I've never read. Esther was the daughter of Mordecai. She persuaded King Ahasuerus, her husband, to spare her people, the Jews, from annihilation at the hands of Haman, a prince of the king's realm."

"Don't ask Victor anytime soon," the troll repeated. "That is Jocko's opinion. That is Jocko's very strongly held opinion."

In her mind's eye, Erika saw Christine lying on the floor of the master-suite vestibule, shot four times through her two hearts.

"That isn't what I want your opinion about," she said, getting to her feet. "Come with me to the library. There's something strange I need to show you."

The troll hesitated. "I who am came out of he who was only a few days ago, but I who am Jocko have had enough strange for as long as I live."

She held out a hand to him. "You are my only friend in the world. I have no one else to whom I can turn."

Jocko sprang off the floor and stood en pointe, as if about to pirouette, but still hesitated. "Jocko must be discreet. Jocko is a *secret* friend."

"Victor has gone to the Hands of Mercy. The staff is at the back of the estate, in their dormitory. We have the house to ourselves."

After a moment, he came down from his toes, slipped his hand in hers. "It's gonna be a very, very funny hat, isn't it?"

"Very, very funny," she promised.

"With some little bells on it?"

"If I find a funny hat without bells, I'll sew as many on it as you want."

CHAPTER 43

CORRIDOR AFTER CORRIDOR, laboratory after laboratory, room after room, in stairways and lavatories and storage closets, a perfect hush has fallen over this place.

With all of its windows bricked up, the building admits no sound from the world outside.

Here and there, brainless bodies lie in groups. They are all EXEMPTS. No one moves who can be seen.

Chameleon follows the tantalizing spoor of the TARGET until those pheromones come to an end at the workstation in the main lab, with no sign of the person who cast them off.

Dim memories of this enormous room stir in Chameleon's mind. It seems to have no recollections prior to these.

Memories do not interest Chameleon. It lives for the future, for the infuriating smell of TARGETS.

Frenzies of violence thrill the pleasure center in its forebrain as intense sex might thrill it if it were capable of sexual activity. Slaughter and only slaughter stimulates its orgasm. Chameleon dreams of war, because for it, war is continuous ecstasy.

Suddenly, on the desktop computer and on an eight-by-six-foot screen embedded in a wall, images appear.

The screens show a broad avenue, tens of thousands of people, dressed alike and ordered into precise ranks, marching in cadence to loud music.

In every fifth row of the stiff-legged marchers, every person carries a flag. The flag is red with a white circle. In the circle is a man's face.

The face is familiar to Chameleon. It has seen this man a long time ago, has seen him often and in this very lab.

The camera pulls back to reveal colossal structures flanking the twelve-lane avenue. They are all of bold design unlike any of the scores of typical-building layouts programmed into Chameleon to assist it in navigating an average office high-rise or church, or shopping mall.

On some of these immense edifices are portraits. The face of the man on the flags is rendered in paint or in mosaic tile, or is etched in stone.

None of these images is smaller than ten stories high. Some are thirty stories.

The music swells, swells, then recedes to a background level. Words are being spoken now, but Chameleon is not interested in what is being said.

The marching hordes on the screens are not real people, merely images. They cannot be killed.

Crawling among the many machines, Chameleon seeks what lives only to be killed.

For a while it smells nothing but the lingering pheromones of the TARGET that was recently here but has gone. Then a new scent.

Chameleon turns its head left, right. Its two ripping claws scissor with anticipation, and its crushing claw opens wide to grip. Its stinger extrudes from under its carapace.

The scent is that of a TARGET. In the hallway but approaching.

CHAPTER 44

ABRUPTLY THE RAIN FELL AWAY behind them and the two-lane blacktop state route lay dry ahead. By driving out of the storm, seemingly swifter than nature in a rampage, Carson enjoyed the illusion of even greater speed than she had actually managed to squeeze out of the Honda.

She raised the bottle of never-sleep-again cola from between her thighs and took another swig. She recognized the signs of noncritical dehydration caused by caffeine: dry mouth, dry lips, a faint ringing in the ears.

In the passenger seat, playing imaginary drums with imaginary drumsticks, Michael said, "Maybe we shouldn't have exceeded the recommended dose for the caffeine tablets. Already I have NoDoz nostrils."

"Me too. My nasal passages are so dry, it's like I'm breathing air that came out of a furnace, it has just a little burn to it."

"Yeah. Feels dry. But this is still Louisiana, so at a minimum it has to be ninety percent humidity by state law. Hey, you know how much of the human body is water?"

"If it's the time of month I retain it, I'd say ninety percent."

"Sixty percent for men, fifty percent for women."

She said, "There's proof—women have more substance than men."

"It was an answer on *Jeopardy!*"

"I can't believe you watch TV game shows."

"They're educational," he said. "Half of what I know, I learned from game shows."

"That I *do* believe."

Moss-draped live oaks on both sides of the road formed a tunnel, and the headlights flared again and again off what might have been colonies of phosphorescent lichen on the fissured bark.

"Do you have to drive so fast?"

"Fast? This heap of Vicky's isn't good for driving anywhere except in funeral processions."

Carson's cell phone rang, and she fished it out of an inside coat pocket.

"O'Connor," she said.

"Detective O'Connor," a woman said, "this is Erika Helios."

"Good evening, Mrs. Helios."

When he heard the name, Michael popped up in his seat as if he were a slice of bread in a toaster.

Erika Helios said, "I believe you may be aware of who my husband really is. At least I think he suspects you know."

"He *knows* we know," Carson said. "He sent two of his New Race assassins after us yesterday. Cute couple. Looked like dancers. We called them Fred and Ginger. They blasted their way through my house, nearly killed my brother."

"Sounds like Benny and Cindi Lovewell," Erika Helios said. "I'm of the New Race, too. But I don't know about Benny and Cindi being sent after you yesterday. Victor killed me the day *before* yesterday."

To Michael, Carson said, "She says Victor killed her the day before yesterday."

"Who're you talking to?" Erika asked.

"My partner, Michael Maddison."

Erika said, "I know it sounds unbelievable, someone telling you she was killed yesterday."

"Thanks to your husband," Carson said, "there's nothing we find hard to believe anymore."

"I'll believe any damn crazy thing," Michael agreed.

"Victor sent my body to the dump. Do you know about Crosswoods Waste Management, Detective O'Connor?"

"It's right next door to the tank farm where he's gonna crank out six thousand of you folks a year."

"You *are* on top of things. I figured you would be, if Victor worried about you. Nobody worries Victor."

"Mrs. Helios, how did you get this number?"

"Victor had it. I saw it on his desk pad. That was before I was dead. But I have a photographic memory. I'm an Alpha."

"Are you still dead?" Carson asked.

"No, no. Turns out, most of us he sends here are for-sure dead, but a few of us who seem to be dead . . . well, there's still a trace of life energy in us that can be brought back to full power, so we can heal. They know how to save us here at the dump."

"Who is they?"

"Those of the New Race discarded here but alive again. I'm one of them now. We call ourselves the Dumpsters."

Carson said, "I didn't know you people had a sense of humor."

"We don't," Erika said. "Not until we die and drop our program and then come alive again. But this may be gibberish to you. Maybe you don't understand about our programs."

Carson thought of Pastor Kenny Laffite coming undone at his kitchen table in the parsonage, and she said, "Yeah, we know about that."

"Oh, and I should have said, I'm Erika Four. The wife with him now is Erika Five."

"He moves fast."

"He's always got Erikas in the tanks, just in case the latest one goes wrong. Flesh is cheap. That's what he says."

"Thank God for NoDoz and triple-threat cola," Carson said.

Erika Four said, "Excuse me?"

"If I wasn't pumped with caffeine to the eyebrows," Carson said, "I wouldn't be able to keep up with this conversation."

"Detective, do you know you can't trust anyone in the police department, so many of them are Victor's people?"

"Yeah. We're aware."

"So you're on your own. And here in the parish where the dump and the tank farm are located, every cop and most of the politicians are replicants. You can't win this."

"We can win this," Carson disagreed.

Nodding so rapidly that he looked like an out-of-control bobble-head doll, Michael said, "We can win. We can win."

"His empire is imploding," Carson told Erika.

"Yes. We know. But you still need help."

Thinking of Deucalion, Carson said, "We've got some help you don't know about. But what do you have in mind?"

"We've got a deal to propose. The Dumpsters. We'll help you defeat him, capture him—but there's something we want."

CHAPTER 45

VICTOR NEVER ENTERED the Hands of Mercy directly. Next door to the hospital, which now passed as a warehouse, a five-story office building housed the accounting and personnel-management departments of Biovision, the company that had made him a billionaire.

In the garage under the building, he parked his S600 Mercedes in a space reserved for him. At this hour, his was the only car.

He had been put off his stride by the business with Erika Four on the phone and Christine not knowing who she was. In moments like this, work was the best thing to settle his mind, and perhaps now more than ever, numerous issues required his attention.

Near his parking space was a painted steel door to which only he possessed a key. Beyond the door lay a twelve-foot-square concrete room.

Opposite the outer door, another door could be operated only by a wall-mounted keypad. Victor entered his code, and the electronic lock disengaged with a *thonk*.

He stepped into a six-foot-wide, eight-foot-high corridor with a concrete floor and block-and-timber walls. The passageway had been excavated secretly by members of the New Race.

Huge responsibilities came with any attempt to pull down an existing civilization and replace it with a new one. The weight on his shoulders might have been intolerable if there had not been perks like secret passageways, hidden rooms, and concealed staircases, which allowed a measure of *fun* in every day.

He had found such hugger-mugger thrilling ever since he was a boy growing up in a rambling house built by a paranoid grandfather who included in his design more blind doors than visible ones, more unknown rooms than known, more secret passages than public hallways. Victor thought it said something admirable about him that he had not lost touch with his roots, had not forgotten from where he came.

At the end of the corridor, another keypad accepted his code. A final door opened into an ordinary file room in the lowest realms of the Hands of Mercy.

These days, no work was conducted on this level. A regrettable incident had occurred here, the consequence of sloppy work by some of his Alphas, and forty had perished. He passed through a dimly lighted area, where unrepaired destruction loomed in the shadows.

In the elevator, on his way up to the main lab, Victor heard music by Wagner, and his heart stirred at the majesty of it. Then he realized someone must have activated *The Creed,* the short film that played once every day throughout the facility for the inspiration and motivation of the New Race staff. But only Victor knew the procedure whereby the computer could be directed to feed the film throughout the Hands of Mercy, and he was curious as to how it had been activated.

When he entered his laboratory, he stood before the embedded wall screen, charmed as always by the marching legions, by the city of tomorrow with its immense buildings that dear Adolf had imagined but had failed ever to erect, by the monuments to himself that would, when the city was built, be much more grand than these examples.

With a team of his people, he had created this realistic glimpse of the future through computer animation. Soon would come the moment when the Wagnerian score faded and in his own voice the Creed would be delivered.

He went to his workstation, intending to sit in his chair to enjoy the last of the film. But arriving there, turning to face the screen from across the room, he saw a portion of the floor ripple, about twenty feet away, and he thought with alarm, *Chameleon.*

CHAPTER 46

TOWARD THE END of a long incline, out of the darkness to the right of the roadway, a white-tailed doe bounded into the headlights and froze in fear.

Ignoring speed limits and periodic roadside pictographs of the silhouette of a leaping antlered buck, Carson had forgotten that at night in rural territory, deer could be no less a traffic hazard than drunken drivers.

Being a city girl out of her element was the lesser part of the problem. Having spent the past few days immersed in the twisted world of Victor Helios Frankenstein, she learned to fear and to be alert for extraordinary, preposterous, grotesque threats of all kinds, while becoming less attuned to the perils of ordinary life.

In spite of her complaints about the Honda, she had pressed it to a reckless speed. The instant she saw the deer in the northbound lane, she knew she was maybe five seconds from impact, couldn't lose enough speed to avoid a disastrous collision, might roll the car if she braked hard.

Speaking on behalf of the Dumpsters, Erika Four said, ". . . but there's something we want," just as the deer appeared.

To free both hands for the wheel, Carson tossed the cell phone to Michael, who snared it in midair as if he'd asked for it, and who at the same time reached cross-body with his left hand to press a button that put down the power window in his door.

In the split second she needed to throw the phone to Michael, Carson also considered her two options:

Pull left, pass Bambi's mom by using the southbound lane and south shoulder, but you might startle her, she might try to complete her crossing, bounding hard into the Honda.

Pull right, go off-road behind the deer, but you might plow into another one if they were traveling in a herd or family.

Even as the phone arced through the air toward Michael's rising hand, Carson put all her chips on a bet that the doe wasn't alone. She swung into the southbound lane.

Directly ahead, a buck bolted from where she least expected, from the darkness on the left, into the southbound lane, *returning* for his petrified doe.

Having tossed the phone from right hand to left, having snatched the pistol from his shoulder rig, Michael thrust the weapon out the window, which was still purring down, and squeezed off two shots.

Spooked, the buck sprang out of harm's way, into the northbound lane, the doe turned to follow him, the Honda exploded past them, and hardly more than a hundred feet away, a truck appeared at the top of the incline, barreling south.

The truck driver hammered his horn.

Carson pulled hard right.

In an arc, the truck's headlights flared through the Honda's interior.

Feeling the car want to roll, she avoided the brakes, eased off the accelerator, finessed the wheel to the left.

The truck shot past them so close Carson could hear the other driver cursing even though her window was closed.

When the potential energy of a roll transferred into a back-end slide, a rear tire stuttered off the pavement, gravel rattled against the undercarriage, but then they were on pavement once more, and in the northbound lane where they belonged.

As Carson accelerated, Michael holstered his pistol, tossed her cell phone back to her.

When she caught the phone and as he put up the window in his door, she said, "That settles it. We'll get married."

He said, "Obviously."

Remembering the dog, she said, "How's Duke?"

"Sitting on the backseat, grinning."

"He is *so* our dog."

When Carson put the phone to her ear, the former Mrs. Helios was saying, "Hello? Are you there? Hello?"

"Just dropped the phone," Carson said. "You were saying you wanted something in return for helping us."

"What are you going to do to Victor if you can get your hands on him?" Erika asked. "Arrest him?"

"Nooooo," Carson said. "Don't think so. Arresting him would be way too complicated."

"It'd be the trial of the millennium," Michael said.

Carson grimaced. "With all the appeals, we'd spend thirty years giving testimony."

Michael said, "And we'd have to listen to a gazillion really bad monster jokes for the rest of our lives."

"He'd probably get off scot-free anyway," Carson said.

"He'd definitely get off," Michael agreed.

"He'd be like a folk hero to a significant number of idiots."

"Jury nullification," Michael said.

"All he wanted was to build a utopia."

"Paradise on Earth. Nothing wrong with that."

"A one-nation world without war," Carson said.

"All of humanity united in pursuit of a glorious future."

"The New Race wouldn't pollute like the Old Race."

"Every last one of them would use the type of lightbulb they were told to use," Michael said.

"No greed, less waste, a willingness to sacrifice."

"They'd save the polar bears," Michael said.

Carson said, "They'd save the oceans."

"They'd save the planet."

"They would. They'd save the solar system."

"The universe."

Carson said, "And all the killing, that wasn't Victor's fault."

"Monsters," Michael said. "Those damn monsters."

"His creations just wouldn't stay with the program."

"We've seen it in movies a thousand times."

"It's tragic," Carson said. "The brilliant scientist undone."

"Betrayed by those ungrateful, rebellious monsters."

"He's not only going to get off, he's going to end up with his own reality-TV show," Carson said.

"He'll be on *Dancing with the Stars*."

"And he'll win."

On the phone, the former Mrs. Helios said, "I'm hearing only half of this, but what I hear is you aren't handling it like police detectives anymore."

"We're vigilantes," Carson acknowledged.

"You want to kill him," Erika said.

"As often as it takes to make him dead," Carson said.

"Then we want the same thing. And we can help you, those of us here at the dump. All we ask is don't just shoot him. Take him alive. Help us kill him the way we want to do it."

"How do you want to do it?" Carson asked.

"We want to chain him and take him down into the dump."

"I'm with you so far."

"We want to make him lie faceup in a grave of garbage lined with the dead flesh of his victims."

"I like that."

"Some of the others want to urinate on him."

"I can understand the impulse."

"We wish to buckle around his neck a metal collar with a high-voltage cable attached, through which eventually we can administer to him an electric charge powerful enough to make the marrow boil in his bones."

"Wow."

"But not right away. After the collar, we want to bury him alive under more garbage and listen to him scream and beg for mercy until we've had enough of that. *Then* we boil his marrow."

"You've really thought this through," Carson said.

"We really have."

"Maybe we can work together."

Erika said, "The next time he comes to the new tank farm—"

"That'll probably be before dawn. We think he'll retreat to the farm from New Orleans when the Hands of Mercy burns down."

"Mercy is going to burn down?" Erika asked with childlike wonder and a tremor of delight.

"It's going to burn down in . . ." Carson glanced at Michael, who checked his watch, and she repeated what he told her: ". . . in eight minutes."

"Yes," the fourth Mrs. Helios said, "he'll surely flee to the farm."

"My partner and I are already on our way."

"Meet with us at Crosswoods, at the dump, before you go to the farm," Erika said.

"I'll have to talk to our other partner about that. I'll get back to you. What's your number there?"

As Erika recited her number, Carson repeated it to Michael, and he wrote it down.

Carson terminated the call, pocketed the phone, and said, "She sounds really nice for a monster."

CHAPTER 47

ALTHOUGH HE DESPISED HUMANITY, Victor was biologically human. Although intellectually enlightened beyond the comprehension of others in the Old Race, he remained more physically like them than not. To Chameleon, Victor qualified as an approved target.

If he had not created Chameleon himself, Victor wouldn't have known the meaning of the rippling floor. He would have thought he had imagined it or was having a transient ischemic attack.

Even now, knowing where to look, he could not easily discern Chameleon against the surface across which it moved.

On the desktop computer and on the big screen across the room, stirring, heroic visions of the New Race future continued to appear, but now Victor's voice rose, reciting the Creed: *"The universe is a sea of chaos in which random chance collides with happenstance and spins shatters of meaningless coincidence like shrapnel through our lives. . . ."*

Chameleon was wary in its approach, although it did not need to be so prudent and had not been programmed for caution, as it was virtually invisible and capable of speed. Most likely, it was being careful because this was its first hunting expedition. Once it had killed, it would become bolder.

"The purpose of the New Race is to impose order on the face of chaos, to harness the awesome destructive power of the universe and make it serve your needs, to bring meaning to a creation that has been meaningless since time immemorial. . . ."

Victor casually backed deeper into the embrace of his U-shaped workstation.

Chameleon advanced as much as Victor retreated, and then another five feet, until it was only fifteen feet away.

It was a half-smart killing machine because its ability to blend with its environment gave it a great advantage that didn't require it also to be truly smart. Victor's intention was to manufacture tens of thousands of Chameleons, to release them on the day the revolution began, as backup for the brigades of New Race warriors as they began killing the Old.

"And the meaning that you will impose upon the universe is the meaning of your maker, the exaltation of my immortal name and face, the fulfillment of my vision and my every desire. . . ."

The granite top of the workstation bumped against the back of Victor's thighs, halting him.

Chameleon scuttled to within twelve feet and paused again. When it was still, Victor ceased to be able to see it even though he knew precisely where it stood. The ripple effect occurred only when the vicious creature remained in motion.

"Your satisfaction in the task, your every moment of pleasure, your relief from otherwise perpetual anxiety, will be achieved solely by the continuous perfect implementation of my will. . . ."

Keeping his eyes on the spot where he'd last seen the clever mimic, Victor eased sideways, to a bank of three drawers on his left. He believed that what he needed was in the middle of the three.

Chameleon neither reproduced nor ate. For the duration of its existence, it drew upon its own substance for energy. When its weight declined from twenty-four pounds to eighteen, Chameleon weakened and died, though of course it had no awareness of its fate.

Computer models suggested that each Chameleon, released in an urban environment, would be able to kill between a thousand and fifteen hundred targets before expiring.

"Through you, Earth and everything upon it will submit to me, and as the whole of Earth serves me, so will it serve you, because I have made you and sent you forth in my name. . . ."

Chameleon began to move closer—one foot, two feet, three—as Victor pulled open the middle drawer and felt through the contents, his stare focused on the would-be assassin.

Just eight feet away, Chameleon stopped. When it decided to move again, it would surely close the remaining distance and rip into its target's legs, his torso, clip off his fingers when he struggled to resist, as it climbed frantically toward his face.

Victor glanced down into the drawer. He saw the bottle of pale-green fluid and plucked it out as he returned his attention at once to where Chameleon had been.

No ripple deformed the floor.

Victor extracted the stopper from the bottle.

Chameleon scuttled forward.

Victor splashed half the contents of the bottle on himself as he quickly sidestepped to his right.

Because the fluid contained New Race pheromones kept in the desk in the unlikely event that Chameleon escaped from its sack in the freezer, the lethal mimic halted short of attack. Victor no longer smelled like a target but instead like one of the New Race.

"You live because of me, you live for me, and my happiness is your glory...."

After a long hesitation, Chameleon turned and crawled away into the laboratory, seeking targets.

Victor had not allowed himself anger while the threat remained, but now he felt his face flush with fury. He was eager to know how Chameleon had escaped its cold prison and who should be punished for allowing it to roam free.

At the computer keyboard, he directed the audio-video system to terminate *The Creed.* The Hands of Mercy fell silent, and the images of the Frankensteinian future vanished from the computer as well as from all other screens in the building.

Instead of displaying the basic menu, however, the computer presented four digits—07:33.

The Dresden clock. Seven and a half minutes, and counting down.

Because he had expected to destroy the Hands of Mercy only in the event of the most extreme and irreversible biological calamity, and because he wanted none of his creations to be able to countermand his decision to destruct once the countdown commenced, the clock could not be stopped. In little more than seven minutes, Mercy would be a seething hell of fire.

His anger gave way to a cool and practical consideration of the circumstances. Having survived two centuries, he could count on a well-exercised survival instinct.

The linked bricks of incendiary material placed throughout the walls and ceilings had been developed by the world's third-most tyrannical government, refined by the world's second-most tyrannical government, and brought to exquisite perfection by the world's *most* tyrannical government. This was a pyromaniac's dream fuel.

In the event those governments ever fell and those regimes were in danger of being brought to justice, the press of a button would ensure that their concentration camps, which they denied existed, would burst instantly into flames of such white-hot intensity that even the guards would be unable to escape. The temperatures produced by this incendiary material were not equal to the average surface temperature of the sun; but this stuff would produce the second-hottest fire in the solar system, virtually vaporizing all evidence.

Victor hurried to a cabinet near his workstation and pulled open a door, revealing what appeared to be a large suitcase. Data-transmission cables connected the luggage to outlets in the back of the cabinet. He quickly disconnected all lines.

The Hands of Mercy would be reduced not to rubble and char but instead to ashes as fine as thrice-milled flour floating in a pool of molten bedrock no less hot and fluid than lava from a volcano. Not one splinter of bone or any other source of DNA would survive for forensic pathologists to analyze.

The suitcase contained backup data files of every experiment ever conducted in the Hands of Mercy, including work done within the past hour.

The countdown clock read 06:55.

Carrying the suitcase, Victor hurried across the lab toward the hall door, Chameleon forgotten, the entire staff forgotten.

He had been enamored of the incendiary material now awaiting detonation, and he had been impressed with himself for having the contacts to acquire a large volume of it. In fact, he had kept on his computer an e-mail sent to his supplier, the most tyrannical dictator in the world, expressing his gratitude, saying in part, ". . . and if it could be revealed that your three nations worked together to perfect this effective and reliable material, the revelation would make fools of cynics who claim your good selves are not capable of international cooperation."

As Victor knew too well from centuries of disappointments, the worst thing about the sudden relocation of the enterprise following a catastrophic occurrence was the irretrievable loss of correspondence and other mementos that reminded you of the *personal* side of a great scientific undertaking. His work was not always solitary and somber. He built many friendships over the years, and there were balmy days in places like Cuba and Venezuela and Haiti and the old Soviet, when he had taken the time to share laughter and memories with longtime friends and discuss the important issues of the age with new friends of like mind. In the firestorm to come, so many small but precious things would be destroyed that he risked a disabling seizure of nostalgia if he dwelt too much on the forthcoming loss.

When he stepped out of the main laboratory, something to his right, about sixty feet farther along the hall, drew his attention. It was big, perhaps as large as four men, with six thick insectile legs, like the legs on a Jerusalem cricket much enlarged, and a riot of other anatomical features. Numerous faces appeared to be embedded in the body, some in the oddest places. The face nearest to where a head belonged—and obviously the most dominant of the group—rather resembled Werner.

From this reprehensibly undisciplined creature came a dozen or two dozen voices, eerily childlike, all of them chanting the same grossly offensive word: *"Father . . . Father . . . Father . . . Father . . ."*

CHAPTER 48

IN THE LIBRARY of the Helios mansion, Erika Five said, "I found it by chance yesterday."

She slid her hand along the underside of a shelf and flicked the concealed switch.

A section of bookshelves swung open on pivot hinges, and ceiling lights revealed the secret passageway beyond.

Jocko said, "This feels bad to Jocko. You want Jocko's opinion. Opinion is—*not good*."

"It's not just the passageway. It's what lies at the other end of it that's the bigger issue."

"What lies at the other end?"

Crossing the threshold, she said, "Better you see it than I tell you. I'd color my description, no matter how I tried not to. I need your unbiased opinion."

Hesitating to follow her, Jocko said, "Is it scary in there? Tell Jocko true."

"It's a little scary, but only a little."

"Is it scarier than a dark, damp storm drain when you don't have your teddy bear anymore?"

"I've never been in a storm drain, but I imagine one would be a lot scarier than this."

"Is it scarier than Jocko's teddy bear being full of spiders waiting for bedtime so they can crawl in his ears when he sleeps and spin a web in his brain and turn him into a spider slave?"

Erika shook her head. "No, it isn't that scary."

"Okay!" Jocko said brightly, and crossed the threshold.

The floor, walls, and ceiling of the four-foot-wide passageway were solid concrete.

The secret door in the bookshelves closed automatically behind the troll, and he said, "Jocko must really want that funny hat."

The narrow corridor led to a formidable steel door. It was kept shut by five inch-thick steel bolts: one in the header, one in the threshold, three in the right-hand jamb, opposite the massive hinges.

"What's locked in there?" Jocko asked. "Something that might get out. Something not supposed to get out."

"You'll see," she said, extracting the bolts one by one.

"Is it something that will beat Jocko with a stick?"

"No. Nothing like that."

"Is it something that will call Jocko a freak and throw dog poop at him?"

"No. That won't happen here."

Jocko did not appear to be convinced.

The steel slab swung smoothly away from them on ball-bearing hinges, activating lights on the farther side.

The subsequent twelve-foot-long passageway ended in a door identical to the first.

Scores of metal rods bristled from the walls, copper on Erika's left, steel or some alloy of steel on her right. A soft hum arose from them.

"Uh-oh," said the troll.

"I wasn't electrocuted the first time," Erika assured him. "So I'm pretty sure we'll be okay."

"But Erika is luckier than Jocko."

"Why would you say that?"

The troll cocked his head as if to say, *Are you serious?* "Why would Jocko say that? Look at you. Look at Jocko."

"Anyway," she said, "there's no such thing as luck. The universe is meaningless chaos. That's what Victor says, so it must be true."

"A black cat crossed Jocko's path once. Then it came back and clawed him."

"I don't think that proves anything."

"Jocko found a penny in the street after midnight. Ten steps later, Jocko fell down an open manhole."

"That wasn't luck. That was not looking where you're going."

"Landed on an alligator."

"An alligator in the storm drain? Well, all right, but it is New Orleans."

"Turned out to be two alligators. Mating."

"You poor thing."

Indicating the rod-lined passageway, Jocko said, "You go first."

As on her previous visit, when Erika entered this new corridor, a blue laser beam scanned her from top to bottom, to top again, as if assessing her form. The laser winked off. The rods stopped humming.

Reluctantly, Jocko followed her to the next steel door.

Erika extracted five deadbolts and opened the final barrier, beyond which lamplight swelled to reveal a windowless, twenty-foot-square space furnished as a Victorian drawing room.

"What do you think?" she asked the troll.

In just the second day of her life, Erika had arrived at a crossroads. Perplexed and irresolute, she needed another opinion of her circumstance before she could decide what she must do.

Jocko did a little moonwalk on the polished mahogany floor and said, "Smooth." He squinched his toes in the antique Persian carpet and said, "Soft."

Putting his peculiar nose to the William Morris wallpaper, he inhaled deeply, savored the smell, and said, "Paste."

He admired the ebonized-walnut fireplace and licked the William De Morgan tiles around the firebox. "Glossy," he said of the tiles.

Cupping his left hand around his left ear, he leaned close to one of the lamps that featured fringed shades of shantung silk, as if he were listening to the light. "Wednesday," he said, but Erika did not ask why.

He jumped up and down on the wingback chair—"Springy"—studied the deeply coffered mahogany ceiling—"Abundant"—squirmed under the Chesterfield on his back and made a peeping sound.

Returning to Erika, he said, "Nice room. Let's go."

"You can't just ignore it," she said.

"Ignore what?"

She pointed to the focal point of the chamber, an immense glass case: nine feet long, five feet wide, and more than three feet deep. It stood on a series of bronze ball-and-claw feet. The six panes of beveled glass were held in an ornate ormolu frame of exquisitely chased bronze.

"It seems to me like an enormous jewel box," Erika said.

After smacking the flaps of his mouth, the troll said, "Yeah. Jewel box. Let's go."

"Come take a close look at the contents," Erika said, and when he hesitated, she took his hand and led him to the mysterious object.

A semiopaque reddish-gold substance filled the case. One moment the contents seemed to be a fluid through which circulated subtle currents, but the next moment it appeared instead to be a dense vapor as it billowed against the glass.

"Does it contain a liquid or a gas?" Erika wondered.

"One or the other. Let's go."

"See how the gas or liquid absorbs the lamplight," Erika said. "It glows so prettily throughout, gold and crimson at the same time."

"Jocko needs to pee."

"Do you see how the internal luminosity reveals a large, dark shape suspended in the middle of the case?"

"Jocko needs to pee so bad."

"Although I can't see even a single small detail of that shadowy form," Erika said, "it reminds me of something. Does it remind you of anything, Jocko?"

"Jocko is reminded of a shadowy form."

Erika said, "It reminds me of a scarab petrified in resin. The ancient Egyptians considered scarabs sacred."

This seemed like a quintessential H. Rider Haggard moment, but she doubted the troll would be able to appreciate a literary allusion to the writer of great adventures.

"What is . . . scarab?"

"A giant beetle," she said.

"Did you hear? Jocko needs to pee."

"You do not need to pee."

"Better believe it."

Putting a hand under his chin, turning his head, forcing him to meet her stare, Erika said, "Look me in the eyes and tell me true. I'll know if you're lying."

"You will?"

"Better believe it. Now . . . does Jocko need to pee?"

He searched her eyes, considering his answer, and tiny beads of sweat appeared on his brow. Finally he said, "Ah. The urge has passed."

"I thought it might. Look at the shadow floating in the case. Look, Jocko."

Reluctantly, he returned his attention to the occupant of the big jewel box.

"Touch the glass," she said.

"Why?"

"I want to see what happens."

"Jocko doesn't want to see what happens."

"I suspect nothing will happen. Please, Jocko. For me."

As if he were being asked to press the nose of a coiled cobra, the troll put one finger to the glass, held it there a few seconds, and then snatched it away. He survived.

"Cold," he said. "Icy."

Erika said, "Yes, but not so icy that your skin sticks to it. Now let's see what happens when I touch it. . . ."

She pressed a forefinger to the glass, and within the luminous substance, the shadowy form twitched.

CHAPTER 49

"FATHER... FATHER... FATHER..."

The Werner thing progressed clumsily, knocking against the east wall of the corridor, then colliding with the west wall, staggering back four or five feet before advancing seven or eight, as though its every movement required a majority vote of a committee.

This creature was not only an abomination, but also a vicious mockery of everything Victor had achieved, intended to deride his triumphs, to imply that his life's work was but a crude burlesque of science. He now suspected that Werner wasn't a victim of catastrophic cellular metamorphosis, not a *victim,* but instead a *perpetrator,* that the security chief had consciously *rebelled* against his maker. Indeed, judging by the composition of this many-faced travesty, the entire staff of the Hands of Mercy had committed themselves to this insane commune of flesh, reducing themselves to a mutant mob in a single entity. They could have but one reason for re-creating themselves as this lumbering atrocity: to offend their maker, to disrespect him, to dishonor him, to make of him a laughingstock. By such a vivid expression of their irrational contempt and scorn, these ungrateful wretches expected to confuse and dishearten him, to *humiliate* him.

Flesh is cheap, but flesh is also treacherous.

"Father... Father... Father..."

They were meat machines who fancied themselves philosophers and critics, daring to ridicule the only intellect of paramount importance they would ever know. Victor was transforming the world, and they transformed nothing but themselves, yet they thought this miserable degradation of their well-crafted forms made them his equal, even his superior, with license to jeer and insult him.

As the Werner thing ricocheted from wall to wall and staggered backward in order to stumble forward, Victor said to it, to all of them tangled within it, "Your pathetic bit of biological theater means nothing to me, discourages me not at all. I haven't failed. *You* have failed, you have failed me, betrayed me, and you have also failed to discourage me in the slightest. You don't know who you're dealing with."

His outrage thus expressed, Victor spoke the death phrase, the words that would shut down the autonomic nervous systems of these anarchic fools, reducing their mocking many-faced grotesquerie to a heap of lifeless flesh.

The Werner thing kept coming, in its tedious fashion, ranting the one word that it knew—that they *all* knew—would most infuriate Victor.

He had little more than six minutes to escape the Hands of Mercy and get out of the neighborhood before the place flared into a molten imitation of the sun. The coming conflagration would obliterate the Werner thing, answering their blasphemy with purifying fire.

The elevator lay between Victor and the shambling mob-in-one. The stairs seemed more advisable.

Carrying the suitcase that contained every minim of his historic work in Mercy, he hurried away from the Werner thing, slammed through the staircase door, and raced down to the lowest level.

Through columns of light and pools of shadow, past the rubble that stood as a monument to a previous bad day in Mercy. Into the file room.

The keypad, his code. One digit wrong. Enter it again. Each tap of a finger eliciting a tone.

He glanced back. The Werner thing had not followed him. It would not get out this way, and no other doors functioned. The Jabberwock was doomed. Let it die mocking him with its many mouths, he didn't care.

Into the corridor with concrete floor, block-and-timber walls. First door closing automatically behind him as he reached the next. Keypad, code again. Right on the first try. The small concrete room, the final door, always unlocked from this side.

The S600 Mercedes sedan looked magnificent, a carriage fit for any royalty and even adequate for him. He opened the back door, but thought better of putting the precious suitcase in such an unsecured place. He went to the back of the car and locked the case in the trunk.

He closed the back door, opened the driver's door, got behind the wheel. The key was in his pocket, and the touch of a finger to the keyless ignition fired the engine.

He drove up to the street and turned right, away from Mercy.

Rising wind pummeled the streets with pellets of rain that bounced like stones off the pavement, and flotillas of litter raced along brimming gutters. But rain ten times heavier than this would have no quenching effect on the incendiary material soon to ignite in his lost laboratories.

So spectacularly would the old hospital burn that no one in the city—or in the nation, for that matter, sea to shining sea—would ever have seen anything to rival the ferocity of the blaze, and they would never forget those white-white flames so bright as to be blinding. Structures across the street from Mercy might also catch fire, and the five-story building next door—owned by his Biovision—would without question be destroyed, which would make him a source of interest to the media and maybe even to authorities.

Considering that the previous day William, the butler, had bitten off his fingers and been terminated, that within the past hour Christine had experienced an inexplicable interruption of function before Victor had shot her to death, he must face the possibility that others on his household staff might be of dubious psychological and/or physical integrity. They might not merely be unable to provide the high quality of service he expected but might also be unable to maintain a credible humanoid form. He could not go home again, at least not for a while.

Logical analysis wouldn't allow Victor to avoid the conclusion that some of the two thousand of the New Race seeded throughout the city might soon begin to have problems of one kind or another. Not all of them, surely. But perhaps a significant fraction, say 5 percent, or 10. He should not remain in New Orleans during this uncertain period.

Because of the widespread nature of the crisis, Victor suspected a problem with the creation tanks at the Hands of Mercy. He knew that his genetic formulations and flesh-matrix designs were brilliant and without fault. Therefore, only a failure of machinery could explain these events.

Or sabotage.

A thousand suspicions suddenly plagued him, and with renewed anger, he feverishly considered who might have been secretly scheming to ruin him.

But no. Now was not the time to be distracted by the possibility of a saboteur. He must first decamp to a new center of operations, of which there was only one—the tank farm. He must strive to insulate himself from any connection to whatever events might occur in the city during the days ahead.

Later there would be time to identify a villain in his life, if one existed.

In truth, mechanical failure was more likely. He had made numerous improvements to the creation tanks that had been installed at the farm. They were three generations more sophisticated than the version in operation at the Hands of Mercy.

Heading for the causeway that would take him twenty-eight miles across Lake Pontchartrain, Victor reminded himself that every setback of his long career had been followed by more rapid and far greater advances than ever before. The universe asserted its chaotic nature, but always he imposed order on it once more.

Proof of his indomitable character was as evident as the clothes he wore, here and now. The encounter with Chameleon, the subsequent confrontation with the Werner thing, and the flight from Mercy would have taken a visible toll of most men. But his shoes were without a scuff, the crease in his trousers remained as crisp as ever, and a quick check in the rearview mirror revealed that his handsome head of hair was not in the least disarranged.

CHAPTER 50

WARILY CIRCLING THE GLASS CASE mounted on the ball-and-claw feet, halting on the farther side of it from Erika, Jocko said, "Not jewel box. Coffin."

"A coffin would have a lid," Erika said, "so I assume there's not a dead man in it."

"Good. Jocko knows enough. Let's go."

"Watch," she said, and rapped a knuckle against the top of the case, as she had done on her previous visit.

The glass sounded as though it must be an inch thick or thicker, and from the spot where her knuckle struck the pane, the amber stuff inside—whether liquid or gas—dimpled much the way water dimpled when a stone was dropped into it. The sapphire-blue dimple resolved into a ring that widened across the surface. The amber color returned in the ring's wake.

"Maybe never do that again," Jocko suggested.

She rapped the glass three times. Three concentric blue rings appeared, receded to the perimeter of the case, and the amber color returned.

Regarding Erika across the top of the case, Jocko said, "Jocko feels kind of sick."

"If you get down on the floor and look under the case—"

"Jocko won't."

"But if you did, you'd see electrical conduits, pipes of several colors and diameters. They all come out of the case, disappear into the floor. Which suggests there's a service room directly under us."

Putting both hands on his belly, Jocko said, "Kind of queasy."

"Yet the mansion supposedly doesn't have a basement."

"Jocko doesn't go in basements."

"You lived in a storm drain."

"Not happily."

Erika moved to the end of the case farthest from the door. "If this were a casket, I figure this would be the head of it."

"Definitely nauseated," said Jocko.

Erika bent low, until her lips were a few inches from the glass. She said softly, "Hello, hello, hello in there."

Within the amber shroud of gas or liquid, the shadowy form thrashed, thrashed.

Jocko scrambled away from the case so fast that Erika didn't see how he had ascended to the fireplace mantel, where he perched, arms wide, holding tight to the framing bronze sconces.

"It scared me, too, the first time," she said. "But I'd only been beaten once at that point, and I hadn't seen Christine shot dead. I'm harder to scare now."

"Jocko is gonna vomit."

"You are not going to vomit, little friend."

"If we don't leave now, Jocko vomits."

"Look me in the eyes and tell me true," she said. "Jocko is not sick, only frightened. I'll know if you're lying."

Meeting her stare, he made a pathetic mewling sound. Finally he said, "Jocko leaves or Jocko vomits."

"I'm disappointed in you."

He looked stricken.

She said, "If you were telling me the truth—then where's the vomit?"

Jocko sucked his upper and lower mouth flaps between his teeth and bit on them. He looked abashed.

When Erika wouldn't stop staring at him, the troll opened his mouth, let go of one of the sconces, and stuck his fingers down his throat.

"Even if that worked," she said, "it wouldn't count. If you were really nauseated, truly nauseated, you could throw up without the finger trick."

Gagging, eyes flooding with tears, Jocko tried and tried, but he could not make himself regurgitate. His efforts were so strenuous that his right foot slipped off the mantel, he lost his grip on the second sconce, and he fell to the floor.

"See where you get when you lie to a friend?"

Cringing in shame, the troll tried to hide behind the wingback chair.

"Don't be silly," Erika said. "Come here."

"Jocko can't look at you. Just can't."

"Of course you can."

"No. Jocko can't bear to see you hate him."

"Nonsense. I don't hate you."

"You hate Jocko. He lied to his best friend."

"And I know he's learned his lesson."

From behind the chair, Jocko said, "He has. He really has."

"I know Jocko will never lie to me again."

"Never. He . . . I never will."

"Then come here."

"Jocko is so embarrassed."

"There's no need to be. We're better friends than ever."

Hesitantly, he moved out from behind the chair. Shyly, he came to Erika, where she remained at the head of the glass case.

"Before I ask for the opinion I need from you," she said, "I've one more thing to show you."

Jocko said, "Oy."

"I'll do exactly what I did yesterday. Let's see what happens."

"Oy."

Once more, she bent down to the glass and said, "Hello, hello, hello in there."

The shadowy shape stirred again, and this time the sound waves of her voice sent scintillant blue pulses across the case, as a rap of her knuckle had done before.

She spoke again: "I am Queen Esther to his King Ahasuerus."

The pulses of blue were a more intense color than previously. The shadowy presence appeared to rise closer to the underside of the glass, revealing the barest suggestion of a pale face, but no details.

Turning to Jocko, Erika whispered, "This is exactly what happened yesterday."

The troll's yellow eyes were wide with fright. He gaped at the featureless suggestion of a face beneath the glass, and what appeared to be an iridescent soap bubble floated from his open mouth.

Lowering her lips close to the glass once more, Erika repeated, "I am Queen Esther to his King Ahasuerus."

Out of the throbbing blue pulses raised by her words, a rough low voice, not muffled by the glass, said, "You are Erika Five, and you are mine."

Jocko fainted.

CHAPTER 51

BY PHONE, Deucalion told them to drive directly to the main gate of Crosswoods Waste Management. "You'll be met by an escort. They're a Gamma and an Epsilon, but you can trust them."

The long rows of loblolly pines broke for the main entrance. The ten-foot-high chain-link gates featured green privacy panels and were topped with coils of barbed wire to match the fence that flanked them.

As Carson coasted to a stop, she said, "They're of the New Race. How can we possibly trust them? This makes me nervous, very uneasy."

"That's just the caffeine."

"It's not just the caffeine, Michael. This situation, putting ourselves in the hands of Victor's people, I'm spooked."

"Deucalion trusts them," Michael said. "And that's good enough for me."

"I guess I know which side he's on, all right. But he's still strange sometimes, sometimes moody, and hard to figure."

"Let's see. He's over two hundred years old. He was made from parts of cadavers taken from a prison graveyard. He's got a handsome side to his face and a caved-in side tattooed to conceal the extent of the damage. He's got two hearts and who knows what other weird arrangement of internal organs. He's been a monk, the star in a carnival freak show, and maybe a hundred other things we'll never know about. He's seen two centuries of war and had three average lifetimes to think about them, and he seems to have read every book worth reading, probably a hundred times more books than you've read, a thousand times more than me. He's lived through the decline of Christendom and the rise of a new Gomorrah. He can open doorways in the air and step through them to the other side of the world because the lightning bolt that animated him brought mysterious gifts with it, as well. Gee, Carson, I don't see any reason why he should seem strange or moody or hard to figure. You're right—it must just be that he's setting us up, he's been lying all along about wanting to nail Victor, they just wanted to lure us to the dump so they could eat us for breakfast."

Carson said, "If you're going to go off on rants, you can't have any more NoDoz."

"I don't *need* any more NoDoz. I feel like my eyelids have been stitched open with surgical sutures."

In the headlight beams, the gates of Crosswoods began to swing inward. Beyond lay the darkness of the dump, which seemed blacker than the moonless night on this side of the fence.

Carson let the Honda coast forward, between the gates, and two figures with flashlights loomed out of the darkness.

One of them was a guy, rough-looking but handsome in a brutish kind of way. He wore a filthy white T-shirt, jeans, and thigh-high rubber boots.

In the backsplash of the flashlights, the woman appeared to be movie-star gorgeous. Her blond hair needed to be washed, and her face was spotted with grime, but she had a beauty so intense that it would have shone through just about anything except a mud pack.

With his flashlight, the man showed Carson where to park, while the woman walked backward in front of them, grinning and waving as if Carson and Michael were beloved kin not seen since everybody had to flee the Ozarks one step ahead of the Bureau of Alcohol, Tobacco, and Firearms task force.

Like the man, she wore a filthy white T-shirt, jeans, and thigh-high rubber boots, but the unattractive getup somehow only emphasized that she had the body of a goddess.

"I'm beginning to think our Victor is less a scientist than he is a horndog," Carson said.

"Well, I guess it doesn't cost him any more to make them curvy than to make them flat."

Switching off the headlights and then the engine, Carson said, "We're taking all our guns."

"In case we have to protect our virtue."

Carson said, "Now that we're planning on you having my babies, I'll protect your virtue for you."

They got out of the Honda, each with two handguns holstered and an Urban Sniper held by the pistol grip, muzzle toward the ground.

The man didn't offer his hand. "I'm Nick Frigg. I run the dump."

Close up, the woman impressed Carson as being even more gorgeous than she had appeared from the car. She radiated a wildness but also an affability, an animal vitality and enthusiasm that made her hard not to like.

She declared with energy, "Marble, mutton, mustard, mice, mule, mumps, muck, manhole—"

Nick Frigg said, "Give her a chance. Sometimes she just has trouble finding the right word to get started."

"—mole, moon, moan, mush, mushroom, moth, mother. *Mother!* We saw the mother of all gone-wrongs tonight!"

"This is Gunny Alecto," Nick said. "She drives one of what we call our garbage galleons, big machine, plowing the trash flat and compacting it good and solid."

"What's a gone-wrong?" Michael asked.

"Experiments that have gone all wrong down at the Hands of Mercy. Specialized meat machines, maybe some warrior thing now and then was supposed to help us in the Last War, even some Alphas or Betas that turned out not like he expected."

"We bury them here," Gunny Alecto said. "We treat them right. They look stupid, stupid, stupid, but they kind of come from where we do, so they're sort of weird family."

"The one tonight wasn't stupid," Nick said.

An expression of awe possessed Gunny's face. "Oh, tonight, it was all different down the big hole. The mother of all gone-wrongs, it's the most beautiful thing ever."

"It changed us," said Nick Frigg.

"Totally changed us," Gunny agreed, nodding enthusiastically.

"It made us understand," Nick said.

"Heaps, harps, holes, hoops, hens, hawks, hooks, hoses, hearts, hands, heads. *Heads!* The mother of all gone-wrongs talked inside our heads."

"It made us free," Nick said. "We don't have to do anything we used to have to do."

"We don't hate your kind anymore," Gunny said. "It's like—why did we ever."

"That's nice," said Carson.

"We used to hate you so bad," Gunny revealed. "When Old Race dead were sent to the dump, we stomped their faces. Stomped them head to foot, over and over, till they were nothing but bone splinters and smashed meat."

"In fact," Nick added, "we just did that earlier tonight with some like you."

"That was before we went down the big hole and met the mother of all gone-wrongs and learned better," Gunny clarified. "Man, oh, man, life is different now, for sure."

Carson shifted her grip on the Urban Sniper, holding it with both hands, the muzzle aimed at the sky instead of toward the ground.

Casually, Michael did the same with his Sniper as he said, "So where is Deucalion?"

"We'll take you to him," Nick said. "He's really the first, isn't he, the first man-made man?"

"Yes, he really is," Carson said.

"Listen," Michael said, "we've got a dog in the car. Is he going to be safe if we leave him here?"

"Bring him along," Nick said. "Dogs—they love a dump. They call me dog-nose Nick 'cause to help me in my job, I have some canine genes that give me a sense of smell half what a dog's is but ten thousand times what you smell."

When Michael opened the back door of the Honda, Duke bounded out and raised his nose to the rich night air. He regarded Nick and Gunny warily, cocked his head left, then right.

"He smells New Race," Nick said. "And that worries him. But he smells something different about us, too."

"Because we've been down the big hole," Gunny said, "and had our heads talked in by the mother of all gone-wrongs."

"That's right," Nick said. "The dog, he knows."

The Duke of Orleans tentatively wagged his tail.

"He smells like a good dog," Nick said. "He smells the way I'd want to smell if I didn't have just some canine genes but was all the way a dog. He smells perfect for a dog. You're lucky to have him."

Carson gave Michael a look that asked, *Are we crazy to go with them into this dark and lonely place?*

He read her clearly, because he said, "Well, it's dark and it's lonely, but we've been through crazy for three days, and I think we're coming out the other side tonight. I say trust Deucalion and the Duke."

CHAPTER 52

ERIKA CARRIED JOCKO from the windowless Victorian drawing room, along the secret passageway.

When the troll passed out, he passed *way* out. He fell so deep into unconsciousness that during this short vacation from awareness, he must have had a room with a view of death.

As limp as rags, his body draped over her cradling arms. Head lolling, mouth open, flaps flopping, he held an iridescent bubble between his teeth, and it didn't pop until she settled him in an armchair in the library.

Jocko remained the antithesis of beauty. If any child were to come upon him accidentally, the unfortunate tyke might need years to regain control of his bladder and would be traumatized for life.

Yet Jocko's vulnerability, his effervescence, and his touching perseverance endeared him to Erika. Somewhat to her surprise, her affection for the troll grew by the hour.

If this mansion were a cottage in the woods, if Jocko frequently broke into song, and if there were six more of him, Erika would have been a real-life Snow White.

She returned to the windowless drawing room. From the threshold, she stared for a moment at the shapeless shadow nesting within the radiant reddish-gold substance.

The care taken with the decor suggested that Victor came here regularly to sit at length with the creature in the glass casket. If he spent little time in this room, he would not have furnished it so cozily.

She closed the steel door and engaged the five deadbolts. At the end of the hall that bristled with rods, she closed the next door and bolted it, as well.

When she returned to the library, where the pivoting section of bookshelves rotated into place, concealing all beyond it, Erika found that Jocko had regained consciousness. Feet dangling well short of the floor, arms on the arms of the chair, he was sitting up straight, clutching the upholstery with both hands, as if he were on a roller coaster, nervously anticipating the next plunge.

"How do you feel, Jocko?"

He said, "Pecked."

"What does that mean?"

"Like, say, ten birds want to peck your head, you try to protect yourself, their wings flutter against your hands and arms, flutter-flutter-flutter against your face. Jocko feels fluttery all over."

"Have you ever been attacked by birds?"

"Only when they see me."

"That sounds horrible."

"Well, it just happens when Jocko's in open air. And mostly in daylight, only once at night. Well, twice if bats count as birds."

"There's a bar here in the library. Maybe a drink will settle your nerves."

"Do you have storm-drain water with interesting sediment?"

"I'm afraid we only have bottled water or from the tap."

"Oh. Then I'll have Scotch."

"You want that on the rocks?"

"No. Just some ice, please."

Moments later, as Erika gave Jocko his drink, her cell phone rang. "Only Victor has this number."

She thought that Jocko's voice had a note of bitterness in it when he muttered, "He who made he who I was," but she may have been imagining it.

She fished the phone from a pocket of her slacks. "Hello?"

"We're leaving New Orleans for a while," Victor said. "We're leaving immediately."

Because her husband sometimes found questions impertinent, Erika didn't ask why they were leaving, but said simply, "All right."

"I'm already on my way to the tank farm. You'll go there in the bigger Mercedes SUV, the GL550."

"Yes, Victor. Tomorrow?"

"Don't be stupid. I said 'immediately.' Tonight. Within the hour. Pack two weeks' clothes for yourself. Get the staff to help. You've got to move fast."

"And should I bring clothes for you?"

"I have a wardrobe at the farm. Just shut up and listen."

Victor told her where to find the mansion's walk-in safe and explained what she should bring from it.

Then he said, "When you go outside, look to the northwest, the sky is burning," and he terminated the call.

Erika closed her phone and stood in thought for a moment.

In the armchair, Jocko said, "Is he mean to you?"

"He . . . is who he is," she replied. "Wait here. I'll be back in a minute."

French doors opened from the library to a covered terrace. As Erika stepped outside, she heard sirens in the distance.

To the northwest, a strange luminosity played through the low storm clouds: throbbing, wildly flailing forms of light, as radiant and fiercely white as spirits might be, if you were one who believed in such things as spirits.

The burning sky was a reflection of an unimaginably hot and hungry blaze below. The place where she was conceived and born, the Hands of Mercy, must be on fire.

The rain driving through the trees and spending itself on the soaked lawn made a sizzle something like fire, but here the night had no scent of smoke. The washed air smelled clean and fresh, and the fragrance of jasmine came to her, and in this moment, for the first time in her brief but event-packed existence, she felt fully *alive*.

She returned to the library and sat on the footstool in front of Jocko's armchair. "Little friend, you have followed the secret passageway to the hidden room and seen all those lock bolts on the two steel doors."

"Jocko isn't going there again. Jocko's been in enough scary places. He wants just nice places from now on."

"You have seen the hidden room and the glass casket, and the shapeless shadow alive within."

Jocko shuddered and drank some Scotch.

"You have heard it speak from the casket."

Unsuccessfully trying to make his voice deeper and rougher and menacing, the troll quoted, "'You are Erika Five, and you are mine.'"

In his natural voice, he said, "There's something in the glass box that's at least fourteen hundred times too scary for Jocko. If Jocko had genitals, they would've shriveled up and fallen off. But Jocko could only faint."

"Remember, I took you there so I could ask your opinion about something. Before I ask, I must emphasize that I want to know what you *truly* feel. Truly, truly."

Clearly somewhat embarrassed but nevertheless meeting Erika's stare forthrightly, the troll said, "Truly, truly. No more Jocko-needs-to-pee-Jocko-is-gonna-vomit. That's the old me. Good-bye to that Jocko."

"All right, then. I want your honest opinion about two things. We don't know what that shapeless shadow is. But based on what you've heard and seen, is the thing in that glass casket just another thing—or is it malevolent?"

"Malevolent!" the troll said at once. "Malevolent, malignant, venomous, and potentially very troublesome."

"Thank you for your honesty."

"You're welcome."

"Now my second question." She leaned toward Jocko, riveting his gaze with hers. "If the thing in the glass case was made by some man, conceived and designed and brought to life by some man, do you think that man is good . . . or evil?"

"Evil," Jocko said. "Evil, depraved, wicked, corrupt, vile, vicious, rotten, hateful, totally unpleasant."

Erika held his gaze for half a minute. Then she rose from the footstool. "We've got to leave New Orleans and go to the tank farm farther upstate. You'll need clothes."

Plucking at the picnic tablecloth that he had fashioned into a sarong, Jocko said, "This is the only clothes Jocko ever had. It works okay."

"You'll be out in public, at least in the Mercedes."

"Put Jocko in the trunk."

"It's an SUV. It doesn't have a trunk. I've got to find you clothes that make you look more like a normal little boy."

Amazement made yet another fright mask of the troll's face. "What genius would make such clothes?"

"I don't know," Erika admitted. "But I've got an idea who might. Glenda. The estate provisioner. She shops for everything needed here. Food, paper goods, linens, staff uniforms, holiday decorations. . . ."

"Does she shop for soap?" Jocko asked.

"Yes, everything, she shops for everything."

He put aside his empty Scotch glass and clapped his hands. "Jocko would like to meet the lady who shops for soap."

"That's not a good idea," Erika said. "You stay here, out of sight. I'll talk to Glenda and see what she can do."

Getting up from the armchair, the troll said, "Jocko is feeling like he better twirl or cartwheel, or walk on his hands. Whatever."

"You know what you could do?" Erika asked. "You could browse the shelves in here, choose some books to take along."

"I'm going to read to you," he remembered.

"That's right. Choose some good stories. Maybe twenty."

As the troll moved toward the nearest shelves, Erika hurried to find Glenda.

At the door to the hall, she paused and looked back at Jocko. "You know what . . . ? Also choose four or five books that seem a little dangerous. And maybe . . . one that seems really, really dangerous."

CHAPTER 53

THE POWERFUL ENGINE transmits vibrations through the frame of the car.

The tires on the blacktop raise vibrations that are likewise transmitted through the vehicle.

Even in the plush upholstery of the backseat, these vibrations can be felt faintly, especially by one made sensitive to vibrations by the tedium of semisuspended animation, in which there was, for so long, little other sensory input.

Like the freezer-motor vibrations in the liquid-filled sack, these are neither pleasant nor unpleasant to Chameleon.

It is no longer tormented by extreme cold.

Nor is it any longer tormented by its powerless condition, for it is no longer powerless. It is free, free at last, and it is free to kill.

Currently, Chameleon is tormented only by its inability to locate a TARGET. It has detected the scents of numerous EXEMPTS, and even most of them were dead.

The sole TARGET located in the laboratory suddenly became an EXEMPT just seconds before Chameleon would have killed it.

Frustrated, Chameleon cannot account for this transformation. Its program does not allow for such a possibility.

Chameleon is adaptable. When its program and real experience do not comport, it will reason its way toward an understanding of why the program is inadequate.

Chameleon is capable of suspicion. In the lab, it continued to maintain surveillance on the one who transformed. It knew the man's face from the past and from the film, but because of the transformation, it thought of him as the PUZZLE.

The PUZZLE had gotten busy, busy in the lab, rushing this way and that. Something about the PUZZLE's frantic activity made Chameleon more suspicious.

In the hallway, the PUZZLE encountered a thing unlike any creature in the extensive species-ID file in Chameleon's program. This thing, large and moving erratically, looked not at all like an EXEMPT, but it smelled like one.

The PUZZLE had run from the building, and because Chameleon had no whiff of any TARGET, no reason to remain there, it followed.

On the way out of the building, Chameleon detected faint traces of a TARGET's scent under the EXEMPT scent of the PUZZLE.

Interesting.

Once they were in the car and in motion for a while, the PUZZLE seemed less agitated, and as he became calmer, the TARGET scent slowly faded.

Now there is only the scent of an EXEMPT.

What does it all mean?

Chameleon broods on these events.

On the backseat, looking exactly like the backseat, Chameleon waits for a development. It confidently anticipates that there will be a development. There always is.

CHAPTER 54

ERIKA PHONED GLENDA, the estate provisioner, at the dormitory and asked for a meeting immediately in the staff lunchroom. This was in the south wing on the first floor, and it could be entered either from the south hall or from an exterior door.

In a few minutes, Glenda arrived at the exterior door. She left her umbrella outside and came into the lunchroom, saying, "Yes, Mrs. Helios, what is needed?"

A sturdy New Race woman with short chestnut-brown hair and a scattering of freckles, wearing an off-duty jumpsuit, she appeared accustomed to lifting and toting. As the sole shopper for the estate, her job included not just browsing the aisles of stores but also the physical labor of transporting goods and stocking shelves.

"I've been out of the tank little more than a day," Erika said, "so my downloaded data hasn't yet been complemented by enough real-world experience. I need to buy something right away, tonight, and I hope your knowledge of the marketplace will be helpful."

"What do you need, ma'am?"

Erika brazened through it: "Boys' clothing. Shoes, socks, pants, shirts. Underwear, I suppose. A light jacket. A cap of some kind. The boy is about four feet tall, weighs fifty or sixty pounds. Oh, and his head is big, quite big for a boy, so the cap should probably be adjustable. Can you get me those things right away?"

"Mrs. Helios, may I ask—"

"No," Erika interrupted, "you may not ask. This is something Victor needs me to bring to him right away. I never question Victor, no matter how peculiar a request may seem, and I never will. Do I need to tell you why I never question my husband?"

"No, ma'am."

The staff had to know that the Erikas were beaten and were not permitted to turn off their pain.

"I thought you'd understand, Glenda. We're all in the same quicksand, aren't we, whether we're the provisioner or the wife."

Uncomfortable with this intimacy, Glenda said, "There's no store open at this hour, selling boys' clothing. But . . ."

"Yes?"

Fear rose in Glenda's eyes, and her previously placid face tightened with worry. "There are many articles of boys' and girls' clothing here in the house."

"Here? But there are no children here."

Glenda's voice fell to a whisper. "You must never tell."

"Tell what? Tell whom?"

"Never tell . . . Mr. Helios."

Erika pressed the battered-wife sympathy play as far as she probably dared: "Glenda, I am beaten not just for my shortcomings, but for any reason that suits my . . . maker. I am quite sure I would be beaten for being the bearer of bad news. All secrets are safe with me."

Glenda nodded. "Follow me."

Also off the south hall on the ground floor were a series of storage rooms. One of the largest of these was a twenty-by-eighteen-foot walk-in cooler where a dozen of the highest-quality fur coats were stored—mink, ermine, arctic fox. . . . Victor had no sympathy for the antifur movement, as he was engaged in the much more important antihuman movement.

In addition to the rack of coats, there were numerous cabinets containing clothes of all kinds that would not fit even in Erika's enormous closet in the master suite. By having a series of wives who were identical in every detail, Victor spared himself the expense of purchasing new wardrobes. But he did want his Erika to be at all times stylishly attired, and he did not expect her to choose from a limited garment collection.

From several drawers in the farthest corner of the room, Glenda nervously produced children's clothing, article after article, both for boys and girls, in various sizes.

"Where did all this come from?" Erika asked.

"Mrs. Helios, if he learns about it, he'll terminate Cassandra. And this is the only thing that's ever made her happy. It's made us all happy—her daring, her secret life, she gives the rest of us a little hope."

"You know my position on being the bearer of bad news."

Glenda buried her face in a striped polo shirt.

For a moment, Erika thought that the woman must be crying, for the shirt trembled in her hands, and her shoulders shook.

Instead, Glenda inhaled deeply, as if seeking the scent of the boy who had worn the shirt, and when she looked up from it, her face was a portrait of bliss.

"For the past five weeks, Cassandra has been sneaking off the estate at night, to kill Old Race children."

Cassandra, the laundress.

"Oh," Erika said. "I see."

"She couldn't wait any longer to be told the killing could at last begin. The rest of us . . . we so admire her nerve, but we haven't been able to find it in ourselves."

"And . . . what of the bodies?"

"Cassandra brings them back here, so we can share in the excitement. Then the trash men who take other bodies to the dump, they take the children, too, no questions asked. Like you said—we're all in this quicksand together."

"But you keep the clothes."

"You know what the dormitory is like. Not an inch of extra space. We can't store the clothes there. But we can't bear to get rid of them. We take these clothes out some nights, take them over to the dormitory and, you know, play with them. And, oh, it's very wonderful, Mrs. Helios, thinking of the dead kids and listening to Cassandra tell how each one happened. It's the best thing ever, the only good thing we've ever had."

Erika knew that something profound must be happening to her when she found Glenda's story disturbing, even creepy, and when she hesitated at the prospect of dressing the poor sweet troll in the clothes of murdered children. Indeed, that she should think *murdered* instead of merely *dead* had to be an indication of a revolution in her thinking.

She was torn by something like pity for Cassandra, Glenda, and the others on the staff, by a quiet horror at the idea of Cassandra stalking the most defenseless of the Old Race, and by compassion for the murdered, toward whom she had been programmed to feel nothing but envy, anger, and hatred.

Her actions on behalf of Jocko crossed the line that Victor had drawn for her, for all of them, in the aforementioned quicksand. The curious sense of companionship that had developed so quickly between her and the little guy should have been beyond her emotional range. Even as the friendship grew, she recognized that it might signify a pending interruption of function like the one that William, the butler, had experienced.

She was allowed compassion, humility, and shame, as the others were not—but only so that Victor might be more thrilled by her pain and anguish. Victor didn't intend that the finer feelings of his Erikas should benefit anyone but himself, or that anyone else should have the opportunity to respond to his wife's tender attentions with anything other than the contempt and brutality with which he answered them.

To Glenda, she said, "Go back to the dormitory. I'll select what I need from these and put the rest away."

"And never tell him."

"Never tell him," Erika confirmed.

Glenda started to turn away, but then she said, "Do you think maybe . . ."

"Maybe what, Glenda?"

"Do you think maybe . . . the end is coming soon?"

"Do you mean the end of the Old Race, once and forever, the killing of them all?"

The provisioner searched Erika's gaze and then turned her face up to the ceiling as tears welled in her eyes. In a voice thick with fear, she said, "There's got to be an end, you know, there's really got to be."

"Look at me," Erika said.

Obedient as her program required, Glenda met her mistress's eyes again.

With her fingers, Erika wiped the tears from the provisioner's face. "Don't be afraid."

"It's that or rage. I'm worn out by rage."

Erika said, "An end is coming soon."

"You *know?*"

"Yes. Very soon."

"How? What end?"

"In most cases, not all ends are desirable, but in this case . . . any end will do. Don't you think?"

The provisioner nodded almost imperceptibly. "May I tell the others?"

"Will knowing help them?"

"Oh, yes, ma'am. Life's always been hard, you know, but lately harder."

"Then by all means, tell them."

The provisioner seemed to regard Erika with the nearest thing to gratitude that she could feel. After a silence, she said, "I don't know what to say."

"Neither of us does," said Erika. "That's how we are."

"Good-bye, Mrs. Helios."

"Good-bye, Glenda."

The provisioner left the storage room, and Erika closed her eyes for a moment, unable to look at the many items of apparel strewn on the floor around her.

Then she opened her eyes and knelt among the clothes.

She selected those that might fit her friend.

The garments of the executed were still garments. And if the universe was not, as Victor said, a meaningless chaos, if it were possible for anything to be sacred, surely these humble items, worn by martyred innocents, were hallowed and might provide her friend not only with a disguise but also with protection of a higher kind.

CHAPTER 55

DUKE LED THEM across a wide earthen rampart, between vast pits of trash, through the dump, as if he knew the way.

With the moon and the stars sequestered behind ominous clouds, Crosswoods for the most part lay in darkness, although a few small fires burned out there in the black remoteness.

Carson and Michael followed the dog, in the company of Nick Frigg and Gunny Alecto, who with flashlights picked out potholes and places where the crumbling brink might be treacherous, as if every detail of this terrain was engraved in the memory of each.

"I'm a Gamma," Nick said, "or I was, and Gunny here—she's an Epsilon."

"Or was," she said. "Now I'm reborn freeborn, and I don't hate anymore. I'm not afraid anymore."

"It's like we've been living with bands of iron around our heads, and now they're cut away, the pressure gone," said Nick.

Carson didn't know what to make of their strange born-again declarations. She still expected one of them suddenly to come at her with no more goodwill than a buzz saw.

"Sign, sink, spoon, spade, soup, stone, spinach, sparkler, soda, sand, seed, sex. *Sex!*" Gunny laughed with delight that she had found the word she wanted. "Man, oh, man, I wonder what it'll be like the next time the whole dump gang gets sexed up together, going at each other every which way, but none of us angry, nobody punching or biting, just doing all the better kind of stuff to each other. It should be interesting."

"It should," Nick said. "Interesting. Okay, folks, right up here, we're gonna go down a ramp into the west pit. See the torches and oil lamps out there a ways? That's where Deucalion's waiting."

"He's waiting out there by the big hole," Gunny said.

Nick said, "We're all going down the big hole again."

"This is some night," Gunny declared.

"Some crazy night," Nick agreed.

"What a night, huh, Nick?"

"What a night," Nick agreed.

"Down the big hole *again*!"

"It's sure a big hole."

"And we're going down it *again*!"

"We are, for sure. The big hole."

"Mother of all gone-wrongs!"

"Something to see."

"I'm just all up!" said Gunny.

"I'm all up, too," Nick said.

Grabbing at Nick's crotch, Gunny said, "I bet you are!"

"You know I am."

"You know I know you are."

"Don't I know?"

Carson figured she was no more than two conversational exchanges from either bolting back to the car or emptying the Urban Sniper into both of them.

Michael saved her sanity by breaking the rhythm and asking Nick, "How do you live with this stench?"

"How do you live *without* it?" Nick asked.

From the top of the rampart, they descended a slope of earth, into the west pit. Trash crunched and crackled and rustled underfoot, but it was well-compacted and didn't shift much.

More than a dozen people stood with Deucalion, but he was a head taller than the tallest of them. He wore his long black coat, the hood thrown back. His half-broken and tattooed face, uplit by torchlight, was not as disturbing as it ought to have been in this setting, under these circumstances. In fact, he had an air of calm certainty and unflinching resolve that reminded Carson of her father, who had been a military man before becoming a detective. Deucalion projected that competence and integrity that motivated men to follow a leader into battle—which apparently was what they were soon to do.

Michael said to him, "Hey, big guy, you're standing there like we're in a rose garden. How do you tolerate this stench?"

"Controlled synesthesia," Deucalion explained. "I convince myself to perceive the malodors as colors, not smells. I see us standing in a weave of rainbows."

"I'm going to hope you're pulling my chain."

"Carson," Deucalion said, "there's someone here who wants to meet you."

From behind Deucalion stepped a beautiful woman in a dress stained and crusted with filth.

"Good evening, Detective O'Connor."

Recognizing the voice from the phone, Carson said, "Mrs. Helios."

"Yes. Erika Four. I apologize for the condition of my dress. I was murdered little more than a day ago and buried in garbage. My darling Victor didn't think to send me here with a supply of moist towelettes and a change of clothes."

CHAPTER 56

AFTER LEAVING THE CHILDREN'S CLOTHES with Jocko in the library, Erika went to the master suite, where she quickly packed a single suitcase for herself.

She didn't clean up the blood in the vestibule. She should have wrapped Christine's body in a blanket and called the New Race trash collectors who conveyed corpses to Crosswoods, but she did not.

After all, if she went to a window and looked northwest, the sky would be on fire. And worse was coming. Maybe it would still matter if authorities found a murdered housekeeper in the mansion, or maybe not.

Anyway, even if the discovery of Christine's body turned out to be a problem for Victor, it wasn't an issue for Erika. She suspected that she would never again see this house or New Orleans, and that she would not much longer be Victor's wife.

Only hours ago, she handled with aplomb—if not indifference—such macabre episodes as a butler chewing off his fingers. But now the mere presence of a dead Beta in the bedroom disturbed her both for reasons she understood and for reasons she was not yet able to define.

She put her suitcase at the foot of the bed, and she chose a smaller piece of luggage in which to pack everything that Victor wanted from the safe.

The existence of the walk-in vault had not been disclosed to Erika during her in-tank education. She learned about it only minutes earlier, when Victor told her how to find it.

In one corner of his immense closet, which was as large as the formal dining room downstairs, an alcove featured three floor-to-ceiling mirrors. After Victor dressed, he stepped into this space to consider the clothes he wore and to assess the degree to which his outfit achieved the effect he desired.

Standing in this alcove, Erika spoke to her reflection: "Twelve twenty-five is four one."

A voice-recognition program in the house computer accepted those five words as the first part of a two-sentence combination to the vault. The center mirror slid into the ceiling, revealing a plain steel door without hinges or handle, or keyhole.

When she said, "Two fourteen is ten thirty-one," she heard lock bolts disengage, and the door slid open with a pneumatic hiss.

In addition to tall upper cabinets, the vault contained lower drawers, all measuring the same: one foot deep, two feet wide. Each of three walls held twelve drawers, numbered 1 through 36.

From Drawer 5, she withdrew sixteen bricks of hundred-dollar bills and put them in the small suitcase. Each banded block contained fifty thousand dollars, for a total of eight hundred thousand.

Drawer 12 offered a quarter of a million dollars' worth of euros, and she emptied it.

From Drawer 16, she withdrew one million worth of bearer bonds, each valued at fifty thousand.

Drawer 24 revealed numerous small gray-velvet bags featuring drawstring closures tied in neat bows. In these were precious gems, mostly diamonds of the highest quality. She scooped up all of the bags and dropped them in the suitcase.

No doubt Victor maintained offshore bank accounts containing significant sums, held by such an intricate chain of shell companies and false names that no tax collector could link them to him. There he kept the larger part of his wealth.

What Erika collected here, according to Victor's instructions, was his on-the-run money, which he might need if the current crisis could not be contained. Listening to him on the phone, she'd thought he should use the word *would* instead of *might,* and *when* instead of *if,* but she'd said nothing.

With the suitcase, she returned to the mirrored alcove, faced the open vault door, and said, "Close and lock."

The pneumatic door hissed shut. The bolts engaged. The mirror descended into place, bringing with it her reflection, as if it had previously taken her image into the ceiling.

In the garage, Erika stowed both pieces of luggage in the cargo space of the GL550.

With a large cloth tote bag in which to carry their books, she returned to the library. In his new attire, Jocko looked less like Huckleberry Finn than like a mutant turtle from another planet, out of its shell and likely to pass for human only if everyone on Earth were struck blind.

Although the faded blue jeans looked all right from the front, they sagged in the seat because the troll didn't have much of a butt. His thin pale arms were longer than those of a real boy, so the long-sleeved T-shirt fell three inches short of his wrists.

For the first time, Erika considered that Jocko had six fingers on each hand.

He had adjusted the expansion strap on the back of the baseball cap to its full extension, making it big enough to fit him, and in fact making it too big. The cap came over the tops of his gnarled ears, and he kept tipping it back to see out from under the bill.

"It's not a funny hat," he said.

"No. I couldn't find one here, and the funny-hat store doesn't open until nine o'clock."

"Maybe they deliver earlier."

Stuffing Jocko's selection of books in the tote bag, she said, "They don't deliver like a pizza shop."

"A pizza would be a funnier hat than this. Let's get a pizza."

"Don't you think wearing a pizza on your head would attract more attention than we want?"

"No. And the shoes don't work."

Even after taking the laces out, he had not been able to fit his wide feet comfortably in the sneakers.

He said, "Anyway, Jocko walks way better barefoot, has a better grip, and if he wants to suck his toes, he doesn't have to undress them first."

His toes were nearly as long as fingers and had three knuckles each. Erika thought he must be able to climb like a monkey.

"You're probably well enough disguised if you stay in the car," she said. "And if you slump in your seat. And if you don't look out the window when another car's passing us. And if you don't wave at anyone."

"Can Jocko give them the finger?"

She frowned. "Why would you want to make obscene gestures at anyone?"

"You never know. Like, say it's a pretty night, big moon, stars all over, and say suddenly a woman's smacking you with a broom and a guy's beating your head with an empty bucket, shouting 'What is it, what is it, what is it?' You run away faster than they can run, and you want to shout something really smart at them, but you can't think of anything smart, so there's always the finger. Can Jocko give them the okay sign?"

"I think it's better if you keep your hands down and just enjoy the ride."

"Can Jocko give them a thumbs-up sign? Attaboy! Way to go! You done good!"

"Maybe the next time we go for a ride. Not tonight."

"Can Jocko give them a power-to-the-people fist?"

"I didn't know you were political." The tote bag bulged with books. "Come on. We've got to get out of here."

"Oh. Wait. Jocko forgot. In his room."

"There's nothing in your room that you'll need."

"Be back in half a jiffy."

He snatched up one of the laces from the sneakers and, holding it between his teeth, somersaulted out of the library.

When the troll returned a few minutes later, he was carrying a sack made from a pillowcase, tied shut with the shoelace.

"What's that?" Erika asked.

"Stuff."

"What stuff?"

"Jocko's stuff."

"All right. All right. Let's go."

In the garage, at the GL550, Jocko said, "You want me to drive?"

CHAPTER 57

JUDGING BY THE QUALITY of their excitement and the content of their conversations among themselves, Carson decided that most if not all of the people with torches and oil lamps were Epsilons, like Gunny Alecto, and were workers at the landfill.

In addition to Erika Four, however, five others of the New Race, left for dead at Crosswoods but later resurrected, were Alphas—four men and a woman—who had been terminated by Victor for one reason or another. This was the group that called themselves the Dumpsters.

Carson and Michael had been unnerved when one of the Dumpsters proved to be Bucky Guitreau, the district attorney. He wasn't the one they had killed in Audubon Park, and he wasn't the original and fully human Bucky. He was instead the *first* replicant intended to replace Bucky. He'd been replaced himself by a second replicant, the one she and Michael had killed, when Victor decided that number one wasn't a sufficiently gifted mimic to pull off the impersonation of the district attorney.

Apparently, all of these Alphas had been returned to life longer than Mrs. Helios. They had found water to wash themselves, and they wore reasonably clean if threadbare clothes, which perhaps they had salvaged from these many acres of refuse.

Although she was the most recent to have been pulled back from the brink of oblivion, Erika Four had been appointed to speak not only for herself but also for the other five Alphas, perhaps because she had been their tormentor's wife. She knew Victor well, his corrupted character and temper. Better than anyone, she might be able to identify the weakness most likely to render him vulnerable.

Deucalion towered behind Erika, and as she brought Carson and

Michael up-to-date, the landfill workers edged closer. None of what she said was news to them, but being the intellectual lower caste of the New Race, they seemed to be easily enchanted. They were rapt, faces shining in the lambent firelight, like children gathered for story hour around a campfire.

"The workers here have known something strange was happening under the trash fields," Erika said. "They've seen the surface rise and resettle, as if something sizable was traveling this way and that in the lower realms. They've heard haunting voices filtering up from below. Tonight they saw it for the first time, and they call it the mother of all gone-wrongs."

A murmuring passed through the Epsilons, whispered exclamations. Their faces revealed emotions that they of the New Race should not have been able to feel: happiness, awe, and perhaps hope.

"It started as a failed experiment, left here for dead, but in fact not fully dead," Erika continued. "A lightning strike in the dump enlivened it. Since then, it has evolved to become a wondrous being, an entity of indescribable beauty and profound moral purpose. Sometimes an Alpha, presumed dead even by Victor, may yet contain an incandescent filament of life for a few days after an apparent death. If attended properly, that filament can be prevented from fading entirely, and encouraged to grow brighter. As it brightens, this life force spreads through the Alpha, returning him to consciousness and full function. What these Epsilons call the mother of all gone-wrongs, we call the Resurrector, for as it was revived by lightning, it now revives us by sharing its own intensely bright life force."

So closely gathered were the Epsilons that their torches and oil lamps encircled Carson with shimmering orange light, and in this one small portion of the landfill, the night was as bright as a dawn sky painted with the sun's celebratory brush.

"Not only does the Resurrector restore the body, but it also heals the mind," said Erika Four. "From our programs, it strips out all of the encouragements to envy, hatred, and anger, and deletes as well the prohibitions against compassion, love, and hope. Tonight, it revealed itself to the landfill workers—and released them from all the programmed emotions that oppressed them, and gave to them the full range of emotions they had been denied."

Skin prickling on the back of her neck, Carson recalled Gunny Alecto's words: *The mother of all gone-wrongs talked inside our heads.*

Michael shared her reservations. "No offense. But no matter how beautiful it might be, I'm basically freaked out by something that can get inside my head *and change me.*"

In the quivering torchlight, on the broken half of Deucalion's face, reflections of flames infused false life into the tattooed patterns, which seemed to flex and crawl across the awful concavities and the broken planes, across the knotted scars.

He said, "It waits for us now in the tunnel. I went down a short while ago—and felt I was in the presence of a being that has no thinnest thread of malevolence in its weave. It will project certain thoughts to you . . . but it won't enter your mind against your wishes."

"As far as you know," Michael qualified.

"For two centuries I've had to bear witness to all forms of human wickedness," Deucalion said. "And cobbled together, as I was, from the bodies of sociopathic criminals, burdened with the brain of the vilest kind of murderer, I have a certain . . . sensitivity to the presence of evil. There is none in this Being."

Carson heard the capital *B* that he put on the final word. And though his confidence somewhat reassured her, though her disquiet didn't swell into apprehension, she had misgivings about going into the tunnel to which he referred.

Erika Four said, "The Resurrector will help us bring Victor to the justice he deserves. Indeed, I don't think we can bring him down without the assistance of this entity."

"If he flees here tonight or in the early morning," Deucalion said, "as we expect he will when he learns of the fire at Mercy, we will have an opportunity that we must not fail to seize."

Under the reflected torchlight in his eyes, the more profound light of his embodied storm throbbed as it sometimes did. Carson wondered if, in his mind's ear, he heard the sky-splitting crack of the thunderbolt or recalled the terror of his first minutes of unholy life.

"I believe the moment is rushing toward us," Deucalion said. "You need to meet the Resurrector, so we are ready and waiting for Victor when he arrives."

Carson looked at Michael, and he said, "So . . . it's down the big hole, this is some night, some crazy night, I'm just all up."

CHAPTER 58

SOMBER THOUGHTS DISTRACTED Victor from his driving, and the deserted state route, winding through lonely darkness, contributed to his bleak mood.

Always before, when setbacks forced a change of venue on him—from Germany to Argentina, to the old Soviet, to China and elsewhere—he had been furious at the associates who had failed him and at Nature for her jealous guarding of the secrets of molecular biology and her stubborn resistance to the incisive blade of his singular intelligence, but he had not lost hope.

The short-lived project in Cuba, so promising, came to ruin because of one stupid peasant, a rabid cat, a treacherous set of stairs, and a wet bar of soap left on one of the treads for no reason that made sense. Yet he and Fidel remained friends, and Victor persevered in another country, certain of ultimate triumph.

The interesting facility in North Korea, with the generous funding by a consortium of forward-thinking governments, should have been the place where the ultimate breakthroughs at last occurred. At his disposal was a virtually infinite supply of body parts from self-pitying political prisoners who preferred being carved up alive to enduring further prison meals. But how could he have foreseen that the dictator, a strutting rooster with a harem, would end up shooting the speed-grown clone of himself that Victor created at his request, when said clone developed a passion for his dangerous look-alike and extravagantly tongue-kissed him? Victor had escaped the country with his testicles only because he and the dictator had a mutual friend, one of the most admired movie stars in the world, who had brokered peace between them.

Yet *still* he had persevered and had suffered neither one day of doubt nor one hour of depression.

The total destruction of the Hands of Mercy affected him more negatively than any previous setback in part because he had been much closer than ever before to triumph, within easy reach of the absolute mastery of flesh, its creation and control.

In truth, the fire itself and all the losses were not what shook his confidence. The identity of the arsonist: That's what brought him this low. The return of his first creation, the crude and lumbering beast who should have spent the past two centuries frozen in polar ice, seemed even less possible to him than that a gay clone could have undone him on the very brink of a glorious success.

He realized that his speed had fallen under twenty miles per hour. This had happened twice before. Each time he accelerated, his mind drifted, and his speed fell again.

Deucalion. What a pretentious name.

Deucalion in Patrick Duchaine's kitchen, turning away from Victor and—just gone. Merely a trick, of course. But quite a trick.

Deucalion, penetrating the Hands of Mercy without setting off an alarm.

In just a few days: Harker giving birth to some monstrosity, William chewing off his fingers, Christine confused about her identity, Werner's catastrophic cellular metamorphosis, the apparent incorporation of the entire Mercy staff into the Werner thing, the freeing of Chameleon, Erika Four destroying the Karloff experiment in psychic control, now Erika Four supposedly back from the dead, those two detectives somehow escaping Benny and Cindi Lovewell, two superb assassins . . . The list of unlikely incidents went on and on.

It all meant something.

So many things could not go wrong spontaneously.

A pattern waited to be discovered. A pattern that might well reveal a conspiracy. A cabal.

Occasionally Victor thought that he might have a mild tendency toward paranoia, but in this instance he knew his suspicion must be correct.

This time, the setback felt different from all before it. What brought him to the brink of ruin this time was not just a bar of soap on a stair or an amorous clone. A symphony of troubles required an orchestra of enemies and a determined conductor.

This time he might have to prepare for the worst.

Again he became aware that if the Mercedes lost more speed, it would be coasting.

Ahead on the right loomed a rest area. He drove off the highway, braked to a stop, and put the car in park.

Before he rushed heedlessly to the tank farm, he needed to brood about these recent events. He suspected that he was going to have to make the biggest decision of his life.

He'd driven out of the storm, but as he stared at the dwindling cones of his headlight beams, the rain caught up to him again, and a groaning wind.

Although Victor's powers of concentration were legendary among all who had worked with him, he found himself repeatedly distracted by the nonsensical apprehension that he might not be alone in the car. He *was* alone, of course, not just in the car but alone in the world to a degree that he did not need to contemplate right now, when his mood was already dark.

CHAPTER 59

FOLLOWING THE DUMPSTERS and the landfill workers to the big hole in the west pit, Carson thought the procession appeared medieval. The vast reaches of the dump lay in a black pall, as though civilization remained centuries away from the electric era. The torchlight, the oil lamps, the atmosphere of a religious pilgrimage that arose from the sudden reverential silence of the group as they approached the entrance to the subterranean chapel of the Resurrector . . .

Although armed with two handguns and an Urban Sniper, Carson felt defenseless in the face of this unknown.

They arrived at a tunnel, approximately eight feet in diameter, angling down into the depths of the pit, which apparently the Being, the mother of all gone-wrongs, had opened to present itself to them earlier this same night.

Before they had set out, Carson asked Nick Frigg how deep the trash was piled. She was surprised to hear they were standing on almost ten stories of garbage. Considering the substantial acreage dedicated to the dump, the Resurrector could have excavated many miles of corridors, and Frigg confirmed that they had explored an elaborate network of passageways that were but part of the entity's construction.

The tightly compacted trash forming the walls of the passageway appeared to have been sealed with a transparent bonding material of sufficient strength to prevent collapse. Rippling currents and whorls of torchlight glistered across the shiny surface.

She imagined that the Resurrector had exuded this glue, which seemed to imply that its nature was in part insectile. She couldn't easily accept that the busy burrowing architect of this labyrinth and the compassionate transcendental Being that lacked a thread of malevolence in its weave were one and the same.

As they entered the tunnel, Carson expected the stink of the trash field to intensify and the air to become thick and bitter. But the glimmering sealant on the walls apparently held back the methane that otherwise would have suffocated them, and a draft flowed up from below. She had no more difficulty breathing here than on the surface, and the malodor was if anything less offensive.

When she glanced back at dog-nose Nick, his nostrils quivered and flared ceaselessly, and he smiled with pleasure. To his enhanced olfactory sense, the path of this pilgrimage was perfumed with a singular incense. Likewise for the Duke of Orleans.

The gradual slope of the tunnel took them perhaps ten feet below the surface by the point that they had walked a hundred feet from the entrance. Here, the passageway turned sharply left and widened into a spacious gallery before seeming to curve down at a steeper angle.

In this gallery, the Resurrector waited, initially at the limits of their lights, half-seen and mysterious.

The width of the chamber allowed the procession to spread out, with a clear view for each. Carson glanced left, right, and saw that everyone but she and Michael appeared deeply affected by the presence before them, not enraptured but certainly content, at peace, many with smiles on their faces, eyes shining.

As they came side by side in a line, the Being before them approached, shadows sliding away from it as the light seemed to enrobe it in spun gold.

To her surprise, a sense of well-being came over Carson, and the foreboding to which she had clung swiftly dissipated. She knew as surely as she had known anything in her life that she would be safe here, that the Resurrector was benevolent and a champion of their cause.

She understood that this entity was broadcasting calming psychic waves of reassurance. It would never violate her sanctity by coming inside her mind, but was speaking to her in this manner as she might speak to it in words.

Telepathically, without seeming to use language and seemingly without images—for none flashed through her mind—the Resurrector somehow inculcated in her an understanding of how they would enter the tank farm, how the New Race working there would be disabled, and how Victor might be captured, his reign of madness and his kingdom of terror brought finally to an end.

During all of this, Carson slowly grew aware that she could not describe the Resurrector in any specific detail. Her sense was that before her stood a thing of such unearthly beauty that angels could not outshine it, a beauty humble in its every part yet so majestic in its complete effect that she was not merely enchanted but also uplifted. Here was a beauty both of form and of spirit, a spirit of such immaculate intention and righteous confidence that Carson's own not inconsiderable courage, hope, and resolution were inspired to new heights. This was her sense, yes, but if asked to describe the form that aroused such soaring emotions in her, she could not have said whether it had two legs or ten, one head or a hundred, or none at all.

She squinted, straining to make out even general contours, a basic biological architecture, but the Resurrector proved to be so gloriously radiant that it shimmered just beyond the ability of her senses to define it. The torchlight in which the entity now stood seemed to cloak it in mystery more than had the shadows from which it first approached them.

Carson's initial foreboding welled in her again and quickened into fright. Her heart began to race, and she heard her ragged breath catching, catching, catching in her throat. Then in a blink, and only *for* a blink, she saw the Resurrector as it really was, a blasphemy, a hideous offense against nature, an abomination from which the mind recoiled in desperate defense of its sanity.

One blink of paralyzing truth, and then again the radiance, the perception of beauty beyond the mind's capacity to fully understand, exquisite form without definition, virtue and righteousness in the flesh, kindness embodied, love materialized . . . Her fright washed away in a tide of benevolence. Her heart settled to an easy beat, and she found her breath again, and her blood did not run cold, neither did the nape of her neck prickle, and she knew that regardless of the form of the Resurrector, she was safe, she was safe, and it was a champion of their cause.

CHAPTER 60

JOCKO IN THE BIG CAR. Not driving. The day would come. All he needed was the keys. And a booster pillow. And long sticks to work the floor pedals. And a reliable map. And somewhere to go.

Until then, riding was good. Being driven was nice.

"Jocko's first car ride," he told Erika.

"How do you like it?"

"Smooth. Comfy. Better than creeping through the night, scared of brooms and buckets."

Rain rattled on the roof. Wipers flung big splashes off the windshield.

Jocko sat dry. Racing through the rain but dry.

In the night, wind shook trees. Shook them hard. Almost as hard as the crazy drunk hobo shook Jocko while shouting, *Get out of my dream, you creepazoid, get out of my dream!*

Wind slammed the car. Hissed and grumbled at the window.

Jocko smiled at the wind.

Smiling felt good. It didn't look good. He smiled at a mirror once, so he knew how not-good it looked. But it sure felt good.

"You know what?" he said.

"What?"

"How long has Jocko not twirled or backflipped, or nothing?"

"Not since you've been sitting there."

"How long is that?"

"Over half an hour."

"Amazing."

"Is that your record?"

"Got to be. By like twenty-seven minutes."

Maybe having clothes relaxed Jocko. He liked pants. The way they covered up your flat butt and the knees that made people laugh.

After the crazy drunk hobo stopped shaking Jocko, he shouted, spraying spit, *What the hell kind of knees are those? Those knees make me* SICK*! Never saw knees make me* SICK *before. You freak-kneed creepazoid!*

Then the hobo vomited. Just to prove Jocko's knees really were sick-making.

Erika was a good driver. Focused on the road. Staring hard.

She was thinking about driving. But something else, too. Jocko could tell. He could read her heart a little.

His first night alive, he found some magazines. In a trash can. Read them in an alleyway. Under a lamppost smelled like cat pee.

One article was called "You Can Learn to Read Her Heart."

You don't cut her open to read it, either. That was a relief. Jocko didn't like blood.

Well, he liked it inside where you needed it. Not outside where you could see it.

Anyway, the magazine told Jocko how to read her heart. So now he knew something troubled Erika.

Secretly he watched her. Sneaking looks.

Those delicate nostrils. Jocko wished he had those nostrils. Not those particular nostrils. He didn't want to take her nostrils. Jocko just wanted nostrils like them.

"Are you sad?" Jocko asked.

Surprised, she glanced at him. Then back at the road. "The world is so beautiful."

"Yeah. Dangerous but pretty."

"I wish I belonged in it," she said.

"Well, we're here."

"Being and belonging are different things."

"Like alive and living," Jocko said.

She glanced at him again but didn't reply. Stared at the road, the rain, the wipers wiping.

Jocko hoped he hadn't said something stupid. But he was Jocko. Jocko and stupid went together like . . . like Jocko and ugly.

After a while, he said, "Are there pants that make you smarter?"

"How could pants make anyone smarter?"

"Well, these made me prettier."

"I'm glad you like them."

Erika took her foot off the accelerator. Eased down on the brake. As they stopped on the pavement, she said, "Jocko, look."

He slid forward on his seat. Craned his neck.

Deer crossed the road, in no hurry. A buck, two does, a fawn. Others came out of dark woods on the left.

The trees shook in the wind, the tall grass thrashed.

But the deer were calm under the trembling trees, in the lashing grass, moving slowly but with purpose. They almost appeared to drift like weightless figures in a dream. Serene.

Their legs were so long and slender. They walked like dancers danced, each step precise. The grace.

Golden-brown coats on the does. The buck was brown. The fawn was colored like the does but with white spots. Tails black on top, white underneath.

Narrow, gentle faces. Eyes set on the sides of their faces to provide a panoramic view.

Heads held high, ears tipped slightly forward, they stared at the Mercedes, but only once each. Not afraid.

The fawn stayed near one of the does. Off the road once more, no longer directly in the headlight beams, it capered in a circle in the half-light, in the wet grass.

Jocko watched the fawn caper in the wet grass.

Another buck and doe. Rain glistening on the male's antlers.

Jocko and Erika watched in silence. There was nothing they could say.

The sky black, the rain rushing, the dark woods, the grass, the many deer.

There was nothing they could say.

When the deer were gone, Erika drove north again.

After a while, she said softly, "Being and belonging."

Jocko knew she meant the deer.

"Maybe just being is enough, it's all so beautiful," Jocko said.

Although she glanced at him, he didn't look at her. He couldn't bear to see her sad.

"Anyway," he said, "if somebody doesn't belong in the world, there's no door they can throw him out. They can't take the world away from him and put him somewhere different. The worst thing they can do is kill him. That's all."

After another silence, she said, "Little friend, you never stop surprising me."

Jocko shrugged. "I read some magazines once."

CHAPTER 61

VICTOR WAS in the dark night of his soul, but he was also in a Mercedes S600, arguably the finest automobile in the world. The suit he wore had cost over six thousand dollars, his wristwatch more than a hundred thousand. He had lived 240 years, most of the time in high style, and he had known more adventure, more thrills, more power, and more triumphs of a more momentous nature than any man in history. As he considered his current situation and the possibility that he might die soon, he found that making the fateful decision he needed to make was easier than he had expected when he parked in this rest area. He had no choice but to take the most extreme action available to him, because if he died, the loss to the world would be devastating.

He was too brilliant to die.

Without him, the future would be bleak. Any chance of imposing order on a meaningless universe would die with him, and chaos would rule eternal.

He used the voice-activated car phone to call the household-staff dormitory at the estate in the Garden District.

A Beta named Ethel answered, and Victor told her to bring James to the phone at once. James had been third in the hierarchy of the staff, behind William and Christine, who were now both dead. He was next in line to be the butler. If Victor hadn't been so pressed by the events of the past twenty-four hours, he would have appointed James to his new post the previous day.

When James came to the phone, Victor honored him with the news of his promotion and gave him his first assignment as butler. "And remember, James, follow the instructions I've just given you to the letter.

I expect absolute perfection in everything a butler does, but most especially in this instance."

AFTER LEAVING HIS UMBRELLA on the terrace and after thoroughly wiping his wet shoes with a cloth that he brought for that purpose, James entered the house on the first floor, by the back door at the end of the north hall.

He carried the mysterious object that had obsessed him for the past two hours: a crystal ball.

After proceeding directly to the library, as Mr. Helios had instructed, James carefully placed the gleaming sphere on the seat of an armchair.

"Are you happy there?" he asked.

The sphere did not reply.

Frowning, James moved it to another armchair.

"Better," the sphere told him.

When the crystal ball initially spoke to him, two hours earlier, James had been minding his own business, sitting at the kitchen table in the dormitory, stabbing his hand with a meat fork and watching it repeatedly heal. The fact that he healed so quickly and so well gave him reason to believe he would be all right, though for most of the day, he had felt all wrong.

The first thing the sphere said to him was, "I know the way to happiness."

Of course, James at once expressed a desire to know the way.

Since then, the crystal ball had said many things, most of them inscrutable.

Now it said, "Salted or unsalted, sliced or cubed, the choice is yours."

"Can we get back to happiness?" James asked.

"Use a knife and," the sphere said.

"And what?" James asked.

"And fork."

"What do you want me to do with a knife and fork?"

"If peeled."

"You're making no sense," James said accusingly.

"A spoon," said the sphere.

"Now it's a spoon?"

"If halved and unpeeled."

"What is the path to happiness?" James pleaded because he was afraid to demand an answer and offend the sphere.

"Long, narrow, twisting, dark," said the sphere. "For the likes of you, the path to happiness is one mean sonofabitch of a path."

"But I can get there, can't I? Even one like me?"

"Do you really want happiness?" asked the sphere.

"Desperately. Doesn't have to be forever. Just for a while."

"Your other choice is insanity."

"Happiness. I'll take happiness."

"Yogurt works with. Ice cream works with."

"With what?"

The sphere didn't reply.

"I'm in a very bad way," James pleaded.

Silence.

Frustrated, James said, "Wait here. I'll be right back. I've got something to do for Mr. Helios."

He found the hidden switch, a section of the bookcase pivoted, and the secret passageway was revealed.

James glanced back at the sphere on the seat of the armchair. Sometimes it didn't look like a crystal ball. Sometimes it looked like a cantaloupe. This was one of those times.

The sphere was a crystal ball only when the magic was in it. James feared that the magic might go out of it and never come back.

In the secret passage, he came to the first door and removed all five steel bolts, as he had been instructed.

When he opened the door, he saw the corridor that Mr. Helios had described: copper rods to the left, steel rods to the right. A low, ominous hum.

Instead of going farther, James ran back to the start of the passageway, pushed the button to open the bookcase door from this side, and hurried to the sphere.

"What is the path to happiness?" he asked.

"Some people put a little lemon on it," said the crystal ball.

"Put lemon on what?"

"You know what your problem is?"

"What is my problem?"

"You hate yourself."

James had nothing to say to that.

He returned to the secret passageway, but this time he took the crystal ball with him.

VICTOR HAD ASKED JAMES to phone him when the task was completed. Alternately consulting his world-class wristwatch and the dashboard clock of his magnificent sedan, he thought the new butler was taking too long. No doubt, awed by his promotion and by the realization that he would be speaking more often with his maker, James approached his mission with excessive care.

As he waited for the butler's call, the conviction again rose in him that he was not alone in the Mercedes. This time, he turned to look in the backseat, knowing full well no one was there.

He knew the cause of his edginess. Until James completed the task he had been sent to do, Victor remained mortal, and the world could be denied the shining future that only he could create. As soon as the butler reported completion of the job, Victor could proceed to the farm, face whatever threat might wait there, and be confident that the future would still be his.

CHAPTER 62

CHAMELEON SUSPECTS DECEPTION.

Once again, the PUZZLE smells like both an EXEMPT and a TARGET. The scent of an EXEMPT is far and away stronger than that of a TARGET, but the second scent is definitely present.

The car has been stopped for some time. Yet the PUZZLE does not get out. It sits in silence behind the wheel.

After a while, the PUZZLE makes a phone call. Chameleon listens, hears nothing incriminating.

But the PUZZLE talks about hidden doors and passageways, a hidden room. This suggests but does not prove bad behavior.

Chameleon assumes that EXEMPTS are incapable of bad behavior. But its program is not clear on this point.

It is permitted to act on assumptions, but they must be Class A assumptions, which in a rigorous application of logic, must conform to at least four of five proofs. This assumption is Class C.

Chameleon is capable of impatience. It has been a long time between kills.

It remembers clearly three kills. They occurred during its testing phase.

The pleasure is intense. The word Chameleon knows for the pleasure that comes from killing is *orgasm*.

Its entire body spasms. In orgasm, it is as fully in touch with its body as it will ever be—but, strangely, at the same time seems to escape its body and for a minute or two is not itself, is not anything, is only pleasure.

After the phone call, the PUZZLE sits in silence again.

Chameleon was a long time in the cold. A long time in the imprisoning polymeric-fabric sack.

Now it is warm.

Under the pleasing scent, the infuriating scent.

Chameleon wants an orgasm. Chameleon wants an orgasm. Chameleon wants an orgasm.

CHAPTER 63

UNDER THE DUMP, Carson and Michael and Deucalion followed the landfill workers and the resurrected Alphas along a passageway that branched off the main course. It would lead them out of the landfill and under the tank farm next door.

Ahead of them, torchlight ignited faux fire across the glazed curves of the tunnel. Because they were at the end of the procession, an inky gloom pooled behind them.

The Resurrector was far in front. Perhaps it had already entered the main building at the tank farm.

Carson had no concern about the darkness at her back. Here, in the warren of their monstrously strange accomplice, they were safer than they had been in a long time.

"What it does telepathically," Deucalion said, "is project its inner nature in order to screen from us its physical appearance, because it would be impossible for most people who see it to believe it's benign."

Like Carson, Deucalion and Michael had been suspicious of the telepathically projected image and had been strong-willed enough to peer through the Resurrector's radiant veil to the truth of its form. Deucalion had seen it twice, once for perhaps half a minute.

Michael achieved only the brief glimpse that Carson had seen. In spite of his tendency toward cynicism, he was convinced that the creature could be trusted, that it was allied with them. "If not, it could have killed us all back there, as big and powerful as it is."

"None of the landfill workers saw through its disguise or even suspects there is one," Deucalion said. "I doubt that the Alphas, Erika Four and the others, have any suspicion, either. They and the Resurrector are of the same flesh that Victor engineered for the New Race, and perhaps that renders them more susceptible than we are to its masquerade."

"I was plenty susceptible," Michael said. "I felt as if I was in an anteroom of Heaven, getting a pep talk from an archangel while waiting for judgment."

"Why make a thing that looks . . . like that?" Carson wondered.

Deucalion shook his head. "That it should look like that was not Victor's plan. Physiologically, it's a gone-wrong. In its mind, in its intentions, it's a gone-*right*."

The tunnel ceased to pass through compacted trash. Abruptly, its walls were formed of earth, coated with the glossy material that had sealed over the trash in the main passageway and in the first part of this one.

The Resurrector was a digger of considerable industry.

"Will he really come here?" Carson wondered.

"He will," Deucalion assured her.

"But Erika Four says she's called him twice. He knows she's up here somewhere, reanimated. He knows something unprecedented must be happening."

As Deucalion looked down at her, the light of the centuries-old storm throbbed through his eyes. "He'll come nevertheless. He's got too much invested in the tank farm, a new crop birthing in less than twenty-four hours. Mercy gone, this is his best bet. He's arrogant and insanely certain of himself. Never forget the pride that drives him. Perhaps in all of history, there has been only one other whose pride was greater than Victor's."

Maybe the caffeine tide pulsing through Carson was brewing up new symptoms or maybe sleep deprivation torqued her mind in spite of the NoDoz-cola cocktails. Whatever the cause, a fresh anxiety began to pluck at her. She was not a seer, not a Gypsy with one eye in the future, but a prickly intuition warned her that even if Victor died in the next few hours, the world he wanted to make was a world of which others dreamed, as well, a world in which human exceptionalism was denied, in which the masses were regimented drones who served an untouchable elite, in which flesh was cheap. Even if Victor received justice and a grave in garbage, Carson and Michael were going to be making a life together in a world ever more hostile to freedom, to human dignity, to love.

As they reached the hole that had been bored through concrete block and into the basement of the main building at the tank farm, Deucalion said, "The first time I saw the Resurrector, before you two arrived, it told me—rather, it impressed on me in that wordless way it makes you know things—that it expects to die tonight, here or at the landfill."

Michael let his breath out in a hiss. "That doesn't sound like our side wins."

"Or," said Deucalion, "the creature may know that, in winning, sacrifices will have to be made."

CHAPTER 64

THE BLUE LASER SCANNED JAMES, approved of him, and switched off the security feature that would have fried him crisp if he had been an unwelcome intruder.

Carrying the crystal ball, he went to the second steel door. He put the sphere on the floor while he pulled the five lock bolts from their slots.

"Try prosciutto," said the crystal sphere.

"That's ham."

"It works with."

"With what?"

"I know the path to happiness," said the sphere.

Voice tight with frustration, James said, "Then *tell* me."

"Paper-thin."

"What does that mean?"

"Serve it paper-thin."

The thick door swung open. James had been forbidden to enter the windowless Victorian drawing room. On his way out, he must leave the steel doors open, the exit route unobstructed.

He remained obedient, even in his current state of distraction.

Anyway, he had no interest in that room. Not when happiness might be within his grasp.

The crystal sphere said nothing on the way back to the library.

From the library desk, James phoned Mr. Helios and reported that the task had been completed precisely according to instructions.

The moment James hung up the phone, the sphere said, "You were not made for happiness."

"But if you know the path . . ."

"I know the path to happiness."

"But you won't tell me?"

"Also works with cheese," said the sphere.

"So I'm not worthy of happiness. Is that it?"

"You're just a meat machine."

"I'm a person," James insisted.

"Meat machine. Meat machine."

Furious, James threw the crystal ball to the floor, where it shattered, spilling a mass of slimy yellow seeds and revealing its orange inner flesh.

He stared at it for a while, uncomprehending.

When he looked up, he saw that someone had left a book on the desk: *A History of the Troll in Literature*. He picked it up with the intention of returning it to its proper place on the shelves.

The book said, "I know the path to happiness."

With renewed hope and excitement, James said, "Please tell me."

"Do you deserve happiness?"

"I believe I do. Why shouldn't I deserve it?"

"There may be reasons."

"Everyone deserves happiness."

"Not everyone," said the book, "but let's talk about it."

CHAPTER 65

AS THE GL550 RACED NORTH in the rain, Jocko hoped for more deer. While he hoped, he thought about some things.

Sometimes Jocko thought about big issues. Usually in two-minute segments. Between activities.

Big issues like why some things were ugly, some weren't. Maybe if everything was beautiful, nothing would be.

People saw one thing, they swooned over it. They saw this other thing, they pounded it with sticks.

Maybe there had to be variety for life to work. Swoon over everything, you got bored. Beat everything with a stick—boring.

Personally, Jocko would be happy to swoon over everything.

Jocko sometimes thought why he had no genitals. All Jocko had was that funny thing he peed with. It wasn't genitals. He called it his swoozle.

Fortunately, it rolled up. Folded away. When not in use.

If it didn't fold out of sight, crazy drunk hobos would vomit about that, too.

One thing Jocko tried *not* to think about. About how he was the only one. Only one of his kind. Too sad to think about.

Jocko thought about it anyway. Jocko couldn't turn his mind off. It spun and somersaulted like Jocko.

Maybe that was why no genitals. No need for them. Not when you were one of a kind.

Through all this thinking, Jocko secretly watched Erika.

"Do you think about big issues?" Jocko asked.

"Like what?"

"Like . . . things you don't have."

She was quiet so long. Jocko thought he screwed up again.

Then she said, "Sometimes I wonder what it would be like to have a mother."

Jocko slumped in his seat. "Jocko's sorry. Sorry he asked. That's too hard. Don't think about it."

"And what's it like to *be* a mother? I'll never know."

"Why never?"

"Because of how I'm made. Made to be used. Not to be loved."

"You'd be a great mother," Jocko said.

She said nothing. Eyes on the road. Rain on the road, rain in her eyes.

"You would," he insisted. "You take care of Jocko real good."

She kind of laughed. It was kind of a sob, too.

Way to go. Jocko speaks. People weep.

"You're very sweet," she said.

So maybe things weren't as bad as they seemed.

Letting their speed drop, she said, "Isn't that Victor's car?"

Or maybe things were worse than they seemed.

Rising in his seat, he said, "Where?"

"That rest area on the right. Yes, it's him."

"Keep going."

"I don't want him behind us. We have to get there separately from him, or I can't sneak you in."

Erika pulled into the rest area. Stopped behind Victor's sedan. "Stay here, stay down."

"You're getting out? It's raining."

"We don't want him coming to us, do we?" She opened the door.

AFTER RECEIVING CONFIRMATION that James had done as instructed, Victor took a few minutes to consider how he would approach the tank farm.

Some of the New Race who lived and worked at the farm might be breaking down in one way or another. He would need to be cautious, but he refused to be scared off. These were his creations, products of his genius, inferior to him in every way imaginable, and they could no more frighten him than one of Mozart's concertos could have terrified the composer, than a painting by Rembrandt could have sent the artist screaming into the night. They would submit to him or hear the death phrase.

He foresaw no chance that anything like the Werner abomination would greet him at the farm. Werner had been a singularity. And where was it now? Vaporized with everything else in the Hands of Mercy.

No rebellion against Victor could hope to succeed, not only because his power was that of the mythic gods, but also because the smartest of the Alphas was an idiot by comparison with its maker, he on whom the centuries took no toll.

Erika Four, an Alpha, would be no match for him. He had killed her once with only a silk necktie and the power of his hands, and he could kill her again if the bitch had in fact been revived. An Alpha, a woman, and a wife—she was three times inferior to him. He would delight in the opportunity to punish her for the impudence of those two phone calls. If she thought she had been cruelly treated in her first life, in her second he would teach her what cruelty really was.

He had no fear of going to the tank farm. He *seethed* with desire to be there and to rule this new kingdom with a ferocious discipline that would allow no repeat of the Hands of Mercy.

As he reached to release the parking brake, a vehicle appeared on the highway, approaching from the south. Instead of passing, it parked behind him, flooding the interior of the sedan with light.

His mirrors presented too few details, so he turned in his seat to look through the back window. Erika Five was behind the wheel of the GL550, which he had ordered her to drive to the farm.

Staring back at her, furious with her because she looked like the impudent and insulting Erika Four, Victor saw nothing in the backseat, but he heard something move there. In the instant, he knew why he had felt that he was not alone: *Chameleon!*

The New Race pheromones with which he had doused himself would provide hours of protection. Except that . . . in moments of exertion when a light sweat might be broken, in moments of rage or fear, his true scent would grow riper and might be detected under the New Race disguise.

Victor flung open the driver's door and plunged out of the car, into the night. Into the *rain*. The downpour would fade the scent of his own pheromones, but it would more effectively wash away the odor of the New Race, which was only sprinkled on his suit.

He should have slammed the door, locked it remotely, abandoned the sedan, and gone to the farm with Erika. But he no longer dared approach the open driver's door, because Chameleon might already have scrambled into the front seat.

Worse, it already might be out of the sedan, on rest-area pavement immediately around him. The ceaseless dance of raindrops on the blacktop would entirely conceal the telltale ripple of Chameleon in motion.

Inexplicably, Erika seemed to have gotten out of the GL even an instant before he had vacated the S600. At his side, sensing trouble, she said, "Victor? What's wrong?"

ERIKA TOLD JOCKO, *Stay down.*

She said it like a scolding mother. She would be a good mother. But wasn't Jocko's mother. Nobody was.

Jocko raised his head. Saw Erika and Victor together. Instantly soaked by rain.

More interesting was the bug. The biggest bug Jocko ever saw. Half as big as Jocko.

This one didn't look tasty. Looked bitter.

In the storm drain, bugs came close to Jocko. Easy to catch. Bugs didn't know his big yellow eyes could see them in the dark.

Something wrong with this bug. Besides being so big.

Suddenly Jocko knew. The way it sneaked. The way it started to rear up. This bug would kill.

Pillowcase. On the floor. In front of his seat. Slip the knot in the shoelace. Inside—soap, soap, soap. The knife.

Quick, quick, quick, Jocko in the rain. Capering toward Erika and Victor. *Don't pirouette.*

CHAPTER 66

THE BUG DIDN'T WANT TO DIE.

Neither did Jocko. Everything going so well. Soap. His first ride in a car. Someone to talk to. His first pants. Nobody hit him for *hours*. Soon a funny hat. So of course a giant killer bug shows up. Jocko luck.

Two ripping claws. One crushing claw. Six pincers. Stinger. Reciprocating saw for a tongue. Teeth. Teeth behind the first teeth. Everything but a flame-spitting hole. Oh, there it was. A bug born to be bad.

Jocko dropped on it with both knees. Stabbed, slashed, ripped, tore. Picked the bug up, slammed it down. Slammed it again. Slammed it. More stabbing. Fierce. Unrelenting. Jocko scared himself.

The bug squirmed. Tried to wriggle away. But it didn't fight back, and it died.

Puzzled by the bug's pacifism, Jocko got to his feet. Maybe the sight of Jocko paralyzed it with terror. Jocko stood in the driving rain. Breathless. Dizzy.

Rain snapping on his bald head.

Lost the baseball cap. Ah. Standing on it.

Erika and Victor seemed speechless.

Gasping, Jocko said, "Bug."

Erika said, "I couldn't see it. Until it was dead."

Jocko triumphant. Heroic. His time had come. His time at last. To shine.

Victor skewered Jocko with his stare. "*You* could see it?"

The cap's expansion strap was hooked around Jocko's toes.

Wheezing, Jocko said to Erika, "It was . . . gonna . . . kill you."

Victor disagreed: "It's programmed to spare anyone with the scent of New Race flesh. Of we three, it would have killed only me."

Jocko had saved Victor from certain death.

Victor said, "You're of my flesh, but I don't know you."

Stupid, stupid, stupid. Jocko wanted to lie down in front of one of the cars and drive over himself.

"What are you?" Victor demanded.

Jocko wanted to beat himself with a bucket.

"*Who* are you?" Victor pressed.

Trying to shake the cap off his foot, panting, Jocko said without the desired force: "I am . . . the child of . . . Jonathan Harker."

He raised the knife. The blade had broken off in the bug.

"He died . . . to birth me. . . ."

"You're the parasitical second self that developed spontaneously from Harker's flesh."

"I am . . . a juggler. . . ."

"Juggler?"

"Never mind," said Jocko. He dropped the handle of the knife. Furiously kicked his foot. Cast off the cap.

"I will need to study your eyes," said Victor.

"Sure. Why not."

Jocko turned away. Skip, skip, skip forward, hop backward. Skip, skip, skip forward, hop backward. Twirl.

AS SHE WATCHED the troll pirouetting across the blacktop, Erika wanted to hurry to him, halt him, give him a hug, and tell him that he was very brave.

Victor said, "Where did he come from?"

"He showed up at the house a little while ago. I knew you'd want to examine him."

"What is he doing?"

"It's just a thing he does."

"I'll find answers in him," Victor said. "Why they're changing form. Why the flesh has gone wrong. There's much to learn from him."

"I'll bring him to the farm."

"The eyes are a bonus," Victor said. "If he's awake when I dissect the eyes, I'll have the best chance of understanding how they function."

She watched Victor walk to the open door of the S600.

Before getting into the car, he looked again at the skipping, hopping, twirling troll, and then at Erika. "Don't let him dance away into the night."

"I won't. I'll bring him to the farm."

As Victor got into the sedan and drove out of the rest area, Erika walked into the middle of the roadway.

Wind tore the night, ripped rain from the black sky, shook the trees as if to throttle the life from them. The world was wild and violent and strange.

The troll walked on his hands, down the center line of the highway.

When she could no longer hear the S600 above the wind roar, Erika glanced back, watching the distant taillights until they were out of sight.

The troll capered in a serpentine pattern, lane to lane, pausing now and then to spring off the pavement and kick his heels together.

Wind danced with the night, anointed the earth with rain, inspired the trees to celebrate. The world was free and exuberant and wondrous.

Erika rose onto the points of her toes, spread her arms wide, took a deep breath of the wind, and stood for a moment in expectation of the twirl.

CHAPTER 67

AS THE LANDFILL was encircled by a formidable fence, so was the tank farm. Instead of three staggered rows of loblolly pines, there were clusters of live oaks festooned with moss.

The sign at the entry gate identified the resident corporation as GEGENANGRIFF, German for *counterattack,* Victor's little joke, as his life was dedicated to an assault against the world.

The main building covered over two acres: a two-story brick structure with clean modern lines. Because every policeman, public official, and bureaucrat in the parish was a replicant, he'd had no trouble with building-code requirements, building inspections, or government approvals.

He opened the rolling iron gate with his remote control and parked in the underground garage.

The experience at the rest area had blown away the last clinging doubts that made him wary of returning to the farm. He'd been spared from a murderous creation of his own, Chameleon, by the mutant being that had evolved out of Jonathan Harker, who himself was one of the New Race. To Victor, this strongly suggested—nay, confirmed beyond question—that the entire New Race enterprise was so brilliantly conceived and so powerfully executed that within it had evolved a system of synchronicity that would ensure that errors in the project, if any, would self-correct.

Carl Jung, the great Swiss psychologist, had theorized that synchronicity, a word he invented for remarkable coincidences that have profound effects, is an acausal connecting principle that can in strange ways impose order on our lives. Victor enjoyed Jung's work, though he would have liked to rewrite all the man's essays and books, to bring to them a far greater depth of insight than poor Carl possessed. Synchronicity was not integral to the universe, as Carl believed, but sprang up only during those certain periods in certain cultures when human endeavor was as close to fully rational as it would ever get. The more rational the culture, the more likely that synchronicity would arise as a means of correcting what few errors the culture committed.

Victor's implementation of the New Race and of his vision for a unified world was so rational, was worked out in such exquisitely logical detail, that a system of synchronicity evolved within it while he wasn't looking. Something had gone wrong with the creation tanks at the Hands of Mercy without any indication to Victor, and before more imperfect New Race models could be produced, Deucalion appeared after two centuries to burn down the facility—an incredible coincidence indeed! Deucalion assumed that he was destroying Victor, when instead he was preventing more flawed models of the New Race from being produced, forcing Victor to use only the vastly improved creation tanks at the farm. Synchronicity had corrected the error. And no doubt synchronicity would deal with Deucalion, as well, and clean up other minor annoyances—Detectives O'Connor and Maddison, among others—that might otherwise inhibit Victor in his ever more rapid march toward absolute dominance of all things.

With Victor's unstoppable drive for power, with his singular intellect, with his cold materialism and his ruthless practicality, and now with synchronicity on his side, he had become untouchable, immortal.

He was immortal.

He took the elevator from the parking garage to the tank fields on the main floor. When the doors opened and he stepped through, he found the entire staff, sixty-two of the New Race, waiting for him, as throughout the ages commoners have gathered along streets to bask in the glory of passing royalty or to honor great political leaders whose courage and commitment those drudges of the proletariat could never hope to match.

Having stood in the rain while the synchronistic Harker mutant had killed Chameleon, Victor was disheveled as no one had ever seen him. On any other day, he might have been keenly annoyed to be seen in a sodden and rumpled suit with his hair disarranged. But in this hour of his transcendence, the condition of his wardrobe and hair did not matter, because his elevation to immortality was clearly evident to this audience, his radiance undiminished.

How they goggled at him, abashed by his wisdom and knowledge, mortified by their ignorance, overawed by his godlike power.

Raising his arms and spreading them wide, Victor said, "I understand the awe in which you hold your maker, but always remember that the best way to honor him is to bend more diligently to his work, give of yourselves as never before, commit every fiber of your being to the fulfillment of his vision."

As they came forward, Victor realized that they intended to lift him high and bear him to his office, as throughout history so many enraptured crowds had borne returning heroes through streets to halls of honor. Previously, he would have chastised them for wasting his time and their own. But perhaps this once, considering the momentous nature of the day's events and of his ascendance to the company of the immortals, he would indulge them, because allowing them to attend him in this way, he would surely be inspiring them to greater efforts on his behalf.

CHAPTER 68

JOCKO IN DESPAIR. Rain-soaked. Feet pulled up on the passenger seat. Thin arms around his legs. Baseball cap turned backward.

Erika behind the wheel. Not driving. Staring at the night.

Victor not dead. Should be but not.

Jocko not dead. Should be but not. Total screwup.

"Jocko is never gonna eat another bug," Jocko said.

She just stared at the night. Said nothing.

Jocko wished she would say something.

Maybe she would do the right thing. Beat Jocko to death. He deserved it. But no. She was too nice. Typical Jocko luck.

There were things he could do. Put down the power window. Stick his head out. Power the window up. Cut off his head.

Erika said, "I'm programmed for obedience. I've done things I knew he wouldn't approve of—but I haven't actively disobeyed him."

Jocko could take off his T-shirt. Tear it in strips. Pack strips in his nose. Roll up his cap. Stuff it down his throat. Suffocate.

"Something's happened to me tonight," she said. "I don't know. Maybe I could drive right by the farm, maybe just drive and drive forever."

Jocko could go into woods. Prick a thumb. Wait for wild pigs to smell blood, come and eat him.

"But I'm afraid to pop the parking brake and drive. What if I can't pass the place? What if I pull in there? What if I'm not even able to let you go free on your own?"

Jocko raised one hand. "May I say?"

"What is it?"

"Jocko wonders if you have an ice pick."

"Why do you need an ice pick?"

"Do you have one?"

"No."

"Never mind."

She leaned forward. Forehead on steering wheel. Closed her eyes. Made a thin, sad sound.

Should be possible to commit suicide with a tire jack. Think about it. Think. Think.

"May I say?"

"Say what?"

"See Jocko's ear?"

"Yes."

"Is ear hole big enough, he could fit in the end of your tire jack?"

"What in the world are you talking about?"

"Never mind."

With sudden determination, she released the parking brake. Put the 550 in gear, drove out of the rest area.

"Are we going somewhere?" Jocko asked.

"Somewhere."

"Will we go past a high cliff?"

"No. Not on this road."

"Will we cross any train tracks?"

"I'm not sure. Why?"

"Never mind."

CHAPTER 69

AS VICTOR CONSENTED to the attentions of the adoring crowd, he realized that in addition to the staff of the tank farm, Deucalion was also present, and Detectives O'Connor and Maddison, as well.

How brilliant he had been to foresee that very soon synchronicity would restore balance to his world, correct all errors by the mechanism of astonishing coincidence. The very presence of his first-made and the detectives confirmed his elevation to the status of an immortal, and he looked forward to seeing by what meaningful coincidence they would be killed.

He still carried a pistol in a shoulder rig, under his suit coat, but it would be beneath him to shoot the trio himself, for he was now not merely the singular genius he had always been, but also such a paragon of reason and logic that the most powerful forces in the universe operated for his benefit. Self-defense was a necessity of the common herd, of which he had never been a member and from which he was now even farther removed. Synchronicity and no doubt other recondite mechanisms would come to his assistance in dazzling and unexpected ways.

Many hands lifted him off the floor, and he thought his people might carry him seated upright on their shoulders, like a Chinese emperor of old was transported aloft in an ornate chair, might carry him to his office where the great work would continue, greater even than everything he had heretofore accomplished. But in their zeal, in their earnest enthusiasm to celebrate their maker, they pulled him supine, and two phalanxes of bearers supported him between them, on their shoulders, so he faced the ceiling unless he turned his head to one side or the other. Their grips on his ankles, legs, wrists, and arms were firm and their strength was more than adequate to the task, because he made his people strong and engineered them with endurance, the endurance of good machines.

Suddenly his bearers were on the move, and the many others crowded close, perhaps hoping they might be able to touch him or hoping that he might turn his head toward them and look upon them, so they could say years hence that they had been here on this historic day and that he had met their eyes and knew them and smiled. The atmosphere was festive, and many seemed jubilant, which was not a mood easily achieved by the New Race, considering their programming. Then Victor realized that they were future-focused on the triumphs their master would achieve in this new facility, looking forward to the day—now so much closer—when the relentless killing of the hated Old Race would begin. This must be the source of their jubilation: the prospect of genocide, the scourging from the world of every last human being to ever have spoken of God.

Evidently they had more in mind than just transporting him to his desk, because although his office was on the main floor, they carried him down two flights of stairs as effortlessly as across flat terrain. They must have some special honor in mind. And though Victor had no need for the approval of their kind, had no desire in fact for the approval of anyone, he was now committed to the tedium that such a ceremony would no doubt involve.

But then something occurred that made the moment interesting again: the celebratory atmosphere faded, and a hush fell upon the crowd. It seemed to him that reverence was the mood of the moment, which of course was more suited to an occasion when such as they would honor one of Victor's exalted position. Reverence indeed, for torches were lit, apparently saturated with a spiced oil that produced a fragrance as pleasant as that of incense. Warming to his role as the object of devotion, he turned his head left and right, allowing them to see his face more than just in profile—and during one of these dispensations of his grace, he saw Erika in the crowd, smiling, and he was disposed to smile at her, as well, for she had brought with her the creature born of Harker, which had saved him from Chameleon, although at the moment, that dwarfish mutant was not to be seen.

Now they entered a passageway of raw earth glistening as if with lacquer, and he was reminded of the raw earth of yawning graves in a prison cemetery so long ago, dickering with the hangman at the brink of the hole. He was reminded of the raw earth of mass graves across the world over the years, where the executioners allowed him to cull from the doomed herd those for whom he might have a use in his experiments. How grateful the rescued always were to him, until that moment in the lab when they realized why they had been saved, and then they cursed him, unable to appreciate, in their cow-stupid way, what an opportunity he had given them, this chance to be part of history. He used them hard and used them well, whether as laborers or subjects of experiment. No other scientist ever born could have used them half as well. And therefore their contribution to posterity was immensely more than they could have made by their own wits.

From the passage with earthen walls, they proceeded into a most unusual corridor. Overhead, not a foot in front of his face, spread an inventive decoupage of crushed cracker boxes, myriad cereal boxes, flattened soup cans, packages that had once contained antihistamines and suppositories and laxatives, tangles of frayed rope, a worn-out slipper, red-white-and-blue political posters proclaiming the right, the need, the duty to vote, a soiled platinum-blond wig, crushed skeletons of long-dead rats, a garland of red Christmas tinsel as sinuous as a boa, a doll with a smashed face and one staring eye, the other socket empty.

After the doll's face, he lost sight of the lacquered montage past which he was carried, and saw instead a thousand faces exhumed from his memory, broken faces and startled faces and bloody faces and faces half peeled back from the bone, the faces of men and women and children, those whom he had used and used so well, and not merely a thousand but two thousand, multitudes. They didn't frighten him, but filled him with contempt, for he despised the weak who would let him use them. They thrilled him because he had always been thrilled by his power to bring others to the realization that they were nothing but meat, to strip from them their fragile defenses, their trust in justice, their childish illusions that they mattered, their delusions of meaning, their idiot faith, their hope, and even their sense of self, until in the end they *wanted* to be nothing but meat, unthinking meat and sick of life.

When faces from the past stopped cascading through his mind, he found that he had been carried out of the passageway into a gallery with a floor curved like a bowl. This seemed to be their destination, for here they stopped. When they brought him off their shoulders and put him on his feet, he stood bewildered because every face in the crowd was now that of a stranger. "So many faces," he said, "tumbling through my mind like blown leaves moments ago. . . . Now I can't recall one of them or who they were. Or who you are." A terrible confusion overcame him. "Or my face. How do I appear? What name do I go by?"

Then out of the crowd stepped a giant, the right half of this face badly broken and the damage only half disguised by an intricate tattoo. Looking at the wholesome side of the face, he sensed that he had known this man before, and then he heard himself say, "Why . . . you are one of my children . . . come home at last."

The tattooed man said, "You were never a madman during any moment of your diabolical work. You were wicked from the moment of your first intention, rotten with pride, your every desire venomous and unwholesome, your every act corrupt, your arrogance unbridled, your cruelty inexhaustible, your soul bargained away for power over others, your heart empty of feeling. You were evil, not mad, and you thrived on evil, it was your sustenance. Now I will not permit you to escape awareness of the justice you receive. I will not let you escape into insanity, because I have the power to hold you to the reality of your vicious life."

The giant put a hand upon the head of the insane, and at the touch, the madness blinked away, and Victor knew again who he was, where he was, and why he had been brought here. He reached for the pistol under his jacket, but the giant caught his hand and broke his fingers in a crushing grip.

CHAPTER 70

ERIKA FIVE WHEELED the SUV to the curb and stopped a few yards short of the entrance to the tank farm, Gegenangriff, Inc.

What little character the building possessed was faded by the darkness and the rain.

"How nondescript the place looks," she said. "Why, it might be anything or nothing much at all."

The troll was sitting up straight in his seat. Usually busy with elaborating gestures or making meaningless rhythms, his hands were still, folded on his chest.

"Jocko understands."

"What do you understand, Jocko?"

"If you have to take him in there. Jocko understands."

"You don't want to go in there."

"It's okay. Whatever. Jocko doesn't want you in trouble."

"Why do you owe me anything?" she asked.

"You were kind to Jocko."

"We've known each other only one night."

"You squeezed a lot of kindness into one night."

"Not that much."

"The only kindness Jocko ever knew."

After a mutual silence, she said, "You ran. You were faster than me. I lost you."

"He wouldn't believe that."

"Go. Just go, Jocko. I can't take you in there with me."

His yellow eyes were no less eerie and no less beautiful than when she had first seen them.

"Where would Jocko go?"

"There's a whole beautiful world."

"And none of it wants Jocko."

"Don't go in there and let him carve you up," she said. "You're more than meat."

"So are you. So much more than meat."

She couldn't look at him. It wasn't the ugliness that was hard to take. His vulnerability broke both her hearts, and his humility, and his brave little soul.

"The pull of the program is strong," she said. "The command to obey. Like a riptide."

"If you go in, Jocko goes in."

"No."

Jocko shrugged. "You can't choose for Jocko."

"Please, Jocko. Don't put this on me."

"May I say?" When she nodded, he said, "Jocko could know what it's like to have a mother. And you could know what it's like to be one. It would be a little family, but still a family."

CHAPTER 71

IN THE SUBTERRANEAN GALLERY, Victor stood at the center of the crowd, determined that this ignorant rabble would never hear him ask for mercy or concede the truth of their accusations.

He realized that the employees of the landfill were here. And several Alphas he had terminated, somehow revived.

Erika Four came to him out of the mob, stood face-to-face and met his eyes, and was not cowed. She raised a fist as if to hit him, but lowered it without striking. "I am not as low as you," she said, and turned away.

And here was Carson O'Connor, Maddison standing behind her with a hand on her shoulder, a German shepherd at her side. She said, "Don't bother lying to me. I know my father saw something that got him on your case. You ordered your zombies to kill him and my mother."

"I killed them both myself," Victor said. "And he begged like a little boy for his life."

She smiled and shook her head. "He begged for my mother's life, I'm sure. He would humble himself for her. But he never begged for his own. Rot in hell."

THE BOOK TAUNTED JAMES as much as did the crystal ball. He paced the Helios-mansion library with growing frustration.

"I know the path to happiness," said the book.

"I swear, you say that one more time, I'll tear you to pieces."

"I will tell you the path to happiness."

"So tell me."

"You better have a drink first," said the book.

In a corner of the library was a wet bar. James put the book down long enough to pour a double shot of whiskey and toss it back.

When he picked up the volume once more, it said, "Maybe you would be better off just going back to the dormitory."

"Tell me the path to happiness," James insisted.

"Go back, sit at the kitchen table, and stab your hand with the meat fork, watch it heal."

"Tell me the path to happiness."

"You seemed to be enjoying the meat fork."

Through his exchanges with the magic book since he downed the whiskey, James had been looking in the backbar mirror, not at the volume in his hands.

By his reflection, he discovered that both voices were his and that the book, as perhaps the crystal ball before it, did not talk at all.

"Tell me the path to happiness," James insisted.

And in the mirror he saw himself say, "For you, the only path to happiness is death."

THE MONTAGE of decoupaged garbage flowed over the walls and the floor of the huge subterranean gallery. The place was more mysterious than any Victor had known before.

In the center of the room, a grave had been prepared: ten feet long, six feet wide, twenty feet deep. Beside this excavation stood the immense pile of garbage that came from it, a festering heap of rotten materials of sundry kinds.

After they chained his hands behind his back, as they escorted him to the grave, he spoke the death phrase, but none of them fell dead. Somehow they had been freed.

Nick Frigg, boss of the dump, buckled a metal collar around Victor's neck, and Victor did not beg.

A lowly Epsilon attached a cable to the collar.

Victor supposed that the cable ran all the way to the surface, drawing juice from the dump's main power.

"I will not beg," he told them. "You owe your existence to me. And when I die, so will every creature I have made."

The crowd stared at him in silence. They neither called him a liar nor asked him to explain.

"I am not bluffing," he warned them. "My altered body has its cables winding through it, as you know. I receive an electric charge regularly, store it in power cells within my torso, convert it to another life-sustaining energy as I need it. Many of you know this to be true."

He saw that they did know.

"When I die, those cells will be tapped to send a signal that will be relayed by satellite to everyone made of New Race flesh, to every meat machine that walks. And you will fall down dead."

They appeared convinced. Yet not one spoke.

Victor smiled, anticipating triumph in spite of their silence. "Did you think a god would die alone?"

"Not a god as cruel as you," Deucalion said.

When several in the crowd cried out that he should be cast into the pit, Victor promised them a new beginning, reparations, freedom. But they would not listen, the fools, the ignorant swine.

Suddenly, from behind the mountain of garbage beside the grave, a creature of great radiant beauty appeared. Oh, graceful it was, its form exquisite, its nature mysterious yet beguiling in every aspect, and he could see that the crowd, too, was in awe of it.

But when he appealed to it, asking it to persuade the crowd to have mercy, the Being changed. Over him now loomed a beast that even he, Victor Frankenstein, in his ferocious quest for absolute control of human biology, could never have imagined. This thing was so hideous, so monstrous, so suggestive of chaos and violence in every smallest detail that Victor could neither repress a scream nor prevent it from escalating wildly.

The beast approached. Victor retreated to the brink. Only when he fell into the foulness at the bottom of the grave did he realize with what putrid materials his last bed had been so richly prepared.

Above, the hateful presence began to push the heaped garbage back into the pit from which it had been extracted. Every foulness imaginable rained down on Victor, drove him to his knees in the even greater foulness under him. And as an avalanche of suffocating filth poured onto him, something spoke within his mind. Its message was not in words or images, appeared instead as a sudden dark knowledge that was at once translatable: *Welcome to Hell.*

ERIKA FOUR WATCHED as the radiant and enchanting Resurrector moved back from the great landslide of garbage that it had instigated, and Deucalion threw the switch that delivered a death jolt to Victor at the bottom of his final resting place.

She looked around at all the New Race and said, "Peace at last," and they replied as one, "Peace."

Half a minute later, the Resurrector and everyone in the gallery fell dead as stones, except Deucalion, Carson, Michael, and Duke, who were not creatures of the New Race flesh.

IN THE SUV in front of the tank farm, Erika Five had a sudden premonition of death, and reached out to Jocko.

From his tortured expression, she knew that the same premonition had stricken him, and he grasped hold of her.

In the instant that they clasped hands, the storm that had thus far been without pyrotechnics abruptly exploded with lightning. The sky flared violently, and the focus of Nature's sudden fury seemed to be the GL550. Barrages of thunderbolts slammed into the pavement around the vehicle, so numerous and so perfectly encircling that from every window nothing could be seen of the night or the land or the tank farm, only a screen of light so bright that Jocko and Erika bowed their heads. And though neither of them spoke, they both heard the same three words and somehow knew that the other had heard them as well: *Be not afraid.*

DEUCALION TURNED to Carson and Michael. "You pledged to fight at my side, and fight you did. The world has gained a little time. We destroyed the man . . . but his ideas did not die with him. There are those who would deny free will to others . . . and there are too many willing to surrender their free will, in every sense of its meaning."

"Busting bad guys is easy," Carson said, "compared to fighting bad ideas. Fighting ideas . . . that's a life's work."

Deucalion nodded. "So let's live long lives."

Making the *Star Trek* greeting sign, Michael said, "And prosper."

Picking up Duke as if he were a lap dog, the giant cradled the shepherd in his right arm and with his left hand rubbed its tummy. "I'll walk with you to the surface, bring Arnie from Tibet, then it's good-bye. I need to find a new retreat, where I can say my thanks, and think about these two hundred years and what they've meant."

"And maybe we could see the coin trick once more," Michael said.

Deucalion regarded them both in silence for a moment. "I could show you how it's done. Such knowledge would be safe in your hands."

Carson knew that he meant not just the coin trick, but all that he knew—and could do. "No, my friend. We're ordinary people. Such power should remain with someone extraordinary."

They walked together to the surface, where the wind had blown and the rain had washed the first light of dawn into the eastern sky.

IN THE WINDOWLESS VICTORIAN ROOM, the reddish-gold substance, whether liquid or gas, drained from the glass casket, and the form that had been a shapeless shadow resolved into a man.

When the empty case opened like a clamshell, the naked man swung into a sitting position, then stepped onto the Persian carpet.

The satellite-relayed signal had been a death sentence to all the other meat machines made by Victor, but by design it had not killed this one, but instead freed him.

He walked out through the open steel doors that would have kept him contained if by mistake he'd been animated before he was wanted.

James lay dead in the library. Upstairs, he found Christine dead in the vestibule of the master suite.

The house was quiet and otherwise apparently deserted.

In Victor's bathroom, he showered.

In the mirrored alcove in the corner of Victor's walk-in closet, he admired his body. No metal cables wove through it, and he did not bear the scars of two centuries. He was physical perfection.

After dressing, he took a briefcase to the walk-in safe. There, he discovered that some valuables were not where they should have been. But other drawers offered all that he needed.

He would leave the mansion on foot. He was so wary of having any connection with Victor Helios that he would not even use one of the cars merely to abandon it at the airport.

Before he left, he set the Dresden countdown for half an hour. Both the house and the dormitory would soon be ashes.

He wore a raincoat with a hood, aware of the irony of departing in garb reminiscent of the great brute's current costume.

Although he was the very image of Victor Frankenstein, he was not in fact the man, but instead a clone. By virtue of direct-to-brain data downloading, however, his memory matched Victor's, all 240 years of it, except for the events of the past eighteen hours or so, which was the last time Victor had conducted a memory update for him, by phone transmission. He was like Victor also in that he shared Victor's vision for the world.

This was not precisely personal immortality, but an acceptable substitute.

In a fundamental way, the recently deceased and this recently born individual were different. This Victor was stronger, quicker, and perhaps even more intelligent than the original. Not perhaps. Most definitely more intelligent. He was the new and improved Victor Frankenstein, and the world needed him now more than ever.

CHAPTER 72

THIS WORLD IS A WORLD of stories, of mystery and enchantment. Everywhere you look, if you look close enough, a tale of wonder is unfolding, for every life is a narrative and everyone a character in his or her own drama.

In San Francisco, the O'Connor-Maddison Detective Agency not long ago celebrated its first year. They were a success almost from the day they opened for business. A hand laid on him by a tattooed healer has brought Arnie out of autism. He works in the office after school, doing some filing and learning hard-boiled lingo. Duke adores him. Seven months from now, a baby will complicate the sleuthing. But that's what they make infant carriers for. Hang the kid on the chest or sling him from the back, and there's no reason not to keep pursuing truth, justice, bad guys, and good Chinese food.

In a small house on a large property in rural Montana, Erika has discovered a talent for motherhood, and she is fortunate to have, in Jocko, a perpetual child. Thanks to what she took from Victor's safe, they have all the money they will ever need. They don't travel, and only she goes into town, because they don't want to have to deal with all the brooms and buckets. The local birds, however, have gotten used to him, and he's never feeling pecked anymore, in any sense. He has a collection of funny hats, all with bells, and she has developed a contagious laugh. They don't know why only they survived, of all those made of New Race flesh, but it had something to do with the lightning. So every night, when she tucks him in, she makes him say his prayers, as she does, too, before she sleeps.

At St. Bartholomew's Abbey, in the great mountains of northern California, Deucalion resides as a guest, while he considers becoming a postulant. He enjoys all the brothers, and has a special friendship with Brother Knuckles. He has learned much from Sister Angela, who runs the associated orphanage, and the disabled children there think he is the best Santa Claus ever. He does not try to envision his future. He waits for it to find him.

ABOUT THE AUTHOR

DEAN KOONTZ is the author of many #1 *New York Times* best-sellers. He lives in Southern California with his wife, Gerda, their golden retriever, Anna, and the enduring spirit of their golden, Trixie.

Correspondence for the author should be addressed to:

Dean Koontz
P.O. Box 9529
Newport Beach, California 92658